Lone ...

Paullina Simons was born in the Soviet Union and emigrated to the United States as a child. She has lived in Italy, England, Kansas and Texas, and now lives in New York with her husband and some of her children. She has recently published a memoir, *Six Days in Leningrad*, and will soon publish her second children's book, called *Poppet Gets Two Big Brothers*. *Lone Star* is her twelfth novel.

Praise for Paullina Simons

Tully
"You'll never look at life in the same way again. Pick up this book and prepare to have your emotions wrung so completely you'll be sobbing your heart out one minute and laughing through your tears the next. Read it and weep—literally."
Company

Red Leaves
"Simons handles her characters and setting with skill, slowly peeling away deceptions to reveal denial, cowardice and chilling indifference . . . an engrossing story."
Publishers Weekly

Eleven Hours
"*Eleven Hours* is a harrowing, hair-raising story that will keep you turning the pages late into the night."
Janet Evanovich

The Bronze Horseman
"A love story both tender and fierce." *Publishers Weekly*

Tatiana and Alexander
"This has everything a romance glutton could wish for: a bold, talented and dashing hero [and] a heart-stopping love affair that nourishes its two protagonists even when they are separated and lost."
Daily Mail

The Girl in Times Square

"Part mystery, part romance, part family drama . . . in other words, the perfect book." *Daily Mail*

The Summer Garden

"If you're looking for a historical epic to immerse yourself in, then this is the book for you." *Closer*

Road to Paradise

"One of our most exciting writers . . . Paullina Simons presents the perfect mix of page-turning plot and characters." *Woman and Home*

A Song in the Daylight

"Simons shows the frailties of families and of human nature, and demonstrates that there's so much more to life, such as honesty and loyalty." *Good Reading*

Bellagrand

"Another epic saga from Simons, full of the emotion and heartache of the original trilogy. Summer reading at its finest." *Canberra Times*

By the same author

FICTION
Tully
Red Leaves
Eleven Hours
The Girl in Times Square
Road to Paradise
A Song in the Daylight

The Bronze Horseman Series
The Bronze Horseman
Tatiana and Alexander
The Summer Garden
Children of Liberty
Bellagrand

NON FICTION
Tatiana's Table
Six Days in Leningrad

Paullina Simons

Lone Star

HARPER

Harper
An imprint of HarperCollins*Publishers*
1 London Bridge Street,
London SE1 9GF

www.harpercollins.co.uk

This paperback edition 2015
1

First published in Great Britain by
HarperCollins*Publishers* 2015

Extract from "The Love Song of J. Alfred Prufrock" taken from *Collected Poems*
© Estate of T.S. Eliot and reprinted by permission of Faber and Faber Ltd.

A catalogue record for this book is
available from the British Library

ISBN: 9780007441631

Printed and bound in Great Britain by
Clays Ltd, St Ives plc

MIX
Paper from
responsible sources
FSC **FSC® C007454**
www.fsc.org

FSC™ is a non-profit international organisation established to promote
the responsible management of the world's forests. Products carrying the
FSC label are independently certified to assure consumers that they come
from forests that are managed to meet the social, economic and
ecological needs of present and future generations,
and other controlled sources.

Find out more about HarperCollins and the environment at
www.harpercollins.co.uk/green

To Natasha, my first resplendent light

To my two stalwart brilliant sainted patient indulgent editors, Anna Valdinger for all the big stuff and for keeping my wine safe, and Denise O'Dea for perfecting every line with her sharp eye, much thanks – PS

There will be time to murder and create,
And time for all the works and days of hands
That lift and drop a question on your plate;
Time for you and time for me,
And time yet for a hundred indecisions,
And for a hundred visions and revisions.
T.S. Eliot, "The Love Song of J. Alfred Prufrock"

Part One

Chloe and Mason and Hannah and Blake

We're not serious when we are seventeen.
One fine evening, full of pints and lemonade,
In rowdy cafes with their dazzling chandeliers,
We stroll under the linden trees in the park.
Now you're in love, till August anyway.
You'll make her laugh, you'll write her poetry
At night you wander back to the cafes
For more pints and lemonade …
We are not serious when we are seventeen,
And when we have green linden trees in the park.

Arthur Rimbaud, "Romance"

1

Insanity's Horse

CHLOE SAT ALONE ON THE BUS RIDE HOME ACROSS THE TRAIN
tracks, dreaming of the beaches of Barcelona and perhaps of
being ogled by a lusting stranger. She was trying to drown out
Blake, Mason and Hannah verbally tripping over one another as
if in a game of drunken Twister as they loudly argued the pros
and cons of writing a story for money. Threads of songs played
their crowded lyric notes in the static inside her head. *Under the
boardwalk like no other lover he took my hand and said I love
you forever*—all suddenly overpowered by Queen's matchless
yawp *Barcelonaaaaaaaaa...!*

She placed her palm against the glass. The bus was almost
at their road. Maybe then this psychodrama would end. Outside
the dusty windows, made muddy by the flood of recent rain,
past the railroad, near a clearing of poplars, Chloe spied a fading
billboard of a giant rainbow, which two white-suited workmen
on ladders were papering over with an ad for the renovated
Mount Washington Resort in the White Mountains.

She had just enough time to glimpse the phrase on the soon
to be obscured poster before the bus lunged past it. "Johnny
Get Your Gun." This left her to contemplate, alas *not* in perfect
silence, the philosophical meaning behind a rainbow being
papered over.

Just before the bus stopped, she remembered where the sign
was from. It was an ad for the Lone Star Pawn and Gun Shop in

Fryeburg. Remembering it didn't answer Chloe's larger question, but it answered the immediate one.

"What idiot thought a rainbow was a good symbol for a gun store?" Hannah's mother had said. Soured on men and life, she had pawned her engagement ring there. Got seventy bucks for it. Took Chloe and Hannah for lobster in North Conway with the money.

They all got food poisoning afterward. So much for rainbows.

Is that what they called karma?

Or was it simply what happened next?

On the dot of 3:40 in the afternoon, the small blue bus pulled up—extra carefully and slowly—to the pine trees at the beginning of Wake Drive, a dirt road past another dirt road marked with a rock painted with a black whale. Four kids jumped off into the dust.

Because it was the merry month of May, and almost warm, they wore the clothes of the young out in the boonies—denim and plaid. Though to be fair, that's all they ever wore, blizzard or heatwave.

In what universe could a five-minute speech by Mrs. Mencken about the annual Acadia Award for Short Fiction at the end of English period right before lunch—when there wasn't a soul in class who was paying attention to anything but the rumble in their empty stomachs—result in Blake and Mason deciding they were suddenly writers and not trash collectors?

"Character is everything," Chloe said doggedly into the dirt. "Character *is* story."

The mile of unpaved road at the end of which they lived was all downhill between dense pines. It meandered through the thick forest, getting narrower, crossing the train tracks, hugging the small lake, ending in pine needles and disarray, not a road anymore, just dust, and that's where they lived. Where the road ended.

Chloe and Mason and Hannah and Blake. Two couples, two brothers, two best friends. A short girl, a tall girl, and two brawny dudes. Well, Blake was brawny. The scrappy Mason was all about sports the last few years, ever since their dad had his back broken. Mason was a soccer midfielder and a varsity shortstop. Blake got the lumbering body of a man who lived in a rural town and could do anything: lift anything, build anything, drive anything. Blake's wavy, bushy hair hadn't been cut in months, his beard was weeks overgrown. The brown Timberlands were grimy. The belt was six years old. The extra large plaid shirt was his dad's. The Levi's were hand-me-downs. His light brown eyes darted around, dancing, laughing, full of good humor.

Next to him, his smaller brother looked like a child of prissy aristocracy. Mason's hair was shaggy straight, but it was meant to be shaggy. It was designer shag. Unlike Blake, who rolled out of bed, hair slept on, and ran to school, Mason woke early and worked hard to make his hair just so. The girls loved his hair, and tortured Chloe about it. Oh Chloe, they chirped, you're so lucky, you can run your hands through it any time you want. Mason shaved every day, and did not wear plaid. He wore black and gray T-shirts. He was monochrome and his jeans were washed yesterday. On his feet were sneakers. He didn't cut wood, he played ball. He didn't look like Blake's brother, with his compact lean build, intense blue eyes, and his serious, gentle face. Plus, unlike Blake, he was a boy of few words. When he quietly held Chloe's hand, it was always with kindness. He didn't pull on her, yank her, demand action from her. He was a gentleman. Not that Blake didn't *try* to be a gentleman with Hannah. Just that he was a lot like the German Shepherd he once owned. Panting, unapologetically getting mud on everyone's floors, dripping ice cream and tomato sauce all over, loping wild through the day. You couldn't help but feel exasperated affection at his constant antics.

And next to Blake walked Hannah.

Though Chloe herself found Hannah to be slightly androgynous with her tall, boyish body—straight hips, straight waist, small high breasts, short hair always slicked back away from her face—other people, boys especially, did not agree. Her face was opalescent and scrubbed clean, with symmetrical, correct, in-balance features and a gaze as straight as her narrow hips. Her eyes, brown and unblinking, were serious and appraising, making Hannah look as though she were engaged—as though she were listening. Chloe knew it was a ruse: the steady stare allowed Hannah to be lost inside her head. She wore makeup she could ill afford, but strived to look as though she just splashed water on her face and, voila, perfection. With fluid grace Hannah strolled like a ballerina.

At the long mirror in her room she had practiced her arabesques and soubresauts, hoping one day she would stop growing and her parents could afford ballet classes. She finally got her lessons in the divorce settlement, but by then she was five-ten and too tall to be lifted into the air by anyone but Blake, who was definitely not a ballet dancer.

With a detached elegance, Hannah walked and talked as if she didn't belong in tiny Fryeburg, Maine. She fancied herself barely even belonging in this country. She wore ballet flats, for God's sake! Even when she schlepped a mile through the mud and pine needles. No butch Timberlands for her. Hannah walked with her shoulder blades flung back, as though wearing heels and a Chanel blazer. She carried herself as if she was too good for the place that by an unlucky accident of birth she had found herself living in, and couldn't *wait* until the moment she was sipping wine on the Left Bank and painting the Seine with other artistic, beautiful people. Her big round eyes were permanently moist. She evaluated you before she cried, and then you loved her. That was Hannah. Always crying to be loved.

Chloe in stark contrast was not moist of eye or long of limb. She didn't care much about not being tall when she wasn't with Hannah. But next to her reed-like friend, she felt like an armadillo.

One of Chloe's best physical features was her brown hair, straw-straight, shining, streaked with sunlight. There was nothing she did to make it great. It just was. Every day washed, brushed, clean, unfussy, thin-spun silk falling from her head. She wore no makeup, to differentiate herself from the senior girls who were all about the heavy eyeliner, the flimsy tanks, the one size too small jeans and three-inch (or higher!) mules in which they clodded through the Fryeburg Academy halls, always in danger of falling over or tripping, and perhaps that was the point. Sexy but helpless. Both things were anathema to Chloe, so she kept her body to herself and walked in sensible shoes. Where was she going that required getting dressed up? Bowling? Italian ices? Swimming in the lake? Gardening? Exactly. And she heard the way the boys talked about the girls who dressed the way, say, that hateful Mackenzie O'Shea dressed. A lifetime of meds wouldn't be able to erase the trauma for Chloe if she thought boys talked about her that way.

Her face, unblemished and fair, suffered slightly from this pretend plainness, but there was no hiding the upper curve of her cheekbones or her wide-set eyes that tilted slightly upward, always in a smile. She had inherited the Irish lips from her father, but the eyes and cheeks from her mother, and because of that, her face, just like her body, wasn't quite in proportion. The ratio of eyes to lips was not in balance, just as the ratio of body to breasts was not in balance. There was not enough body for the milk-fed breasts she had been cursed with. There may have been a genetic component to the comical chaos inside her—to her math abilities colliding with her existential confusion—but there was simply no cosmic excuse for her palmfuls of breasts.

Chloe blamed her mother.

It was only right.

She blamed her mother for everything.

Look at Hannah. Everything on that girl was assembled as if hand-picked. Tall, lithe, lean, eyes mouth hair nose all the right size, not too big, not too small, while Chloe spent her life hiding under minimizer bras and one-size-too-big shirts. She was afraid no one would take her seriously if they thought of her as a body instead of a person. Who'd ever listen to her explanations about the movements of the stars or migrations of mitochondria or beheadings in a revolution if they thought she was just a pair of boobs with legs. Too heavy-breasted to be a ballerina and too short to be a bombshell.

That Mason didn't agree—or said he didn't—only spoke to his poor judgment.

The bus had been dropping them off on the same rural road for thirteen years. Kindergarten, elementary school, middle school, fancy high school.

Soon there would be no more blue buses, no more lurching afternoon rides. In a month they would all be graduating.

And then?

Well, and then, there was this:

"Don't be hating on my story already, Chloe," said Blake. "It just began. Give it a chance. It's a good story. You'll see."

"Yeah, Chloe," echoed Mason. Being ten months younger than Blake, he looked up to his older brother, though he did not necessarily disagree with Chloe, as evidenced by his cheerful wink. She took his welcome hand as they strolled past old Mr. Leary out on the lawn, surrounded by every bit of garbage scrap he owned, trying to make it look less garbagey so he could sell it.

"Blake, dear boy," Mr. Leary called out, "you said you'd come by after school and help me with my block saw. I still can't get the dang thing to turn on."

"Sure thing, Mr. Leary."

"Block saw?" muttered Mason. "What does that codger need with a block saw? It's soft dirt all around him."

"He wants to build a bomb shelter," Blake said out of the corner of his mouth, smiling at the old man as they ambled by. "That's why he's collecting the cinder blocks."

"What's a block saw?" asked Chloe.

"Who cares," said Hannah. "A bomb shelter? Guy's a freak."

"Blake, not now?" The craggy man persisted. "I have some snacks for you and your friends. Donuts."

"Thank you, sir, but not now."

Because now Blake was busy. He had to clear the brush from the dusty path of his own winding life.

All the trouble began when Blake turned eighteen last July and was allowed to enter the Woodsmen Day competition at the Fryeburg Fair. He entered five contests. Tree felling, crosscut sawing, axe throwing, log rolling, and block chop. He lost the crosscut and the log roll and the block chop, and you'd think he'd remember that and be humbled—that he lost three out of five—but no. He beat the best time that year on tree felling by six seconds, coming in at twenty-three seconds flat, and he set a Fair record on the axe throw with six bullseyes in a row.

You'd think his head was the bullseye: it swelled to four feet in diameter. He strutted down the dirt roads and through Academy halls like an Olympic gold medalist. Chloe would remind him that the Fryeburg Academy—which all the local kids attended for "free" through a tax deal between the school and the state of Maine—was one of the most prestigious preparatory high schools in the United States. "No one here gives a toss about your axe toss, I promise you," Chloe would say to him, but you'd think he were deaf.

It was right after that Blake and Mason entered the business competition for Mr. Smith's tech class—and they won! Mason was used to winning, with his dozen sports trophies lining the dresser, but Blake became impossible. He acted as if he could do anything. Like, for example, write.

It wasn't that they didn't deserve to win. The project was: "Create a successful business." Who knew that Blake and Mason would take the thing they had been doing part-time and turn it into a winner. With their dad's ancient truck, they had been going to houses around the lakes in Brownfield and Fryeburg and asking if, for a small fee, the residents would let them cart their trash away. Now, most people in this part of Maine aimed their shotguns to point the brothers in the direction of the exit to their property, but there were some—widows, the feeble-minded—who agreed to pay them a few nickels to cart away their old refrigerators, non-working snow blowers, rusty rakes, newspapers, chainsaws. The boys were strong and worked hard, and after school and on Saturdays, they would drive around and try not to get killed while they made a few dollars. After placing an ad in the *Penny Saver*, they discovered there was already a national junk company called 1-800-GOT-JUNK. This only fired up their cutthroat spirit. They flattered Hannah into designing their logo: THE HAUL BROTHERS HAULING SERVICES. "WE HAUL SO YOU DON'T HAVE TO."

It looked pretty good. They got a decal made, slapped it on their father's truck, painted the truck a hideous lime green—Blake said because it was the color farthest removed from the color of the crap they were hauling—used their rudimentary buttering-up skills to get Chloe to create a profit and loss statement, and figured out that if they worked full-time, hired two more guys, and bought another truck with a lift, they would make six figures at the end of three years. Six figures! They had an advertising plan: Yellow Pages, the *North Conway Observer*, local ads on TV, three radio spots—and then their dad's Chevy died.

It was over twenty years old. Burt Haul had bought the V8 diesel powerhouse in 1982, before he knew he'd be having sons who a generation later would need it to start a fake business. Burt loved that truck so much that even after the accident that nearly ended his life, he refused to let it go and spent his own scarce money rebuilding it. "I drove your mother home from our wedding in that truck," Burt told his sons. "The only reason I'm alive today is because of that truck. I ain't parting with that thing."

But now the truck engine was like Mr. Leary's gas-powered block saw. Defunct.

No one had money for a new truck, even a used one. Burt and his boys were being shamefully carted around in Janice Haul's Subaru. Were they even men?

Hannah and Chloe tried to console their disappointed boyfriends by reminding them that their business wasn't *really* a business, it was just a business on paper, which is no kind of business at all. But Blake and Mason had fallen too far into the trap of a dream. Chloe knew something about that. The Haul boys had been so sold on their own pseudo-company that they decided to drop out of school in the middle of senior year and work until they got the money together to buy a truck, figuring that in their line of work a high school diploma was about as useful as watering grass during a downpour.

It was a challenge for the girls to keep their boyfriends in school. It was Chloe who had finally hit on the winning combination of words: "Do you think my mother and father would ever allow me to hang out with high school dropouts?"

That worked, though not as instantly as Chloe had hoped, alas.

So ... the senior year passed, truck still broke, and Janice not only had to drive to work and shop for the family, but share her inadequate station wagon with two restless boys with divergent friends, interests and schedules. To make money, the boys shoveled snow, cut grass, did shopping for the infirm, Blake mostly, because Mason was at varsity. Fast forward to today when they were hopping off buses and yammering on about dreams. You had to hand it to them. Those two were single-minded in their pursuits. *All* their pursuits.

"Chloe, speak up. Listen to what I'm saying. Why isn't it a good story?" Blake always got irked by her tight-lipped approach to his shenanigans.

"Because so far you haven't told me anything I'd want to read," she said.

"I haven't stopped speaking!"

Chloe opened her hands in a *my-point-precisely*. "Who are the main characters?"

"It doesn't matter who they are. Can I finish before you judge?"

"You mean you *haven't* finished? And I'm not judging."

"You so judge. That's your biggest problem."

"I'm not—"

Blake put his finger out, nearly to her mouth. "The premise of my story is—are you listening? Two dudes run a junkyard."

"That part I got."

"They do say write about what you know."

"I. Got. That. Part."

"Two dudes run a junkyard and one day they find something awful."

"Like what? All you cart away is Wise potato chips and Oreo wrappers."

"And condom wrappers." Blake grinned, slowed down, and threw his big arm around Chloe's shoulder.

"Hannah, control your boyfriend." Chloe pushed him away. "But okay, even still. Where is the story?"

"Can there be anything more full of story possibilities than a ninety-year-old woman throwing out a Hefty bag full of used condoms?" Blake laughed.

"Not used condoms," Mason corrected him. "Condom wrappers."

Chloe glanced at the silent Hannah for support. "Can we move on? What else have you got?"

"We don't know yet," Mason said. "Hannah, you think it's good so far, don't you?"

"So far there's nothing!" That was Chloe.

"He wasn't asking you!" said Blake.

They had ten minutes before they reached home to hammer it out. It wasn't enough time. Blake pulled them off road, away from home and onto the train tracks that ran through the woods and divided their small part of the lake from the better, larger part. Arms out, backpacks on, they balanced on the rusty tracks and skipped on the ties.

Writing a story for money! What a thing. Acadia's first prize was ten thousand dollars. Chloe knew the Flannery O'Connor Award for Short Fiction had been around longer and was certainly more prestigious, but it paid only a thousand dollars, and you had to write at least forty thousand words for it. No matter how bad one was at math, dividing forty thousand words into a thousand bucks was an awful return. "All work and no pay," said Mason, and laughed for five minutes at his own joke.

But here—ten thousand dollars for a novella. Blake didn't even know what a novella was until Chloe told him. To the brothers, a sum that large was the lottery. It was a new truck and the start of their own business. It was the rest of their lives. They acted as if they found it lying under a tree in a suitcase. All that was left to do was count the money.

And little naysay-y Chloe was not allowed to even *mention* that:

1. They had no story.
2. They were not writers.
3. There would be at least five hundred other applicants, who a. might have a story and b. were writers.
4. One of those applicants might be Hannah who most certainly had stories, a number of them.
5. A new truck was more than ten thousand dollars.

Chloe couldn't help herself. She had to say something. If only she could learn to keep quiet, like Hannah, or Mason, things would be so much better in her life.

"Who are the junkyard boys?" she asked.

"We are. Blake. Mason. We're ambling along, asking for no trouble, and suddenly—wham! Trouble comes."

"Wham," said Chloe.

"Blake's right," Mason said. "We've found some awful things."

"Like what?"

"Dead rats."

"Rats are good," she said. "But then what? Someone not wanting dead rats in their house is hardly a story. It's more like a truism."

"We found some jewelry too once."

"Jewelry is good. Then what?"

"Okay, maybe not jewelry, then. Something else."

Chloe glanced at Hannah, walking on the side of the tracks, away from the three of them, barely listening. Blake jackhammered away at Chloe's concrete skepticism. "They discover something awful. Something that changes everything. Mason, what can they find that is so monumental and terrible that it changes everything?"

"True love?" Chloe smiled.

"It's not that kind of story, my dear Haiku," Blake said with twinkling amusement. "This is a man's story. No room in it for lurv, no matter how terrible and true. Right, cupcake?" Jumping off the rail, he jostled Hannah along the pebbles.

"Right," she said.

Mason had new suggestions. "We found an old suitcase once. It was full of snakes. And once we found a live rabbit."

"Yes," Blake said. "He was delicious. But Chloe is right. We need a story, bro." He smacked his forehead. "Got it. How about a human head in the trash?"

Chloe didn't even blink this time. Almost as if she'd seen a human head in the trash before. "Nice," she said. "And then?"

Blake shrugged. "Why do you care so much what happens next?" he asked.

She could tell he wasn't taking it seriously. What the boys did for a living—that was work. Here, all they had to do was come up with a few words and place them in the sweet order that assured victory. Blake was convinced it was child's play.

"You're right, we're all Philistines with our slavish devotion to plot," Chloe said. "Be that as it may."

"Yes. The writer drones on about what happens next and as soon as you the reader guess what's coming, you either fall asleep or want to kill him."

"So the trick is what? Never give the reader what she wants?"

Blake shook his head. "No. Give her what she didn't even know she wanted." He acted as if he knew what that was.

They turned for home. "They find a human head," he went on, as he and Chloe ambled down the narrowing pine path leading home, Hannah and Mason behind them. A few hundred yards downhill, the dirt road tapered to one lane on which a truck or a car or people could pass—one at a time. "But not a skull." Blake glanced back and widened his eyes at Hannah. "A *head*. That's been recently separated from the body. It still has *flesh* on it. And they don't know what to do. Do they investigate? Do they call the cops?"

"I think they should investigate," Mason said, running up. "Investigations are fun."

"There's danger in it."

"Danger is good," Hannah said from behind. "Danger is story."

No, Chloe wanted to correct her uncorrectable friend. Danger is danger. It's not story.

Blake went on ruminating. "What if asking too many questions of the wrong people puts them in mortal danger?"

Chloe wondered if there was any other kind.

"Someone needs to shut them up. But who?"

"Obviously those who separated the head from the body."

"But why would someone separate the head from the body?" Mason asked.

"I don't know yet. But I really think we got us something here. Haiku, what do you think?"

"I say keep working on it." Chloe used her most discouraging tone.

"Wait! I got it!" Blake exclaimed. "What if they find a suitcase? Yes, a mysterious suitcase! It's blue. Oh my God, I got it. That's my story." Blake stopped and turned to the girls, beaming, his whole face flushed and thrilled. "*The Blue Suitcase*. What do you think?" He clapped. "It's flipping awesome!"

Hannah smiled approvingly.

Chloe caught herself shrugging. "It's a good title for a mystery," she said. "But a title is not a story. What's in the suitcase? Once you figure out that part, Blake, *then* you'll have yourself a story."

Blake laughed with characteristic lack of concern for details. He was a big picture guy. "James Bond always goes to a foreign country to solve mysteries and catch the bad guys," he said. "Some fantastic exotic locale full of drink and women and danger."

Chloe made a real effort not to rub her forehead. She had a lot of practice hiding exasperation from her mother, but this was on a different scale altogether. "James Bond is a government spy. He kills for money. He doesn't rummage through the trash for severed heads."

"Foreign country!" Mason exclaimed. "Blake, you're a genius."

Blake's entire peacock tail opened up in kaleidoscope green.

"But wait," Mason said. "You and I have never been to a foreign country."

Blake blocked the girls' way, smiling meaningfully at them. "Not yet," he said.

The girls remained impassive. Only Chloe twitched slightly. Oh no! she thought. He doesn't mean …

"We'll go to Europe with you," Blake said. "Mason's right, I *am* a genius. The answer to our mysterious suitcase is in Europe. Oh man, this is going to be fantastic. And we've only been at it for five minutes. Imagine how good it'll be when we spend a few days on it." Blake thumped his flannel plaid chest. "We could win the book prize."

"What book prize would that be, Blake?" Chloe said.

"I don't know, Chloe. The prize they give the best book of the year. The Oscar for books. The Grammy, the Emmy."

"The Pulitzer?"

"Whatever. That's not the important part. To write something people will love, *that's* the important part."

Chloe leaned in to Hannah. "Did your crazy boyfriend just say he wants to go to Europe with us?"

"I'm sure that can't be right," Hannah, her expression frazzled, whispered back. "I'll talk to him—"

Blake pulled Hannah away from Chloe. "Hannah, when are you two flying to Barcelona?"

"I don't know," Hannah replied. "Chloe, when are we flying?"

"I don't know," mumbled Chloe.

"Mason, that's where we go, bro. Barcelona! Our story will climax there." Blake laughed. The brothers high-fived and bumped shoulders.

"I thought you said it wasn't *that* kind of story," Chloe cut in.

"If it ends in Barcelona, Haiku, it'll have to be a story for all seasons. Isn't that where they have the running of the bulls?"

"Oh dear God. No. That's Pamplona."

"Wait," Hannah said. "Blake, you're not *seriously* thinking of coming with us?"

"We're done thinking. We're coming, baby!"

Mason looked shocked. "We're going to Europe? You're bullshitting me."

"Mason, do I come up with the best ideas or what?"

Mason was at a loss for words.

"Blake ..." Finally Hannah became actively engaged in the conversation. "Think about it for a minute. You're not serious about writing a story, are you? The contest is open to all Maine residents. That's a lot of competition. Just from our school, there'll probably be at least a hundred entries. Everyone on our literary magazine is submitting a story."

"Hannah, have you *read* the literary magazine?" said Blake, swinging his arms around, bouncing down the road. "It's called *Insanity's Horse*, for heaven's sake." He laughed. "Just for that title alone, those fools should be disqualified from participating. Do you remember the magazine's April thought of the month? *The pastiche of the pyramids implementing primal passion is a prolix representation of all phallic prose.* I got your phallic prose right here. Yeah," he said, merry and intense. "I'm not worried."

How did this happen? One minute ticked by, and before it was up, Blake and Mason had climbed aboard the girls' slow-chugging teenage dream.

Hannah stopped listening. She pulled on Chloe to slow down. "Now I *really* have to talk to you," she said. "Come by before dinner?"

"Is it about Barcelona?" Chloe looked up into Hannah's flat expression.

Hannah blinked. "No and yes. Do you have your passport yet?"

Chloe didn't reply.

"Chloe! I told you—it takes two months to get a passport. Come on. Do you want to blow it?"

"Of course not. But that's easy for you to say—you're eighteen. I have to ask my parents to sign for my passport."

"So?"

"Well, I'll have to tell them I'm going first, won't I?"

"I can't believe you haven't told them!"

"Yeah, well." Chloe couldn't believe a whole bunch of things.

Blake was in front of them, panting, eyes blazing, his body heaving. "So what do we have to do to get a passport?"

"Go to the post office," Hannah said. "But take Chloe with you, because she doesn't know how to get one either."

"I know how. I just …"

Hannah batted her lashes. "Are you guys really going to come with us? Because don't get our hopes up and then not come. That'd be mean."

"I never disappoint you, pumpkin, do I?" Grabbing the slender Hannah, Blake pretended to dance with her and stepped on her feet. She yelped.

"Blake, you do know where Barcelona is, right?" Hannah said, her arms around his neck. "In Spain. And you know where Spain is, right? In Europe. As in—on another continent. As in, you need not just a passport, which costs upward of a hundred bucks, but also a plane ticket, and train tickets, and maybe, oh, I don't know—some lodging and food money."

Mason began to look doubtful, but Blake shrugged with gleeful indifference. "You know what they say, babycakes." He squeezed her. "You gotta spend money to make money. It's like the ten grand I'm getting for my story. We can't start our own business till we win this thing. And we can't win this thing till we do this other thing."

"This other thing," said Chloe, "meaning horn in on my lifelong dream?"

"Exactly. Mase, let's jet. We gotta go get ourselves some passports. We have no time to lose." As they sped up, their boots kicked up dust in a bee cloud. "Where's this post office, anyway?" Blake called back.

"Are you joking? You've never been to the Fryeburg post office?"

Hannah poked Chloe. "You've never been there either, missy."

Chloe poked Hannah back. "Yes, I have, stop it."

Blake pulled on his brother. "Let's hoof, bro. Should we pick you up, Chloe?" The Hauls lived three houses up from Chloe, around the pond through the scraggly pines and birches.

"Yeah, Chloe," Hannah said, sticking a finger into Chloe's back. "Should they pick you up to go get your passport?"

"It's okay," said Chloe, swatting Hannah's fingers away. "I'll have my mom take me."

The girls gazed after their young men, and then resumed walking. Hannah shook her head—in distress? In wonderment? Chloe couldn't tell. "I guess I'll be going to Spain with my boyfriend and your boyfriend, but not with you."

"Har-de-har-har."

"You think I'm being funny? You can't start your adult life being such a chicken, Chloe. What are you afraid of? Be more like me. I'm not afraid of anything." She said it as if she didn't mean it.

But all Chloe heard was *be more like me*. Ain't that a kick in the teeth, she thought, stiffening. They were almost at the clearing in front of Chloe's green bungalow. Hannah slowed down, as if she wanted to linger, but Chloe sped up as if that was the last thing she wanted. "I have to be diplomatic," she said. "I need their permission to go. I can't just present them with an I'm-going-to-Europe vaudeville routine."

"If you don't start acting like an adult, why should they treat you like one?"

How much did Chloe *not* want to talk about it. It wasn't that Hannah was wrong. It was that Hannah always said obvious things in such a way that made Chloe not only think her friend was wrong, but that she wanted her friend to be wrong.

"I'll talk to them tonight," she said, hurrying across her pine needle clearing.

"I wouldn't tell them about Mason and Blake just yet."

"Ya think?"

Since Mrs. Haul and Lang went shopping on Fridays, Chloe had a feeling that her silence on the subject might be short-lived.

"Okay," Hannah said, "but start slow. Don't make your mother go all Chinese on you. You always make her nuts. First dangle our trip, then wait. The boys might be pie in the sky anyway. Where are they going to get the money from? It'll pass, you'll see."

Chloe said nothing. Clearly Hannah had no idea who her boyfriend was. There was no talking Blake out of *anything*. Short fiction indeed! And as if to prove Chloe's point, Janice Haul's Subaru came charging toward them from around the trees, Blake rolling down his window, slowing down, honking.

"We're off to get our passports!" he yelled. "See ya!"

Chloe turned to Hannah. "You were saying?"

"All right, fine. But don't tell your mom about them yet."

"What did you want to talk to me about?" Chloe asked. Only a flimsy screen door separated Chloe's mother's ears from Hannah's troubles.

Hannah waved her off. "Just you wait," she said, all doom and gloom.

2

Sweet Potato

"I'M IN THE KITCHEN," HER MOTHER CALLED OUT AS SOON as Chloe opened the screen door. A statement of delightful irony since they lived in a winterized cabin that was one room entire, if one didn't count, which Chloe didn't, the bathroom, the two small bedrooms and the open attic lost where Chloe slept.

I'm in the kitchen, Lang said, because this month she was baking. Last winter, her mother was scrapbooking so every day, when Chloe came home, she would hear: *I'm in the dining room*.

The previous fall, her mother decided to become a seamstress and told Chloe that from now on she was sewing all of her daughter's clothes, *in the craft room*.

When she was tracing out the family tree on her new Christmas-present software, Lang was *in the computer room*.

During the summers, Lang said nothing, because she was outside, fishing and tending her vegetable garden, voluminous enough to supply tomatoes to all eight homes around their part of the lake. Bushels of zucchini and cucumbers went with Chloe's dad to work.

Chloe's mother Lang Devine, née Lang Thia of Chinese descent from Red River, North Dakota, reinvented herself constantly into something new. She had wanted to be a dancer when she was young, but then she met Jimmy and wanted to be a wife. After many years as a wife, she wanted to be a mother. And after many years as a mother of one, she wanted to be a mother of two.

Jimmy's favorite, he said, was when Lang took up tap dancing. He built her a wooden platform; she bought herself a pair of black Capezios size 5, some CDs and taught herself how to tap dance. That was noisy.

And not as delicious as baking, which was the current phase, and Chloe's favorite after gardening. Jimmy Devine liked it, too, but groused that he was gaining two pounds a week because of Lang's buttery hobby. Chloe thought her dad might teasingly mention the extra pounds Lang herself had put on around her five-foot frame, now that she wasn't tap dancing. But no. Just last week, Jimmy said as he dug into Lang's cream puffs (made with half-and-half, not milk, by the way), "Sweet potato, how do you bake so much and yet stay so thin?"

And Chloe's mother had tittered!

How to explain to both her parents that it was unseemly for a grown woman of advancing years, married for nearly thirty, to titter when her husband paid her a half-hearted compliment by calling her the name of a red starchy root vegetable?

This afternoon Chloe walked in slowly, set down her school bag, pulled off her boots, and walked down the short corridor, past her parents' bedroom, past the bedroom that no one ever went into anymore, past the bathroom, into the open area to put her lunchbox on the kitchen counter where it would be cleaned and prepped for tomorrow. Something smelled heavenly. Chloe didn't want to admit it, because she didn't want to encourage her mother in any way. What her mother needed was a tamping down of enthusiasm, not a fanning of the fire. Her mother and Blake shared that in common.

"Doesn't that smell divine?" Lang giggled, turned around, and with floury hands, patted Chloe on both cheeks. "I only make divine things for my divine girl." One of the few things

Chloe tolerated about her mother was that she was short, making even Chloe seem tall by comparison.

Chloe brushed the white powder off her face. "Whatchya makin'?"

"Linzer tarts."

"Doesn't smell like Linzer tarts." Chloe glanced inside one of the pots on the stove.

"Raspberry jam. I made it from scratch this afternoon for the tarts. It's still warm. You want to try?"

Chloe did want to try, so much. "No, thank you," she said. "I'm full."

"Full from lunch four hours ago?"

Lang got out some orange juice, a yoghurt, unboxed some Wheat Thins, opened some cheddar cheese, washed a bowl of blueberries, and set it all in front of Chloe sitting glumly at the table. She brought the long wooden spoon half-filled with warm jam to Chloe's face. Chloe tasted it. She had to admit it was *so* good. But she only admitted it to herself. She wouldn't admit it to her overeager mother. "What's for dinner?"

"I'm thinking ratatouille."

"What?"

"You'll see. It's a vegetable stew, I think. But it could be a condiment." She chuckled. Honestly, why did Chloe have to be the only serious one in her house?

"Dad needs meat."

"Yes, don't worry, we'll feed the carnivore some pork chops. I found a spicy new recipe. With cumin. How was school?"

Chloe desperately needed to talk to her mother. She didn't know where to start. That she didn't know *how* to start was more vital. She tried not to be irritated today by her mother's earnest round face, unmade-up and open, high cheekbones, red mouth, smiling slanting eyes, affectionate gaze, her short black hair straw straight like Chloe's. Tell me everything, her mother's welcome expression said. We will deal with everything together. Chloe tried hard not to sigh, not to look away, not to wish however fleetingly for Hannah's mother, the thin, pinched, absent-minded and largely absent Terri Gramm. "School's good," she said.

That's it. School's good. Nothing else. Open book, look down into food, drink the OJ, don't look up, don't speak. Soon enough, the hobby called. Jam would have to be cooled, the Linzer tarted, the ratatouille stewed.

Trouble was, today Chloe *needed* to talk to her mother. Or at least begin to try to talk to her. She needed a passport. Otherwise all her little dreams were just vapor. She had kept her dreams deliberately small, thinking they might be easier to realize, but now feared she hadn't kept them small enough.

"Are you going to write a story too?" her mother said. "You should. Mrs. Mencken told me about the Acadia prize. Ten thousand dollars is *amazing*. I bet Hannah is going to write one. She fancies herself to be good at anything. You will too, of course. Right?"

Now who wouldn't be exasperated? What kind of a mother knew about things that happened *that* day in fourth period English, before her child even had a chance to open her mouth? Chloe managed to contain her agitation. After all, her mother had unwittingly offered her the opening she needed.

"You discussed it with Hannah and your boys?"

"Not necessarily," Chloe replied. Disgusted is what she was. "Why would you say that?"

"Because you took nearly forty-five minutes to walk home from the bus. It usually takes you fifteen. What else are you doing if not discussing the Acadia Award for Short Fiction?"

Again, easy to suppress a giant sigh? Chloe didn't think so. She sighed giantly. "I'm not going to do it, Mom. I've got nothing to say. What am I going to write about?"

Lang stared at Chloe calmly. For a moment the mother and daughter didn't speak, and in the silence the ominous shadows of hollowed-out fangs essential for a story were abundantly obvious.

"I mean," Chloe hurriedly continued, "perhaps I could write about Kilkenny. But I can't, can I? Because I didn't go. Maybe you can write that story. I don't think there's an age limit on entrants."

When Chloe was eleven, her parents had gone to Ireland without her. They said it was for a funeral. Pfft. Their trip formed the foundation of much, if not all, of the resentment of Chloe's teenage years. A blown-up photo in a heavy gold leaf frame of the Castlecomer glens hung prominently *in the hallway*.

Lang continued to stare calmly at Chloe.

"You don't need Kilkenny to write a story," Lang said. "There are other things. Or, you make it up. That's why they call it fiction."

"Make it up from what? I'm going to make up a story about something so dramatic that it will win first prize?"

"Why not? Blake is."

How did her mom know this!

"I've seen nothing. But Blake has seen rats and—" She stopped herself from saying *used condoms*.

"You have an imagination, don't you?"

"No, none. I need a story, Mom. Not musings about what it's like to live on a puddle lake in Maine."

"Puddle lake? Have you glimpsed the stunning beauty outside your own windows?"

In the afternoons, the glistening lake, blooming willows and birches trimming the shoreline, the railroad rising on the embankment did occasionally shine with the scarlet colors of life. That wasn't the point.

"I can't write about skiing or bowling, or learning to drive," Chloe continued. "I need something substantial. And I have nothing." Why couldn't she talk about herself without allowing a whiff of self-pity to waft through her smallest words? The one ashen tragedy in their life she could never write about. And Lang knew that. So why push it? Besides, her mother had once informed her that the Devine women were too short to be tragic figures. "We can be stoics, but not tragics," Lang had said a few years ago, when it seemed to everyone else that the very opposite was the only thing true. "Make it up, darling," Lang repeated, unperturbed by her daughter's tone. "You're a very good writer."

"Mom, I don't want to be a writer."

"Neither does Blake. Yet look at him."

Chloe watched her mother walk to the printer *in the computer room* behind the sofa and peel off several sheets of paper. Lang slapped the rules of entry for the Acadia contest on the table.

"You have five months to come up with a story and write it. It must be original. It must be fiction. And after it wins, it will be published by the University of Maine Press. Properly published! In book form and everything. That's very exciting, isn't it?"

"Did you not hear me?"

"No. By the way, I got you the pens you wanted." Lang produced three packages of blue pens, gel, ballpoint, and fountain, and laid them in front of Chloe.

"I also took the liberty of getting you a notebook. Several different kinds to choose from. I thought you might need one if you're going to write a story that's going to win first prize. The Moleskine is very good. Has soft paper. But you try them all."

Chloe stared at the pens, at the four notebooks. Had she actually mentioned that she needed a pen? One blue pen!

"Mom, listen to me."

Lang sat down, elbows on the table, staring at Chloe with complete attention. She looked so pleased to be told to do what she had already been doing.

"I want to write something, I do. I just don't think I have ... look, here's what we were thinking."

"Who's we?"

"The four of us."

"The four of you were thinking all at once?"

"Well, discussing."

"That's better. It's always good to be precise if you're thinking of becoming a writer."

"Which I'm not, so."

"What are you four up to now? Let's hear it."

"We're thinking of going to Europe."

Lang stayed neutral. She didn't blanch, she barely blinked. No, she did blink. Slowly, steadily, as if she was about to say …

"Are you *crazy*?"

There it was. "First listen, then judge. Can you do that?"

"No."

"Mom. You just said you wanted me to write."

"You have to go to Europe to write? Did Flannery O'Connor go to Europe? Did Eudora Welty? Did Truman Capote?"

"Actually, he did, yes."

"When he wrote *Other Voices, Other Rooms*, his first novel, he'd been to Europe?"

"I don't know. We're getting off topic, Mom."

"*Au contraire.* We are very much *on* topic."

"Mason and Blake need to do research."

"So they're going to *Europe*?"

Chloe made a real effort not to facepalm, a real, true, Herculean, McDonald's supersize-sandwich effort not to facepalm, because there were few things her mother hated more than this brazen gesture of exasperation and frustration.

"Hannah and I have been talking about the trip for a while."

"I thought you just said you wanted to go for Blake and Mason? Make up your mind, child. Either you thought of it on the railroad tracks, or you've been planning it for years."

"How do you know we were on the tracks?"

"I saw you." Lang pointed out the window. "Right across the lake."

Both things were true. Chloe and Hannah *had* been dreaming of going for years, but Blake and Mason just thought of it today. Lang sat and watched her daughter like a bird watching the world. One never knew what the Langbird was thinking until she sang.

"Isn't going away to college enough for you?" Lang said quietly.

Chloe clasped her hands. She didn't want to look into her mother's face. She knew how hard it must have been for her parents to let her go away to school. "I've been dreaming of Europe since I was little," she said, almost whispered. "Way before college."

"Sometimes circumstances change, and we have to dream a different dream," said Lang. There was only a breath after that, and no change in expression to reflect the colossal wreck from which life had had to be recomposed, rebuilt from the ashes, Capezio shoe by Linzer tart. "College away is a big step, not to mention an enormous expense, even with the scholarship they're giving you."

"I know, Mom. Exactly. And then work and study and more work and study, and when else could I ever do it?"

"Oh, I don't know, let's see, how about—four years from now? Or never. Either way is good with me."

"That's what I want for my graduation present," Chloe declared boldly. "A trip to Europe. You went to Europe."

"It was for a funeral!"

"So what."

"Graduation present. Really. I thought you wanted a laptop."

"I'll use our old one. I'll take the desktop."

"You certainly will not. All my family-tree files are on it."

"I thought you were baking now? Oh, and yes, the files are permanently embedded in that one desktop computer. You're right. They can never be moved."

"Do you know what happens after you make a choice to be sarcastic to the woman who gave you life?"

Chloe softened her tone. She knew that talking to her parents about anything was a fifteen-part process that would begin with an idea being promptly rejected and then followed up by a string of days during which her mother enumerated in Tolstoyan prose why whatever it was Chloe wanted was the *worst* idea. After a *War and Peace*-length volume on why they couldn't get a dog, or a tattoo, or a third earring, or go to Europe, the real decision would be handed down. She didn't get a tattoo. Or a dog. Or a third earring. What was happening here was just preface. The real meat of her mother's argument was still to come.

But this time Chloe wanted a different resolution. This time she wanted her way, not Lang's way. "Mom, what's the big deal? I'll be eighteen when we go." *When*, not if. What a clever play on words! What a clever girl.

"Yes, because that solves all the problems. And don't use the word *when* with me, young lady."

Ahh! "What problems? There are no problems. We want to go to Europe for a few weeks. We'll walk around, visit beautiful churches, eat delicious food, go to the beach, experience things we've never experienced before—"

"That's what I'm afraid of."

"And then come home," Chloe continued, "and Blake will write a beautiful story that will win first prize."

"The boy has many skills. Do you think writing is one of them?"

"He thinks he does and that's all that matters." Chloe was defiant, but she didn't have the answers. To her friends, she was usually the person her mother was being to her right now. The devil's advocate, the sucker of joy. There were a thousand reasons why everything Blake and Mason wanted to do was a terrible idea. Oh God. Had Chloe already turned into her mother at seventeen? Facepalm!

"And by the way," Lang said, "Europe is a big place. It's not Rhode Island. Or Acadia National Park. Where in Europe were you four thinking of visiting? You mentioned church and beach. That could be anywhere."

"Barcelona."

Her mother groaned. "Barcelona. Really. *That's* your idea. Of all the places, *that's* where you want to go?"

"We've never been to Spain. And it's on the water."

"So is Maine. And you've never been to Belgium either."

"Who wants to go to Belgium? What kind of story can one possibly write about Belgium? Or Maine?"

Lang shook her head. "There is so much you don't know."

"That's why I want to go to Europe. So I can find out."

"You're going to learn about life lying on a filthy beach? Okay, riddle me this," Lang said. "Where do you plan to sleep?"

"What do you mean?"

"Am I not being clear? You're planning to go with your boyfriend, your best friend and her boyfriend. Where are the four of you going to sleep in this Barcelona?"

Chloe tried not to stammer. "We haven't thought about it."

"Haven't you." It was not a question.

"Probably a youth hostel or somewhere like that."

"So in a dorm with fifty strangers all using the same bathroom facilities, if there are any?"

"We don't care about that. We are young, Mom. We're not like you. We don't care about creature comforts. Where we sleep. What we eat. What we wear. It's all fine. So it's not the Four Seasons. So what? We'll be in Europe. We'll buy a student Eurail pass for a few hundred bucks, sleep on trains if we have to, to save money."

"Why would you need to do that?" Lang's already narrow dark eyes narrowed and darkened further. "You just said you were going to Barcelona. Why would you need to sleep on trains?"

"In case we wanted to see Madrid. Or maybe Paris." That was Hannah's idea. Hannah, the Toulouse-Lautrec artiste.

"Paris."

"Yes, Paris. Isn't France next to Spain?"

Her mother folded her hands together. "Chloe, I tell you what. Go away and think carefully about all the questions I'm going to ask you next time you sit down and say, Mom, I want to go to Barcelona. Everything I'm going to ask you, ask yourself, find an answer, and come prepared."

"Like what?"

"Nope. That's not how it works. You figure out the solutions to the problems. Oh, and by the way, one of those problems is telling your father. Let's see how you surmount that."

Chloe became deflated. "I thought maybe you could tell him."

"That's likely."

"Don't be sarcastic, Mom."

"I'm not being sarcastic. I'm being snide. You know I'm actually going to tell him as soon as he walks in the door."

"Perhaps he'll be more reasonable than you," Chloe said. "Maybe Dad remembers what it's like to be young. Oh, wait, I forgot, you can't remember, because you were born old. Born knowing you'd have a kid someday whose dreams you'd spend your entire life harpooning."

"I'm harpooning your dream of going to Barcelona?" said Lang. "The dream I didn't know you had until five minutes ago?" She raised her hand before Chloe could protest, defend, explain, justify. "Where are you going to sleep, Chloe? Why don't you first work on giving your father the answer to *that* pesky question. Because it'll be the first thing he'll ask. Then worry about everything else."

Her parents didn't yell, they didn't punish. They were simply hyperaware of every single thing Chloe said and did. She got a new ribbon at the high school book fair? They knew. She once almost failed a biology test? They knew. She wore black eyeliner? Oh, they knew. She and Mason danced too close at one Friday night canteen? How they knew. They had no life except to live vicariously through hers. And the only thing that was expected of her, aside from not flunking out of school, was not to let down half a billion Chinese mothers by going to a Barcelona beach to have unfettered sex with her boyfriend.

"Going to Barcelona is also an education, Mom," Chloe muttered. She *really* didn't want to face her dad's questions. What was she supposed to say? We're going to get two rooms, and the girls will stay in one room, and the boys in the other? What kind of naïve fool for a parent would believe that?

"Yes, an education in boys," said Lang. "What are you going to tell us, that you'll get two rooms and you and Hannah will stay in one and the boys in the other?"

There you go. Didn't even have to say a word.

"Your plan," Lang continued, "is to rove around Europe for a month with your boyfriend on your hard-earned college savings. This is something you're seriously proposing to your father and me?"

Dad is not here, Chloe wanted to say. She didn't know of whom she was more afraid. Dad never really liked Mason, that gentle kid. She didn't know why. Everyone loved him. "We could go to Belgium, too, if you want."

"Are you weak in the head? Why would I want this?"

"You mentioned Belgium. I could bring you back some chocolates."

"Your father gets me a Whitman's Sampler every Valentine's Day. That's enough for me."

"Belgium is safe."

"Is Mason safe?"

"Hannah will be with me. She's nearly a year older. She'll protect me."

"Chloe," said her mother, "sometimes you say the funniest things. That girl couldn't protect a squirrel. She can't protect herself. I trust Mason more than I trust Hannah."

"See?"

"More, which is to say nothing. How much is two times zero? Still zero, child." She raised her hand before Chloe could come back with a wisecrack. "Enough. I have to slap these Linzers together and then get dinner on. Your father will be home soon. Go to the *music room* and practice."

"I'm going to be eighteen, Mom," Chloe repeated lamely.

"Yes, and I'm going to be forty-seven. And your father forty-nine. I'm glad we established how old we are. Now what?"

"I'm old enough to make my own choices," said Chloe, hoping her mother wouldn't laugh at her.

To Lang's credit, she didn't. "Can you choose right now to go play a musical instrument," she said. "Piano or violin. Pick one. Practice thirty minutes."

"Hannah wants to talk to me before dinner."

"Well, then, you'd better jump to it," said Lang, her back turned, an icing sugar shaker in her hands. "What Hannah wants, Hannah gets."

3

The Perils of College Interviews

CHLOE SPRINTED FROM HER HOUSE ACROSS THE FLOWERBEDS and brush to Hannah's next door.

Since the divorce five years ago, Hannah's mother had been involved with revolving boyfriends, and consequently their yard never got cleaned up. "Why can't she do it herself?" Lang would demand. Blake and Mason offered every month to help, but Terri didn't want to pay them to do it. And she didn't want them to do it for free because that was asking *men* for a favor. So she lived surrounded by unkempt backwoods, in wild contrast to Chloe's parents' approach to their house and their rural life. Lang allocated part of every day to weeding, mowing, cleaning, planting, raking, leafing, clearing, maintaining. The birches and pines were trimmed as if giraffes had gotten to them, and all the pine cones were swept up and placed in tall ornamental wicker baskets, and even the loose pebbles were picked up and arranged around the flowerbeds and bird houses and vegetable gardens. It was quite telling that Terri and Lang lived next door to each other for almost twenty years and yet didn't know each other's birthdays. Lang never said a thing, and kept Jimmy from saying anything, but Chloe could tell by her father's critical expression when he spoke of "that family" that he looked forward to the day Hannah might become a friend of the past. There are two kinds of people in the world, Jimmy Devine said. Those who try to make everything they come in contact with more beautiful—and then there is Terri Gramm.

Before Chloe knocked, she stopped by the dock and stared out onto the lake, the railroad across it, the bands of violet mackerel sky. She imagined a lover's kiss in the Mediterranean breeze, the mosaics of streets, parades down the boulevards, music, ancient stones, and evening meals. Beaches, heat, flamenco, bagpipes. Passion, life, noise. Everything that here was not. She imagined herself, fire, flowing dresses, abundant cleavage, no fear. Everything that here she was not. Her heart aching, she knocked on Hannah's porch door.

Hannah's mother was on the couch watching *Wheel of Fortune.*

"Hello, Mrs. Gramm."

"Hi, honey." Terri didn't turn her head to Chloe. "Are you staying for dinner?"

"No, my mom—"

"I'm joking. We got nothing anyway."

Hannah pulled Chloe into her bedroom and slammed the door.

"Did she say no?"

"Of course she said no."

"But was it no, we'll see, or was it no like never?"

"It was no like never."

"But then she started asking you all kinds of questions?"

"Yes."

"So it's yes. They never ask anything unless it'll be yes eventually. Give her a week to think about it. She has to talk to your dad."

"You think I'll have a better chance with him?"

"No. But he might give you money."

"For Barcelona?"

"We'll figure it out. We have bigger problems right now."

"Bigger than my mom saying no?"

"Yes." Hannah was biting her nails. Perfect Hannah with her perfect teeth was biting to the nubs her ugly nails at the end of her perfect long fingers. "How likely is it, do you think, that Blake and Mason are actually going to go?"

"A hundred percent." Chloe pulled her friend's twitchy hand out of her mouth. "Stop doing that. Don't you know what Blake is like?"

Hannah didn't reply. She was too busy bloodying the tips of her fingers.

Chloe plopped down on Hannah's lavender bed. The girl turned up her music which was already plenty loud. She did it so her mother couldn't hear her, but the result was that Chloe couldn't hear her either. Hannah had a barely audible soprano, like a low hum, and over the high treble strands of Metallica's "Nothing Else Matters" she was nearly impossible to make out.

She lay on her bed next to Chloe. "Chloe-bear, I'm in trouble."

"What?"

"I have to break up with him and I don't know how to do it."

"With Blake?" Chloe sat up. She was horrified.

"No, with Martyn."

"Who?"

"Stop it. Be serious."

Chloe stopped it. How to tell Hannah that she *was* serious? Who the heck was Martyn? She hoped her pitiable ignorance didn't show on her face. She scrunched it up knowingly, trussed her eyebrows, nodded. "Why, um, do you have to break up with him?"

"He was going to give me money to go to Barcelona, because he knows I don't have enough, but if Blake is going, he won't give me any money."

Chloe blindly navigated the maze before her, hands out in front. "So don't tell him Blake is going." Who the hell was Martyn?!

"Except … he was going to meet us in Barcelona for a few days."

Chloe weighed her words. "Martyn was going to meet us in Barcelona for a few days?" As if repetition would make Hannah's words make sense.

"I didn't want him to, Chloe, believe me, but I don't have enough money to go, and I thought, what's a couple of days, when we're going to be there two weeks, right?"

"Martyn was going to meet us in Barcelona."

"Don't be mad. I was going to tell you he was coming. I was just waiting for the right time. Please don't be mad." Hannah briefly leaned her head into Chloe's head, and then clapped her hands business-like. "No, that's it. I'm going to end it. It's for the best," she said. "He is getting too serious, anyway. We need to break up, not go on vacation."

"Martyn was going to meet us in Barcelona." Chloe couldn't get past this one point.

"He doesn't want me to go without him. He's afraid I'm going to meet someone, have a fling. He is intensely jealous."

"Martyn is jealous."

"Yes, so jealous."

"Um, does Martyn know you have a boyfriend? Maybe he can be jealous of him." Poor Blake.

"He's not worried about him."

"Well, you're not, why should he be? So this Martyn is afraid you'll have a fling in Europe with someone other than your boyfriend?" Chloe opened her hands. "What kind of girl does he think you are?"

"Can you *please, please* be serious? I know I need to break up with him. But then where do I get the money to go?" She wrung her hands, twisted her sore and bitten fingers. The usually unruffled Hannah looked ruffled.

Chloe was afraid to ask the follow-up question. There were so many questions, she couldn't sort out their order of priority. She was thinking of Barcelona. But she was also thinking about Blake. "Hannah, if you have someone else, why do you string Blake along? Why don't you break it off with him, and do what you want?"

"Don't talk nonsense, Chloe," Hannah said. "Did you not hear me just now when I said I was going to end it with Martyn?"

Chloe heard all right. "Do you even still want to go to Barcelona?"

"More than anything."

"With Blake?"

"I'd prefer to go with just you." Hannah pulled Chloe in for a hug. "Like we planned. Do you think we can talk Blake out of going?"

Chloe shrugged. "Perhaps you can dissuade him by telling him if he goes, then your secret lover won't give you any money for Europe."

In a humph Hannah turned her back to Chloe.

"I thought you had money," Chloe said quietly. "I thought we were both saving."

"We were. We are. But Chloe, I'm not you. I can't walk around in the same extra-large T-shirt. I need spring clothes, I need summer clothes."

"What do you want, a new skirt or Barcelona?"

"Both."

"You don't have money for both. Pick."

"Both!"

Hannah's back curved into a ball.

Chloe sighed, kneading her comforting palm between Hannah's shoulder blades. "Who's this Martyn anyway?"

"Don't joke."

"I mean"—Chloe cleared her throat—"how come *he* has money to burn?"

"He's a professor. He's got plenty of money."

Martyn, Martyn, Martyn. Chloe tried to remember the first names of their teachers at the Academy. In any case, Hannah said professor, not teacher. Jumping up, Hannah started to pace and talk, began to tell Chloe things she couldn't hear. It occurred to her that perhaps this was the reason she didn't know about

Martyn. Hannah told her, but Metallica was playing and through the strands of living life their way, Chloe had missed it.

Hannah grabbed Chloe's hands. "What am I going to do? It'll crush him."

"Do you *want* to break up with him?"

"I have to. He's become way too emotionally involved with me."

"What about Blake?"

"Will you forget Blake! I have a real problem and you bringing him up every five seconds is not helping me."

Chloe tried to regroup, find something else to say that sounded less hectory. "Um, how long has the Martyn thing been going on?"

"October."

"*Last* October?"

"Yes, since my college interview. Chloe, why are you being so obtuse? Is this deliberate? Is this your way of judging me? You're making it hard to talk to you."

Now Chloe remembered. She had driven Hannah to Bangor for her University of Maine admission interview. Chloe had been accepted without an interview so she waited outside while Hannah went in. Hannah walked out with a man, who shook her hand or, rather, took her hand and held it. Hannah introduced Chloe to a very tall, grandfatherly gentleman, soft spoken and modest in manner. Surely that wasn't Martyn?

Chloe thought no more about it, except in January when Hannah asked to be driven to Bangor again because the admissions office needed to go over a couple of things.

That couldn't be the man Hannah needed to break up with. Chloe had it wrong. It couldn't be him because he was …

"Hannah, I'm sorry, but how old is Martyn?"

Hannah studied the lilac bedspread as if the answer was written on her sheets like a cheat sheet. "Sixty-two," she said.

Chloe jumped off the bed.

"Sit down. What are *you* getting all riled up about?"

"Hannah!" Chloe couldn't sit. She could barely focus on Hannah's aggrieved face. "Please tell me you're not involved with a man forty years older than you. Please." Was Chloe the only one who thought this was gross?

"Okay," Hannah said. Metallica segued into Nirvana. Come as you are. As a friend. "Forty-four years," she corrected Chloe.

Come as you are.

Chloe didn't know why she should feel so affected by this. Hannah on the other hand was flushed, blinking rapidly, breathing through her mouth, as if she was catching the strands of the plot on her tongue and was about to jump on her computer and write a story for the ages. "He's very much in love with me," she said musically. "I didn't realize he would fall so deep. He's a widower and has been very lonely. At first he told me it was just for company. He knew we couldn't last. He's the one who told me it wouldn't last!"

"But you've only seen him the few times I've driven you to Bangor," Chloe said dumbly. "Right? I mean …"

"Don't be naïve. We've been meeting every Tuesday at the Silver Pines Motor Court. And some Saturdays. He finishes teaching early on Tuesdays."

Chloe's expression must have been a sight.

"That's why I didn't tell you," Hannah said. "I didn't want to be judged, and I was afraid you'd spill the beans to Mason, and then Blake would find out."

Where had Chloe been that she hadn't noticed Hannah's twice-weekly disappearance? What did Hannah tell Blake about her regularly scheduled absence from their already convoluted life? How could *he* not know? Chloe had been busy squirreling away her own secrets from Hannah, and perhaps was grateful for a few days a week when she didn't have to look away every time Hannah waxed about the University of Maine they would both be attending in the fall. But what was Blake's excuse?

Tonight Chloe had nothing to say about Hannah's dilemma. She remained stuck on the geezer's age. He was thirteen years older than her father! Yet Hannah seemed unconcerned with this most startling detail: that she was sleeping with Cain and Abel's uncle. Hannah sighed as if in a romance novel. "It's extremely flattering to be loved like that," she said. "So intensely. Oh Chloe! Do you know what it's like to be loved so intensely?"

"Oh, sure." Chloe stared into her hands as if they loved her intensely. "Quite a situation you've gotten yourself into, girlfriend," she said.

"Don't you think I know that?" For a moment, Hannah looked ready to cry. Yet Chloe knew that to be false, for Hannah didn't cry. She only appeared to look to be ready to cry.

"I gotta go," Chloe said, rising. "Hey, look on the bright side. My parents probably won't let me go anyway."

"How is that the bright side?" said Hannah. "We've been dreaming of Barcelona since we were eleven."

4

Paleo Flood at Red River

It was dark outside and her father's black Dodge Durango was parked in the open clearing by the time Chloe left Hannah's and made her way through the brambles between the two properties.

It was a warm evening. Through the open window she could hear her mother's soft voice and her father's booming one. Chloe slowed down. Treading quietly over the pine needles that crunched under her feet, she inched up to the screened-in window in the *living room*.

"It's out of the question."

"That's what I said."

"Why would she want to go *there*?"

"She says because she hasn't been."

"What kind of a reason is that?"

"She says because we went to Ireland without her."

"If I hear one more word about Ireland!"

"Shh. I know."

"I hope you were forceful, Mother. I hope you said no."

"I was forceful. I said no."

"But what?"

"But nothing."

"No, I can see by your face it's something. What?"

"She's insisting."

"So? We're going to allow the child to make the decisions?"

"She said something about turning eighteen."

"Oh, so she's going to play *that* card!"

"That's what I said."

"Why does she *really* want to go?"

"I don't know, Jimmy."

"What's in Barcelona?"

"Nothing. It's not Fryeburg, not Brownfield, not Maine."

"So why doesn't she go to Canada? We'll drive her to Montreal. It's only a few hours away. In another country. We'll leave her and Hannah there, then pick them up a few days later."

"Yeah. Well. I haven't told you the half of it."

There was rustling, cooing, small giggles. "You haven't heard *my* half of it, sweet potato. It'll give you and me a chance to stay in a hotel. Like newlyweds."

"Jimmy, don't be bad."

More rustling. Even some grunting.

"Jimmy, come on …"

Sweet God. Chloe couldn't even eavesdrop on her parents' conversation about *her* without it becoming a study in her own mortification.

"But seriously," her father said. The cooing had stopped, thank God. "We can't let her go."

"I agree. How do we stop her?"

"We'll just tell her she can't go."

"I look forward to our spicy pork chops tonight over which you tell her."

"I've never liked that Hannah. Why couldn't that no-good father of hers have gotten custody instead?"

"I think the answer is built into your very question."

"That Terri is a piece of work. Doesn't she know what's going on with her own kids? I hear Jason is always in trouble up in Portland. By the way, the raccoons got to her garbage again."

"I saw. I smelled."

"Did you talk to her about cleaning it up? Or am I going to have to?"

"She told me this morning the animals have to eat, too."

"I'm going to shoot them next time I hear them near her cans. They're a rabid nuisance."

"Jimmy, carry the potatoes. She better come home soon. Dinner is ready."

"Should I go get her? Did you drive her?"

"No, I didn't drive her to Hannah's house. It's forty yards away."

There was silence. "I didn't drive her, Jimmy. She's fine. She's next door." Chloe heard the pot being placed on the table.

"So what are we going to do?"

"Talk some sense into her. She listens to *you*. You're her father."

"If she listened to me, she'd never ask for something so stupid."

"It's not stupid, Jimmy, it's just kids being kids."

"I never did nothing like that."

"Okay. We did some stuff too."

"Not like that."

"Worse. We were young, too."

"Hmm."

"You remember Pembina? The paleo flood in the Red River in '77? All right, Mr. Comedian. I know you remember. We were so bad. We didn't need to go to Barcelona."

"We never needed to go anywhere, sweet potato."

"Get the drinks. I'll go get her."

Pembina was where Lang was from. Pembina, North Dakota, less than two miles south of the Canadian border. The Red River is slow and small. It doesn't have the energy to cut a gorge. It meanders through the silty bottomlands. Yet every few years it floods catastrophically through the marsh at its delta. It causes immense destruction. In 1977, the river flooded, and the National Guard was called in to help the locals cope. Jimmy Devine, National Guard, met Lang Thia, whose father was a prominent local businessman who made hearing aids.

Her mother didn't need a hearing aid. She came to the window near which Chloe was hiding and said into the screen, "Chloe, come to the table. Dinner is served."

With a great sigh, Chloe peeled away from the wood shingles and walked, head hung, to the door.

5

The Irish Inquisition

LANG TURNED ON THE LIGHT ABOVE THE SMALL RECTANGULAR table. They sat silently, their hands folded. They blessed their food. Jimmy said amen. Chloe asked him to pass the potatoes. Jimmy poured Lang a jasmine ice tea. Lang poured Jimmy a beer. They cut into their pork chops. The silence lasted two or three minutes. Jimmy had to get some strength before he began, though he looked pretty strong already. He was a big Irish guy, blond-haired once, now gray, blue-eyed, direct, no nonsense. He was funny, he was easy, but he also had a temper, and he never forgot anything, neither a favor nor a slight. It was almost his undoing, the merciless blade of his memory. Sometimes he had to dull it with whiskey. Sometimes he had to dull many things with whiskey. Tonight Lang eased him into Chloe's summer plans by letting him eat for a few minutes in peace while she grilled Chloe on irrelevant matters.

"Did you do your homework?"

"I didn't have any. It's senior year, Mom. No one gives homework anymore."

"Then what do they give you a fourth quarter grade for?"

"Showing up mostly."

"So no tests, no quizzes, no overdue projects, no missing labs, no oral presentations, no incomplete class assignments?"

"Not to my knowledge, no."

"Enough nonsense," said Jimmy, having fortified himself on meat. "What's this your mother tells me about Barcelona?"

Her father looked straight at her, and Chloe had no choice but to stare back. "Did my mother tell you that she wants me to enter into a story contest? Ten thousand dollar prize."

"She mentioned something about that, yes. I don't see how the two are related."

"I have nothing to write about."

"Come to work with me for a day or two. You'll get three books out of it." Jimmy Devine was the Fryeburg chief of police, like his father and grandfather before him. Fryeburg, Maine. Pop. 3500. Settled in 1763 by General Joseph Frye and incorporated in 1777, exactly two hundred years before the bad luck of the paleo floods two thousand miles away, and now Chloe sat impaled on the stake of parental disapproval.

"Really," she said, irritated. "Books on what, breaking up domestic arguments and littering?"

"Nice. So now even my work, not just your mother's, is denigrated?"

Chloe regrouped. "I'm not denigrating, Dad. But our hearts are set on Spain. Hannah and I have been talking about it for years."

"You told your mother you thought of going just today. So which is it? An impulse or a lifelong dream?"

Chloe didn't reply. They were denigrating *her*!

"How in the world can Hannah afford Barcelona?" Jimmy asked. "Her mother is at the bank every other day asking for an overdraft increase. And your friend, who abandoned you to do Meals on Wheels by yourself on Saturdays because she claims she has a job, often skips out on the one lousy four-hour shift she has at China Chef. So where's her half of the money going to come from?"

Chloe hated that her dad knew everything about everybody's business. It was terrifying. She stopped eating and stared at her father, the last bite of pork chop lodged in her dry throat. Did he know *why* Hannah was skipping out on China Chef? Oh God, please, no. A demoralized Chloe couldn't withstand even two minutes of modest interrogation.

"Why do you want to go so much? Tell your mother and me."

Chloe said nothing. Her entrails in knots, she felt like a scoundrel.

"Is it because we went without you that time to Kilkenny?" Jimmy said. "You're lucky you didn't go. Funerals are not for kids."

And just like that the three of them were swallowed up by silent oceans. Jimmy awkwardly picked up his fork only to drop it. Lang nursed her jasmine tea. Sickened by the ghastly turn of the already difficult conversation, Chloe tried to right the course.

"It's not about that. It's not about funerals," Chloe said. "It's not about anything. It's just awesome Spain. Why do you think I've been taking Spanish these last six years? I'm the only senior still taking a language. That's why. Dad, I'm not a child anymore."

"If you're such an adult," said Jimmy, "then what are you talking to us for?"

"I need your help with the passport."

"Oh, *now* she needs us," Jimmy said. "Just a signature. No help, no advice. No money. You have everything now, big girl. You've got it all figured out."

"I don't, but … it's just a few weeks in Europe, Dad. Lots of kids do it."

"Who?"

"I don't know." Chloe stumbled. "Lots of kids." No one from her school.

"It's the worst place, by the way, to have a vacation," Lang cut in.

"Why is it the worst place? It's the best place! Have you been there, Mom?"

"I don't need to go to Calcutta to know I don't want to go to Calcutta."

"Calcutta? Can we calm down? It's Barcelona! It's on the sea. It's nice. It's fun. It's full of young people."

"Did I hear your mother correctly?" Jimmy asked. "The two junkyard wildings down the road want to go with you?"

Well, at least it was out there. The pit in her stomach couldn't get any bigger. "Why wildings? It's Blake and Mason. You like them."

"Don't put words in my mouth or feelings into my heart."

"You *do* like them. Mr. Haul is still your friend. Despite everything." Chloe took a breath. "You help him out with money, you lend him your truck, you barbecue with him. You exchange Christmas presents. Mom gives them tomatoes."

"What does that prove? Your mother gives tomatoes to everyone, even the Harrisons who tried to kill Blake's dog. And in my line of work, I'm forced to talk to a lot of unsavory characters."

"Mr. Haul is not one of them. And Mom and Mrs. Haul are friends."

"Don't get carried away," said Lang. "I drive to ShopRite with her. She is not the executor of my will. So don't hyperbolize."

After a pause, Chloe said, "Now who's hyperbolizing?"

"I don't know why *anyone*, especially my daughter, would want to go to Spain of all places," Jimmy said, getting up from the table, as if done with the conversation he was himself continuing. "Do you think there's any place more beautiful than coastal Maine? Than the White Mountains of New Hampshire?" He snorted as he scraped the remains of his dinner into the trash. "You have staggering beauty outside your own door."

"That's what *I* told her, Jimmy."

"Would that I had a chance to compare," said Chloe.

"I'm telling you how it is."

"So I have to take your word for it? I want to see for myself, Dad!"

"Where did this crazy idea even come from? Lang, did you know about this?"

"Jimmy," said Lang, "she doesn't know anything about Barcelona. If she did, she wouldn't want to go. Believe me."

How did one not raise one's voice when confronted by a mother such as Chloe's mother? "Mom," Chloe said slowly, which was her equivalent of a raised voice. The slower the speech, the more she wanted to shout. At the moment, she was positively hollering. "I know you *think* I might not know anything about Barcelona. But what in the world do *you* possibly know about Barcelona?"

"Chloe! Be respectful to your mother."

"*That* wasn't respectful?" If only her parents could hear how Hannah talked to her mother.

Lang raised her hand. She was still at the table, across from Chloe. "No, no. Chloe makes a valid point. Clearly she thinks Barcelona has virtues Maine doesn't."

"I think it because it's true," Chloe said. "It has stunning architecture. Art. History. Culture."

"You think we don't have architecture?" Jimmy bellowed.

"Houses are not the same as architecture, Dad!"

"Don't shout! Since when do you care about architecture? It's the first time in my life I've heard you use that word. Now you want to go halfway around the globe to learn more about house design?"

Chloe found it difficult to speak through a clenched mouth. "Art. Culture. History."

"So go visit Boston," Lang said, pushing away from the table. "There's a big city for you. It has Art. Culture. History. It has *architecture*."

"Maine has history too." Jimmy tried not to sound defensive about his home state. "What about the Red Paint People?"

"Dad, okay, history is not why I want to go to Spain."

"Why then?"

"I bet it's to lie on the beach all day," said Lang.

"And what's wrong with the beach?"

"You can lie on a beach in Maine!" Jimmy yelled.

"Chloe! Look what you did. You've upset your father. Jimmy, shh." Walking over, Lang put a quieting hand on her husband.

Taking hold of Lang's hand, Jimmy continued. They both stood a few feet away from Chloe, near the sink, united in their flummoxed anxiety. Chloe continued to sit and stare into her cold, half-eaten chop. "What about York Beach?" he said. "We've got five hundred miles of spectacular sandy coastline. How many miles does Barcelona have?"

"Is it warm?" said Chloe. "Is it beachy? Is it Mediterranean?"

"Do you see?" Lang said. "She doesn't even know where Barcelona is. It's on the Balearic Sea, for your information."

Chloe couldn't help herself. She groaned. Clearly, in between grilling swine and sugar-dusting Linzer tarts, her mother had opened an encyclopedia and was now using some arcane knowledge to … Chloe didn't know what.

"Mom," Chloe said, so slowly it came out as *mommmmmmmmmm*. A raw grunt left her throat. "The Balearic Sea is part of the Mediterranean. Look at the map. Don't do this."

Undeterred, her mother continued. "They didn't even have any beaches fifteen years ago. They built them for the Olympic Games. That's your history right there. Don't pretend you're all about the Barcelona sand. Maine has had beaches for five hundred years."

Chloe blinked at her mother. Lang blinked back defiantly. "Mom, so what? What does that have to do with anything? What does *that* have to do with me going or not going?"

"Don't raise your voice to us," Jimmy said. "So if it's not for the beach, why do you want to go? Do you want to prove something?"

"I don't want to prove anything. To anybody," Chloe said through closed teeth. "I. Just. Want. To. Go. That's it. You want to know why Barcelona and not Rome or Athens or some other place? Okay, I'll tell you. Because while you were gallivanting through the glens of Kilkenny and I stayed with Hannah and her mom, Blake bought me a magazine."

"Oh, well, if Blake bought you a magazine ..."

"A *National Geographic*," Chloe continued through the sarcasm. "There was an article on Barcelona in it. It sounded nice. So Hannah and I said to each other we'd go when we graduated."

"So you want to go to Barcelona to punish us, is that it?"

Chloe wanted to scream. "Why would I want to punish you?" she said. "Do you want to punish *me*? Is that why you're doing this? It's not about you. It's not about anything. Hannah and I fell in love with it when we were kids. We thought it would be fun to go when we grew up. And here we are. All grown up. Her mother is letting her go. Her mother is treating her like an adult. And yet my mother and father are still treating me like I'm eleven years old!"

"Can you act like an adult," Lang said, "and stop being so melodramatic?"

No one spoke for a moment. Then her father did.

"All I know about Barcelona," he said, turning toward the sink, "is that in Spain, the drivers are considered the worst in the world." His back was to his wife and daughter. He didn't, wouldn't, couldn't face them as he spoke. "It's a well-known, established fact. The worst drivers in the world."

Putting her soothing hand on Jimmy, Lang glared at Chloe, as if to say, do you see what you've done?

Chloe opened her hands. "I won't be driving, Daddy. I promise." Her feeble voice oozed with pity and penitence. The fight had gone out of her.

"You'll be walking, though, won't you," Jimmy said, "while others are driving, poorly." He lowered his head.

"Not even, Jimmy," said Lang, caressing her husband's squared back. "Didn't you hear her? She'll be lying on a brand-new beach. Admiring the architecture."

6

Mottos

EVERYONE HAD A MOTTO. CHLOE'S MOTHER'S WAS: "CAST your bread upon the water."

Her grandmother's was, "How I envy the handicapped in their wheelchairs who can push themselves around. They don't know how lucky they are."

And Chloe's? Once, to go miniature golfing, Courtney and Crystal arrived at Chloe's green cabin wearing slinky hot pink dresses and clangy bangles. Lang took one squinted glimpse at the two and stage-whispered to Chloe, "Where are they going to, a parade at a bordello?"

That became Chloe's motto: To avoid at all costs such an assessment by anyone's mother, including her own, or by, God forbid, a boy.

Okay, no, that wasn't Chloe's motto. That was her wish. You know what Chloe's motto was?

On the blank canvas of your life with bold colors paint.

Maybe not so much a motto as an unattainable goal.

Chloe just wanted to know who she was. Not who she wanted to be. But who she actually was.

Up in the loft attic open to the living room, she lay on her bed with the ballerina-pink fluffy down quilt and soft pillows, clutching a tattered 1998 *National Geographic* to her chest, the one with the precious Barcelona article in it. When Polly, the old wizened woman who owned the Shell gas station in

Fryeburg, decided to go into the used book selling business, running it out of her garage, Blake, out with his dad one afternoon, picked up a worn copy of the magazine. He paid two dollars of his allowance to buy it for Chloe when she was eleven and he was twelve. Reading about Barcelona burst her heart into a flame.

She'd read the article so many times since then, she had it practically committed to memory. *Redeeming touch of madness. Millionaires on motorbikes, witches caked in charcoal dust, pimps and uncrowned kings. Miro, Picasso, Dali, firebombed girls in whorehouses.* Just think about that! *Firebombed girls in whorehouses.* Barcelona has been inventing herself for a thousand years. With her parents talking below her in their tiny bedroom next to the front door, a nearly defeated Chloe caressed the cover of the magazine, pressed to her breasts, kneaded it like a rosary, prayed to God, please, please, please, and strained to hear the snippets of their parenting. From up here, it was just rising and falling pitch, up down, questions, quiet replies, voices, tempers, tides. For some reason her father's voice was muffled, unclear. Her mother's alto rose through the rafters.

Jimmy yelling suddenly and Lang yelling back. The walk down that long dirt road from the school bus is responsible for Barcelona, she says, and Jimmy yells, are you crazy, Mother?

"Better she go with the boys, Jimmy. Blake keeps everybody safe. He'll keep her safe."

She can't hear her father's response. Only Lang's voice is clearly heard.

"I don't want her to go, either, husband."

"You know she's leaving, Jimmy. You know that, right? She's leaving home in three months. For good."

"Okay, I'll tell her she can't go."

"Don't be sick with worry, Jimmy. She'll be fine. Disaster won't fall on us twice."

Now Chloe hears her father's voice. "Not on *us*," he says. "On *her.*"

Chloe crept on her hands and knees to the railing, as if crawling on all fours would make the attic floor less creaky. Her Barcelona magazine on the planks in front of her, she pressed her face between the slats. They didn't want her to go. She expected nothing less. Her parents weren't Terri Gramm. They were never going to say, oh, sure, honey, Barcelona with the Spanish boys and your two horny boyfriends and topless beaches and incorrigible Hannah. And you, our only child, who's never been anywhere without us, not a problem, you go, girl.

Chloe wanted so desperately to graduate, to be self-reliant, to sign her own applications, to take herself out of state, to travel on her own, to be *grown up*, that it was a physical ache throughout her whole body. A throbbing. What do I have to do, her body cried, to be taken seriously, to be thought of as a fledged human being, not just a fledgling? What do I have to do? It is so painful to live like this, thwarted, dependent.

Her ear was wedged between the slats, listening for a possible seachange.

What else could Chloe say to persuade them? Mom! she wanted to cry. I want to be the girl who later in life when she was old could say, yes, when I was young I traveled by myself on a train through Spain. I don't want to be the girl who will tell her kid, no, I've never been anywhere, except North Dakota where I was born, and Maine where I married your father, and Kilkenny one time when somebody died, somebody who with his wanton recklessness ended up wrecking my careful life.

But Chloe couldn't say that, just as she couldn't say that maybe in Barcelona she would have sex with her boyfriend. Or that she might sunbathe topless on the man-made beach, built just in time for her Olympian topless body.

As she sat with her ear to the empty air below, she cupped her hands under her breasts and bounced them up and down. She wanted to sunbathe topless in front of Hannah, so that in this one way, she could come out slightly ahead, because Hannah bested her in everything else. Hannah was always playing a game of one-upmanship. Why couldn't Chloe play just this once? Hannah was passive-aggressive, a constant downer, not a smiler, an inveterate shopper who made Chloe spend more of her allowance than she ever wanted to, to try to keep up with blouses, skirts, dresses, the latest boots and gloves. The size 2 girl who was always dieting, who told everyone she was fat, the long-limbed girl, aristocratically mouthed, and small-pointy-breasted. What other city could offer Chloe this particular intangible? Bathing topless on the beach in front of their two boyfriends and a city full of strangers, so she could win. How small. How stupid. And yet how completely essential. Could she do that in York, Maine? How could Chloe's noblest desires fly side by side with her soaring pettiness?

Hannah, who was loved through and through by Blake, and still, it wasn't enough.

Chloe fell asleep on the floor, her head pressed into the railing. She was woken up at one in the morning by her mother, who helped her into bed.

Please, Mom, she whispered half-asleep, reaching out to touch her mother's face, or maybe she only thought she whispered. You wanted to be a dancer once. Let me do this one thing for me, but also for you. Let me live what you never lived, far away in whirling dancing noise and nights of magic flowers until the world blows up.

7

Olivia the Dancing Pig

CHLOE DIDN'T KNOW HOW BLAKE HAD MANAGED IT, BUT BY the time her mother dropped her off in front of the Academy bus circle the next morning, every single person she met on the way to homeroom knew about their impending Catalonian Bacchanalian sexcapade. That must have been how Blake painted it, judging from the arched eyebrows and the innuendo smiles.

"Who do you think you are, Isabel Archer?" was what her mother had asked her as she pulled into the parking lot.

Chloe looked at her blankly. Lang stared back. She folded her plump arms. "You have no idea who Isabel Archer is, do you? What do they even teach you? Finest prep school in the United States indeed. Go learn something before you graduate."

Her friends Taylor, Courtney, Regan, Matthew, his sister Miranda, and four girls on the cheer squad—who for some reason were hypnotized into believing Chloe did not despise them—all cornered her between her locker and the door of the physics lab.

"When are you going?"

"Did you already buy your plane tickets?"

"Can I see your passport?"

"Can you bring it to school tomorrow?"

"What's the weather like in Barcelona?"

"Do you think your Spanish is good enough?"

"Does anyone speak English over there? Because frankly, Chloe, your Spanish isn't that good."

"And Mason doesn't speak Spanish at all," bubbled up Mackenzie O'Shea. There wasn't a girl in six counties Chloe hated more than Mackenzie with her twisty body and twisty pigtails and mouth full of Bubblicious gum. One time in Science she popped the huge bubble wad in her mouth, and the gum burst from her cheeks to her chin and she got gum in her hair. In front of everyone. That was an excellent day.

"Where are you going to stay?"

"I can't believe your dad is letting you go. My dad would never, and he's not even the chief of police." That was Mackenzie.

"Are you allowed to drink over there?"

"Really, you shouldn't drink. You're not used to it. You'll vomit. Like that other time." Still Mackenzie.

"Don't they drive on the wrong side of the road?"

"I thought the capital of Spain was Madrid. Are you sure it's not Madrid you're going to? Because I don't think Madrid is on the beach. Blake tells us you're going to an Olympic beach. He's wrong, isn't he?"

"My aunt's second cousin went to Madrid. She said it was dusty."

"It wasn't Madrid, genius. It was Mexico City."

"Same difference. Very dusty. And crowded."

"Is there skiing there?"

"Do they take American dollars?"

"How would you even change dollars into pesos? Or are they on the euro now?"

"What's a euro?"

"Blake and Mason are not going to like it. They get very sunburned. Mason especially." Still fucking Mackenzie.

Not a word was required of Chloe, or even desired.

"You must be thrilled," Taylor said as they took their seats in Physics. "To travel through Europe with Mason. It's a dream."

Chloe heard Mackenzie's high-strung voice from behind her. "Mason is not a city guy. He's a ballplayer. A skier. He's not gonna like it."

"Don't be a fool, Mackenzie," said Taylor, sparing Chloe a crackling response. "You think varsity players don't like traveling?"

"Not Mason. He doesn't like empanadas or that weird Spanish food they have over there. Tapas or some shit. He likes burgers. Steak."

"I swear, I'm going to deck her," Taylor whispered.

"Get in line," Chloe whispered back, and after class implored Mason to control his brother who couldn't keep his big mouth shut about anything.

"Like I can control him," Mason said, kissing her and running off.

"Are you *so* psyched?" was the first thing Blake said to her as they took their seats in Health.

"About what?"

"Barcelona, dumblehead."

"Do I seem excited to you? Did you tell your parents?"

"Of course. They couldn't be happier. They can't believe you girls were thinking of going on your own. Dad said Chief Devine would never allow it."

Chloe mumbled unintelligibly.

"Mom said she wants us to protect you from the big bad Europeans." Blake laughed.

"Why'd you have to go tell everybody?" Chloe was churlish. "You and your big mouth. What if my parents say no?"

"Haiku, you funny." Blake patted her arm as he flipped open his spiral notebook. "You didn't think your mother would just buy you a plane ticket to Spain, did you? The woman didn't let you take the school bus until your senior year and even now still drives you in the morning. She was hardly going to run to Liberty Travel in North Conway. They need to think it over."

"Yes. And then say no."

"They loves you. Why would they say no to the one they loves?"

Blake knew nothing. Lang was gearing up to say no. She was making heavenly lemon pound cake when Chloe got home from school, a consolation dessert if ever there was one.

"For your information, Mom," Chloe said, having fortified herself with a shallow knowledge of Henry James's monumental novel and worked on her riposte all day, "Isabel Archer came into a fortune. That will hardly be me. Are you afraid some broke European is going to sweep me off my feet because he is angling for my five hundred bucks?"

"Is that your fantasy?" Lang asked. "To be desired by dangerous men for your meager dollars?"

"Of course not!" She was with Mason, the cutest boy in the Academy halls.

"Then why did you say it so wistfully?"

"I'm not Isabel Archer, Mom. You know who I am? Olivia, the dancing pig. She has a painting of Degas's ballerinas on her wall, but she's never going to be either Degas or a ballerina, is she?"

"So now you're a pig dreaming of being a ballerina?" Lang slid a plate of pound cake in front of her daughter. "What are you doing, Chloe? Are you placing all your hopes on what may lie just around the next bend in the river? You think you can drift on the train from Spain to France not knowing where your next stop will be in the fervent hope that you'll come closer to an answer to that most profound of human questions?"

"And what question is that, Mom."

"Who you are, of course."

Was there ever a mother more infuriatingly on point than her mother!

Hannah was out. Mason was at varsity. Blake was helping Mr. Leary with his concrete-buster block saw. So Chloe scribbled down some notes for a Social Studies oral essay on women's rights as interpreted by Pearl Buck and watered the garden.

To her surprise, her father came home early.

"Chloe-bear," Jimmy said. "Your mother and I are not going to talk to you about Barcelona anymore. You know how we feel. We know how you feel. Until we have something to speak to you about, we are going to call truce and talk about other things. Deal?"

"You should've told that to Mom," Chloe said. "Because she's been going on about Henry James and Huck Finn all afternoon."

"She told me. That's why I'm saying this now. Excuse me." Jimmy moved Chloe out of the way. "Your mother and I are going for a walk."

"You're what? Why?"

"Isn't it obvious?" her father said. "Because we need privacy to talk about you, and at home you're always eavesdropping."

No words more frightening could have been spoken mildly by a gruffly amiable man, who placed his badge and his service weapon on the hall table and donned his spring parka. Lang put on her suede shoes and a Pittsburgh Pirates baseball cap she had bought at a garage sale even though she'd never heard of the Pirates and thought they were a football team. Off they went, arm in arm, her mother stout, her father expansive, into the hills around the lake.

They were gone an hour.

At dinner they talked of television shows, movies, her graduation party, college. Should she ship her heavier items like a television ahead of time, or should they buy a TV on the other side? And what about a car. She'd definitely need one. How did she feel about a used VW Beetle? Perhaps red? Not a word about Spain was spoken.

The next afternoon, the pattern was the same. Lang made oatmeal raisin cookies, Jimmy came home early, and they vanished through the birches. The third day Chloe began to doubt everything. How important was Barcelona anyway? Why did she have to be so obstinate?

Where could she go that might be more acceptable to her parents? She had read about Innsbruck, the heart of the Alps, white with fresh snow. Picturesque gardens, musical chambers, Roman marvels, Bavarian creams. Her clothes, down coat and all, always on, even in bed.

Ugh.

She spent her entire life living in snowed-in valleys surrounded by mountains. She skied, snowboarded, sledded. She skated right on her lake. She played wild, nearly violent games of ice hockey with her friends. Every four years she and Mason pretended they were Olympic skaters, spinning and salchowing over the thick ice. But Chloe and Blake were actually speed skaters and every winter when they weren't ice fishing, they spent from sunup to sundown in racing abandon. Chloe owned more parkas than jean jackets. She knew what to do for frostbite. She had read Jack London's terrifying "To Build a Fire." More than once.

Why would she go anywhere else but Barcelona? Why would she ever want to?

8

Empty Wells and Vernal Pools

CHLOE ASKED TO BORROW HER MOTHER'S CAR TO DRIVE Hannah to Bangor. She made up some story about dorms and housing applications.

Lang only half-listened. "Are you ever going to tell her?" she asked.

Hannah was headed to Bangor to break up with the grandpa who loved her. He might not make it out of the afternoon alive. Did she really need Chloe adding to her woes? "Of course. But not right now."

"You've been saying that since April. Tell her on the way."

"I will. Soon."

"Now's the perfect time. Um, Hannah, guess what? Our trip to Bangor reminds me of something. That sort of thing. You know she'll find out eventually."

"Of course she'll find out eventually, Mom." Duh.

"Perhaps when she moves into a UMaine dorm and instead of you her roommate is a tall black chick?"

"Yes, like then. And don't say chick, Mom. Ew." If Chloe ground her teeth any more, she'd have no teeth left. Why couldn't her mother be like Hannah's mother? Terri never asked questions, never hounded, never scolded. Chloe wasn't one hundred percent sure Terri knew where her daughter was accepted to college. She was just so chill and lax about things.

"Why won't you tell her, child? What are you afraid of?"

Why did everybody keep asking her this! What *wasn't* she afraid of. That Hannah would not forgive her. That she couldn't explain it. When she tried to explain it to herself, she could not, so how was she going to explain it to her best friend, and to Mason?

"Have you told Mason at least?"

Chloe didn't reply.

"Oh dear Lord. Chloe!"

"Mom! Can you please not stress me out? Am I not wound up enough? I tell you what, sign my passport application, and I'll tell everybody everything in Barcelona."

"Chloe, you haven't told your boyfriend you're leaving for San Diego?"

"Mom, he'll find out soon enough! He's got his last varsity game coming up. He's been in training for three weeks. I didn't want to bother him. And I only just decided."

"A month ago."

"A few weeks ago." She stuck out her hand, trying not to shake from exasperation. "Please can I have the keys?"

"I'm telling you right now, I'm not doing it," Lang said, opening her purse. "You're not hopping on a plane to California and leaving me to mop up your mess."

"Let me go to Barcelona and I'll tell them myself."

"Don't threaten me, young lady, I won't stand for it."

"The keys. Mom. Please."

In the car, while Hannah was angsting away about Martyn, Chloe wasn't listening, her focus elsewhere. Had there been silence in the car, she might have attempted a confession. A pretend casual tone. No big deal, Hannah. I know you're thinking we're going to UMaine, but did I mention this other place I applied to, three thousand miles away from Bangor, our whole wide country away? A Spanish city with beaches, warmth, no mountains, no snow. Like Barcelona, but in the States.

"Have you applied for your passport yet?"

Chloe snapped out of it. "How can I apply? They haven't said I can go."

"Tell them in a firm and convincing manner that you're going and that's all there is to it."

"Yes, right, okay. Do you know what my mother has been doing?" Chloe said. "Buying me books. *Frommer's Guide to Spain's Coastal Cities. Fun Facts about Barcelona. To Barcelona with Love. DK Guide to Spain's Most Beautiful Churches.*'"

"That's nice. She's being helpful."

"You mean impossible. She says to me, see, honey, you don't have to go anywhere, you can just read books about it."

"True, your mother is always advising me to read more," Hannah said. "She says you can live other lives through books, experience travel, love, sorrow."

"She's buying me books so I can see Barcelona from the comfort of my recliner while she makes me éclairs and rum babas."

"Yeah," said Hannah. "You have it so tough."

Chloe drove. She didn't want to say how much she envied Hannah her parents' spectacular non-participation. Divorce did that—shifted priorities.

"They make unreasonable demands on me," Chloe said.

Hannah turned down Nirvana. "I wish somebody would make a demand on me."

Grandpa is making demands on you, Chloe wanted to say. How's that going? "I thought you liked that they never asked you for things," she said instead.

"Turns out, I want to be asked for something."

"Like what?"

"Anything," Hannah said. "Just to be asked." She turned to Chloe. "Why are you so tense? Look at the way your hands are clutching the wheel."

Chloe tried to relax, really she did.

"I'm the one who should be tense," said Hannah. "You have no idea how upset he's going to get."

Chloe thought long and hard about her next question. "He's generally in good health, right?" she asked. Like his heart?

"Oh, yes," Hannah said. "Believe me, there's *nothing* wrong with him."

"Ew, gross. Not what I meant. But okay."

"What'd you mean?"

"Nothing."

Hannah was looking too pretty for someone who was about to break up with a nonagenarian. Almost seemed mean. The poor fellow was going to be feeling like shit anyway, why rub it in his face, the youth, the slim feminine attractiveness, the long legs? Hannah even wore a skirt, as if headed to church. Linen skirt as short as the month of February. Navy blue sparkly ballet flats. A cream top. Face deceptively "unmade-up," yet fully made-up. Eyes moist.

Chloe couldn't pay too much attention to Hannah's appealing exterior while driving down a zigzaggy two lane country road, but from a surreptitious corner of her eye, Hannah was looking delectable, not forlorn.

"Hannah, why are you looking so pretty if you're ending it with him?"

She beamed. "He likes to look at me, that's all."

"But you want him to like to look at you *less*, don't you?"

Hannah didn't reply, busy eating her fingers, twisting her knuckles.

To everything there is a season. That was another one of her mother's mottos. This was emphatically not the season for college confessions. This was a time for lovers. Chloe cleared her throat.

"Can I ask you about Blake?"

"What about him?"

"Don't you like him?"

"I love him, what are you talking about?"

"Well, then, why …"

Hannah waved at her. "You won't understand, Chloe. You and Mason are so perfectly aligned."

"You think so?" Chloe wouldn't have minded talking about it.

"But it's different with me and Blake. He's so sweet, but ..." Hannah paused, chewed her nails, stared out at the pines passing by. "Besides the physical, we have little in common. Don't get me wrong. The physical gets you pretty far. With Blake, believe me, almost the whole way. If it was the only important thing, we'd be in great shape. But aside from that, what do we have? All the things I like, he couldn't care less about, and all the things he likes I don't get at all."

"Blake's so into you. He likes everything you're into."

"What do I care about junk hauling, or building things, or helping old people, or fixing band saws? Or fishing? And what does he care about Paris and museums, and classic literature, and pretty clothes?"

"There are other things ..."

"Yes, we've done them." Hannah sighed dramatically. "Do you think that boy will ever live away from his dad? He still helps him into the boat, for God's sake. He wants to start a junk business. I mean, what am I going to do with someone like that?"

"He also wants to write a book," said Chloe.

Hannah waved in dismissal. "He and a million others. Me, I want to travel the world. I want to learn three languages. I want to live in a big city. You and I both do. It can't end with Blake any other way but this way."

"But that's the thing," Chloe said, her gaze on the road. "It's not ending. If you ended it with him, that'd be one thing. But you're not."

Hannah turned to Chloe, frowning disdain on her displeased face. "How do I do that? And then what? What do I do with *us*?" She made a large air circle, embodying by the broad sweep not just herself and Blake, but Chloe and Mason too. "We are all four of us together every day. We have one life. If I break up with him, what happens to the four of us? Do you even think before you speak? I mean, could you break up with Mason?"

"I don't want to."

"But if you did?"

They didn't talk for a while. The road was narrow, the pines tall, the ride long, what was there to say? Except what a hypocrite Chloe was, what a deceiver. She decided she would tell Hannah about San Diego on the way home, her heart falling through her abdomen at the thought of it.

Chloe underestimated the open and public heartbreak a man near retirement age could display on the walkways of Orono, near the river on the University of Maine campus, when his eighteen-year-old lover told him it had to end.

Chloe stayed as far back as possible. She couldn't believe Hannah would do this on the avenue where students and faculty strolled on a warm May evening. But his reaction was so extreme that perhaps this was why Hannah had chosen the public square for his flogging; she had hoped he would keep it together. At first they walked arm in arm, overlooking the flowing waters, the mountains beyond. He smiled at her, squeezed her arm. They made quite a picturesque couple against the backdrop of the snow-capped Appalachians.

Hannah spoke. He stopped walking. He took his arm away. She gestured, in her small elegant way, and he stood, a pillar of incomprehension. Then he started to weep. Hannah stroked him, embraced him, talked and talked, a filibuster of consolation. Nothing helped the gray man become less stooped.

Chloe had to stop peeking at his despair. It was as if she had caught him in the shower, or them in a different sort of clinch. She became embarrassed, for herself, for him, for the passersby who slowed down, concerned at his distraught exhortations. He grabbed his chest, as if in the middle of heart failure.

After an hour he was still crying! And Hannah was still rubbing him, talking to him, gesturing far and wide.

Chloe understood *nothing* of this kind of emotion. Nothing. It seemed to her that logic must prevail in a grown man's head when he spied himself standing in the middle of the college where he had tenure, bawling because his teenage lover had decided to move on. Not even move on, for Blake was the here and now, just … move sideways. Move back. Move away. How could the enormous common sense of that decision finally— *finally!*—not triumph over him?

Chloe had been keeping an eye on the time—the thing she usually had least of, next to money—but after ninety minutes her eyes left the watch permanently to pitch silent poison darts in Hannah's direction, hoping her friend would sense Chloe's own despair at the tedium of spying on a stranger's excessive distress. Come on, wrap the whole thing up, put it in a doggy bag, take it home. Let's go, let's go, let's go! Chloe kept silently shouting. LET'S GO!

There was pacing, but there was no departing.

A hundred and ten minutes. A movie now. First a tragedy, then a comedy, then a farce, now *Shoah*.

Wait. Something new was happening. The stooped old man nodded. He let Hannah hug him, pat him.

Unfounded optimism. There he was, crying again. He could barely stand on his grieving geriatric legs. Carefully Hannah helped him over to a bench, and sat down next to her soon-to-be-erstwhile lover, continuing to cajole and comfort him.

The girls had a three-hour ride back home.

"Did you see him?" Hannah asked.

Oh, I saw him all right. Saw him, heard him, memorized him. I could play him by heart on the piano, that's how well I've studied him.

"Yes," said Chloe.

How could she tell Hannah about college?

She couldn't. And didn't.

She wanted to ask if Hannah loved Blake half as much. Would she shed a quarter of Martyn's tears when it came time to say goodbye to Blake? Would she miss him an eighth as deeply? What was it called when it wasn't pain, but a fraction of pain? Grimly Chloe closed her hands on the wheel.

"What happens next, Chloe?"

"I don't know, Hannah. What happens next?"

It was going to get dark soon. Her mother would be worried. Nothing to do but drive on. "Remember Darlene Duranceau?"

"Who could ever forget her? Why would you bring *her* up, of all people?"

Chloe shrugged. "I'm trying to make a point about what happens next."

Blake and Mason had dismantled the woman's overflowing garbage heap of house in Denmark, Maine, after she died. She had been a hoarder, hoarding even herself in the end. She kept eating and sitting, eating and sitting, and soon she got so big that she couldn't move off her couch, and she just kept eating and eating and eating, using the couch not just as a bed and a dining table, but also as a toilet, and, eventually, as a grave.

It was winter when she died, and everyone had been snowed in for days. The local market couldn't deliver Darlene's groceries. When the roads were finally plowed, Barry the delivery boy brought Darlene her customary two boxes of Pringles and pretzels. Barry found her. Barry did not recover from this. He had been a shy clumsy kid in Chloe's homeroom, but now he was on major meds, in therapy six days a week and home-schooled by Social Services.

The townies talked about nothing else. What was Darlene's life like before she and the couch became one? What drama in her life had led her to the upholstered end? Was the end a consequence, an answer to a why? Or was it a catalyst? If everything you did led to everything else that would eventually happen, the question was: was Darlene Duranceau the beginning or the end?

After the coroner pronounced her dead, and it was time to remove her from the premises, the EMT workers discovered that she was stuck. From lack of movement, she had developed sores that festered, causing open wounds that oozed into the sofa, which then closed up around Darlene's flesh like lichen to a rock. She had liquefied and then mummified into her furniture. The town cremated her with the couch. No one but the boys out in the schoolyard ever discussed how the funeral home fit Darlene and her Davenport into the relatively narrow opening of the cremation pyre.

How could Chloe add to Hannah's chaos by confessing about California?

She wants to tell her, but she can't.

She can't.

And she doesn't want to.

Hannah will feel betrayed.

What kind of a terrible friend would Chloe be to betray her friend and then tell her about it?

So she doesn't tell her.

She thinks she justifies it beautifully.

Only a guilty mouthful of what feels like open safety pins alerts Chloe to the falseness of her excuses.

"I know the answer," Hannah said. "You know what happened next for Darlene? Nothing."

"Yes. That was the end of Darlene's story. But yours is just beginning, Hannah. That's what I'm trying to say. Take heart."

"Did you see how upset Martyn was?"

"I saw."

"Do you think he's going to be okay?"

"I don't know."

"What do you think is going to happen?"

"It'll be something. Martyn is not Darlene."

"But what if what happens next is you and your sacred striped sofa become one?" said Hannah. "What if when God said flesh of my flesh, he meant flesh of my sofa? The Chesterfield of my flesh? What if Martyn *is* a Darlene?"

"You can't possibly believe that."

There was silence for a while. It was black out. There were no lights on the road except for the car's headlights.

"Blake is the sweetest lover," Hannah said in a small sad voice. "You don't expect that from someone like him, because he's so rough and tumble, but he is super gentle and super considerate. He's always caressing me, kissing my back. He's always trying to make me happy."

"You're lucky," Chloe said, settling into the wheel, stepping on the gas pedal. She didn't think Blake was so rough. For months, when his dad couldn't walk, on account of nearly dying, oh and having a back broken in three places, Blake carried his father to the reclining chair by the sandy shore and set him down into it so Burt could watch the lake and the sky and Blake and Chloe fishing in the boat and skating on the ice. His dad liked to watch the kids having fun, Blake said.

9

Red Vineyard

"Teach me, Haiku. Tell me how to begin. Tutor me in beginnings."

Blake plopped down across from her in the nearly empty learning center, scruffy, smiling, slapping his notebooks onto the heavy wooden table between them. His pens rolled toward the window. Chloe watched them, and he watched her watching them. Without breaking eye contact with her, he stopped them from falling to the floor and then he spoke. "What's been the matter with you today?" When she didn't reply, he went on. "Is it because of Barcelona? Don't worry. They'll say yes. They've been talking to my mom. Asking her if she thinks we're trustworthy." Blake laughed. "I told her, lie, Ma, say yes!"

She smiled half-heartedly but couldn't look at him. She pretended she was super distracted by Very Important Thoughts. About pi and Ovid and Pearl Buck. The tutoring center at the Academy was a large first-floor classroom with twenty-foot windows and long wooden tables behind which girls like herself sat and waited for students who needed help in math, hard sciences, English, you name it.

Although final exams were getting close, the place was nearly empty. She'd had just one student all afternoon, an apathetic freshman from Delaware named Kerwin, whom she schooled in irrational numbers like pi. "You can't have an infinite string of zeroes in a pi exponent," Chloe told Kerwin, "because then the fraction would end. And what do we know about pi? It's transcendental. It cannot end." Her mother had once taught her about pi. Something about divinity and infinity. The soul is divine, her mother had told an anguished Chloe. Don't worry. The soul has no end. Like pi. An infinite thing cannot end.

Kerwin wasn't getting it. And Chloe wasn't at her best. Her mind kept wandering. To distant beaches, imposing cathedrals, white stucco resorts in the hills, Hannah walking arm in arm with Blake through the halls, cozy as all that, as if Martyn had not happened, as if the last eight months of tawdry Tuesdays and Saturdays at the Silver Pines had not happened, Hannah making out with Blake between Health and Gym, discussing the prom with him between English and Science, fretting about her mango dress matching his peach cummerbund at the prom, and all the while Blake going on and on about Barcelona, and all the while sadness seeping on and on into Chloe's heart. How could Hannah pull off such nonchalance? Chloe couldn't tell why this bothered her as it did. Usually she tried not to ask herself too many why questions.

Now, pretending she hadn't heard Blake ask about beginnings, Chloe turned to the window, to continue to daydream about Iberian dragons rampaging through the streets. Across the field she could almost make out Mason's breathless shape on the baseball diamond. He was just a panting dot in golden dirt. It was the only time she saw him panting, perspiring, on fire. When he was out in the field.

"Yoo-hoo, Haiku ..."

She blinked and dragging herself back to reality turned to a quizzical, smiling Blake. He was clad as usual in plaid and flannel and cotton and denim, his stubble four days old, his wild hair three days unbrushed and two months streaked by the spring sun. "I just need to know what's in my suitcase," he said.

"In our play we reveal what kind of people we are," Chloe told Blake, quoting Ovid. "So first figure that part out."

He looked wholly unimpressed. "You're putting the cart before the horse."

"No …"

"You are. Believe me. First I write. Then I figure out what it all means. Which, by the way, is the opposite of the insane horse crowd. They put portents on paper first and then use a mallet to beat it into a story."

"You have it all figured out, don't you? What do you need me for?" She sounded just like her father.

He leaned forward as if confiding. "I don't have anything figured out. What would *you* put inside it? How would *you* start it? Look what I have." He pulled out a three-subject spiral notebook to show her. He had divided his notes into sections: story, characters and the last one for thoughts, notes, lists, tidbits.

"I write and write," he said, "but I still don't know the most important thing."

Ain't that the truth, thought Chloe. She studied the grain in the table. He was too carefree and earnest to be saddled with her pity. "You do kinda have to know what's in the suitcase if you're writing a mystery."

"Who said it's a mystery?" He shook his head. "No. See, it's the best thing of all. It's an unexpected thing. You think you're reading one kind of story, and then—POP, it's another."

"Like not a mystery?"

"You *think* it's a mystery, but it's really a Western." He laughed. "Or you're ready for a mother–daughter drama, but it's really a two-man play about the meaning of trees. A thriller becomes a musical, a coming of age story is now the return of the native, science fiction turns out to be a war story."

"Wait," Chloe said, "a *musical*? How can a story on paper have music in it?"

He grinned as if he were about to doff his black hat. "That's the trick, isn't it?"

They were leaning forward over the table. The only other people in the room were three other tutors and a proctor. Outside it was deep spring, warm colors, tulips and grass, outdoor sports and new running shoes, the courtyard full of girls in light summer frocks, the kind she never wore, blowing up in the wind. She could see the three cream-brick dormitories, Payson-Mulford, Webster, and Hastings, arranged in a semi-circle of unchaperoned fun. Every Friday night before curfew, drunken madness. Next to Hastings a fence, a back gate, and a cemetery. Before the fence a tent. And under the tent, a barbecue grill and three picnic tables.

There once was a story with music in it at one of those tables.

Blushing at a hot lick of a nearly forgotten memory, Chloe quickly cantered away from the aching nostalgia of the picnic bench near Hastings, thinking we'll never be that drunk again, her tongue-tied gaze colliding with Blake's amused and amiable stare.

"What?"

"Nothing." She stared at his large, scuffed hands, folded together in calm Zen across the table.

"Tell me why we *must* go to Europe," he said.

"To find the blue suitcase, I suppose."

"Why Barcelona?"

"The question is not why Barcelona," she replied, gazing out the window. A thousand open questions, invisible to the naked eye, apparent to every living soul. "The question is why anywhere else?"

"Exactly. Who else would know this but you?"

She was trying to answer her own riddles in the unfinished English essay, a treatise on feminism and freedom in Pearl Buck. "You *would* write about Pearl Buck," said her English teacher, whose insinuations Chloe didn't appreciate, but it was too late to change her topic. You *would* get all As, Chloe. You *would* have an extra eraser, your neat notes from last year, the report handed in three weeks before deadline, and a yes from all the schools you applied to. Universities of Pennsylvania and Maine. John Kennedy Jr.'s alma mater, and Einstein's. Every Boston school worth going to, Duke too, and San Diego, that misty Spanish renaissance on Mission Bay. You *would*. Chloe hated those two words.

It fed too cleanly into the digested and mealy narrative about her, the stereotype she despised and had tried all her life to change. She didn't want to *not* do well. She just didn't want to be known as the girl with the Chinese mother who did well.

You *would*.

My mother is fifth-generation American, Chloe would answer to every suggestion of the supposed intellectual blessings of her ethnicity. She is more American than I am, since my father's father was born in Ireland and his mother somewhere in the Baltics. *My* mother, on the other hand, makes peanut-butter and jelly sandwiches. She frequently forgets to buy soy sauce. Does that sound Chinese to you? And yet how else to explain her own relentless quest for excellence? Every revolutionary date, every candidate for president, every battle in the Civil War, every Law and Act, every polynomial and integral domain, every *tomorrow, and tomorrow, and tomorrow* all the way to dusty death had to be not just memorized but internalized?

Pearl Buck wrote about the Chinese woman from a hundred years ago, but she could've been writing about Chloe's mother and father. Jimmy Devine wanted a docile lamb who would be happy to contain herself within his four walls. Pearl Buck said that a woman full of energy and intelligence could not be contained within any man's walls, but then Pearl Buck, the obedient daughter of a Christian missionary in China, had never met Lang Devine. She can't be held there, Pearl Buck wrote, even if the walls were lined with satin and studded with diamonds. Chloe disagreed. Her mother's wood cabin walls weren't lined or studded with anything but photos of Chloe.

Pearl Buck seemed to think that Lang would soon discover she was living within prison walls. Chloe begged to differ.

Even children were not enough for some women. She may want them, Pearl Buck wrote, need them, and even have them, and love them, and enjoy them. But they wouldn't be enough for her. "Nobody likes children, Chloe," her mother would often say. "But we have them anyway." Chloe was almost sure Lang was joking. Because for some women, children were everything.

Some women didn't know anything about politics. It took all their effort to be wives and mothers. Well, Ms. Buck opined, that may be sufficient for *some* women, but their husbands certainly found the time to occupy themselves, not only in their chosen fields and with being husbands and fathers, but also apparently, with other women as well. Just ask Terri Gramm next door who worked sixty hours at L.L.Bean to pay the mortgage while her husband honeymooned in Maui with the assistant baker from Dunkin' Donuts.

Chloe swore she would grow up to be a different kind of woman, not Terri, not Lang, not the donut-maker-helper.

But what kind of woman?

She had no idea. Chloe had the answer to everything, except the important things.

"Don't worry about what's in the suitcase for a moment," she said to Blake in a voice thick with longing. "And the answer to the why will come. Just start at the beginning. Start with something true and real. Begin with your two main characters, the junk dealers."

"If you're going to make fun," Blake said, "I'm going to give them another livelihood."

"I'm not making fun. Tell me about them."

Eagerly Blake opened the notebook to the second section. Character. Pages were filled in pencil in a slow and careful hand, too slow, too careful for Blake. Her delighted skepticism must have been apparent on her face. Without affront, he said, "Did you know, Miss Smartass, that Van Gogh sold only one painting in his entire lifetime?"

She marveled into his grinning face, tedium forgotten, even Barcelona and parents and Hannah's other lover forgotten for a moment. "The surprise here," she said, "is that *you* would know anything about Van Gogh."

"Come on, Haiku, you know I'm a font of useless information."

She broke a pencil. "Are you implying that you will also sell only one thing in your lifetime, say your purported story? Or could you possibly be equating yourself with Van Gogh's talent?"

"Neither." Blake was unperturbed by her teasing. "*Red Vineyard* was not even his best painting."

"It was pretty good, let's say that, but again, how is that relevant"—she wagged her finger in a small pi-circle at him and his notebook— "to what's going on here?"

"All I'm saying," Blake said, "is that if Gerald Ford can be a male model, then yours truly can be a writer."

"Another metaphor *entirely*, but at least more apropos."

"And did you know that Einstein did not or could not speak until he was nine years old?"

"How in the flipping world is *that* relevant?"

"Maybe I'm a late bloomer like him."

Chloe smiled. He was being so cute. "Maybe. But the thing that's actually relevant about Van Gogh is that he painted the *Red Vineyard* not while standing at the window looking out at it, but solely from his memory and imagination. Take that away and mull it, Einstein."

Blake took it. He mulled it. "Maybe *The Blue Suitcase* will be my *Red Vineyard*," he said, his own voice deep with longing.

"Or you could try writing something like *Breath* by Samuel Beckett," Chloe said, straight-faced. "It's one of his lesser known plays. It lasts thirty seconds and has no actors and no dialogue." Her eyes twinkled.

And Blake, bless him, laughed, as Chloe had hoped he might. "Yes!" he exclaimed. "It's called an intermission."

And Chloe laughed.

The proctor shushed them. "Mr. Haul, I'll thank you to keep your voice down."

"What if I'm a writer?" Blake said to her, lower and leaning in. "I could be a writer, no?"

It must have grated on him that Chloe didn't think he could do it. And she didn't even think that. Well, all right, she did. She did think that. But so what? What did it matter what she thought? God.

"Figure out what's in your suitcase," she said, "and you will be a writer."

Blake sat contemplating her. His face was inscrutable.

"What?" She became discomfited. She hated not knowing what people wanted from her. She didn't like to disappoint.

"What do you think should be in it?"

"It's your story."

"But if it was *your* story."

Chloe shrugged. "This one lady I deliver Meals on Wheels to, all the way in Jackson, lives in a yellow shed. I'm not kidding, it's a shed off the main property, which is huge, but the shed is tiny, and it's painted yellow, and she sits in a chair outside this canary box all day and watches the road, the cars, the walkers. She's right past the covered bridge to Jackson. She's ninety-two. She tells me that she prays to Jesus every day that today will not be the day she dies because she wants to be buried with all the jewelry her husband had given her, but she's afraid her kids will never go for it once she's dead. She tells me she's trying to figure out how to get buried alive so she can decide what goes with her. She'd probably put her jewelry into this vanished case."

"What's her name?"

"Lupe."

"I need to meet her ASAP," Blake said. "Are you and Hannah doing Wheels tomorrow? Mason and I will go with you."

Chloe didn't know what to say.

He was so excited, he skipped right over her lying silence. Then it was time to go.

They ran for the late bus, heaved on, said hi to Freddy the thoroughly vetted and tested union driver. Chloe sat next to the window, Blake next to her, their backpacks squeezed between their legs. Freddy waited another minute for stragglers. Chloe spotted Mason still in his baseball uniform, walking down the path from the fields, with a team of catchers and cheer girls flanking him with their pom poms and their camaraderie. He saw the bus, waved to Freddy, yelled something facing the girls while running backward, then turned and sprinted with his gear and school books to the blue bus. In the twenty seconds it took Mason to jump on, Blake had gotten up and moved over one seat. Mason took the vacant spot next to Chloe. Blake sat with his back to the windows, his feet stretched out. He nearly tripped Mason with his sticking-out black Converse hi-tops.

A panting, sweating Mason kissed Chloe. "Sorry I'm all gross," he said, wiping his face with the sleeve of his jersey.

"No, I like it." It was nice to feel an exerting Mason wet on her skin. It was only after sports that she felt it.

"Mase, we're going with the girls tomorrow," Blake announced. "Meals on Wheels. To get awesome deets for our story."

Holding Chloe's hand, Mason shook his head. "No can do, bro. End-of-year varsity barbecue tomorrow. Sorry. But the three of you go. Have a blast."

Twisting her mouth this way and that, Chloe looked out the window. How does she tell Blake that Hannah hasn't gone to Meals on Wheels with her in months?

10

Lupe

HANNAH'S WHEREABOUTS ON SATURDAY AFTERNOONS WAS explained by none other than Hannah herself who, as soon as they came pounding on her door to tell her about tomorrow, said, Chloe, what are you talking about, I haven't been doing Wheels with you in months. You know I've been working the lunch shift at China Chef, trying to save up for our trip.

Blake's kinetic gaze slowed down to take in Hannah, and then Chloe for a puzzled moment longer. "Why wouldn't you just tell me that?" he asked.

"I haven't done it for a while myself, I forgot," stammered Chloe, throwing Hannah a rebuke dagger with her eyes.

"What's the matter with you?" Hannah whispered, dragging her inside the house. "You know I've been working most Saturdays."

"Do I?" Chloe said, pulling her arm away from Hannah and walking back outside. "I thought you were working on Tuesdays too. Shows you what I know."

At nine the next morning, Blake knocked on her door.

"Good morning, Mrs. Devine. Good morning, Chief."

"Good morning, Blake," Jimmy said from the breakfast table, hands around a coffee cup. "How have you been? Looking forward to graduation?"

"Oh, absolutely, sir. Thank you. Very exciting. Yes." Blake always talked to her father as if about to be arrested.

"Listen, I have a tree by the water that's rotting, a willow."

"Say no more. I'll take it down for you. Do you have power out there?"

"By the lake? No."

"I'll bring my axe and my gas-powered chainsaw. Today after I bring Chloe home?"

"Anytime you can, Blake. It's a big tree, though. If you help me knock it down, you can keep half the wood."

"Thank you very much. My dad would like that. He gets cold cramps at night."

"How's he been?"

"Not too bad. Back keeps bothering him, you know."

"I know," Jimmy said, staring into his coffee cup.

"Yeah, well, um. Is Chloe ready?"

Chloe was ready.

Lang pulled her into *the vestibule*, that is, the very same short hall Blake had taken over with his broad flannel-clad frame. "You two have fun," Lang said, "but come back before six."

"Okay," Chloe drew out. "Wheels is from eleven to one, and you know that, so." She broke off. "That's well before six. What's up?"

"Moody is coming tonight for dinner," Lang said reverentially, as if announcing the arrival of Queen Victoria. Moody was Chloe's terrifying grandmother. "I hope you don't have any prior engagements."

Why would she? It was only Memorial Day weekend, when the kids from six towns would be gathering for the fireworks in North Conway, staying out, hanging around by the outlet shops, miniature golfing, eating ices, listening to the free bands in the old town square, making out, maybe other things. "Prior engagements? Who talks like that, Mom?" was all Chloe said. Moody was coming to dinner! Blake pretended to study the picture of Castlecomer on the wall.

"I just want to make sure you'll be home."

"So you talk like Edith Wharton? Why do *I* need to be home? Why is she coming?"

"She wants you to drive her to the cemetery to visit Uncle Kenny."

"Ugh, no!"

"Yes. Plus she wants to talk to you."

There it was. Chloe's teeth set against each other as if in battle. Her antennae shot up, spring-loaded. "About what?"

"Am I Moody? How do I know?"

"I can tell you know."

"Go. Just be back."

"Mom! Is it about Barcelona?"

"Go!"

This was a futile conversation, and the fact that Lang allowed it as long as she did only spoke to Lang's own anxiety about her mother-in-law's upcoming visit. It was the first time in three years Chloe's grandmother would be coming to their house. Chloe glanced over at her dad, to gauge his reaction to his mother's arrival, but he was head down, buried in the newspaper.

"Blake, ready?" Chloe wanted to storm out of the house.

"It was nice to see you, Mrs. Devine. Have a great day. Chief, I'll be by later to help you with that tree. I'll bring some rope too."

"Wait," Jimmy said and got up. He handed Blake the keys to the Durango. "Take my truck. It's easier to get in and out of than the Subaru."

"Yes, it is, thank you very much, sir."

"Dad, you're giving Blake your truck?"

"Hardly giving."

"You don't lend it to Mason!"

"When Mason takes you to deliver food to the infirm instead of parking with you behind Subway, he can have my truck."

"Thank you, sir. I won't let you down in that regard, or any other."

"I know, son."

"One quick thing—where do you keep the siren lights? Somewhere in the truck?"

"Get out of here, Blake, before I change my mind."

"Yes, sir."

Six cold meals and six hot meals were delivered to St. Elizabeth's on Main Street, the Devines' parish church, by Petey, the Meals on Wheels delivery boy, who did not like to be kept waiting. Wheels didn't usually deliver on Saturdays, but a dozen homes depended on Chloe, and that was the only day she could work.

"I'm surprised you still want to go," Chloe said to Blake as he opened the Durango door for her. She was in a dismal mood. Moody was coming!

"I told you I would. I must meet this Lupe."

"I don't even know if she's on the schedule today. Petey gives me a list. We should hurry. Sometimes she cancels. She doesn't want me to go all the way out there just for her. Blake, what are you doing, what are you looking for?"

Blake was searching through Jimmy's truck. "Looking for those damn siren lights. I want to slap them on top of the truck when we get on the highway. You said we should hurry. Turn the suckers on. Scare the shit out of the cars in front of us."

"No! You can't use them, Dad will throw you in jail for sure."

"It'll be worth it."

On the way to the church, Chloe wanted to tell Blake she was happy for his company but didn't know how to phrase it without sounding like an idiot, so she didn't. She liked it when Hannah used to come with her. Chloe drove, Hannah navigated, though she was awful with directions, but they had some laughs getting lost. And the old people enjoyed seeing the girls. Chloe got dressed up a little, wore jeans without holes.

But today Blake was driving her. It was better. Until he said, "So why didn't you tell me Hannah doesn't come with you anymore?"

Chloe fake-studied the map. "You know, you should teach Hannah how to drive."

"*You* should teach Hannah how to drive. I tried."

"So did I."

The two of them chuckled. "Let's just agree she's a reluctant learner," Blake said. "But it's in *your* best interest to teach her, not mine."

"It's in *your* best interest to teach her, not mine."

"What are you, four? Stop mimicking me. Do you want to be driving her around Bangor when you two start college, the way I drive her around here?"

Chloe was very, very busy with the map. "Maybe she'll get a car and I won't have to."

"Where's she going to get a car from?" Blake said. "If she has any money saved up, it'll be spent on empanadas in the Ramblas."

So he was reading up on Barcelona too. That made Chloe smile, until she recalled Moody. Thinking of her grandmother coming for dinner and, oh God, going to the cemetery made Chloe tighten her spine, squeeze shut her lips and reveal to Blake nothing about her other anxieties: the lack of their funds, the lack of permission, the lack of passport, the lack, the lack, the lack.

She said, turn here, but Blake was already turning. He could find the dirt roads around Fryeburg and Brownfield blindfolded. He seemed to have an innate ability not to get lost even when the rural roads were unmarked. His navigation skills were pretty impressive. When she praised him, he replied by asking why she was dressed so nicely. She pretended she wasn't dressed especially nicely; how to explain that the old people enjoyed looking at her? But the thing that was great about Blake was that no question lingered in his hyperactive brain for long, and often, when the answer was a few seconds in coming, he would make up his own reply, which was what he did now.

"The young girl," he said in a dramatic voice, "who got all dolled up to feed the elderly vanished one Saturday afternoon.

Where did she go? Perhaps her ironed jeans were found in the pond nearby?"

"Why would I lose my jeans in the pond?"

"That's what I'm trying to get to the *bottom* of, Haiku," he said, and guffawed.

He was so silly.

"What does *my* denim have to do with *your* story?"

"I don't know yet," he replied. "I'm merely collecting information."

"So I'm not even the *end* of your story, just a random detail?"

"Nicely punned. I said I don't know. Look in my notebook—no, not that section, the one in the back that says descriptions. See if there's anything you like."

He had written out fifty pages of notes on lakes, junk he had found, birds building nests during spring—and the garden by her house! He was incredibly prolific. Every minute observation was in his spiral.

"Why is my garden here?" In his random musings, he had written about her wine-red tulips, the coral knockabout roses, the orange nasturtium and the hot pink azaleas blooming outside her windows.

"Never know what I might need."

"Before I vanish," Chloe said, closing his notebook, "you might want to have me do something amazing or idiotic."

"Losing your pants is both, don't you think?" He poked her in the arm as he drove. "Why are you all freaked out about Moody? She's your grandmother, not Freddy Krueger."

"That's what you think." Chloe sighed. Everyone in the large Devine family lived in fear of Moody. She could not be argued with, or negotiated with. She could not be reasoned with. She believed what she believed, said what she said, commanded what she commanded. I've seen too much to bother arguing with the likes of you, was Moody's standard reply to anyone in her family who dared raise a squawk in opposition. Only Chloe's father had spoken out against her, and the result of that was that mother and son had been on the outs for the last seven years, since Uncle Kenny died.

The old people became notably enthusiastic when they saw that a tidied-up Chloe did not come alone. "Who is the young man?" Mrs. Van Mirren said with a meaningful smile.

This is Blake, Hannah's boyfriend, Chloe would say to Mrs. Van Mirren, Ms. Rivers, Mr. Mann and Mr. Warner. They asked where Hannah was. They asked about Mason. They asked when the prom was, and when Europe was. They gave her money. Five dollars, two dollars, seventy-five cents. They would not take no for an answer. This is for your trip, they said. Take pictures. Write things down. Don't forget. Life is long. You won't remember if you don't write things down or take pictures. Are you excited about college? We'll miss you when you go. We love you. Blake, we love this girl. Take another dollar.

Lupe was last, because she lived the farthest, in New Hampshire, in a tiny hamlet called Jackson, ten miles from North Conway.

Just as Chloe had told Blake, outside a yellow painted storage shed sat Lupe, in a wooden chair planted outside her front door. In the window box under her one white window bloomed purple nasturtiums. "I planted those for her," Chloe said. Lupe, shriveled like a bald bird in water, gummed a smile and waved. She was white from top to bottom, white hair, white shirt, white bracelets, white pants, white socks, white shoes. As usual, she wore most of her jewelry. If not all her jewelry. Three necklaces, a cross, a dozen jangling bracelets on each wrist, and rings on every finger. When she waved to Chloe and Blake, she trilled like a wind chime.

"Izh thish Mashon?" she said, as if she didn't have her dentures in.

"No, Lupe, it's his brother. Blake."

While Lupe was vigorously shaking Blake's hand and appraising him, Chloe pulled out Lupe's lunch, the last one in the hot box, and stepped inside the woman's one-room *house* to get a tray and some silverware. Though who was Chloe to tease Lupe about the size of her habitat?

"Lupe, Blake came with me because he's entering a story contest." She set the food on a tray in the old woman's lap. "Did you read about it in the paper? The Acadia Award for Short Fiction. I told him about your box of jewelry." Chloe poured Lupe some ice tea, put a napkin near her elbow.

"And what, he got interested? He wants it?"

"No, no." Blake looked mortified. How amusing!

"Young man, I'm joking. Instead of looking for my jewelry, you should find yourself a sense of humor. It would come in more handy."

"Um, yes, ma'am."

"Where's your brother today?"

"At practice."

"Blake is Hannah's boyfriend," Chloe said.

"Who? Oh, Hannah." The old woman studied Blake intently as she ate. The fork trembled in her shaking hands.

Blake smiled. "I know. She's too good for me, Lupe."

"That's not quite what I was thinking."

Chloe pulled on Blake's denim sleeve, and the two of them perched on a nearby bench and kept the woman company while she finished her lunch.

"Has your mother agreed yet to let you go?" Lupe asked.

Chloe shook her head, keeping mum on Moody's imminent visit.

"She will, though, don't you think?" Blake said. "I keep telling her."

Lupe shrugged. "The odds are about even. Don't count on it, but don't discount it. I've met mothers before. I was one myself until my sons got too wise for my help. Mothers can be an unpredictable bunch." She took a swig of her ice tea, shielding her eyes from the sun.

"Let me ask you something," she said to Blake after he had scintillated her with stories of his story, even offering her a peek at his journal. "You say you want to go to Barcelona for research."

"That's right, ma'am." And to Chloe, out of the corner of his mouth, added, "And for other things."

"Call me Lupe. But can't the answer you're looking for be found right here in New Hampshire and Maine?"

"I don't think so."

"Sure it can. Answers are found everywhere. And in anything. You just have to know where to look."

"Barcelona will make for a far more interesting story, don't you agree? Rather than writing about boring old North Conway." North Conway, the biggest town in two counties was a two-mile stretch of a straight rural highway. Fifteen traffic lights and Applebee's dueling it out with Burger King. Pizza Hut against KFC, Baskin-Robbins against Carvel. There were one or two antique shops, an outlet mall, an L.L.Bean, and gas stations. That was the town. And China Chef, of course, purveyor of hot and sour soup that Hannah supposedly placed on people's tables. How do you find the answer in a town like that?

Lupe insisted. "You can. You can find answers anywhere."

"I'd like to find them in Barcelona," Blake said, and Chloe was proud of him for not being *too* intimidated by a ninety-something woman. Forgetting herself for a second, Chloe almost made a joke. Leaning to Blake, opening her mouth, she almost, *almost* said—we should introduce Lupe to Martyn, don't you think? They're about the same age—before slamming her hand against her mouth. What was wrong with her!

Blake must have liked Lupe because he talked to her for longer than any of the others. And she must have liked him because she kept asking him to do small chores for her. She pointed out that her chopped wood was too far from the fire pit. It was all the way in the back, near the river. Chloe and Blake carried the chopped wood and the iron rack to the front of her yellow house. They set it up near the fire pit, stacked the wood on the rack, covered it with a blue tarp. Lupe looked pleased by their efforts, especially Blake's. She asked him to build her a fire. She's my last one, Chloe told Blake, as they collected some branches for kindling. She always keeps me here. She's lonely, he said, and she likes the company. I don't mind. "Lupe," he called to her, "do you know that your fire pit is eroding on one side? The stones have broken off."

"I know," she said. "Who's going to fix it, me? Or my children in California?"

Blake motioned toward the mansion-like house. "Who lives there?"

Lupe shrugged. "A family. They don't help me. They got their own problems. The husband is sick. He just don't know it yet. Or don't want to admit it."

"How do *you* know?"

"Can you tell the difference between a healthy man and a sick one? They're like two different species."

To this, Blake bowed his head without reply. He knew the difference well. His own father had been a Hercules before the disaster that almost claimed him, and now was a husk.

"Maybe I can help you fix it," Blake said to Lupe. "I'll go to the quarry, pick up some stones."

The woman shook her head. "Why don't you come by after school next Thursday? I have a doctor's appointment and no way to get to it. Usually I call for a taxi. Maybe you can drive me. I'll pay you for your time, and then we can go to the quarry together. Pick out the stones. I'll pay for them too."

"*You're* going to go to the quarry?"

"I'm ninety-two," she said. "I'm not dead."

On the way home Blake rained on Chloe with questions that at first sounded like research but perhaps weren't. How long had she been visiting Lupe? When did the husband die? Why did she go to these twelve homes and not others? Why did she stay for five minutes in one home, but forty minutes with Lupe? What happened if she saw something suspicious? What if the people behaved erratically? What if they hurt her?

He had been slightly concerned about Mr. Gibson, a blind man with long scraggly gray hair who had grabbed Chloe's hand and wouldn't let go, not letting her leave or feed him. Blake gently, but not too gently, pried Mr. Gibson's dinosaur fingers off Chloe's white wrist.

"He's fine," Chloe said. "He's just lonely. Like Lupe."

Blake was off again about Chloe and her pants vanishing.

"Give it a rest, Blake. I'm not your project, I'm not your story."

"But if you disappeared," he went on, speeding invincible in her father's siren-less off-duty truck, "that would be quite a story, wouldn't it?"

"No! It's only a story if there's a reason why I disappeared." She paused. "Also what does my disappearance have to do with your blue suitcase?"

"Maybe everything," he said.

"You leave me out of your lunacy, Blake Haul."

"It's fiction," Blake said. "In fiction, you can have everything to do with my lunacy. Isn't that what you told me? I can use my imagination and have it all turn out exactly how I need, how I want." Fiendishly he rubbed his hands together while driving with his knees. His expression was for once both serious and remote, as if he was thinking about something else entirely.

Covering her face, Chloe groaned.

It was a good afternoon.

11

Moody

SHE RAISED HER GAZE FROM THE TRASHY GOSSIP MAGAZINE, from sordid uncouplings and inappropriate attire of beautiful strangers, and focused the red dot of her anxious brain on her mother. Rather, focused on her mother's back, while her mother's studious front was forming tiny spicy Mediterranean meatballs with feta and fennel.

"So why's she coming?"

"You shall see."

"Why can't you tell me?"

The eminently sensible Lang pointed out that if she told Chloe, then Moody wouldn't need to come over.

The eminently sensible Chloe opened her hands to say, exactly! But it was done to her mother's oblivious back. "I'm making meatballs," Lang said. "Do you want to help me?"

"If I help you, will you tell me?"

"You *will* help me," said Lang, "and I won't tell you a thing."

"It's about Barcelona, right? She's got some plan?"

"It's about a man with a horse. Come here and help your mother."

Their house had once been Moody's summer retreat. Lochlan Devine built it with his own hands for his young bride back in the fifties so she could have a home by the lake as she had dreamed. Twenty years later Moody gave it to Jimmy and Lang as a wedding present.

"Why would she suddenly be visiting us again?"

"She says it's been too long."

"Tell me why so I can prepare myself."

"Prepare yourself for what?"

Chloe wanted to provoke her mother. "She told me last Thanksgiving that she doesn't come to us anymore because she's mad we still blame Uncle Kenny for everything."

"Well, that's just silly," said Lang, looking at no one.

Her father spoke his first sentence of the afternoon. "We do blame my brother for everything," Jimmy said.

"Jimmy, shh." Lang turned to Chloe. "Stop stirring the pot, young lady. Your grandmother wants to help, that's all."

"Help who?"

"Did we ask for her help?" Jimmy said.

"Yes, Jimmy, we did," Lang said, one hand on her husband's shoulder, one hand straightening out the errant lamp shade behind him. She had been feverishly cleaning as if preparing for an open house viewing.

"*You* did," Jimmy said. "Not me. Chloe is right. My mother shouldn't come if she's still angry."

Lang leaned her tranquil solemn face into a sitting and grim Jimmy. "She is putting away the bygones and coming for your daughter."

Jimmy sat coldly. "They're not bygones," he said.

"Come on. We agreed."

"You agreed. I'm resigned to it. Big difference."

She kissed his forehead. "You promised you would be civil, kind, polite."

"No. I promised only that I'd be silent," Jimmy said, standing up. "And you're not letting me keep my promise, woman." He went outside to do some yard work.

The next three hours crawled by in epic time, in Thackeray time, every day lasting a thousand tragic pages. Blake stopped by to cut down the rotting willow. Mason stopped by. Hannah stopped by. Then her friends left to go have fun in North

Conway with other young people who didn't have horror-movie
grandmothers. Jimmy left to go pick up his mother and bring her
back to their house.

Finally six o'clock arrived like the executioner's hour.

Sometimes Chloe thought of her grandmother as Zeus in his
Athenian Temple, gargantuan and fierce. Sometimes Moody was
like Tamerlane of Mongolia, murderous and crippled. Sometimes
Chloe saw Moody as Siddhartha, half the size of China, wise but
terrifying in his omnipotent silence.

On Memorial Saturday, Moody was just a kettle-sized white-
haired woman. She had been married to Lochlan Devine since
just after the war until his death, fifty years, four of them pretty
good. She had given him six children, five surviving, all boys,
though what she wanted was two measly daughters. Everybody
knew it because she never missed an opportunity to say it.

She was nearly deaf in both ears, but denied she was hard
of hearing in even one. She grew odd white fuzz on her face.
She liked to drink whiskey and eat caramels and strange spicy
sausages she said were from the old country. She smoked
unapologetically. She spoke fluent English in a loud, heavy and
indeterminate accent. She had occluded sight, which prevented
her from driving, though didn't prevent her from complaining
about not driving. Hence her life's motto about envying the good
fortune of people who could push around their own wheelchairs,
which she repeated again tonight as she walked through the
front door. "They don't know how lucky they are," Moody said.

Behind his mother, Jimmy walked in without a word,
dropped his keys on the side table and went to sit down. Lang,
dressed in church clothes, fussed like a tumbleweed. After
Moody hugged Chloe, she blurted without so much as a half-
blind appraisal, "Why do you always look so dour, child? What
is this awful thing you're wearing? You're a beautiful girl. Why
are you hiding yourself from boys? Or is it one boy in particular
you're hiding yourself from? It won't work. They all know what's
inside the hefty bags you wear for clothes. Come, let's go. I'm not

even taking my coat off despite your mother's efforts. Take me to the cemetery. Don't protest, better go quick before it gets dark. You don't want to go to the graveyard at night, do you? I jest. Of course you don't. Believe me. So let's go pick some flowers from this famous garden of yours, and get to it. Jimmy, give your daughter the truck keys. You haven't suspended her license for speeding—or other violations—have you?"

"You mean like Dad didn't suspend Kenny's?" Jimmy said, gesturing at the keys to Chloe. "Yeah, Chloe's still driving. She's also not speeding, or otherwise violating the good laws of all sane people."

Moody stared coolly at Lang.

Lang glared at Jimmy.

Chloe rolled her eyes and quickly took her grandmother out of the house.

Chloe never saw her mother as respectful to anyone as she was to Moody, and her father as silent. Lang didn't sit until Moody sat. There was no eating, drinking, or speaking, until Moody ate, drank, and spoke. Every other question out of Lang's mouth was, do you have enough salt? More ice? Enough cream on the mashed potatoes? I made chocolate profiteroles for dessert, and fresh coffee, but I also have decaf, or some brandy, if you like. Of course I have whiskey. Would you like some now? Are you cold? Would you like a shawl? You're too hot? Chloe, open all the windows. And bring in the floor fan from the shed.

Her mother sat in adoration. As if Moody had waltzed in, in light cloth, sans sandals, and beyond her stooped shoulders trembled two wings. That's how Lang behaved around her husband's mother. Not so much the husband.

"I fixed the screens," Jimmy said in a stiff tone meant to convey he had built the Maginot Line—between himself and his mother.

Moody shrugged, as if his fixing the screens was an achievement on par with brushing his teeth. "Good," she said. "Because I don't enjoy mosquitoes."

When Lang would pass Moody's chair, she'd place her hand gently on the white-haired woman's shoulder, patting her. It would be amusing if it weren't so exasperating. All the while Jimmy gazed upon his wife with a pungent mixture of compassion and hostility.

A stressed and anxious Chloe was sullen and silent, like her father, though, she guessed, for different reasons. She and Jimmy sat gray like the unfallen Berlin Wall and stared at their food, at the darkening lake, warily at Lang and Moody across from them making small talk. Chewing her lip, counting to 741 by unlucky thirteens, Chloe tried to be still, to not think. The evening blossomed with the smell of mint and quivering fresh water.

"Moody, how are your flowers doing?" Chloe went over to her grandmother's every spring and planted beautiful things in the raised black soil.

Moody made a face. "The flowers bring bees," she said. "Which I also don't enjoy, having grown up in a bee farmer's house. Especially the blood orange tulips that came up a few weeks back. Pretty, but the bees! Never seen anything like it. Don't plant those again."

"Tulips are perennial, Moody. They come up on their own."

"Well, plant something else. Something that doesn't attract bees."

"You want me," Chloe asked slowly, letting it sink in, "to find flowers that don't attract bees?"

Nothing sunk in. "No bees is what I want," Moody said. "How you get there is your problem."

Chloe's scalp tingling, her skin shivering, she clawed at an old bite on her forearm. Was the grand diminutive woman *ever* going to get to the point of her visit?

There was much food and meaningless conversation before

there was finally no food and a meaningful one. After coffee with Baileys, and a second helping of profiteroles (or was it a second helping of Baileys?) Mudita Devine, née Klavin, mother of six sons, oldest one deceased, Lochlan's widow, fluttering Clarence Odbody clockmaker, opened her mouth.

"So your mother tells me you're wanting to go to some damn fool city in Europe."

It wasn't a question. It was just a beginning. And what a beginning! Chloe nodded.

"Why?"

Before Chloe could reply, Moody cut her off. "I don't care why. Neither do your parents." Her mother across from her and her father next to her didn't have time to nod. "The question is, is this a good idea?"

Chloe knew better than to even pretend to answer.

"Your mother and father don't think so. You plan to go with your friends? That boy you've been hanging around with?"

"Mason. Yes. I've grown up with them, Moody."

"Did I ask how long you've known them? Did I ask their names? What does any of that matter to me? You could know them five minutes or fifteen years. None of it matters. What matters is they're boys, and you want them to join you girls in some tomfoolery."

"Not …"

"Chloe." Moody raised her hand. "You'll have plenty of time to speak briefly. Your time has not come yet. Let me ask you this. In broader terms, beyond the few weeks you're hoping to grab on a beach, have you given any thought to what you want to do with your life?"

Now could she speak? Chloe glanced from her mother to her father. She answered. Yes, she said. She has thought about it. She was thinking of going into law. She was thinking of majoring in history.

"So what I'm hearing is you want to major in history, yet your first inclination is to head to a Barcelona night club?"

Chloe must have looked flummoxed. "It makes me wonder," her grandmother said in explanation, "how serious you are about your life."

"Moody, I'm not even eighteen ..."

"Do I not know how old you are?" Moody exchanged a glance with Lang. "So to your parents, you declare that you're almost eighteen, as if you're so grown up that you can make your own decisions. Yet now you remind us of your insignificant age to excuse why you can't be serious about the road before you."

A squirming Chloe kept quiet.

"So which is it? Are you **eighteen** or are you eighteen?"

Chloe had no answer, except yes. She couldn't look up.

"I thought so. Look at me, child. That's better. Your mother tells me you've had your heart set on Europe."

Not Europe, Chloe wanted to bleat. Barcelona. She wasn't even brave enough to defend her one small dream to her grandmother.

"You can decide to visit any European country," Moody continued. "There are nearly two dozen to choose from. You have a few precious weeks before college. An opportunity of a lifetime. And you choose—Barcelona?"

Why was this so frightening? Her heart drummed in her chest. "Yes."

Moody raised her strong, wrinkled hand. "Still not your turn, child." Her gaze was unwavering, which was more than Chloe could say for her own. She'd rather look at her mother! What torture this was.

"Your parents tell me that Hannah talks a good game, but has not yet produced enough cash for your Iberian adventure. And the young men, having come into your dream belatedly, are even more broke. Is this true?" Moody stopped Chloe from replying. "I have a proposal for you," she said. "A proposal I've talked over with your parents, and they agree. A way for you to get what you want. That's why I came. Do you want to hear about it?"

Chloe couldn't hear anything above the thumping in her chest. A way for her to get what she wanted! was all she heard. What could Moody possibly have in mind? That Lang and Jimmy go with them to Europe to chaperone? That they go to Canada instead, as her dad had suggested? Moody was speaking, but Chloe—bouncing up and down on the trampoline beat of her excited heart—missed the important part, and she knew she had missed it because the three adults around her had fallen silent.

Chloe blinked. "I'm sorry, can you repeat that? I don't think I heard right."

Moody sighed. "Riga," she said impatiently. "*Riga.*"

"I don't know what Riga is."

"The capital of Latvia. Also, where I was born."

"Ah." Chloe nodded, as if acknowledging that she vaguely already knew that.

The three adults waited for Chloe's reply. Chloe waited for an explanation.

"Honey, so what do you think?" asked Jimmy.

"Of what?"

"Of your grandmother's plan."

"I don't understand. You want us to go"—Chloe struggled—"to Riga?"

"Yes."

"No! Why?"

"I have family near Riga," Moody said. "I want you to visit them. I told them a lot about you. You can bring them a letter from me, and a package."

"You know, Moody, there's something we have in this country called the United States Postal Service—"

"Not interested. And don't be fresh. Also, there is an orphanage in a Latvian town called Liepaja. The town has had a painful history with the Communists, and since the fall of the Soviet Union, the young people there have not been doing so well. Many American families sponsor children from Eastern Europe to come live, study, and eventually work in the United

States. Your parents have been thinking of sponsoring such a child."

"Don't look so shocked, honey," Jimmy said. "We meant to talk to you about it. We just didn't get a chance to." He glared at his mother who ignored him.

"Your parents would like you to visit this orphanage in Liepaja. Maybe you can find them a suitable boy. Age doesn't matter, but it must be a boy. Older is better. Not too old. Six or seven. The four of you kids can stay with my relatives. It will make them happy and stretch your lodging budget. Riga is a wonderful historic city. You'll love it. A win-win, if you ask me."

Chloe shook her head. Lose-lose is what it sounded like. Worse, Moody wasn't finished. There didn't seem to be a finality to her words.

"And," Moody continued, "after you finish helping your parents, I'd like you to do something for me."

"Other than visit with your family?"

"You have it wrong. They're doing you a favor, not the other way around. You won't be forced to stay in places unsuitable for a young lady." The old woman kneaded her creased and square hands. "A long time ago, before the war, I had a best friend like you and a sweetheart like you. When war broke out in Poland, we knew we were going to get squeezed by the Russians on one side and the Germans on the other. We ran from Riga and hid out in the countryside. Our plan was to get to the Baltic Sea, make our way to one of the Scandinavian countries and board a ship bound for the west. But we didn't realize how much of the continent Hitler and Stalin already had in their grip. We were in Kaunas, northwest of Vilnius, when we got caught by the Soviets and taken to the Jewish ghetto. We were there two years, until 1941 when the Germans came. We all thought we were lucky we weren't in Vilnius because there was a massacre there, near Ponary. Everyone died. They put us on a train bound for the Bialystok ghetto. A year later there was an uprising, crushed of course. But by that time, most of the Jews had been taken to a transit camp nearby. Do you know the name of that transit camp, Chloe?"

"Of course not."

"Treblinka."

No one spoke for a moment.

"What about you?" the girl asked her grandmother.

"I'm not Jewish," Moody said. "Though I reckon that meant little to the Germans. What might have meant more is that I made boots for them. Footwear for the German soldier. I was quite good. Perhaps that helped me." She spoke matter-of-factly, looking only at her gnarled hands that once had made boots for the Wehrmacht. "How little I understood life. I really believed after the war I would find my friends, see them again. I didn't know then that Treblinka was like pancreatic cancer. No one survives."

Chloe didn't know what to say. Questioningly she opened her hands.

"After Latvia, I'd like the four of you to travel by train and visit Treblinka. Bring my love some red roses. There must be a mass grave around there. After that, you can do what you like. You might want to visit Warsaw, or Auschwitz in southern Poland, but that's your business. You have three items on the to-do list. Liepaja for your mother and father, Riga for my family, and flowers in Treblinka for me. You do those things, and I will help pay for your trip."

"I have my own money, Moody," Chloe mumbled in response, as if that was the only thing she'd heard.

"Oh, sure you do," Moody said. "But you know who doesn't have their own money? Hannah. You know who else? Blake and Mason. I hear their mother plans to tap into her life savings to buy them the plane tickets. You can't travel through Europe on the kindness of strangers, Chloe."

"You're going to pay for all of us to go?"

"Well, let's just say you're not going to be staying at the Ritz-Carlton. You'll bring your own money for food, for incidentals. But your travel expenses and your lodging expenses, yes, I will take care of."

Chloe shook her head. "Moody, I don't want to go to Riga." Or to an orphanage! She scowled at her stoic mother, at her father sitting like a sad sack next to her. "My friends will never go for it." Chloe was thinking of Blake especially. "They'd rather not go at all than go to Poland."

"Child, I think you're mistaking what this is," Moody said. "Is this how your mother allows you to speak to her? This isn't a negotiation. It's a proposal. Take it. Or leave it. You want Barcelona? Fine. You'll have to get to it through my home country. And through Poland. Barcelona through Treblinka."

"But …"

"Or you don't go."

Chloe frowned, perplexed, maddened, upset. "Why would you pay for my friends to go with me?"

"It's my graduation present to you," Moody said. "You've been largely absent from my life these last few years"—she glared at Jimmy who glared right back—"and I would like to fix that. I'm not as young as I used to be. I don't want your father's irrational anger at me to stop you from taking this historic trip. And without your friends you can't go."

"Not irrational, Mom," said Jimmy.

"Oh, yes," Moody said. "Chloe is your daughter, like Kenny was my son, like you're my son. Why can't you understand that?"

"Chloe is a very good daughter," said Jimmy.

"You're not such a good son," Moody said. "What son can stay angry at his mother? Kenny wasn't a good man, but he was a good son. Better than you. He didn't stay angry for seven years. That's a sin, you know. It's bad luck."

"We've had about all we can handle of that, thanks to him," Jimmy said as if spitting. "Us, Burt, Janice, their boys. Bad luck well and truly covered, Mom."

"Listen, if I spoiled him, all right, but I spoiled all you kids.

He wasn't special. You wanted me to love him less than you? He was still my son! I had it rough growing up. I wanted it to be easier for my own children. Why is that so hard to understand?" She raised her hand. "Stop arguing with me, Jimmy. I'm done with it. We've yelled all we can yell. Help your child, spoil your child, or take me home. That's *your* choice."

Chloe could see her mother making intense beseeching eyes at her father from across the table. Head bent, Jimmy wasn't looking at anybody.

Moody turned her attention back to Chloe. "I advised your parents not to keep you from going. Even though you are only eighteen or already eighteen or whatever it is you say, I told them that you should at least try to look for the answer to the fundamental question before you."

Chloe hated questions before her. "What question is that?" she asked in an exhausted voice.

"What meaning does your finite existence have in this infinite world?"

Chloe didn't think her Uncle Kenny asked himself this question once, and he probably was never harangued like this. Maybe he should've been. Maybe that had always been her dad's point when he railed at his mother.

"You keep telling your mother and father you want to see things with your own eyes," the old woman said. "So go see them. Do you only want to see the water and the waves?"

Yes?

"Do you only want to hear the cathedral bells?"

Um, yes?

"What about examining for five minutes your place in the world, what it means to be alive? What it means to be dead?"

"Enough, Mom," Jimmy said in a voice more exasperated and tired than Chloe's. "Unlike some others we won't mention, Chloe gets it." Jimmy turned to his daughter. "It's not ideal, Chloe-bear," he said, putting his arm around her. "It's called life. You endure a lot of stuff you don't care about, but then, if you're lucky, you get what you want." Jimmy's eyes caught Lang's for a glimpse.

Chloe took a few minutes to compose herself before she spoke. "Moody, Mom, Dad, do you guys have any idea how far Riga is from Barcelona?"

Moody smiled with a full set of dentures. "Yes," she said. "A train ride away across Europe, just like they did it in the war days."

12

Peacocks

THAT NIGHT UP IN THE ATTIC LANG SAT ON CHLOE'S BED. "Your father doesn't want you to be upset. He thinks we were too hard on you. Some police chief! He's gone soft in the head, I tell you. The fight has gone out of him."

"I wonder why," Chloe muttered. Lang said nothing.

"We don't want you to be disappointed," she said when she spoke again. "Dad and I don't fully understand why you want to go, but then we're not meant to, are we? I almost wonder if you yourself know. And that's all right too. If you think you need to go to Barcelona to discover what you want and who you are, then who are your father and I to stand in your way? Your acceptance of Moody's generous terms is wise. I know you're worried about your friends not wanting to go to Latvia, but I think they're going to surprise you. Besides, what choice do you have, really?"

"Not go?"

Lang nodded. "That will make your father happy," she said. "In any case, everyone agrees the boys should go with you. Burt, Janice, Moody. They'll keep you safe. Your father and I won't argue this anymore. If you must go, then better with them. Soon you'll be far away, and they'll still be here saving up for that junk-hauling truck they won't be able to afford because they've spent the summer frittering away their money in Barcelona with you."

"You mean in Poland with me. In Latvia with me. Trudging through graveyards and death museums. And orphanages. What fun."

Lang remained unfazed. "Europe is your parting gift to your friends. Now you can say goodbye to them the way you're meant to. Abroad. And I hope when you come back, you'll see one or two obvious things in a different way. Though I told Moody and your father, I wouldn't count on self-discovery. I barely count on you coming back in one piece."

"Nice, Mom."

Lang patted the pink quilt above Chloe's leg. "This is our gift to you, letting you go. Your dad and I are proud of you. You've been a good girl. We wanted to reward you for not disappointing us the way other parents have been disappointed."

"Like Terri?"

"Not Terri. I think she's rather fond of her daughter. And Terri works the hardest in that family. That's why she doesn't give a damn about the raccoons and dinner and Hannah's homework. When you have to care desperately about bringing home the bacon, you're hardly going to be bothered about who cooks it or what species eat it."

"Who do you mean, then? Mason and Blake? But you love Janice."

"There you go again, putting words in our mouths and feelings into our hearts. I didn't say Janice. I don't mean anybody in particular. I'm just saying. We thank you for not letting us down."

"Not letting you down how? By not dying?" Chloe was disappointed in herself. With her mother, and only with her mother (and maybe a little bit with Blake), she sometimes had trouble hiding her tortured heart.

A composed Lang said nothing.

For a few minutes, neither of them spoke.

"Just stay safe, all right?" Lang said quietly. "As safe as you can."

"Mom, why do you want me to find you a strange boy?" Chloe whispered.

"Not strange," Lang said. "Just someone who might need a little help. Someone you think your father and I might like. We're not adopting him, Chloe. We're sponsoring him. What are you worried about?"

"I'm not worried."

Lang got up. "In this one way I echo Flannery O'Connor," she said. "For the last eighteen years, my avocation has been raising peacocks. This requires everything of the peacocks and very little of me. Time is always at hand. Especially now that the last surviving peacock is leaving."

The conversation was over. Lang smoothed out Chloe's blanket and bent down to kiss her head. "How was the cemetery?"

"Fine. Moody insisted on putting *my* flowers on Uncle Kenny's grave."

Lang sighed as she took the railing to descend the steep attic stairs. "Why not? I do."

13

Uncle Kenny from Kilkenny

WHEN CHLOE WAS ELEVEN HER UNCLE KENNY DIED. HE was a wild one, lived small, died small. He was cremated and a portion of his ashes were interred in Fryeburg's rural cemetery, while the rest was flown to Kilkenny to be buried in the family plot next to Lochlan. Chloe's parents flew to Ireland for his burial. Chloe got excited. Then she found out she wasn't going.

They were gone a month.

"Must have been some funeral," she said when her parents returned, all flushed and refreshed, as if they'd been on a honeymoon. They showed her photos of Dublin and Limerick, of glens and castle ruins, of moors and churches and pubs with names like the Hazy Peacock and the Rusty Swan. They began inexplicably to refer to the time away as a "trip of a lifetime."

Chloe didn't know what that meant, but she did internalize it.

Seven years later no one spoke of that trip of a lifetime, or of Kenny, or Kilkenny, or glens, or moors. Most of the pictures of Ireland had been taken off the walls of their wood cabin and stored in a box in the shed her father had built for the specific purpose of storing boxes with photos of Ireland in it, and of other mementos. One black and white Castlecomer dell remained in a frame in the hall.

A colossal vat of frightful things was stirred up by Kenny Devine's vagrant life and subsequent (or consequent?) demise.

The Chevy truck he crashed his speeding swerving rattletrap into belonged to Burt Haul.

On the way home from work, Burt had stopped at Brucie's Diner to pick up some meatloaf on Monday special. It was eight in the evening in July, not yet dark. It was warm, glorious, chirping.

Burt survived because his truck, built like a Humvee, had been in second gear. The same could not be said of Kenny or his Dodge Charger. Eyewitnesses, unreliable but myriad, clocked his miles per hour at somewhere between seventy and a hundred and twenty. He had no chance.

Burt lived, but barely. He suffered three broken vertebrae, a punctured lung, and five broken ribs. His kneecap, hip and femur were crushed almost beyond repair. It was upon visiting Burt in the convalescent facility that Moody first noted how blessed were those who could push around their own wheelchairs. Burt couldn't.

His livelihood depended on his truck and his able body. When he wasn't driving the school bus, he was a handyman. After four months in recovery, he found himself on a disability pension, still unable to walk. Janice Haul got a job at the attendance office at Brownfield Elementary School, but it barely paid half the bills. Little by little Burt improved, but was never the same. He couldn't sit behind the wheel of a bus anymore, his fused and compressed vertebrae barking so loud they required handfuls of Oxycontin to quieten, and how well could anyone drive a school bus numbed up on Oxy?

Until Burt got well enough to return to work, he was replaced by a Brian Hansen, a recent Vermont transplant, and apparently an excellent driver.

Jimmy Devine's animosity toward his brother, whose reckless existence had set into motion the spinning wheels of fate, was so violent that it ate apart the bond with his own family. He blamed Moody for never reining Kenny in, for indulging him, spoiling him, coddling him, paying his tickets, his suspended license fees, his legal bills, bailing him out of jail, buying him new wheels, allowing him to live in her basement and to drink her liquor. "Not just a good man's back, but a whole family has been shattered, all because you could never say no to your firstborn son," was one of the accusations Jimmy hurled at his mother, way back when. Burt and Jimmy and their families had been close before the accident, then less so, and then hardly at all. Burt blamed Jimmy for his ruined life, for knowing that Kenny should've never been allowed behind the wheel and yet doing nothing. "How much more could I do?" Jimmy argued in his defense. "Kenny's license had been permanently suspended!"

And then, three years later, after another tragedy, Jimmy blamed not only Kenny for all the misfortune, but also Burt for not being man enough to get up every morning and drive the bus. It didn't matter to Jimmy the pain Burt was in. Living three houses apart, the Hauls and the Devines stayed barely civil, even though Lang kept pointing out in feeble attempts to effect a truce between the men that Burt had done nothing wrong. "It's not his fault he has a weak back, Jimmy."

"Nothing wrong," Jimmy said, "except stroll out of Brucie's Diner with his arms full of meatloaf at precisely and absolutely the worst moment. Nothing wrong except not go to work, and ruin everybody's fucking life."

"He's suffering too, Jimmy."

"That's why I said *everybody's* fucking life, Mother."

Chloe and Moody stood shoulder to shoulder near two graves in the small rural cemetery under the pines as tall and gray as emerald redwoods. Chloe placed all the flowers they had brought in front of a black granite tombstone that read "JAMES PATRICK DEVINE, JR. 1998-2001."

Moody made her put half of them on Kenny's stupid grave.

They stood with their heads bent. Moody held on to Chloe's arm.

"Do you come here with your mother?"

"Sometimes."

"How often does she come?"

"I don't know." The gravesite was beautifully tended, weeded, neatened, full of flowering azaleas, faded lilacs, knockabout roses. "Often, from the looks of it."

"Your dad?"

"When Mom forces him."

Moody nodded. "You have to forgive Uncle Kenny," she said. "It's not his fault he was born with bad genes and couldn't walk straight. Not everybody can make a life like your mom and dad, child. Not everybody can push his own wheelchair. Some aren't so lucky."

"Yes. Like my brother."

"Yes. Like him. But he was lucky to be loved. That love is better than hate for my Kenny. No question he did wrong. But it wasn't all his fault. Sometimes catastrophic things just happen. And your father doesn't understand that."

Moody bent her head deeper. Chloe too.

"He understands," Chloe said. "But that's not what happened here. A catastrophic thing didn't just happen."

They stood.

"What was the poem you used to recite to Jimmy? He knew it by heart. You and he were so cute with it. Do you remember?"

"No."

"Something about Santa, and vampires. Come on. You do remember. Tell your grandmother. It's a sin to lie to old people."

"I don't remember, Moody." Chloe ground her teeth. She didn't tell, though she well remembered.

I wonder if Santa Claus is real
The Easter Bunny
The Tooth Fairy too
I wonder if ghosts really say boo
I wonder if leprechauns collect pots of gold
I wonder if vampires ever grow old.

Little Jimmy, who used to yell YES for the first five and an emphatic NO to the last, had been conceived around the time of Uncle Kenny's death. Her parents had been trying for little Jimmy all of Chloe's life. For all she knew, *she* was supposed to be little Jimmy and they had been trying for nine years before she was born and for eleven after. In some ways her mother was very much a Chinese mother. Two decades of trying for that one highly valued masculine child. Jimmy lived for three very good years. Their little cabin in the woods was full of noise and tricycles and paint on the walls and mess everywhere, and Lang didn't care, and Jimmy didn't care. Jimmy came home at six o'clock sharp every night, punctual as Big Ben. Lang called the Fryeburg police station a dozen times a day. Jimmy, you won't believe what your son just said, Jimmy, you'll never guess what your son just did.

When it was time for little Jimmy to go to nursery school, he was so excited to be taking the big boy school bus. He would jump with joy off the curb when he would see the blue bus pulling up to take him home. One early afternoon Brian Hansen's wallet had fallen into the footwell. He noticed it when he was in the parking lot, about to pull up to the waiting kids. He bent down to retrieve it. He was driving so slowly. He thought he could take his eyes off the road for just a second. But Jimmy was little and his bones were greensticks. They were no match for a school bus, even a small one, even a slow one.

Lang was at ShopRite buying fruit snacks and juice boxes. Big Jimmy was in a meeting about police logistics for the upcoming summer festival. Chloe was in ninth grade math, dreaming of a tuna sandwich she was about to eat for lunch.

Had Uncle Kenny not broken Burt's back, Burt would have been driving the blue bus as he had been driving it for thirteen years. Burt would have never taken his eyes off the road. But Kenny did break Burt's back. And with Burt out of action, the town had hired an out-of-towner with "very good credentials" to drive over the little ones to and fro.

Afterward, Burt didn't care how bad his back was. Though big Jimmy said it was one fucking day too late, Burt stuck a syringe of cortisone into his thigh three times a week and got behind the wheel of the bus until the town gently retired him, because every time he went over a pothole, he cried out in such anguish that the little kids shrieked in terror. Fryeburg had to either repair the town's potholes or golden-shake Burt's hand. The second option was cheaper.

On Jimmy's tombstone: "THE LORD GIVETH AND THE LORD TAKETH AWAY."

Other repercussions: three years ago, Mason comforted Chloe by taking her hand one summer night and becoming her boyfriend.

Still other repercussions: instead of Barcelona, Chloe was headed to an orphanage in Latvia. Damn Uncle Kenny to all hell.

After it happened, Lang did not come out of her house for five months. Then she bought a sewing machine, learned how to stitch herself bright new clothes and staggered on. She bought a heat-gun and heat-cured paints and took up painting lifesize dolls, the height of a small girl, or perhaps a boy. She made fifty of them, and then sold them on consignment, immersing herself instead in gardening with Chloe. The money from the fifty dolls was still dribbling in. And now Lang was giving some of it to Chloe to go to Latvia to search for another lifesize boy.

14

The Meaning of Typos

YOU HAD TO GIVE IT TO HER. LANG TRIED. BY HERSELF SHE took Chloe to apply for a passport. Turned out both parents had to be physically present to sign the application. Chloe, of course, knew why her mother would prefer her father not come, but said nothing.

With Jimmy in tow, Lang quickly filled out the application form while Chloe, bored and hungry and anxious because her mother was anxious, tried to distract her father. The scene would've been funny if her mother wasn't so stressed out. Her dad, bless him, was barely paying attention to the words Lang was writing down, but when it came time to sign, he moved Lang's hand away from the paper so he could sign his name by the X at the bottom, and casually glanced over the document.

"Mother," he said, "why are you so careless? You're as bad as the incompetents in the school records department. Look, you've misspelled her name." He turned to the postal clerk. "Dave, get us another application. My wife here doesn't know her own daughter's name."

"Sure thing, chief."

"Thanks, buddy. Careful this time," Jimmy told Lang. "Want me to do it?"

"No, your handwriting is terrible. I'll do it."

"At least I know how to spell."

"Who can tell? No one can read it."

He watched her.

Lang gestured to Chloe, who once again tried to distract her father with idle chatter about the upcoming prom, graduation, her dress, a limo, a chaperone. Lang said her pen was running out of ink; could Jimmy go get her another?

He went, but as soon as he returned, he peered over the top of her rounded shoulder.

"Lang! You did it again. What's the matter with you? I don't know what's wrong with your mother today, Chloe. Dave, sorry, I need one more application."

Lang sighed and straightened up from the counter. Chloe stepped away. She made eye contact with Dave and shook her head, as if to signal him to wait, but also to scram because all kinds of crap was about to go down inside the peaceful Fryeburg post office on a weekday afternoon.

Lang placed her hand on her husband's chest, on Chloe's father, Jimmy Devine. "Jimmy," she said mildly. "Wait."

He waited.

"I didn't misspell it, Jimmy," Lang said. "Look."

She thrust Chloe's birth certificate into his face. Jimmy stared, perplexed. Plain as noon, printed in black, with a raised seal from the state of Maine confirming the official nature of the words was "Divine." Preceded by "Chloe Lin."

Jimmy understood nothing. "For eighteen years you knew the registrar's office misspelled our kid's name and you never told me?"

"Oh well." Lang patted him. "Nothing we can do about it now. Let's sign and go."

"Nothing we can do about it?" he bellowed. "Of course there's something we can do about it."

"Not in time for her to get her passport for Europe."

"She can't have a passport with her name misspelled in it, Mother," Jimmy said in his best no-arguments-will-be-entertained chief-of-police voice. "A passport is good for ten years. But a mistake like this is forever. No."

"Jimmy."

"No! I said we will fix it and we will fix it."

Lang did not raise her voice. "It's not misspelled, Jimmy," she said. "That's what I told the lady to write."

"What lady?" He was dumbfounded.

"The lady at the hospital who came to take the baby's name for the birth certificate. I told her to write *Divine*."

"Well, the idiot clearly didn't hear you correctly. She needs to be fired. Chloe is not going to have the wrong name on her passport because of a typo."

"It's not a typo, Jimmy. I spelled it out for her. I told her to write D-I-V-I-N-E."

There was commotion at the post office. A man was taping a box shut, the plastic ripping off loudly. The metal door to the postmaster's quarters slammed, a phone trilled, somebody laughed.

Jimmy was mute.

"It's not a typo," Lang repeated. "I wanted her to be Chloe Divine."

"You made a mistake."

"I wrote Divine on purpose."

"But our name is Devine! With an E!"

"I know that. But not her name."

Jimmy stammered. "What are you saying, woman? That you deliberately gave my daughter a different last name from her father?"

"Same name. One letter different."

"That's a different name!"

"No. Just one different letter."

"A different *name*!"

"Jimmy."

Jimmy was hyperventilating.

Chloe hid her amusement. She knew her mother was being disingenuous, for no one knew the power of a letter or two better than Lang, who could have been Lin, which meant beautiful, or

Liang, which meant good and excellent, or Lan, which meant orchid, but instead she was Lang, which meant sweet potato. Lang knew the difference between Devine and Divine very well, which is why she changed it in the first place, why she wrote it with an I, why she kept it from her husband for nearly eighteen years. She knew. Divine: altogether marvelous and lovely, celestial and glorious, of the gods, with the gods, exquisite, heavenly, limitless and great. *Divine*.

15

She Will Be Loved

AT THE END OF JUNE, CHLOE WENT TO HER PROM. IT WAS held in the glass ballroom at the Grand Summit Hotel in Attitash, at the foot of the White Mountains. All the boys dashing, all the girls beautiful. Chloe tried not to judge through her mother's eyes: who was on parade at a bordello? A few would've fit that description. Mackenzie O'Shea in particular. The trouble with Mackenzie was that she thought herself to be quite a tasty morsel. Chloe couldn't figure out why Mackenzie annoyed her so much. Plenty of girls at the prom were dressed much sluttier.

Mason did his best to match his cummerbund to Chloe's funky pewter jewelry and silk silver dress, but he was more granite than metal. Hannah, of course, was a tall glass of water in a clingy mango dress, almost like a slip, with shoulder straps and a bare back, but Hannah had nothing to reveal under her dress except skin, no folds, no fat, no breasts, no sags, nothing unseemly, nothing out of proportion, nothing to make her self-conscious. Her dress was low-cut, but because she was so slim, she didn't look slutty, she looked royal. Chloe, on the other hand, couldn't wear anything low-cut for obvious reasons, and she couldn't wear anything too high-necked because then she looked like a retiring female politician. She couldn't wear an open-back dress because she required a full-back bra to contain what she normally contained under three or four layers of clothing. Summer was always a challenge. She opted for lifeguard bathing suits—red and two sizes too tight—that slammed anything that might bounce against her sternum. Unfortunately, bathing suits were not a dress option for the prom.

After searching for most of her senior year, Chloe finally found something she could wear—a flapper dress, vintage and hand-beaded in glass. It had a cascading fringe, a straight fall and an almost modest V-neck. She wriggled into a square-necked black Spanx slip to cover up her cleavage, and after putting on black eyeliner and black satin sandals, was generally pleased with her almost Audrey Hepburn–like appearance. She left her hair mirror-shiny and down, and wore a red lipstick and a red rose corsage to contrast with the silver beads. She also contrasted well, she thought, against Mackenzie's pink tutu of a dress, against the girl's infuriatingly long legs and cheap stilettos. Mackenzie's straps looked ready to snap at any moment—on her shoes *and* her shoulders. What a mess that girl was. Why didn't the boys think so?

While Hannah and Taylor and Courtney spent the day fussing with their hair and makeup, Chloe was done by one. She then sat on her manicured hands and waited, dreaming about Europe and fretting about traveling from Riga to Barcelona.

"It's two thousand miles by train, Chloe," Blake had said to her. "What's the big deal? In July a band of men travel two thousand miles up the French Alps on their bikes. It takes them three weeks. You're telling me we can't do the same sitting on a train?"

Chloe had been wrong about Blake. As soon as he heard of the new plan for Europe, he produced maps and atlases, guides on the Baltics, a Latvian–English dictionary, several *National Geographics* about flying around the Baltic Sea, the 1915 partition of Poland, and a story on the last of the Polish Jews. Absurdly, he acted more excited about going to Riga than to Barcelona. He told her he had always wanted to visit Vilnius. Chloe corrected his geography, told him Vilnius was in Lithuania, not Latvia, and he corrected her right back, telling her that you couldn't get to Poland from Latvia without first going through Lithuania and the Gates of Dawn. Jostling Hannah, shaking her like a bear shakes a rabbit in his mouth, play punching Mason, filling his notebook with pages and pages of notes and facts and stories and asides about Riga and Vilnius and Warsaw, a thrilled Blake acted as if it was paradise already.

For the prom Jimmy lent the four of them his Durango, and Blake drove them to Grand Summit. Initially they had planned to rent a white limo and go in style, like some of the other kids. But now that they had the expanded trip to the post-Communist world and three weeks of travel to budget for, no one wanted to plonk down eight hundred bucks on a limo. To save money, Blake and Mason even said they would forego tuxes, until Janice put her foot down, thank God, and paid for their tux rental herself.

The girls had seen their boys in suits once before, at a funeral, before Chloe and Mason started dating, but tonight was different. Mason, of course, was groomed like a country-club lawn, but even Blake made an effort to comb his hair and trim his stubble. It was funny how he tried to fit his all-over-the-place self into a black tux and patent leather shoes. Though he looked handsome, he didn't look as if he were born to it. After the first fifteen attempts to fix his crooked bow tie, Hannah gave up.

Chloe and Mason had been nominated for prom queen and king. The king and queen were voted on as a pair, and Chloe knew she was holding Mason back from winning. Without her he would have been prom king for sure, but she was never going to be prom queen, not even in a dress with beads shimmering and clinking like champagne glasses. It's an honor just to be nominated, cooed Taylor, trying to stay positive.

The week the nominations had come out, Chloe had found an anonymous note stuffed into her locker. *How does it feel to know you are keeping that boy from winning what is rightfully his?* Chloe threw the note in the trash, but she thought about it now, on the dance floor with Mason. She couldn't ignore the sense that other girls were appraising them, and concluding that she wasn't good enough for *that boy*.

Fed up with their imaginary glances, Chloe excused herself. In the bathroom, she took off her dress and squirmed out of the suffocating Spanx. Her liberated breasts rose up in rebellion out of their gunmetal V. With cleavage on display, she looked much less like Audrey Hepburn and more like a squat Sophia Loren. Perhaps this was a more fitting look for an almost prom queen.

She strode out into the ballroom where Mason was waiting. The way he smiled at her, it was worth it to overlook for tonight one of her mother's more critical mottos against revealing clothing.

Mason was a great and special boy. Although he wasn't much of a dancer, tonight he kept up with Chloe song after song, dancing alongside Blake and Hannah, doing the Macarena, seeing how low he could go under the limbo stick. Pretty low, it turned out. Lower than Blake, even. She touched his face as they danced. She kissed him. On the dance floor she was almost allowed to do this. The Academy's six vile lunch ladies had transformed themselves into equally vile prom chaperones. They waddled between the tables like malevolent mallards, quacking. What are you doing? You're sitting too close. No public displays of affection, go dance, but respectably. Are you finished with your dinner? You haven't touched your steak, your mother and father will be pleased to see their hard-earned money going into the garbage. Fix the straps on your dress, young lady, Miss Divine, your dress is riding inappropriately low. Miss Divine, I'll thank you to keep your hands on the table, not on your boyfriend's lap. Mr. Haul, please remove your paws from your date's bare back. Miss Gramm, do you have a shawl you can throw on? You look cold. Miss Divine, do *you* have a shawl you can throw on? Mason, honey, you look wonderful tonight. As you were, dear boy. As you were.

Although the occasion was jolly, Hannah seemed less jolly than usual. When they had a minute to themselves on the dance floor, Chloe pulled Hannah close. Keith Urban's "You'll Think of Me" was playing.

"What's the matter with you?" she said to her friend.

"Nothing. Why? Do I seem off?"

"Little bit."

"No, I'm fine." She patted Chloe. "It's all good."

"You look beautiful."

"You too. Very va-va-voom." Hannah sighed. "He's threatened suicide, you know."

"Who?"

"Martyn, of course. Says he can't handle it. What am I going to do? How am I going to go to UMaine, knowing I'll run into him?"

"I don't know," Chloe replied, a little too loudly and brightly, as if delighted by the possibility that Hannah might consider not going to UMaine.

"Maybe I should just join the Peace Corps."

"What?"

"Why not? I'm an idealistic young person. I'd like to visit Ecuador. They travel all the time. I'd meet new people. Experience different cultures."

"Um, are you selfless and unobtrusive?"

"Yes."

"You know they don't get paid, right? They're volunteers. It's not like joining the army."

"I won't need any money. I'll be in Ecuador." Hannah's long arms draped over Chloe's neck. She smelled of Dior Poison. It drowned out Chloe's gentle musky scent. Chloe patted Hannah's bare back. She could feel the blades of her shoulders, like wooden fence boards.

"The Peace Corps has been in the news lately," Chloe said. "And not in a positive light. They may have forgotten their initial objectives."

Hannah chuckled, pulled Chloe closer, ran her hand over Chloe's hair. "Silly girl," she said. "I love how you're always trying to talk me out of bad choices. Don't worry, cutie. I'm not serious about the Peace Corps. Besides, I can't *not* go to UMaine. I'd never leave you there by your lonesome. So don't worry. You want to go find our boys?"

A pasted-on smile greeted Hannah when the girls disengaged. "Cheer up," Hannah said as the girls made their way through the taffeta and satin jungle, searching for their dates. "Like you said, we're not Darlene Duranceau. Everything's still ahead of us."

They got separated. Chloe remained at the edge of the pulsing, strobe-lighting floor. Somewhere on the other side of the ballroom, near white walls and glass doors, reflected in black windows and royal mirrors, Chloe glimpsed Mason, his spiky hair, smiling mouth, delight, bow tie, surrounded by a flurry of shiny silk snowflakes, a lake of reflected satin and soft flesh. In other words, encircled by the cheer squad, blonde hair and soprano giggles all. They were trying to ensnare him in their ribald karaoke routine. In the strobes Mason was being girl-handled, teased, laughed at, pawed. It all throbbed across in fractions of real time, two seconds of black followed by a neon explosion. Chloe couldn't even be sure it was him. It could have been nothing more than a flash of athletic-field memory. After school, she sits in the bleachers and does her homework, while on the field Mason pitches and flirts with the flirty girls. But mostly he pitches, and mostly Chloe reads, and it's only for a fraction of an image between blinks and pages that Chloe thinks, is there something there or is it just adolescent fun? She barely even thinks it. She feels it, and in only two or three beats out of a whole minute of her heart.

"Chloe," a voice says. She blinks and comes to.

Blake was in front of her, smiling, appraising her with his familiar eyes, soaking up her shiny baubles, glittering beads, perhaps other luscious things.

"Have you seen Hannah?"

"She's looking for you. Seen Mason?"

"He was over there." Blake waved to the glassy parquet. David Bowie started up. Almost involuntarily their bodies moved up and down and sideways to the pulsing one-TWO, one-TWO of "Let's Dance."

As they were already gyrating, they gyrated toward each other, looking around for Hannah, for Mason, Chloe trying to make her breasts bob less (not easy) and make her tacked-on smile less uncomfortable. Her ears ringing like the bells of Notre Dame, Chloe wished she could check her watch. David Bowie was so loud. Oh my God, she thought, am I really that old? Is David Bowie *too loud* for me at seventeen? Let's dance.

Maroon 5 came on, kinder, softer, better, lights flashing, bodies inching closer, and she and Blake inched reluctantly closer with apologetic smiles. Sorry there's no one else to dance with to Adam Levine, their awkward expressions read. Then he opened his arms. She raised hers and stepped up to the Blakeplate. Placing one hand into his, she rested the other on his large tuxy shoulder. She felt the pressure of his palm low around her waist, felt his open fingers not just resting against the back of her flapper dress, but holding her.

"Look, I shaved," he said into her ear. "Do you see?"

She saw.

"Do you like it better like this, or normal?"

What was the thing to say here? "Either way's fine."

"Do you know this song?"

"What?"

He leaned down, toward her, close. "This song, Chloe," he screamed into her perforated eardrum. "'She Will Be Loved.' Do you remember it?"

She knew it well. Everybody knew it. The boys and girls sang it as they played volleyball in gym, as they ran up and down the stairs, as they spring-cleaned the front lawn for field day, as they devoured their sandwiches at lunch. They sang it, they knew it. "She Will Be Loved." She pretended she didn't hear him or that it was too loud to reply that of course she remembered it. She nodded in the general direction of his shaggy curly head.

"Are you excited!?"

"About what?"

"I don't think I've ever been as psyched about anything in my whole life. Riga! Vilnius! Warsaw!"

And *Barcelona*, she wanted to add to his litany of paradise, but there was no point—he wouldn't hear her. She tried to catch the floating threads of his voice. He was repeating his avid approval of her idea last week that they should each keep a journal in Europe and at the end of the trip share them with one another. At least, that's what she thought he was saying. The music was so relentless. Where was the prom queen who didn't belong to him? He searched for the eighteen-year-old every day for miles. Your dress is pretty, Blake might have said. Very sparkly. You and Mason light up the floor.

"What did you say?" she yelled. Her heart was full.

"You smell so good," he said, his head near her perfumed earlobes. "What is that?"

"Jovan Musk," she yelled back. "And Love's Baby Soft!"

Where was Mason? She flew across the bodies, searching for this mysterious Mason, and found him entombed in a bevy of loathsome beauties dazzling him with their best cheer moves. Come hither, said the spiders to the fly.

"He's not happy," Blake yelled, warm breath in her face, his eyes merry. "No boy likes that kind of attention. Makes him feel like a hog at a fair."

In a moment of swoony weakness, Chloe leaned her cheek against Blake's black lapel. His big hand tightened around hers. His palm opened wider against her back.

She caught herself, and blessedly "She Will Be Loved" ended.

In silence the four of them chased dreams with time to lose in the empty ballroom. They were the last to leave. The overhead lights had been switched on. "A Hundred Years to Live" turned off in sync with the honk of Mackenzie's dad's rickety Buick. The waitresses were clearing the last of the teacups and the janitors were dragging black trash cans around. Most of the white balloons had run out of helium and floated down to the floor in tired gasps.

Chloe watched a red balloon twitching under a table. She and Mason didn't win. Was he disappointed? He didn't say. But he also didn't say something corny like, don't worry, you're still my queen. He wasn't a corny guy. Chloe appreciated that. Mackenzie had invited them all to her house for an after-prom sleepover. They didn't go. Chloe wasn't allowed, and Hannah didn't want to. Go if you want, Chloe had said to Mason. I won't mind. Are you sure? he asked. The briefest of glares from Blake interrupted him. Mason's just kidding, Blake said. Yes, I am, said Mason. And now here they all were.

"They're going to throw us out."

Hannah, wrapped around Blake, her head thrown back, looked up at the lights. "Let them try."

Mason was next to Chloe. He was perspiring, and his bow tie had come undone. His tux jacket off, his hair wet from dancing, still slightly out of breath, he sat glazed, staring across the deserted dance floor, squeezing and unsqueezing Chloe's hand. He was staring into the space by the wall where a short while ago he had been flanked and fondled by smiling shining soon-to-be-extinct nimble-bodied cheer queens.

Only Blake remained fully animated. Yeah, yeah, yeah, he sang, yeah, yeah, yeah.

"I don't know what you're so happy about," Mason said to him. "Once high school's over, our life as we know it is over. Everything familiar slides across the floor, out those double doors, and vanishes."

Blake cheerfully thumped his brother on the shirt sleeve. "Duuude, no. Wrong attitude. The magic is just around the corner."

Chloe pulled on Mason's hand to redirect his attention from the spectral past to the material her. Obligingly he leaned over and she kissed him to make him forget whatever it was he couldn't.

"I hope we find some good souvenirs," Mason said. "Everyone is dying of jealousy that we're going. I want to bring something back for them."

"Like the clap?" Blake asked.

"*That's* what you hope to get out of our adventure?" said Hannah. "Cheesy trinkets for your dumb friends? Perhaps a fridge magnet from Auschwitz?"

"Let's see if his friends can spell Auschwitz," muttered Chloe.

"I'm afraid," Mason said, "that the best part of my childhood is done. That when we come back, we won't be kids anymore. Won't see each other anymore." Slowly he turned his head to stare at Chloe.

In shame she looked away.

"You and I will be kids forever, bro," said Blake.

"And we'll be only two hours from here, Mase," said Hannah. "It's not like we're going cross-country. You'll drive up one weekend, we'll come down the next. You'll see. It'll be awesome."

Now it was Mason who looked away. "Will it?" His dull voice faded into the white tablecloths.

Blake nudged Chloe, his black patent foot pushing the satin heel of her sandal. Nudged her, eyeing his brother, as if to say, don't give up. Do something. Say something.

Not knowing what to say, Chloe stared up at a lonely blue balloon clinging to life. It had drifted off and hid around a glittering chandelier. Soon Spain. What would it be like? Noises of cities, flickering lights, midnight music, endless dancing, now and forever. A raucous man to swoon and sing the words, *I want you to be queen*. I want to tremble and laugh, Chloe thought, I want to cascade down the waterfall like a goddess, to see the substance of my fortune, to find the answer to my prayers. I want to see things I've never seen. Holy nights, intoxicating nights. I want to feel things I've never felt.

"I just figured out what's in my blue suitcase," said Blake. "Oh God. Of course. How could I have not seen? It's fantastic. But don't even ask. I won't tell you. You'll have to read to the end to find out what happens next."

Part Two

Johnny Rainbow

One half of me is yours, the other half yours
Mine own, I would say; but if mine, then yours,
And so all yours.
William Shakespeare, *The Merchant of Venice*, 3.2

16

Modern Travel

Chloe

Chloe truly hoped, really and truly, that the bulk of the twenty-one precious days in life-changing lands would be better than the travel to said lands because the travel sucked. If Dante lived now, what a book he'd write about the road to hell. Long, full of delays, unforeseen and expected trouble, stultifying waiting, wrong seats, terrible food, numb swollen legs, aching back head knees neck throat and throbbing glands—and not any glands that would be fun, at least theoretically, to have throbbing.

She had never traveled before, except in a car with her parents, and this wasn't at all as she imagined, or as the movies made it out to be. It wasn't in the least romantic. This was more like being stuck for nineteen hours in motionless traffic on the highway, except less comfortable, because instead of being inside a car, it felt as if the car were on top of Chloe. The carry-on backpack that weighed ten pounds when they left the house now felt like a hundred and ten. One of the wheels on the old suitcase was busted, so Chloe had to half-drag, half-carry it. Then it ended up being over the luggage limit by six pounds. It was either pay a hundred more dollars or lighten the load by one umbrella (she hoped it wouldn't rain), two bottles of shampoo (how important was clean hair, anyway?), and two books (who had time to read?).

Before Chloe could lighten the load she was asked a *ton* of questions of punishing stupidity. Did you pack this yourself? She didn't know what to say. Yes? But also—no. Her mother helped her. Was she allowed to mention she had a mother?

Did anyone *else* help you with your bags?

"Do you mean pack them? Or carry them?"

The lady pinpointed her contemptuous gaze on Chloe. "Just answer the question, young lady."

"I want to. I just don't know how to."

"What don't you get? Did anyone help you with your bags?"

"Pack them or carry them?" Mason helped her to carry them. Hannah helped her pack. Not just Hannah, but her mother and father, and Blake threw in a notebook, damn it. If it weren't for his notebook, she could've kept her umbrella.

"Oh my God, I can't do this today," the lady said. "Either. Or."

"No," said Chloe, sweat running down her aching back.

The woman looked ready to punch Chloe in the head.

They had left home at nine in the morning for a 6 p.m. flight out of Logan. They had a four-hour drive to Boston, a burger lunch, and a wait in line. It was scary saying goodbye to her mother. Chloe acted like she was cool with it, but inside she was all stuttering ambivalence. What if something went wrong? Who would fix it? What if she lost her suitcase? What if she was robbed? What if all her money was gone? What if she couldn't find Varda's house? What if no one spoke English?

What Chloe dreaded most was the worst of all possible scenarios: a desperate need for a mother and no mother.

They had been right, her parents. Damn. She *was* too young to go anywhere. She could make it to the water slide in North Conway, twenty-eight miles away, but that was about it. She could deliver hot meals to old people. In the airport when Lang asked if she would be okay, Chloe said, of course, barely looking in her mother's direction. Do you want me to stay? Lang asked. No, we'll be fine, Blake piped up in his booming voice. Don't worry. We'll take care of her. Where was Chloe's dad? He wanted to come, but couldn't fit in the truck. Where was Terri Gramm? At L.L.Bean, unpacking the fall windbreakers. That's why Hannah was real-calm, not fake-calm. She was already adult and on her own.

Hannah had bleached her hair before they left. It was Marilyn Monroe blonde now, squeaky straight, very short, and brushed back severely off her face. The electrified blonde bob made her look even more exotic. Hot damn.

They were late taxiing off, and Chloe imagined all horrors, and she meant *all* horrors, lurking under the belly of the plane while she bit her nails on the runway. How does a plane fly at night? How can the pilot see? Does the plane have headlights, like Mom's car? But there are no roads. She kept her terrified musings to herself, gnawing on her nails to stop herself from running screaming from her seat. Hannah sat across the aisle with Blake. Mason was one seat in front of Chloe. They couldn't even sit together. Mason kept writing notes to Chloe on tiny plane napkins and passing them back, as if in Science class. *Whatcha doin? You excited? You hungry? You love me? I can't wait. Look up, I'm smiling at you. Look between the seats, I'm blowing you a kiss. You think we can get postcards when we get to Riga? I want to send one home.*

To that last one, she wrote back on her own tiny napkin. *Who do you want to send postcards to?*

Dunno, came his answer. *Kids at school.*

What kids?

Dunno. All of them. With a heart at the end.

In the car on the way to Logan, Chloe and Hannah had talked about two butch-looking girls they'd seen holding hands at L.L.Bean, and Chloe said out of nowhere, I bet Mackenzie is a lesbian, and Mason said, why would you say that, and Hannah said, Mason, what do you care if Chloe thinks Mackenzie is a lesbian. And even Blake said, yeah, bro. And Mason said nothing. Why did she remember this? Now he was sleeping. Chloe knew this because he stopped writing her love napkins.

Across the aisle Hannah kept her eyes closed while Blake chatted away, leaning his head against the middle seat, whispering, stage-whispering, joking, laughing, poking her, expounding, trying to get her to open her eyes and look into his notebook. Hannah wouldn't play. Blake, she kept repeating. I want to sleep. But how can you sleep? This is so exciting.

Blake.

Wake up.

Blake.

Wake up.

"Blake!" That was Chloe, hissing. "Shut up."

Chewing the cap off his pen, Blake feverishly wrote in his journal, occasionally glancing over at Chloe. You okay? he kept mouthing.

What are you writing? she whispered. He held it up, as if by its cover she'd know. It's my "back" journal, he said. That's what the Russians call it. For everything else but the main story.

How would he even know that? What Russians?

Chloe didn't want to tell him she wasn't okay, because there was no way to explain why she wasn't, since she didn't herself know, and so she nodded and closed her eyes, and then quickly opened them again because she didn't want to miss the food trolley. Chloe loved to eat. Hannah missed it. She didn't care about food at all. She once said to Chloe, maybe if you stopped with all that cereal and milk, your boobs wouldn't have grown so big.

The lights were turned off, the movies came on, the headphones came out. Most people slept, or played computer games, or leafed through magazines. Chloe tried to read a book, *A Connecticut Yankee in King Arthur's Court*, but couldn't concentrate. She left to go to the bathroom, and Blake somehow hurled himself over a fake-sleeping Hannah and followed Chloe down the aisle.

"You can't sleep either, right? It's too exciting."

"It's many things," she said.

"Exciting is definitely one of them, right?"

"Many things."

"But exciting is one of them?"

It was pretty far down the list. Chloe didn't say it. They waited for the bathroom.

"I think I packed too much stuff," he said. He sounded so chipper. "Too many T-shirts and jeans. Where are we going to do laundry? I didn't bring twenty-one pairs of jeans. Mase and I brought five hundred dollars spending money. You think that'll be enough?"

"If you don't eat, yes."

He laughed. Sleeping people opened their eyes and glared.

"I'm glad we're staying with your grandmother," Blake said, only a notch quieter. "She'll feed us."

"She's not my grandmother," said Chloe. "My grandmother is in Fryeburg. Moody. You know her."

"What about the other one—in Peking?" He tilted his teasing head.

Why? Why?

"It hasn't been called *Peking* in over twenty years, one," Chloe said, swatting him like a harassing fly, "and two, my mother's mother's mother's mother never set foot in China. How many times do I have to say it?"

"What? No. I've never heard this story. Do tell."

They didn't want to go back to their seats so they loitered near the food cart and verbally abused the awful cookies to pass the time.

The flight dragged on. When Chloe thought they must be halfway around the world, in Singapore or someplace, they finally landed—but not in Riga. In Paris. Hannah was excited, but did they see Paris? No. They saw a Parisian airport. Four-hour layover. They wandered around, washed their faces, split two breakfast buns and two coffees, perused the duty free, put on some makeup (girls) and examined the liquor bottles (boys), then checked how much time they had left: three more hours. Having slept on the plane, Mason was refreshed, having fake-slept, Hannah sore and silent. Blake was exactly the same as he had been seven hours earlier, fourteen hours earlier, nineteen years earlier.

They bought a newspaper and Hannah pretended she could read French. Five minutes of mocking her passed the time. It would have been longer if she'd had a sense of humor. They checked out the naughty magazines, not even decorously covered up by brown paper. They were so progressive in Europe, Blake said, so *advanced*. Bless them, said Mason.

The girls were getting more and more impatient. "You're looking at it all wrong," Blake said. "It has to take a long time to get where we're going, because we are leaving our old life behind. By the time we arrive in the new world, we are reborn. It's *supposed* to take a long time, don't you get it?"

"This is torture," Hannah said. "What's wrong with you that you don't see it?"

"This is fantastic," Blake said. "I've never been on a plane before. Or in an airport terminal. Never met a French person. Or seen a French blue magazine." He winked with delight. "I'm writing down my impressions in the back journal. Who has time to be ornery?"

Hannah asked if Blake could write down his impressions silently, mutely, off.

Blake didn't think he could. On the flight from Paris to Riga, the brothers sat together and the girls sat in front of them. The guys kept throwing paper over the seats, pulling the girls' hair, whispering, laughing.

Questions of Punishing Stupidity Part II: Customs control.

Are you bringing anything into Latvia? Are you carrying contraband? She didn't even know what contraband was. How could she know if she was carrying it? Are you carrying drugs?

What is your business in Latvia?

What is your destination?

The Latvian customs control were philosophers! Did they mean today? Where was she headed after she left the airport?

Or did they mean the destination from which she would fly home? Or the destination to which she was headed in five short weeks, not in Riga, not in Maine, not in Spain, but far far away, in a distant land of saints, palms and stucco. What was her destination indeed, damn them.

Mason

Last month when Blake and I went to fix Lupe's rotted-out pantry shelves, she said to us that we all float on a boat down a river of Truth that keeps dividing and dividing into tributaries that reunite, and once we reach the sea, we die. We spend our whole existence arguing with each other about which tributary leads to the main stream. "But they all lead to the same place," she said.

I saved it for later to understand. The later is now. Because I'm trying to look out the window, and all the others are doing is arguing.

Lupe also told Blake that a wise man does three things. First, he does himself that which he advises others to do. (I don't know if I do that.) Second, he doesn't do anything that contravenes the Truth. (What is this river of Truth?) And third, he is patient with the weaknesses of those who surround him. (I am definitely not that.) She said Blake was all three.

Blake says he loves that woman. But I don't know if I agree with her. He keeps borrowing Mom's car to drive over there and take her to the doctor. There's always yelling at home now because the four of us are trying to make do with one car and a loaner, a beaten-up jalopy with pistons that misfire in two of its four lousy cylinders. Blake causes strife in our house. I ask you, how wise is that? And how tolerant of it am I? He says Lupe needs a new fire pit. I tell him Mom needs her car, Dad needs a new back, and I need to get to a varsity reunion. Everybody needs something.

I thought that in Europe there'd be no yelling. Silly me. Here I am, in the cab from the airport, my face to the window. Please tell me I will find something here other than strife.

Hannah doesn't like to travel. Oh, she talks a good game about how she's going to travel all over the world for some job, translating or something, but I truly believe it's a fantasy. She hates to go anywhere. I don't know why she wanted to go to Europe with Chloe. When Chloe told me she and Hannah were heading to Barcelona, I wanted to remind my girlfriend of the few days the previous winter when the four of us went to Franconia to ski. The lift had broken after our first run. There was a blizzard, followed by an avalanche. We were snowed in for four days, with no power, no TV, no radio. Hannah nearly went mad, and we were an hour away from home.

No one lost a limb. No one starved. No one froze. We were just stuck. It hadn't gone as we planned. But we had a fire, we shoveled snow, we went sledding and snowboarding until they came and cleared the road. We sang songs, and ate cans of Campbell's soup from the cupboard, stale cereal, almonds, pretzels, pork rind, and talked about life. We played Scrabble and charades and cards, and Risk. It wasn't glorious skiing, but three of us thought it was fun. Not Hannah. She said it was the worst four days of her life.

Blake laughed it off. He thinks she's a sugar plum and a candy cane and doesn't take anything she says or does seriously. I tried to counsel him. She wasn't joking, I said. She was utterly unmoved by my beautiful Franconia.

Getting from Boston to Riga is another good example of what I mean. We did have to wait a long time. So what? The seats weren't the most comfortable. So what? The food wasn't as good as Burger King. But so what, and what is? We are on a three-week joyride together. To Europe! That's amazing. During the Franconia snow-in, we were with our mom and Chloe's mom. You know, to keep an eye on things. Make sure we didn't get out of hand, and um, out of some things, and into other things. This time we're motherless, and the girls still aren't happy. Chloe keeps calling Riga her penance. I hope she is joking. And Hannah doesn't care about anything but Barcelona. She also thinks we're going to swing over to Paris for a few days. If I didn't know that Hannah doesn't have a humorous bone in her body, I'd swear she was joking. To explain why we couldn't "swing over to Paris," Blake tried to show her the map, to talk through the twenty-one days of our trip with her, every one accounted for, but she ignored him. To pay her back, Blake and I now ignore every mention of Paris. It's like we can't hear her. Every time she says Paris, we say, what? She says PARIS, and we say, what? She says Paris!!! We say, what?

I can't tell you how much that annoys her and amuses us.

It's warm in Riga, and the fields are pretty. Maine has more pine. Here, everywhere I look, the grass is uncut. The roads have no shoulders and no sidewalks. I'm sure when we get closer to the city, there will be sidewalks. Right? There have to be some sidewalks somewhere, no?

Hannah is an ice queen. I'd never say anything to my smitten brother. I know she's beautiful and all. But my God. She's sitting in a Latvian taxi, looking at her feet. She's not even looking out the window. I say, Hannah, look, Riga.

And she says, so? It's a city. I've seen cities before.

But you've never seen Riga, right?

The worst part is, she got Blake to sit in the middle because she said she wanted to sit next to a window, and now she's not even looking out of it! If I was Blake, I'd be pissed. Heck, I'm pissed already, and I'm not even Blake.

At least Chloe loves stuff. Once she stops being anxious and, granted that's easier for me to write than for her to do, but once she stops, she loves stuff. She loves going to the movies and to water parks, loves talking and fishing, and though I don't like fishing, I like that she likes it. She loves skating and plays a mean four-player hockey game. And she's a fast skater, too. Not as fast as Blake, but fast for a girl. I can buy her an ice cream or a burger, and she eats it with gusto. She likes driving, and she sings when she drives. She sings when she gardens, too. She never yells at other drivers. And she is so pretty. She doesn't like people to think that, sometimes not even me. Says she doesn't want me to objectify her, or some shit like that. I still like looking at her, and when she lets me, I like touching her. She's got the silkiest hair of anybody I've ever met. And other soft nice things too. I wish she'd let me touch her more often. Sometimes it's hard to get her alone. Ever since Dad's truck broke, it's been a bitch to get together just the two of us. Blake and Hannah somehow manage, because on top of everything else, I'm always at varsity. Poor Blake. He's the most in-deep-trouble dude in Maine, because not only does he not know how unlucky he is, but he thinks he's lucky.

Things I'm most stoked about: 1. Seeing the Alps on the way to Spain. 2. Barcelona. 3. Being alone with Chloe. Miles of beaches, cheap hotels, food, drink, night. Maybe a room to ourselves. I can't wait. A last hurrah.

Hannah

I miss him. I'm a million miles away and yet all I can think about is him. Last time we saw each other he kept begging me to let him come visit me for a few days in Spain. I said, how could you possibly, I'm going with Blake. He didn't care. He said maybe I could get away for a few hours. Where would I tell Blake I'm going, I asked him. To a Barcelona bed with me, he said.

I want to be a good girlfriend for Blake here in Europe, give him these few weeks as happy memories. He's been good to me. And I've been good to him, of course.

Mason has never seen anything or been anywhere, so he's acting like Riga is da bomb. It's annoying. I didn't even know Riga was a capital city until Moody told me. I had barely heard of Latvia. This isn't where my future lies. I'm going to study to be a trilingual interpreter. I will wear beautiful clothes and go to state dinners in the capitals of the world. Not Riga. Other capitals. I will meet important diplomats, shake their hands and flirt with them. I will get fluent in Spanish and French. Where is my French book? I want to study my subjunctive conjugations while we pass Riga by.

Tomorrow Chloe is going to the orphanage and the boys to the Old City. I'm tempted to send them all off without me, so that I can get over the jetlag, write, practice my Spanish and French, and my English elocution. I'll say I'm not feeling well. I'll allude to some womanly problems. That always works. I've actually been feeling off lately, that's not a lie.

Blake

Everything is amazing. Traveling was great. I want to travel all the time. I love planes, I'd never been on one, but how amazing! Packing was fun, carrying stuff, helping the girls, the ride to Boston; I wish we had time to spend a few days in Boston, looking around, walking around. When I grow up and have my own business and can take off work whenever I want, I'll go to Boston once a month for a long weekend, just to walk around and see the sights. Maybe Chloe can go to Harvard Law School and Mason and I can go visit her. The airport was awesome. I had four burgers because I knew I might not eat for a few hours. The check-in lady weighed my bags to see if they were over, but she should've weighed me, because I was over. Ha! Four burgers, two large fries, a large shake, and a Hershey chocolate pie. And a Coke. I was full up, man. She forgot to weigh me. Poor Chloe hardly ate at all, on account of being such a nervous flyer. Her bag was too heavy. She said it was because of my journal, but I told her it was because of her three pairs of shoes.

Hannah is the most seasoned traveler out of all of us, which isn't saying much, because we've never been anywhere, but she's been to Quebec once, and to Niagara Falls. Before her 'rents imploded, they took her and Jason to Chicago, and once to see Elvis's house in Memphis, because her crazy cheating dad is an Elvis freak. She took five years of Spanish and three years of

French, as she keeps reminding us. So she's an expert, she says, and doesn't need to be awake. I love how calm she is.

Poor Chloe! Mason wasn't sitting next to her and he was snoring to boot, and Hannah was meditating or whatever, but Chloe really needed to talk to somebody to calm down, and she had no one. She would've been less steamed if she'd talked to somebody. She just needed a few jokes and some banter about bullshit.

I'm so psyched about Riga. Who else but me is going to write about Riga in the competition? I'm going to season my story with the spice of Europe, baby, and I'm going to choose my words extra carefully, and they'll be dazzled. I'll have Chloe read it before I send it, so she'll be dazzled too, and she'll say, I didn't know you could write, Blake, and be all impressed. Look at how awesome your story is, she'll say.

17

Carmen in Carnikava

Chloe

She loved the city in the distance. She loved the traffic on the roads (though she loved it less on the bridge they were failing to cross), and the vivid colors of the buildings. She even liked the unfamiliar sounds of Latvian: half-Slavic, half-guttural.

She was ashamed she was such a bad and unprepared traveler. Having no one to turn to, since neither Hannah nor Mason knew anything about Riga, Chloe turned to Blake, who walked arm in arm with his back journal, and it so happened that his journal on this particular Saturday was filled with tidbits about Latvia! He was infuriating. Why was he always the one looking things up, knowing things? What did Riga have to do with his story? "Everything," he said. "The story keeps morphing, my dear Haiku. The chrysalis is becoming a butterfly. Did you know for example that Riga is a hotbed of spy activity? I'll use that detail in my book."

"What do Latvian double agents have to do with the suitcase found in a dead woman's yard?"

"We don't know where the suitcase was found," he declared. "Don't assume anything."

"Your hero goes to Riga to find his answers?"

"Also, don't assume he's the hero. He may be the anti-hero. But yes, he goes to Riga. Just look at this place!"

She did. She was startled by the black church spires rising up outside the taxi windows, and she was startled by Blake. His cheerful immersion in the details of their travel and his commitment to his unformed opus were completely at odds with the Blake Chloe had grown up with. He was confounding. Hannah was no help. She accepted the new Blake the way she had accepted the old Blake, with neutral amusement.

Now, stuck in traffic on the bridge over the Daugava River, Chloe was forced to listen to Mr. Eager plan their itinerary like he was some kind of expert on all things Latvian.

"We'll go to the Central Market. We can't leave Riga without seeing it. And the Riga Museum. Also the Opera House. And, Chloe, I can't wait to try the Black Balsam—how about you? No, I'm not going to tell you what it is. You'll find out soon enough." Leaning forward between the seats, he poked her in the arm. "There's also a bakery that's to die for, you know how much you like pastries, wait, I'm looking for the name of it ..."

Hannah, of course, in her dry way, rained on all things, especially the bakery. "Well, it can't be any better than the bakery in Bangor, near UMaine," she said. "They have the most divine cream puffs. I drool when I think about them, and I don't usually like sweets. And can the Riga Museum really compare to the Field Museum in Chicago? Same with the Opera House. It might be okay by Latvian standards, but compared to Carnegie Hall? And you know what I think? Beer is beer. Heineken, Bud, Black Balsam. It's just beer, Blake. Plus Chloe doesn't even like beer. Let's not talk about it like it's Dom Pérignon."

Mason, looking and sounding annoyed, asked Hannah if she'd ever actually had Dom Pérignon.

"I'm just saying," said Hannah.

"Didn't think so," said Mason.

Blake didn't care. Sitting between Hannah and Mason in the back, he leafed through his notebook, his bedhead banging the roof of the cab. "Chloe," he asked absent-mindedly, "when did you take Hannah to a Bangor bakery? You had cream puffs and didn't tell me? Were they really that good?"

Chloe was at a loss. On the radio, the Latvian music, full of balalaikas and cymbals, syncopated through the cab.

"I don't know," she said. "I don't remember." She stared at the outlines of the city through the window. "Moody's aunt lives so far outside Riga. When would we even get to a bakery?"

"Don't worry," Blake said. "We'll find a way. This bakery is a must-see."

Chloe was hungry, sleepy, slightly irritated by the long ride, the slow-moving traffic. "Well, it definitely can't be tomorrow," she said. "We have to go to Liepaja." The air whistled out of her balloon. Across the wide river, the Old City tempted her, its blue and pink walls, its green and yellow roofs, the colored stone, the purple domes, the pale light of the late afternoon northern sun. Riga seemed to be holding its breath before the raucous Saturday night ahead. Like Chloe was holding her breath before the next twenty days, before the rest of her life.

"We don't *all* have to go to Liepaja," said Blake.

Hannah heartily agreed.

"Chloe, I'll go with you if you want," Mason said from the back seat.

"I thought we would all go," said Chloe. "Wasn't that the plan? To live through everything together, like always?"

"We don't have enough time." That was Blake. "Hannah will go with you, Haiku. Mase has to come with me. We're going to the war museum, bro, the Powder Tower. Manly things that dainty girls aren't interested in. We're writing a story. This is the work part of our trip. While Chloe is in Liepaja looking for a boy, you and I have to find nefarious goings-on in Riga."

"No!" said Hannah. "Why do I have to go to Liepaja? I'd rather go to Riga with you. But not to a bakery. What's the point of going to a bakery if Chloe's not coming with us? I'm not going to eat any of that cream-filled starch. I'll be five hundred pounds before the trip is over." Spoken like a true size 2.

Chloe couldn't help herself. "If you don't like the pastries, Hannah," she said, "then why were you wolfing down so many of them at the Bangor bakery?"

"She makes a good point, turtle, why?" said Blake.

"I was much thinner then."

As if that answered anything.

"And what do you mean you're not coming with me?" Chloe knew she sounded petulant. "*Somebody* has to come with me."

"Yeah, Hannah," Blake said. "Chloe can't find a boy on her own." He pulled Chloe's hair. "She needs help."

"Leave me alone," Chloe said.

"I'll come with you, Chloe," said Mason.

"You can't, bro. What did I just say?"

They were finally out of the city, over the bright, freshly minted bridge. The countryside went from urban to rural in the space of two city blocks and a farm. Inside the cramped cab, their tired chatter faded.

"What's the name of the town we're going to again?"

"Carnikava," Blake said. "Chloe, why do I have to tell you where *you're* going?"

"Not Carnikava," the cabbie said. "Tsarnikava."

Blake studied the map. "Says here Carnikava."

"Tsarnikava!" the cabbie yelled.

After five tense minutes, Chloe spoke again. "How far is ... Tsarnikava from here?"

"Twenty kilometers!" the cabbie said. "Maybe ... twenty ... FIVE!"

"Thank you!" she shouted back. She glanced back at Mason. His eyes were closed. He hated stridency, yelling. How did one yell thank you in Latvian? You'd think Chloe would've thought to pack a Latvian–English dictionary. Just to learn how to say thank you, or where is ...? or how much?

"*Paldies*," said Blake.

Oh, great. So *he* knew how to say thank you. She retreated into herself, her gaze on the fields. How could her grandmother have an aunt still living? It made no sense. "Chloe, did you say your family were bee farmers?" Blake asked.

"I never said that." *Did* she say that? She couldn't remember.

"You did say that. I bet they have awesome honey. I can't wait."

"Did you say *beer* farmer?" Mason deadpanned.

"Yes, that's right, bro. *Beer* farmer. You got it." They started roughhousing over Hannah. Chloe felt better. Maybe they could leave the aunt's house after one night, stay in a Riga hostel? She thought this, but then she checked the meter. The price was ratcheting up like a champion swine for sale at the Fryeburg Fair.

47.

She swivelled her head to stare meaningfully at her three companions but none of them could convert the number into dollars, not even the brilliant Blake. Chloe had thought about nothing but the trip for months, but now she felt unprepared. The numbers on the wretched meter kept clicking upward. 51. Her anxiety level rose with each digit.

"What's the currency here?" she bleated.

"Latu," the cabbie said. "One latu, almost two dollar. One, two. Easy." He laughed, opening a big-lipped, inadequately dentured mouth.

Chloe spun around, eyes big. Blake, sitting in the middle, stared at the meter—55 now—and laughed.

"Next time, take train," the cabbie said. "Without bags, easy. One latu to Riga. One latu."

59. 60. 61. Yeah. Maybe next time they would take the train.

The trees got taller, pinier, the countryside flatter, the yards more florid. There were farms and peat bog, and swamps. There was a dusky mauve color to the long-limbed conifers. The rural roads were poorly marked. It took the cabbie a while to find the address. For a few miles he drove down a long potholed avenue lined with birches. The small houses, mostly made of stone, were set deep inside the verdant foliage. They were neatly kept, had flowers and greenhouses. The landscape was nearly indistinguishable from Maine. Except for the shadow of the rangy White Mountains and the abundance of lakes, Carnikava and Fryeburg seemed more closely related than Moody and Varda. Chloe hoped no one else would realize that. That they traveled five thousand miles only to see their own backyards.

Chloe made some ironic remark about the beaten down nature of the landscape, and Blake said, "Beaten down?" He sounded prickled for some reason, as if she'd offended his very own Latvia. "May I point out that the road here, while narrow, is paved? Can you say the same for the dirt path you live on?"

Did he say this to be funny or to make her ashamed?

"Why choose?" said Blake. "And please note the trash cans put out onto the road. Are you familiar with this custom? A garbage truck comes to your house and picks up your trash, so you don't have to haul your week-old garbage in your mother's Subaru to the landfill fifteen miles away."

"All right, all right," Chloe said.

She wasn't sure they were at the right house because there wasn't a number on the small stucco cottage painted in sky blue. But out on the road there was an onyx-haired woman, her arm around a skinny adolescent girl, both standing at attention near a peach tree and a wooden gate. The girl waved madly before the cab stopped. They climbed out of the narrow car onto the narrow road, grateful to stretch out and careful not to disturb the droopy branches of an apple tree draping over the hedge and fence. Mason and Blake retrieved their suitcases from the trunk and Chloe paid the fare (77 latu! Nearly $140. She tried not to think about it).

Cautiously they approached the old woman and her young charge, who were still waving but also eyeing the Americans' abundant luggage with skeptical wonder. Chloe thought that it couldn't be the right house. The strong, serious woman couldn't be Moody's aunt, couldn't be twenty years older than Moody, who was in her mid-eighties. This woman didn't look seventy.

"*Es esmu* Varda," the woman said. "*Es esmu* Varda." She hugged Chloe, muttering incomprehensible things. She banged

Chloe's chest and said *"Jūsu vārds ir* Chloya." The young girl next to Varda, demure rather than desperate, despite her name—Carmen—didn't stop hugging either, except she was hugging Blake and Mason, two young men not remotely related to her. Perhaps she was more like a Carmen than *Chloya* had first allowed.

"I speak English," the girl said with an accent. "I learn in school. I translate. Grandmother says she very happy you come. She waited for you long time. She want to know your friend names. And why you bring so much suitcase?"

"It's not so much," said Chloe. "One suitcase each. We *are* traveling for three weeks."

"Grandmother says too much suitcase," the girl repeated.

Varda had hair blacker than any hair Chloe had ever seen. It was without a strand of gray. She had black eyes, a weathered, saddle-colored face. Her hands were gnarled claws, tanned, strong, veined, scarred with old injuries. Some of the fingers were crooked, as if they had been broken and then healed poorly. She wore a plain gray dress and old brown suede shoes that she obviously had just scrubbed, for they looked damp. She had dressed up to meet the Americans. The tween by her side, too. Carmen had put on a peasant dress, scraped half the mud off her moccasins, and braided back her long sandy hair. She stood enveloped in a sickly cloud of cheap cologne.

Varda said something to the girl, emphatic and loud.

"She says to tell you she not Mudita's aunt," the young Carmen said. "She says you confused."

The old woman pounded herself in the chest, and said what sounded like "Septic dank."

"She says she sixty-nine," said Carmen. *"Sešdesmit devītā."*

Blake snickered. Chloe flailed out her arm to get him to stop the adolescent nonsense.

"How did you get this so very wrong, Haiku?" said Blake, leaning down from behind to whisper into her ear. "You'd think you'd remember the number sixty-nine."

"Duuude, cut it out," whispered Mason, shoving him. "You're not allowed to make that joke after eighteen."

"You wrong, bro," Blake said. "Cause I just did."

Carmen, having taken a shine to Mason, oozed over and attached herself to his side. "How do you like Latvia? How long will you stay? Why so little? Three days not enough. We have much to show you. There is summer festival in Jurmala this week. You can't leave without seeing Jurmala. Where are you going after? Why Poland? Poland ugly. Where else? Vilnius? No. Riga much better. Latvia beautiful. We have beaches. Do you want to go swimming? Jurmala festival right on water." Carmen said this all rapid-fire while threading her hands around Mason's polite arm. How did he draw them in like this, even on the other side of the world, like bears to honey? Even the Latvian bears couldn't keep their grubby paws off him. Remembering the Fryeburg Academy cheer squad wiped the benevolent smile off Chloe's perspiring face.

"Isn't she a little young to be so touchy-feely?" Chloe whispered to Mason after he'd managed to disengage.

Rolling his suitcase through the gate, he smiled. "She's almost fifteen, she told me. Do you remember us at fifteen?"

Shaking her head, Chloe looked away. He talked about being fifteen like it was seventy years ago.

The single-story cottage was clean but cramped. There was stuff everywhere. Samovars, platters, silverware, tablecloths, steins, cups, canning supplies in the living room, gaskets and covers on the floor by the television, and, on the stretches of paneled walls, family photos.

Hannah and Chloe would be sharing a room with Carmen. The room had one bed and a stretch of wood plank floor. "I sleep with you," Carmen said. "I take the floor. I don't mind. You guests. You have my bed. I sleep with dog."

"You live here?"

"Yes, this my room, my bed," Carmen said. "My mama and papa are down hall. They not here, they work at market. We very honored you come to our house. Grandmother wants to know if you will drink vodka. She knows in America young people don't drink."

"Young people drink," Mason said. "They're just not allowed to."

"Grandmother wants to make toast at dinner."

A stinky, shaggy mongrel barreled into the bedroom and sank into the laid-out bedding, smelling everything up with his mangy fur and rancid dog breath. His name was Patton. Hannah looked very disapproving of his presence in her bedroom.

The boys got the glassed-in back porch. There was an old wicker couch for Blake and a long chair for Mason, since he was shorter than his brother. The sun set in front of Varda's house. Which meant, it rose in the back. Which meant that tomorrow morning, bright and early, Mason and Blake would be wakened by sunrise.

"What time is sunrise around here?" Mason asked Carmen.

"Is very beautiful, sun," she replied. "We close to water, and sun has extra special color here."

He pointed to the glass walls, the glass doors. "What time does the beauty come in the morning?"

"Around 4:00. You want me to wake you so you can see sunrise?"

"I don't think that will be necessary," said Mason.

From the porch the young people stepped down into the backyard. The house was normal-sized, but it was attached to a very large piece of property. It almost looked like a farm, with a fence and untrimmed hedgerows around it. The garden was a working orchard. Row upon row of apple and peach trees bloomed. Fragrant blackcurrant bushes bent like willows with heavy black berries. There were beds the length of streets filled with holy vegetables. Roses blossomed chaotically in one of their three greenhouses. Chloe didn't see bees anywhere.

"Come," Carmen said to the four of them. "I want you to meet Otto. My grandfather."

"I thought he was dead!" whispered Mason, nudging Chloe.

"Haiku knows nothing, bro!" Blake whispered back.

Near the vines of blackcurrant on one of the paths close to the house, the kids found a thin, silent and completely bald Otto, sitting on a wooden bench, drinking a gallon-sized stein of beer. "I bet that's Black Balsam," Blake said excitedly. Wearing an old, grossly oversized army uniform, Otto sat surrounded by hundreds of pieces of wood of varying widths and lengths; they lay on the ground by his feet like a fallen-down forest. He would take a gulp of brew and then pick up a few of the pieces. He was concentrating on making something and barely acknowledged the new arrivals. He glanced at them, grunted in their direction, maybe even nodded to Chloe, but generally remained silent and unimpressed.

"So that's Otto?" Blake whispered. "The famous bee farmer? What's he doing?"

"Looks like he's all farmed out," said Mason.

From the steps of the house, Varda yelled something in Otto's direction. He ignored her too, paying careful attention only to the sticks in his barely functioning hands. She yelled again.

The young people backed away from the warm, stenchy beer Otto was exhaling. "So many awful smells," Hannah whispered to Chloe.

Mason turned to Carmen. "Is this bee-farming season for your grandfather? Because it is in Maine, where we come from."

"Here too," said Carmen. "But what it have to do with Otto?"

"Isn't he a bee farmer?"

Carmen laughed. "Who says this? The only time my *vectev* catches bee is when he eat watermelon and it sting him, and he slap it dead. My *vecmamina* grow bees."

Blake gave Chloe a mocking shove. "Can't you get one thing right? So Otto is not the *beer* farmer."

Carmen lowered her voice. "Don't let grandmother hear you," she said. "You don't understand. Women do everything here. I'm flower girl. I grow flowers. But I will be just like grandmother.

She drive wagon in the old days, but she still harvest flax, pile grain, tend cows and chickens. She shovel sawdust, and grow vegetables and sell them in open market. She load vegetables in her wagon. Papa drive our truck now. We bought new truck."

"Must be nice," Mason and Blake muttered enviously in unison.

"It's very nice," Carmen agreed. "She also split wood herself with axe. And yes, she farm bees."

Before Chloe could ask anything else, she had to know. "Carmen, um ... what's flax?"

Carmen laughed. She pointed to a long row of tall-stemmed blue flowers that stretched down a hundred densely planted feet.

"That's flax. It's seed. Use for food and to make clothes. Flax is linen."

"Oh." Chloe couldn't believe she didn't know this. "So, what does Otto do?"

Carmen put her hand on her grandfather's sloped shoulder and kissed his bald head. "As long as I know him, this."

"Yes, but what is that?"

"Drink beer. Make picture frames."

"Make picture frames to sell?"

"No. You will see in house. Grandmother so tired of picture frames. But he won't stop. You can't tell him what to do. Because he was in war." Carmen smiled. "Grandmother says Otto was in war, got shot, got medal, and after medal, was done. So now every time he bring her new picture frame, he does it so proud and she yell at him, what do you want, medal?"

They all stared at Otto. Chloe wanted to hug him. Although he didn't look the huggable type.

"I wish he spoke English," Blake said.

Hannah said, "What war did he fight in?"

Carmen stared uncomprehendingly at Hannah. "*The* war," Carmen said, opening her hands. Then, raising them high: "*The* war. Is there any other?"

Varda was shouting at them from the porch.

"She ask us to come inside," Carmen said, pulling on Mason's arm. "Dinner soon. And you so sweet, mosquitoes will eat you alive. She want to spray you with vinegar."

Mason

I'm not *un*comfortable. But I don't understand what anyone is saying to me. Old Otto keeps pointing at the food in front of me and repeating the same thing over and over, even though he sees I don't understand. He thinks the solution is to shout it. Carmen, who sat me by her side, has barely turned my way. She can't translate everything at once, and she is busy running interference between Varda and Chloe. So I have an old man, in whose house I'm staying for free, yelling at me at the dinner table. I'm afraid to eat, afraid to look at anyone, afraid to gesture. What do I do? I sit like an idiot and smile at him like a moron, and nod every once in a while. He remains adamant. I pass him the dish of gruel in front of me, but he swats it away, grabs the ladle and pours three helpings of mud into my bowl. It looks so gross. But what if I don't eat it and then find out it's the national dish of Latvia? Who can I ask? Blake, because he's got no sense, is eating the mud, the gruel, the cabbage, the sausage, the bread, everything. Why is the bread black? I asked for some white bread, and they all laughed.

The part I liked was how Varda stood up at the head of the table. I thought she was going to make a toast, but then she pressed her hands together and I thought, oh good, maybe grace, and she said, *Pienācis mans Kungs.* Sounded like *beer nutty manse coons.* Maybe not grace, then.

While Blake eats, he chats happily to Hannah, as if everything is right with the world. He's got his arm around her, he's stroking her hair, and she's nodding and shaking her head. Those two are having an intimate dinner date, while I'm being attacked by Otto in a crowded room in a foreigner's house, and no one sees and no one cares. I think Otto is saying shishkebob. But what's in front of me doesn't look like shishkebob. It looks like a camouflage-colored stew made of gray peas and zucchini. I hate regular green peas and I hate zucchini. I can't eat it. Whenever Chloe's mother offers it to me, I can't even fake it.

"It's not zucchini," Chloe says to me across the table when she gets a break from Varda. "It's gray peas, pig snout and sauerkraut. Eat it."

Is she joking? What I want is the thing that looks like meat pie down the table, right near the romantic couple giggling away, their heads touching. I glare at them, to no avail.

Carmen finally directs her attention to me. "Otto wants to know if you think it delicious," she says. "He keep asking: delicious? *Garsigi?*" The girl spoons something onto my plate and I raise my hand to say NO MORE, but she thinks I mean more and gives me another helping. I ask what it is. Herring in milk, she says.

Help!

Chloe is wrapped up with Varda, who is feeding her eggplant and poppy-seed cake and rubbing her back and stroking her hair. I feel bad for Chloe, because she doesn't like to be touched. Carmen would like to talk to me, but without her, Varda and Chloe wouldn't be able to speak. What are Blake and I going to do tomorrow in a city where no one speaks English? I know coming here is the price we had to pay for getting to Europe, but I'm starting to doubt if it was worth it. Am I going to be able to eat in the next three days? It's not *all* going to be alligator soup and lizard eggs? Aren't there some kind of hospitality rules against this sort of thing? Don't you condemn yourself for all time if you serve your poor starving guest pig snout and sour porridge?

Blake

The food is fantastic! The meat pie, the poppy-seed cake. The peach preserves. Everything is out of this world. The whole house smells sweet like burnt jam. A little like Chloe's house.

I really wish Otto spoke English. He's awesome. He sits at the table in a vintage army uniform about three sizes too big and keeps trying to get Mason to eat some food, but Mason would rather be stabbed through the eye than eat a muffin with grated carrot. He's a fool. It's so good. Varda wanted me to learn how to say it, but I just wanted to eat it. The dark bread is good, the freshly churned butter. Carmen served us herring boiled in milk. She said it was a delicacy. I can see why. It was super tasty.

Varda's house is cozy, and she is so happy to have Chloe with her. You can tell she loves Chloe even though she's never met her before today. Chloe asked me how I knew this. And I showed her the photos all over Varda's house. They're all of Chloe. There are also some of her many cousins, but mainly of her. Moody must have sent them. And Otto has made a frame for each one.

Through Carmen, Varda keeps asking Chloe if we can stay longer. Stay, stay, she keeps saying while kissing her, hugging her. Chloe, who doesn't usually get pawed like this, is enamored by the affection. I know she wishes her own mother hugged her more. Varda seems to be a different breed of woman entirely.

My poor bro can't find anything at Varda's table to eat. He'd probably opt for two weeks trapped in the snowed-in ski lodge with Hannah than another night here.

I almost don't want to go anywhere tomorrow. I want to try to talk to Otto and play with his dog. Please, God, let it rain. He's got a German Shepherd named Patone. That's the only word Otto said to me. His dog's name. Patone. He's such a great dog. I want to take him for a walk but don't know how to ask if he's got a leash. Maybe tomorrow I'll ask Carmen, if she ever stops making googly eyes at Mason.

Chloe leaned over to rain on my parade and said, you do know he's saying Patton, right? Not Patone. Patton, the greatest war commander the world has ever had.

I know who Patton is, I said, quite grumpily.

If you know who he is, then why did you say Patone?

She's impossible. I don't care. I can't stop petting the dog, whispering to it. When God created you, I whisper to it, He told you to sit by the front door of your house and bark at anyone who walks past or comes in. For that God is giving you a lifespan of twelve years. Nine if you're unlucky. I asked Carmen how old the pup was. It was almost eleven. I leaned toward the dog. You don't have much time, I whispered, shooing it away. There's the garden. Don't just sit here. Go do something fun. Dig a hole. Rearrange the flowers. Lick somebody. Go.

Poor Chloe. No one wants to go with her to the orphanage tomorrow. She doesn't want to go herself, so how can she expect us to? I know someone *has* to go with her, but I need Mason with me, and Hannah doesn't want to do it. I spent all dinner trying to persuade her to go. She says she'd rather take a tour of Stalinist architecture in Riga than go to an orphanage. I told her that could be arranged, and I'm not kidding. She is going to get a tour of Stalinist architecture. But seriously I don't know what to do. Do I offer to go with Chloe myself? And how is that supposed to work? Mason and Hannah will wander around Riga, the blind leading the blind, while Chloe and I travel on a train across Latvia? They don't know what they're saying. When I suggested all four of us go, Mason and Hannah laughed at me. She can't go alone, I repeated. They didn't offer a solution. They didn't say, okay, I'll go. They didn't say, you should go. They just stared at me like I was sour porridge.

Why can't she go alone? said her best friend and my girlfriend.

Hannah

Carmen was just asking me in English how I get my hair so blonde and straight, and everybody was looking at me, and suddenly Blake starts telling Carmen that the flowers Chloe grows back home are really pretty. And then everybody started looking at Chloe and Blake, and no one wanted to talk about my hair. I was so annoyed. I said the flowers are just as pretty if you go to the country store on Saturday and buy a bushel for ten bucks. You don't have to spend your Sundays on your knees.

I don't want to talk to anybody right now. All I wanted was to have tomorrow to myself, and it looks as if I'm going to have to go with Chloe to the stupid orphanage. Why can't I be stronger? I keep saying I don't want to, but Blake just won't listen. Men.

Why can't Mason go? Mason, I said, she's your girlfriend, you *have* to go. Blake and I will walk around Riga, have lunch in a café maybe. Blake, I cooed, some time alone together, don't you want that? And he said, ah, cutie, but I have to blah blah blah.

I turned to Mason for support, and he said, you heard my brother. I can't. We have to blah blah blah.

Mason's already getting on my nerves. This is only our first day here. How are we going to last another twenty days?

Chloe would let me stay back. She can go by herself. I know she can. I want to ask her, but she's been busy with her aunt all night. I've been staring at Otto while waiting for her to finish talking. Otto is completely ignored by his wife. He could keel over, and she wouldn't pause to breathe between words. What could she possibly be telling Chloe? In fact, Otto's fallen asleep at the table and is tilting over onto Mason, who looks terrified. It's so funny. Five more degrees and Otto will be on the floor. Maybe he'll be more comfortable there. He can put his head on the dog. Better not, that mongrel smells like the swamp. Varda passed Otto no food, poured him no drink, didn't address him once, and still hasn't looked at him, and now he just struggled up and shuffled away, and she never even glanced in his direction. She gazed at the meat pie longer than she gazed at her own husband. I wish I could ask her about it. What I want to know is: did Varda and Otto begin like other people? Did they begin like my own parents, before they hated each other, or like Chloe's parents, who never stop talking, bickering, discussing, relating, or even like Blake's mom and dad, who were normal before Burt got hurt, although now they're a little clogged up? Burt is like Otto in some ways, peripheral to the daily life of his family.

Anyway, Otto disappeared, but Chloe continued to talk to Varda through Carmen, who was too busy to make eyes at Mason, and so Blake had time to harass me all night about the orphanage and his prize-winning pig—I mean, story.

When I tell other people about Chloe and me, they cry. Like Martyn. When I told him, he went all sentimental. That's the sweetest thing I ever heard, he said. Lifelong friends, who ever gets such a thing? Okay. Yes. Great in theory.

But look at us. We can't go to Europe without the boys. We can't go to Europe without each other. We can't go to college without each other. We are rooming together our freshman year, as if we're identical twins. There's no way out.

I'm really tired of the way Chloe acts sometimes, all mousy, and small, and helpless. Oh Mason, can you help, oh Blake, can you help, let's push the boat out, can you help, I want to build a bench, can you help, I have unlaced ice skates, can you kneel down in front of me and help, who's going to come with me to the orphanage, help help help.

I think she could be using her helplessness and her body to get guys to do stuff for her. Except she hides her body, so my theory falls apart slightly. Okay, maybe using not her body, but definitely using her helplessness, which is like her inner body. She told me once that she hid her boobs because she was afraid if guys saw them, they wouldn't notice how smart she was. She's not *that* smart. She didn't even know the currency of Latvia.

That's it, I'm refusing. Mason can go, or Blake, I don't care. The way I see it, if you can't ask your boyfriend to schlep with you across a foreign bog, then what are they good for? I don't think Chloe has ever once asked herself what she would like in a boyfriend. Or what the important things are that some boyfriends like, say, hers, might do. For example, does a boyfriend buy you things? Does he pick flowers to bring to you? Does he maybe do other things to you, things you'll soon find you can't live without? I would say and *do* say to her, Chloe, you know how this is supposed to work, right? This is prime hormonal time.

He's not supposed to kiss you on the cheek at the screen door of your house. She and Mason have been "dating" since they were fifteen, right after Blake and I hooked up, and in that time, I've never heard them say one cross word to each other. They laugh, they talk, they discuss things, they never argue. Once they were almost going to disagree, when Mason said that *Field of Dreams* was his favorite film and it clearly wasn't hers. But Chloe just said, Mase, aw, I love that you love that film so much. And for his seventeenth birthday she got him a *Field of Dreams* baseball cap that he slept in for six months after.

I mean, is that normal, to go out with someone and not have one teeny argument? For example, he doesn't want to go with her tomorrow. So what does she do? Nothing! She asks *me* to go. She doesn't get upset with her boyfriend. Mason is late, that's fine. Mason is sick and doesn't go to Meals on Wheels, that's okay. Mason dances with the entire cheerleading team, not a problem. What does Mason have to do to get a rise out of Chloe?

She argues more with Blake than with Mason. She argues more with Blake than with anyone. They're always at each other. If it weren't for me and Mason, I don't think those two would ever willingly hang out. Everything he does annoys her, and her criticism bothers the crap out of him. Their personalities clash and have always clashed. He doesn't want to go here, she doesn't like to eat there, it's not the eighteenth hole, it's the sixteenth, *Gone with the Wind* was absolutely Margaret Mitchell's only book, *Dodgeball* was stupid, "Una Palabra" from *Man on Fire* means "One Word" not "One Act." On, and on, and on. Ad nauseam.

And he, to torture her, calls her "Haiku", even though he knows it drives her crazy.

Why can't Blake go with Chloe to the orphanage? Why do I have to?

18

Cherry Strudel

Chloe

So apparently for boys, the sun brightly shining in at four in the morning is like sleeping with an eye mask, because Blake and Mason didn't stir until Hannah and Chloe kicked them awake at eight. Carmen's mother Sabine, who had arrived with bread, fresh eggs, and thick-cut bacon, in her energetic Latvian way was already frying up a feast for eight people.

Sabine and her husband Guntis took the things Varda grew and sold them at the market. That was how the family made its living.

Guntis set up the stalls, and ran the unsold produce to sell it on the pigfeed market at the end of the day. Varda had told Chloe all this and more last night at dinner.

"So not only *is* there a dad," Blake said to Hannah when he'd heard, "but he's a good one. See, Hannah, men aren't all bad."

At odds with yesterday's disrespect was Sabine's reaction to Otto. She and Guntis had been away last night in Valmiera, trying to get a contract from a local seed farmer. But though there were guests from America, the first thing Sabine did when she walked into the kitchen, her arms full of squash, was go outside to find her father. Chloe watched them through the glass door. The woman put her arm around Otto, leaned down, hugged him, kissed his head. They spoke. He smiled! Otto looked positively benevolent in the morning sun, looking up adoringly at his daughter. He was wearing the same baggy uniform as yesterday and the sticks were in his hands.

Over breakfast, Blake planned his and Mason's day in Riga. He was sunny like the morning, rumpled, unshaved, wearing a plaid cotton shirt with the sleeves rolled up, jeans, and cowboy boots. It was supposed to hit ninety in Riga this afternoon, but according to Blake a long-sleeve shirt was what Latvian weather called for.

"You sure you're not underdressed?" Chloe asked. "You might want to bring your parka. You know, just in case."

"Tell that to the cold rain in Liepaja," he said. "Because that's where *you'll* be in your sleeveless pink blouse."

Chloe asked Hannah to hurry up because they needed to leave. It was Sunday and the trains might be running poorly. She read in one of Blake's books that sometimes there was trackwork. And Liepaja was a long way away, over two hundred kilometers, not that anyone had any idea how far that was. You could've said seventy cubits, and they'd be none the wiser.

Hannah, who was not speaking to anyone this morning, shot Blake a lethal glare.

"Hannah, honestly, you don't have to go with me," Chloe said. "Blake, I know you're trying to guilt her into going. Stop it. It's fine. I'll go by myself." Chloe didn't mean it. She'd never been on a train by herself.

She'd never been on a train.

Mason said he would go. But first he asked Carmen if the family went to church on Sundays. It was nine in the morning. He would go with Chloe after church, he said.

"No, you're coming to Riga with me, bro," Blake said.

"Church was at six," said Carmen. "Market opens at nine. We already went."

"You woke up at six o'clock?" said Hannah.

"No, we woke up at four. To water fields and harvest vegetables. But church at six."

Mason looked disappointed he had missed it.

Blake elbowed him. "Mase, it's in Latvian."

"So? God is God." Mason seemed happier this morning. He ate ham, and even tried the black bread, which he said was not the *worst* thing he'd ever tasted.

Having cooked, Sabine cleaned up and talked to her parents in the manner of a hectic, harried spitfire. Black-haired and black-eyed, she looked like Varda, a little taller, a little thinner, her face already weathered, her skin scarred with work, the hem of her dress fraying.

"How old is your mom?" Chloe asked Carmen.

"Thirty."

Chloe tried to hide her American shock. "Wow. Huh. She doesn't look thirty." Chloe took a long sip of her coffee. She looked fifty. What did the world do to you to age you like that before your time? Her mother—despite everything—didn't look as old as Sabine. "She must have had you young."

"She was fifteen. She had older sister. Killed in wagon accident before Mama was born. Then Grandmother lucky to have Mama when she was almost forty."

"And now you all live in this house?"

"Yes. Grandmother wants Mama to have another baby. But Papa says it will be with another woman because Mama too old."

"Ah. I think your father is joking, no?"

Carmen didn't reply. But Chloe, having absorbed the proximity with which Carmen had been nesting near Mason even at a casual breakfast, suddenly understood some things.

"Did you hear what that girl just told me?" she whispered, pulling Mason into a corner of the kitchen, pretending to look for a butter knife.

"No." He was eating a ham sandwich so heartily, he hadn't bothered to swallow. "What she shay?"

"Mase, a little distance, please. I'm seeing that girl in a new light."

"Why?" He grinned. "She so nice."

Chloe rolled her eyes.

"She's just a kid," he said.

"Yeah, like us. Just—keep away, that's all. I worry for Carmen's future if this is what she's like already." Chloe started collecting her wallet and book to read on the way to Liepaja, but Carmen stopped her.

"Mama says too late to go," the young girl said. "When you woke up so late, we thought you not go."

"Late? We woke up at seven-thirty."

"Too late. Liepaja train runs once a day."

"That can't be true," Chloe said. "It says the trains run from Riga. Our guidebook said. Blake? Right?"

"They run from Riga," said Carmen. "Once a day. Once there, once back. You missed train there. Try again tomorrow. You have to wake up early if you want to go. Grandmother says she didn't want to wake you after long travel. But she wake you tomorrow."

Seven-thirty was too late to wake up?

"Much too late," said Carmen. "If you serious about Liepaja, you wake up at five, and then really hurry."

"What time would we need to wake up if I wanted to take my time?" Chloe said, dazed. She turned to Blake and Mason. "Guys, did you hear?"

Blake shrugged. "What can we do? You'll come with us to Riga. We'll find out what time the Liepaja train is for sure. You'll go tomorrow."

"You won't see Riga today. It's going to rain," Carmen said. She seemed delighted by this. She was dressed in a pretty frock and had flowers in her hair and pink gloss on her lips. "You can stay here. Come with us to market. We can play cards. There is beach nearby, I can take you."

"I thought you said it was going to rain?" Chloe said suspiciously.

"If it stop," the girl said without a beat. "We can talk about how you can adopt me instead of some Liepaja boy. They dangerous. They get into all kinds of trouble. But not me. I come with you to America." She smiled at Mason.

All right, Chloe thought, let's just drink some chamomile tea and chill the crap down.

"My parents want to sponsor a male child," she said, disbelieving Carmen about the trains. How would Carmen even know? When did she ever take a train? Rain! Look what a beautiful day it was. There wasn't a cloud in the sky. The girl simply did not understand boundaries. And Mason, harmless and friendly, wasn't going to inform Carmen of them. He loved the attention. He never informed anyone of the boundaries.

"Okay, quick, let's go to Riga," Chloe said to Blake.

"Only one train a day from Riga to Liepaja," Carmen repeated. "Everybody in Latvia know this. Otto know this."

Sabine said a bunch of words.

"Mama says orphanage will not be close to station."

"How does she know?"

Rapid fire from Sabine's mouth.

"Because," Carmen said, "Mama says kids all runners. You don't want them close to train station. You will have no orphans left."

Chloe, Hannah, Mason and Blake had a meeting outside in the garden, with Patton underfoot and Otto nearby, already drinking beer, his rough hands shaking through his miter cuts. Blake watched the old man, chewed his lip uncertainly, and then opened his journal. They revised the countdown of their days. Where was this extra day of unexpected delay going to come from?

"How long do we absolutely *have* to stay with Varda?" Blake asked Chloe.

"Three days. Minimum." She didn't tell him what Moody had told her, that she better not stay one minute less than five days.

"Does yesterday count?"

"Yesterday's gone," Mason said.

"Okay, not helpful. Chloe?"

"I don't want to stay in Latvia an extra day," Hannah said, "just because Chloe couldn't be bothered to check out the train schedule."

"You didn't check out the train schedule."

"I didn't have to."

"I didn't have to either."

"Yes, you did."

"No, I didn't."

Blake interrupted. "Hannah, no one was going to get up at four in the morning today, even if the train made a special stop at Varda's house to pick you girls up. Let's go to Riga, and then get to bed early tonight, so you can get up as early as you need to. Mase and I will go to Jurmala. Frommer's says it's a must. The day after, the four of us will get a tour guide for Riga, and the following morning we'll head out to Poland."

"Except this day, the day you're standing in presently, in Otto's yard, doesn't exist on your little schedule," Hannah said. "It exists in reality. Here." She waved her hand. "But not in your chart of meaningless numbers. You didn't budget for stay-in-the-house-and-Mason-flirts-with-Carmen-all-day day."

"I'm not flirting with Carmen."

"He's not flirting with Carmen," said Chloe. Ugh.

Blake put away his notebook. "We'll have to make it up down the road," he said. "In Poland somewhere. Nothing we can do about it now."

"Except not go to the orphanage."

"Hannah!" Chloe and Mason shouted. Hannah stormed off.

"Thanks a lot," Blake said. "Only one of us is going to have to grovel, and it's not going to be the two of you, wiseacres."

Inside the house Sabine was talking again with great urgency, as though it was the only way she knew how to speak. She pointed to some distant location and pushed Carmen forward.

"Mother says I should come with you to Liepaja," Carmen said to Chloe with a saucy smile. "They do not speak English at orphanage."

"Of course they do," Chloe said. Someone had to be able to translate the sponsorship papers for the Americans.

"Mother says I should come with you," the girl stubbornly repeated.

Hannah nudged Chloe in the back. "Yes let her come!" she whispered. Chloe turned around and fixed her friend with the stare she had learned from her mother. The stare that said you better shut your mouth when you're speaking to me.

"You are being a really bad friend right now," Chloe said. "Really really bad."

"Okay, fine." Hannah raised her hands in frustrated surrender.

Chloe turned her sights back on Carmen. "Carmen," Chloe said, "the boys are not going with us to Liepaja. Only Hannah and I are going. You know that, right?"

After that, Carmen lost interest.

Mason

The orphanage is dividing us. No one listens to me when I keep quoting Lupe saying and saying that together we travel down one river, we all meet up at the end, why worry about the tributaries. I feel guilty for not going with Chloe. I feel guilty for wanting to go with her when my brother clearly wants and needs me to go with him. Wait, that's not actually true. I don't *want* to go to an orphanage. I want Hannah to go, and I don't care if she doesn't want to. The more she doesn't want to, the more I want her to. There's a word for that, isn't there? Schadenfuckingfreude.

The commuter rail station was in stony Carnikava, a mile away or, as they say in this part of the world, something something kilometers.

Blake and I wore boots, Chloe flat sandals. Hannah of course wore some impractical thing like ballet flats a size too small, and defended them by saying, ballerinas practice eight hours jumping on their toes in these, and I can't walk to a small village?

After two sheppeys of walking down a paved road, she began to complain of breaking blisters and open sores and general exhaustion. It was barely noon.

The trains to Riga ran once an hour on Sundays. We had just missed one and had to wait fifty-five minutes for the next. On the platform we bickered about why it didn't occur to anyone to bring a schedule? Why didn't the station house have a schedule? Where was the ticket seller?

The train was late. Blake was drenched in sweat in his plaid shirt by the time we climbed aboard, and then it had no air-conditioning and was crammed with hundreds of under-deodorized Latvians taking a Sunday trip to the big city.

We got off at a big old Communist-style train station, which is to say that the station was built in pre-Communist times, taken over by them, and never renovated. Everything was falling apart: bricks, windows, frames, stairs. I said to Hannah, look, here's that Communist architecture you wanted to see so much. She ignored me.

Blake wanted us to spend a day together, just me and him, researching things, taking notes, making observations. But every time he opened his journal, Hannah groaned. So you know what we did?

We went where Hannah wanted to go. We marched through the Old City as if it meant nothing, through a park, past the Riga Canal, on which it would've been so nice to stop and meander, to the white Opera House. It was an impressive building. Maybe we could check out the Daugava River after? No. Hannah wanted to buy some dresses, wanted to go to the World War I zeppelin hangars of the Central Market. Chloe wanted to walk in the park by the winding canal. Blake wanted to find some spies. No one wanted to do what I wanted to do, which was go inside a great big old church called St. Peter's with the gray spire. Chloe said she'd go with me while Blake went skirt-shopping with Hannah, but Blake didn't want to split up the group. Chloe said to him, why not, you don't care about splitting up tomorrow.

I said, Hannah, if we go to your stupid market, why can't we go inside my stupid church? But then they all made fun of me for wanting to go inside a stupid church. So I dropped it.

You know how Blake dealt with having to spend all day with his girlfriend? By talking to me and Chloe about *The Blue Suitcase* and looking for places to eat and mostly ignoring her. Hannah didn't want to eat, or have a beer, or be in the sun. Fair enough, it was really hot out, like HOT. Like Maine sometimes gets. Not New Hampshire. It's always cool in the White Mountains. I miss them.

Blake said that according to his guidebook, Rigensis was the best bakery in Riga, so we had to stand in line, no matter how long it was. The bakery was between the Daugava and the Riga Canal in the Old City. The line looked to be two furlongs and one zork. The last man standing told us it was an hour wait. Chloe said it must be good if people were willing to stand in the heat on a Sunday afternoon for a Napoleon and a cherry strudel, but Hannah said she wasn't one of those people. Blake told me not to worry, we'd go to the bakery tomorrow when the girls were in Liepaja.

Chloe said she really wanted a cherry strudel and Hannah said, yes, but do you really *need* a cherry strudel?

Blake and I exchanged a weary glance. Let her eat what she wants, Hannah, Blake said. We're on vacation.

All the more reason to watch your figure, Hannah said. Don't you think?

Hannah is right, Chloe said, deflated. Last thing I need.

The three of us started to walk away, but Blake didn't move. Dude, we gotta go, we said. He didn't move. What are you doing? He was standing in line.

I'm getting myself a cherry strudel, Blake said. Who's with me? Chloe, you want one?

So we all waited.

Aside from Hannah whining about her shoes, the sun, the heat, the smell, the walking, the heat, how she didn't have a good enough pair of sunglasses to see the colored buildings, and how she didn't want to have warm beer, even though it's nearly impossible for us to drink back in Maine, blisters, saying she didn't like raisins so why would she eat an apple strudel with raisins, oh and did I mention the heat, and being bored with every topic of conversation anyone brought up, making the rest of us want to scream, and I'm not a screamer, we had a good day. Was Hannah always like this? We've been hanging out a long time. She was fun once. She used to ice skate and come sledding. She used to like ice cream. But not anymore. You'd think Blake would be fed up, but no. He says, baby, come on, look at the cobbled Old City, isn't it pretty? Want to walk down to the river? Don't you love the way the Opera House and the canal divide the Old City from the new? Which do you like better, the old or the new? Want a sweet pretzel? An ice cream? He's got his hand on her back, caressing her, and she says, please, can you not touch me, I'm hot like glue, and he just smiles and pats her and says I'm glued to you, and continues talking and laughing, and touching her.

I'll give one thing to Hannah—the strawberries at the dumb market she dragged us to were unbelievable. Juicy, sweet, like nothing I've ever had, even in Maine. We bought two baskets, devoured them between the four of us, and bought two more. Blake had strawberry juice all over his plaid shirt. Chloe said his shirts always looked like this, and that's why he wore them plaid: so no one could see the stains. Ignoring her, he wondered if we could work strawberries into our story. The girls groaned. I remembered Lupe telling him anything can be worked into the plot, and Blake laughing and saying, that's right, baby, because the whole world is my research.

Maybe it's not the orphanage that's dividing us.

Blake

It's like a dream. I have a constant feeling that I'm going to blink and wake up by my window at home overlooking the lake, with the zipline, which runs from the oak branch over the lake to a post on our deck, tempting me. Yet, here I am, here we are. Walking on narrow cobblestoned streets, sitting on screeching trains, the sound of metal on metal telling me I'm not asleep. I pretend I'm doing my research because I don't want them to know how bowled over I am—they'd laugh at me. Mason asked if I wanted to rent a row boat on the big river, and I said, I row every day on our lake, why the hell would I want to row here? As if I'm some kind of rube. But Chloe pointed out that she, not I, rows on our lake. We debated this thorny issue at some length as we gaped around the ancient town, while Hannah put on her been there, done that air. I don't want her to think that I'm walking around Riga with my mouth open because I'm unsophisticated. So I say intellectual things like, did you know that the Dome Cathedral altar and the cross-vaulted walkways were built in ornate Romanesque style but the steeple and the eastern pediment in Baroque style? But that's not what I'm feeling. What I'm feeling is wow.

We sat for a few minutes in the cloister of the Dome Cathedral, the courtyard all glowing and sunlit. I thought it was a little bit like magic. But then Hannah said she wanted to go buy some clothes, and Mason said, you want to go to a mall, is that it? Like the outlet center in North Conway? I didn't say anything, but the illusion of heaven was broken. Chloe had said she wanted to get a cherry strudel and to walk by the little river (she meant the canal), but Hannah wanted a dress from the Central Market so she said some mean thing to Chloe, which I can't remember, but I remember thinking it wasn't nice because Chloe looked so pretty. She wasn't wearing six layers of shirts as she usually does. She wore one pink blouse. Her thin white arms were bare. Hannah of course looked ready to be in a photo shoot, with her bleached slick hair and snazzy miniskirt. She has so many clothes, why does she need one more of anything?

I just want to stumble around and be stunned by the whole thing. But I pretend to have a plan. To visit the museums dedicated to spies, to the barricades, to the occupation of Latvia. Really, I want nothing. Truly. Except to just be. I don't want to think about plot, or about Latvian history. I just want to walk around and be amazed, and then maybe fall into a chair in Livu Square and have a Black Balsam ale. It's beer but like real liquor. Strong. Besides, when I said I wanted to go to the war museum, Hannah said no. She wanted to go to some art gallery. It's a beautiful day, said Chloe, why do we have to go inside some stuffy gallery? There's an embankment here, and a café. Or how about the jetty over there in the middle of the Daugava? People are walking on it. Must be quite a view of the Old City from there. So beautiful. Beautiful? Hannah said. It's hot like a sauna. It can't be hot and beautiful? said Chloe. And Mason said, have you actually ever been to a sauna, Hannah?

On every corner someone is painting the cityscape or playing music or selling amber, which is apparently the national gem of Latvia. I almost want to start painting myself. I've never seen amber before. Chloe told me that amber is pine resin that stiffens at the bottom of the Baltic Sea before it's washed ashore. How do you know, Hannah asked, and Chloe replied that Varda had told her. Varda had given Chloe an amber necklace as a gift. She's wearing it now. It looks so pretty, the deep orange against her pink blouse. She usually never wears colorful clothes. The Latvians love amber because they worship the sun and the color of the stone reminds them of their favorite star, Chloe tells me. Maybe there's amber in your blue suitcase, she suggests, and Hannah groans and tells her not to encourage me.

"You don't have to encourage me," I said. "I already know what's in it." But I won't tell them.

I had wanted this day to be just my brother and me, but it's nice to have the girls. I wish we could agree on something. Mason wanted to see inside St. Peter's, but Hannah didn't want to. Yes, I forgot, Mason said. You want to go to a mall.

Once you see it—the narrow stone streets, the colorful buildings breathing down the winding alleys, the stately river that belongs in a capital city, the restaurants, the music, the beer, the people—it's not just yours anymore. It's ours. I didn't mind the walk down to the Riga Canal with my bro and our girls, the cherry strudel we shared. The strudel, by the way, was completely worth the wait. My only regret is we didn't get more of it. Hannah refused to have even a bite, but Mase, Chloe and I ravaged it like lions a zebra. Nothing was left except the cherry jam on my shirt. All that's left is to eat your shirt, Chloe said. I told her to be my guest. In Maine, the cherry trees rain down their pink blossoms for a week in the middle of May. The ground is covered with pink mist; it's like walking through cotton candy fog. That's the color of Chloe's blouse.

While we were strolling down the river, she needled me about the contents of my blue suitcase, and I said, don't you want to find out when you read it? And she said no. I knocked into her with my shoulder, but she kept saying no. I just want you to tell me what's in it. Where is the fun in that, I said. Who said anything about fun, she said. It's not like trying to find a word in English that rhymes with silver or purple. Oh, I said, you're right, that would be fun. And so we tried to find a rhyme in Riga for silver or purple, but we couldn't do it. Some words just don't exist, Chloe told me.

Hannah interrupted us, caught up to us to say she couldn't walk anymore because the mosquitoes by the canal were causing blood blisters on her arms. So we left.

When we were in Central Market and out of earshot of Mase and Chloe, I asked Hannah what the matter with her was. She was acting all sore, like she was shoveling manure, not wandering around cool old hangars looking at patchwork dresses and paper flowers that looked more real than actual flowers. They were pretty spectacular. Chloe bought a flower to take back to Varda but then put it in her own hair. It was a purple hibiscus. Nothing rhymed with that. What about my blood blisters, Hannah said, and Chloe laughed and said that almost rhymed. Hannah didn't find it funny at all. It takes a lot to impress her.

Maybe cream pastries at a Bangor bakery.

Hannah

I can't do this for another three weeks. I can't do this for another three minutes. They're being awful to me. Is this my punishment for not wanting to go to the orphanage? We missed the train today, and I said, thank heavens, thinking we wouldn't have to go at all, and they were mad at me all day.

Is Latvia my penance? Apparently one of the Letts' favorite things to do is remember past suffering. They have six national mourning days a year, that's what Chloe told me. Weird people, weird language, weird house, weird food. I don't even want to talk about the food, jars of jam and bushels of peaches everywhere. The whole house reeks of cooked peaches. Like Chloe's house after her mother decided to go into the canning business. Maybe that's why Chloe likes it. She won't admit it, but it reminds her of home.

The old man is weird. He keeps staring at me. I tried to tone it down dress-wise, but he keeps staring anyway. Does his wife know what a lech he is? I don't want to wear my nice clothes around him. And where can we do laundry? The red cherry filling had dripped all over Blake's only decent shirt. When I said this to little Carmen, she stuck out her hands to Blake. Take off your clothes and give them here she said. I wash them. Where, in the river, I asked. And she took me to the laundry room. A big, big room with two washers and two dryers! A sink, running water, counter space to fold the clothes, pins, detergent, lines for hanging anything that couldn't be machine dried. Almost professional. I didn't say what I was thinking which was, I was frankly surprised they had electricity in Latvia.

After we had missed the train to Liepaja, I wanted to save us a day by hurrying to Riga and seeing everything today instead of two days from now. How much could there be to see, anyway? But they all said no. Blake said we were getting a tour guide on Tuesday and allowed no argument. Then he asked Carmen to ask Otto if he needed help with his miter cuts. He said the man's hands trembled so bad that his forty-five degree cuts were more like thirty-nine or fifty-one degrees. Nothing lined up. But Carmen put Blake in his place. She said, Grandfather know how to measure it, know how to saw it. He do it his whole life. But his hands shake. After you leave, his hands will still shake. He okay. He happy do it his way, even when it comes out all crooked. I loved seeing the chastised look on Blake's face.

But instead of going straight to Riga, we first traipsed to some open market to see where Varda and Sabine sold apples and pies. I don't know if I've ever seen Blake more excited. Look at all this stuff they're selling, he kept saying, earthenware, jams, dresses, fruits, look at the size of the plums, look at the tomatoes. Like he's never seen a tomato before. I was mildly amused by a whole pig, but before I could comment, Varda bought it. She said it was for dinner tonight. I thought Mason would throw up.

So we didn't get to Riga until the afternoon, and everyone was crabby with me. Whatever I said I wanted to do, they were like, no. It was revenge, I know it. No matter what I proposed. Art gallery, no. Take in an opera? No. We promised Varda we'd be back for dinner, Chloe said. Go get a glass of wine? No. They kept trying to foist Black Balsam on me. It was hideous. It was like bitter mud but less sweet. Of course Blake loved it. He can't believe we can drink here, that anyone will sell us alcohol. After the boys and Chloe got tipsy on this black liquid dirt, they wanted to stumble around and marvel at buildings. Like the castle or the yellow fortress. I keep telling them how beautiful Paris is; they don't want to hear it. They're walking around Riga as if it's Paris. Blake says that Riga, Vienna, and Brussels were all built in the same art nouveau style. Yes, Blake just used the words art nouveau to me. The world is upside down. I said, do you even know what art nouveau is, and he said, do *you*? Then he proceeded to tell me what it was. He said in German, the word they use is *jugendstil*, which means *youth*. He said UNESCO listed Riga's collection of *jugendstil* buildings as unmatched anywhere else in the world. I refused to believe this was true. He argued with me about this through Livu Square like I was Chloe: like I cared.

Why another church, I asked Mason. We just went to the Dome Cathedral. He had no answer. He said there were forty-two churches in Riga center, and shouldn't we try at least one more? They also sell kaftans, around here, I said to him. Do you want to try one of those too? He had no response. Blake told me to stop arguing. What about Mason, I said. And what about you and Chloe? He's got some nerve.

Mason and Chloe held hands the whole day, but Blake held his Frommer's guide and his journal, and had no hands for me. When I asked him to put it down for just *one goddamn minute*, he said it was time to catch the train back, that we promised we'd be back by seven.

I don't understand why Chloe is acting the way she is. She never wanted to come here. She's been beautifully miserable for two months, ever since Moody proposed this crazy idea. I thought she and I would see eye to eye on the whole Eastern Europe thing, bond over our dissatisfaction, but for some reason she's pretending to like it. She's got to be mad at me. Why else would she be acting all happy, skipping, tugging on everybody's sleeve, wanting ice cream and Napoleons and strudels. It's an act. Chloe, who can't be persuaded to pinch even one of her dad's Miller Lites, is drinking Black Balsam and smacking her lips about how delicious it is! And also, I mention this in passing, she is wearing a pink blouse. Yes it's over jeans, but on her feet are thong sandals, and she has painted her toenails red. Chloe. Toenails. Painted. Red. What's happening to the world? She has put on a little makeup, as if she's trying to look pretty for Latvia. It's weird, frankly.

Whatever, I don't care. I told her she shouldn't be eating those strudels anyway. I was being constructive. I was *trying* to help. Of course she took it the wrong way. And the boys took her side! Blake said, we're on a Roman Holiday. We eat what we want, drink what we want, do what we want. Eat the Napoleon, Chloe, he said. Eat two strudels. We stood in line an hour to buy a stupid pastry! Can you imagine? On a beautiful Sunday afternoon, to stand in line, like we're in Russia or something, like the Berlin Wall never fell, to get a Napoleon. To eat an eight-hundred calorie dessert and get fat, and for this we wait an hour.

With the baked goods in hand, we walked forever to the canal because Chloe wanted to, and strolled excruciatingly slowly under the trees by the water, eating pastries. All the insects were out, and again I'm the bad guy.

Blake is driving everyone crazy with his story research. I could scream. I've been quiet about it, letting Chloe express our mutual skepticism, but now she's suddenly pretending she's on board. Suddenly *I* have to be the voice of reason. He's never going to win it because there'll be a thousand entries, including a hundred from the Academy, and no matter how good his story is—someone else's will be better. I wish somebody would remind him of this. Chloe used to, back in Maine, but here, she's asking him questions, discussing things, fake-listening. Tell me about these spies, she says. Why are there so many secret agents, double agents in Riga? What do they want with a blue suitcase?

That's the question, he says. The old lady dies, and the innocuous blue suitcase in her bedroom vanishes. Who took it?

Riga spies? says Chloe.

We're ambling down the river promenade, the others eating cherry strudel and listening to Blake tell us about the size of the engine in the truck he's going to buy with the prize money. The lunatics have left the asylum.

"Blake," I say, as gently as I can, "don't you think there will be *so* many other story entries? I mean, don't you think you should … I don't know. Not divvy up the bear until the bear is dead? The chances of winning are minuscule. There's bound to be one better than yours, no?"

And he says, "Lupe told me never to compare myself with other people because, she said, there would always be someone worse and someone better than me, and I would become either vain or bitter. Just keep your eye on the prize, she said."

Who in the flipping world is Lupe?

I smile, elegantly, politely. I walk next to him, gaze at my gait, my ballet flats, my legs in my miniskirt. I'm hot, I'm trying not to sweat, and I don't listen to a word he says anymore.

I'm thinking about Martyn. I wonder how much he misses me.

It's brutally hot out. And humid like Houston. So unpleasant to walk around. We should be at a beach in Barcelona, not here. At least I look good. I caught my reflection in the shop windows; a thin wan girl stared back, a slender profile. Cheekbones. Tiny denim skirt, green T-shirt, lavender belt. Chloe caught me looking at myself, smiled, and said, "The question the philosophers ask is, when you walk past a shop window, do you a. look to see what's inside, b. look to see what's in the window, or c. look at yourself? We know what your answer is."

Why did this annoy me? "Oh, and I suppose you never look at yourself?"

"No, my answer is all three," she replied.

On the way back we had no one on our train, and it still stunk like a skunk. I can only imagine how fun it's going to be tomorrow.

Back at Varda's they fed us well. *Pienācis mans Kungs*, Varda said again with open hands. We ate half a pig tonight. I have to admit it was delicious. Sabine was there, with her husband Guntis. He was also making eyes at me when no one was looking. They all got dressed up. Guntis wore a tie! Sabine wore a red jacket over her peasant dress.

You ask if I have a future with Blake.

Exhibit number one: By the canal under a tree on a bench I'm studying the schedule for the Opera House, piano recitals, cello concertos. And Blake, Mason, and Chloe are barefoot on the grass, hopping on one foot to see who can do it the longest. With cherry strudel all over their faces. And then they run over to the bench where I am sitting and paw me with their sticky hands, yanking me up and trying to make me skip as well.

I'm a young woman, I said to them. And you are children. I do not skip.

Exhibit number two: He never stops eating. He eats at every place we stop. No, that's not correct. He seeks out places to stop so that he can eat. Leave it to me, he says. I know where I'm going. And it's always to a café. He had cold beet soup with chopped egg in it. He had a potato pudding with bacon, and fried rye bread with garlic, and then tried to kiss me! He drank that Black Balsam. And at Varda's, he ate the pig and sardines, and sour porridge, and dried pork in a bun. He had blood sausage! And mushrooms with onions. That man has an iron stomach. Nothing fazes him. A few years ago, he actually ate some webcaps. He thought they were white mushrooms. He was in the woods with some of his dirtbag friends after a rain, getting up to no good, I'm sure, drinking, maybe even smoking, looking for some other kind of mushrooms, I bet, though Blake would never admit it. But he was clearly impaired because he'd been picking mushrooms since he could suck his thumb and never before mistook fatal for edible. His friends nearly died. Three of them were in the hospital for months. Major kidney damage. One of them is still on dialysis. One got lucky and had a transplant.

But Blake? I'm not saying he didn't throw up, and for weeks had a reduced appetite, and even a headache once, he swore. What I'm saying is, the man ate fool's webcap, the most poisonous toadstool in the world, and walked away with a stomachache.

He should write about *that*. He's got a lot he can write about. He doesn't need hidden treasure in an old lady's suitcase. He has a poisoning, a fateful accident, a sick dog, a critically injured father. But who listens to me? That's why I say nothing, even when he asks. Because he thinks he knows everything.

We should have brought some cherry strudel to Carnikava. Because Mason and I decided that we're not crazy about Latvian food. It's all pickled. Everything. I tried to ask Carmen about it tonight, but she didn't know what I was talking about. As in, of course it's pickled. What else would it be? I mean, everything is pickled. The cabbage. The sausage. The tomatoes. The eggs, for God's sake. Who pickles eggs? Latvians, apparently. The potatoes tasted pickled, but that's because they were doused with pickled cabbage and pickled tomatoes and pickled pickles.

I know, I know. Preservative, schmervative. I don't care. Mason doesn't care. He wants Burger King. I'd like a steak. Or a paella. How soon until we can have some tapas and empanadas? There's an entire Poland to get through first, and I bet they like things pickled there, too. I blame the Communists.

19

Zhenya

Chloe

The girls got up at sunrise to catch the commuter train to the city. The Liepaja train was leaving Riga at six in the morning. The boys dared think they could continue to slumber and not see the girls off. Silly boys.

Chloe didn't want to remind Hannah how unsophisticated she really was, how she'd never been on a train before yesterday. She was nervous to travel just the two of them. She wished the boys were coming with them.

The Liepaja train was nothing like yesterday's rambling, falling apart commuter rail from Carnikava to Riga. It wasn't rows and rows of wooden seats. Oh, to be sure, the Liepaja train, built sometime before the Glorious Bolshevik Revolution, was also falling apart, but the cars on this train were divided into small compartments with seating for eight. Hannah informed Chloe that first class had white linen on the seats and only six people per compartment, but cost three times as much. Chloe and Hannah could not afford first class. Fortunately, the train wasn't full. In their stall there was only a mother with a baby, but at the next stop, in Jelgava, a teenage girl got on. She was around their age and spoke no English but was provocatively dressed, as if the two went hand in hand.

Clearly the strumpet wasn't headed to an orphanage, because today even Hannah had dressed down. She was neat but covered up. Hannah could look elegant wearing a man's shirt, Chloe thought, whereas she herself had only two speeds: matron or slut. Elegant was not an option. Today, so as not to provoke the orphans or the pastor at the Lutheran daycare center, Chloe chose matron. She wore khaki pants and a long-sleeved, lightly checkered blue shirt, buttoned up to her throat. She twisted her hair into a schoolmarm bun. Her makeup, fleeting at best and hastily applied at 4 a.m., had melted off after ten minutes in the stifling broiling oven of the carriage. Her shirt and bra stuck to her body and the socks to her feet, as if she'd stepped into a Chloe-sized puddle. She sat and tried to read, but outside was countryside and marshland, distant hints of sea, farms, silos, dirt roads passing by. She stared out the window and daydreamed of being a stilt-walker caked in charcoal dust on the Ramblas in Barcelona.

They seemed to stop every other minute. Jelgava, Dobele, Broceni, Saldus, Skrunda. The train would pull into the well of a station and then shut down its engine. After an eternity, it would start rolling again. The mother and her baby left; an old man and his wife replaced them. Then they left. For a while it was just three people in the cabin: Chloe, Hannah, and the strumpety chick. Then the girl left, to go be a harlot elsewhere. Chloe's mother would have had a few choice things to say about her. Hannah was oblivious. She was sound asleep.

The train chugged west, until there was no more west, just the sea, and finally after three hours the train stopped. The white signs outside read Liepaja. Chloe wished she knew something about Liepaja. She should've read up on it. She should've asked Blake. Now it was too late. The chipping green stucco station with its cracked red brick windows awaited.

Immediately noticeable was the drop in temperature. Chloe had ignored the gradual cooling on the train. She had stopped feeling hot but was still damp; then she was damp and comfortable; then damp and slightly chilly. Now, getting off the train, she wasn't chilly. She was cold. It was overcast and very windy and about to rain.

"What happened to the weather?" said Hannah, wrapping her frowning arms around herself. "Holy crap, it's like a tornado. Why is it freezing? It must be fifty degrees!"

Didn't Blake say something about this? Chloe wished she'd listened more carefully. She hadn't believed him, even this morning when he told her to bring a jacket. What are you, my mother, she'd said to him.

"You didn't want to walk in Riga either," Chloe said, "and it wasn't cold there."

"It was crazy hot," Hannah said. "Besides, I didn't want to walk to where you three were headed. A mosquito-infested canal."

The girls sprinted to the end of the platform, looking for a taxi. Chloe's poorly secured bun was no match for the gale. Gone was the thought of walking to the orphanage two miles away on Labraga Street.

They jumped into the first cab they could find. It smelled disreputable and was driven by a man who not only could not speak a gasp of English but, judging by his expression as he studied the piece of paper they showed him with the directions, couldn't read a lick of Latvian either.

Liepaja was gray and wet and nearly deserted. For some reason it took a long time to drive two miles in no traffic to Labraga Street, where the cabbie pulled over by a small, leafy park. He demanded from the girls a small fortune. Thirty-two latu. Wasn't that nearly sixty dollars? Chloe protested. "Too much. No."

He raised three fingers, then two, and repeated what sounded like *trees met with Vivi*. Chloe opted for dumbness and blindness. She counted off five latu. He scratched out 32 on an old coffee-cup lid and thrust it in her face.

"Just give him the money and let's go," Hannah said.

Chloe gave him two more. "Seven latu," she said. "But that's it."

He got loud. Hannah was already out of the cab, but the driver was grabbing at Chloe's shirt sleeve, shouting his incomprehensible blackmail.

A door opened. A tall man draped in black cloth came down the stoop from the beige building, shouting at the driver and pointing down the street. He pulled Chloe firmly from the cab.

"How much did you give him?" he asked in accented English.

"Seven latu."

"Too much. He's abusing you." He yelled at the cabbie again, who screeched away, gesticulating and yelling back.

The man introduced himself. He was Reverend Kazmir, the director of the daycare and the pastor who had opened the home for children eleven years ago. He was serious and had a lot of thick, gray, well-groomed hair for an old man. He made Chloe feel self-conscious about her own uncharacteristically messy coif.

After he ushered them inside, he told them that when the Communists retreated back to the dying Soviet Union they left in their leprous wake a complete disintegration of a wonderful city, pockmarking it with vast unemployment and an even vaster drug habit. "Drugs are a very big problem in Latvia, I am ashamed to admit," the reverend said.

Chloe told him it was nothing to be ashamed of, but she had to admit she was slightly frightened. How was she going to find a boy for her parents in a town like this? Her father was the chief of police. Order was what he craved. But drugs were chaos. Here, the adults smoked, shot up their arms full of H, had drug-addicted children, and then tried to escape, except there was nowhere to run to. Often their only escape was prison, where they were shipped off, almost happily, leaving their children behind. The kids went to school, haphazardly at best, and afterward some of them came to Kazmir's place. He and his assistants helped them with homework, taught them to paint and pray. But mostly the reverend organized photographs and folders documenting their life stories, which he then sent to a non-profit group in Dallas that arranged Eastern European sponsorships and adoptions.

Hannah, impatiently tapping on the table while the reverend talked, abruptly asked when they could see these supposed children. Chloe knew her friend's problem. She shared it herself.

The girls were famished. They'd had a hunk of bread and a cup of tea six hours ago. While Hannah had slept on the train, Chloe didn't want to leave her friend alone and traipse off to the dining car. And when they got off the train, the extortionist cab was right there.

The reverend shook his head and patiently explained how the procedure worked while the girls twitched and starved. This was not a zoo. Chloe and Hannah did not walk by the cages where the children sat on display. The girls would remain in his office and he would bring them the files of the available children. They would take their time and look through the photographs, bios and personal notes. If they found someone potentially suitable for Lang and Jimmy, a room would be set up where they could meet this boy or girl face to face. Then the reverend left.

"I'm so hungry, I'd eat pickled bread at this point," Hannah said as they waited for him to come back with the files. "Please, I beg you, choose someone quickly. It's all the same. Don't dawdle. Pick someone, anyone. Because after, we'll still have to meet him, and you know there'll be loads of paperwork. We don't have all day."

"Actually, we do have all day."

"The quicker you choose, the quicker we can get out of here. What time is it now?"

"Eleven, I think."

"What time is the train back?"

"We just got here!"

"I know when we got here. I'm asking when the train goes. I don't want to miss it. There's only one a day, right?"

"It's at five. You're not the only one who's hungry, you know."

"I know. But it's harder for me. I don't have any fat stores."

The reverend returned carrying not files but a tray. On the tray was a pitcher filled with dark drink, sandwiches, some fruit, and some (pickled!) salads. There was herring and even a cheesecake.

Chloe wanted to cry, she was so grateful. For this she would sponsor all of the children and an adult or two as well.

"I thought you might like a little refreshment after such a long journey," the reverend said. "Why don't you start, and I'll be back in a few minutes with the folders. Please try the *kvas*. It's our national beverage. Made from bread. It's very good."

"It could be made from lead at this point," said Hannah, pouring the drink so quickly she spilled some on the sandwiches. It was good. Thick like a meal. Before the reverend returned, the sandwiches were gone, the cheesecake gone, the raspberries, potato salad, the herring and most of the bread. Only sauerkraut remained, lonely and acidic in the corner by the discarded crusts.

Lowering the stack of paper to the coffee table, the reverend glanced with amusement at the empty tray, then at the girls. "After a meal such as this, a nap is needed, don't you think?"

Chloe couldn't agree more, having gotten up at the godless hour of dawn. Hannah was nodding, too!

"What are *you* nodding for?" Chloe grumbled, quite drowsy. "You didn't watch *me* sleep for hours on the train."

"I wasn't sleeping, I had my eyes closed."

"Yeah, sure."

"Really. I wasn't sleeping."

Why did that irk Chloe? Hannah wanted to have it every which way. Sleep on the train, yet be tired now. Chloe couldn't be the only one tired, oh no. Hannah had to be hungrier, and sleepier. And thinner. Ugh.

Chloe spread out the folders on the coffee table and opened them one by one. Hannah leaned back against the cushions and closed her eyes. Chloe yanked on her linen sleeve. "You're not here to nap. You're here for moral support, and to help me. Let's go, missy."

Apathetically leaning forward, Hannah studied the faces of the children and the notes in their files. "This is my favorite," she said. "Kristine: seven years old. When she grows up, she wants to be a cleaning lady. Pick her."

"What did I tell you? Ignore the girls. Only boys."

"Are you serious? Why?"

Chloe turned to stare meaningfully at Hannah.

"Ah, okay," Hannah said. "How old?"

"The age Jimmy would be now, I guess." Chloe leafed through the folders. "Around seven."

"How about this one? Nicole: six years old. The one place in the world she wants to visit is a swimming pool. Pick her."

"I told you, no girls."

"She's cute, though."

"If it's a girl, move on. Find a boy."

"Wow. And you said you weren't Chinese. Don't like the girls, do you? Yup, Chinese through and through."

Hannah

Chloe told me not to look at the girls, but it's only the girls that interested me. I didn't care a whit for the boys. After seeing the sweet Kristine with her big dreams of becoming a cleaning lady, I searched through the girls. And why not? I didn't come here on a job. I'll admit, some of them looked as if they'd be following in their parents' footsteps soon if they weren't already. I asked the reverend if all of them were orphans.

"Not at all," Kazmir said, presiding over us behind his big desk. "Many of them have parents. Sometimes the parents are in prison since they can't find other work besides dealing drugs. But the children can leave here and go home at any time. However, here we have food. It's warm in the winter." He paused. "The drug laws have become very strict in Latvia. Sometimes the parents, even when present, have six or seven other children to take care of. There is no adult supervision. Being here is better than wandering the streets. We offer them art, singing lessons, Bible study, sports, English. By the time these children are twelve or fourteen, they're expected to work, make money. Many drop out of school at fourteen. Some turn to drugs." He pressed his troubled hands together in supplication. "We have sixty-five children here. Most are good kids, don't worry. They just need a little help."

"Don't we all," I said.

Here's what I remember. I was twelve years old and a couple of my friends called me to hang out. Sure, my mother said, as long as one of their parents can pick you up and drive you back. Not a problem, I assured her. She and Dad weren't even divorced yet, but he was out. I called Chloe to see if she wanted to come with me. I heard her mother yelling in the background while she put her hand over the phone. Abruptly she hung up without even replying to me. But through my windows I heard her mother yelling. The whole lake heard. Are you out of your mind? It's eight o'clock on a school night and you're twelve years old. Where do you think you could possibly be going? What universe do you live in? She stayed home. I went out. I pitied her. Poor Chloe. I'm so grown up, I thought, and she's going to be a baby forever.

Janna, from a family of eight. Sounded almost like my name. Janna, Hannah. She was six. Her card said: "She really wants to live in another place." Perfect. Like me.

Daniela liked pizza. Well, who doesn't? And how did Daniela know anything about pizza? And if she knew about pizza, how come we've been fed nothing but cabbage the last three days? I bet it would be pickled pizza, I thought, and laughed out loud, incurring a glare from Chloe and a disapproving blink from the reverend.

"Please can we sponsor a girl?" I asked Chloe. "Look at this cute one. Marina. She is eight. She loves ice cream. She wants to help people. She wants to be close to Jesus. Please pray for her."

"Hannah, you and I are not sponsoring her. My parents are. And they want a boy."

"Tell them you couldn't find a good one. Look here. Valeria is eight. She doesn't know what she wants to be but she wants to go to Livu Waterpark."

The reverend told me that if I wanted to, I could also sponsor a child. I got absent-mindedly excited. "Oh yeah? What would I have to do?"

But I didn't hear his answer. Because I found a girl.

Zhenya. She was nine years old. Her favorite story was Lazarus being raised from the dead. She wanted two things: to go to Russia and to help her grandmother. When she grew up she wanted to be a policewoman. She asked you to pray that no one beat her up.

I turned away from Chloe and the reverend. I stood up and walked to the window for a few moments. The street was drizzly with rain, windy, wretched. My back was still to them when I asked the reverend to repeat what it would take to sponsor a child. "How much every month?"

"Sixty dollars. With extra around the holidays. Or extra simply if you have extra. But the minimum is sixty. You pay the Dallas company, not us. They wire the money to us. That way you don't have to worry about converting into latu. Of course you can always invite your sponsored child to the United States for a visit. For many of them it's the trip of a lifetime, as you can imagine. And then, if you wish, your parents can sponsor them to come live with you. You can be their host family. Almost like your American foster care, but with foreign children …"

I stopped listening. "When can I see her?" I stared at the picture of Zhenya's wan little face.

"Hannah, you don't have sixty dollars a month!" Chloe said behind my back. Always the naysayer. "You're going to college. You have no money for books. You don't have money for a whole Latvian."

"I'll make money," I said. "And if you and I both sponsor her, it'll be only thirty dollars a month." I whirled around. "What do you say?"

"That you're not helping me find a boy is what I say. Why are you getting so hung up on the girls?"

"Not plural. One girl in particular. Reverend, can we see her?"

"Who?"

I handed him Zhenya's folder.

He shook his head. "She's not with us anymore."

"Where is she?" I didn't want to hear his answer. I was so disappointed.

"I don't know. Sometimes they vanish. We pray it's because everything is better at home. Usually they return to us after a few weeks."

I took the folder from him, almost snatched it, stared at Zhenya's white face, her severe, uneven bangs. Why did he still have her folder if she had vanished?

"You're right, we should transfer her folder out of the current file. May I have it, please?"

I didn't give it back. "Can't you call her house? Make sure? Find out?"

"No one has a telephone."

"Can we go to her house?"

"Hannah!" This was Chloe, raising her voice at me. "We are not going to somebody's house. Geez. Give the reverend back his folder and then sit down and help me. Look at these boys. Which one, you think?"

I didn't want to help her anymore. I would have helped her, if she helped me. But I had come with her, and she was ungrateful. If the reverend hadn't fed me, I would've starved. And now she shouted me down when I expressed the slightest interest in something that was important to me instead of fawning, as always, about something that was important to her.

The reverend was staring at me too, so I sat down and tuned out. Uh-huh, I said. Yeah, him. And him too. I didn't care. Zhenya was the only child I saw in front of my eyes, her squeezed-together face, her motley hair. The rest didn't matter.

Chloe

How she wished Mason had come with her. Or Blake. Or even her mother! Leave it to Hannah to make Chloe wish for her mother on her first overseas trip.

Chloe didn't understand why Hannah would become so difficult when the smallest thing was asked of her. She was sitting and sulking because a girl whose face she glimpsed for thirty seconds and whose bio she just read was no longer at the orphanage. Thirty seconds. And Hannah couldn't understand why Chloe didn't just drop everything and run to this girl's house! Yes, her story was poignant. But the ten boy stories in Chloe's lap were no less bitter.

Maksim, age seven. His favorite Bible story was when Jesus healed the blind.

Reverend Kazmir said Maksim was blind.

Erik, age nine. Looked like a cherub. Wanted to be a cook on a ship when he grew up. Liked pandas.

Arturs, also nine, wanted to be a firefighter and loved French fries.

Intars, age six. Didn't know what he wanted to be when he grew up. He wanted to belong and to learn to believe in God.

Kostays, age eight. When he wished upon a star, he wished for lots of money to buy food.

Vladimir, age ten. Liked to walk around. He hadn't given much thought to his plans, but he knew he'd like to have some money. At school, he liked the breaks best.

Denis, age six, asked you to pray for him to be more reliable.

Vova, age eleven, liked salads. When he wished upon a star, he wished for his brother to get out of prison.

Raymonds, age six. Liked cucumber soup and potato chips. An only child. Summer was his favorite season because there was no school. When he grew up he wanted to become a cop or a mechanic. When he wished upon a star he wanted to learn how to swim.

"That's the one," Chloe said, handing Raymonds's file to Reverend Kazmir. "That's the little guy." His last name was Fyodorov. He had a round face, an impish smile, black hair, round friendly eyes. He was the one. You know how you just know?

"Oh, I know," Hannah said. "That's how I feel about Zhenya."

Please, please, Chloe thought, closing her eyes. Please, unlike Zhenya, let Raymonds be available for my mother and father.

"Ah, Ray. Good choice. He is a sweet boy. He's out playing in the back. It's break time. Would you like to come watch him play for a few minutes before you meet him? That way you can see how he is with other children."

Chloe jumped up. "These things written about them in their folder, are they accurate?"

"Of course."

"Then I don't need to watch him play. He's the one. When can I meet him?" She turned to Hannah. "Are you coming?"

Like a queen, Hannah slowly lifted herself out of her spot on the sofa. "Oh, so for *your* chosen child, we bolt instantly."

"I wouldn't call what you're doing bolting, but yes," said Chloe. "Do you know why? Because mine is still here, still available, oh, and we're not here to sponsor a child for *your* mother. You don't think she's got enough to deal with?"

"Not for my mother, are you crazy? For me."

"Are you crazy?"

"Tell me you wouldn't go chasing after Raymonds all over Liepaja if you found out he wasn't here."

Chloe stomped out of the reverend's office. She wasn't sure she wouldn't.

Raymonds was too shy to come near Chloe. Her visit with him was brief. He didn't take his curious Cocker Spaniel eyes off her, but didn't approach her, either. He spoke no English, but gave her a high-five before she left. Back at the reverend's office, Chloe spent a long time filling out the paperwork. Did the reverend have some more photographs of him? Could her parents write letters to him? Would he be studying English? If her parents wanted to bring him to the United States, how would they go about it?

"Now? That's not possible."

"No, later. For a visit." A long visit, Chloe thought. She wasn't sure her parents would be able to part with him once they'd met him.

Hannah paced, looking out the window. "What if they wanted to actually adopt Raymonds?" she asked. "What then?"

"It's possible," the reverend replied. "We can arrange adoptions through our Dallas partners. They screen the sponsors for adoption eligibility. It has happened." The way he said it indicated that it happened rarely. "Americans want little babies," he said. "We have bigger children, unfortunately."

"Just the right size," said Chloe, putting her hand out into the empty space where Ray's little black head might've been. Or Jimmy's. She glanced at her watch and gasped. It was 4:15. Their train was leaving in forty-five minutes. The reverend called for a cab and paid for it upfront, four latu, not thirty-two. After saying goodbye to him, they left in a hurry.

In the cab, Hannah leaned toward the driver.

"Do you speak English?"

"Little."

"Can you take us here?" She showed him an address on a scrap of paper.

"Hannah!"

"Shh."

"Not for four latu," the cabbie said.

"How much?"

"Another four."

"Okay. I'll pay."

"Hannah, what are you doing?"

"Nothing. We won't be late for the train. I promise."

"You do understand that the train is at five."

"I just want to drive by her place. To see where she lives."

"Why?"

"Because. Why did you want to see Raymonds?"

"Because my parents are going to sponsor him," Chloe replied slowly as if speaking with the deranged.

"Maybe I can convince my mother to help me sponsor Zhenya."

A defeated Chloe fell back on her seat. "You do understand that if we miss the train, there isn't another one until tomorrow night?"

"We'll make it."

Liepaja was flat, granite and looked abandoned. The rain had stopped, but the wind swirled the residual mist in the air like icy pollen. Chloe's face and shirt were damp after a minute of walking down the steps to the cab. Apartment buildings rose up out of the grass, looking like the urban project tenements Chloe had seen on the evening news. Dilapidated concrete boxes, six stories high.

Zhenya didn't live in one of those, "Thank God," said Hannah, when they stopped next to a small brick house with bars on the windows. On the front patch of brown grass stood a mangled, rusted but functioning see-saw and on this see-saw balanced two girls. One of them must have been Zhenya because Hannah's face softened as if she'd encountered a long-lost sister. "There she is," she whispered, pressing her face against the dirty glass of the cab, fanning her hand on the window. Chloe wasn't sure if Hannah was waving hello, or wiping the dust away to see the girl better.

There she was indeed. The girl's hair was matted, and she wore someone else's clothes: someone bigger, taller and maler. She was barefoot in the icy vapor, her arms white sticks, poking out of the greasy, dirty T-shirt.

The cabbie said something that Chloe didn't understand, but Hannah, having suddenly acquired the gift of Latvian

comprehension, said, "No, no. Drive on. I just wanted to see."
She rolled down her window. The girls on the see-saw guardedly
studied the people in the cab. Hannah smiled and waved. An
uncertain Zhenya waved back.

Chloe was flummoxed. "Hannah, stranger danger, what are
you doing? They're going to call the cops. What are you seeing?"

"Just a girl," Hannah said. "Who asked me to pray that she
wouldn't be beaten."

"Not you specifically."

"Yes, me specifically. I was the one who heard. Therefore, me.
Blake should've come with us. He'd understand. He could write
about her. She could be his vanished girl."

"What does urchin Zhenya have to do with his treasure, his
Latvian spies?"

"Maybe they're searching for the treasure but they find her
instead, in that house. And they find the suitcase, too."

"In her house?"

"Perfect place to hide it. Maybe Zhenya is the treasure. Did
you ever think of that?"

How little Chloe understood about life. Her friend had acted
like an adult at eleven, twelve, thirteen. Sometimes Hannah's
mother didn't even look up when a car came through their dense
wood to pick up her daughter and take her somewhere. Hannah
could have said she was out with anybody, and often did.
Hannah, already a beautiful young woman, mature, appealing,
the most grown up of them all. Yet here she sat, her cheek to
the Latvian glass, waving to a neglected kid on a see-saw. A
thousand questions, all answers invisible to the naked eye.

Hannah

We arrived at the station with barely ten minutes to spare. Unlike
the morning, it was mad packed with irate travelers, a crash of
rhinos, all shoving and yelling their way to the one platform.
Chloe and I couldn't find two seats together. I know she blamed

me because I wanted to take a look at that girl. My little Zhenya. All the compartments were full. After racing back and forth, we finally found three single empty seats in one cabin.

The five other seats were occupied by an obese middle-aged couple, a father traveling with his small son and a professor in a tweed suit by the window, reading *A Brief History of Time* by Stephen Hawking, in Latvian probably. There was one empty seat between the small boy and the professor, and one on each side of the lard consumers, who had wisely chosen to sit in the middle two, hoping to deter anyone from sitting next to them. It almost worked. But we were stuck. We tried to ask them to move over so that we could sit together, but they just stared at us as though we were the elephants. Just as well, because I refuse to sit next to enormous foreigners. And I know that Chloe likes the window. Besides, I wanted to sit next to the professor. He looked smart and handsome. Maybe he spoke a bit of English. I could find out.

Chloe breathed a big sigh of relief when we made the train. But not me. I half-hoped we'd miss it, and be forced to stay in Liepaja one more day, and maybe tomorrow the weather would improve, and I could walk to Zhenya's house and if she was there I could ask her if she wanted to go with us to the beach. I'll buy you a lemonade, I'd say. And cotton candy if there's a boardwalk like the one in Revere, where there's a Ferris wheel and fireworks in the summer. I'd ask Zhenya if she wanted to see Revere Beach, maybe go on a roller coaster with me. We have a lake where I live, I'd tell her, and the water is warm in the summer, and there's lots of fish. And in the winter, we could ice skate on it. Chloe could teach you how to speed skate when we're back from college for Christmas break. And I swear to you, I'd never let you out at night.

20

Thorn Forests

Chloe

She squeezed in by the window near the massive woman. She felt so claustrophobically cramped. Too many strangers in one confined space. Like spending hours in a packed and broken elevator. At least there was a window. Across from her, Hannah was primping her Marilyn Monroe hair next to the professor, who did not look up from his book, not even at bleached Hannah.

Running her hand over her tousled hair in a weak attempt to smooth it out, Chloe pressed her face to the glass and closed her eyes. She recalled wide open spaces, swimming in her lake, and Raymonds's little round face, she recalled rocking the boat with Blake to see if they could tip it over while his father waved at them to stop from his sick chair and her mother yelled, I have ice tea, row back, you've been out there for hours.

Her mother and father would be proud of her, Chloe thought. She did well today. Coming here wasn't the waste of time she'd feared it would be. Quite the opposite, really. What had Blake and Mason been up to? How much longer? Maybe she could doze, wake up in Riga. She took a breath, her hands clutching the paperback, and opened her eyes. On the platform, people carried backpacks, suitcases, pushed trolleys and strollers. A pregnant woman was saying goodbye to a man in a suit. They were erotically making out. An old woman carried a toddler in her arms. A man in a military coat with lots of stars on its shoulder straps was shaking the hand of an obscured young man, perhaps his son. A baby was crying. A young woman comforted him. The conductors were yelling, gesticulating. There was a loud stream in Latvian of one endless announcement after another.

Fifteen minutes behind schedule, the train engines finally spun into action, and Chloe permitted herself a small smile. Yes, it was smelly. And awfully crowded. And soon to be hot. Her shirt was still damp from the rain, and all the windows were closed and she couldn't find her ticket to show the conductor. But at least the train was moving. Soon this would be over. What station was next, Skrunda?

Not a minute after the conductor left, the door opened again and into their stuffy, overcrowded cabin stepped in the dreaded eighth passenger, a young dude. No! It was impossible! There was no room here; couldn't he see that? It was as clear as the scowl on her face. A sharply inhaling Chloe despised him from the moment he slid open the door, smiling widely, and stepped inside to look for a seat. He was not only tall and had to bend his head to fit through the glass door, but he carried with him a crapload of stuff, enough shit to warrant his own cabin. Besides the oversized green duffel and a backpack, he wore a bulky leather jacket and a pretentious black beret. And on his back, to top it all off, was a guitar. Chloe nearly groaned. A guitar!

The luggage shelf above their heads was full. Fat people needed big suitcases. Father and son had a suitcase each, the professor a carry-on. There was no room for a man-sized duffel, no room for a man-sized guitar, no room for a man. The guitar looked old and beat-up, and had no case. Nice way to take care of an instrument, Chloe thought. But when she spun around, she saw that the strings were brand new. She didn't know which detail made her most hostile. All of it.

This interloper, at whom Chloe was too upset to look at directly, assessed the situation in the cabin. "Hello there," he said in a low easy melodic American voice. Cool and casual and friendly. Like a sing-song. A fed-up Chloe stared out the window, ignoring him. Undeterred, the insolent intruder continued to speak. But now he was speaking in what might have been Latvian to the bulky pair next to Chloe. He sounded falsely polite.

And then, just when Chloe thought things couldn't get any worse, things got worse. Because after the trespasser had finished speaking, the chunky Lett chuckled. Chloe couldn't believe the woman didn't see right through him. The lady heaved herself up and, pulling her husband with her, slid over one seat! The eighth seat, right next to Chloe, became available!

Chloe glared in his direction, hoping her internal screaming might dissuade him.

Nope. Just the opposite. Grinning at her with his mouthful of teeth like a simpleton, he took one long gallop through the compartment and was by her side, his duffel, backpack, guitar, jacket, pompous beret, everything. Was his black hair short or was it slicked back in a ponytail? He would have a ponytail, wouldn't he? Oh yes. There it was.

"Hi," he said to her, dropping the duffel to the floor. "Sorry about all my stuff. Would you mind?"

"Mind what?" Chloe barked. Her mother wouldn't be pleased with her manners. How did he know she spoke English? She could be a bosomy Lett herself.

"Um, scooting over just a wee bit?" he said. His large eyes were twinkling. He probably thought they were dark chocolate in color. "You're in my seat. Maybe you could move a smidge, and then I'd fit right in." He grinned. "I'm good at fitting into tight spaces." He didn't just say that! "I'm skinny, you see," he went on.

She didn't see. She didn't see anything. Chloe flung herself at the window. She wanted to fling herself *through* the window like a waxwing slain. Hannah, who a moment ago had been unsuccessfully trying to engage the professor in conversation, had forgotten all about physics and was avidly gesturing to Chloe, in a back and forth pattern through the air, as if to say, *let's switch seats!*

Chloe wanted nothing more than to switch: cabins, cars, countries. But why should Hannah get what she wanted? Chloe wasn't getting what she wanted. Peace. Quiet. No personal space invaders next to her. Imperceptibly she shook her head.

"Wow, it's crowded," the guy said. No shit, Sherlock. "This may be the last available seat on the whole train. Believe me, I looked and looked."

"It wasn't crowded this morning," said Hannah, suddenly the queen of small talk! Having struck out with the professor, she was appealing to the marauder from across the aisle. His skinny denim-clad legs stretched out to Hannah's ballet flats. Chloe tucked in her own feet, feeling exposed in the strappy sandals. She didn't want him to spot her red painted toenails. But there was no way around some other things—like her khaki thigh touching his denim thigh. The grossness of the whole thing. She wished her hair wasn't such a dire mess. Oh, who cared.

He didn't smell like the fat foreigners, but he looked as though he might. He stood the body of his guitar on top of the duffel, holding it by the neck like a cello. Every few seconds he would strum it. At first Chloe thought it was accidental, but no. He was strumming it. Spreading wide his net to catch his prey with his little perfect fourths and his stretched-out legs and his evenly trimmed black stubble. How Chloe wished she hadn't taken music theory her senior year. All the useless information she had learned in that class still fresh. What did Mr. Lecese know about strumming stubbled ponytailed bandits on Latvian trains?

The conductor opened the door and grunted at the unwelcome arrival. "*Billetes?*"

"One moment." The guy reached into his back pocket, and his elbow poked Chloe in her breast! He stopped, didn't even say excuse me, moved away slightly, and passed her the guitar. "Can you hold it for a sec? I have to find my pass."

It wasn't as if he asked her for a favor, expecting perhaps a no. Had he ever *heard* the word no? He acted as if he hadn't. First he pushed his guitar at her, already standing up, and then he asked her to hold it. Perhaps the unspoken threat was, either hold my guitar or be elbowed again in your ample bosom.

He took something out of his wallet that did not look like a ticket or a Eurail pass. The conductor glanced at it, glanced at him a moment longer, nodded quickly, his hand almost going to his temple in a salute, and backed out of the cabin. The guy stuffed everything back into his wallet, and sat down.

"I'll take my guitar now," he said.

She turned to the window and checked her watch for the time. It was only five-thirty! The train wouldn't get to Riga until after eight. Chloe couldn't figure out why God was punishing her, tried to think of other things. Yet the boy's presence next to her was enormous and could not be denied. He crowded out all her other thoughts. She couldn't close her eyes. She couldn't read her book. Trying not to breathe, she stared grimly out of the window, her mouth in a clamshell.

For a few minutes, the compartment was almost silent. The professor was reading Hawking. The father was reading the paper and the boy was playing a handheld video game. The male half of the stout couple was napping, while the female half was attempting to involve guitar boy in conversation. Apologetically glancing at the woman while trying to catch Chloe's eye, he said in English with a rueful smile, "I speak only the most basic Latvian. I wish I could explain that to her." Oh, he fancied himself to be quite the smiler!

What are you telling *me* for, Chloe thought. Tell her. She zeroed in on the passing farms outside, pretending to be deaf, to be a non-English-speaker and to have no peripheral vision.

"Right?" Hannah butted in. "They keep talking to us in Latvian, too, but we don't understand a word."

"Who's they?" the boy said, pointing to his left. "These two?"

"No, no. I mean in general." She smiled. Hannah! In the Academy yearbook she was voted the least likely to smile. This was not a joke. This is what it actually said about her in the yearbook. Chloe wanted to share it with the ticketless traveler, but remembered just in time she didn't want to speak to him. To avoid any possibility of further conversation, she forced herself to open her book.

"What are you reading?" he promptly asked. "Let's see."

"It's nothing." To be half-civil, she showed him. *The Way of All Flesh* by Samuel Butler.

"Pretty funny book," he said, as if he'd read it. "I like its depiction of father and unredeemed son."

He'd read it!

"I haven't finished it, so I wouldn't know about the unredeemed part," Chloe said pointedly. "Hope you didn't just ruin the book for me."

He laughed. Listen to him, all mellifluous and throaty. "No, no. The parenting stuff in it is hilarious. Butler writes that if you want to control your children, keep telling them constantly they're being very, very naughty. My father must have read it." He shrugged. "Want to know what I'm reading?"

How did one politely say, no, not in the least, not even slightly.

"Yes, what are you reading?" chirped Hannah.

The rotund woman to his left not only continued to beseech him in a low Myrtle Wilson voice, but was tapping on his sleeve to get his attention.

"I'm sorry," he finally said to her in English. "My Latvian is not good enough. I don't understand what you're saying."

She said something in Latvian.

"*Es nerunāju loti labu latviešu,*" he said. "*Es atvainojos.*"

Hannah looked so impressed! Chloe couldn't figure it out. Here is a straphanger, one tenth of the age of the dude she's stepping out with behind the back of her current boyfriend, who is not just any boyfriend, but Blake! Blake, her devoted squeeze, and Hannah's suddenly all aflush because some guy can speak a few words of a foreign language—the language of a country she doesn't even like! Blake has a guidebook too, Chloe wanted to blurt out.

It was hot. Chloe's damp shirt was pressed against the shoulder of his leather jacket. After a few minutes he mercifully took the jacket off, but not before flinging his arms and elbows and hands in all directions. Women, Chloe wanted to yell in alarm, guard your boobs! Under the leather, he wore a plain black fitted tee with the white star of Texas above the pocket. Was he from Texas? Words could not express how much she didn't care.

"Oh! Are you from Texas?" Hannah asked.

"Nah, it's the one state I've never been to." Yes, the jacket was off, but the rest of him, long, lean, arms akimbo, was still way too warm and way too pressed against Chloe. The neck of his guitar kept banging against her knees, and his huge green duffel took up the floor space where her feet needed to be. Crossing her legs, she turned her body window-ward, but no sooner had she done this than he thrust his book at her.

"Look what I'm reading," he said.

It was the *U.S. Army Survival Handbook*. Whatever.

"Oh?" said Hannah. "Why are you reading that?" Even the Lettish Myrtle was curiously mouthing the words of the title to herself, perhaps trying to translate.

"Always good to know stuff, don't you think?" he replied to Hannah, but was turned to Chloe. He opened the book to show her. "Did you know, for example, that you should always travel through the jungle wearing a long-sleeved shirt to avoid cuts and scratches?" Approvingly he touched her checkered forearm with his octave-length fingers. "Ah, but you're damp. That's no good. Your clothing must stay dry. Says so right here."

She pulled her arm away and heaved herself at the window. He was practically talking to the back of her shoulder. "And you shouldn't grasp at brush or vines when searching for the trail because they might have irritating spines or sharp thorns."

"Good to know," Chloe said. Irritating was right.

"The black briar is dangerous, wouldn't you agree? When you're trying to find your way?"

"Guess so."

"And don't pick any mushrooms in the woods," he continued. "Many will be poisonous."

"Yeah, we'll be sure not to pick any mushrooms while we're in Riga," said Chloe.

He laughed, his teeth gleaming. "Yes, you better not. Though by the Daugava near the Old City, they simply pro-LI-fe-rate after a rain, which is almost every day."

"Funny, hasn't rained once since we've been here," Chloe said.

He appraised both girls. "How long?"

"This is our fourth day," Hannah readily replied.

Was that really true?

"Tomorrow is our last day," Chloe said—because *that* was the important part.

His eyes were on Chloe, amiable like a brown bear's. "So what were you two doing in Liepaja? Not many American girls head to Liepaja on their own."

For some reason Chloe felt puffed up for a second to think that she was the kind of brave girl who would head to Liepaja on her own.

"How would you even know to go there?" he asked. "It's only in the last ten years that the city's been open to tourists. How did you hear about it? Did you like it?"

"We didn't see much of it," Hannah confessed. "But what were you doing there?"

Chloe pretended to read.

"Oh, I was …" he trailed off, his hand swirling in the air. "I met my father there. In Liepaja, they keep records on the Poles, Russians, Bulgarians who went missing during the war. Very poor records, as it turns out."

"Your dad is looking for them? Why?"

"That," the boy said, "is a very good question. Damned if I know."

"Is that why *you're* in Latvia?"

"One of the reasons. I'm on my way to Italy, actually. Need to make a little money in Riga first. Are you girls visiting family?"

"How in the world do you make money in Riga?" Hannah asked.

"Lots of ways." He raised his eyebrows and made a scabrous chuckle. "I give tours, for one."

"Of Riga?"

"Sure. Of Riga, of Jurmala. Why are you so surprised?" He glanced over at Chloe. "Are you surprised, too?" he asked her, all charm and smiles and destruction.

"I wasn't listening. What?"

"Well, it *is* a very absorbing book you're reading," he said. "I'm Johnny, by the way," he said. "Pleased to meet you. And you are ..."

"Chloe." They were sitting too close for Chloe to turn her head and look him in the eye. His face was barely a foot away from her face. She half-nodded in his general direction, keeping her eyes on his denim-clad knees and the pointed black leather toe of what looked to be a very snazzy cowboy boot. Lucchese perhaps? Wow. Leather jacket, beret, an ancient guitar with new strings. What the hell.

"Hi, Chloe," he said. "Would you like to book a tour of Riga with me? I'm very good."

How good could he be? Didn't he just tell her he couldn't get out of a briar patch? "No, thank you."

"Hi, Johnny, I'm Hannah," Hannah said, reaching across and extending her graceful hand to him. "Chloe, let's not be hasty. We actually were thinking of hiring a guide for tomorrow, remember?"

No steely daggers out of Chloe's eyes would dissuade her friend from talking. "Johnny can give us a tour," Hannah continued. "Are you expensive?"

"Like a piece of steak. But I'm very good. A filet mignon." Every word spoken through two rows of exposed teeth.

"Hannah is a vegetarian, so there you go," said Chloe.

"No, I'm not! And he's not being literal, Chloe," Hannah said in a patronizing tone. "I think a tour would be great, Johnny. Tomorrow is our last day. We haven't seen very much."

"Where are you headed after this?"

"Poland. Then Barcelona. We're traveling for three weeks." Hannah said it as if to impress him. "What about you?"

"I'm not traveling to Barcelona."

Hannah giggled! "No, silly," she said, all coquettish. "How long have you been on the road?"

"On and off about two years, I guess."

Hannah whistled. Even Chloe blinked in wonderment. She couldn't help a small question. "In Latvia for two years?" she asked.

He looked so happy she'd asked him anything. He turned his whole body to her before he answered. "No. In Latvia almost one, though."

"What have you been doing in Latvia for a whole year?" asked Hannah.

"This and that," he said, volunteering nothing further. "Where are you girls from?"

Was it Broceni and then Dobele or Dobele and then Broceni? How long was this going to continue? As the train lurched on, Hannah told Johnny everything there was to tell about them, and then some more stuff. She told Johnny where they were from, where they were staying, when they came, and even why.

Chloe concentrated on the fields and the rivers, wondering why Hannah was suddenly so garrulous. For God's sake. Normally you couldn't get her to share important news with her closest friends. Like her affair with the Noah of Bangor. Now she was blabbing as if Johnny was her therapist.

With the professor next to her fretting in disapproval, Hannah asked Johnny questions about trains, and comfort, and Riga. Every time he would answer Hannah, he would glance at Chloe and smile. His thigh kept pressing against her thigh in a way that was galling.

They were only at Broceni. Damn it. Dobele and Jelgava still to come. Why wasn't anyone getting off? To think that she might have to sit squeezed like this against him until Riga. She glanced at her watch. Why was her stupid heart beating so fast?

He stopped talking and, with his army manual open on his lap, dozed off. Hannah kept gesturing to Chloe, who finally turned her head from the window. "What?" she said, pretty loud.

Johnny's head drooped forward.

"Shh," said Hannah. "Well?" She pointed in the general vicinity of him.

"The worst," Chloe mouthed. The train pitched sideways, and his head bobbed sideways, toward her. His clean shiny hair was touching her shoulder. She cleared her throat and shifted in her seat, to rouse him, to force him to change his position. Oh, he changed it, all right. By slumping even further to the right. The boy was practically drooling on her arm! "Why are you talking to him so much?"

"Why aren't you? I'm making chit-chat."

"Weird how I didn't hear you volunteering any chit-chat about Blake and Mason."

"He didn't ask." Hannah grinned as he had grinned, like a Cheshire cat. It was hopeless.

He woke up a while later, stretched his ridiculously long body, like a sapling twig, one of his arms nearly hitting Chloe on the head, sat up, leaned forward, pulled out a silver flask from his duffel, swigged it and offered it to her!

"Um, no, thank you."

Hannah of course grabbed it. She coughed a little, surprised by its high alcohol content.

"Stoli." He smiled. "Good, right? Excuse me, I'll be right back." He asked Chloe to keep an eye on his stuff, got up and vanished. He was gone a fairly long time. When he returned he was awake, flushed and full of energy. He fitted in snugly between the lasciviously smiling zaftig woman and an ill-disposed Chloe, turned to her, and said, "So what are you doing after?"

"After what?" She tried not to snap, but failed.

"Do you mean later?" Hannah said. "What are we doing later?"

"No, I mean after all this. Did you just graduate high school? Are you headed to college?"

Lucky for Chloe, Hannah took that one. "Chloe and I are going to the University of Maine, up in Bangor," she said. "Do you know where that is?"

But Johnny, who had been looking at Chloe when Hannah replied, didn't answer, blinking with awareness at the shadow passing across Chloe's face.

Hannah kept on and on at him about things. "Where are you headed in Italy?"

"Tiny place. Tarcento. Do you know it?"

Of course Hannah didn't know it. Why even ask?

"I'm going to visit my mother," Johnny said. "She's staying in Tarcento, and I'm on my way to say goodbye to her before I fly to Columbus, Georgia. Fort Benning. First OCS. Then the 75th Ranger Regiment."

Ah. Maybe that's why the conductor had half-saluted. But how would he know that from the travel pass?

"You're going into the army?"

"Not just the army. I'm going to be a Ranger!"

Hannah was drowning in a pool of amazement. "You're enlisting? That's awesome. Where are you going to be deployed? Afghanistan, wow! Aren't you scared? Are the Rangers like an elite force? Special operations, you say. Your family must be proud of you, no? When do you leave for overseas?" She giggled again. "I know you're overseas now, I meant Afghanistan. November? That seems so soon. So Ranger training is not that long? Do you get a weekend pass when you're at Fort Benning?"

Chloe listened to this, drowning in her own pool of amazement.

He smelled of cigarettes, possibly something carbonated, there was a man smell, but also a stale smell, not necessarily unpleasant, but unfamiliar and not altogether pleasant. But … not altogether unpleasant, either.

Could Hannah sustain this level of excitement at every new fact about himself the boy shared? Johnny, while fielding Hannah's questions, kept smiling at Chloe. "Where are you from, Chloe?"

"Maine—like my friend said. We live next door to each other. Like she said."

Why did that amuse him, please him?

"Where are you really from?" His fingers circled around her face, uncomfortably close to it, one heave of the train and his pointing digit would graze her cheek.

"You mean, where is my mother from?"

"Or father."

"North Dakota," Chloe said, stubbornly refusing to participate with him. "And Maine. Is that what you wanted to know?"

He pointed to his own elfin face: high forehead, square jaw, prominent cheekbones. "Do you see? My mother is Indonesian." He thought they were kindred spirits! How precious of him. Well, Chloe would put paid to that immediately.

"Yeah, I'm not from Indonesia."

"Where in North Dakota?"

"Pembina."

"Really. There's an army base close by."

"I know," said Chloe. "My dad was stationed there. That's how he met my mom."

"Aha," Johnny said. "So your dad was a military man?"

"He was in the National Guard for a few years. He's the chief of police now." He was less impressed by this than she'd hoped he would be. Smiling, though. Thoroughly entertained.

"Chloe's mother is originally from China," Hannah said.

"Nooo," Chloe drew out. "My mother is originally from Pembina, North Dakota. And her mother. And her mother's mother. And her mother's mother's mother. And …"

"I get it," Johnny said. "Your mother's from Pembina."

She didn't want to be telling him any of it. "Back when North Dakota was a territory," she told him anyway, "and not a state, over a hundred and sixty years ago, the missionaries from Canada went to China and brought back eight girls and two boys. The children were nine or ten at the time. They lived in the missionary compound, near Dauphin, north of Lake Manitoba, but when they were old enough, some of the children went south for warmth. They stopped at Pembina, two miles south of the border, declaring it warm enough."

Johnny laughed. "Only a true Chinese would deem Pembina on the 48th parallel to be warm enough," he said.

How did he know this!

"So where in the States do you live?" Hannah asked while he was still laughing.

"Oh, I've lived everywhere."

"Except Texas," Chloe pointed out.

"Correct! Except Texas. And North Dakota. Tell me, is Pembina close to Manitoulin Island? That's where I'd want to escape to, if I could."

Chloe suppressed a mocking chuckle. "Manitoulin Island is nowhere near there."

"It's near Canada, though, right?"

Chloe would not catch his twinkling eye. "Canada is the second largest country in the world. So technically yes. But a thousand miles from Pembina."

"What is distance anyway, right?" he said. "Just a blink. A number on the page, nothing more. Manitoulin's got a place called Misery Bay. Isn't that the best name? How could one not want to go there?" He leaned in to Chloe, like a kid, already familiar and undaunted by her hostility, oblivious to it. He inhaled the air around her and said, "You smell nice." He tilted his head, this way and that. "Like a girl. You smell ..." He inhaled again. "Like lavender and vanilla."

For a moment Chloe caught his smiling eye. He blinked, slowly. She blinked slowly back. When she replied, she felt slightly heady, as if she'd been winded. "You're telling me I smell like fabric softener?"

And he, without missing a beat, said, "I don't know, what's fabric softener?"

Chloe sighed and stared at her watch, as if by staring, she could somehow will the time to go faster. Had they passed Jelgava yet? She couldn't believe it. She had missed Jelgava.

"Jelgava is next," Johnny said. "You should get off there another time. It's got a most splendid castle. Like Versailles, but bigger. You like castles, don't you, Chloe?"

"I don't know," she said. "I've never seen one."

"Latvia has castles?" Hannah was surprised.

"Latvia has lots of castles," Johnny said. "Kings and queens and dukes and princes lived here for many centuries. Chloe, really? You've never seen a castle?" Like a whiskey burn, that was the low-register timbre of his husky voice.

How long was this insipid chinwag going to continue?

"What's your full name?" He had been addressing Chloe, but Hannah replied.

"Hannah Gramm."

"Uh-huh. What about you, Chloe?"

"She's Chloe Divine. With an i not an e."

"You're Chloe *Divine*?"

"What's so funny?" said Chloe. "What's your name?"

"I'm Johnny Rainbow," he said, grinning wide.

"Your name is Johnny Rainbow," she said, "and you're laughing at *my* name?"

"Because yours isn't real."

"And yours is?"

"Sure."

"If yours is, then mine is."

What he might have said was, she wasn't *for* real. Except she knew she was. Maybe she feared he was right. In any case, since she knew almost for certain that she was Chloe Divine, she had to conclude that the mirage was not her, but the strumming vagabond next to her named Johnny Rainbow.

"Your family name is Rainbow?"

"Your family name is Divine?"

"Yes."

"Then yes for me, too."

An incredulous Chloe snorted. "Come on, what's your *real* name? No one is called Johnny Rainbow."

"What's your real name? No one is called Chloe Divine."

"Yes, they are. Me. My dad."

"Her mother changed one letter on her birth certificate," Hannah piped in. "So she's actually the only Divine."

"I bet she is." His smile was ridiculous and insubordinate. He was so good-natured, it was impossible to stay mad at him, to remain hostile to him. "Brilliant! Even better. Well, then, my mother changed one letter too."

"Which one?"

"V. She changed it to a W."

Chloe blanked as she tried to figure out what he meant. He was making it tough for her to concentrate because he was too close, his teasing eyes dancing, roaming.

"We used to be Rainbov," he explained. My mother was afraid the V made me seem too Russian."

"You're Russian?"

"I said *seem*."

"You're having us on," Hannah exclaimed. "Your name was not Johnny Rainbov."

"Of course not. Johnny is an Americanization. I was Ivan."

"Ivan Rainbov."

"Correct."

And Chloe laughed.

Ah! Vanish the beguiling idle gypsies of this world, wasting my golden flames on your common impulses. The PA came on. The announcement said something about Riga. Thank God. Almost there.

"Girls, I have a proposal for you," said Johnny. "It's a great plan. Want to hear?"

Hannah

The boy is so cute and harmless and full of charm. I don't know why Chloe has taken such a dislike to him. He's like a puppy. Plus he's easy on the eyes, I won't deny. She's being so rude. She was turned to the window the entire time he was making conversation. And why shouldn't he talk to us? It makes the time pass. I said that to her when he left the cabin for a minute. What's the matter with you, I said, it's just to make the time pass, and she said, and I think she was quoting somebody, the time will pass either way, and I replied (I think quoting somebody too), yes, but not as rapidly.

I asked if he was crowding her. Clearly he was, trying to squeeze into the narrow space between a hostile Chloe and a huge woman with a proportionately huge crush on him. I don't see Chloe giving *her* the evil eye, like she's been giving me. I said that to Chloe, and she gave me an even worse evil eye and said, "She's not my friend, and she's not going out with Blake, and do you *not* see the difference?"

"No, I don't see the difference, Miss Judgy Pants," I said. "I don't see what the big deal is. The ride will be over soon and we'll never have to talk to him or see him again." I think Chloe misunderstands me. I'm not interested in him. He reminds me of my brother, the same slovenly I-don't-care-about-anything air about him. But he's cuter than Jason, he's got a winning smile, and he's not surly, like Chloe. I must talk to her when I get a chance, tell her that no boy, even one as sweet as Mason, likes sulky girls. Plus aren't we here for the experience, I said to her, and this is one of them, meeting strangers, striking up conversations.

The one possibly problematic thing is the favor he's asked of us. But I said to her, I know it's not the sixties anymore, but can we all just chill a tiny bit? Why so rigid, so tense, so planned? Why can't we just float where the river takes us, for damn once?

Chloe thinks the boys might be upset. She is wrong. They'll be fine.

Blake

I am without words. And until the girls came home it had been such a good day. Mason and I spent the day in Jurmala. The girls would've loved it. The sun was out, everybody on the Majori beach, loud music everywhere, great food. We swam, drank Black Balsam, found some stuff for the girls. Jomas Street near the beach was an endless buffet of cafés, restaurants, shops, street vendors, and live performers on every corner. I almost wish we could go back there tomorrow to show the girls.

I bought Hannah a purse mirror, covered in amber. Mason couldn't find anything for Chloe, though he kept looking at a lot of amber jewelry, small vases, picture frames, postcards of the beach. He bought some things, but nothing specifically for her. I showed him an amber-colored knit beanie she would've liked. "For Chloe, because it's cold up in Bangor," I said to him. For some reason he wasn't as impressed with the beanie as I was. She's got plenty of hats, he said. He found her some caramels instead.

The sand was white and cool, the beach wide and long. The Riga Gulf at the end of July was slightly warmer than the Atlantic off the coast of Maine, but only just. It was hot out. We didn't want to leave. We had dinner there; Mason found a sausage and potato pie he quite liked from a street seller. I bought three helpings of a herring, beet and apple salad. It was crazy good. We bought some pierogi, we thought with potato, but it was with cabbage. I laughed so hard watching Mason struggle with it in his mouth that a little of the cabbage came out my nose. We got in maybe half an hour before the girls. Varda and her family had already eaten, but Sabine was warming up some food anyway. She said the girls would be starved for sure when they got home.

The girls were many things when they strolled in, around nine. Starved was one of them. The other thing they were was not alone. They dragged a homeless person in with them. I don't mean this facetiously. I don't mean this to be droll. I'm not even using hyperbole the way I do in my prize-winning story, to emphasize a point. I mean this in the most literal sense. My girlfriend and my brother's girlfriend brought to Varda's house a vagrant with a ponytail who asked if he could stay the night because he had nowhere else to go and no money.

He shook my hand! He shook Mason's hand. "Hi, I'm Johnny," he said.

I asked to see Hannah outside under the peach trees for a moment.

"What's the matter?" she said sweetly. "He needs a floor for the night. And for that he's going to give us a free tour tomorrow! It's a great deal for us. He's supposed to be excellent. There's even a boat ride. His tours usually cost fifty latu."

"Are you crazy? We're not going on tour with him!"

"Why not? You said yourself we were going to hire a guide tomorrow. It's serendipity." She frowned. "Why are you upset? I don't understand."

"You don't understand? *I* don't understand!"

"I thought you'd be pleased. I saved us a hundred dollars."

"I don't care about the money."

"It's not your money, that's why. But Chloe cares."

"So whose idea was this? Chloe's?"

"Johnny's. I told you. He asked us—a place to sleep in exchange for a tour—and we said yes."

"He asked you and you said yes," I repeated.

"Yes."

"Did he ask you before or after you told him that you were both traveling with your boyfriends?"

"Blake, it's not like that. Come on. It's just an adventure. A new bend in the river."

"You invited him without asking Varda first?"

"Well, how were we going to ask her? Just think about what you're saying. We were on a train. And Varda doesn't care. Look at her."

True. Through the windows, I saw Varda cozy with Johnny in the living room, chatting to him (in Latvian?), a drink already in his hand!

"Hannah," I said, "there are thousands of men on the streets of Europe who have no place to go."

"We can't save everybody," Hannah said. "Not even Zhenya. But we can help this one."

"Who the hell is Zhenya? Another bum?"

"No. I'll tell you later. I'm starved. Do you want to come and sit with us while we eat?"

"Where did you find him, at the orphanage?"

"Of course not. I told you, we met him on the train. It's no big deal. After tomorrow you'll never have to see him again. Blake ..." Questioningly, she pulled her arm away from my grip. "What's gotten into you?"

I don't know what got into me. Clearly something, otherwise why would I be acting like such a jerk? The guy had a ponytail of wavy black hair pulled back tight off his face. He had designer stubble and a beret! Who in the world wears a fucking beret? He brought with him a guitar, a smell of smoke and alcohol, white teeth always on disgusting display, and produced flowers and a bottle of Black Balsam to give to Varda as a gift. Maybe if he used the money he'd just spent on gifts to get himself a bed at a hostel, he wouldn't be here.

He pretended to be polite. He spoke English. Varda brought out a place setting for him and he sat at the table—at the head!—Carmen on one side of him, Varda on the other. Sabine and Guntis had gone to bed. Otto was outside. Mason sat by Chloe. I had no choice but to fit next to Hannah and fume in silence. He clearly also spoke a little Latvian, because he opened his hands and said, *"Pienācis mans Kungs."*

"Oh dude," Mason said. "They've been saying it for three days. What is that?"

Johnny smiled as if he knew everything. "That's the Lutheran prayer. *Come, my Lord.* That's *all* they say. They never add the rest of it. *Come, my Lord, light my way to salvation.*"

"I knew it was a prayer!" Mason exclaimed, and I muttered that it was hardly the riddle of the Sphinx, but no one heard.

He told Mason and me, as if we cared what he thought, that we had two very fine girlfriends, and that Maine was a great and noble state. He told us he had once worked a summer in Wiscasset.

"That's on the water," I said. "We're inland."

"Near the White Mountains," Mason added. "What were you doing in Wiscasset?"

"Yeah, a long way from home for me," he said. "But a couple of years ago when I was out looking for this thing or that, and had the summer to kill, I hitched to Wiscasset." He smiled. "Got a job as a worm-digger."

Chloe shuddered, trying not to show her disgust. Why did that bring me joy?

"Oh yeah, baby," he continued happily. "Wiscasset is the worm capital of the world. I'm talking bloodworms *and* sandworms. I was paid fifty cents for each one I dug up." He shrugged. "Made okay money. But had to stand all day knee-deep in fetid goopy silt out in the mudflats. I was black like tar all summer, and smelled like rotting earth and black worms. So you can imagine how well I did with the ladies." He grinned. "I made nearly two hundred bucks a day, though. Saved up my money, and came here."

"And he's been in Europe for two years!" Hannah said, as if it was all just so hopelessly romantic.

Chloe spoke to me. "Blake, would someone pay fifty cents for a worm?"

"If you were a bait fisherman, you would," said Johnny.

I cut in. She was asking me, not him. "The better and bigger the worm, the better and bigger fish you'll catch." I looked away from him. And from her, looking at him.

"I've never met happier people than I did in Wiscasset," Johnny said, eating ravenously. "Except maybe my grandparents.

Are they happy like that in your town, too? In Wiscasset everyone lives as if they've won the lottery of life. I couldn't stay there, but boy did I envy them that did."

We said nothing. He told us he needed the floor for just one night because tomorrow he was leaving early. His first guided tour was at eight in the morning, and he had two others before he could fit us in. "I could give you a private tour, as promised, or you can join me on one of my other tours. Don't worry," he added, with a winsome smile, "in two hours I will show you more things in Riga than all the other tour guides can show you in six."

I hated him from the moment I saw him.

"Thanks," I said, "but we already hired a guide. Gave him a deposit. Can't back out now."

Mason looked disappointed. "You sure, bro?" he said to me. "You sure we can't cancel? Johnny says he'll do it for free."

Mason and I had booked Gregor that morning, before our train to Jurmala. I wanted to inform my brother that whatever Johnny was doing, it sure as hell wasn't going to be free, but I didn't. "We can't cancel, Mase," I said. "I gave the dude a deposit."

"Who did you book?" Johnny asked.

"A guy. You wouldn't know him."

"I know all the tour guides in Riga," he said, eating so heartily he might have really been homeless. "Who?" When I told him it was Gregor, he smiled into his cabbage. "Good luck," he said.

"What does that mean?" Did that come out rude? I didn't care.

"Nothing. He's very knowledgeable. You'll see."

Varda served Johnny. He thanked her, listened to her, replied in Latvian, complimented her sausage pie, her vinegar porridge. She chuckled like a schoolgirl. He was ingratiating and infuriating.

I've never had such a visceral reaction to a complete stranger. I was so upset with the girls that I almost couldn't listen to Chloe's story about the orphanage. She said she'd found someone for her parents, a little boy named Raymonds, but she could barely get the words out before Johnny started telling us about Liepaja and what a shame it was that they hadn't stayed longer in that long-forgotten city.

Why would the girls do this? Why would they pick up a strange guy and involve him in any way in our life? We had been so happy together. He could be a murderer. He might rob us in the middle of the night, cut our throats, leave with Moody's money and our passports. Sure, he seems friendly. The Boston Strangler wore a suit for most of his life. He was the most polite man, right up to, and maybe even after, the moment he obtained unforced entry into the homes of the women he assaulted and strangled. They let Albert DeSalvo inside their homes, I wanted to shout. What does politeness matter in cases like this? Vigilance is what's firmly required.

No one paid a lick of attention to me. Varda and Carmen had taken their eyes off my adorable brother and were now flitting around the Ponytail like hummingbirds. They clucked around him like chickens around a rooster. More *kvas*? More vodka? More food? Want a light? We don't care, smoke in the house.

I tried to catch Chloe's eye, but she wouldn't play. Chloe was quiet and neutral. That meant nothing. Chloe is quiet and neutral when she's got nothing to say, and also when she's got everything to say. It's her default position: she retreats into herself to observe and contemplate. From the outside, she looks the same. She smiles lightly, glances at everyone methodically, eats normally, nods her head like the steady hands of a clock counting out the hours. Tonight, the only sign that something was perhaps askew was that the clock hands of her gaze were stopped on him the entire time he talked. And let me tell you, he talked *plenty*.

Mason and Hannah weren't helping matters by conducting what was almost an interrogation. "Bro, did you hear?" Mason turned to me excitedly. "Johnny's going to join the 75th Regiment. Special Ops. The Rangers!"

"Stupendous," I said. I didn't hear Rangers. I heard basic training and then possibly maybe somewhere down the line, the pipe dream of Rangers. I heard Afghanistan. I heard six thousand miles away. He told us he was off to Fort Benning as soon as he returned Stateside.

I couldn't help myself. I said, "And when would that be?"

Hannah glared at me. I cleared my throat. "I mean, how long do you plan to stay in Europe?"

"Only a few more weeks, man."

"Us too!" exclaimed Hannah.

"Settle down," I said to her. "You're not joining the army."

"Johnny is on his way to Italy to visit his mother."

Varda and Carmen clucked approvingly.

Mason asked where his dad was.

"He's remarried," Johnny said. "Lives in the States."

Hannah wanted to know if he was an only child.

Johnny shook his head. "I wish. I have two older sisters and a younger brother."

Hannah immediately disclosed that she had a twenty-two-year-old brother, and then pointed out the obvious—that I had a brother. Chloe said nothing.

Johnny turned to Chloe. "And how old is your brother now, Chloe Divine?" he said, smiling. Why the hell did he have to use her full name like that?

No one said anything for a moment. I was so annoyed, I didn't process his question properly. Why would he even mention Chloe's brother? For a moment the entire table fell mute because no one knew what to say.

"How—how do you know I have a brother?" said Chloe, neutral, and yet I knew—not neutral.

Johnny pointed over her shoulder to the walls of the dining room. Young Chloe and young Jimmy abounded in Otto's distorted, misaligned frames.

"What's the matter?" He acted all puzzled. "What did I say?"

Carmen leaned over to Johnny's slick head and whispered something into his exposed ear. For one long moment, Johnny stared at Chloe with his bottomless black eyes. She did not raise her own eyes from her plate. "There are some losses from which you never recover," he said. "That's what my dad keeps telling me. I'm sorry."

Chloe tried hard to stay composed.

"Haiku," I said, to distract her, "can you pass me the *kvas*?"

And Johnny reached over before she could get to it, and handed it to me. I had no choice but to say thanks.

He vied for her attention. "Why does he call you Haiku?"

Lifting her gaze finally, Chloe smiled into what I hoped was my utterly unamused face. "Because he's the perfect walking shining example, the prime embodiment of too little information being a dangerous thing. He thinks he is being clever."

"I am being clever," I said.

"See, you're not. Want me to tell you why?"

"You've told me a thousand times. I stopped listening."

Chloe turned to Johnny. "He calls me Haiku," she said, "because he knows my mother is Chinese, and he thinks he's given me a funny nickname to reflect my heritage."

"But a haiku is not Chinese."

Chloe smiled at Johnny, and then from across the table smiled at me. "*That's* the point," she said.

I didn't laugh. "That's what makes it even funnier. Is it my fault none of you pedants have a sense of humor?"

"Johnny, has your mother always lived in Italy?" Hannah piped in, diverting him to herself.

"No, just for the last few years," he replied, offering no details.

"So who have you been living with?"

"Well, for the last two years I've been in Europe," he said, downing the entire tall glass of Black Balsam. "But before that, I lived with my dad, and with my grandparents when my dad had to travel for work."

"You're already two years out of school?" Hannah asked.

He nodded. "I'm nineteen in a couple of weeks," he replied. "Graduated when I was seventeen."

I had already turned nineteen. Did anyone stare at me like I was the bomb?

So he came to Europe when he was younger than we are, and two years later he was homeless. Was there a lesson there? Why didn't he go to college? Why didn't he go back to the States like normal people and get a job, even as a worm-digger? Why didn't he enlist when he turned eighteen? If he had, we wouldn't be sitting here appraising him now.

Hannah, having found a kindred spirit, a child of divorce, inched away from me and closer to him. I could tell she felt an instant affinity with him, even though at the Academy every fifth family is separated, and she's not all elbows on the table, head in her hands with them.

Mason didn't want to talk about divorce. He wanted to talk about the Rangers. "Is it hard to get into?" he asked. As if he planned to join them himself. He wanted to know how long the training would be, and what was required of new recruits.

"When I was sixteen," Johnny told him, "there was a man living down the road from my grandparents who was a retired Ranger. Clemente. He was sixty, ancient, but still strong like a bull, and he trained all the kids in the neighborhood who were thinking about the Ranger program. He knew a lot of shit, pardon my language, ladies. He was phenomenal. If you passed his kickass neighborhood training school, you were one hundred percent ready for Benning. He was one tough motherf …" He trailed off, delicately. "The way he tortured us, you'd think he was getting paid for it. But he wasn't. He did it because he was a sadist and he liked it. We had to swim five hundred yards in fifteen minutes. Run two miles in fifteen minutes in a hundred-degree heat while wearing a thick jacket and long jeans. He had us doing forty push-ups in two minutes. Kids dropped like flies. That was the idea. I almost did. But I stayed. I wanted to prove to him that I was tough too, that I could do it. He taught me how to fight, and how to fire a weapon—"

"You know how to fire a gun too?" Hannah said, nearly squealing.

I nearly groaned.

Johnny grinned. "I come from a long line of gunslingers," he replied.

Chloe spoke. "Were you trying to prove something to Clemente, or to your dad?"

"Very good, Chloe Divine," Johnny said with a smile.

I interrupted them. "Is there a difference between Rangers and Navy SEALs?" I asked. "Because I heard, and I could be wrong, that the SEALs are tougher."

Staring at me for a moment, a puzzled Johnny said nothing. Then, his gaze clearing, he opened his mouth and laughed. "You're right, Blake," he said. "I agree the SEALs are badasses, but this is what I have to say about it. The Rangers have to do all the things the SEALs do, except we have to do it on only one meal a day, while the SEALs never stop stuffing their faces. So you tell me. Which is harder?"

Do you see why I hate him?

Mason

The dude the girls brought home is awesome. The thing that impresses me most is I don't know how he could be a tour guide. He's not from Latvia, wasn't born in Latvia, doesn't really speak Latvian, though he made quite a go of it to win over Varda. He's got panache. But also—he knows his shit. The girls went to Liepaja to find a small boy and brought back a fully grown dude. Blake has his hackles up, but I don't get why. I agree with Hannah, this is exactly what you're supposed to do when you travel. Meet different people, go off the grid. I liked him immediately. The stuff he knew about Liepaja, I don't even know how he knew it. He told us that in the Soviet era, Liepaja was not on the map. On any map. "Find an old map of Latvia, or Poland and vicinity, and you won't find it on there. And yet it's the single largest port on the Baltic Sea." He repeated it in case we didn't hear. "The single largest port on the Baltic Sea. The sea that contains Copenhagen, Leningrad, Kaliningrad, Helsinki, Stockholm, Tallinn. And little Liepaja is larger than all of them. And yet it wasn't on the map. Imagine that."

"Maybe it wasn't that important," said Hannah.

"Just the opposite," Johnny said. "It was indispensable to both Hitler and Stalin. When it was in German hands during the war, it was Stalin's main bombing target in the region. And it was the first city in the Baltics Hitler had occupied." Johnny smiled. "Of course, Hitler being Hitler, the first thing he did was eliminate all of Liepaja's Jews."

"When you say all of them ..."

"I mean all of them," said Johnny. "There were seven thousand Jews in Liepaja before the start of the war, and when the Soviets 'liberated' it, on 9 May 1945, they counted thirty."

"How do you know that?" Hannah exclaimed. Even she was impressed, and she knows nothing about history and cares even less.

That's what I mean by obscure knowledge. Why would a kid from America, penniless, homeless, starving, traveling on the cheap, know something that esoteric and that specific, and yet so fascinating? Maybe that's why Blake doesn't like him. Because Blake is also full of odd bits of trivia. Just different kinds. He knows how to do a lot of stuff, and sometimes he knows things about bees, or fish, or even the best river for fly fishing in Idaho, which on balance is as crazy as Johnny's knowledge that Liepaja was first invisible and then destroyed in the war. With only ruins of old forts remaining, he told us, the Soviets built a new concrete city on these, and kept it off the map until 1991.

"But why?" Blake demanded. "Why would they do that?"

Johnny continued eating. "They built underground nuclear-weapon warehouses," he said, mouth full. "Sixteen nuclear submarines. They needed the port. Liepaja is virtually ice-free during the Arctic winter because of its relatively high altitude. The winter is mild, usually doesn't get below twenty-six degrees Fahrenheit, minus two to three Celsius." He stopped eating for a moment. "Man is mortal," he said. "But mankind is immortal. And yet Liepaja is proof positive that the Soviets and the Americans managed to find a way to make mankind mortal, too. It's all on display in Liepaja, the secret stores of the Soviet nuclear arsenal that was kept in the Karosta forts for forty years and hidden from the world."

"How do you know all this?" Blake asked.

"About the temperature?"

"About nuclear weapons!"

Johnny shrugged. "I know a little bit of shit," he said. "Useless, but vast."

"Blake," said Chloe, "it's like you knowing that Taiwanese funeral processions usually include a stripper. You just know, right?"

Blake wasn't in the least amused, but Johnny roared with laughter.

Later, he became fascinated that Chloe's parents would know anything about the Liepaja orphanage. I could see poor Chloe didn't know how to answer. She said that her father's mother was originally from Latvia, was related to Varda, and her parents wanted to sponsor a child from Moody's birth country.

Johnny listened, and then said, "But Varda is not related to your grandmother." We all fell quiet. "Varda is related to her only by marriage. It's Otto who is your family. Otto and your grandmother were cousins. Almost like siblings. Born and raised under the same roof for eighteen years before the war. They're nearly the same age."

How did he know this?!

Johnny shrugged. "Everyone, everywhere is dying to tell you things," he said. "Dying to tell you everything. All you gotta do is listen."

Carmen furrowed her brows at Chloe. "Chloe, I tell you this your first night here. Grandmother told you. You have it wrong, she said. Otto and Moody like brother and sister."

So that odd fish of a man was Chloe's only real link to her grandmother's past! Unbelievable.

To change the subject, Johnny asked the girls why they hadn't partaken of the white-sand Liepaja beaches. Before they could answer, Blake jumped in.

"What do we want with cold northern beaches when we're headed to Barcelona?"

"Oh yeah, that's right," Johnny said, tutting into his food. "Hmm."

"What?" Blake snapped.

"Nothing. It'll be fine."

"What will be fine?" Hannah asked. "Have you been to Barcelona?"

"I've been everywhere."

"Of course you have," Blake muttered. Poor bro. He had been priding himself on researching Barcelona and all the great things we could do there. Poor Chloe. She'd been dreaming of Barcelona half her life.

"Thing is," Johnny continued, "you really don't want to go there in August."

"Why? We're used to the heat."

"It's not the heat," she said. "Most stores, markets, restaurants shut down in August. Everyone's away on vacation. Oh, I'm sure you'll find a few things open. They love the *guiri* in that city."

Guiri were tourists that the locals could spot half a town away. Blake had told us about them. We apparently were not allowed to look like *guiri*. But clearly, coming to Barcelona in August was a blatant *guiri* move.

We had no choice, Hannah told Johnny. We couldn't go earlier because we were working to save money for the trip, and we couldn't go later because some of us are starting college.

"That's right." Johnny studied Chloe. "University of Maine, as I recall."

Chloe, true to form, said nothing. Of course I said nothing. Blake said nothing because he was still seething about the *guiri*.

Johnny excused himself and left the room, and we were alone in the dining room.

"Are you sure we can't cancel our tour guide and go with Johnny, Blakie?" Hannah said. "He owes us, so it'll be free."

"It won't be free. And we've already paid the other guide. No. He's on his way, and we're on our way. Besides, I suspect he's a con artist. He'll lure us into some alley and rob us. Assault us."

Chloe looked as if she was nodding in assent but then said, "This is not your story, Blake. This is real life. You can't make up details about him just because they suit you."

"How does getting robbed suit me? Explain that."

Before Chloe could explain, Johnny returned. "Y'all sure lug a lot of stuff with you."

"What's it to you?" Blake said. I elbowed him in the ribs. He ignored me.

"Well, what it means to me," Johnny said, "is I can't find a place on the floor of the porch to perch. Maybe we can move your suitcases out for one night? Otherwise I'll have to sleep on the floor with the girls." He smiled. Blake inhaled sharply. "But more importantly," Johnny went on, "it'll mean something to the thieves who haunt the trains from here to Spain. If you take a sleeper car on one of your legs to Barcelona, I'd sleep on top of the suitcases if I were you. It won't guarantee no robbery. But at least you might wake up *as* you're being robbed."

"And who's going to rob us?" Blake wanted to know. "People who travel the trains, um, like yourself?"

Johnny laughed. He winked at the girls, and went out into the backyard, leaving the four of us stumped and wary, even me. We saw him through the porch, kneeling in the dirt talking to Otto. He talked to the old man for a long time. We were all crazy curious what they talked about. And in what language?

Before turning in, Johnny thanked Varda for the hospitality and the girls for inviting him. ("Inviting him?" Blake demanded. "I thought he invited himself.") He shook our hands, and said he was going to be up real early and would probably not see us again. He said it was fun getting to know us a little bit. He wished us well on our travels. He told us to stay safe.

We slept poorly with him on the porch with us. He was an extremely restless sleeper. Blake had the couch, I was by his side in the long chair, and Johnny was on the floor. I heard him get up at least four or five times in the night and go out into the yard. Once, near blue dawn, I peered through the glass to see what he was doing. I think he must have been smoking by the shadowy rows of fat tomatoes. His head was down in his hands and his long narrow back was turned to me.

21

The Guider of Guiri, the Singer of Songs

Chloe

Gorgeous Livu Square, beautiful day. Street performers, crowds, humid sunshine. Chloe didn't want to do anything except breathe in the air and maybe have an ice cream near the red roofs and the sparkling blue walls.

But no.

Blake had booked Gregor.

Gregor turned out to be an uptight dick in maroon loafers, who majored in geology at some fancy university Chloe had never heard of. Geology and tourism, he told them. "Geo-tourism." What an ass. She had been accepted into the best schools too, she wanted to tell him. The best of the best. Did she bore him with her resume?

"Oh yeah, he's much better than Johnny would've been," she whispered to Blake.

"That's right. One bazillion points of light better."

That was at ten in the morning. Blake changed his tune by noon. Gregor tortured them by never, and she meant *never*, stopping speaking. He led them on a walking tour that included that hideous example of Socialist Classicism, the Latvian Academy of Sciences built in Stalin's pompous empire style. The four of them sounded an objection, said they didn't want to go, but Gregor wouldn't hear of it. "I have a plan, ladies and gentlemen, to show you everything important in Riga in the most sensible and effective way possible. The building is on our way. We simply must see it. It's the heart of our city." He convinced them it was for the best, sort of like a rectal probe. All poor Mason wanted was to see inside the black dome of St. Peter's. "We will get to it," said Gregor, adding, "*if* there's time."

"Oh, so for Stalin there's time, but Jesus is a maybe?" Mason hissed.

"Shh."

They followed Gregor around like slaves. He walked five steps ahead of them at all times and never ceased yammering. They bleated gently like lambs that they desired to partake of the Jewish ghetto. Gregor said no. He said it was completely destroyed in the war.

"Why does everyone keep referring to it as *the war*?" Hannah whispered to Chloe, doggedly keeping up behind Gregor. "There've been other wars, no?"

"No," Gregor said, who overheard. "Maybe other wars, but they are all completely inconsequential."

The Freedom Monument, the factory that made Stolichnaya vodka, streets and streets of art nouveau. They toured inside the Opera House, up and down the marble stairs, but were not allowed to stop to get a schedule of events. Gregor said there was no time, not if they wanted to see the Orthodox Cathedral—which under Soviet rule had been used as a planetarium—or the famous Riga Hostel. ("Why do we have to see that?" "And why couldn't the hobo you dragged in yesterday stay there instead of with us?")

"Do you know how much blood has been spilled on Latvian soil?" Gregor asked, but rhetorically; he didn't even wait for his own answer before launching into a comparison of Lutheranism and Catholicism and a discussion of the magnificent Tower of the Holy Spirit.

He had no need to stop for food or a drink, and was irritated when the girls cried bathroom break and vanished for twenty minutes into an adorable hidden alley with little shops that sold summer dresses. They each bought something flash, but had to roll it up and hide it in their backpacks so Gregor wouldn't yell at them. He was worse than Chloe's mother.

On and on and on, stories about Old Town and Riga Castle and what used to be a vibrant and active Jewish quarter, "the way it was in Vilnius and Warsaw and Krakow and Trieste."

"Where the hell is Trieste?" Chloe whispered.

"There are no Jews anywhere," Gregor said, "that's my point, because they're all dead. Especially in Poland. Though to answer your question, Trieste is in Italy. That's how far down the destruction of the Jewish population extended. I used to be a tour guide in Krakow and Warsaw. I know those cities well. If you go to Krakow, by all means stop by Auschwitz, but you should also try the salt mines if you have time, and Oskar Schindler's enamelware factory. That's a must-see in Krakow. Even more than Auschwitz probably." He told them stories and historical anecdotes, legends, lies, myths and provocations, how the riverbeds dried up and that's why the tram line now ran through what used to be a river.

"In Riga?"

"No, in Krakow. I was talking about Krakow."

You know what they didn't get?

Silence.

You know what else they didn't get?

Peace and quiet.

And you know what else?

An ice cream. A cherry strudel. A conversation among themselves. A potato pancake. A fifteen-minute rest at a table in Livu Square. But they did, however, receive a lecture on Livu Square as Gregor stormed past it. "There was no square here before the war," he said, "but one of the bombardiers leveled three city blocks, and suddenly opened up this lovely area. After the war, the city council decided to leave it and rebuild around it. Isn't it wonderful? You can sit, browse the local painters, have a coffee, listen to the musicians, but not now, ladies and gentlemen, now we must hurry, no stopping."

He bored them into submission with his staccato Germanic delivery and four hours later still had not shut his trap. When he talked, he demanded complete silence and would not let them interrupt or move until he stopped spouting whatever nonsense it was he was spouting. "Can I just have your attention, please, for two more minutes until I finish?" All eyes had to be on him, and he invited no questions. "Ask me questions as we walk to the House of the Blackheads, but please, walk quickly," he said.

He finally abandoned them just after three, and even then reluctantly. As soon as he left, they ran screaming to the meandering park enfolding the Riga Canal, got drinks, food, ice cream, found a green slope to perch on, spread out on the grass under the trees beside the calm and languid water and spent a blissful hour ragging on Gregor.

Though Blake also found it hard to shut up about Johnny. "What kind of a pseudonym is Johnny Rainbow? Like, what's he hiding?"

"Do you think it's not his real name?" said Hannah.

"Of course it's not. It's so dumb and fake. He probably thinks he's being clever."

"Blake, give it a break," said Chloe. "Gregor was much worse. Let it go."

"She's right, man," said Mason. "Let it go. Johnny was an okay dude. I know you didn't think so. But we did a nice thing for someone. Because of us, he had a place to sleep and he didn't get robbed. That's it. It's over. Let's talk about tomorrow and Gdansk. How long do you think it'll take us to get there?"

"And most important, is Treblinka near Gdansk?" Hannah asked.

The four of them stared at the map, spread out in front of them on the grass like a picnic blanket.

"I don't see the death camps marked on your Rand McNally masterpiece of Poland, bro," Mason said.

"Where is this Treblinka? Does it even exist?" Hannah asked. "Because I want to get it over with as quickly as possible and go to Barcelona."

"Gee, really?" said Chloe. "And here I thought you wanted to linger in Poland."

"I don't," the bleached-blonde said, deaf to irony.

"Hannah's right about one thing—we need to be mindful of the time," Blake said. "We don't have a day to spare. Barcelona's a long way away."

"Chloe, please, do we really have to go to Treblinka?" Hannah asked. "Wouldn't you rather go to a beach or a castle than Treblinka?"

Blake carefully folded the map. Mason carefully studied the folds.

"Why are you being like this again?" Chloe said after a strained pause. "Yes, we really have to go to Treblinka."

Both brothers made clucking conciliatory noises. Everything will be okay, they cajoled the girls. We'll have plenty of time. And we'll be together. Isn't that the whole idea? Chloe and Hannah reluctantly agreed that it was.

There was uncertainty about distance and trains that affected Hannah, made her uneasy. Chloe could see that. She wanted to tell her friend that everything was uncertainty. Gypsies. Demons. Aurochs and angels. But Hannah wanted certainty. Did Hannah even hear the story Johnny had told them over herring the night before? Chloe recounted it now. He had told it as proof that they should fire Gregor and hire him instead. He said that the Latvians harbored hostility toward the Germans and Russians that stretched back a millennia. So though a sign might say DOGS ARE NOT ALLOWED TO RUN WILD in all three languages—Lettish, German and Russian—the last two languages would be tarred out. The Latvian thinking was, if a man can't read Lettish, his dog has an excuse for running wild. They had laughed then, and they laughed again now when Chloe retold it. All except Blake. "I don't know why you're telling us his stories," he said. "Who cares?"

Chloe tried again. "Johnny also said that if you ask a Lett for directions in Russian, they'll give you the street name in Russian, but when you get there, the Russian and German will be tarred out." Blake almost smiled that time.

He was much happier than he was last night. He pored over the map, tracing the journey ahead of them. Gdansk was but a blip on the northern water, Krakow somewhere south, and Barcelona a distant dot a continent away. "Don't worry, it's not really that far," Blake said to Hannah by way of comfort. "Europe is the smallest continent."

"Blakie, don't kid," Hannah said. "You're always kidding. Johnny said Barcelona was really far."

"What does he know? You know he's not really a tour guide?" Blake nodded. "He's actually a mentally ill homeless person. Last week he thought he was the head of the joint chiefs of staff for the United States Armed Forces. You are so gullible. Wise up."

"Oh, because you're so smart," said Chloe.

"Smarter than you."

"Really? What about when you decided to borrow your dad's welding torch to melt the ice on your mother's Subaru? Do you remember what an epic fail that was?"

"Define epic fail. The ice did melt."

"Yes, and half the car with it!"

"I didn't say there weren't some unintended consequences." Blake looked so proud of himself. "But God gave man the power of fire. Hence the acetylene torch. It's a sin not to use the power God gave you."

"You were grounded for a month."

"It was a manly grounding. I was grounded for being manly."

"Yeah, okay." Chloe licked her ice cream, dazed and dreamy, sitting up on the grass with her knees drawn up in her light summer dress.

"And what about you, genius?" Blake said to Chloe, flicking her leg. "Remember the Nativity play? Gold, *Frankenstein* and myrrh, you said. Do you remember?"

Hannah and Mason joined in. Yeah, yeah, we remember that. We peed ourselves laughing.

"It was elementary school! I was ten!"

"More like eleven," Blake said. "And what about when you sang 'America the Beautiful' for the Academy talent show? 'Purple *mountain's magazines* above the *fruit that's plain.*' How old were you then?"

"That was elementary school too. And I was, um, six."

"No way."

"Yes way."

"Genius."

"You genius," Chloe said, tickling him. "What about when your father nearly killed you because you decided to carve up his brand-new concrete driveway with the pneumatic chainsaw?"

"He'd gone outside the edge! I was helping him. Besides, it's in the name. It's a pneumatic *concrete* chainsaw. It's a saw that cuts through concrete. I had no choice but to use it."

"Because you're so smart. It has a noise level of eighty-eight decibels. You nearly went deaf."

"What?"

"You nearly went—oh, I'm not playing anymore."

Blake laughed and laughed and Mason said and what about the time Blake swung on the zipline he'd just hooked up and crashed into a tree and broke his leg in five places, that was smart, and Chloe was about to get to the chocolatey end of her ice cream cone at the very bottom, her favorite part, and she was murmuring and thinking up something else to tease Blake with, and then she heard someone calling her name.

Chloeeeeee. Chloeeeeeeeee.

She was wearing a green and yellow dress, floral, cotton jersey, easy on (easy off), elastic waist, no zippers, no sleeves. A neckline. Her breasts were somewhat camouflaged by hibiscus flowers (she hoped!), and her thin arms had burned a little in the Riga sun. She didn't mind. Better burn slightly here than blister in Barcelona. Her hair was shiny and loose like a hippie at Woodstock, her nose freckled, her lips parched. They had drunk some *kvas* and Black Balsam, were light-headed, had been trying to sober up, watching parents with their kids on the grass, couples arm in arm on the walkways, young and old, the very colors of life dancing scarlet and blue, everything saturated with muffled music and the whistles of men. For a moment Chloe thought her eyes had caught fire.

She looked down to the river, at the small wooden boat drifting slowly near the grassy knoll where they were lounging, and there was Johnny at the helm of this craft crammed with tourists. With a microphone in one hand, a camera in the other and a beret on his head, he was waving to them and calling out. "Guys! Hey! Guys!"

"Ignore him," Blake muttered. "Maybe it's not us he's waving to."

Hannah waved back. For a moment, Chloe stood warily. She turned to Blake. "What were you saying about him being a mad general?"

Hannah had already scrambled up from the grass and walked down to the waterline to hear Johnny better. He was barely ten feet away. Chloe followed her.

"How was Gregor?" he yelled. He didn't even have to use a microphone. "You look like you're still recovering from him." Happily he turned to his boatful of people. "Ladies and gentlemen, are you enjoying yourselves?"

A throaty hurrah was his reply.

"This is my third tour," he yelled.

Hannah asked where he got the boat from.

"Oh, I know a guy." He grinned. "I'm singing in Livu Square after this. Will you come?"

From behind, Blake was pulling on the hem of Chloe's sundress. "Say no, say no, say no."

"Stop pulling on me."

Johnny turned toward his group and resumed his narration. The canal was quiet, and Chloe could easily make out his low tenor, his perfect diction. "Riga is one of the wettest capitals in the world," she heard him saying. "It rains or snows in Riga nearly half of all the days of the year. Drought is one of the few climate conditions that Latvians do not experience. So enjoy this rare dry and sunny day, ladies and gentlemen. Please note the white wagtail singing on the elm branch over there. The wagtail is the national bird of Latvia and is one of the most striking birds in the world. Plus it sings beautifully." Johnny smiled, turning to the embankment. Chloe could almost swear his beaming smile was for her. "Not as beautifully as me, but still quite beautifully."

"Oh, so he sings too?" said Blake. "Is there anything this wonderchild doesn't do? Doesn't make enough scratch for a place to stay, but oh, sings and gives tours and charters boats."

"Maybe today is his first day at work," Hannah said.

"What was he doing before that?"

"Why don't you ask him?"

"No, thank you." Blake pitched his voice half an octave up. "The conifer and birch forest covers most of Latvia," he intoned in imitation. "The rest is low-lying plains. Makes farming difficult because of the drainage problems, but not impossible. Riga has nearly a million people, almost half the population of Latvia, and blah, and blah, and look at how smart I am."

"Stop it," Hannah said. "Let's hail a cab and go see a castle. Johnny said there were castles all over Latvia, right, Chloe?"

"Oh, well, if Johnny said," said Blake. "Though there is actually a castle on the outskirts of town that once belonged to Prince Krapotkin. Built in the thirteenth century. Would you like to go there, my lady?"

"Stop teasing, I'm serious."

"Me too."

"No, you're not, you're eating a sausage sandwich."

"That's just to absorb the Balsam in my gut."

"So let's take a train ride to a castle," Hannah said. "Chloe, yes?" Hannah's languorous bones looked reclothed in new linens.

"No, I want to stay right here and not move until it gets dark," Mason said, lying on his back, looking up at the clear sky. "I want to see this canal with all the city lights reflecting off the water. I want to see the night light show of a big city. Why does it have to get dark so damn late? I've never seen a big city at night. And then I want to step inside an evening cathedral."

"Mase, Hannah, stop the circus, you too," Chloe said. "Up, both of you. No castles, no city. Varda is waiting for us. It's our last night. She's making a special dinner."

"What, raw ox tongue?" said Mason. "You know, Homer Simpson says there are some things that are not meant to be eaten."

Chloe pinched him. "Varda asked me this morning if Johnny would be coming back."

"And you said of course not, right?" Blake said. "We're never going to see him again is what you told her, correct?"

"Something like that."

"But we've never seen a castle." A pale complaint from Hannah. Chloe stared down the river after the vanishing boat.

"Pumpkin," Blake said, "this is the beginning of our trip. There are lots of castles in Spain. We'll see them all. Eye on the prize, baby. Barcelona has human castles," he went on. "They're called castells. The people stand on top of one another, sometimes five people tall, and build a castle. We can't leave Barcelona without seeing the castellers do their magic."

"But I want a real castle, Blakie."

"How about I take you to the Castle of Cardona, a medieval fortress in Catalonia, would you like that?" He nuzzled her. "So much to look forward to."

After a while, they found a bin for their trash and began a slow amble out of Riga. They looped one last time through the Old City before heading to the train station. Chloe could barely move her legs. She was wiped out after Gregor and the Black Balsam. She could have fallen asleep on the grass embankment and dreamed of the wooden launches bright with sunlight and wild with wagtails.

Nearing Livu Square they heard the amplified strands of an acoustic guitar, playing a hyped-up, jazzed-up, rock-out version of a half-familiar pop song. The voice accompanying the music slowed Chloe down, unsyncopated her step. She stumbled over the cobblestones.

She had heard many buskers around Riga, with harmonicas, guitars, and banjos, with castanets in their hands and beer in their throats. This wasn't that. This was something else. Hannah and Mason heard it too. Blake's eyes didn't leave his Frommer's guide.

"What a voice," Hannah said, her eyes widening. "Let's go check it out."

"Sounds like a concert," Blake said, glancing up. "There were many in Jurmala yesterday. Listen to the sound. There's an amp, speakers. Sounds semi-pro. It won't be free. It's not in our budget. Besides, like Chloe said, we have to catch a train back."

They talked as they walked, pushing past Rockabilly House. Inside Livu Square, all tinged with pink and yellow Teutonic buildings and olive and white spires enclosing brick patios and cafés and cream umbrellas, a vast crowd had gathered in the center on a patch of green near a lonesome pine. Ignoring Blake's protests, they snaked their way through the tourists toward the music and the voice. The singer was warbling something familiar, but in a new arrangement. It took Chloe another half-verse and the beginning of a chorus to recognize the tune as "Fell in Love with a Boy" by Joss Stone. Except he sang fell in love with a girl. His heart was still beating. He was just looking for something new. Oh, that's what it is, Chloe had just enough time to think, before the voice *demanded* she kiss him by the canal even though he knew that love was fleeting — and then the voice climbed an octave or three and soared above the pine and over the spires and the art deco buildings. It lifted and flew across three bridges and to the sea. That's how strong the voice was, how long it held its note, how far it scaled the limits of humanity. The tone was sunny, a wave of satin, but it brought with it intoxication, impatience, torment. Chloe stopped moving. Rather, she couldn't take one more step.

"Are you all right?" said Hannah. "You've gone all white."

"Did you hear that?" She stumbled forward. She must be all right, because her heart was still beating. She was surprised and yet not surprised when they made it close enough to the eye of the hurricane to see Johnny Rainbow standing at the mic with his beat-up guitar, his black wavy hair out of the ponytail, shiny, messy, wild like his voice. Two black speakers were on each side of him, groaning under the strain as he belted out the last oooh, the last ahhh, carrying the lyric edge up and down, round and round, repeating and repeating.

Chloe stood breathless.

He was astonishing.

And he didn't need her slack-jawed endorsement. He was freed from human approval. There was no oblivion for him ever again among strangers because all the silver strings in all the world trembled as he sang. The Apollo was bending every backbone to his red electric will.

Surely she had failed to hide her shock at being seduced (or poisoned?) by his glossy unhumble filament of sound. She remembered something from childhood, drummed into her memory, now almost forgotten. *When that which is perfect is come, that which is in part shall be done away.* That's what she felt as she stood like a pillar. She had never heard anything like Johnny's voice. Not in real life. Freddie Mercury at the height of his powers had a quality like his, the surplus melodic tenor, the staggering operatic range conquering every beating heart by the next lilting kiss at the riverside. It was not his gift to give to her. It was Chloe's gift to receive from him. It was a sacrament of wine and gold. She was so high her nose nearly bled.

Her past annoyance at him, her initial irritation, her confusion at his friendliness, her relief and regret at his being gone, all that had vaporized. Awe replaced it. A deep pink wonder like tears of warm milk. She lowered her head, staring at the cobblestones, afraid someone close to her would recognize what she was feeling. No wonder he was so cocky, so unafraid. No wonder he wouldn't take no for an answer. Who could ever say no to him?

"He's got some pipes on him," said Hannah, and an equally impressed Mason made a concurring urgh. Chloe said nothing.

"If he's so good," said Blake, obviously unimpressed, "why does he need to sing on street corners? If I had a good voice, I'd be in school for it, or giving concerts for money."

Even as Blake spoke, locals and tourists streamed past him to throw money into Johnny's overflowing beret, and into a wooden box, sturdy like a safety deposit, with a slit for an opening, a barrel-sized box into which clapping gawkers gladly stuffed latus and dollars and euros. Thank you, thank you, he said, continuing to sing, to smile, to bow. Chloe wanted to put all of her money into his box. It'd be like putting her paleo flood heart into it.

"You were wrong about him, dude," Mason said to Blake. "You thought he was having us on, but he does give tours, and he sure does sing. He's awesome. He does everything."

"Everything? What else does he do?" People shushed Blake. Johnny was singing the Beatles. He heard the news today. And afterward the sky was full of diamonds. No one had time for Blake's pronouncements.

"Are we ever going to get going?" he said, rather roughly, after another half-hour had passed.

Chloe couldn't move. She was mesmerized by Johnny's flying claim that he would love to turn her on.

"Blake, come on," Hannah said. "Why would we go? Just listen to him."

"Haven't we heard enough? We're going to miss our train."

"We'll catch the next one, dude," Mason said. "Let's enjoy."

Like the Grumpalump, Blake stood back near an ivory umbrella while the three of them pushed forward, to the front. When Johnny saw them, he waved and smiled, and Chloe swelled, self-conscious and delighted.

They listened to a handful more songs. "Love Is the Drug." "I'm Only Happy When It Rains." "Bless the Broken Road." And Zeppelin's "Whole Lotta Love," which brought down the sky and the square and the river. Chloe had never heard such applause before, for anybody. All the Latvians and Asians obviously knew and loved that song, as if they'd all grown up on Led Zeppelin. Johnny was going to give them every inch of his love, and they embraced it and clapped and hollered for him, as if he had just given it to them. It was bewildering, his extravagant voice and their reaction to his singing. Both were so out of bounds.

Chloe would have listened to him for another two or twelve setlists. It wasn't enough. Nothing was enough. Johnny! she wanted to yell. Who *are* you?

"Wow, dude," Mason said, after Johnny had finished. Most of the groupies had finally cleared out, though not before loitering around Johnny and his equipment, pointing, touching, asking all kinds of technical questions in broken English, almost as if they too were trying to understand what had just happened. If they could only learn what kind of condenser microphone he used, perhaps with autotune built in and some midichlorians, then it would all make perfect sense. Oh, it's a Bluebird mic. That's the best there is. There you go. It's all about dollars and cents. You spend thousands of dollars on a mic, you too can sing. Afterward they smiled in satisfaction. That's what they wanted to hear.

Answering their questions, he was patient and gracious, like a benevolent king. Yes, the Gibson Hummingbird is mic'd too, separately. Otherwise it would be drowned out by the vocals. Because everything was drowned out by the vocals: Riga, river, life. Yes, it has its own amp. Yes, there is a generator, because sometimes it's difficult to find an electrical outlet in the middle of squares, and the cables aren't long enough. Yes, he has been singing since he was little. Thank you. Thank you. Thank you. No, I don't have a phone. No, I don't live in Riga. No, I'm only here until tomorrow. No, I'm not from Texas. Yes, of course I'll look you up next time I come. Yes, give me your number.

Finally it was their turn to be groupies. Johnny shook Mason's hand. He tipped his head to a suddenly shy Hannah, tipped it a little longer to a mute Chloe. He was sweating, exotic, hyper.

"Yeah," he said, tying back his wet unruly hair. "Helps to make the daily nut, no question." He pried open the wooden box. It was full of bills.

"How much do you think is in there?" Hannah asked.

Casually glancing inside, Johnny felt around the paper money. "Probably four hundred latu. Maybe more."

"You just made eight hundred dollars?" Hannah gasped.

Johnny nodded, still panting. "Today was a pretty good day. Did you tip Gregor? Just kidding. That Germanic bore never gets any extra. I tell you what, though, they don't come out like this in the rain. I can't make any money when it rains and the streets are empty."

He wiped his face and neck on a towel. "I'm soaked, excuse me." He pulled off his wet T-shirt, grabbed another black tee from his duffel. He was skinny like a string, but a string that did forty push-ups in two minutes, and fifty sit-ups, and ran two miles in fifteen minutes with his mic, his bag and his guitar. He was a steel string. He wasn't tanned, but his skin looked as if in another time, another place it could tan well. On his heart he had a blue tattoo of the star of Texas. Chloe didn't want to ogle. But she did. He had other tattoos. He had large geometric designs on the insides of both forearms, all the way into the crook of his elbows. They all pretended to look the other way to give him the illusion of privacy. Though as Chloe had thought: there was no more oblivion for this boy.

"Where did you learn to sing like that?" That was her asking him a question. She had finally found a tinny voice.

"My mother sang. My father sang."

"Professionally?"

"My mother, yes. For a time. Until she ruined her voice. She wanted me to be a singer like her. Though this is probably not what she had in mind." Johnny was bent over his cables. She couldn't see his face.

"Oh." She didn't know what to say. "And your dad?"

"He didn't ruin his voice. But he did stop singing when he stopped playing guitar."

She stayed back, watching him wrap his audio cords around his hand and elbow, waiting for another syllable to fall from his mouth.

He offered her a tidbit of his life. "My grandfather once told me that his uncle had a voice like mine. That was a century ago. Apparently the man could sing like Enrico Caruso."

"Enrico who?"

"Never mind. Drove all the girls wild."

"Who did?" muttered Chloe. "Caruso?" She blushed and hoped no one noticed.

Johnny stacked up the amps, speakers, the generator, and all his wires. Broke down his equipment in less than twenty minutes, like a pro. The mic stand was aluminum and retractable. He dropped the stand and both mics into his duffel. Mason asked about the other equipment.

"The Bluebirds are mine. But the rest I borrow from a guy I know. Fabius. I gave him a percentage of the receipts."

"What about when you're in Vilnius or somewhere and Fabius isn't around?"

Johnny shrugged. "Usually I can find someone who'll rent me the gear for a few hours. There's music in every city. But if not, then it's just me and the guitar. I pop the Bluebird on a stand and sing into it as if it's plugged in."

The three of them, except for Blake, kept whirling around Johnny in little circles.

"So what are you up to next?" Mason asked.

"Not much. Drink a little beer. Smoke a little. Eat maybe. Hang. Chill. What about you guys?"

"We're heading back to Varda's. It's our last night."

"Yeah, mine too."

Hannah joined in. "Where are you headed next?"

"Poland."

"Us too!" She sounded like his cheer squad.

"That's right. I remember." He smiled at Chloe. "You're still set on Treblinka?"

"Of course," she said. "You?"

"Well, having been there before, I'm not set on Treblinka. But I did get roped into a private tour of all six death camps for a group of eager beaver professional tourists."

"How'd they find you? Do you advertise?"

"Advertise? No. My uncle knows them."

Mason exchanged meaningful glances with Chloe, with Hannah. No one glanced at sulking Blake.

"How long does a tour like that take?"

Johnny shrugged. "A few days. We start in Warsaw, make our way south to Krakow. Maybe eight days for all six, including travel."

That's too long, Chloe thought bitterly.

Johnny smiled as if he could read her mind. She really *really* hoped he couldn't. "I can't remember, are you seeing only Treblinka? Or did your grandmother make you promise to see them all? Because you could come with me on my tour if you wanted. There's definitely room."

"We're seeing just the one," Blake cut in. "Maybe Auschwitz, too, if we have time, but we're not sure yet. So we definitely don't need a tour of all six. And Auschwitz has its own guides. Thanks anyway. Come on, guys—train."

Mason lifted his hand to stop his brother. Hannah lifted her hand to stop her boyfriend. Only Chloe stayed motionless.

"Blake, hang on, dude," Mason said. "We were just saying how we don't know how to get to Treblinka."

"A tour guide in Gdansk will tell us," Blake said.

Johnny scrunched up his face in disapproval. "Why are you going to Gdansk? It's all the way north and really far from Treblinka. You should come with me. It'll be easier for you." Johnny raised his hand but not his voice. "Wait, Blake, wait. Hear me out. You don't have to come with me for all six. Just come for the one day I go to Treblinka."

Hannah nearly jumped in place. "That's a really good idea!"

"It really is, bro."

Chloe pressed her lips together to keep quiet.

Blake shook his head. "No. We're going to Gdansk. We already decided."

"You're adding days to your trip." Johnny's tone was unfazed. "It's going to take a long time to get to Warsaw as it is. And then you've got quite a way out of Poland to Spain. I wouldn't be wasting my time on Gdansk if I were you."

"Bro, he's right," Mason said. "We want to make sure we have as long as possible in Barcelona."

"Though I will repeat," said Johnny, "a week in Barcelona in August is plenty."

Blake stiffened as if he wanted to punch him.

It was time for Chloe to speak up. "Blake," she said softly. "We shouldn't go to Gdansk if we don't have to."

"We made our plans, Chloe," Blake said.

"Listen, dudes and dudettes," Johnny said. "It's no skin off my nose either way. I am simply offering. I'm hiring a charter bus from a guy I know in Warsaw." He bowed slightly. "What can I say, I know a lot of guys. The bus sits ten plus the driver. Five of them, plus me, plus four of you. It's ideal. And it'll save you the trouble of getting to Treblinka by train, and that's trouble, believe me. I'm just trying to help. Do whatever you want, of course. You don't have to pay for the tour or anything. I still owe you one." He smiled. "Though another dinner at Varda's would be delightful. I'll bring the drink and dessert this time—I'm flush." He shook his wooden box. All the equipment black and heavy was stacked into a Fisher Price red wagon with a beige plastic handle.

Chloe stood, hoping and praying someone else would leap up and invite him to go with them to Varda's, so she wouldn't have to. Quick, her insides kept yelling, quick, before he changes his mind. Hannah and Mason made excited eyes at Blake, who glared back in rank resentment. "Johnny, we need a minute."

"Take all the time you need, dude. I'll go get myself another beer. Anyone want one? It's on me. Oh, and I'll grab some dessert from Rigensis for Varda."

"The line was over an hour at the bakery," Blake said.

"Don't worry." Johnny winked. "I know a guy. Be back in ten. Can you watch my stuff?"

He left them with his red wagon, his duffel and his box of money. The only thing he took with him was the guitar. They were left alone in the becalmed Livu Square. It was nearing seven. The sun was still high in the sky, the air was warm, redolent with spilled hops and pickled cabbage and wild purple.

Everything was the same. Nothing was the same. Chloe couldn't look at Mason, couldn't look at Blake, couldn't look at Hannah.

"Have you lost your minds?" was the first thing out of Blake's mouth.

"Blake, come on, man," Mason said. "It'll help us. We don't know where to go, you have to admit that. And he does. Look, we were headed to Gdansk. That's proof right there that we need a tour guide."

"Like herpes we need him."

"Blakie," said Hannah, "it's just for a few days. If we don't like it, we can always bug out."

"I don't like it now."

"Bro … come on."

"Blakie … come on."

Chloe said nothing. She didn't have to.

It was one Blake against three swooning teenagers with puppy-dog eyes over Johnny's marmalade skies. Everyone knew Blake stood no chance, even Blake. He spat before he walked away to be by himself, while they waited for Johnny to come back with the beers and the boxes of pastries, and then ran to tell him the good news, the great news. We can go with you, we will go with you.

Blake may have been immune to Johnny's magic, but no one else was. His voice was what made Chloe trust him completely. It was an offering from God, gold rain thrown from blue heights, it was like grace. It was impossible to overstate the effect that his singing had had on her. What was the matter with Blake that he couldn't warm to the boy-man who chanted sobs of poetry like the Gregorian monks at the resurrection? It was quite a feat on Johnny's part, to make Blake come out looking like the bad guy. But, truly, it was as if they all had stepped inside the Cathedral of Notre Dame during Pentecost high mass, witnessed astral greatness, and Blake was the only one left unmoved.

They raised their beers to each other. Blake refused his, so Johnny drank it. They perched on the stone wall by the Guildhall, quenched their thirst and chatted agreeably, Mason and Johnny like old friends, Hannah and Chloe sitting shoulder to shoulder, admiring. Blake was the fifth wheel, surly and ungracious.

"Hannah, go make your boyfriend feel better," Chloe whispered.

"How am I supposed to do that?"

"How? Use your feminine wiles. Tell him something warm, something he wants to hear."

"He's being ridiculous and childish. I'm not going to kowtow to that. That's enabling his immaturity. Not going to happen. You go make him feel better if it's so important to you."

Blake

"So what's your plan for getting to Warsaw, dude?" Johnny asked me, as if we were friends.

"I don't know. What's *your* plan for getting to Warsaw?"

"Mine is to take the 7 a.m. bus to Vilnius, and then a train out of Vilnius to Warsaw. What about you?"

"We're not taking any buses, so …"

"Oh, so you've looked at the train schedule?"

Through clamped teeth: "Of course I've looked at the train schedule."

Johnny smirked. From his olive drab Mary Poppins bag he produced a thick worn book, ripped up and faded. European Rail and Bus Timetable, August 2004.

"I hope this is where you check your train times."

"No, we have the Travelers' Railway Map of Europe." It was easier to read, but I didn't want to tell him that.

"Pig nonsense." He leafed through my book dramatically, for humor, I assume, though I was not in the least humored. "There is no direct train from Riga to Gdansk. Or Riga to Warsaw. So what do you want to do?"

That couldn't be right!

"What would *you* do, Johnny?" asked Hannah.

I didn't even give my girlfriend a scolding glance. "There's got to be a train," I said. "There simply has to be."

"It's ludicrous, I know. But that's the way it is. As the crow flies, Warsaw is only five hundred miles from here and yet there's no direct train."

I tried not to make my hands into fists. I asked for my useless book back.

"It'll take me," Johnny continued, "if I'm lucky and make all my connections and don't run into any bus delays or construction or accidents, until midnight tomorrow to reach Warsaw. And that's with taking the bus to Vilnius. You could take several trains to get to Vilnius. First you'll have to take a train to Daugavpils that runs only once a day, in the evening. Which means you'll have to stay overnight in that border town. I myself don't recommend it for a number of reasons, one being it'll take you an extra day. Did you budget two days to go five hundred miles?" He smiled winningly. I wanted to poison him. I wanted to put salmonella in his hair.

We were deflated. We hated the bus. "Blakie, please don't tell me we have to take the bus," Hannah said in a whine.

"You absolutely don't have to, Hannah," said Johnny. "Take the train to the border. You can stay overnight in a hostel in Daugavpils. But pick a place carefully, because some have a rat problem. Also, make sure you get up in time to catch the 5:30 train to Vilnius, because the next one is not until a full day later. You will, however, have a three-hour layover in Vilnius. Blake did say yesterday he wanted to see the Gates of Dawn. Blake, you'll have three hours to gaze at Ausros Vartai before you board the 11:20 to Warsaw. With two train changes, it'll take you eleven more hours. I'll be halfway done with my five-city tour, but you'll be just getting into Poland. Welcome to Eastern European travel."

No one had a word to say. Especially me.

"It doesn't make sense," said Chloe. "How can a bus be faster than the train?"

"The bus sits fifty people instead of five hundred," Johnny explained to her, too patiently by my reckoning. "So when it stops at the border, it takes less time for passport check."

"Isn't it all part of the EU?" I said.

Johnny nodded slowly. "It is, my good man, it is. But so what? You're not a member of the EU, are you? And neither are half the people on that bus. Not even me. They have to check everyone's papers at the border. That's how it is. They'd have to check us on the Canadian or the Mexican border, right? So a bus makes passport control faster, the train slower. But it's up to you. Me, I must to get to Warsaw by tomorrow night. I have no choice, because the next morning at eight, me and my five world travelers are driving to Majdanek."

What choice did we have? Clearly we had to go with him. I refused to agree to it, though. I couldn't accept it, especially not after he started lecturing me about how early to get to Riga tomorrow to buy the bus tickets since they frequently sold out. "You can't leave Carnikava later than five in the morning. Or you won't make it."

"What about you? Will you make it?" I was so fed up with him.

Johnny smiled at me and nodded. "Blake I'm gonna split, all right? I still have to get the gear back to Fabius. This was fun. Good luck with Gdansk."

My whole group nearly had a mutiny, as if I'd screwed everything up. What is wrong with all of them? Chloe especially. We were having such a good time ganging up on poor tedious Gregor, laughing, relaxed, and they had to go and ruin everything. Not me. Them. It was finally the way it was meant to be, the way I had pictured it in my head, us together, having fun, being kids. My idea of fun is not picking up a derelict off the street and hitching our barely shining star to his fake destiny. I don't care how well he knows Baltic travel, I don't care how well he sings. He is not part of my story, he is not going to appear in anything I write, or in my life. No one can talk me out of my dislike for him. Not even Chloe. Especially not Chloe. Though to her credit, she was the only one who tried, the only one who came over, to try to talk some sense into me, I suppose.

"What's the matter with you?" she said.

"Nothing. What's the matter with *you*?"

"Nothing."

She poked me lightly in the arm, in the chest. She pinched me, pretended to pull the hairs out of my forearm. Tickled me a little, though she knows I'm not ticklish. "Come on. Why is he getting up in your grill? It'll be fine. It's good luck."

"Oh, it's some kind of luck, all right."

"Let me finish. It's good luck to find somebody who can make the next few days a little easier for us. All we want is to get to Barcelona. And he's helping us do that quicker. You should be pleased."

"Do I look pleased?"

"Well, no. But he's about to leave. And without him, what are we going to do?"

"Gee, I don't know. What was our plan before him? Because we didn't know this paragon of guiding excellence until yesterday, and yet as I recall we had a plan."

"Yes, our plan was to go to Gdansk!" Chloe exclaimed, peering up at me. I felt a little ashamed, but not so much that I stopped hating him. "We were going to wander around, hoping to find someone who might point us in the direction of a mode of transport that would take us to Bialystok and Treblinka. And we did find that someone. Except we found him in Riga. That's the only difference. And he's telling us to go with him to Warsaw."

"Like a demon whisperer."

"Blake! You'd prefer to navigate blindly through Polish forests on foot, watching Barcelona vanish before our eyes, instead of taking a seat on a private bus he's offering? A free seat, I will add."

"Nothing is free. Guaranteed. Especially not this."

She squeezed my arm. I sighed theatrically, like a girl. I moped. What could I do? I had to go with the majority.

I didn't want to admit that Chloe was right, but most of all I didn't want to admit that Johnny was right, that my strategy of going to Gdansk was clearly idiotic. I was annoyed that my own brother didn't share my irritation; quite the contraire, he also had a schoolboy crush on the dude, even worse than my girlfriend. And his girlfriend. But I was used to Hannah making a fool of herself with other guys. I wasn't used to my brother making a fool of himself. I especially wasn't used to Chloe making a fool of herself. I stared at her, and she stared back, all mild and kind and beseeching. I desperately wanted at least her to be on my side, to give me balance, strength in numbers.

What an illusion. He opens his mouth, and the whole world faints. They look at him the way Carmen first looked at my brother, and now looks at Johnny. But after he shuts his trap, then what? What else has he got?

Oh, sure. He's got a thick tome of numbers, a bus, friends in high places, a driver, and a tour all planned. How convenient. How did he engineer it? I don't believe in coincidence. Not in my life, not in my book.

Lupe would have a lot to say about this. I can almost hear her gravelly voice in my head. There is no hate without fear, she'd say. Hate is fear crystallized, fear objectified. We hate what threatens our selves, our dreams, our plans, our freedom, our place in the world, our place in the hearts of the people we love. We fear first. Then we hate.

And I know just what I would say to her in response. Lupe, I'd say. My troubles are just beginning.

Mason

Chloe somehow made my brother see reason, and he agreed to travel to Warsaw with Johnny. We pulled the loaded red wagon a long way past the Riga University and through the now shuttered thieves' market.

"He's not coming back with us and sleeping on our porch again, is he?" Blake asked me.

Perhaps Chloe didn't make him see reason enough.

"Dude, he's got nowhere to stay."

"He just made a thousand billz singing about love and drugs and every inch of him being inside your girlfriend. A whole lotta love he was gonna give her. You remember that, right? He could rent us a suite at the Grand Palace Hotel, if he wanted to."

"Blake, what's gotten into you? What do you propose, that we meet up with him tomorrow at dawn?"

"Or not. I'm good either way."

I left Blake's side and caught up with Johnny pulling his wagon, the girls flanking him. I hoped they were having a better time of it.

"Still, what a talent," Hannah was saying. "Is there a school you could go to for that?"

Johnny smiled. "Like a school for talent?"

"Performing arts or something."

"Maybe like the High School of Performing Arts?" he said.

"Something like that."

"Exactly like that. The one in New York. Remember they made a movie about it? *Fame*."

"Never heard of it."

"I'm gonna live forever." He opened his mouth and belted it out, holding the forever forever. It took a moment or two before Chloe and Hannah recovered.

"There you go," Hannah said, clearing her throat. "Why didn't you go to that place?"

"Who says I didn't?"

"Did you?"

"Sure. Why not?"

"Well, did you or didn't you?" Blake said, too loudly from behind.

"I did," Johnny replied without turning around. "We're just talking, man. No reason for the 'tude."

"No, 'tude," Blake said, abashed but still hostile.

The girls continued with Johnny.

"Did you have to audition?"

"The only way you can get in."

"So you had to sing?"

"I tried a tap dance, but I was terrible."

"You graduated from the High School of Performing Arts?" That was Chloe.

"I didn't say that." Johnny asked me to pull the wagon while he lit a cigarette. "I said I got accepted. It didn't work out for me, going there."

We all expressed strong disbelief.

He shrugged. "Not the singing. I hated their uniforms. I kept leaving the school at hours that were convenient to me but inconvenient to their curfew Gestapo. I didn't want to live by their rules. It's not as if I didn't know how to sing. My mother had taught me a few tricks. Anyway, they slapped me on the wrist a couple of times. But then, I may have smoked a joint on school premises." He chuckled. "Perhaps shared that joint with a few of my eager new friends. Perhaps received money for said joint. So … Rule B37 or something. Expulsion."

Expulsion! We didn't know what to say. The couple of kids who got expelled from the Academy went away for a good long time. They were so dangerous, we had seven assemblies in a row about them. How not to do the things they'd done.

"Your dad must not have been happy with you," Chloe said. As if Johnny's mother was inconsequential. Or maybe because mothers always forgive their sons. I know our mother does.

"My father has not been happy with me since the day I was born," Johnny told Chloe. "I can hardly live my life trying to please him. I'll be dead before it ever happens. I could become a general of the Third Army and have an Order of the British Empire pinned to my chest, and he'd say, but why not president and commander?"

Chloe wanted to talk more about his family, but Hannah was intrigued by other things. "So what'd you do when they expelled you?"

"I couldn't be out on my own yet. I was only sixteen. I had tutoring at home. That didn't go well. I had some other problems. My mother wasn't doing great. So my father shipped me off to his parents for a while. I went. Glad not to be in his house. Thought I'd have an easier time with my grandparents. Boy, was I wrong. They were pretty sharp. Plus they weren't working. Their whole job became keeping an eye on me."

"And that was bad?" Hannah said thoughtfully.

"The worst."

"Is that when you went to Europe?"

"You didn't want to go to college or anything?" Chloe asked.

"Is there such a thing as a college for singing?" Hannah said.

"There is," said Chloe. "Juilliard." Johnny was quiet, his friendly smile a little withered under the barrage of questions. Chloe shrugged. "Juilliard is very competitive. Almost impossible to get into."

"Is that so?" said Johnny.

"Yes. Your Ranger combat force is easier to get into."

"That may be true," he said. "But I got into Juilliard."

"You got into Juilliard?" That came out more as, "You got into Juilliard?!!?"

"Sure, why not?" He seemed so blasé about an impossible thing.

"Did you audition for that too?"

"Well, I wanted them to take my word for it that I was awesome, but they refused. They said I had to sing."

"What'd you sing?"

"I don't remember."

This time Chloe did not let it go. "You got into Juilliard *last year*, and you don't remember what you sang? I don't believe you."

"It was two years ago, but if you must know, I sang my great uncle's favorite song. 'E lucevan le stelle.' From Puccini's *Tosca*. Happy?"

The girls watched him pull the wagon as if he were driving a tank through the fields.

"Are you on leave?" Hannah asked.

"Sure, why not?" said Johnny. "Permanent leave."

"You left Juilliard?"

"It was a mutual decision," he said evenly. "They asked me to go, and I said okay."

"Oh goodness!" Hannah was incredulous—and disappointed for him.

"Why did *they* kick you out?"

"I couldn't stand their rules. It's a college, for God's sake. Not kindergarten. But they were like, you can't do this, you can't do that. Can't, can't, can't. Can't smoke, can't use bad language. So I said fuck you. Lit up while I said it. And left."

"They kicked you out for cursing?"

"Nah, they kicked me out for—" He stopped talking, his Gibson bouncing on his back as he walked. "It doesn't matter. It's all bullshit," Johnny said. "This is what I wanted to do. Sing on the streets. This is where I wanted to be. Europe. I don't need to go to Juilliard. I'm in Berlin, Riga, St. Petersburg, Kaliningrad, Sofia, Prague. I've been to Paris, Rome, Brussels, Madrid. I've been everywhere. Barcelona, too. I sang in Innsbruck during an Alpian blizzard. People still stopped and put money in my box. They didn't say, did you study at fucking Juilliard? Because if you didn't, we won't give you a euro. No. They hooted, whistled, asked for an encore, and snowed their foreign currency on my damned expelled head."

I watched the pensive expression on Chloe's face. It was less entranced. She took my hand.

"If you can't stick it out in a light-discipline school like Juilliard," she said to Johnny, "what makes you think you'll make it in Ranger school? I don't know much about either, but something tells me these rules you hate, curfew, smoking, drinking, might be a little stricter in the latter."

Johnny nodded approvingly. "Indeed, Chloe Divine. I'm hoping the Rangers will teach me how to follow orders. It's never too late, don't you think?"

"Too late for what?"

"It's never too late to be what you might have been," said Johnny.

We walked into a narrow, foul-smelling alley. Johnny knocked three times on a rotting double door before an odd man, hairless, tattooed and strung out, cracked open one side, glimpsed Johnny through his frantic eyes and said, "I ain't got no more. Come back tomorrow."

"I'm returning your gear, man. I don't want anything. I have money. You want some?"

"I don't want your money, I ain't got no more, I told you," the ruined dude repeated, his inflamed eyes darting suspiciously from me to Blake to the girls.

"I don't need anything. I'm giving you billz for borrowing your gear. Look." Johnny stuck a handful of crumpled notes into the guy's epileptic hand. "There's more where that came from." Asking us to wait a sec in the alley, he wheeled the wagon inside. The doors closed behind him. I heard a large metal lock slide across. It was quiet. The four of us stood, trying not to breathe through our noses, shifting from foot to foot.

"So *this* is where musicians live," Blake said. "In alleys full of piss and crank."

"Some musicians clearly live here," Hannah said, coming to Johnny's defense. "Because Johnny had great equipment when he played. Why are you so judgmental? You're worse than Chloe. Writers shouldn't be so judgmental, Blakie. Makes it hard to create real characters, to sympathize with actual people. Observe, don't judge."

"Ah, yes," Blake said, "because what's sorely needed here is for me to sympathize with a hundred-pound junkie with track marks on his arms."

"Johnny is not a hundred pounds!" Hannah exclaimed.

"I meant the other dude," Blake said slowly, frowning at Hannah.

Johnny was gone ten minutes or so. He reappeared alone, gear gone, bald guy gone, box of money also gone. He was flushed, happy, smiling. His guitar was now in a black velvet hard case.

"Let's roll," he said. "Everything's cool."

"Who was that guy?" Hannah asked Johnny as we filed out behind him.

"That's Fabius. He's an old friend. Lends me his rig when I need it. I bought the case from him." He showed her. "Hummingbird needs a swanky cage, don't you think?"

"He's a musician?"

"Used to be."

"What's he up to now?"

"Little bit of this, little bit of that. He got his hand injured. Stopped playing bass."

"Looks like his hand is not the only thing he injured," Blake muttered next to me, and then louder said, "How do you know so many people in Riga?"

Johnny smiled, trying to dazzle Blake with his teeth. "This isn't my first rodeo. How do you think I can give a tour here?"

My brother remained coldly undazzled. "I don't know. Maybe you read up on Riga the Internet."

Johnny almost put his friendly arm around Blake, but thought better of it. "I would've, my friend, you're right," he said. "Problem is, our bee-farming, Nazi-killing hosts don't have Internet service."

"Now who's being judgmental?" Blake whispered to Hannah as they fell back.

"Well, he's not my boyfriend," Hannah said, taking Blake's arm. "I can't tell him not to be judgmental."

We walked down the long, straight Marijas Street on our way to the train station. We were all exhausted, except for Johnny, who bounced along the pavement. We could barely keep up. The three of us walked behind him and Chloe, the two of them in front of us, side by side. We watched them. With the old Gibson slung on his back like a rifle, Johnny strolled with Chloe down the treeless city street, a spring in his step, chatting. I strained to hear, but couldn't grasp the threads of their unspooling conversation. Blake nudged me, pointing at them.

"This doesn't bother you?"

"What?"

"That."

I shrugged. It didn't really bother me. I could see that Blake thought it should. But Blake and I are different people, and we feel different things. I'm not going to apologize for the way I am. I don't expect him to apologize for the way he is.

"Don't get so bent out of shape, man," I said to him. "It's not a big deal. We're going to be together for the next couple of days. People are going to talk to each other. What do you want me to do? Knock out somebody's teeth every time Chloe says hello to them?"

"Not somebody's," Blake said. "His."

Hannah

Oh my goodness, but does Blake ever have a bug up his butt over a nice guy who's doing us all a big favor. The rest of us don't know how to thank him, while Blake walks around as if he's planning to kill him in his sleep. I don't know what's wrong with him. I've never seen him act like this. He is normally the most affable guy. Too affable. Nothing bothers him. He's super chill all the time. Suddenly he's Genghis Khan. It must be an alpha male thing. I don't get it, but I hear that happens sometimes.

The thing is, Johnny is so friendly, so polite, so non-confrontational, so sixties about the whole life thing, that it makes Blake seem like an asshole, and though we all know he's not, he sure seems like one today, all stomping and cranky and sniping, making comments, huffing, rolling his eyes. Chloe is right: Johnny sings like he has a host of angels in his throat while Blake mutters obscenities under his breath. (I didn't make that line up about the angels, Chloe came up with that one, I'm just using it here, because she so rarely comes up with something clever, I want to give her credit when it's due.) I swear, Blake liked him less after he heard him sing and realized he was a freaking prodigy. We on the other hand all fell in love with him a little, hearing his fly voice raise Roxy Music from rock to opera. I didn't think it was possible, to take that rough and tumble song and sing it like they do at Lincoln Center, but Johnny did it. Love is the drug indeed. Yet my Blake is deaf to it.

Somehow Chloe got Blake to agree to travel to Poland with Johnny, I don't know how. I didn't think he'd budge. When he's being unreasonable and pigheaded, he usually doesn't, and the more unreasonable he's being, the less he budges. But she got Blake to do it. I meant to ask what she said to him but I forgot.

The only thing that bothers me a tiny little bit, and I hate to even put pen to paper and admit it, is every once in a while when I look at Johnny, or hear him talk, or watch him when he doesn't think I'm watching him, I find him staring at or talking to Chloe. I mean, it's polite and casual, but I do wonder what's behind his crazy melted eyes. A little thought flashes by. Could he like her? I know she hated him at first. She's impressed with his singing now, but that's not enough to turn someone's opinion around. Just look at Blake. What troubles me a little is not that Chloe might like Johnny, because other than Blake, who doesn't? But that Johnny might like Chloe.

Like earlier on the train when we were coming back to Varda's, he somehow finagled a seat next to her. Blake glared at Mason as if to say, you gonna stand for that? But Mason, calm as all that, just planted himself right across from Chloe and ignored Blake. Or later, at the cramped dining room table, once again Johnny managed to squeeze into the seat next to her. Mason on one side of her, Johnny on the other. It's probably a coincidence, and they didn't look at each other much during dinner, or talk to each other, but every time Chloe spoke, Johnny, no matter whom he was talking to, stopped, turned, listened, and reacted only to her. When she spoke, he never ignored her.

I'm sure it's nothing.

When we told Carmen and Varda that Johnny was a singer, they got so excited. Sabine said her husband Guntis fancied himself a singer too, and maybe they could do a duet. I smirked. After dinner, Johnny took out his guitar and played them a song. Varda and Carmen cried. But no one cried harder than Otto.

Guntis said nothing, but he sure didn't ask Johnny to harmonize after that.

I don't know what song it was. Johnny sang in another language. I assumed it was Latvian, but when I asked him about it later in the yard, he said it was an old Russian war song called "Varshavyanka" or something like that. "I've learned that people around these parts like not just the Beatles but war hymns too," he told me.

"I don't know," I said. "The foreigners sure liked Led Zeppelin earlier."

He nodded. "Yeah, Zeppelin is definitely a crowd pleaser."

"Why is the old man still weeping? It's been a half-hour since you sang."

"Because he used to sing that song on the Dvina with his squadron as they marched downriver to fight the Germans in the Battle of the Baltic," Johnny replied.

I persisted. "But how would you possibly know a song in Russian? Especially a war song?"

"Most Russian songs are war songs." He laughed.

"That's not what I'm asking."

Before he answered me—though I was the one who stood in front of him—his eyes sought out Chloe, who sat on a bench nearby. He wanted to make sure she was listening! Or was that my imagination? I should be a writer. Johnny said, "I know a bunch of songs. I know Italian and French songs, and even Spanish songs. I can sing you 'Barcelona,' if you like."

"But Russian war songs?" That was Chloe. I knew it! I knew she was eavesdropping.

He took a step in her direction, even though it had been our conversation, and talked to her instead of me, as if it was theirs, not ours. "Even Russian war songs," he said, gazing down at her. "I learn them phonetically."

We glanced over at Otto. He was still sniffling. Johnny left us and walked over to his chair. Crouching next to the old man, he put his arm around him and talked to him quietly, every once in a while patting Otto, squeezing him, nodding. I couldn't hear what they were saying, but since I know Otto doesn't speak English, I had to assume that he and Johnny were speaking Latvian. Latvian that Johnny had insisted to the fat lady on the train he did not speak. What a mystery he is, what a puzzle of contradictions.

"Carmen, why is your grandfather crying like that?" I asked the girl when she came down the porch steps into the yard.

"Grandfather said he hadn't heard that song since 1944 when he lost most of men he fought with. He said Johnny broke his heart."

"Oh. What language did your grandfather talk to Johnny in?"

"Russian," Carmen replied. "Johnny doesn't speak very good Latvian."

But he spoke good enough *Russian*?

"He told grandfather his own grandfather taught him song when he was little boy and he never forgot."

"His grandfather was Russian?"

"No. He said he was American."

As we packed up, I went outside to get my ballet flats, which I'd put out there to dry, and found Otto still sitting in his lawn chair, hands on the armrests, staring into the blackness, singing the refrain of the "Varshavyanka" over and over under his breath. I listened for a few moments and then left quietly, feeling I was intruding on something I didn't understand. Like Johnny.

22

All Things Are Numbers

Chloe

Chloe woke before the rest, when it was still blue out, right before dawn, cleaned herself, scrubbed herself, put on makeup, fresh clothes, obsessively brushed her hair, to make it smooth, make it shine. She left it loose and down and fake-casual, pinched her cheeks for color, bit her lips for tint. She put on a dress, but then decided she was overdressed for the train and changed into snug jeans. Also black Doc Marten boots, and a soft fitted T-shirt with a scoop neckline that fell just above the swell of her breasts. The T-shirt was deep blue with white flowers on it, and the Doc Martens were brand-new, never worn. The mascara clumped but also popped her eyes, like it was nighttime and she was going dancing. She hummed a few bars of "Love is the Drug" as she got ready and when she peeked out of the tiny bathroom window, Johnny was already outside, dressed, having a cigarette, his black hair pulled tightly into a ponytail, his stubble dark against his young pale face. He was gamine, maybe gaunt, and his lack of a tan, despite his travels in the European summer sun, slightly unsettled Chloe. Something about it was off, and she couldn't pinpoint why. But she forgot about the paleness of his face when she walked outside. He was so friendly, and his face colored, became animated when he saw her.

"You're up early," he said.

"Not as early as you are."

"I don't sleep much. A few hours is enough for me."

"Is that how you've always been?"

"According to my mother," he said. "I drove her nuts. Would never nap. Always wanted to be out and about, running, playing. Never sat still."

"Your sisters too?"

"Nah. Not even my brother. Tomboy is as placid as a sloth. Mom and Dad concluded it was just me." He smiled. Clearly he liked being this way and not the other, controllable, way.

Chloe stood awkwardly, trying to figure out what to do while he smoked. Even Otto wasn't up yet. It was humid, slightly muggy, not quite warm. "So how are you going to make it in the army, if you can't sit still?" she asked.

"Why do you have to sit still in the army?"

"Don't you? Don't they make you stand at attention while they inspect your bed or something?"

He nodded cheerfully. "They also make you do twenty-mile obstacle courses. Clemente sure did. I'm hoping to be so tired from the running that I'll be relieved to stand still. Besides," he added, "I travel a lot by train. I better know how to sit still on one of those, no?"

Chloe didn't know if that was a yes or a no. The first time they were on a train together from Liepaja, he got up twenty times to her and Hannah's once. The second time they were on a train together, coming back to Carnikava last night, in a forty-minute ride he must've gotten up six times, vanishing and reappearing.

Now Blake appeared in the dewy, post-dawn garden, bleary but already hostile. A hostile Blake was such a paradox. "Are you ready?" he said to Chloe, barely acknowledging Johnny. "Our train is in an hour."

"Yeah, but no one else is even up yet," she said.

"Everyone is up and dressed and ready to go, while you're lollygagging. Hannah cleaned the whole kitchen for Varda."

Blake said this accusingly, as though it was Chloe's job to clean the kitchen.

"Hannah cleaned the kitchen?" Chloe cast Johnny a guilty glance and started inside. "That's new."

It also wasn't true. Hannah had wiped down the area next to the sink. Everything else in the kitchen was being scrubbed down by Carmen and Varda.

The women fussed and bickered, getting sandwiches ready for the American kids to take on the road. Carmen wouldn't leave Johnny's side. "Don't forget to say goodbye to Grandfather," she said to him. "He upset if you leave without saying goodbye. He outside now, making you picture frame."

"I wouldn't dream of leaving without shaking that man's hand," said Johnny.

"Grandfather wants to know who you knew in the war," Carmen said. "He said you can't sing that song like you do without knowing someone in war."

"My grandfather fought in the war too," Johnny said. "Didn't everyone's grandfather?"

Chloe's grandfathers didn't. Lochlan Devine was born blind in one eye and thusly avoided the draft, though he did work the desk at the Boston headquarters of the Army Corps. Her mother's father, Hulin Thia, whom she had never met, was too young for one war in 1941 and too old for another in 1950. No one in her family had fought in Vietnam. Her father served in the National Guard. In North Dakota, where he had been stationed and where he had met her young mother, no one marched along undammed rivers singing "Varshavyanka."

At 4:57 a.m., as they were collecting the last of their stuff and giving Varda a goodbye hug before racing out the door to catch their 5:30 train—the train they absolutely had to catch—Hannah fainted.

She had been hurrying around the kitchen looking for her lost ballet flat under the table and banged her ankle on the leg of a chair. "I'm fine, I'm fine," she said, putting her head down on the table, and the next thing you know—she was on the floor and Chloe was yelling for Blake.

There was a gray commotion.

Johnny stared at his watch.

"We have to go," he said. "We'll miss the train."

"We can't go without Hannah," Blake said, crouching by his girlfriend's supine body.

"Let me put it another way," Johnny said. "*I* have to go. Whatever happens, I can't miss the train."

"We'll catch the next one."

"There is no next one. I told you. There's no next train, no next bus. I have to be in Warsaw tonight. I thought I explained it."

"Maybe Papa can drive you," Carmen said. "He's got his truck."

Papa Guntis did have his truck, but neither he nor the truck was home. "He can come back," Carmen said.

"How will you get in touch with him?"

"He comes back for lunch sometimes," the girl happily replied.

Johnny stared at Chloe, also crouching by Hannah's side, at Carmen smiling eagerly as if hoping none of the guests would leave, at Blake's back, at Mason standing by, and said, "Is anyone in this entire house listening to me?"

Hannah came to. Sickly white, she kept repeating she was fine and just needed a glass of water. Three people lunged for the sink. Her hands shook as she took it. Johnny, fidgeting, making calculations, made a joke of it; he said his hands shook all the time too when he needed a drink and yet he never fainted.

"Blake," Mason said. "Johnny's right. We gotta go, man."

Blake shot his brother a look to say, what do you want me to do about it? My girlfriend is still on the floor.

"Mason, Chloe, let's the three of us run ahead," Johnny said. "We'll hurry, they'll follow. That way we can hold the train. Carmen, quick, call a taxi for Blake and Hannah."

"How?" Carmen said. "I never called taxi."

"Do you have a Yellow Pages?"

"Yellow Pages?"

"I give up." Johnny waved it all away and motioned to Chloe and Mason. "Come, it's our only chance."

Blake straightened out. "What?" He had slept on his wet hair and it was crazy curly this morning.

"He's right, bro," Mason said. "Otherwise, we'll miss it for sure. I'll take your suitcase. You just help Hannah with hers."

Blake leveled a killer look at his brother. "We're going to split up?"

"For twenty minutes, yes," Johnny said. "Come on, Mason."

"Let's wait just one damn minute," Blake said. "She'll be ready to go soon. We'll catch the next train. There's one an hour later."

Johnny smirked. "When we're on the train—if we ever get to the train—remind me to explain chaos theory to you," he said. "But until then, I *have* to make the 5:30. You might not have anywhere to be, but I *have* to pick up the tour bus in Warsaw, *Poland*, first thing tomorrow morning."

"You think five minutes right now is going to make you miss your bus tomorrow?"

"Chaos theory, dude," Johnny called back as he motioned for Chloe and Mason. "One day maybe I'll introduce you to my grandmother. She'll tell you that *all* things are numbers. Guys, you ready?"

Varda got Hannah some more water while Blake stood paralyzed and watched Johnny with his duffel and Chloe with her wheeled suitcase and Mason with two suitcases spirit out of the house.

Chloe hurried down the shrubbery walk, out the gate and walked as fast as she could down the road. She was torn. She didn't want to look at Blake's face, which was full of injustice and blame, or at Hannah's sloped back over the table. She felt guilty about Blake and angry at Hannah, but mostly what she felt was that if they let Johnny get on that train without them, they would never see him again. And so she denied what was behind her and followed only what was in front of her, which was army boots, and jeans, and a gray tee, a cased guitar, a green duffel and thick black hair tied back, smiling coffee eyes, full lips, and communion with breathless darkness.

They walked too quickly to chat, to discuss Hannah, to say anything. They panted as they struggled down the road with their bags.

They were more than halfway to the train station. It was 5:16. Mason suddenly stopped, pulled off his rucksack and started frantically rummaging through it, muttering.

"Mase, what's wrong?" Chloe said, slowing down. "What'd you forget?"

"Whatever it is, it's not important," Johnny said, barely even glancing back. "Gotta keep moving."

"It's very important," Mason said. He closed his eyes and deeply deeply sighed. When he stood up, his head was hung low. He didn't look at Chloe.

"What, Mason? What is it?"

"I'm really sorry, Chloe," Mason said. "I have to go back."

Johnny and Chloe stopped walking.

"Mason! What'd you forget?"

"I can't go without it."

"Mason, what in the world could you have forgotten?" she whispered.

"I, uh, I forgot my passport."

Johnny appraised him. "Why didn't you just say so?"

"Too busy looking for it."

"You take your passport out of your backpack?"

"Not usually. But I must've last night. I'm such an idiot. I left it on the table by my chair."

"Blake will get it," Chloe said.

"And if he doesn't? And why would he?" He waved Chloe down the road. "Chloe, hurry, go with him. I'll catch up."

"Mason, it's 5:18."

"I know. I'm sorry." He couldn't look at her. "Let me run. Maybe the train will be late."

"They usually are. But seriously, hurry, dude," said Johnny. "We'll slow them down as much as we can. We'll spill the contents of Chloe's bag."

Mason hurried. Picking up the two suitcases, he sprinted down the road as if he were running a mile for sadistic Clemente.

Johnny and Chloe glanced at each other. "We're *all* going to miss the train if we wait another second," he said to her. "We've got ten minutes, I'm going to run. Can you try to keep up?"

He picked up her suitcase, his own duffel, and they ran.

Mason

The disorder inside me and the chaos in my life is because I haven't been punished enough. I broke all kinds of laws and received no justice. My soul has been paying the price. And now my life pays the price.

How could I forget it? Johnny knew I was lying, I don't know how, like he's got a sixth sense or something. As long as Chloe believed me, I don't care. Dudes know when other dudes are lying. Of course I had my passport with me. What I didn't have with me was the little fake-gold statue I had left on the table on the porch, a statue of a ballplayer in a batting stance with the words, "World's Best Hitter" engraved on the pedestal. I know I should've just let it go, but I couldn't. I can't.

Blake was shocked to see me. Hannah was still at the table, finishing a buttered roll, and Blake was coaxing her up.

When I walked in the door, he immediately looked behind me. "Where are they, outside?"

"I forgot something …" I trailed off and, before I could lie to him, too, ran to the porch, grabbed the souvenir, stuffed it quickly into my bag and said a little prayer begging for forgiveness. In the kitchen, Hannah was wobbling to her feet and Blake was helping her, pulling her and her red suitcase out of the dining room.

"Where are they?" Blake repeated.

"Holding the train for us," I said, looking past him to Hannah. "Hannah, you think you can walk?"

"Absolutely," she said. "I'm one hundred percent. Let's do it."

With Varda and Carmen clucking, coming in for one last hug, with Blake seething, we finally left for good, I hoped. I pulled two suitcases; Blake pulled Hannah's, his other arm wrapped around her. I could hear him muttering, hurry, hurry and damn it, damn it.

But no matter how we hurried, damn it, there was no way we could traverse a mile with Hannah stumbling like a newborn foal. We did pretty well. It took us twenty-three minutes. The ticket seller said the train had been fifteen minutes delayed. Some girl had dropped the contents of her backpack onto the platform. Such carelessness. Train just left. Five minutes ago.

I tried to console Blake. It's all right. We'll catch the next one.

Without speaking to me or Hannah, Blake paced up and down the platform, perhaps hoping that Chloe had let Johnny go on his own and was waiting for us. Hannah and I stood dumbly.

"You think he's mad?" she said. "He looks mad."

"Not at you." I sighed. "You couldn't help it."

My brother stopped and stood at the other end of the platform from us, staring onto the train tracks. We had another forty minutes to wait until the next train. There was no hurry. I should've left Hannah, walked over to him, talked him down, but you know what happens when you're guilty? You're fucked. You can't figure out the right thing to say. Every word that comes out of your mouth condemns you. Every word that doesn't come out of your mouth condemns you.

Hannah and I sat down on a bench.

"How are you feeling?" I asked.

"Light-headed, but better," she replied. "The bread helped."

"Bread always does."

She looked pasty, a little shell-shocked.

For over twenty minutes, Hannah and I were at one end of the platform and Blake was at the other. Finally he made his way back to us, grabbed a water bottle, drank from it. It was a mild, cloudy morning, quiet and warm. There should've been nothing wrong. So we missed a train. So what.

"Why did you leave them?" Blake said to me. "I can't believe Chloe got on the train without us. But why did you leave them?"

"I told you, I forgot something. Dude, it's fine. It'll be fine. They'll either be waiting for us in Riga or—"

"How could you let her go?"

"What was I going to do? They said they would hold the train. And they tried. You heard the man. Train was delayed. We just couldn't get here fast enough."

"Oh, so it's our fault."

"I didn't say it was anyone's fault." We didn't look at Hannah, and she didn't look at us. I certainly didn't look at Blake. And he didn't look at me.

"Oh, it's somebody's fault, all right," Blake said. He wouldn't sit down. The three of us stared straight ahead, him, me, Hannah, all staring at the tracks. "Whatever it was you forgot, why didn't you just leave it?"

"I couldn't." I was about to open my mouth and lie to my brother, but he spared me the fraud by his frustrated coldness. He turned his face away before I could lie. I didn't know what he was most angry about. That I would let her go without me. That she would go. That Hannah fainted. Why choose, he might say if I asked him. I didn't ask him.

We missed the train by exactly the time Hannah's fainting delayed us.

Except for the fact that Chloe wasn't with us and, granted, that was a big except, there should've been not that much wrong. At that point five minutes seemed so minor, especially to deal with something as important as fainting. Blake and I spared Hannah a probing inquiry into what caused her to faint in the first place.

Okay, Hannah had fainted. It couldn't be helped. And, sure, I'd forgotten my golden idol. It couldn't be helped. And, yes, Johnny and Chloe were on the train without us. It couldn't be helped.

The next train was twenty minutes late and took another fifteen to leave Carnikava station. It then crawled along the track, taking an hour and fifteen instead of fifty minutes to get into Riga. We didn't get there until nearly 8:30. So five minutes of fainting became two hours of obstruction. Here it was, Johnny's chaos theory in action, showing us its fanged true face. And that was just to get to Riga. Because the vaunted bus to Vilnius was, of course, sold out for the nine o'clock and the noon. There were no seats available until after three.

We looked for Chloe and Johnny at the bus station, but anemically. We knew they wouldn't be there.

We had a six-hour wait. Done with Riga, I wished I could go to sleep so I wouldn't have to think about all the things I'd done wrong. Yes, I'd left Chloe, but I knew I would've felt just as guilty if I'd left Hannah and Blake behind. I almost felt better I was with my brother, although judging by his severe lack of goodwill, he didn't agree.

We tried waiting it out in the bus station, but it was unbearably hot, so we stashed our suitcases in lockers and wandered over to the air-conditioned Latvian Museum. We sat on a bench in the cool air in the lobby. Blake said that this might be a good time for me to go look inside St. Peter's church, since I wouldn't get another chance. He shook his head when I asked if he would come with me.

"So you want to split more of us up, is that it?"

He didn't reply. I didn't go. Even though I could've used a visit to a church. We went and bought more sandwiches and drinks for the bus. What could we do? Hannah hadn't meant to faint. It just happened. Five minutes. Forty-five minutes. Six hours.

And then Blake said, "And what do you think will happen to our Warsaw train connection when we get to Vilnius at eight at night?"

No one had an answer. No one at the Riga bus station knew anything about the timetable for the trains from Vilnius. Some lady who overheard and almost spoke English suggested that we go to Minsk first and from Minsk to Warsaw. But that couldn't be right. We didn't even know where Minsk was. She said the trip took twenty-seven hours. That could *not* be right! That's not what Johnny had told us. We tried to find an Internet café, but couldn't locate one close to the station and didn't want to risk missing the 3:15.

"Blake," I said to him, when Hannah had gone to the ladies' room and we had a moment to ourselves, "come on. Don't be sour. It's going to work out. We're a few hours behind them. We're all going to the same place. We know the name of our hostel in Warsaw. We have a room booked. We'll meet them there."

"I'm glad you think it's all going to work out," he said.

"You want to know what I think?" I said. "I think that if you let it affect everything, it's going to own everything."

"Ah," my brother said. "Which *it* exactly are you referring to? There seem to be so many *its* that affect fucking everything."

The bus was hard. Hannah didn't look good. Blake kept his arm around her and stared out the window. I sat behind them, my remorse blinding me to the green outside. It was all my fault. We are guilty about everything in front of everybody and everyone, I kept repeating to myself.

Blake

Everything that could go wrong has gone wrong. I wanted to take notes, make observations, chat, eat, but I couldn't even eat. Me, losing my appetite. That's how bad things are.

It's a conspiracy against me. Mason is right—I have to find a way to get past this. Because right now it owns everything. Except I'm still living it, and getting past something you're in the middle of is hard. What do the philosophers have to say about that? Take it on the chin? Grin? Bear it? Oh, I'm grinning. I'm bearing.

The 3:15 bus. Can we just talk about this for a second? Bus! This is our European adventure with our $500 Eurail tickets that are no good on Latvian or Lithuanian trains, and I'm on a Communist Greyhound, cramped next to Hannah who first needs the window, then needs the aisle and then needs the bathroom every half-hour and yet there is no bathroom on this luxury bus, because the luxury version was sold out, and this is the economy version. "Oh, it's better, it's cheaper. It only costs thirteen latu, sir." I would've gladly paid double so Hannah could actually go to the bathroom instead of repeating, ad nauseam, I need the bathroom. Blake, what do I do, I need the bathroom. She asked the driver to stop three times. The third time, the driver, suddenly finding his English, said, "People who are sick should not be traveling. They should be home. In bed."

"Hey, leave the girl alone," I said.

"I'm not sick," Hannah said to the driver. "I'm just not feeling well."

Ah. Yes. A fine difference indeed.

Mason sat behind me next to a woman who was too big for her seat, and I wanted to tell the driver that maybe people who take up two seats shouldn't be traveling either, but I didn't. Mason had his eyes closed, listening to his brand-new iPod, a graduation gift from Mom and Dad, mouthing along inaudibly, and I wanted to sit next to him and ask him again what he was thinking, letting Chloe go by herself, but what's he going to tell me that I don't already know?

To write was impossible: the bus had no suspension. A healthy person would puke. We were being thrown up and down and sideways for hours. The bus was supposed to arrive in Vilnius around eight at night, but of course, there was traffic or an accident or roadwork, there was Hannah asking the driver to stop the bus so she could throw up by the side of the road because there were no well-appointed restrooms in the countryside. The fourth and last time we stopped, about twenty miles from the Lithuanian border in Daugavpils, there were some proper facilities. We all took a pit stop. It was around seven, almost the hour we were supposed to be in Vilnius. I asked the bus driver how much longer. He said usually another three hours but it depends how many times your friend makes me stop the bus. Mase and I stomped away and walked around the bus station, waiting for Hannah.

After thirty minutes the bus driver found us and said that if the lady wasn't on his bus in exactly five minutes, he was leaving without us.

Those damn five minutes again!

"You can't leave without us," I said. "We have a ticket."

"I rip up your ticket. Go try to get refund. Five minutes, I said. Everybody waiting. They ready to kill me. I ready to kill me. It not right. People will miss their connections."

Yes. People like us. I knocked on the bathroom door in a panic, but Hannah didn't answer. "Hannah, please," I said. "They're going to leave without us."

No answer.

I knocked louder. She flung the door open, her eyes manic.

"What do you want me to do?" she said. "I feel *horrible*."

"He said he'll leave if we're not on the bus in five minutes."

"So go. Get on that bus."

"Hannah …"

"I can't go like this. I've never felt this bad. It must be motion sickness."

She slammed the door. Mason and I stared at each other.

The bus left without us.

We had no choice but to stay overnight in Daugavpils. I couldn't hide my disappointment. I didn't even try. Daugavpils instead of Vilnius!

We would have to wake very early the next morning to make sure we were on the 5:30 train to Vilnius. We might have a little time there before the train for Warsaw left at 11:20. That's what I was reduced to. Being grateful that I might eke out an hour in Vilnius.

I didn't want to be testy with Hannah. It wasn't fair to her. I loathed most of all not her fainting, not her vomiting, not her holding us up, or even making us miss our bus, but Johnny being right.

He was right to bolt as he did. In my head, I mocked and re-mocked his parting words to us. "While you're waiting for your connections, watching your whole trip melt away like ice in the tropics, just remember your ninth-grade physics, especially the definition of chaos theory," he said. Bastard. I don't give a shit about his theory. When I asked Mason about it, he said cryptically, "Everything unravels." That's all he said.

I wish I could stay mad at Mason. But I can't. He's my brother. I know he's doing his best, even if he is constantly screwing up.

"Blake, please don't be mad at me," Hannah said in Daugavpils when she finally left the bathroom. "I can't help that I feel all funky."

I might have patted her for reassurance; I don't know. It was an accident, I said. Shit happens. An unfortunate thing. People hurt themselves, faint in response to pain. It's normal. And then throw up for six hours straight. I'm sure that's normal, too. I probably didn't come off as one hundred percent sincere.

"So we stay in Daugavpils instead of Vilnius," Hannah said. She didn't look good. She was crazy pale. "What's the big deal? After we missed our train this morning, we knew we'd have to stay overnight somewhere."

I stared at her coldly, warily, as if she were about to sting me. "No big deal?" I said. "Hannah, I'm not mad at you for feeling sick, but please, don't piss me off by not understanding why I would want to stay in Vilnius, not Daugavpils. I explained it to you enough times. It makes me feel as if you're not listening to me. Vilnius was my only consolation for this day of disaster. Vilnius is one of the cities you want to visit before you die. Vilnius is a historic capital, beautiful, full of rivers, and museums, and war. And restaurants. If we had time, I'd want to stay in Vilnius for a week. You do see a difference, don't you, between this one-horse border town and one of the cultural centers of Europe, a Jerusalem of the north?"

Hannah was left unimpressed by my soliloquy, which in turn left me unimpressed with Hannah. "Who told you this?" she said. "Frommer's?"

"*National Geographic*, if you must know," I said.

"So clearly you already know everything you need to about Vilnius," she said. "You've read all about it, my little armchair traveler." She ruffled my hair. "Why go see it?"

"Why see anything?" I said, pulling away from her hand. "Why see Treblinka, or Krakow, or even Barcelona, or the Alps? We can just read about them."

"Oh, I heartily agree with you about Treblinka."

I had to drop it, because although I wanted to provoke her, I didn't want to have a fight. It's not a fair contest to fight with a girl who at any moment might blow chunks. And I was being mean to Daugavpils. It was actually shockingly big for a tiny city. It had boulevards and parks, long streets and outdoor cafés, and graffiti on tenement walls. I looked it up in Frommer's. It's the second largest city in Latvia. One-horse town indeed. It's twenty times bigger than North Conway. It is two hundred times bigger than Fryeburg. It just wasn't Vilnius.

The three hostels we found in Daugavpils were full. "How can they be full?" I said. "There are no people here." A narrow, rundown, Bolshevik joint, advertising itself as three-star accommodation and serving mostly commuters, wanted a hundred latu from us, nearly two hundred dollars. Even Mason became agitated. None of us had ever stayed in a hotel that expensive. Scratch that. None of us had ever stayed in a hotel, period. With our vats of knowledge gleaned from skimming Chloe and Hannah's celebrity magazines, we thought the Ritz-Carlton on the French Riviera commanded those kinds of prices, not a fleabag on the wrong side of the tracks in a provincial town. (Which is where people like us lived, Chloe would say, if she were here. But she wasn't.) We had two choices. Cough up or look for another place.

"Or sleep on the piss-soaked bench at the station," offered Mason. Then, seeing Hannah's glare, he added, "Just kidding." But who was he kidding? We three knew he would've preferred to sleep on that bench than pay two hundred dollars for a room. Mason was nothing if not frugal.

We paid two hundred dollars for the room. It came out of our money—the money we had worked for and saved—not Moody's money, which was all with Chloe. After paying, the three of us became stunningly bad-tempered.

Across from our luxury palace we found a cheap café.

"Why did you faint, Hannah?" I asked after we sat down and ordered. I tried not to sound churlish.

"People faint, Blake."

"Not you."

"Bro's right," Mason said. "You've never fainted."

"Just because *you* haven't seen me faint doesn't mean I haven't."

"When have you fainted, bird?" I asked.

"Not in front of you, but I have."

"When?"

"When I was a kid. What's the point of this interrogation anyway? Even if I've never fainted, I fainted this morning, didn't I?"

"Yes."

"So what are you getting at?"

"Nothing."

"What are you implying?"

"Nothing."

"That I didn't actually faint?"

"No, no, you definitely fainted," I said. "The question remains, though: why?"

"Why do people faint, doctor? I don't know. I hit my ankle. I was in sudden pain. I fainted." She was annoyed, but not as annoyed as I was. And then she aimed for the balls. "I thought you might be relieved," she said, "that we didn't have to travel with Johnny, whom you don't seem to care for."

"While that is certainly true," I returned, "instead of relieved, imagine that we might actually be worried about Chloe."

"No one's worried, bro," Mason said. "Just you."

"Amen," said Hannah.

"Well, you two *should* be fucking worried," I said to Mason and Hannah. "That you're not is worrying in itself." I glared at my brother.

Mason said nothing, but looked twisted with guilt.

I said nothing more. I stopped obsessing about Hannah's vomiting, though I continued to obsess about Chloe being thrust against the worst human being on the planet. My gut was so full of anxiety about Johnny's nefarious nature that I couldn't fit even a sandwich in there with it.

To avoid talking to Hannah and Mase, I took out my travel guides, opened the map on the table, moving aside the food, the beer. I didn't know what I was looking for, tracing the roads, from the Latvian border to Warsaw, almost as if I would have liked to rent a car and race to Poland down the paved highways. All futility. I paid the bill and closed my guidebook. I didn't want to oversleep and miss our train. That was the one thing I could still control. Or we'd be three days behind, and then we might never find her.

Hannah

I am never getting on a bus again as long as I live. That was the worst thing that's ever happened to me. The boys are both mad at me, but I don't care. I would rather hitch the rest of the way than set foot on a bus again. The most miserable three hours of my life were spent between Riga and Daugavpils. As soon as the bus ditched us, I felt better. A coincidence? I don't think so. I wasn't sure *how* we were going to get to Warsaw but I knew for sure it wasn't going to be by the worst transportation mode ever invented by man, and I didn't care beyond that. We sat too far in the back because all the front seats were taken, and the entire time I was just praying, don't throw up, don't throw up, don't throw up. I know this is not ideal. We could've already been in Vilnius. But it is what it is. So what if we're one day behind Chloe? We'll make up that day along the way. I smiled fetchingly. Perhaps by not going to Treblinka?

Blake snapped at me not to joke, but I don't know what he meant, I wasn't joking at all.

Blake snapped at me. I couldn't believe it.

I know he's mad, but it's not my fault. It's the bus's fault. We weren't supposed to take a bus. That wasn't in the plan. Ours was a train vacation; the bus is hateful. I know Blake agrees with me, but he's being stubborn at the moment, as if I ruined things somehow.

It's not great, I won't dispute it. The one daily train to Vilnius isn't until 5:30 the next morning.

"Blake, don't be upset. The train to Warsaw doesn't leave Vilnius until eleven. We'll definitely make it."

"You sure about that?" he said. "So far, not a single thing has gone as planned."

I wanted to ask him if he meant today or the whole trip, but I didn't. I was feeling well enough to travel by train but not well enough to argue.

The large expensive hotel room turned out to be the size of a walk-in closet. It had barely enough floor space for one double bed, which only fit because it was pressed into the corner. Didn't the hotel clerk tell us for a hundred latu we got two beds, not one? No one felt up to going downstairs and arguing. The room was high up, and through the window we could see the station, the dozens of train tracks beyond it, the lights. We had a bit of a view.

"Come on, you guys, it's an adventure," I said. "Let's go find a place to eat." I can't believe I was suddenly the cheerleader. Me.

The little café close to the hotel served decent sausages and potatoes. Mason was famished, but I just had some clear chicken broth, bread, and a cream cake. Here's how I know something was wrong. Blake bought himself a sandwich and only finished half of it. Blake didn't finish a sandwich. And when I asked him about it, he said he wasn't hungry. He didn't have the Blake twinkle in his eye. He looked like a different Blake without that twinkle.

The brothers kept talking, but not about me, about how I fell and hurt my leg, but about Chloe. Where is she? What do you think has happened? Are they already in Warsaw? We planned on Gdansk first, they said, so Chloe will have to sweet-talk her way into our hostel reservation two days early. Or was it only a day early? Neither I nor the boys could tell anymore. I could see they were worried about finding her, Blake especially, because they wouldn't shut up about it. Mason was like, of course we'll find her, dude, and I was like, Mason's right, where could she possibly get to, can we talk about something else? And Blake said, I just want to go to sleep. He didn't want to talk about anything. We set two alarms and asked the desk guy to wake us up at 4:30 and he looked at us weird and said, "Four-thirty in afternoon?"

Blake and I lay down in the bed together, and Mason took our only blanket and half of our pillows and squeezed in on the floor next to his brother. Blake and I were fully dressed in T-shirts and shorts. It was night, and we had a bed. That was the first time those two things had combined in one moment in our three years together. Night. And bed. There had been night before, without bed. In trucks, back seats, an abandoned barn. And there'd been bed before, without night. A few times when our parents were out. Now in Daugavpils there was night. There was bed.

And there was Mason.

I wanted Blake to hold me, to spoon me, but he turned his back to me. He said he was hot. He didn't even sleep under the sheet. What's wrong with him?

There was no bathroom in the room (a hundred latu and no bathroom?) and I had to get up three times in the middle of the night to use the facilities down the hall. Blake got up with me each time and waited outside the bathroom to make sure I was okay. It's fine, I kept telling him. Stay in bed. But there was a strange man sleeping on the floor in the corridor near the bathroom. He was either sleeping or dead. He smelled awful, of not washing and of drink. Or perhaps decomposition. I was glad Blake was with me. Sometimes I think I deserve better than him. But sometimes I think he deserves better than me. Every once in a while I think I haven't treated him as well as I should have. I thought this especially when I was in the bathroom at three in the morning, throwing up all of my insides, while he stood like a Buckingham Palace guard outside my door next to the unconscious drunk.

23

Lost Children

Chloe

She kept hoping they would appear, pleading with the conductor not to pull away just yet. But they didn't. The train pulled away. Trying not to fidget, Chloe sat next to the window, Johnny to her left.

"Don't worry," he said. "Your friend didn't look well. She'll be okay, but she probably needed a few extra minutes. They'll catch the next one." He opened his European Timetable book, looked up some numbers. Binomials? Irrationals? Sequential algorithms for living a better life? "Yeah, it's not looking great for their bus. The early ones get sold out quick. But if they can catch the 3:15, they can stay overnight in Daugavpils and then catch the train to Vilnius in the morning. So they'll be a day behind us." He paused. "Provided, of course, they don't miss that 5:30 a.m. to Vilnius."

"Why would they miss the train?"

"I don't know. They missed it today."

"Well, Hannah is not going to be fainting tomorrow, is she?"

Johnny closed his book of numbers. "Let's hope not."

Why would he say that? Why wouldn't Hannah be feeling better? She had banged her ankle, not torn her Achilles' heel.

"Blake and Mason know to be careful, right?" he said. "Some of the hostels are sketchy."

Chloe didn't know if Blake and Mason knew to be careful. They never had to be careful before. "How do you know?"

He shrugged. "Let's just say I learned the hard way not to miss the bus from Riga to Vilnius. After I'd missed it once, I thought, so what. I'll take the evening train to Daugavpils, stay overnight, get up and go the next morning. I was so cocky."

Was? Chloe thought. "So what's wrong with the hostels? We're booked into a three-star one in Warsaw. It got great reviews on a travel website."

"Yeah," he drew out. "Do you know the saying seek and ye shall find? Many who stay in the hostels take that commandment fully to heart. Drunks and addicts seek to lift the lids of the communal toilets to see what they shall find inside the tanks."

Her eyes round with alarm, Chloe tried not to sound scandalized. "Um, what are they looking for under there?"

"You name it. Drugs taped to the lid. Bottles of vodka sunk into the water. The junkies hide stuff in the toilets, hoping to retrieve it at some future date, but other junkies find the goods first. Then they stab each other in fights over the contents."

"When you say stab each other ..."

Johnny said nothing for a long moment. "With any luck the hostels near the station will be full and your friends will get a hotel room instead. Are you hungry?"

Though she was, she said she wasn't, because she didn't want him to think she had appetites that could not be controlled.

"I'm starved," he said. "Absolutely stahrved." He smirked. "My grandparents would not be happy with me. They tell me never to say that, because I have no idea what that really means. But I can't help myself. That's how I feel, famished. I don't say it in front of them, though."

"Why?" Chloe asked, but she was only half-listening. She was scanning through her brain for details about Mason, trying to make sense of his passport forgetting. It was so out of character. He didn't leave behind his keys, his school ID, his permit, his license, his money. He was the careful one, the most careful one of them all. And if it was his passport he'd forgotten, why didn't he say so immediately? Why did it take four tries to get an answer out of him? She wondered if he had made an excuse to go back. But why would he do that? Perhaps he was just flabbergasted he'd forgotten something as non-negotiable as a passport. She didn't know what to think, all the while catching snippets of Johnny talking about his grandparents, their big house, the food on their table.

The commuter rail arrived at Riga Central right on time, at 6:20. Their bus was at seven. They hurried, Johnny dragging Chloe's suitcase on its busted wheels. She wished she had bought a new suitcase for this trip and said so. She apologized to him for her suitcase. But he shook his head. "Trust me. Be like Paris Hilton."

"Um, in what way?" she said, coloring slightly, thinking only of the graphic video, *One Night in Paris*.

Johnny, thank goodness, meant something else. "Have you seen her walking through the airport after coming back from her travels?" he asked. "No? A shame. Everyone should learn from Paris. She pushes eight suitcases on a trolley. And you think that she's freaking Paris Hilton, she's going to have Louis Vuitton luggage hand-made especially for her. But no. Do you know what she has? Kmart luggage. The oldest and most sorry-looking. Ripped-up suitcases, held together by twine, clasps broken, wheels coming off, mismatched, as if she'd picked them up off the side of the road before the garbage men came. In this heap of awfulness, she carries her Gucci shoes and Prada dresses and Tiffany diamonds. That's how you travel. Humbly." He smiled, opening the door for Chloe into the tiny station café. "The way *you* carry yourself. Without ostentation."

Taken aback by his words, she couldn't think of a riposte at first or a thing she wanted from the café chalkboard. She carried herself without ostentation? She looked down at her Doc Martens. He ordered for both of them. Two coffees and three cheese buns. "On second thought, five buns," he said. "If we miss a connection or are stuck on the bus, we'll be glad for the food."

"Without ostentation," Chloe repeated. "Huh. You mean, like your Lucchese boots in black calfskin leather?"

He laughed. "Touché," he said. "As you see"—he pointed to his current footwear—"I wear my father's old army boots when I travel. Luccheses are for when I perform. But only you would know what they are, Miss Fashion Magazine. You think anyone here knows about cowboy boots?"

Chloe, perversely flattered that he would be impressed by her trivial knowledge of cowboy boots (and it was only because her mother had bought a pair for her dad one Christmas ten years ago and he wore them to this day) said, "Folks here seem to know about Bluebird microphones."

"Yes, the Eastern Europeans do like the western tech," he admitted. "Come, let's hurry. And by the way, it's alligator leather, not calfskin." Winking, he tipped his beret. "A gift."

"For singing?"

"Funny. But no. Maybe. For nothing really. For living."

They made the bus with five minutes to spare, but had to sit in the back. She sat next to the window, he next to her. He didn't ask to sit next to the window, and she didn't offer. His duffel and guitar were stuffed under the seat and between his legs. Her suitcase was in the cargo hold.

"Why do you always hold on to your bag?" she asked him.

"My whole life is the guitar and the duffel. You have to protect the things you can't do without, don't you agree?"

Chloe thought back. "But on the train from Liepaja, you left your stuff with me when you stepped out."

He nodded. "You looked as if you could be trusted. Was I wrong?"

"Well, no. But"—she furrowed—"yesterday at Livu Square you took the guitar when you ran off to the bakery."

"How would it look if I gave you my guitar to hold while I ran off? What would Mason say?"

Oh, Mason wouldn't care about a silly thing like that, Chloe had to stop herself from saying. He'd barely notice.

It took a while to check everybody's passports. The bus finally took off, ten minutes late, which stressed out Johnny, since the transfer in Vilnius from bus to train had to be perfect to succeed. The bus would arrive at 10:45 a.m., and the train to Warsaw departed at 11:20. No time even to get a sandwich.

"How far is the bus depot from the train station?"

"You'd think they would build them next to each other for convenience," said Johnny. "But the Communists preferred the old ladies to cart their suitcases some distance down the Vilnius cobblestones."

"Hey, I'm not that old," she said.

"Old ladies and very young women, then."

Why did that make her blush?

"Why are you blushing?"

"I'm not blushing." God!

"You are, I just saw you. What did I say?"

"I have no idea what you mean. Pastry is good."

"Yes. Did the pastry make you blush?"

"I didn't blush."

"Okay."

After some time had passed he said, "The bus is awful, isn't it?"

She hadn't noticed. She hadn't noticed anything except him sitting next to her.

"Yes, it's pretty bad," she quickly agreed, because she didn't want him to think she was so lost in reverie that she didn't notice the horror of buses in general and of this one in particular. She was slightly let down that he would observe in such subtle detail how the bus lurched, how bad it smelled. He was sweating. She wiped her own brow. She was sweating. The bus had no AC. Fifty people and no AC.

"Do these buses ever have AC?" she asked him.

"What's AC?" he said. "You're in Latvia. Soon you'll be in Poland. Wait till you make your acquaintance with those trains. You won't get AC until you get on a train in Vienna."

"Vienna? I'm not going to Vienna."

"If you want AC, you will."

"Why do I have to go to Vienna?"

"Because Vienna waits for you." He didn't take out his timetable book. "I'd show you the routes, but not now. Sitting in the back of the bus like this, if you do anything but stare ahead, you'll be throwing up for hours. It'll ruin your trip."

Could anything ruin Chloe's trip, even the vomitous bus? She didn't think so.

A woman sprung up from the seat in front of them. Whirled around and stuck her head over the seat. "For your information," she sputtered in huffy accented English, "this bus is a luxury bus. There is a bathroom and cup holders and extra leg room. The AC, as you call it, is on. You'd know if it wasn't on. You know how? You'd be dead from heat stroke." Pointing to a vent up in the ceiling blowing out hot air, she spun forward.

Chloe and Johnny laughed soundlessly. "Do you know Italian?" he whispered, leaning into her head. "Maybe we can talk quietly in Italian."

"You can't insult my country in any language," said the woman in front, not turning around this time. "And for your information, I also speak Italian."

They covered their mouths, trying not to giggle. They were still sweating, nearly pressing their damp foreheads together. Chloe decorously moved away a few inches. Johnny took off his jacket. This time he contained his arms and didn't elbow her in inappropriate soft places. She couldn't take anything off, wearing only her T-shirt, all her warm things packed away.

"I like the color of your shirt," Johnny said, pinching the hem of it between his fingers.

"Thank you. It's labradorite."

"What?"

"Labradorite."

"Is that the color of a Labrador? White? Or black?"

"Well, since it's blue, it's neither. It's iridescent blue. There's a semi-precious gem mined in the Urals, I think, called labradorite."

"I should've known," Johnny said. "All the best things come from the Ural Mountains."

"You've been to the Urals?" He seemed so well traveled.

"No. It's on my list, though. After I come back from Afghanistan."

She was quiet for a few minutes while she composed things to say, to ask, to comment on. One thing she tried hard to get out but couldn't: *What if you don't come back from Afghanistan?* When she turned to look at him, to ask if he was really really going to Afghanistan, he was sleeping, his head tilted toward her iridescently blue shoulder. She stared at him for a long while. Then she became worried that he would open his eyes and find a deranged half-stranger devouring him, inches away from his straight nose, from his soft full mouth. She turned to the window, the pit in her stomach whooshing, sucking her into a vortex of itself, a cauldron that contained odd despair, angst, tension, crackling exhilaration like Bengal lights, a numbing sensation of falling.

Like this she passed the hours from eight to ten, as the countryside changed from marsh to forest, forest to fields of red wildflowers, trees of green, and rivers, rivers, rivers, streaming south from the Baltic Sea. She sat and tried to make herself grow up before he woke up, grow up so she wouldn't see all the new things in her life with her mouth open, wanting to laugh at anything, at everything, at the sun, at idle youth, at her bedazzled impetuous heart.

The bus was ten minutes late getting into Vilnius. They had twenty minutes to make the Warsaw train; a ten-minute walk.

They hurried. It was just the two of them. No one fainted, no one lost their passport. At the station they had enough time to buy her ticket and find their platform.

"You don't need a ticket, Johnny?"

"Nah."

"I have a Eurail too, but it's not valid in Lithuania."

"I don't have a Eurail."

He didn't offer to show her what he had, and she didn't press further, maybe because she was all out of breath as they rushed down the long steep steps to the platform. He carried her suitcase and his duffel.

"What would I do if you weren't with me?" she said.

"My guess," Johnny said, "is that you would walk up to any man at this station and say, dear sir, could you help me, and they would carry your suitcase and possibly you too down the stairs. Oh, okay, *now* you're blushing."

"No," she said, averting her face. "Do you want me to carry your guitar?" To change the subject.

"Guitar's on my back, I'm fine. Glad I got a case. It was getting even more beat up than it already is."

It did look old and beat up. But the strings were new. Last night he had spent a long time sitting by Otto in the backyard restringing it in the near dark.

"Was it a present, like the boots?"

"Guess so," he said, as he gave her his hand to help her up into the train. "It was my dad's. He no longer played. So when he saw I had an interest, he gave it to me."

"Your dad must be pleased that you love his guitar so much, no?" she said, as they found two seats in an empty compartment that quickly and irritatingly acquired four more people before the train left the station. How were they going to banter with four strangers listening? Now it would have to be self-conscious banter.

"I don't think he's pleased with me in general," Johnny said. "I'm not sure if he cares I have his guitar."

They settled in, got as comfortable as they could. A young couple was talking intimately across the aisle. A man traveling by himself was trying to fall asleep, though it was barely noon. On the seat one over from Johnny a middle-aged woman took out her knitting. Another woman opened the door and panted in. She was very large and had with her a cell phone and a pet carrier. Inside the carrier a small dog was yapping. The woman and her dog squeezed in next to Johnny. He leaned toward Chloe's ear, inhaling. "What is it with me and large women?" he whispered. She nearly laughed out loud.

"Next leg I get the window seat," he said.

"No way. Ladies get window seats. And what leg would that be? I thought this train takes us to Warsaw?"

"We have two train changes. One in Kaunas in a few hours, and one in Sestokai on the border a few hours after that."

"How long does the entire trip take?"

"Eleven with luck."

Eleven hours! Lucky indeed. The agitated excitement Chloe felt was similar to when she was three years old and her dad was teaching her how to swim. One afternoon he dropped her into the lake from the floating dock. She squealed and flailed, trying not to swallow (too much) water, trying to stay afloat. That's what she felt like now. Squealing and flailing her arms.

"Hey, whatcha thinking about?" he said, nudging her leg, watching whatever melodrama was playing out on her face.

"Nothing." She wanted to make something up, but couldn't think of a lie fast enough. She tried the truth. "I was thinking of my earliest memory." She told him what it was. He listened.

"Why were you thinking of that? Do you want to go swimming? That'll be hard to do in Poland. Hostels don't usually have swimming pools."

"I'll wait till Barcelona," she said. "Your turn. Tell me your earliest memory."

"All right." He scratched his tattooed forearms. "I was probably younger than three," he said. He smelled of smoke. He kept shifting his long legs to get comfortable. "I was crawling in the grass to catch a Gila monster."

"What?"

"You know, a large, striped, poisonous lizard."

"I know what a Gila monster is, thank you. I'm just wondering why you would do this."

"Ah. Well, like I said, I was two. Plus it was striped. It looked like a little banded crocodile. It wasn't moving at all. That morning I had overheard my sister saying it had the most awful breath. She said it didn't have a butthole and it pooped out of its mouth. My other sister said that was how it killed its prey. By breathing on it. Well, any boy would have to see that for himself, don't you agree?"

"Um, actually, the opposite of agree," said Chloe. "But why were you crawling?"

"Like a soldier after an enemy," said Johnny. "I got so close! Then suddenly I hear what sounds like twenty people screaming behind me, and I turn and see my whole family—parents, sisters, grandparents, uncles—yelling and sprinting."

"What were they yelling?"

"Something dumb like no. But real loud and annoying. So before they caught me, I stood up and ran as quick as I could toward the Gila monster. I really wanted to smell its breath."

Chloe waited, her own hopefully-not-fetid breath paused in her throat. "And? Did they catch you?"

"They did," he said cheerfully. "But only after I fell on top of the lizard." He laughed. "Hugged it with my body, wrestled with it, and tried to prop open its jaws with my fingers. It and I must have weighed about the same at that point. Maybe thirty-five pounds. We were evenly matched."

Chloe's hand was to her mouth. There went all her ambition to react like a grown up. "Did you? Open its jaws?"

"Oh, yes," he said. "Beck and Rach were right. Its breath really was putrid."

"Dear God, Johnny. You opened its mouth and it didn't bite you?"

"Oh, it bit me, all right," he said, his large black eyes dancing. "It was awesome."

Chloe had no words.

"Someone threw me in the pool, maybe my grandpa, because he knew that submerging the attacking lizard in water is the only way to break free of its grip. So in a way my story and your story are the same. Both are about learning how to swim."

"See, no, I don't think our stories are the same."

"Just look at the similarities."

"Did it hurt?"

"I don't remember. My sisters, because they never stop mocking me, tell me I cried like a baby."

The train finally took off.

She tried asking him some more questions. Where was he born? Where was he raised? Did he have a big family?

But Johnny wasn't interested in talking about himself anymore. "I'm sad I didn't get to show you Vilnius," he said. "I wish we had a day here. It's not enough, but it would've been better than what we had. Which was nothing."

"How do you know anything about Vilnius?"

"Your friend Blake knows about Vilnius," said Johnny. "And I assume he's never been here?"

"Yes, but he's crazy," said Chloe. "He spent all of July reading about every single place we might visit along the route to Barcelona." He also read up on stuff that had nothing to do with Europe. Such as, what a vernal pool was (an ephemeral pool of water that provides a brief habitat for beautiful flowers). And the number of the cabin at Chateau Marmont where John Belushi died of a drug overdose (#3). Blake said vernal pools were important, and also it was important to know where a person had died.

"He is very well read," Johnny said. Mocking? Serious?

How amusing Blake would have found the description of himself as well read, if only he didn't detest Johnny. Chloe didn't comment, nor did she volunteer information about Blake's researching Eastern Europe to write his book to win the money to buy a truck to start his junk-hauling business with Mason. Hauls R Us. Haul-away Brothers. Halo Inc. That's what Lupe had said a few weeks ago when Chloe visited last. The boy has a halo. Does your friend Hannah have a halo detector, the old woman had asked Chloe.

"What's so great about Vilnius?" Chloe said instead.

They had nothing but time, so Johnny told her. Quietly he told her all the things he knew about Vilnius. Which turned out to be a lot.

"How do you know all this, Johnny?"

He shrugged. "How do I know anything about anything? I just know."

"But how?"

There was a small sigh, as if he didn't want to lie to her, or lie to a direct question, or perhaps lie to a direct question from her. "My father brought me here with him, to the Baltic states. Two years ago, when I first came to Europe, I came with him. We went to visit my mother first. And then he thought I might like to see thousands of miles of battlefields. That's really all it is to him. The front during the war."

"Oh, so he also thinks there is only one war," Chloe said lightly.

"No. He thinks there's also Vietnam."

"Did he take you there, too?" She chuckled.

"Yup. Summer right before I turned sixteen, we went."

"Really?" She studied him with interest, fascination, as if he were a rare rhesus monkey on loan from a Nepalese zoo. "Was your dad in Vietnam?"

"He thought it would be good for me to get away," Johnny went on. "It was just after all the stupid trouble with Performing Arts. I thought I was being punished. I said to him, haven't I been punished enough? I told him he deliberately wanted to take me away from my friends, from the band I was trying to start. And he agreed! He said yes he was. As you can imagine, I wasn't the best companion."

"Well, you were sixteen." Chloe couldn't imagine going anywhere alone with her mother when she was sixteen. Genital herpes was preferable to hanging with your 'rents at that age.

He smiled. "I think he finally learned. He stopped wanting to take me places."

"Except for Liepaja."

Johnny shrugged. "That was a different thing. He … I was … never mind."

She never minded, but wished he would tell her. "Your mom will be happy to see you, yes?"

"Yes," he agreed. "She's been waiting a long time for me to come visit. This will be only my third time visiting her in Tarcento. I keep telling her it's not exactly near anything or on the way to anything, but her feelings are still hurt. I'll spend a few days with her before I fly back."

Chloe wanted to say his mother was probably right. Two years on the same continent and you only visit your mother twice? Not very good.

"I've been busy," Johnny said, as if she needed an explanation, as if Chloe was the one he didn't come to see. "I had to make my own way. I had no money. Dad wasn't giving me a penny."

"Except the guitar," Chloe said. "A vintage Gibson Hummingbird, no less. And the Bluebird microphone. Oh, and the Lucchese boots."

"Okay, smartass, I told you the boots were from my grandmother."

"Ah."

"And it's not like cash to eat, sleep, to live. I can sell my stuff, but then I won't be able to make any money at all. Right now I'm microphone rich but cash poor." He wasn't offended. He smiled.

"Winters here must be hard for making money. Playing music. Giving tours."

"Last winter it didn't matter," he said in a clipped, evasive tone. He didn't explain why it didn't matter, when most of your work was outside in the blizzards. "My first winter in Europe I spent down in southern Italy. Naples, Sicily. And Spain. That was better."

"Did you stay in hostels?" *Seek and ye shall find.*

"Or with friends. I met lots of dudes along the way, musicians, tour guides, others. I'm tight with one or two restaurant owners. They feed me when I'm in town."

"In Barcelona?"

He moved slightly away. "Don't take this the wrong way, Chloe, but Barcelona is overrated. You'll see. It's packed, stifling hot, expensive, and dangerous. You have to be on constant alert for thieves. The beaches aren't great."

"In Barcelona?" She tried not to sound naïve and open-mouthed. She tried hard to grow up between his comment and her question.

"Not great at all. Built as an afterthought for the Olympics. And now slammed with people. No place to put down a blanket. You'll see."

She turned her gaze away. Barcelona was her dream, why was he raining on it? She looked for the hill with the Three Crosses he had told her about. Instead there was a banjo player by the side of the road, near the train tracks, serenading the passing train. She waved to the banjo player, and when she turned her head, Johnny was watching her fondly, corners of his mouth slightly up, his almond eyes soft. "You like the banjo player, Chloe?"

"I admire his resolve," she replied. The train was rattly, the compartment smelly. Maybe they should have invested in first class travel. Someone could come, serve them. Everything would be scented with perfume, and the people would be better dressed and talk less loudly on the phone. The woman next to Johnny, with the yapping terrier, was trying to outbark the dog and succeeding. The knitting woman and the exhausted man were grousing at her. Chloe didn't have to understand them to know what they were saying.

As if he could read the distaste on her face, Johnny smiled. "Wait till we get on a Polish train. What a treat that'll be for you."

Chloe sighed. "Do you think my grandmother knew this when she made me come here?"

He shrugged. "Last time she was on a train, she was probably in a freight car meant for fifty people but carrying two hundred standing in their own filth on the way from a destroyed ghetto to a Nazi work prison. I don't know if she was thinking about your comfort."

Chastened, Chloe steered the conversation away from Moody and back to Johnny. Under the white noise of the loud Lithuanian in the tiny compartment, they tried to converse. He told her about his family. Lots of cousins and uncles. They lived all over. Virginia, California, Georgia, New York. She told him about her family. She had eight cousins on her father's side. Half of them lived in Fryeburg. She didn't see her mother's family much. As in at all. No, she had never been to North Dakota. A few times, her mother's mother had come to Maine to visit. Last time was for little Jimmy's funeral. Then she died. Chloe could tell Johnny wanted to ask about little Jimmy, but there were too many people listening. He didn't and she felt relieved. She really didn't like talking about it.

He told her about his friends. Lots of acquaintances but few close friends. The closest friends he had were Richie and Mel with whom he had a band for five minutes and then they fell out over nothing, Johnny couldn't even remember what. Chloe didn't have to tell him about *her* friends. He knew. But she told him about some of her other friends, about Taylor and Madison and Regan and Megan, and also about the cheer squad who thought they were her friends, but whom she did not care for, especially that Mackenzie. This for some reason amused Johnny no end, and they spent way too long on slutty Mackenzie, until suddenly the fat woman with the dog stood up and started shouting at the knitting woman. The woman grabbed her animal cage, her cell phone and stomped off through the sliding door down the corridor. A new woman immediately appeared in her place, a tiny quiet bird. Now

Johnny and Chloe were the only ones talking. Everyone could hear them. Chloe didn't like that. Almost everyone spoke some English around here.

Johnny didn't care. He kept asking her about Hannah and Mason and Blake, asking and asking.

"Johnny, what am I not telling you? Are you dancing around your actual question? What do you want to know?"

He wanted to know why they had paired up the way they did.

"That's just silly. Can you picture Mason and Hannah together?"

"Why not?" he said. "The varsity star ballplayer and the model."

"Well," she said, "that's not how it was, okay?"

"So how was it?"

"Not like that." Now she was the one who was clipped and evasive.

He asked how she and Mason had started up. It sounded ridiculous when he put it that way. Started up. Like a car. "I don't remember," Chloe said. "We were at a party. And then went bowling. Or roller blading."

"Wait," he said. "You don't remember how you started dating your high school sweetheart?"

"We were always together anyway," Chloe said. "One day, there was more." She *really* didn't want to talk about it, in the daylight, in a compartment rife with stink and strangers. She didn't want to tell Johnny that three years ago the grave was unquiet, the wind did blow and rain did fall. She needed comfort, and Mason was the one who had comforted her.

"What about Hannah and Blake?"

"They started about the same time."

"Who first?"

"What do you mean?"

"I mean, who started going together first, you and Mason or Hannah and Blake?"

Chloe said she wasn't sure. She said she didn't remember. She didn't want to talk about it! "It wasn't as if we could just play musical brothers," she said. "They weren't interchangeable, Mason and Blake."

"That is certainly true," said Johnny.

"Go easy on Blake," Chloe said with a small sigh. "He's not usually the way he's been."

"Which is how? Ornery? Tendentious?"

"Yes. Not usually like that. I don't know what's wrong with him."

"Don't you?"

"No." She shrugged. "It's weird."

"Anyway. You were saying. Mason and Hannah?"

"I wasn't, but okay. Mason was too young for Hannah. I don't mean age-wise, I mean … maturity-wise. He was—is—really into sports, and she isn't at all."

"And you?" Johnny appraised her Ural gem shirt, her thin white arms, her flushed face. His scrutiny forced her to turn to the window. The fields, the trees, the rivers, raced away beyond. Lithuania wasn't as heavily forested as Maine, and it didn't have mountains like New Hampshire. Flat fields stretched across green plains. Clouds floated in the blue skies. White flowers blanketed the grasses like cotton.

Suddenly Johnny widened his eyes and laughed. Everything was clear, he said. "I forgot, your dad is chief of police, isn't he?"

"So?"

"Well, that would explain why Mason is so respectful around you." Johnny shook his head. "My sisters weren't allowed to date until they were almost out of college."

"Why, is *your* dad the chief of police?" Chloe snapped. "And Mason is not respectful. Why would you say that?"

"It offends you that I said your boyfriend is respectful? For the love of God, why?" Johnny smiled. "Chivalry truly is dead."

Chloe didn't know why that offended her. Maybe because it

made Mason seem courteously distant, and the fact that Johnny, who'd known them for all of two days, could see it bugged her.

She sprang to Mason's defense. "He's a very good boyfriend," she said. "He behaves like a gentleman. He's in an unfamiliar house. Otto scares him. He was trying to be extra polite so he wouldn't accidentally insult our hosts."

"You're saying back home Mason is not polite?" Johnny was smiling like he was teasing. And she kind of heh-heh smiled back, but remained tight-lipped. At home Mason was also polite. Also respectful. Chloe remembered what she had written in Mason's yearbook. It had taken her a long time to find the right words. *High school sucks but you made it so much better. You're literally my best friend, and the best boyfriend. I love you so much, because you're the best, funniest, cutest boy ever. I hope we can stay together for a long time. Thanks for making my life not suck. I love you, babe.*

Why did she write she hoped they could stay together? She was going to San Diego. She knew what happened to long-distance sweethearts. And yet she couldn't imagine her life untethered from the people she had grown up with. That was the truth. What she wrote in Mason's yearbook, that was the last tether.

Here on the train, she tried to remember what Mason had written in her yearbook so she could submit to Johnny this further proof of Mason's devotion, but could not.

She did, however, remember what Blake wrote. *A lawyer or a florist, that or something else, anything, everything, the gold drum is beating and the cannon is firing for you. I can't wait to see what you do next.*

Because there was no pressure with recalling Blake's words. God, it was so obvious! Johnny was confounding her and she couldn't think. Frowning, she avoided his eyes. They were dark, impenetrable, today the iris and the pupil nearly the same color. It was hard to see inside him. Yet he was able to see inside things that weren't him. Here was Chloe failing to figure him out, and here was Johnny figuring out things that were not meant to be figured out in the slightest. Chloe didn't want to explain Mason. She didn't want to explain Hannah. She didn't want to tell Johnny about Hannah's Silver Pines restlessness, or why Blake and Hannah started going together and were now pretending to be happy. She didn't want to tell Johnny about college, or that this twenty-one-day trip was like the last thing you did before you loaded the rest of your bags onto the moving truck waiting downstairs. Is this what Johnny was intuiting from their waning teenage intimacy?

"You know what it is," he said. "You four seem more like brothers and sisters than boyfriends and girlfriends."

Oh, that pricked her. Why did so many things he say feel like sandpaper on her skin, making her constantly want to explain, defend? Shut up and sing, she wanted to say. She couldn't figure out why the conversation wasn't easier. He wasn't meaning to offend, was he?

"No, that's not true," she said. "Why do you say that? We're comfortable together, sure. That's because we've known each other for so long."

"You don't seem that comfortable together," Johnny said. "Familiar, yes. But not comfortable."

She said nothing.

"I could be wrong," he said.

"You're completely wrong." She dropped the subject. But here was the thing. He didn't drop the subject. As the train sped on toward Kaunas, he kept inquiring about her quiet life, as though she were Phileas Fogg and not Chloe.

"What did your mom do before she met your dad?"

"She was a dancer."

"Really?"

"Is that surprising? She studied hard. Imagine, in Pembina, North Dakota, a fifth-generation Chinese-American woman dances because she thinks it's her ticket out."

"Was she good?"

"She was good."

"But then she met your dad."

"Yes, and stopped dancing."

"She does a lot of other things now, it sounds like."

"Not dancing."

His eyes mined her face. "Does this upset you? She can't be a mother and a dancer."

Why couldn't she be both, Chloe wanted to say.

Johnny was fascinated by Lang and Jimmy and the green cabin in the pine needles in the clearing. She couldn't understand it. Why couldn't Johnny see how small her life was?

"Excuse me for a moment," she said, standing up. She bolted from the compartment. Making her way down the narrow single-file corridor, she slid open the heavy door and stood between the train cars, wind blasting her face and tangling her hair. Johnny sat too close to her, all over her personal space, and stared at her too intently. The conversation panicked her, made her skin clammy, her throat dry. There was no water, and no AC, and no respite, and there was no way to change the subject. He was too single-minded; he would not be diverted. She had to find her inner voice, tell him to stop asking her things. She briefly and insincerely wished she hadn't run to the station with him, but stayed with her safe friends instead. They never asked her things. She marched forward but felt battered and knocked down. She could not get away.

What was she going to do for the next nine hours, changing trains, eating, drinking, talking, sitting, all with *him*? And what if she needed to go to sleep? Was she going to fall asleep with her head on his shoulder? Was he going to watch over her as she slept?

It wasn't fair to Johnny that Chloe was so inept at dealing with boys other than Mason, other than Blake. It wasn't his fault she lived on a sheltered lake, protected from all sides by parents and flowers and pines and old friends, friends like family. Why in the world did he listen to her stories about it like it was better than Barcelona?

She carried so many illusions about the city of dreams she hadn't yet seen with her own eyes. What if it didn't exist, this mythical place of sacrificed virgins and roses? She had decided to give Johnny a day of her life, but what else would he take from her besides?

Unfamiliar thirst darkened her veins, a pitted hunger her abdomen.

The train hadn't stopped, but there were two new people in their compartment when she returned to her seat. It was full up. Eight for eight. There was a British man and a French woman who spoke briefly to one another and then opened their books.

Johnny was in her seat next to the window, his *U.S. Army Survival Handbook* opened. "Law of adverse possession," he said when she demanded her seat back. "You move, you lose." He waved his book around. "Do you realize that with the help of this manual, we could get lost, jump off the train, make our way through the woods with almost nothing, and be okay, find our way?"

She pulled him by his slender but steely forearm. He didn't budge.

"Have you found your way?" she asked. "Come on, shift."

"No, but I have no fear with the manual of life in front of me."

Finally done teasing her, he moved. Relieved, she assumed her rightful place next to the window. The glass was a place to hide. "Uh, why would we jump off the train?"

"Just saying."

"What about if we remain *on* the train? Does your dumb book tell us how to procure food on fast-moving public transportation?"

"Yes, indeed." He pretended to turn to page 230. "It says right here, wait an hour, get off at Kaunas, buy some extra sandwiches at the coffee shop at the station to tide yourselves over until Sestokai." He grinned at her, and she returned it with a youthful smile of her own. There was something about Johnny Rainbow that pierced her heart with both sorrow and gladness, cut apart the place which all of herself came from. She didn't know what it was. His friendly smile, his elfin face, his pulled-back hair, his dark stubble, his face young and yet grown up, full of youth, yet having seen too much, his calm eyes full of some preternatural somber knowledge, all of it swaying her, frightening her.

It's just the motion of the train, she convinced herself, as his shoulder bumped her shoulder.

People were listening, no matter how quietly they talked. The gentleman who'd been trying to get some rest since Vilnius said to Johnny, "Do you mind?" after Johnny laughed especially loud at something Chloe had said.

"Do I mind what?"

"Keeping it down. I am trying to sleep."

"I'm not telling you not to sleep," Johnny said.

"I can't sleep with you so loud."

"So move to another car."

"You move to another car."

Johnny opened his hands. "Dude. Tell it to the conductor. Complain to him about my laughing."

The man cursed under his breath.

"You should feel grateful," Johnny said. "In the car next to us, they've been drinking for hours and singing songs completely out of pitch and out of time. You want to sit in that car instead?"

"I made a polite request."

"You've been hissing since Vilnius. This car doesn't say no talking. It doesn't say no laughing. And this car is definitely not a sleeping car. I know that for a fact. Because the sleeping cars are down the corridor and cost more money. You should've gotten a berth there."

The guy shut up, but after that, it was hard to be cute, to giggle, to talk nonsense.

Johnny asked her to take out her journal and pen. In it he wrote, *The man needs to get laid*. She barely stifled a laugh. *Let's play a game*, he wrote. He drew a tic-tac-toe board. She beat him seven times. Okay, what else? He drew a hangman. They played for five minutes. Got bored.

How do you know how to speak Russian, she wrote.

Oh, we're playing the Socratic game, he wrote. *Okay. My dad studied it in school. Taught me.*

Where did he go to school?

Somewhere exclusive and elite on the Hudson River. You got two questions, now I get two. Who do you want to be when you grow up?

A lawyer, she wrote. *Or maybe a florist. Because I love the law. But flowers are so pretty.*

He laughed out loud, and four people woke up, including the grumpy unlaid gentleman.

Don't do that, he wrote. *Don't make me laugh. You'll get us thrown off the train for mirth.*

How bad would that be, thought Chloe.

He smiled at her, and that brought her happiness. When they passed the pen back and forth, his long flexible fingers scraped against hers. His pads were rough and calloused from playing guitar. She wanted to touch the bony knuckles on his hands. She wanted to place her little white hand over his. *What do you want to be when you grow up*, she wrote.

And he wrote back, *Alive.*

The Red River flooded, he wrote. *Pembina got wrecked. Your dad was sent up to help people out of homes that were like boats.*

Yes, she wrote.

So he rescued your mother? Why was Johnny smiling?

Yes, so?

That is so great.

It is? Why?

Was it love at first sight?

Eww. I don't know. Weirdo. This was her parents they were writing about! Talk about awkward. As if her parents could ever be young, or in love.

While she wrote down things, he studied her in a way that was almost prehensile, almost as if he were grasping her with his hands, outlining her cheeks and nose and lips with his fingers.

How did your mom and dad meet? she wrote.

She was a music teacher at my aunt's school. My aunt introduced them.

Like set them up on a date?

Exactly like that.

Did your dad like your mom's singing? she wrote. Kind of like I feel about your singing. Like I'm dropped abandoned into all the colors of the crayon box.

I think he liked her face, wrote Johnny.

Is your mother pretty? Chloe was certain she must be.

She was a beauty queen.

A beauty queen for real?

A real bona fide, no kidding beauty queen. She won Miss New Mexico. She was third runner-up Miss America.

What??

Oh yeah.

Why didn't he look more proud when he wrote that?

A beauty and a singer.

Yes. You'd think she had everything. Johnny stopped looking at Chloe.

Didn't she? Chloe wrote. *Didn't she have everything?*

You'd think so.

Your dad must have been smitten.

You'd think so. She watched him blink. He wasn't smiling when he wrote down his answer. *My dad wasn't young when he met her. He was older. She was twenty-three. He knew other women before my mom. She was always jealous. She thought he loved them more. She'd ask, do you love me? Would you give your right arm for me? And he'd say, I'm thinking, I'm thinking. She never thought that was funny. She'd ask, would you run out onto the breaking ice for me? And he'd reply, the question is, dear Ingrid, would you run out onto the ice for me?*

Chloe didn't know what to ask next. That made her sad and she couldn't say why. Maybe because he looked sad.

Tell me your favorite song, he wrote.

Dunno, she wrote. *"She Will Be Loved" by Maroon 5?*

Why is there a question mark? Don't you know?

She almost giggled, suddenly bashful. She was unsure of her own opinion, watching his hands as he held the pen, writing things in her journal, words she would keep, like a recording of their trip, etched on lined paper, for her posterity, for her forever.

The train chugged along, windows grimy, fields outside, rivers, flatlands, marshes, pine forest, sometimes all at once. She wished they could have walked around Vilnius. Why did she suddenly want that? To stop writing, to start talking. To walk together, maybe down the street, to a park while he told her things. This headline approach wasn't working for her. She wanted all her nerves exposed by his reckless voice.

Who sings it to you?

No one, she wrote, frowning. *I just like it.* Little Jimmy gone less than a month, her mother had forced her to go to an end-of-year karaoke barbecue on the Academy common. The kids dragged out the karaoke machine, and all took turns pretending to sing the pop songs of the year. No one sang "She Will Be Loved" to Chloe. Accessible to all, it was just sung into the balmy June air. There were other songs sung that night under the Maine stars. "I Will Survive," the perennial karaoke favorite. "Total Eclipse of the Heart," another. "Piano Man." "Paradise by the Dashboard Light."

The memory of the last one plucked Chloe out of the blue tumult of the Lithuanian moment and dropped her into the blue tumult of the Maine moment. A dozen boys were on one side, with Mason, with Blake among them, a dozen girls on the other, with Chloe, with Hannah, the karaoke machine on the ground between them, new hot coals on the fire, parents coming soon to retrieve them, and for nine minutes, at the top of their screeching voices, they harmonized with Meat Loaf about teenage frenzy and adult disillusionment. Those nine minutes to this day remained one of Chloe's favorite memories. Who would love her forever? She needed to know right now. Those nine minutes and the couple of minutes at the hidden-away picnic bench that followed. The minutes she never let herself think about.

Why are you smiling? Johnny wrote.

She shook her head, tried to stop smiling.

Even Hannah had sung along with the girls, and she was usually above such infantile activities. It was later that night that she and Blake first got together. Maybe it was the Meat Loaf song that tipped the scales in Blake's favor. Or was it in Hannah's favor? Blake was certainly the most exuberant of all the boys, swearing he would love her till the end of time.

The wetlands, the marshlands, the pines drifted by.

If you could be anywhere in the world, where would you want to be? he wrote.

Here and now, she wanted to say. But couldn't and wouldn't.

Ibiza, she wrote. She didn't even know where Ibiza was. She had read about it in one of the *National Geographics* Blake had bought for her from Polly in Fryeburg. Ibiza was paradise. *What about you?*

Here and now is pretty good, Johnny wrote. *Like I'm still in junior high on a crowded train.*

She didn't want to show him her pleased face. She showed it to the spruce and elms flying by.

But if not here and now, then Manitoulin Island, he continued. *Check it out. It's in the middle of nowhere surrounded by water. And it's got Misery Bay. Who could ask for anything more.*

I'm hungry, she wrote.

Kaunas is next. There's a park outside the train station. We'll have time to buy food and drink. I'll buy beer and Coke, and you'll buy water and Coke. We'll get sandwiches and potato chips and cookies, and a whipped cream cake that is surely going to melt. You'll forget your daily budget and spend all your per diem on food for the train. My survival handbook demands it. What if the train gets stuck between stations? What if the engine blows out? What if there is a mishap, an accident and we're forced to live in the woods for days? You'll need a cream cake then, won't you?

Chloe read his words, longing for a minor mishap. Then for a few minutes out of the rest of her life she would be forced to live in the woods with him without other eyes on her. Strangers' eyes. Friends' eyes.

Where are you going to learn to be a legal florist? Johnny wrote. *Or is it a floral lawyer?*

And just like that, back in reality, Chloe was cornered. She could either lie to him as she had been lying by omission and commission to her friends, or tell him the truth. She could trust him with the truth as he had trusted her with his guitar. Tottering on the beam between light and lies made her pen fall silent.

Kaunas. The red domes of the Gothic castle swim by her eyes. She sees but doesn't see, is hungry but is not, thirsty but not really. She just wants the minutes to slow down. She'll tell him anything, confess anything, profess anything, just so Enrico Caruso, masquerading as Einstein with his eternally repeating transcendentals, figures out a way to sing a brake onto time.

He watched her conflicted face with amusement. "You'd think I asked you about the meaning of life," he whispered. "Chloe, you do know where you're going to college, don't you?"

She didn't want her answer to appear on irrefutable paper.

Wait, I remembered, he wrote. *Hannah said UMaine, right?*

Chloe's pen hovered in the air.

He took her hand and drew it to the paper. Still she refused to write it. *He took her hand* is what she was feeling. Squeezed it into a ball inside his palm.

Ah, he wrote. *Not UMaine?*

She leaned over to his ear, to his ponytailed head. She was so close to his stubble, she could kiss it if she moved a lyric note forward. "San Diego," she whispered into his cheek.

In confusion and delight, he laughed, banging one loud slap on his black velvet case.

!!! Now I understand everything, he wrote. *It's not they who are detached from you. It's you who is detached from them.*

That's not true!

Why San Diego?

She scratched out his question.

They gave me a full ride, she wrote. *And it's warm.*

It's very far from Maine.

It's warm.

It's far.

I'm not running away, she wrote, defensively. *My mother approves.*

I didn't think you were running away from your lovely mother.

Chloe lost interest in doodling back and forth. Gripping the pen, she pressed her head to the window and wrote nothing.

He grabbed the pen from her. *Do they know?*

She didn't reply.

Oh my God, Chloe. No one knows? Not even Mason?

Mason can't keep a secret. Was Chloe going to scratch out the whole thread of this conversation? Easier to just rip out the pages of the journal and stuff them down her throat.

You don't think? wrote Johnny. He drew pictures of bass clefs and treble clefs over and over, as if thinking. *When do you plan to tell them?*

Dunno. After Barcelona?

Johnny shook his head in mock disapproval. Maybe not mock.

Listen to me, he wrote after a few minutes had passed. *I know you're afraid to tell them, to tell Mason. Don't be afraid. Tell him. It'll be fine. You'll see.*

How do you know?

I know.

How?

I just know.

You don't think he'll be upset?

No.

Why not?

He won't be upset, wrote Johnny, *because he doesn't love you.*

She sprang from her seat as if scalded, turned and faced him. Six other people getting ready to change trains were awake and grimly staring at her, about to make a scene. Johnny, hands slightly open in quiet question, sat silently, his blinking mild eyes on her. Red in the face and panting she stood without words. He raised his hands in surrender. "Don't be mad at me," he said. "Be mad at him. He's the one who doesn't love you." She yanked her bag down, clamped her mouth shut and stood facing the door. She said nothing.

They were off the train and in line for sandwiches at the Kaunas station when she finally spoke. "Why would you say that?" She tried not to sound upset and failed.

"I'll tell you when we get our food and sit down."

Chloe was suddenly not hungry. But they bought sandwiches and walked outside, deep into the rambling green park across the street. They found a secluded bench. "It isn't true," she said. She didn't open her smoked ham and cheese baguette.

He opened his. "So why are you so bent out of shape, then?" He ate heartily.

"Because it isn't true!" She had to get up again, up and around, to face him, to face him standing.

His mouth was full as he tried to chew and swallow before he spoke. "If I say you're a gazebo, will you also get this mad?"

"I'm not mad. And it's not the same. You're ... you're casting aspersions."

"Not at all. Listen to me. Are you listening?"

"No."

"Can you sit down?"

"No."

"Mason is a nice boy," Johnny said. "He is polite. We've established his good manners. Treats you with respect, blah blah. But you misunderstand his motives. He is not easygoing and indulgent of your anxieties and whims because he's in love with you. He is indulgent because he isn't."

She was still standing, stiff at attention. One should be on one's feet when receiving news like this.

"Just think of all the questions in your head, about him, about the way he acts. What I told you is the answer to them all. That's how you know I'm right. It's hardly news," Johnny added. "It's been in front of you all along."

Chloe sat down. She stopped talking to Johnny as she opened her sandwich and ate listlessly in gloomy thoughtful silence. "But he's so good to me," she said quietly when she was done eating. "He calls when he's supposed to. Remembers my birthday. Holds my hand. Walks me to the door."

"Never oversteps his bounds?" Johnny asked.

"Never!" she said triumphantly.

"That's how you know," said Johnny. "Who ever loved within bounds?"

She threw out their trash and returned to the bench. They had only a few minutes before boarding the train.

"How many hours to Sestokai?" she asked, wishing despite the latest calumny that the train would be slow and that their compartment would have no people so she could talk alone to him, sit alone with him.

"Just over three. Hey, wanna smoke a joint with me?"

She was dumbfounded.

"You've piffed before, right?"

"Pfft," she said. "Of course. Hundreds of times."

"You don't say."

"Dozens and dozens. I mean, yeah. Who hasn't? You have some with you?"

"Always."

She swallowed and came clean. "Maybe you didn't hear me when I told you I was the police chief's daughter. No one, and I mean no one, does drugs in front of me. Or even talks about drugs."

"So the answer is no?"

"Police and chief and daughter. The answer is no."

"Okay, don't tell your dad. So do you want to smoke with me or not?"

She watched as he opened a zip-lock gallon bag—inside which was another gallon bag, inside which was another gallon bag—and pulled out and unrolled a red jewelry roll. Inside were several (many?) pre-made joints of varying thickness. He pulled out a thin one, and flicked on his lighter. "Ready?"

She had smoked once, a couple of years back, when she was sixteen. Taylor's friends were going on about it, and Chloe didn't want to be even more the nerd. She took a puff, nothing happened, she took another, felt light-headed, said that's enough, and that was that. But she hadn't told Johnny the complete truth.

"It's not about my dad, really," she said, watching him take long drags on the joint. Though it was true, no one brought out drugs in front of her. "You want to know why I don't?"

"Sure." He took a deep inhale, closed his eyes, and waited. To hear her, to exhale.

"Because I'm afraid of death," she said.

He laughed. "It's pot, not heroin."

"All the same," she said. "That's why I don't. That basketball player who took one hit of cocaine, had a heart attack and died? That will be me."

"What basketball player? One hit of coke and death? Poor asshole. Clearly he was doing it wrong."

At sixteen, it hadn't been a great and glorious high for Chloe. But Johnny was smoking deliciously now, his eyes rapturously closed, his head back, his wavy ponytail swinging. He was tantalizing. She reached for the joint. "Give it here," she said with a small resigned sigh. Maybe grass was better now, greener, she thought as she put it in her mouth. And maybe, just maybe— she closed her eyes and took one toke and another, holding the joint in her mouth for a moment and passing it back to him— this would be the closest she'd ever get to touching his great and glorious mouth.

She thought she heard him quoting the manual about survival, and he was—about clear plastic bags layered inside one another, hiding the smell of all pertinent vegetation. "Because"— and here he laughed—"said vegetation has such a strong and recognizable scent, that sometimes nosy and stupid police officers in foreign countries smell it, search you, find it, and then make all kinds of trouble for you, all because you carried a little vegetation for strictly leisurely use."

"What kind of trouble?"

"Oh, some juvy pissing annoying trouble. All kinds of hassle for absolutely fucking nothing. Never mind, it's all over with now."

Chloe dimly remembered Reverend Kazmir talking about the new and improved Latvian drug laws. Had some bad things happened to Johnny?

The joint was almost done, the train was leaving in ten minutes. "I know what you're thinking," Johnny said. "That this amount I got on me seems like more than I might carry under normal circumstances for personal use, but that's only because I'm traveling from country to country and don't want to be stuck scrounging to acquire some ganja, snow or mud from sources unknown after being on trains for a thousand kilometers, do you know what I mean?"

Here was the thing. When that sentence began, Chloe knew what he meant. But by the time it ended, she no longer had any idea. He started swimming in front of her eyes, doing the backstroke, and she was swimming in circles in front of his circles. Her feet no longer felt on solid ground, and the feet weren't so solid either.

He said something like we have to go and she said something like where. He was pulling her up except she was swaying. He said they had to run or they would miss it, and she laughed so hard because she couldn't run, but also because, miss what?

She was pulled by him in a zigzag across the street to a big building and then he left her wandering the concourse and ran off. She wondered how he could be running when she couldn't even drift in a circle. He came back, said, come on, they're holding the train, but hurry, and try to look normal. Or they'll have us arrested. You don't want that, do you? God knows, I *can't* have that. So please, Chloe. Just walk straight, and blink like a normal person. She tried to say I am walking straight, but the words were meandering and she couldn't get them out.

He got her inside the train, set her down by the window, sat next to her, but too close. Not because she didn't want him close but because she was spinning and needed the space to spin freely. As the train gathered speed, she too gathered spinning speed, and remembered all too clearly why she had smoked only once and never again. It was because of this. She couldn't sit up, stand up, talk. She couldn't understand what Johnny was saying. All that kept going round and round inside as she went round and round outside was, please let this end, please let this end, please let this end, and then somewhere deeper still, not spinning, not moving and not fading was the raw regret that this is what she had instead of what she wanted, which was to be present for every second of the dance in the garden with him after vespers. What she got was nothing.

"CAUTION: Do not use poisonous vegetation," the book had clearly said, his manual for living. Johnny had all the survival techniques down. He used all his senses. He remembered where he was. He vanquished fear. He improvised. He acted like a native, lived by his wits, knew basic skills. He valued living.

He did value living, right? He wasn't dying while he was living, was he?

Loud music on the train from down the corridor. Raucous laughter. The fermented yeasty smell of beer. Then fighting. She hears but doesn't see. Every time she pries open her eyes she is spinning spinning, her head bobbing.

Yet his stubborn arm is around her.

She wishes she were more present in the moment in which his long tattooed arm cradles her. But here's the conundrum, and she understands it, even as she rolls in the air, and he tries to weigh her down. Just with his hand, not his body. For shame. The conundrum is this. If she weren't spinning out of orbit— nauseated, dizzy, unable to sit straight or open her eyes—his pale copper arm wouldn't be wrapped around her lapis lazuli shoulder. He touches her because she is not present enough to sit without being untouched. She is absent from her body. If her soul and body are in one place, his hands are to himself. If she is here, he is far away.

Yet the way she is now, she cannot feel as a girl does, cannot react as a girl does. So what good is it? She can't talk to him, or smile, or look out the window or make jokes. She can't laugh. Her rational controllable self is back on the bench in Kaunas, taking the joint from his hands. That was the last moment her conscious Chloe acted from her Chloe free will. When her fingers touched his as he passed her the demon weed on a summer day, and she wanted him to think she was Miss Cool, not a shadow drip full of failings.

She doesn't know how long she lingers in limbo between sleep and light. She is dimly aware of the noises down the corridor getting louder. Dimly aware of his angly black-clad shoulder pressing into her cheek. All she wants is to be herself again.

To make matters more unpleasant, he keeps trying to engage her in conversation, just like before Kaunas. Their compartment is empty. They could be having the most breathtaking discussion. They could be talking about feelings. Chloe could finally tell him what she has been unable to articulate, about the boxes her parents had built to hide little Jimmy from themselves and from her, containers like coffins the size of Lang and big Jimmy. Little Jimmy was on the outside and they were on the inside. It took a long while for them to climb out. They chipped and chipped away, whittling the boxes down to the size of little Jimmy. Now they carry the boxes with them wherever they go. Is that what you wanted to know? How you do it? That is how you do it. You either put yourself in a crate or your grief in a crate. And then you nail it shut.

Chloe could tell Johnny about Hannah and her desire to be excited, to be loved. She could tell him why he's wrong about Mason, why he's right about Mason, and she could tell him about Blake and the moment years ago on a picnic bench after Meat Loaf's paradise. She could tell him so many things. They could discuss smart things, too, like vector graphics and pi's senseless procession to infinity. Instead he keeps asking if she wants a drink, a potato chip, a piece of gum, and even that's too intellectual a conversation because her mouth won't cooperate with her brain. It's true what they say. God chose what is foolish in the world to shame the wise.

She opens her eyes. She is lying across three seats. He is opposite her, reading his survival manual. What does it say about stoned girls spread out across your bench? He helps her up. He seems completely normal, as before. She feels slightly better, though woozy and thirsty. As if he knows this, he gives her a drink. Wow, he says. You are something else. She doesn't think he means it as a compliment. She sits like a lump for a few minutes, three or forty, she can't tell. He says soon they'll be in Sestokai. How long was I out, she says. More than two hours, he replies.

Possibly three. Oh the black regret! Three hours. Gone. She won't have another chance to be on the train alone with him. She won't have another chance to sit close to him. This was it. And she wasted it, literally. She found the longed-for diamond hours taped to the lid of the communal toilet, a hot bounty of time, a gift of grace, and flushed them down the bowl, and wasn't even cognizant enough to watch them swirl.

By the time they got off in Sestokai, she was famished. She bought herself another parma ham and cheese sandwich and devoured it on a lonely bench in a small dim park nearby. It was after seven in the evening, sun still out, but shadows long.

"Sorry I'm such a baby," she said.

"It's my fault. I never should've offered. I'm the one who's sorry."

"I took it from you."

"I didn't know you'd react like that. I won't do it again. I was worried for a minute. But then you went to sleep. I hoped after you woke up, you'd be better."

"I am better. Not a hundred percent."

"Chloe," he said, "I don't remember a time in my life when I was a hundred percent. Welcome to the grown up world."

She shook her head. "I know you couldn't possibly feel like that. You couldn't drive a boat or play chords and feel like I felt."

He didn't speak for a moment. "Did you consider the possibility that I can't drive a boat or play or sing unless I feel like you felt?"

"No," she said. "No." She ate. She drank a Coke. She felt human. This was human. The other thing, that was possession. "Speaking of singing," she said to change the unwelcome subject from pathetic self to fantastic him, "what are you going to do after the army? You're not planning to be a career soldier, are you?"

"I'm not planning very much at all."

She turned her head to his grave face. "You sing like no one I've ever heard in my whole life, Johnny. I'm not complimenting you, Johnny, I'm just stating fact. You have the great fortune of never having to figure anything out, like the rest of us dumb mortals. What am I going to be, what am I going to do, how will I live. All that handwringing. It's not for you. You don't have to ask yourself anything. You will be a rock star."

He smiled with rueful pride. "You think?"

"I have no doubt. You've got the goods."

"All the goods?" he said provocatively without glancing at her. "How do you know I haven't been there, done that? Not like a rock star, but like a lone star." Lifting his black tee, he showed her the tattoo on his bare chest.

"Wait," she said, "is Johnny Rainbow your stage name? Like Johnny Rainbow and the Hail of Bullets?"

He was delighted. He slapped his knee. "If I ever again get a band together, you can be sure that will be my name for it," he said. "Johnny Rainbow and the Hail of Bullets. Fantastic. What did you say you wanted to be when you grow up? A creative director?"

"A florist," she said, and he laughed like she was Seinfeld.

They were on the bench, Chloe still feeling like muddy water, gazing at him as he talked. Johnny was telling her about hazel and holly, the best tree fuels for warmth, and about collecting moss and bark tinder to make the strongest fire. A tall man walked by. He said something in another language, extending his hand.

"Sorry, I don't speak Lithuanian," Johnny said.

"Do you have a few dollars for food," the man said in English.

"Oh, look," Johnny muttered, leaning to Chloe, "a multi-lingual beggar." And louder, "No, sorry," barely even looking the bum's way.

The man in rags stopped in front of them. He didn't move.

"Maybe you can play me a song, then," he said, a notch louder, pointing to Johnny's guitar.

Carefully Johnny gave back to Chloe the remains of her sandwich and raised his steady eyes to the foul-smelling man in rags.

Chloe searched up and down the street. It was empty. A few blocks down she could see people, but they were two countries away for all the good they would do them now. Propelled out of her post-stoned mud into something colder and sharper and more real, she became afraid for Johnny's guitar. That's what she thought of first. Johnny's guitar.

"Dude," Johnny said, pointing at the sidewalk. "Those feet of yours, they're meant for walking. Use them. Keep on walking."

"Sing me a song, man, and I'll give you a dollar."

"What did I say? And where's this dollar?"

From the mysteries of his ruined threads, the scrounger produced a torn piece of a crumpled greenback and threw it at Johnny. "Now sing," he said. There was hard menace in his voice.

Casually Johnny flicked the half-dollar off his jeans.

"Johnny, we should go," whispered Chloe, her legs feeling like macaroni.

"No," Johnny replied in his normal voice. "You haven't finished eating, and I haven't finished telling you about bark tinder." To the man, he said, "I have a sore throat today. Not good for singing. Move along."

"I gave you money, so sing."

"No."

"Why?"

"Because I don't fucking feel like it. Get going."

"I don't feel like going," the man said. "And I don't think you understand me." Chloe blinked. In his hands the man brandished a two-foot-long steel pipe.

Chloe didn't gasp. She didn't have time to take a breath.

Johnny grabbed his guitar and swung it over the back of the bench, and then and only then did he push Chloe sideways, forcing her to slide as far as possible away from the beggar, and then and only then did Johnny stand up. Without any preface, his leg kicked out, knocking the steel pipe out of the man's hands and sending it flying twenty feet into the street, where it landed with a thud on the concrete.

"You want to race for it?" Johnny said in his calm voice, as the man's eyes darted wildly from his pipe in the street to Johnny's face. "Go ahead. But you better be quicker than me, because trust me, you don't want me to get to it first."

Mumbling furiously under his breath, the hooligan backed away, and when he was far enough from Johnny, he turned and ran screaming into the street. He grabbed his pipe and hightailed it down the boulevard, screaming the whole way. Johnny sat back down. "Can I have another bite of your sandwich, please? Now, where were we? Have I told you about close contact weapons?"

Chloe inhaled, still staring down the street after the vagrant, the half-eaten sandwich lying dully in her lap. "Um, no, I don't believe you have." She handed him the baguette.

"A knife or a long sharp bone is best," Johnny said, taking a big bite. "A stone polished away on one end to a dull edge can also be useful for puncturing or post-making. But sometimes, at close quarters, do you know what's needed most?"

She shook her head.

"A *sochin dachi* and a *sokuto*. An immovable stance and a foot kick."

"Ah."

"Finish, please. We have to go."

She couldn't stop staring at him with fresh marvel. "Where did you learn how to do that?"

"Do what? Kick a pipe? A baby could do it."

Yet the baby that was Chloe couldn't do it.

The Polish train from Sestokai to Warsaw was stuffed to the ceiling beams with people. Yes, she was awake and aware, but the loud, small, unpleasant others in their compartment precluded conversation, intimate or otherwise. A mother and father kept a sleeping baby next to them and placed two whining dervish children next to Johnny. A nasty-looking woman with underarm hair like a man's sat across from Chloe, smelling awful and constantly reaching overhead to get food and magazines out of her bag, unabashedly displaying her hirsuteness. The light was on in the cabin, and outside was night. There was nothing to look at except her own reflection in the glass. She got out her book, Johnny got out his. The little brats yapped to Johnny in Polish. They pointed to his guitar. He answered them in Polish, shaking his head. "*Proszę. Proszę coś zagrać na gitarze,*" they kept repeating. The kids tried to touch it. Johnny said no. He stared pointedly at the parents, as if inviting them to do some damn parenting, but they kept eyeing their children with a mixture of impatience and adoration.

Outside the corridor there was awful noise. "It's forbidden to drink on Polish trains," Johnny said. "But as you can hear, people manage. Especially on night trains."

Johnny said it sounded like a rave. Chloe barely knew what a rave was. She nodded wisely.

Their door slid open and an old priest entered. He looked around, said something apologetic in Polish to the parents with the sleeping baby. Gruffly, they moved the child off the seat and into a lap so the priest could sit down. The priest said a few words. Johnny leaned to Chloe. "Father said he had the bad luck to be next door."

The door to their compartment opened again and two drunks stuck their heads in. One of them saw the priest and in clipped British yelled, "Fuck me, a priest!" Quickly they closed the door and moved on. The priest had a good laugh about it.

The lights in the compartment and in the corridor kept flickering off. Johnny said it was a bad sign. He said electrical problems were usually followed by more serious problems with the train. What kind of problems, Chloe wanted to ask, but the small kids kept pulling on Johnny's arm. The priest was gazing at the children kindly and Chloe was embarrassed to be so shabby as to resent small children. It didn't make her stop resenting them, but at least she felt bad about it in the presence of clergy.

"Why are you really going into the Rangers, Johnny?" she asked him, pulling on his other arm, directing his attention away from the little monsters and back to her. "Won't it make it hard for you to be what you're going to be?"

"Which is what?" He smiled.

"A rock star, I told you."

"Why are you so funny?"

"Does the army have something to do with your dad? Geez! Those urchins are driving me nuts. Can't you tell them to leave you alone?"

"I tried."

"Can't you play one song for them to shut them up?"

"I'll be playing for the next two hours, then. I can't. Now what were you asking?"

"Rangers. Dad. Is it for him, or against him? Are you going into the army because of him, or despite him?"

"Neither," Johnny said.

"Why can't you just say no? Just say you won't go."

"Don't have that option anymore, Chloe," Johnny said. "I had it once." He sighed. "I got into a spot of trouble, you see, and my dad helped me out. But his price was the army. He had to pull serious strings to get me into OCS. I told him I didn't think the army was for me, but he said it was. He said it was the only thing that could save me."

"Save you from what?"

"From myself, I guess."

"Do you need to be, um, saved from yourself?"

She fully expected him to joke, to say no, but he didn't. He said nothing.

The lights kept flickering. Each time, the kids squealed with delight, and the priest crossed himself. Each time, the drunks next door whooped and hollered.

"What kind of trouble?" Chloe asked—either about the electrical problems or Johnny's—but no sooner had the words left her mouth than the lights flared bright, as if in a last hurrah, and went out completely. The compartment, the corridor, the whole train was thrown into blackness. Chloe inhaled and waited, one second, another and another. The lights didn't come back. They didn't. She waited for her eyes to get readjusted to night.

They didn't.

"Why is it so dark," she whispered, almost rhetorically or inaudibly. She wasn't sure Johnny could hear her, though he was sitting right next to her, his bare arm pressed against her bare arm.

"It's cloudy," he said. "We're not passing through any towns. There are no lights out in the forest, no roads, and no lights on the tracks."

"But how can the train be moving if the power is down?"

"Diesel powers the train."

"Doesn't it power the lights too?"

"What did I tell you about Polish trains? It's a feast. Don't worry. The lights will come back on in a minute."

She sat, the drunken jeers from next door getting so loud in the blackness that she became frightened. The children started to cry. They weren't next to Johnny anymore, but with their parents across the aisle. She could hear the priest muttering prayers in Polish. The drunks didn't seem afraid, just the opposite. "What are they yelling about?"

"They're trying to figure out if they're dreaming," said Johnny. "Or if they're having a drunken blackout. Apparently they can't tell."

They laughed, sang crazy loud Polish songs, broke things, dropped things. It was obnoxious and stupefying. How could this be allowed? The train continued to roll forward. There was no light of any kind.

She closed her eyes. It was black. She opened them. It was black. Closed, open, the world was free of all color.

On her lids were images of light, even through the fear.

"What are we going to do?" she whispered.

"We?" he whispered back. "You can't see light. You can only see what the light lights up."

"Which is everything."

"Not everything," said Johnny.

Images of Riga. The rainbow-lit Old City, lovingly rebuilt, recreated brand-new to look like the old. The blue roofs, the orange doors, the yellow window frames and sepia cobbles, the red tents of the men selling paintings in Livu Square, the lilac tents of the ice cream carts. The sun blinding everything into shade and white, and Johnny in the center, in the pinpoint of the kaleidoscope, in front of his microphone on a telescopic stand, mouth pressed against it (lucky microphone), eyes closed, gutbucket blues flying supercharged out of his throat, holding the note until Chloe felt it, telling her that all of love is forever or all of love is fleeting …

Eyes open or closed? She couldn't feel herself blink. Her mouth parted slightly to take in an inky breath. She reached out to touch his arm by her side, just to be sure of him, but it wasn't next to her anymore. His arm was behind her. She didn't feel his body turn, or even lean toward hers. She smelled his breath barely an instant before his open lips shivered like a tremor on her open lips. She gasped—into his mouth. His hand was in her hair. His tilted face was pressed against hers. He didn't let her take a breath, he kissed her for the length of the dream that was her life, all in that one ebony moment. He kissed her forever and not long enough, terrifyingly long (what if the lights came on what if everyone else could see what if everyone else could hear his mouth bruise hot against her lips what if they could hear her moan what if they could see the shadow of his face against her face what if what if what if what if), and anguishingly brief. Her hands trembled, her arms, her legs; her quivering back was slung low on the seat, her head was thrown back. She felt at any moment she was going to slide down, onto her back, and he would fall on top of her, and crush her with his body (only if she was very very lucky) with all the Poles, the children and the sick, the sinners and the saints, all manner of souls, watching her.

He was first to pull away. The lights came on.

Or …

The lights came on. He was first to pull away.

She opened her eyes, so slowly, unwillingly waking in the winter dawn.

The noise from next door was insulting her senses, but it also made it difficult to speak, so Chloe didn't. She turned to the window, her hands shaking, her lips still wet, still parted. She clamped shut her mouth, clamped her hands into fists, and leaned against the glass. She was so hot. Drops of sweat streamed hot from her throat onto her breasts, her stiff nipples, down to her stomach. Her spine was wet with electric water. Everything on her was wrong and alive.

Maybe she had imagined it. What would it feel like if she had? Would it feel the same? It was so unexpected, so pulverizing. She didn't dare look his way, but from the corner of her half-blinded eye, she glimpsed him reading his survival manual. What did the book say about the kiss of life in an ice-cold space where everything was suspended without gravity? But she was both, floating and flying. And she wasn't ice cold. She closed her eyes and imagined darkness.

For a long time Chloe didn't speak. The train lumbered on through a countryside she couldn't see. Inside, four people were sleeping, three were reading. The eighth had her face pressed to the window. This eighth person, a wraith of a girl, a ghost of the old Chloe, stared into the mystifying blackness thinking everything and nothing. She came here across the world to doom herself. Encore, encore! Was she an angel or a whore? Did she want to wrap herself in heavy cloth or rip the sheer blue cotton off her body? Go abroad, Chloe, and love a boy, not the one you said you loved, not the one you thought you loved, the one who doesn't love you, but fly across the world to find another lover. In an epileptic tremble she bobbed with the train, in her pretend-penitent reverie entwined in his arms and legs, her hands on his bare back, in his black hair, swirling and swirling together to the murky watery bottom, both of them in a shipwreck.

After this train stops at Central Station in Warsaw, what happens next? Where was Blake to tell her? She and Johnny go together down the street, searching for the hostel, their bags in hand, like travelers, like lovers. And tomorrow? When the others come? Can she talk her way out of this one, see her way out, lie her way out? Can she turn her warm breasts away? Was she caught? And what if she wasn't? What was worse?

To not think, not feel, not be. That was worse.

Had his lips touched her? Encore, encore!

"Hannah is beautiful, isn't she?" Chloe said.

"That's what you're thinking about, Hannah?"

"Isn't she?"

"Maybe," Johnny said, neutrally. "It doesn't matter."

"Doesn't it?"

"She's blonde, she's tall, she's striking, yes," he said. "But so what? Beneath the mask of her self-involved serenity is nothing but bitterness and boredom. She is frivolous. She is empty."

Chloe disagreed. "No, not empty." Why was she always defending her friends to him? One wasn't frivolous, one wasn't crabby, one did love her. "She is full of terrors like everybody else. She's trying to find her way, Johnny. Like you. Like me."

He shook his head. "She doesn't know what she wants."

"Do you know what you want?"

"Yes. Do you know what you want, Chloe Divine?" He lowered his voice an octave to rasp out her name. Otherwise nothing from their desultory words tells her if she dreamed the dream of his lips on her or lived it. She doesn't tell him what she wants. Because what she wants is the last ray of sun all gold on the white foamy water. A mad kiss on a red plate. His rough fingers on her aching velvet skin. What if the boy you worship brings you a pitcher of lemonade? Would you drink it? How can you not?

I'm just frozen champagne bubbling and melting against his flame mouth, O Lord. Forgive me. There is a fine but wretched chance he did not touch me and will never touch me again, and clicking my little boots I'll be forced to walk away and live out the rest of my life haunted by what might have been, live out the rest of my life in the shadow of his streetlamp in the middle of pale night.

24

Missing Time

Chloe

On the outskirts of the Old Town in the center of Warsaw—the Old Town built in 1955 because the war that altered the world had leveled the old Old Town entire—there is a hostel nicer than the others, inasmuch as they could conclude when they read about it in Blake's indispensable guide to Poland. It stands on a quiet street two kilometers away from the Old Town. Not in a great central location, but cheap and clean. That was very important. They had booked two nights, reserving a room with four beds, a sink, and a bathroom down the hall, all for about twenty dollars a person, which was preferable to a hotel, which would cost twice that. Of course a hotel would have had a shower in the room. They decided a private shower wasn't worth an extra hundred dollars a night. It was to this hostel that Johnny and Chloe came near midnight.

The desk manager, awakened and hostile, stood in his tatty robe behind the low counter, looking for her name in his book, in which row after row of names had been written out by a careless hand. That he found her name at all was a miracle. She was a day or two early, since they decided to cancel the travel to Gdansk. She could barely sweet-talk her way into the reservation. Beg, more like. The room was on the third floor. There was no elevator. He ordered them to keep it down as everyone else was already asleep. What did he think they were going to be doing, and noisily, too?

Chloe didn't know what he meant by "everyone" because everyone she saw was wide awake and on the stairs and in the hallways, their doors flung open, smoke and smells emanating, the whole place like a foyer to a sewer.

"How can we stay here?" Johnny, the veteran of Daugavpils crack houses, asked about a three-star hostel in the capital of Poland.

"It's midnight. What do you see as our options?"

The room had four grungy beds, one in each corner, narrow like steamer trunks, the old mattresses bare and stained. The sheets, pillows, pillowcases and blankets were folded in careful squares at the foot of each bed. The room was painted deep green with bright yellow trim. It had brown curtains and a warped wood floor. It was dark; three of the light bulbs were out, and one lamp cord was broken. The water didn't run into the sink. It didn't run at all. If it weren't so late, Chloe would have gone downstairs to complain. But she'd given up complaining for the night.

Johnny waited for her in the dirty pink corridor outside the bathroom. After escorting her back to the room, he told her to lock the door and not let anyone in. He took the key. She asked if he wanted her to wait for him in the corridor as he had waited for her. He half-smiled. "What are you going to do, protect me, Chloe?" he said. Then he left.

Yes, she wanted to say. You should always protect the things you can't do without.

She made up her bed, next to one window, and then his bed, on the opposite wall. She sat on the bed with her hands folded. She sat and sat, and when she grew so tired that she couldn't sit anymore, she put down her head, for just a minute. The bed was hard, the pillow hard. She wondered if he was all right, but was too frightened to go outside to check. The trains and the drunk men, the noisy children and the violent beggars, the green weed and the stark absence of her closest friends, it all intruded into the space where there should have been nothing but candlelight and ripe peaches. She waited and waited. She fell asleep.

She woke up in the middle of the night. She bolted up in bed, because she heard a man screaming in the corridor, walking up and down banging on all the doors. She yelped like a mouse, and then adjusted to the night and saw Johnny in his bed, under the sheet, sleeping. She didn't know how he could be sleeping because the man outside was raging as if everyone was about to die. Johnny, she whispered. Johnny, are you awake? He had propped two chairs against the door, one under the handle, one to the side. She crawled out of bed, because the man was now banging on their door, shrieking in Polish. She got so scared she started to cry. Johnny, Johnny. Kneeling by his low bed, she shook him gently. He didn't stir. In a few minutes the man's outraged voice was answered with another loud voice, then two more, and then the man stopped banging on their door, and was dragged away, shrieking. The noise died down. It was four in the morning. Everyone else had gone back to sleep, but Chloe could not. She sat by Johnny's side, not knowing what to do, and then crept into his tiny bed and squeezed in on her side in front of him. He formed a big C and she a little c. She lay awake, her back pressed against his sleeping inanimate front. He never woke up. And she never went to sleep.

Johnny, she whispered. Johnny.

He opened his eyes, sat up instantly, and smiled at her. They were both in his narrow bed. "Good morning," he said. "Why didn't you wake me when you climbed in?"

"I tried," Chloe said. "How did you not hear? There was a horrible hysteric outside our door in the middle of the night."

"Chloe, if I woke up every time an addict yelled in the corridor, I'd be Al Herpin, the man who never slept, wouldn't I?"

"I don't know. Would you? I didn't get any sleep."

He glanced at his watch. "It's seven. Time to go." Still wearing yesterday's clothes, he jumped up. "I have to go get Emil and the tour van. I'm meeting my group at nine."

Slowly she sat up, swooned, and bobbed back down again. "I feel run over," she said. "Like I've been in an accident and my head came off and someone put it back wrong."

He laughed. He was refreshed, clear-eyed, full of energy. He leaned over her.

"I'm a very sound sleeper," he said.

"Um, I noticed. Why was that man shrieking?"

"Someone probably pinched his stash. He was looking to knife that someone."

"So why was he banging on *our* door?"

"I don't know. I was sleeping." He was still by her side. He touched her face with the back of his fingers. "Can you get up? We have to get going. I hope you're a morning person. Otherwise you and I can never be."

What a funny, tear-inducing thing to say. "Johnny, don't joke. I barely got five minutes of sleep. I can't go anywhere."

"You got some sleep," he said. "Because when I came back, you were out."

"You were gone forever."

"Five minutes. And you were out."

"Well, those were the only five minutes I got."

"Chloe, you have to come with me," he said. "You can't stay here by yourself."

"I'm just going to sleep."

"I've slept in alleys that were safer than this place. You'll be robbed. Or worse."

She shook her head. "Nothing could be worse than going without sleep. I'll go with you tomorrow. I can't today. Look at me."

"I'm looking."

"So stay with me," she said, extra quiet.

He caressed her face. "I would. But I can't. I have five people waiting for me to tell them about death. And I've got a guy who needs to get paid for a van rental. We have to find you another place to stay."

"I can't. We prepaid."

"Yeah, that desk guy didn't seem like the type to offer refunds. Oh well. Forget about the money. Money is paper. Your safety is paramount. Let's jet. I'll take you to another place, but we have to hurry."

"What about Blake and Hannah and Mason?"

"This room is paid for. And I don't know the address of the place I'm taking you. I just know where it is. In the afternoon, when you've had some rest, you can come back here and leave a new address with the manager."

"Where am I going?"

"Castle Inn."

"Is it a hotel or a hostel?"

"A hotel," he said, smiling. "Funny how one letter makes *all* the difference. Right in the Old Town, near the River Vistula and the Royal Castle. You want to see a castle, don't you, princess? Quick, and I'll take you there."

Blake

After a trip that was torture, after a terrible, terrifying, cramped, hungry, eighteen-hour hell ride with three changes and numerous delays, we arrived in Warsaw at almost midnight only to discover that Chloe wasn't where she was supposed to be.

The hostel looked a lot less attractive than it did in the photos, as if a little bait and switch was going on, and when we knocked, no one opened the firmly locked door for nearly ten minutes. When a half-asleep gentleman in a robe finally turned the lock, we were ready to give up.

"You have reservation?" he barked. "Why does everyone come at such hours?"

"This is when the train from Vilnius gets in," I said.

"I don't care," he said. "What name reservation?"

I gave him Chloe's.

"Ah, yes. Khloya Deveeny."

"Chloe. Divine."

"Room on third floor. You are paid until tomorrow, but you have to leave by ten."

"Do you have a key?"

"I gave key to her," he said.

"Her who?"

"Khloya."

"Is she upstairs?"

"I don't know where she is," he replied. "I have one key to room, I gave it her. The rest I don't know."

"She's probably in the room, bro," Mason said. "It's late."

"She not upstairs," said the manager. "She left this morning. Not come back all day."

"I thought you said you didn't know where she was?"

"I made mistake."

"She left this morning?"

"Yes. With suitcase."

"With suitcase?"

"Why you repeat what I say? Yes. Left. This morning. With suitcase. And with man with guitar."

Mason and I exchanged a look, his quizzical, mine murderous.

"Where did they go?" Hannah asked.

"Miss, I not know nothing. I give key, they go to sleep, or whatever. This morning, they come down with suitcase, and they not come back."

"Are you sure?" It was his *whatever* I found especially ill-mannered.

"This my place. You think I not know who come and go?"

Hannah made exhausted, unhappy noises. "Can you just let us into the room, please?"

The manager made exhausted, unhappy noises. "Your names are on reservation, otherwise I no let you upstairs, you understand?"

Really, asshole? I wanted to say. This is your great and proud commitment to the safety and security of your guests? Was Johnny Rainbow's name on the reservation? Yet you let him upstairs. Explain that, why don't you? Elaborate on that pinochle, if you will.

"Thank you so much for your consideration," is what I said.

He gave me a key off his master ring, but would not walk us upstairs. We all went, me pulling my suitcase and Hannah's, and Mason helping her up three flights of shabby, stinking stairs.

I don't know what I expected, but it wasn't this. A dank, square room with a bed in each corner, two of them made, two of them with their mattresses still exposed. There was no sign of Chloe, no sign of Johnny, the window was closed, and it was suffocatingly stuffy. I traipsed downstairs to give the manager back his key.

"You really don't know where they went?" I asked.

"You think I lie to you before? If I know, I tell you. I don't know. Give me key. I have to go to bed."

Slowly I made my way upstairs. Inside the room, there was a round table with two chairs. The other two chairs had been dragged and left on either side of the doorway. I stared at them, trying to figure out why they would be there.

"Blake," Hannah said, "are you going to stand there and analyze the room or are you going to help me push our beds together? I can't seem to move them. They're stuck or something."

I went to help her. The beds were stuck. I felt around on the floor by one of the legs.

"The beds are bolted to the floor, Hannah," I said.

She was putting the pillowcases on and didn't turn around. "I don't think we can both sleep in this bed, Blakie," she said. "It's too narrow."

It did look like half of a twin bed.

"It's fine," I said, suppressing a small sigh. "Don't worry about me. I'll sort myself out." I hoped that was true.

Hannah went out to use the bathroom. Mason and I followed her down the hall like dogs. The hallway smelled worse than the one in Daugavpils, and I didn't think that was possible.

"I know you're worried, dude," Mason said, "but it's okay." He smiled. "You saw the two made-up beds. They're as far apart as they can be."

"Well, they are *bolted* into the floor," I said. My back was to the wall. I didn't look at my brother. "And you're the one who needs to be worried about *that* part, not me. What I'm worried about is more obvious."

"Like?"

"Where the fuck are they?"

That Mason had no answer to.

"Exactly."

"Don't get so worked up. There's a good explanation. You'll see."

"Like what?"

"I don't know, do I? Wasn't he supposed to go on tour today? She probably went with his group. Maybe they had to stay overnight somewhere."

"Like where?"

"Another city. He didn't want to leave her alone here. It's not safe. I wouldn't. You wouldn't. He did the right thing. You'll see. Everything will be clear when we meet up with them."

"If."

"If what?"

I waved Mason away. Nothing felt right. The place was a dump. I can't believe we fell for the pretty pictures. Oh, look, close to town. Oh, look, close to the parks and the churches and the museums. Everything at our fingertips and the place is clean, and painted, and for a small increase we can get a room for the four of us, instead of sharing a dorm room with twenty others. A room with a sink!

The corridor floors were buckling, and it smelled bad, of piss and drink, and also like maybe something had died in the walls and was still busily decomposing. I knew that smell. We have all kinds of rodents, squirrels, raccoons, foxes die in the woods near our house. The smell is how we find them.

We were all too tired, frankly, after days on trains to be too bothered. Hannah changed into her sleeping shorts, and I put on a clean T-shirt and sweatpants. Mason took the bed where Chloe had possibly slept, and Hannah the one she had just made up. I lay on the bed that already had sheets on. I didn't know what was worse. To lie down in the made bed he had been in, or to lie down in the made bed he might not have been in.

I stared at the ceiling and out the half-open window overlooking the courtyard where they threw out the trash and the dead animals, overlooking other windows with cats and drying towels in them. I listened for the noise of the city, which had quietened down at two in the morning. I still couldn't sleep.

What was troubling me?

What *wasn't* troubling me. Missing Chloe. Not writing notes for my story. Hating Johnny. Worrying about Hannah. On the train she'd been so withdrawn. Blowing through Lithuania without seeing a half-hour of Vilnius. Our train had been monstrously delayed. We were supposed to get into Vilnius at eight in the morning, but didn't get in until 11:05 with the train to Warsaw leaving at 11:20. I mean, my God, we were in Lithuania, and we didn't even get to walk through the Gates of Dawn! Why even come to the Baltics?

On the train, in the cabins next to us, every single person was deafeningly drunk. They bellowed in blurred voices and called it singing. They laughed like hyenas but then, with their next breath, fought like carrion crows over God knows what, shrieking and screeching. They yelled for the conductor, ran up and down the aisles, got into a shoving match that was going to get out of hand in about five seconds, and then did. A fist flew out, someone's hair got pulled, there was caterwauling, and blood. The women rushed out into the corridor, to calm down the men, we thought, but no. They joined in the mêlée. A whole suitcase got thrown out the window! A suitcase went flying, in the middle of the day. It wasn't even lunchtime yet, and they were this drunk. The conductor said, "They got drunk last night. They stayed drunk."

It went on for hours. No one stopped them, no one even complained. In Kaunas, I asked the helpful, English-speaking conductor why no one did anything about it, and he confessed sheepishly that it was because everyone was afraid of them. Great.

But then it *was* great. We had to change trains in Kaunas, and the rabble-rousers forgot to get back on! We saw them from our windows running down the platform and waving madly. I think the engineer actually sped up when he saw them trying to flag his train down. That was pretty awesome.

The ride from Kaunas to Sestokai was quieter but also less entertaining and therefore interminable. Hannah slept, Mason too. They're like bears, the both of them. They can sleep anywhere. Actually, Hannah can't. Her sleeping surprised me. I tried to work a little bit, write in my back journal, think about my story, but I couldn't. I was too busy staring out the window and thinking about dumb things.

Lithuania is beautiful. For hours I gazed at the pine forests and the rivers and regretted we hadn't stopped in Vilnius. Our Lady at the Gate of Dawn is the only city-gate of the original nine still standing, through all the wars and destruction. The icon of the Mother of God is supposed to have healing powers. People come to it from all over the world to pray. I would have liked to pray for a few things. For my dad's back. To win the truck so Mase and I could start our business. To write this novella about mysteries and stolen treasures and suitcases full of magic things with healing powers. Instead, nothing.

I guess I forgot to pray that we'd find Chloe again because she's not here. Maybe Mason is right, and she left because this place was horrible. But how could she have forgotten to tell us or the robed hostelkeeper where she was going? That wasn't like her. Or was it? Was she really that reckless? What if we don't find her again? I can't even say this to Mason or Hannah; they'd ridicule me, if they weren't snoring. They slept nearly the whole time on the trains, and they're asleep now. Not a care in the world for those two.

Mason

At four in the morning someone was trying to pry open the door. Four in the morning! Blake jumped up and pressed against the door, but the key was turning and a voice, not too loud, but a voice I recognized, whispered, "Dudes, let me in, dudes ..."

It was Johnny.

"It's only Johnny, Blake," I said, relieved, falling back to bed. "Open the door."

It took Blake a few moments to back away, almost as if he didn't want to.

"Where's Chloe?" was the first thing he said; not even a hello.

"She moved to another place because this one sucks ass. She was supposed to come back and leave a note with the address, but she forgot."

"So did she wake up in the middle of the night because she remembered?"

"I guess so. That's why I'm here."

"Why didn't you wait till morning?"

"That's what I told her," Johnny said. "You think I wanted to walk at this hour? She insisted. She said you'd all be frantic." Johnny cast a glance at sleeping Hannah and at me, barely awake, lying in bed, covered up with a blanket. Only Blake, standing up, tense, angry, looked to be remotely frantic.

He was stiff, agitated. I could see this even half-conscious. "Blake, bro, it's all right," I muttered. I don't know why he was so upset. Chloe wasn't lost. I knew she wouldn't be. I thought

Blake would be relieved, like I was, but he took a step toward Johnny. That's when I knew I'd better shake myself awake, try to talk some sense into my brother. He can be so hair-trigger sometimes.

"Why were you and Chloe up at four in the morning?" Blake asked.

"I wasn't," Johnny said. "I was sleeping. But then she woke me up."

Blake, fists clenched, glared at me from across the room and then at Johnny. It was dark; the dim light from the tall window was blue. Johnny raised his hands. "Whoa, dude, what's up?"

"We had no idea what happened to her."

"If you listen, I'll tell you. You see this place, right? She didn't want to go on tour with me, and I didn't think it was safe for her to stay here by herself. Don't you agree? I found her a nice joint. She was supposed to come and leave the address for you."

"Why didn't she?"

"You'll have to ask her," Johnny said. "I'm not Chloe's keeper."

"Why didn't you ask her when you came back from your tour?"

"It slipped my mind," Johnny said. "It's not my responsibility to remind her to notify her friends, is it?"

Johnny and Blake stood at an impasse for a few moments.

"So now what?" Blake said.

"I don't know. Now what?"

I didn't understand what was happening. My eyes kept closing, and their conversation was fuzzy like my eyeballs. I kept losing the thread. Now what? Now we go to sleep. Was there something I was missing?

Next thing I knew it was morning, and I was being shaken awake. I opened my eyes. It was Johnny. "Come on, dude, wake up," he said. "We gotta go if you want to come with me to Treblinka."

I wasn't so sure I did. It took me a little while to get my head clear. Hannah wasn't in the room. Neither was Blake. The sun was coming through the courtyard window in streaks. It was stifling, the air thick and dense.

"Where's Hannah?"

"In the bathroom," Johnny replied. "Throwing up, from the sounds of it."

I assumed Blake was with her down the hall. I needed a shower myself, and a change of clothes, and a big breakfast. Then I could figure out all the right questions to ask. Hannah came back. But she came back by herself.

"Where's Blake?"

"I don't know," she said.

"Blake," said Johnny, "is with Chloe."

Now I was fully awake.

"What?"

"I think your brother had a problem with me going back to Castle Inn and staying with her. You were dead asleep, and he didn't want to leave her alone. So I gave him the address, the directions, and he left. I slept here."

I absorbed this. "Why didn't he wake me?"

"He tried, I think. You were out."

I absorbed this too.

I'm not saying I wasn't unconscious. But I'll give you an example of what was troubling even untroubled me. Two summers ago when Blake's German Shepherd died, it died in the middle of the night. Blake needed me because he couldn't deal with it alone. I was asleep, possibly as deep as I was last night, and do you know what Blake did? He shook me and shoved me, and yelled at me, and woke me. He woke me so that I could stay by his side while his dog died.

That's all I'm saying. He found a way to rouse me. Then, I mean. Not now, obviously.

Hannah

How am I going to get dressed? How am I going to get on a
tour bus? How am I going to leave this gross bathroom? How
am I going to eat, talk, be normal? How am I going to go on
a tour of anything, especially Treblinka? Chloe came to Poland
for Treblinka. This is what her grandmother gave us money for.
What am I going to do? Eventually Chloe and Blake and even
oblivious Mason are going to notice that I'm still throwing up in
the vilest bathrooms all over Europe, where my vomit is probably
the most pleasant thing to happen in them. Eventually they will
ask why, and also why I'm not eating, why I've stopped eating,
and why I look as if I've emerged from the Dead Sea.

What am I going to tell them?

I need to talk to Chloe, is what I need to do. Right now, at
length, and desperately. When I raced out to the bathroom this
morning, Johnny was already awake, sitting up in bed, looking
at maps or I don't know what. The small lamp by the round table
was on. He might have been smoking.

He said to me, "Need the bathroom? It's down the hall."

"I know where it is," I said.

"I'm sure you do," he said.

And when I was in there, I wondered what he meant by that.

I'm so scared right now. I'm so scared. I don't know what's
happening to me. And why was Johnny in the room? I didn't even
ask. And where was Blake? I didn't ask that either. I can't even
be bothered with the important questions. I want to tell Mason
and Johnny that I don't think I can go to Treblinka with them
today, but I don't know how to say it. I have to go so that I don't
have to explain it. But I can't stay here by myself while they're off
gallivanting around Poland, having fun at Dachau or whatever.
There are zombies in the corridor waiting for the bathroom. Who
are these people? They're like cadavers. I hope that's not what I
look like to them. I can't stay here. They'll suck the blood right
out of my veins. Perhaps that's exactly what I deserve.

Please no please no please no please no please no please no
please no please no please no please no please no please no please
no please no please no please no please no please no please no
please no please no please no please no please no please no please
no please no please no please no please no please no please no
please no please no.

Please.

No.

Chloe

Chloe opened her eyes, for a moment unsure of where she was.
It was morning. The ceiling was painted blue, trayed, high above
her. She was quite familiar with the design of the ceiling. A sheet
covered her body. She touched her hair, still damp from the
shower she had taken late last night after Johnny left to run to
the hostel to salvage what remained of her European adventure.

It had taken all her will to force him to get dressed and stop
sitting mute by her knees, to go into the night and rush to the
hostel to tell them about the Royal Castle and the adjacent inn
with the geometrically odd rooms, and Chloe lying in bed in
one of them, overlooking the flowing Vistula. He didn't want to
leave. And she didn't want him to. He went anyway. After all,
this was *Roman Holiday* not *Nightmare on Elm Street*.

Would he come back? Would he come alone, or bring the
whole brood back with him? Would he not come back? He'd left
his guitar. She knew he would have to return eventually. The
guitar was his heart. And one always returned for one's heart,
didn't one?

After her shower, she tried to wait but, spent and ruined, fell
into a troubled sleep, full of vivid, ludicrous dreams of gates and
churches and fields and bombed-out buildings; things she'd never
seen and never dreamt of, and yet there they all were hovering
behind her eyes. In the dreams she had lost her friends and was
wandering around the cathedrals of destruction, praying to find

them, alarmed at the geography of the new city that made up the immense reality of her visions.

Now she woke up, came to, remembered things. Like snowflakes in fire, the dreams melted away. She jumped up out of bed, wearing tiny silk shorts, an even tinier tank top, loose everywhere, and sheer. But at least she was wearing something. She wasn't naked. Because in the armchair by the window sat Blake, staring at her with cold and accusing eyes. For a minute she thought (or prayed?) she was still dreaming. Because at the altar in one of the ancient towns, she had found Blake, and he had carried the same scowl in his formerly happy eyes he was carrying now. Chloe even looked back at the bed, half expecting to find herself still in it, peacefully slumbering, but no, the bed was empty, and Blake really was in the chair.

"Why are you sitting up?" was all she could think to ask. Her arms drew up to her breasts to cover herself. Too late, probably. Too late. She might as well have been naked. That's how she felt.

"*That's* your question? Because I have a few of my own."

"Blake, what … I don't … what time is it?"

"Time to tell me what the hell is happening here."

"I don't know. What's happening with you?" She stood awkwardly by the side of her untidy bed, five feet from Blake's stretched-out feet, in a room lit up by morning. Quickly and, she hoped, furtively, she threw a glance at the two beds. Oh, thank God. The other bed was unmade too, rumpled up last night by Johnny. But when she turned her gaze back to Blake, she saw that he was thinking the same thing. Both beds were unmade, Blake was thinking. This shamed Chloe. She wanted to ask him if he was pleased that the new room she got for them had private facilities instead of a communal narcotics toilet, but he didn't look pleased by much this morning.

"Do you have any idea how worried we were?" he said.

"I know. I'm sorry. That's why I sent him when I realized I forgot." She couldn't even speak his name aloud in the daylight.

"How could you forget to let us know?"

"I don't know, Blake. I just forgot."

"And he was in the room with you until four in the morning?"

She blinked. "Where else was he going to go?"

"How is that your business?"

"We traveled together. What was I going to do, throw him out?"

Blake glared at her incredulously. "Um, yes, Chloe," he said. "That is exactly what you would do. Throw him out."

She rubbed her eyes, her repentance yielding to annoyance. As usual, Blake always managed in seconds to animate her from relative peace to irritation. "I don't know what you're upset about. I said I was sorry for not leaving the new address. I fell asleep and forgot."

"Oh, well, if you *said* you were sorry. What, did you fall asleep for an entire day? The day, the evening, the night, all the way down to four in the morning?"

Chloe swallowed. She didn't want to keep secrets, other than the mammoth ones she was already keeping. She didn't even want to confess that Johnny had gotten her stoned, way back in Kaunas, although what a minuscule infraction that had been.

"I wasn't feeling well," she said slowly. Lies should be spoken extra deliberately. "I think it was the sandwich at Sestokai. I never felt good after I had it. Perhaps a touch of food poisoning. I was bad yesterday. I couldn't go on tour with him."

"Yes, he told me." Blake wouldn't say Johnny's name either. "But you didn't answer my question."

"That's because I don't owe you an answer, Blake," said Chloe.

"Don't you?"

"No. I may owe it to Mason, but not you."

"So there's an answer you owe Mason that you can't tell me?"

"No! I stayed in the room. I slept. I went out for a little while."

"Alone?"

"I was alone all day, so yes."

"He wasn't gone all day on his little tour, was he?"

That was true. He had come back around nine and said to her, come on, let's go out, we'll go have some food, walk around. I didn't get a chance to show you Vilnius, but I'll show you beautiful Warsaw. She had put on a soft coral dress she had bought that day. She put gold clips in her brushed out hair and red gloss on her lips. Jovan Musk was behind her ears and in the swell between her breasts. They went out. They had some food. They walked around. He told her things. He showed her things.

"Where's Mason?" asked Chloe. "Why didn't he come?" Mason would be so chill right now. That's what she needed. Mason to ask her no questions.

"Back at the hostel with Hannah, I assume. Sleeping."

She nodded. She wanted to ask where Johnny was, but didn't dare. Blake didn't look quite up to answering that one. For a few silent moments he sat, and she continued to stand, braless in front of him, in a barely there tank, barely there shorts. She wasn't a warm, peach-colored nude, although the way Blake was staring at her, half-full of condemnation, half-full of other things, she might as well have been. She tried not to move, fearing her breasts were trembling with her every breath, as though she were on the floor trembling from pleasure. She sighed a deep and overflowing sigh. And then, before she could figure out how to control her inappropriately animate breasts or her even more inappropriately erect nipples, the lock in the door turned, the door opened, and Mason and Hannah walked in, rolling their suitcases behind them. They were followed by Johnny. Suddenly the indecorousness of her nipples a few feet away from Blake's face became incidental to the impropriety of her entire barely clothed body scrutinized by Mason and by Hannah. And by Johnny. Though his wordless scrutiny was the least of her problems at the moment.

No one said anything while they thought of something to say.

"Chloe, when will you be ready to go?" That was Johnny, after a prolonged throat-clearing. "Because Emil is meeting us downstairs at eight-thirty."

"What about your group?" She was having a terrible time forcing her arms to remain at her sides and not fly up and hide the self-conscious confession that was splayed across her breast. Covering up would be an admission to every person in the room, the ones who were looking at her and the ones who weren't, that there was something dissolute and unrestrained in every single thing she had done since Mason ran back to Varda's house to find his passport.

Ah. That was something to say.

"Mason, did you find your passport?"

"Yes, yes," he said quickly. He opened his mouth to say something else, then paused.

Blake came out of his trance. His eyes drifted from Chloe to his brother, still standing holding the long handle of his suitcase.

"Mase," Blake said, frowning and confused. "What is she talking about? You didn't leave your passport. I did a final check. There was nothing in that room after I left it. It was passportless, dude."

Do you know why my grandmother sent me to Latvia? Chloe says to Johnny over pierogi and vodka at a dimly lit café after he comes back from Majdanek. Because it's not hot there. She doesn't think I can get into too much trouble in a country where the temperature doesn't usually rise above sixty degrees. There's never been a *Girls Gone Wild* in Riga.

Has there been a *Girls Gone Wild* in Warsaw? Johnny asks.

Inaudibly, Chloe says no.

Johnny shakes his head. Grandmothers know very well you can get into trouble anywhere. My own lived somewhere colder than Poland and she managed to get into a lifetime of trouble.

Really?

Really.

Chloe drinks and thinks. My father says that he and my mother were able to form a lasting marriage only because they both came from the same climate.

Johnny laughs. I love them. I love your parents. Why are they so funny?

He is not so funny, my father, Chloe says. He says people who live in cold climates are physiologically and psychically different from people who live in warm climates.

Johnny smiles. Do you want him to be wrong, Chloe, or do you want him to be right?

I don't know, Chloe wants to say. It all depends where *you're* from, Johnny Rainbow. They drink some more. She asks him to order wine not vodka because she is a lightweight and light-headed. She giggles when he speaks. He keeps telling her things to make her laugh, to make her smile. And when she laughs, he sits and watches her. She drinks some more because she can't withstand the ebony gaze, the caramel scrutiny, the parted mouth. It feels so grown up to sit like this, to drink, to talk, to be alive.

It wasn't an accident, you know, that I sat by your side on the Liepaja train, he says to her after they've been ambling and meandering down the noisy Warsaw streets. He has offered her his arm, and she has taken it.

She says nothing. She can't breathe and listen to his low intoxicated voice all at once.

I was looking for a place to perch, he says, and all the cars were full. There was a seat by a man, a seat by a woman, a seat by a child. And a seat by you.

I walked by once. I glimpsed you through the dusty glass. I kept on walking. Three cars down, I finally found a compartment with three seats empty. I opened the door halfway. But I was thinking of you. You had been glancing up from your book and staring out the window. He smiles, remembering her. You had a sweet spellbound face and hippie hair. You were staring at a field like you'd never seen a field before. And you were hiding your body. He nods approvingly at her colored face, at her coral dress. I couldn't see what you were hiding, but I knew you were hiding it. Chloe stumbles over the cobblestones and grabs tighter onto his arm. She is not hiding anything now in her Polish-bought halter sundress that swings as she walks, that reveals soft skin illuminated by city lights.

He continues to tell her things she is desperate to hear. It wasn't ideal, he says. Your compartment was packed. The woman sitting one away from you, I could tell was drowning in cloying cheap perfume.

How right you were.

Unlike you.

She doesn't look up at him when he says this.

I didn't even know if you spoke English. But I closed the door I had opened, the one that didn't lead to you, and I walked back three cars, and opened another door.

I glimpsed you through the dusty glass, Chloe.

The drinking, the wandering in the warm evening air of an exotic foreign city, the leaning down and smelling her perfumed neck, the murmuring, you smell so musky, so delicious, the shoulder bumping against hers, her arm in the crook of his arm, it's all elegant seduction leading to wanton frenzy. And he hasn't even begun to sing. He's just *talking* her out of her slinky Polish dress and onto her arching back. He's gazing at her, but not kissing her, or circling the soles of her feet with his thumbs, or rubbing the center of her bare spine with the knuckles of his hands. Not yet. They're just walking, full of raspberry wine, full of chocolate wine. He offers her a cold beer on a street corner, and she says no, and he laughs, and she watches him. Do you know, he says, that a girl is fifty percent more likely to love you if she likes the taste of beer and drinks it with you on your first ever night out?

Chloe laughs too and says, is love a euphemism there? That's when he stops walking, and turns to her. No, he whispers. It's not.

He kisses her under a Warsaw streetlamp in a cobblestoned alley, not far from squares and singers and art and cafés open late, and yet a plunging world away from it all. He raises her face to his great black eyes, and presses her woozy-with-wine body in soft spun cotton against his chest.

He tastes of beer and vodka and wine and smoke and strawberry rhubarb pie. He whispers into her mouth wild things, mad things. He hasn't even begun to sing.

She almost needs to be carried back to the inn by the castle, up the stairs to their room, to their high bed by the window.

He throws off his shirt and falls sprawled on the bed. She wobbles in front of him and unzips her summer dress. You look so pretty, he whispers, opening his arms, beckoning her to come near. The dress falls to the floor.

There's no light except for the lit-up Royal Castle by the River Vistula outside their tall windows. Naked she climbs on top of him, her bare breasts, her bare nipples skimming, grazing against his chest. They kiss.

Oh Chloe.

Oh Johnny.

Bare on bare, naked on naked, woman on man, she lowers her breasts to his impatient ardent mouth. She moans, he moans. His hands cup her, fondle her, he licks her, he kisses her. He sucks her nipples until she can't sit up on top of him anymore. She is spinning. He is her narcotic, her opiate, her potion and poison. She falls on the bed, on her back. She raises her arms above her head. He falls on top of her. She is pulsing, and he has barely touched her. But he is pulsing too. Everything red, wine, lust, raspberries, lifeblood flows just under her white and aching skin. I am parched, she gasps. Only in your throat, Chloe Divine, whispers Johnny. Only in your throat. She moans, all foamy. Now he has touched her. Now he is almost singing. Please don't moan, he begs her. Please don't.

Oh God, why.

Because if you moan I will come.

Desperately she tries not to, but she can't help it. She moans. And he can't help it either.

They have so little time. Nothing but frenzied minutes. Don't be mad at me for Mason, he whispers beseechingly. We're just kids, saying the wrong things, doing the wrong things. What I said … it's not true.

Yes, it is.

It's not, Johnny says. You know how I know? Because if he touched you, he would love you. Are you telling me he's never touched you?

He has, but not like this, says Chloe.

And then later: I know you think it makes your relationship with him a lie, but it doesn't. It just makes it your first relationship.

Chloe doesn't care. She listens to the drum of Johnny's tapping fingers, she watches his caressing hands on her. Their heads nod in sync with one another, their bodies move together to the rhythm of love. She clutches his neck, presses her palms against his back. It's clumsy at first. She wishes he could be more gentle, less fevered. They don't know how to walk in step yet, their dance new, syncopated to a disparate beat. In the beginning he stops dancing before the music ends.

Don't fret, Chloe Divine, says Johnny in the briefest of drunk afterglows, don't worry. One day, a man will touch you in wonder, and you'll know I'm telling you the truth.

They stare at each other across the blue air, heavy with varnish, sap, beer, peaches and plums.

Are you that man? she mouths to him, terrified, inaudible, barely moving her lips.

I am, he says, his clammy face lowered into her breasts, his stubble scratching her raw. I'm the one.

He whispers, he kisses her. His mouth is so soft, so sweet. The sweat from his hair and head drips into her face. So this is what it feels like. A lover bringing himself to bear over her. First short dance on the bed, second longer on the floor, the third they stand like horses, like palms, tango like lovers, entwined, embraced, and he whispers, holding her whole bare body to him, your lips are paradise and she moans back her answer but he is panting and sweltering and doesn't hear, so she moans it again, moans it louder until he does.

Lower, Johnny, she moans. Paradise is lower.

25

Roses for a Farm

Chloe

She had hoped that breakfast would cheer the rest of them up, but no. Johnny, however, was invigorated, fresh, brushed, and shaved (down to designer stubble, not bare cheek). He got them coffees and pastries while they waited outside Castle Inn for Emil. He brought melted ham and cheese for the boys, a plum Danish for Chloe, and plain buttered toast for Hannah with water, not coffee. She didn't want to eat even the toast. She said she was still not feeling well.

"I know," Johnny said. "But if you force down a few bites of bread, you'll feel better."

Blake was in quite a pickle. He didn't want to accept breakfast from Johnny, but he was also starved.

Right outside their hotel, horse carriages waited for riders. There was a long line of them, all in a row, horses eating out of feedbags and pooping. It was enough to ruin a healthy person's appetite, and Hannah was not a healthy person. They walked around the corner to a cobblestoned plaza, to get away from the smell. The Pizza Hut had al fresco tables with cute umbrellas. Another time Blake would've found that amusing. Not this morning. The entire Old Town was cobblestoned, and where they were waiting, the buildings were white stucco with red roofs to match the red roof of the Royal Castle. Chloe tried to tell her friends that elsewhere in the Old Town, the buildings were painted all the colors of the rainbow, but no one cared. Mason nodded politely, but his mind was clearly elsewhere.

"Listen, Chloe," he said, "I want to talk to you." He paused. "Blake's not right about the passport. I did leave it. It was under the chair. I had to look for it. He didn't know it was there. He didn't see it."

It took Chloe a second to figure out what Mason was talking about. She patted him on the arm, touched his turned-away face, ruffled his hair.

"Don't worry, Mase," she said. "I believe you." She turned away her own face. They both watched Hannah, bending forward after attempting the toast.

"It must be food poisoning," Mason said. "All that stuff at Varda's. I'm surprised we're all not barfing like her. Who wouldn't get sick?"

The four of them loitered in the plaza, near white steps and smooth walls, while Johnny waited for Emil a little farther down the street near the horses. Chloe tried not to look down the street after him, tried not to look at his denim-clad legs, his gray T-shirt, his twisted-back hair. Last night his hair was out, spraying sweat with every pulse of his body. She moved away from Mason, in shame. She studied the cobblestones. She studied Hannah.

"I don't know what's wrong with me," Hannah said to Blake, who stood like a stoic by her side, his backpack over his jean jacket, his belt buckled, his Timberlands tied, his unsmiling gaze on Pizza Hut. But to Chloe, when Blake walked ten feet away to throw out their garbage and her uneaten toast, Hannah whispered, "I *have* to talk to you."

"And I have to talk to *you*," Chloe whispered back. "But when? Tonight?"

By Hannah's desperate expression, Chloe didn't think her friend could wait until tonight. She didn't know if she herself could wait.

"Where did you get that dress?" Hannah asked, weakly appraising her.

Chloe wore her newly bought coral concoction, flimsy like cotton candy, sleeveless and soft. There was a cinched waist, a halter neckline, and a jaunty bow across the hip. There was cleavage. There was casual loose hair and glossy lips and the flickering eyes of a frantic animal. Chloe knew what she looked like. She had stared at herself in the mirror long enough before she finally dared leave the private bathroom upstairs.

"I went out for five minutes yesterday. There's an outdoor market two blocks over. Maybe we can go tomorrow. You'll find some nice things."

"You felt too unwell to remember to leave us a note," Hannah said, "but well enough to go dress shopping?"

It was obviously the dress Hannah was objecting to. Perhaps it was too nice for a death camp.

Chloe didn't want to show Hannah how light-headed she felt, liquid in the stomach, terrified of the nightmare slowly unfolding, all that, and yet blinded and beguiled. The violet plunder of yesterday hadn't ended things. It barely began them.

While they waited outside in the abundant sunshine, Chloe noticed that Hannah was not wearing makeup. She wore a long skirt with an elastic waist and a borrowed, oversized T-shirt that swallowed her rail body. Instead of looking effortlessly elegant, she looked haggard. Her bleached hair was brushed back. Her face was plain and pale. She looked as if she'd slept through a night of terrors and was still haunted by what she'd seen. She looked as if she hadn't slept.

Gamely, Hannah stood for a few more minutes, leaning against the wall of the building, but finally she squatted down on some stone steps. Chloe perched next to her. She touched Hannah's arm. She put her arm around Hannah.

"Don't do that," Hannah whispered, "or I'm going to break down."

Blake and Mason were near. They couldn't say much.

"Hannah, what's going on? You okay?" Chloe whispered to her friend.

"No," Hannah said. "Not even remotely."

Mason

Emil drove up into the square and parked his beige shuttle bus next to us. Johnny was in full animation mode, chatting to Emil, inspecting the van, making jokes, laughing, slapping him on the back, drinking another coffee, I think his third. Even his stubble looked energetic. You couldn't say the same for us sorry lot. I felt pretty good but everybody else was dragging, Hannah especially. I wasn't sure what to think about Emil. Johnny introduced him, we shook his hand and all, but he was sullen and silent. Shorter than Johnny, and stockier, he was dark of skin, dark of hair and clothes, dark of disposition. He was unpleasant. He wore mirrored sunglasses, so you couldn't see his eyes, and sported an ungroomed beard and messy unwashed hair. He looked as if he'd just struggled out of bed. He wasn't interested in the smallest niceties; he didn't even ask how we were enjoying Warsaw. He didn't give a shit, and acted it. His van looked like the shuttle buses we saw at Logan Airport, except the sign on the side said Warsaw Tours. A second dude jumped out of the van, this one a tiny, skinny guy named Chris, who gave Johnny a huge hug as if they'd been friends forever.

"Johnny! When did you get out?"

"A week ago," I heard Johnny mutter. Then he added, "Joining the army next week. Then off to Afghanistan."

"Duuude!" Chris mock-saluted him, giggling. I couldn't tell how old he was, but he didn't look as if he shaved yet. He was crazy skinny and white and skittish, like a live wire. "Afghanistan! No shit. How'd you manage that? Your dad? Hey, say hello to him for me, will you?"

"He'd disown me if he thought you and I were still tight, man."

Chris laughed. "Word, man, word. Things've been good around here. We're doing good. Emil too. Hey, you need to be hooked up?"

"Nah, I'm all set, thanks. You coming with us today?"

"Nah, I'm just here to say hello to my man Johnny. When Emil told me he took you to Lublin yesterday, I damn near shit my pants. I didn't believe him, I said I had to come see for myself. I actually gotta run, man, an hour late for a day gig, but you take care, Johnny-boy. How long you in town? Maybe I see you tonight?"

They hugged, they fist bumped. "Well, if you want to hang tonight or something, you let me know, I'm still at the same place on Vosznecenka."

"Word, dude."

Chris tipped his cap to us and gunned it down the cobblestones.

"How's he been?" Johnny asked Emil.

Emil's accent surprised me. He looked so foreign, and yet he didn't speak like a Pole. He looked dark as if he could be from the South Pacific, but he spoke in the most elegant Queen's English; not that I would know, I'm just saying he sounded more like Henry Higgins than Eliza Doolittle.

"He's been all right, my man, hanging in there, like the rest of us, trying to stay out of trouble, trying to make a living. We still hang sometimes. Speaking of making a living," Emil continued to Johnny, in a tone that was too loud to be truly private, "we're going to need our money."

"I know. I told you, I'll pay you tonight."

"But I'm not driving down to Krakow with you unless I get my money now. So what are you going to do about that?"

"I'll ask them for partial payment. Don't worry."

"What about them?" Emil nodded in our direction. I pretended I was studying the Baroque architecture of the building we were standing next to.

"They're friends. They don't pay."

"I'm not taking them if they don't pay."

"Dude, I'm the one paying for your wheels. What difference does it make how many seats are occupied?"

"There's three hundred extra kilo on my suspension," Emil said. "You don't think that makes a difference?"

Johnny shook his head.

"I just want my money," Emil said flatly.

"You'll get it. I promise."

"I don't know. Last time you promised me my money, you disappeared for a year."

"You know that couldn't be helped," Johnny said. "But you did hear from me, right? I didn't blow you off. Came all the way to fucking Warsaw, found you. So what are you worried about?"

"You put me in a bad spot, John-boy," Emil said. "I caught a lot of shit because of you. Had to shell out my own dough to cover your little messes."

"I understand. I'll take care of it. Will you relax? We have one more day with them. Now be a proper driver. Smile, tip your cap."

"Fuck that."

While Emil and Johnny were having that conversation, Hannah and Chloe on my left were having a different one.

"How much is this luxury hotel you've booked us into, Chloe?"

"I'm not sure if the dig is on the word luxury or …"

"No dig. I just didn't realize we were so flush with cash that you could double book us."

"Hannah, you've seen the other place, right? We couldn't leave our bags there. We couldn't stay there. I couldn't."

"I'm not sure a few fleas warrant bandying about our precious dollars."

"I'm not bandying."

"Leave her alone, Hannah," said Blake, who overheard. "We couldn't stay in that room, and you know it."

"I'm just saying," Hannah said. "We should try to be a little more economical, that's all."

Perhaps the two conversations weren't so different after all.

Meanwhile five feet away on my right, Johnny and Emil's financial meeting was coming to a close.

Emil: "It doesn't sound to me as if your new friends are loaded up with cash."

Johnny: "I told you, they don't pay. I pay you. That's all you need to concern yourself with. Chill, for fuck's sake."

Emil stalked off to have a smoke. Johnny got out his guitar. He started strumming, then singing, then singing a little louder, strumming a little louder, as he was walking, along the desert, the mountain highways, the dry death valleys …

Ten seconds into the chorus, an older dude in a smart suit rushing by took out a bill that had a 100 printed on it and casually threw it on the ground by Johnny's feet.

"*Dziękuję*," Johnny called after him, still strumming, still singing. "*Dziękuję* very much …"

I wanted to talk to Johnny about yesterday and his trip to Majdanek. But he was singing, and I was listening. I wanted to talk to Blake about why he didn't wake me to go stay with Chloe, but Johnny was singing and I was listening, and the day was so happy and sunny, and the plaza had six cafés on it, and churches, and little shops and people strolling by, and it smelled good, of flowers and bread, but also of horse manure, which wasn't as good, and then Chloe said, "I almost forgot, I have to buy flowers, I promised Moody I'd buy some flowers for Treblinka."

Johnny stopped singing, although he continued to strum. I didn't know "This Land Is Your Land" had so many verses. He'd been singing it for ten minutes. I think he was just making up the lyrics as he went along. There was some shit in there I'd never heard.

"You're going to bring flowers to Treblinka?"

"I promised her."

"My group is going to be here any minute. And then we have to go—they're running late." We had been waiting for them for a long while. "Come with me," he said to Chloe, slinging the guitar onto his back. "There's a stand in the Palace Square that sells cheap roses. We'll be right back," he said to the rest of us, motioning Chloe to come along.

"Why can't we just buy them at Treblinka?" she said, not moving from my side.

"You'll see why when we get there," said Johnny. "There's nowhere to get flowers. Either come, or there won't be any roses."

They walked away, between the narrow white buildings, to the flower stand in the large main square. Chloe's head was down, as if he was talking to her but she didn't want to listen. I took the opportunity to saunter up to Blake and, as casually as a backwards baseball cap, ask him why he didn't wake me to go stay with Chloe in the middle of the night. I thought it would be good if we cleared the air.

I wish I had kept my big stupid unthinking mouth shut.

Blake did a double-take, and got loud. "Are you kidding me?"

"I just want to know, man. You woke me that time—"

He pulled me away from Hannah.

"You're messed up, bro," he said to me. "You're asking *me* why I didn't wake you? Ask yourself why you were flat out when your girlfriend was nowhere to be found in the middle of the night in a foreign city. Why you made your bed, put on your PJs and tucked yourself in under the covers. Go ahead. Ask yourself. I'll wait."

I raised an apologetic hand, began to say I'm sorry, but he didn't wait and didn't let me finish. "Even after Johnny came to tell us where she was. You heard him. I know you did, because you asked him questions, opened your eyes, stared at him. But what you didn't do is get the fuck up. How is that my fault?"

"Blake, I'm sorry."

"You're messed up," Blake said. "What's going on under your very nose would make any other dude's red blood turn to lava, but not you, no. You're too busy having a boy-crush on a bum who's five thousand kinds of trouble, which you can't see because your head is up the ass of that baseball statue you've been caressing in your backpack."

"Blake ..."

"I swear, man, start acting like her boyfriend. You know the only reason he's taking liberties is because he thinks you don't give a shit. I beg you, Mason, don't prove him right on this one, too."

Before I could defend myself, he stormed away, disgusted with me. I was ashamed of myself. Blake was right. What was I thinking? I followed him, wanting to beg him to forget what an asshole I was, but just then, a band of middle-aged backpackers assailed us with beaming smiles and loud voices. It took a few minutes of my mind being very much elsewhere to realize they were the group we'd been waiting for.

Hannah

I don't know what everybody else is so miserable about. It makes them act not nice toward Johnny. Blake and Chloe have really shut down. And it's a shame because he's a remarkable boy. After five minutes in the van on the way to see the ancient horrors none of us particularly wanted to see, he somehow made the whole day better and more interesting.

He is a perfect guide. In every way. He is quick-witted, not an arrogant douchebag like that geo-tourist Gregor. He tells us only what we need to know and doesn't bore us into stupidity with useless extraneous info, just so we can admire how clever he is. He is polite to everyone, even Blake, smiles all the time, and listens to people's questions. He jokes that there aren't any stupid questions, only stupid people.

He's brought bottles of water in a cooler for all ten of us, which is astonishing considering no one else thought of bringing anything except our backpacks. Plus he's easy on the eyes and he sings like that guy from Bad Company, who sounds like he's got a Harley Davidson in his throat. We're lucky that he found Chloe and me, but I'm beginning to think I'm the only one who thinks so. He seems to be upsetting the hell out of everybody. Even Mason, who never gets upset at anything.

Neither does Chloe usually. The reason she and I get along so well is because she's always sunny and optimistic. Even when I'm down, she finds something positive to say. She's the one who says of course we're going to make our train, even when we're clearly not. She's the one who says, no, you won't get a sunburn in Riga, it's too far north, even though my skin is so fair. Yes, that dress looks lovely on you. You're not too tall. You're just right. You're perfect. She doesn't judge me for some of the things I've done, I hope, and she is a good listener, and she's funny. She gets along with everybody. Everybody likes her. She is friendly, like a guy you'd want to pal around with. If Chloe were a guy, she'd be the one you'd invite over for a Saturday afternoon after your wife left you for another man. She'd bring the beer, the humor, the easygoing; she'd make you some food, and put extra beer in your fridge, and fix your screen door if it was broke. She'd feed your dog without being asked, that's Chloe.

I depend on her completely, which is why it's so baffling what's been happening since we got to Warsaw. She has barely talked to me. Blake too. Mason's head is in the clouds, but Mason is not my go-to person. Chloe is. And she's failing me. I desperately need to talk to her, and she keeps making every excuse not to be left alone with me for a second. Here's an example. In the morning we were waiting for the backpackers. For an hour we sat twiddling our thumbs on a wall outside, while Blake and Mason bickered, and Johnny played guitar and Emil smoked. She and I could've talked. But we didn't. She pretended to listen to Johnny sing, not that I blame her, because when he sings, it makes it near impossible to do anything else, even breathe, but come on! Not even for five minutes? If I didn't know any better, I'd say she was avoiding me. My paranoia talking.

And earlier this morning, what was *that* all about? I come back from the bathroom, feeling like crap, looking like crap, and Blake is gone, and Mason is yelling at me to hurry up, like we're going to miss the school bus. After we hooked back up with Blake and Chloe at some new hotel, things only got weirder. Blake and Chloe were grim as if they'd just had a fight, which is par for the course, they're always arguing about something or other, I pay no attention. But they both looked so mad, and no one would explain anything, and every time I asked, they both said, nothing's wrong, nothing! Even Mason didn't look happy. Then I caught Johnny staring at Chloe. She had just woken up, and wasn't looking her best. I was slightly embarrassed for her, and I wanted to quietly tell her to go get herself together, but then I saw Johnny secretly eyeballing her, thinking perhaps that Mason and Blake were so busy being all ticked off that they wouldn't notice. I don't even know how to describe it, the look in his eyes. A profound dazed something.

Then I realized why. She was standing in front of three boys and not wearing a bra! And of all the girls in Warsaw, Chloe really needs to wear a bra. She's not like me, she can't get away with walking around braless in cute little halter tops. The thing is, she knows this well, and usually keeps her 34DD self tightly under wraps. Her mother has done a good job instilling a sense of the respectable in Chloe, and the more she's developed, the more circumspect she's become until you almost can't tell how buxom she is. So for her to be standing, hands at her sides, oblivious to the boobs spilling out of her loose tank was shocking. Had she been sleeping? Then why was Blake sitting in the chair, all dressed? Was he just sitting there looking at her while she slept? How weird. But if she was awake and in that state, that's almost weirder. I finally managed to get her to the bathroom, but as she walked across the room, her breasts swayed back and forth. I blocked the view of her as best I could from Blake and Johnny, and before she went inside, I whispered to her, Chloe, bra! And to thank me, she slammed the door in my face.

So like I said, everybody's testy. I don't know why Blake is not talking to Chloe, or why Chloe is not talking to Mason, or why Blake is angry at his little brother. And yet here we are, ladies and gentlemen, our dream vacation and no one's talking to anyone.

I suppose I could ask Chloe what's bothering her, but I need to talk to her about my situation first. Then we can talk about her. I don't know what she has to be upset about. Everything is so easy for her. Though I have no idea why she's wearing a nice dress to go to a field in the forest. She barely wore a nice dress to her own prom.

"Mason," I asked, before we boarded the shuttle bus, "what's the matter with Blake?"

He shrugged. Which didn't mean he didn't know.

I sat next to Blake, in the front just behind the driver's seat so I wouldn't throw up like before. "Are you okay, babe?" I asked him and took his hand.

He blinked, squeezed my hand in reply, leaned over and kissed me. "I'm great, sugar plum," he said. "Too much traveling yesterday. I hardly got any sleep. I wish we had a day at the beach to recuperate." He kissed my hand. "Never mind. Barcelona soon enough."

"Soon enough," I agreed, eking out a smile, my heart catching when I thought of the day ahead, the week ahead, the months ahead.

Johnny was in the passenger seat next to Emil, twisted around to face us, telling us things. Emil scares me a little bit. He keeps eyeballing me and smoking. He's giving everyone else funny looks but he's eyeballing me. Chloe and Mason sat behind Johnny, across the narrow aisle from Blake and me. Chloe wasn't paying any attention to Johnny even though he was telling us incredible things. She just kept staring ahead, kind of at him, but not really, holding that stupid bouquet of flowers in her arms. Mason looked directly at Johnny, but that didn't mean he was paying attention. Mason has a way of doing that. Pretending he's listening, yet not hearing a word you say. I don't know how Chloe puts up with it. Blake and Chloe are much better listeners. Except they sat barely a foot away from each other in the aisle seats and never looked at each other or spoke to each other. Not once.

"So what were you and Chloe fighting about when we came in?" I asked Blake quietly.

He shook his head. "We weren't fighting. I was upset because she changed hotels and didn't tell us where she was."

"Oh, I agree. That was inconsiderate of her."

"She apologized."

"Did she apologize for paying for two places when we're only staying in one?"

"Let it go, Hannah," Blake said. "That was a smart move. I wasn't upset about that part."

It was as if he wanted me to ask him what he was really upset about. But I didn't. I let go of his hand. "Our cash is not infinite, Mr. Moneybags." Especially mine. And it was about to become a lot more finite. Many things were about to become a lot more finite.

"We brought extra," he said, "for the just in case."

"Not me. I don't have any extra." Though I most certainly do have a just in case.

"I'll cover you, babe. Stop fretting about the money. Money is the least of it." He got a sad, faraway look in his eyes.

The least of what, I wanted to ask. Except I knew.

What am I going to *do*?

How am I going to manage another two weeks before we go back? I can't hide this. I'm sick right now. It's all I can do to not ask Emil to pull over so I can throw up by the side of the peaceful hillock that Mason is admiring. Blake is oblivious to me because he is fixated on the annoying bunch of people around us. And Chloe, I don't even know what she's thinking about. She's staring forward past Johnny as if in a trance.

Does anyone care what's happening to me? Why am I being punished like this? It's not fair.

Stop it, Hannah. Don't cry on a minibus. It's unclassy. And Blake will see.

I turned to the window and wiped my face, and of course Blake, irked up to the eyeballs, didn't see. But you know who did see? Johnny. Sitting at the front, straddling the seat backward, he honed in on me, focused me in his sights. The look on his face was one of compassion, as if he knew. This complete stranger had somehow divined the truth about my desperate situation. His face when he finally looked away was blank. Maybe it's him, not Chloe I should talk to. He's the only one not oblivious to everyone else. His eyes are always raised. How do the rest of us stay so wrapped up in our own heads and lives and hearts and problems that we don't see what's a breath away from us?

Mason

After we left Warsaw and had been driving a while, the villages disappeared. There was almost nothing around us. For miles and miles all I could see outside my window was a dense and desolate pine forest on sandy loam earth. The villages were as sparse as joy. Inside our bus, though, there was raucous amusement. Everybody was talking, laughing, making jokes, asking questions. I'm glad Chloe let me sit next to the window. But I wonder how they're going to quiet down when we get to where we're driving. Sandy loam is good for growing roses, if the soil is properly irrigated. I don't know if anyone is irrigating this soil, but the few poor houses and streets we drove by, many of them have beautiful, large roses around their fences. I mentioned this to Chloe, because she likes flowers, and she was holding beautiful red roses in her hands, clenching them, almost. She blinked and came to, as if that was the last thing she'd been thinking. I pointed out the window. She leaned sideways, against me, to look. Then she said, "I'm surprised they grow so well here. I know how hard it is to grow them successfully."

"I know you do. That's why I showed them to you."

"Yeah. But they need drainage, and fertilizer, and lots of nutrients. This soil looks too dense. Packed too tight."

"Yet they grow."

"Yeah." She turned back to the inside of the bus, away from the sad little huts with their blooming roses.

Between the thick forests lie swamps. I think before the roads were paved, travel through these parts must have been difficult. Sand combined with marsh makes for silty mud, feet deep, through which tire tread gets stuck and burrowed into, like grooves in quicksand.

Johnny said it wasn't far, only sixty kilometers or so, but why does it seem as if we've been driving for hours? I asked him if he'd been here before. He said he had come here a little while back, with his father. He was non-specific. He was telling us about why the Germans built the death camps so close to Warsaw and yet in the middle of nowhere. He said it was to hide what they were doing, and yet be close enough to the Warsaw ghetto to get all the Jews from there to here. Blake asked where the ghetto was, and Johnny told him there was no more ghetto, like in Vilnius, and Blake shot a glare at Hannah and said he wouldn't know about ghettos in Vilnius. Don't fret, said Johnny, there aren't any. Then Blake asked where the Jews lived now and Johnny said there were no more Jews. Not in Vilnius, not in Warsaw, or Krakow, or Trieste, where there had been a large Jewish community. And Blake asked if there were any Jews in Barcelona, and Johnny said there were never many to begin with.

Then Johnny told us—though I don't know if anyone other than Chloe and I heard him—that the railroad that went through here was often used by Poles on their way to Bialystok, Cedlec, Lomza. During peaceful times many rode alongside these trees, paying little attention to the dull landscape of pine, sand, and marsh.

It would be hard to notice the insignificant town of Treblinka amid the heather and dry brush, and its plain, ordinary train station. It would be even harder to notice the spur off the main railroad line, just a pair of tracks vanishing into the dense and lonely woods, pine woods so thick that it almost looked as if the spur had been a long-ago mistake, which the forest crowded over and time forgot.

This spur, said Johnny, leads to a quarry four kilometers inside the forest, a quarry of white sand that was mined for industrial and urban development.

That quarry now is an empty sandlot, he said, surrounded on all sides by forest. The soil is infertile, and farmers don't cultivate it. Nothing grows there. Wasteland has remained wasteland.

"This barren wilderness," Johnny said, "was selected by the Gestapo and approved by Reichsführer SS Heinrich Himmler for the construction of a human slaughterhouse, the breadth and likes of which the world had never seen."

No one heard him but Chloe and me.

Blake

The tour group that hired Johnny and his bus and ominous driver was a peculiar bunch of ducks. They showed up an hour late in full Indiana Jones gear. They had on khaki cargo pants, vests with dozens of pockets, fancy hiking boots, wide-brim hats to keep out the sun, and lots of cameras. Yes, they were all good on the cameras. There were five of them, three men and two women. The men carried an SLR each, a Nikon, a Canon, a Pentax. The camera bag they brought was the size of Johnny's duffel that contained his whole life. In this bag, they had five or six lenses for each camera, flashbulbs, filters, extra batteries, cleaning solutions, a small screwdriver kit, in case, I presume, either the cameras or their eyeglasses went kerflooey, and extra lens caps.

"You sure you don't have a printer in there?" I quipped, thinking I was being witty, and the bald man slapped me on the back and pulled out a black cuboid.

"Canon makes the best one. It's light," he said. "You can carry it anywhere, and it prints pretty well. Would you like to see?"

"Um, no, that's okay."

He stuffed the miraculous prism back in the bag.

They were older than us by some forty years. They were too enthusiastic by half. They included even the truculent driver in their bonhomie, pumped our hands, slapped our backs, asked interminable questions about what and where and how, commented about how wonderful it all was, and then launched into a five-person harmony about who they were, where they lived, what they'd seen so far, and where they were headed.

Apparently they had been friends since high school, just like us. They grew up in Arizona, in Carefree or something. More like care-less, as in, could not. I laughed out loud at my own inward joke, unfortunately not at the most appropriate time as they had just finished telling us that the wife of the fifth wheel with them had recently passed away. They said "passed away" in a hush-hush voice, as if they didn't want the fifth wheel to know. Their names were kitschy and rhymy and alliterative. I thought they were joking with us. Brett and Yvette and Dennis and Denise. I didn't catch the widower's name because he was all by himself and couldn't poetize. They said they *loved* our names, and they *loved* our tour guide's name.

"Johnny *Rainbow*! Isn't it *fantastic*! How did you come up with that? Your mother name you that? Give that woman a medal!"

Denise said, "Give that woman a medal for having a child, period."

And Yvette leaned over my seat to my head and whispered into my ear, "I *love* Denise to death, but she doesn't have any *kids*!"

"You don't have to tell them my whole life story, Yvette!" Denise shouted. "Why don't you tell them that Dennis got snipped while you're at it?"

I looked into my lap. Even my lap was embarrassed.

"How long have you been in Warsaw?" Yvette yelled to us. She was sitting behind Hannah and me, and kept leaning over into every millimeter of my personal space. She was leaning over into personal spaces that even my girlfriend had not visited. The woman was right up my ass, and shouting into it. "We've been here a week already, waiting for Johnny! He's the *best*, so we didn't want to have a death tour until he came, we're *so* happy it worked out, I wish you could've come with us yesterday, yesterday was *amazing*, wasn't it, Brett, tell them, wasn't it?"

You might think that they would marry their opposites, the way people sometimes do if they want to stay married. But no. Brett also leaned over into Hannah's crevices and began shouting.

"It was *incredible*! Johnny said you were going to join us, but you missed your train? Those trains are a bitch, aren't they? We didn't want to travel the Baltic states for that reason! Too much hassle, and we don't want any hassle, we *hate* hassle!"

Across the aisle Denise leaned over to Chloe. "Darlin', did Johnny tell you his chaos theory? He explained it yesterday on the way to Lublin when he told us all about you. We had time. It was like a three-hour tour!"

Dennis broke into an out-of-tune theme song for *Gilligan's Island*.

The widower from the last seat in the back, slightly quieter than the rest, bless him, said, "Johnny's chaos theory is why we felt so bad about keeping you waiting this morning. Totally our fault. I hope it doesn't ruin our day."

"I really hope your theory is wrong, Johnny," said the widower. "Otherwise we're screwed—pardon my French." He took off his hat and fanned himself.

"Why are you fanning yourself?" Emil suddenly bristled, glancing through the rearview mirror. "There's air-conditioning on my bus. It's running on max." The poor overheated man apologized and stopped fanning himself!

"I hope I'm wrong, too, Artie," Johnny said. Artie! That was his name. Please remember it, Blake. You're a writer now. "Chaos theory states that one small change out of the ordinary order of initial things multiplies by geometric expansion all the subsequent things until unpredictability follows. That's why they say that a tennis ball lobbed in error can lead to the collapse of the universe."

"Isn't that the butterfly effect?" Brett said.

Johnny nodded. "It's the double pendulum theory. Minute changes in initial motion result in drastically different patterns of consequences." His gaze kept circling back around to Chloe.

"Wait, what's your name again?" Denise said to Chloe. "Chloe what?"

"Chloe Divine."

"Oh Yvette, isn't that just divine! Aren't they darling, all four of them, simply divine, aren't they? Do they remind you of anyone, Yvette? They're just like we used to be. Aren't they precious?"

"What about me, Denise?" Johnny smiled, but after catching my humorless face looked away, toward Chloe, of course.

"You are the divinest of them all, darling boy!"

"How do you know anything about double pendulums?" Hannah asked Johnny. I wanted to know this myself, but I wouldn't abase myself to ask. That might mean I was interested in his answer.

"I told you, my grandmother is a mathematician."

"Lucky you," Yvette exclaimed. "Your grandma is still alive?"

"Yes," Johnny said. "Grandma taught me more than I ever wanted to know about the laws of mathematics." For some reason he then glanced at Hannah! What a freak.

"Lucky, lucky! And your grandpa?"

Johnny grinned. "He taught me how to fight. Just kidding. How to fish, I mean." But his eyes were all twinkly.

I nearly groaned. He fished, too? I know Hannah wouldn't be that impressed, but Chloe loved fishing. Sure enough, when I glanced to my right, there was Chloe, blinking, all soft in the eye, probably thinking, oh, you fish too …

Bastard.

Trouble was, when I looked over at my brother, to see if he was as disgusted as I was, Mason was gazing at Johnny with Chloe's expression, all doe-eyed and smiley. Oh, you fish too…

I give up. I. Give. Up.

Yvette and Brett, Dennis and Denise, and Artie told us that they'd been traveling together since the last of Yvette and Brett's and Artie's kids left for college. Before they regaled us with stories about which countries they had been to, they regaled us with stories about their children, grown, successful, two of them married, one of them popping with twins, one engaged, one almost engaged but pregnant, so Artie was going to be a grandpa again, and "Oh, how Arlene would have loved to have a little girl after having all them boys!"

Hannah turned to the back of the bus, to face Artie. "Do they plan to get married?"

"They don't know. They gonna have the baby first, then see how they feel."

"What do you think about that?"

"Good, fine. If they're happy, I'm happy. They're my kids, I just want them happy."

Hannah nodded but uncertainly, as if she didn't quite understand or believe it. Johnny stared at Hannah with a mixture of pity and regret, and I wanted to ask him what the hell he was staring at, but Denise, happy not to be talking about the kids she never wanted to have, tapped insistently on my shoulder and resumed telling us about the places the six of them had traveled to over the years, but when Arlene "passed away" (in a whisper) last year, they pledged they were not going to stop just because they lost one of their ranks. "Arlene wouldn't want that, would she, Artie?"

Artie agreed that his deceased wife wouldn't want that.

"So we realized," Denise continued, "that though we'd been to Greece and Spain and Italy, and all round the Mediterranean islands, though we'd spent a month in France and a month in England, we've never been to the Baltic states. We decided there was no later. And being that Arlene was Jewish, we thought we'd honor her memory by going to see the camps in Poland. Artie approved, didn't you, Artie?"

From the back, Artie grunted his approval.

"Though we'll tell you frankly, we don't like the travel here. It's a slog, and the distances are too far. We much prefer the Alps, or Marseilles. We're actually thinking of cutting the trip short and flying to Cote d'Azur for a few days, just to wash the grime off our bodies, relax a little bit by the sea, aren't we, Yvette?"

"I don't know if we'll have time, Denise," said Yvette. "There's a lot to see."

"Yesterday Johnny was so efficient with time," Yvette said. "We can do it if he's with us. He was swinging that pendulum all day, weren't you, dear boy? He swung it back and forth between Sobibor and Majdanek."

"Sobibor was the worst," Brett said.

"Johnny didn't think so!" Yvette said. "He was most affected by Majdanek, weren't you, Johnny?"

"I don't get why," Brett said. "It wasn't nearly as impressive as Sobibor. It was so small. A few barracks, one little gas chamber, all overgrown with grass."

"A lot of destruction for a small place," Johnny said.

"I agree with Yvette," Denise said. "Majdanek wasn't that impressive."

"It looked different from the way my grandfather had described it," Johnny said.

"Different? How? How would your grandfather know? Did he come here?"

"Yes," said Johnny. "He came here."

"Well, according to the guidebook, the camp's been like this for years. He must've come a long time ago. How was it different?"

"He said there were shoes in the barracks and giant cabbages growing in the ashes," said Johnny.

An odd hush fell over the bus.

"What ashes?" Denise said.

"There were no cabbages," Yvette said.

"Or shoes in the barracks."

"Maybe we didn't see everything," Denise said. "Dennis, did you see shoes?"

"I did not see shoes," said Dennis.

"How long ago was your grandfather there?"

"I don't know," Johnny said. "Sixty years."

There was an exhale of relieved air among our seasoned travelers.

"Oh!" Yvette said, "so a *really* long time ago! Well, no wonder!"

And then from the back came Artie's voice. "Sixty years, Johnny?" he said. "Wouldn't that be 1944?"

"I guess it would," said Johnny. "Give or take."

"Give or take what?"

"A few days."

"What was he doing here?" asked Denise. "No wonder he saw cabbages. Probably on the farms all around Lublin. They were destroyed during the war. Are you sure he was in Majdanek?"

"Oh, I'm sure," Johnny said. "Emil, stop the bus."

Emil slowed down and pulled into a dusty half-road by the edge of the forest.

"Why are we stopping?" Yvette said. "Are we taking a bathroom break?"

"Oh, good," said Hannah. "I could use one."

"We're stopping," Johnny said, "because we are here."

"Here where?"

"Treblinka."

Chloe

The two of them walked to get the flowers, half a block away in the Palace Square. A lady on a sunlit corner sold roses under her umbrella. They had been picked fresh that morning. Johnny paid for the two dozen red roses with baby's breath in pink cellophane and then handed them to Chloe as if he were giving them to her. She took them, without lifting her eyes, and said thank you, and he said look at me.

I can't, she whispered back.

Please, Chloe. Look at me.

I can't, Johnny. They're watching us. I can't.

Just raise your eyes to me.

What could she do? Not look at him was one thing she could do. That's not what she did. She lifted her gaze. His blinkless tar eyes stared back at her dumb with love.

Not nearly enough roses for you, he said, his voice catching on all kinds of things.

Johnny, please, she breathed out, like begging.

I want to kiss you right now. He bent his head toward her. I'm going to kiss you right now.

Johnny, please!

She staggered away. He stood motionless. I can't take this, he said.

Me neither.

Khloya Deveeny, what are we going to do?

Nothing. You are going to spend the day telling us about the camps.

I'm not going to tell you. I'm going to show you. I don't mean that. I mean after.

After what?

He didn't say after what. But she knew. After today when he would go to Tarcento and she to Barcelona, and he to Afghanistan and she to San Diego, he to somewhere in his vagrant life, and she most certainly to some place else. She couldn't look at him anymore. Her mouth twisted sharply in an effort to keep her eyes from welling up. We better go back, she whispered.

They were a few buildings away, in full view of the others, who loitered on the street past the horses, waiting for Johnny's tourists. Everybody's eyes were on them. They walked as slowly as they could.

"Was it okay when Blake came back instead of me in the middle of the night?"

"No."

"Were you surprised?"

"I wasn't *not* surprised."

"He insisted he go."

"That sounds like Blake."

"I wanted to come back, Chloe. But he insisted."

"I understand."

"Was he angry?"

"Yes, but ..." Chloe didn't know why they were talking about Blake.

I don't know what I want to say, he said. I guess I'm not saying it very well.

No, Johnny, she said. You're saying it perfectly.

You're tearing me from limb to limb.

And you me.

They took the last steps of their glacial amble, closing in on the others. She clutched the flowers to her chest, as if she and Johnny were walking down the aisle of a long church. By the time she realized this, it was too late. But she didn't know how else to carry flowers! Or how to walk next to a tall beautiful boy if not in a ONE-two-and-three waltz, trying not to weep, to look less alive, to want less, to hurt less with bliss and sorrow. One two and three. One two and three. All things are numbers.

26

Dread

JOHNNY SAID THEY WOULD WALK FOUR KILOMETERS INTO THE woods. They would follow the old spur of the railroad, the spur that had been built by imprisoned Jews to reroute the trains from the main track in Treblinka village to a field in the remote forests. The sign was still there by the side of the desolate road in the gray flatlands. Treblinka, the sign proclaimed, announced, shouted, whispered.

They climbed out of the van at the crumbling, run-down train station. Yvette asked if it was still operational.

"Would you hop aboard a train at a station called Treblinka?" Johnny asked. Yvette wasn't sure how to answer that.

Artie helped her. "The answer is no, Yvette. Say no."

"No."

"Thatagirl."

Mason said that maybe the station had been left shuttered, yet standing on purpose and Chloe agreed. Acidly, Blake said, "You *think*?" Chloe and Mason glared at Blake.

"Anyway, as Johnny told us," Mason went on, "they couldn't continue to use it after the war, could they?"

"Why not?" Denise said. "Tell us, Johnny, you're the tour guide." Johnny, bless him, had to repeat everything he had told Chloe and Mason on the bus. He did it without rancor, but Mason was peeved for him, Chloe could see that. She gripped her roses with one hand, and Mason's hand with the other. Aberrantly, she liked that Mason liked Johnny.

"The sign is a replica," Blake said. "The original hangs in Yad Vashem."

"Where?"

"Jerusalem."

Johnny stared at Blake, amused. "That is correct, and it's fascinating," he said, "that you would know that."

"I know a lot of crap," Blake said with a cold shrug and an even colder stare.

Johnny advised everyone to leave their heavy things behind. "Bring your cameras if you want, but I'd counsel against even that. It's eight kilometers there and back. You don't want to be loaded down." He showed everyone his little Olympus point and shoot. "This is the size of camera you want on long hikes." Chloe glanced over at Blake and saw that he wanted to pitch his own silver Olympus into the trash. Imagine those two having the exact same camera.

"Can't Emil drive us?" Hannah asked. Chloe poked her to keep quiet. "What?" she said. "I'm just wondering."

"No, Emil can't drive into the forest," Johnny said. "Is everyone ready?"

Hannah stared at the path disappearing into the woods. "Why not?" she whispered to Chloe. "Why can't he drive us?"

Chloe hurried ahead to stay closer to Johnny, while doing some math in her head. Eight kilometers was five miles. Two and a half miles each way. Piece of cake. They walked more than that when they went mushroom picking around their lake after a rain. Chloe wanted to whisper that to Hannah, but her friend was in no mood to be chided, no matter how lightly.

They left their belongings in the van, which Emil promptly locked up. He wasn't joining them. He wasn't interested in that stuff, he said, swirling his hand in the direction of the forest. He was going to find some food and have a nap.

"How long, Johnny?" he asked in his regal English.

"About three hours," Johnny replied. They fist bumped.

"Three *hours?*" Hannah mouthed in horror.

The group set off.

"What if we have to go to the bathroom?" she asked, loudly, and then to Chloe: "I sort of have to go now."

Yvette laughed. "The forest is your ladies' room, darling," she said.

Hannah hemmed and hawed. "Wouldn't that be disrespectful?"

Johnny nodded. "Yes, probably best to go now rather than later."

Hannah shook her head. "Is he kidding me?" she whispered, hanging on to Chloe's arm.

It was just past noon. There was no one else on the needly path through the woods. "Well, why should there be?" Dennis said. "There's hardly anything here."

"There are some things here," said Johnny.

"Does anyone know about this place?" Denise asked.

"Yes. Poland and the Jewish Holocaust Committee are thinking of building a permanent museum here."

"There's not even a museum?" Dennis exclaimed.

"There's not even a museum," said Johnny.

"So what's here?"

"Well, there's these four kilometers of the railroad spur. As they rode it in the cattle cars, we're walking it now." He smirked. "Though I'm sure Hannah would prefer it the other way around, no?"

Hannah colored a little. "I'm fine now," she said, taking Blake's hand. "Carry on. You were saying there was a museum?"

"Actually, just the opposite."

"So what's there?" Brett persisted. "A watchtower? A barbed-wire fence? Remnants of the sleeping barracks?"

"Even Majdanek had more," Denise said. "And it hardly had anything."

"Yes, Treblinka has less. You'll see."

"So what are we walking to?" Hannah said. "We're just going to walk down this road, and then walk back?"

"We're walking to what used to be a farm," Johnny said. "Or what is now a cemetery, if you prefer."

They moved in single file along the narrow path, except for Hannah and Blake, who brought up the rear side by side. Hannah, despite her bravado, walked like the injured. Johnny strode in front, black guitar case on his back, followed by Chloe, Mason, and then the Arizona tourists. Johnny was the only one with a small backpack. His had maps in it, a compass.

"Not even some barracks left?" Yvette called from the middle. "Barracks are fascinating to see. I'll never forget the barracks at Sachsenhausen and Buchenwald."

"Living quarters for the Germans, you mean?" Johnny asked.

"No, I mean barracks for the Jews. Like in Majdanek."

"There were no barracks here," said Johnny.

"So what are we walking four miles for?" Hannah said from the rear. "A field?"

"Four kilometers, not miles."

"Same difference."

"Hannah, shh, listen to him," Blake said. Chloe was glad somebody had. Though to think: Blake told Hannah to listen to Johnny. Cats and dogs living together.

"Johnny, I don't get it. How can there not be barracks?" Denise said. "There are always barracks."

"Here's the thing about Treblinka II," Johnny told them, walking backwards so he could face them. "Treblinka I, a few kilometers away, had barracks, because it was a concentration camp. People slept and worked there at the quarry before they died. But that's not the part we're going to. The part we're going to had no barracks. They got off the train, and three hours later their bodies were burning in the pits."

A hush fell over the group, even Hannah. Half a kilometer went by in silence.

"Is the burning pit still there?" Yvette asked.

"No. It's gone."

"But how did they hide the pits from the Jews who'd just arrived?"

"They camouflaged them with exotic landscaping. And they covered the absence of barracks by telling the Jews that Treblinka was nothing more than a transit camp. That they were on their way to better camps elsewhere. A nicer train was waiting to pull in as soon as the dirty one left, and the people had washed and deloused."

"But couldn't everyone smell the human flesh burning?" That was Blake. He had asked Johnny a question. Treblinka, the great equalizer.

Johnny continued to walk backwards while answering Blake. Chloe was worried for him. Careful, she wanted to call out. Careful. You'll trip, you'll fall.

"Oh yes, Blake," he said. "The smell and the smoke from the fires permeated the region for miles. Everyone could smell it, everyone knew what it was. But you saw how sparsely populated the few villages around here are. That was the case sixty years ago too. And most of the villages had Gestapo living in them. No one said a thing. What could they say? Excuse me, that smells mighty suspicious. Let's just take a gander at what you have there?"

Blake nodded in grim understanding.

"Maybe they could've complained," said Hannah.

"To who?"

"Well, I don't know." Chloe thought Hannah wanted to add that she herself always found someone to complain to.

"No one admitted anything, or wrote anything down," Johnny said. "The smoke the Nazis didn't acknowledge, and everything else they hid. They wouldn't even allow the driver to pull the locomotive into the camp. He was ordered to put the train into reverse and back up four kilometers. The locomotive remained in the woods while the cattle cars with the Jews were slowly emptied. When they were done unloading, the conductor took the train back to the main spur. He never saw what was on the load manifest. For all he knew, he was delivering lumber."

Johnny stared at Chloe. She got uncomfortable and looked away. "Your grandmother knew this," he said. "Once you come here, you never forget. She didn't tell you about her past? Many survivors don't. It's too heavy and useless a burden for others."

"She didn't come here," Chloe replied. "Her friends did. Then they vanished. She searched for them for a long time after the war, she said. She was sure she'd see them again. She didn't believe the stories about Treblinka."

Johnny nodded, his eyes still on her. "Many people didn't. The Germans demolished nearly all the evidence. For years Treblinka was called the Forgotten Camp."

"Is there a crematoria here at least?" asked Denise. "Like in Majdanek?"

Johnny shook his head. "There wasn't one. They were burned on a pyre. Well, not at first. At first, after they were gassed, they were buried. But when Himmler visited the camp and saw the black oozing liquid of the decomposing bodies rising up from the shallow mass graves, he became physically ill. He had to be hospitalized. Afterward he ordered that every single body in the pits be dug up and burned. It took a thousand men three months to fulfill his orders. And they didn't get them all. They hoped he wouldn't come back and inspect the camp again."

"How do you know they didn't get them all?" asked Brett.

"Be patient. I'll get there," Johnny said with a small smile. "Chloe, your grandmother wasn't the only one who was skeptical. Lots of people maintained that Treblinka was a myth perpetuated by the Jews, nothing more than a vicious lie. Except for a tiny problem: intact bones kept being unearthed near the field we're about to see, for the next—well, until now, actually. They're still being unearthed."

"We're not going to see bones, are we, Johnny?" Hannah said. "Because I won't be able to stomach that."

"No, don't worry." They continued onward.

"I want to underline," Johnny said, "that the extermination of human beings on this scale is unprecedented in human history. There's been genocide, there's been slaughter, and indiscriminate killing. But there has never been such a pitiless conveyor belt of mass death. For a long while no one raised a voice against it, partly because no one believed it, just like Moody." Johnny blinked at Chloe. She blinked back without breaking stride. He remembered her grandmother's name. He was the boy who seemed to remember everything. Would he remember her?

"The one or two people who had managed to escape," he went on, "and recounted some of what they'd seen here, were dismissed as kooks and liars. Imagine having several trains a day deliver thousands of human beings and have them all be dead by sundown. Yvette is right. No one believed this was possible. Or that Hitler would be insane enough to divert the vast resources from his war machine, a diversion that many people point to as having cost him the war, which he had started and for all intents and purposes won in 1942.

"But it was precisely in 1942," Johnny continued, "at the moment that Hitler felt most invincible that he began his long-planned construction of the six death camps. *Operation Reinhard* required trains, coal, electricity, transport, and building materials. It needed sand and concrete, bricks and mortar, and weapons— and gas! Let's not forget that someone had to manufacture an enormous amount of Zyklon B, and it all had to be shipped to Majdanek or Birkenau, along with benzene, kerosene, wood, metal, weapons, ammunition, and barbed wire. But the diversion of transport trains was probably most instrumental in Hitler's defeat. Instead of bringing his wounded soldiers from the front to the hospitals, instead of bringing food and arms to the front, instead of carrying materials desperately needed to fight the Soviets in the dead of winter, with Poland directly in the path between Group Army Nord and the unstoppable Red Army, Hitler instead used the trains to deliver millions of Jews to their execution. Instead of using the Jews for slave labor, he killed them. All of it boggles the rational mind. It's one of the reasons why no one believed the sporadic reports that arose from the camps and the ghettos. Not Churchill, not Roosevelt. Stalin may have believed it," Johnny said, "but he didn't care. He had his own agenda against Hitler. He was willing to kill twenty million of his men to destroy Germany—and did—because Hitler had betrayed him, not because Hitler was a monster. It was all personal with Stalin.

"The bottom line is that the place we are heading to is unique even among the death centers. The Germans built thirty or forty concentration camps in the occupied territories—and they were all death camps, make no mistake about it. The Jews, and many others, died everywhere. And of course when we see Auschwitz in a few days, the thing that I hope will affect you the most is the sheer size and scope of the slaughter operation there: it had six crematoria and four gas chambers. The Birkenau section was three miles square. An entire twenty-wagon train pulled in comfortably inside it. But even Auschwitz-Birkenau had barracks. What we'll be looking at here is distinct from the others, because what you're about to see had only one purpose. It was an abattoir. It was to kill Jews. The killing wasn't a byproduct of this camp, but its reason for being. There was no other business in Treblinka. They were brought here not to work but to die. That's why there were no barracks. They weren't needed."

"Why didn't they build a crematorium here?" Yvette asked in a much quieter voice. "How did they dispose of the ..." She broke off.

"Because they learned from Birkenau," Johnny replied, "that the ovens were not as economical or efficient as the burning pits. After Stalingrad was lost, and the Nazis realized they were on the clock, they quadrupled their efforts. It's not a coincidence that most of the six million Jews died after the Soviets held Stalingrad in January 1943. No time to futz about with ovens."

"Hannah is right, though," Denise said. "What are we going to see here if there's nothing to see?"

"Well, there is something to see," said Johnny. "There is the leveled field in the middle of nowhere with woods all around it. There is a cemetery. And I brought with me a schematic layout of the camp. I'll show you some of how it happened."

"Isn't there anything there?" Brett pressed on. "Any gas chambers, barracks, station, *anything*?"

"No," said Johnny. "Nothing but the cemetery. You'll have to imagine the rest."

They walked. The woods were dark, even at noon, and smelled of rotting plants, sappy pine needles, undergrowth. Chloe became afraid. If ever she might have had a nightmare about a death camp, she couldn't have conceived of anything more frightening than walking four kilometers deep into the empty woods to a forgotten farm where nearly a million people had died.

"Where is everyone?" Denise asked. "Yesterday there were dozens of people at Sobibor."

"Not here," Johnny said. "I came here once in the middle of winter, and there was no one here then either."

"Well, perhaps that's because there's nothing to see," Brett said, not so gently.

"I disagree with you, Brett," said Artie. "I strongly disagree."

"You have to decide for yourself that question," Johnny said. "It's probably a philosophical one. Why do you walk up Via Dolorosa to Calvary? Is there something to see? Why do you go inside the Roman Colosseum? Anything there? Gettysburg?" he asked. "Now there's a field for you. Is that all you see when you tour Gettysburg?"

"I get your point," Brett said, amending. "But couldn't they rebuild some of it so we could imagine it better?"

"They left it as the Germans left it," Johnny said, "because they thought that would be more telling."

"Who did you come with in the winter?" Chloe asked him.

"My father," Johnny replied. "Everything was covered with deep snow. It was deathly quiet."

"Like now."

"Quieter. No birds. No insects. No other people but me and him. All you could hear was the dead."

"Johnny, stop," Yvette said. "You're making us shiver."

Chloe didn't want to continue walking. She turned to glance at Mason slightly behind her, at Hannah and even at Blake, who kept his eyes away from her, wouldn't look at her directly. Hannah was pale and slow, and definitely looked as if she didn't want to continue walking. Blake had his arm around her. Mason caught up and squeezed Chloe's hand. "We have railroad ties across our pond. We go there all the time."

"It's not this."

They played there as children and teenagers, running on the tracks, pretending the train was just around the corner, and they had mere seconds to jump to safety. That wasn't this. That was child's play. Literally. They skipped on the ties. If you misstepped onto the pebbled sand, you lost. There, they balanced themselves on the rusty rails, pretending they were Olympic gymnasts. Not here. There was no rail here. The tracks had been long demolished. Only the symbols of tracks, ominous wide black ties, ran alongside the path they doggedly trod on. How far was four kilometers? Why did it feel like a day on the trains? Blake wasn't taking any photos. Neither was anyone else. Everyone just wanted to get through it.

Johnny pointed ahead. Finally the clearing.

They walked out into an open field shaped like a polygon, the size of a football field. It was dotted with sharp jagged rocks of varying sizes, like an ocean shore at low tide. In the middle stood a much larger stone, a giant mushroom cleaved through the center. They stopped, huddled, took a drink of water, looked around while Johnny got out his maps. After a short break, too short by the sounds of Hannah's under-the-breath whingeing, they resumed following Johnny, while he told them about what once stood on this ground.

"What you bear witness to here," Johnny said, "are the best qualities of the German personality corrupted in the terrifying distorting mirror of Hitler's Reich. Accuracy, attention to detail, frugality, cleanliness, all good traits in a nation of hardworking people, were instead applied by Hitler to a crime against mankind. The barracks they built right in this corner for their own living quarters were constructed in an orderly line, as if on a well-planned street. They planted birch trees along their walking paths for aesthetic pleasure and some shade. They carefully leveled the roads with white sand from the nearby quarry. They built comfortable laundry facilities for themselves with well-constructed steps leading to the basin. They even built small fountains for the woodland birds. They had a bakery, a barber, a storage shed, a fuel station. There were gardens, flowers, a little petting zoo! They played music, sang sentimental songs, took pictures of one another. Their natural inclination toward order, toward maps and plans and schematics, was worked out to the last detail." Johnny smirked. "Except for small problems here and there," he said. "For example, they didn't have delousing facilities at Treblinka. They had to send the clothes they removed from the Jews to Majdanek for delousing with Zyklon B before shipping them off to Germany."

"They didn't have Zyklon B here?"

Johnny shook his head. "Only at Birkenau and Majdanek. Here they used carbon monoxide, the exhaust fumes from an internal combustion engine. The efficiency in Treblinka was such that the Germans were able to kill more than a thousand people at once. This tiny place whirred at maximum operation for only a few months in 1943, and yet with these limited facilities, no crematoria, and gas chambers much smaller than Auschwitz, they still managed to kill nearly a million people. Just think about the fury and single-mindedness with which they approached the task entrusted to them."

"It's impossible!" Artie exclaimed. "The logistics alone are impossible."

"And yet."

All Chloe wanted was to turn around and run back to the van. She clasped her flowers. She had promised her grandmother. Moody, crazy like a fox. She must have known what the children would see here before they grew up and became adults. As Chloe meandered through the jagged rocks to the large mushroom-shaped stone structure, she didn't think the Poles needed to make it into a proper memorial. This graveyard almost without markers had a sure and absolute stamp of death in every knowing tree branch, in every falling needle, in every flattened ounce of its loamy soil.

Johnny caught up to Chloe and Mason. "To make the façade as real as they could," Johnny told them, pointing to the edge of the field, "they built a fake train station, and spent extra time on it, so that the soon-to-die didn't panic any more than they needed to. It was all about maintaining order. They painted a clock on the fake station, which permanently read six o'clock." With his words, Johnny kept drawing for Chloe invisible things with material weight. "They painted words with destinations. Warsaw, Bialystok, Vilnius. The camp was small, as you see, and they mined the perimeter, and fenced it in, and then fenced off separate sections within the camp. Such as the small cabin with a Red Cross flag on it, where the old and the sick and the weak were taken immediately and shot through the neck above the pit where a fire smoldered. Farther along the fence, only a few hundred feet away, concealed from everything else by fake shrubbery, were the excavation pits, where the ashes and bones of the burned were rolled in wheelbarrows to be buried. Where the *Sonderkommandos* lived, they fenced off that area, too."

"Who were the *Sonderkommandos*?" Yvette asked. The rest of the group had caught up with Chloe and Mason.

"Good question," said Johnny. "They were the unlucky Jews to whom fell the task of turning on the gas, of pulling the gold teeth out of their dead brothers, of removing the jewelry, of carrying the bodies one by one on stretchers to the raised platform onto which they placed them, and of throwing more wood on the fire underneath them."

"What did the Germans do?"

"Supervised. They didn't like to get their hands dirty. They hated uncleanliness."

"What happened to the *Sonderkommandos*?"

"Burned with the rest. Replaced by new *Sonderkommandos*."

They all stopped at a large stone monument with a crack in it like a schism.

Chloe looked around the flat, drab field, the distant trees. "Everything is out in the open," Blake said. "I just don't understand how they could have hidden what they were doing from the people they were killing. It seems so hard to hide the truth." He seemed stuck on this particular point, the deception.

"In the long term, yes," Johnny said. "But in the short term anyone can do it. As I said, they constructed ingenious fences. A barbed-wire fence, camouflaged with long branches of pine. The fence was six feet tall, so when you were naked and stooped in shame, your eyes to the ground, you didn't see the fire grates and the excavation pit. The Germans placed a flowerpot in front of the entrance to the gas chamber. There was a guy, an SS standing guard, whose sole job was to make sure the pot always had fresh flowers in it, to make the entrance to the showers more hospitable. The Jews were told that after their shower, they would get a hot meal and a ticket out. Chloe, do you want to put down your flowers here, on the place where the flowerpot was?" Johnny asked. "We're standing over that spot. We know this because a Treblinka survivor built a very good model of the camp, which is now in the Holocaust Museum in Kigali. They're hoping to move the model here, if ever they open a museum."

"Kigali?"

"Yes, Kigali. Rwanda."

"There's a Holocaust Museum in Rwanda?" Blake asked.

"Apparently a very good one." Johnny pointed to another area in the far corner of the field. "After the Jews got off at the fake transit station, always accompanied by jaunty, uplifting music from a live orchestra, just like in Birkenau, they shuffled to the undressing square. There was no selection process here as at Auschwitz. Everyone went to the same place—the flowerpot. But to get to it, the Jews had to walk the last distance naked down a narrow walkway called The Tube. It was about four meters wide and eighty meters long, hidden by the pine branch fences. The Germans called The Tube *Himmelfahrtstrasse*. The Road to Heaven. Chloe, let's put your flowers down. Do you want to? You're holding on to them as if you don't. Maybe Blake can take a picture for your grandmother."

Blake resentfully lifted the Olympus to his face. Chloe could see he didn't want to be told what to do, by Johnny of all people.

"Or I'd be glad to do it," Johnny said.

"I'll do it," Blake snapped. Carefully, Chloe placed her roses on the ground near the mushroom stone, next to a menorah and the star of David, alongside other dried and wilted flowers. Chloe knew all too well how long graves can remain unquiet, singly or collectively.

After a few minutes of silence, they left the monument and walked away to explore. Chloe kept hoping for other people to come join them, so the place wouldn't feel so eerie, so tremblingly spooky.

"How long was the camp running, Johnny?" Chloe asked him.

"Treblinka opened on July 22, 1942. The first train arrived the next day, July 23. During the first few months, it took the Germans with their disorganized Ukrainian workers about four hours to kill half the people on the train. But as they expanded the gas chambers, they reduced the time between arrival and excavation pit to ninety minutes. After they became a model of efficiency, they were able to liquidate the entire twenty-car train in four hours. While the last of the Jews were being gassed and burned, another fifty Jews washed down and cleared the train, which then left Treblinka to make space for the next one already waiting."

"Why did it close so much earlier than Majdanek?" Denise asked. "Yesterday you told us the Germans barely cleared out of Majdanek before the Soviets arrived."

"Yes, Treblinka closed nine months earlier, in October 1943."

"Why?"

Johnny shrugged. His guitar case rose and fell. "All the Jews were dead. The job was done. So they mined everything, leveled it to the ground, filled in the pits, razed the buildings, carted away the rubble. The fence was gone, the station gone. They planted some new trees, built a fake farm, right over the fake station, planted some fake crops, and hired a real Ukrainian to live here and keep the locals away.

"As it turned out," he continued, "not far enough away. Because with the war still raging, the residents started digging up the surrounding areas in search of valuables possibly left on the bodies. They found only a few jewels, but they did exhume quite a large number of bodies, which, despite Himmler's orders, had remained in the earth. Presented with this evidence after the war, the Germans said bodies, what bodies? We don't know what you're talking about. Ask the damn Ukrainians. We know the place as a sand quarry. Poles and Jews worked in the quarry for our war effort. The rest we have no idea about. That's what they continued to say for many years, and some people believed it, even though the Soviets who had marched through here in July 1944 and the war correspondents who accompanied them wrote unbelievable things about what they had found in the earth. Most of these writings have not been translated into English."

"So how do you know this?" Blake asked.

"A few bilinguals with classified clearance translated many documents to get to the truth."

"But how do *you* know this?"

The guitar rose and fell on Johnny's shoulders. "I know some of the translators."

Before Chloe had a chance to zero in on Johnny, to hone in on his face and the words he had uttered, Hannah spoke. "I don't want to be here anymore," she said. "I'm going to be sick." And then she bent and was promptly sick on the sandy earth.

Everyone looked away.

Shortly afterward, they left.

"Wait," said Yvette. "Johnny, can you take a picture of the five of us with Artie's camera? Guys, wait, come back!" she called to Brett, Denise, Dennis and Artie. "Okay, Johnny? Otherwise, honest to God, no one will ever believe we were here."

The four-kilometer walk back was interminable, but not quiet. Chloe and Mason and Hannah and Blake were quiet. But Brett and Yvette, Dennis and Denise and Artie clucked and chatted non-stop about the fake clock and the fake directions to fake cities, about the pairs of shoes tied together by laces to make them easier to sort for the Germans, and about Artur Gold conducting his orchestral trio through one happy tune after another at the end of the long barrel of a German rifle. Artur Gold, who fiddled until he was gassed in 1943, a few months before Treblinka had shut its doors. They talked about the trains arriving from as far as Holland, France, Italy. To stop them from talking, a tired-looking Johnny told them stories about the trains in a soft voice.

"Denise, Yvette, listen to me, girls. The trains were very important. Without the trains, there is no question, there would've been fewer dead. The Germans knew this—they had been planning the final solution for years—which is why very early on, 1939 and the start of 1940, they moved all the Jews into ghettos near a robust rail system. Krakow, Warsaw, of course. Lublin. They exported them to the camps from as far as Greece and yes, Italy. The trains were all either freight wagons or cattle cars. They weren't the luxury passenger liners Chloe and I rode from Vilnius to Warsaw." He almost smiled, but not really. "Sometimes the trains had ten wagons, sometimes sixty. It's because of the trains I mention so often," Johnny said, "that we know how many millions died in the camps. Because the Germans, as it turned out, didn't keep accurate record books on the deaths of the Jews."

"Go figure," Blake said.

"Yes!" As if Blake and Johnny had shared a secret joke. "Of all the things they liked to record, how many people they gassed was far down the list. But the Polish State Railway kept records. About sixteen hundred trains were commandeered by the Germans, who ran the Polish railroad from 1941 to the end of 1944. Sixteen hundred trains in about eleven hundred days. That's how they counted them. The trains had to be filled to capacity. There was no point in bringing only a half-full train to Treblinka. So sometimes the trains sat in the rail yards, waiting for more 'shipment,' as they called it, to be loaded on. With minimal food and water, many people died on the trains before they got to the camps—and that was also the point. Anyone whom the ghettos and the trains didn't kill, the death camps finished. The shortest train travel was from Bialystok, fifty kilometers away. The longest was from Korfu in Greece. It took eighteen days. By the time the doors on the train from Korfu opened in Belzec, all seven thousand people on that train were dead." Johnny stared at Chloe with ineffable emotion. "That's why I like riding the trains today," he said. "Despite all the inconveniences. I remind myself of what it means to be alive and ride the train, ride it to life, to Barcelona, to Paris, to Trieste, instead of to Lublin, to Auschwitz, to Lodz."

He fell quiet. Mason took Chloe's hand. Blake had his arm around exhausted Hannah. Denise and Yvette started arguing about how much was sixteen hundred trains times three thousand people times eleven hundred days. Brett and Dennis joined in, helping them multiply.

"Oh my God," Blake said. "Will they never shut up?"

"Not yesterday," Johnny said. "Not today. So I'm thinking no."

He turned to them all and walked backwards.

"You're right, Denise, to keep multiplying the numbers," Johnny said. "You're trying to find a mathematical explanation for the thing that's impossible to think about and impossible not to think about. But you won't. Nothing in math or history equals it. Nothing comes close. You can't even really talk about it without reducing it with pale words and woeful arithmetic. Both are inadequate. If you're an atheist, it almost makes sense what happened. This is just the way it is, the unbelievers reason. Such is the merciless barbarity of the world. But if you believe in God, the slaughter of innocents, young and old, is harder to rationalize. What words do you use to reconcile an all loving, all powerful God with the burning pits and the gas chambers and the trains? It's almost enough proof for the doubters that God indeed may be powerless, or indifferent, or non-existent." Johnny waved his hand to the hidden field, to the gathering pines. "Love isn't at the heart of it. The absence of love, the absence of God is at the heart of it. But even so, it remains an unanswerable mystery. Sometimes there is just no explaining the devastating things that happen."

Chloe knew this firsthand to be true, her own small house still recovering from the holocaust of just one extinguished life.

Denise and Yvette clucked in solemn agreement with Johnny, and then resumed multiplying the parenthetical before adding it to the next algebraic equation. To force them to fall quiet, Johnny took the guitar off his shoulders and handed the black case to Chloe to carry. He started strumming and singing a lilting waltz melody. It was so beautiful that Chloe couldn't help herself, she started to cry.

"What song is that?" she asked, surreptitiously wiping her face, hoping no one would see, not even Mason walking next to her.

"The 'Polish Tango,'" Johnny replied. "Do you like it?"

"It's by Artur Gold!" Yvette exclaimed, rushing up to them. "Johnny, that's wonderful. How do you know this song? It's one of his most famous, most beautiful melodies. We were just talking about him."

"Yes, Yvette, I know."

"Can you play any of his others? He had so many."

They surrounded Johnny. "Can you play 'Chodz na Prage'?" Artie asked. "It means 'Come to Prague.' The melody is played as a trumpet call in the Prague section of Warsaw every day at noon, to this day." He smiled tearfully. "My Arlene knew a lot about Artur Gold. She liked that he and I shared a name."

Johnny nodded, continuing to strum. One two and three. One two and three. All Chloe wanted was to hear him sing. That's what she told herself was all she wanted.

"Yes, the Germans took their music very seriously." He spoke in a lilting voice, almost like singing. "And Kurt Franz, the camp commander, ordered that the entire orchestra, which later included dancers and singers, be in full dress, as if at a ball. The men wore starched long white frock coats with blue collars and blue lapels. They put on white shirts, patent leather shoes, and dark pressed pants. After supper, the Germans liked to hear German songs, but during the day when the sky was smoky black and the wind carried the smell of charred and rotting flesh, Artur played well-known Polish evergreens by the fake train station. He played the song I just sang, the 'Polish Tango,' which is my favorite. It's also called, 'It's Not Your Fault That My Heart Is Asleep.'" Johnny paused as he strummed the chorus, walking on one side of Chloe, while Mason flanked her on the other. From the periphery Chloe glimpsed a small smile on Johnny's somber face. Then he stopped smiling. "At the bequest of the commander, Artur Gold also composed 'The Treblinka Song,'" Johnny said. "That one has never been recorded, but thanks to a helpful former Gestapo officer who had served here and was interviewed in secret for the documentary *Shoah*, we have the

rousing melody and lyrics of that song permanently on record."
He began to sing in march time, a Germanic ONEandtwo:

"Wir wollen weiter, weiter leisten

bis dass das kleine Glück uns einmal winkt.

Hurrah!"

"What does it mean?" Chloe asked.

"We want to work, more, more, MORE until the little fortune
finally greets us, hurrah!"

The professional tourists fell back, continuing to debrief and
assess. They walked in non-stop babble, while Johnny dolorously
sang the tango in another tongue, his voice tearing Chloe up and
binding her back together.

"Ty ne winna chto me serce spi."

It's not your fault that my heart is asleep.

Nothing was asleep on Chloe and it was all Johnny's fault.
Johnny, you make all things, even the unbearable ones, a little
bit better.

Oh my God, I love him, she thought, clutching his guitar case
because she no longer carried the roses he had given her. I love
him. What am I going to do?

After four kilometers of black railroad ties and acoustic intimacy,
they finally walked out of the woods to the Treblinka train station
sign, placed there as a historic marker of the unquiet mass grave
to which they had just borne witness. That's where they had left
Emil and his van. By the sign.

The sign was there. Neither Emil nor his van was there.

That's when Brett and Yvette and Dennis and Denise and
Artie finally shut up.

27

Emil

FOR A FEW SECONDS, THEY STOOD MUTE LIKE DOLLS, TRYING to process. No one could infer the immediate meaning of Emil's stark absence. Chloe certainly couldn't. So she rejected meaning in favor of facile explanations of others.

"Maybe he went to get some food."

Vigorously, she nodded.

"He must have been hungry, poor guy," Denise said. "He's been sitting waiting for us for nearly four hours."

Nodded, nodded.

"Or he really needed to use the bathroom," said Hannah. "I know how he feels."

Yes, that was certainly true, nodded Chloe.

"He went to find a phone."

Assent.

"He went to get gas."

Possibly.

"Maybe he had told us to meet him somewhere else, and we forgot?"

Not likely, but not impossible.

"He'll be right back."

Of course he will.

They waited.

Eventually Hannah wailed in frustration. "I need to sit down," she said. "I'm not feeling well." Blake propped her up on a broken stump, a remnant from an old rotted fence. Artie and Brett and Dennis paced, away from the women, talking quietly. Chloe would've liked to know what they were saying. They looked a bit grim. Mason put his arm around Chloe. "You all right?"

She thought he meant about the current situation they found themselves in, but Mason waved to the far and nebulous forest, as if nothing concerned him but what they had just seen.

After a few seconds of inarticulate nodding, Chloe spun around in a perplexed carousel to look for the answers in Johnny. Weren't in him the answers to all things? What was he doing? Maybe his actions could tell her where Emil was.

He stood some distance away from them. He didn't look down the road, or at the four young people or at the five older people. Cigarette dangling from his mouth, guitar dangling on his back, Johnny was engrossed in the train schedule.

"What do you think?" Chloe said to Mason, pointing at Johnny. On her back was his black guitar case. "Should we be worried?"

"Nah," Mason said. "We don't know what he's looking up." He kissed her cheek. "Could be the schedule of his trains to Italy. Isn't that where he's going next? Let's not draw any conclusions."

"Really? None?"

"Chloe, Emil wouldn't just leave us here," Mason said. "Why would he do that? Besides, all of our stuff is on his bus." He stopped speaking for emphasis. Or maybe he just stopped speaking. He paled slightly.

They were on an empty stretch of land in the middle of a desolate plain of pines and brush, a hasty escape away from the glade filled with a million murdered souls, and Emil was nowhere to be found. A shivering Chloe, no matter how much she didn't want to, began to draw some conclusions.

There was an unreal feel to it. The excuses waned. The gazes fell to the ground.

Johnny put away his timetable book and approached them. "There's a six o'clock train out of Malkinia Gorna," he said. "It's three kilometers down the road. It's not even five yet. If we hurry, we can make it. We *will* make it. Because if we miss it, the next train is not until nine, and we don't want to be stuck here for three hours. There's nothing to do and nowhere to eat. And it's going to get dark." He said the last thing with a stress that Chloe didn't need pointed out to her. There were no streetlamps, no houses, no roadside markets. When it got dark, it would get *dark*. And they were a cry away from the killing field. When Hannah cried out, Chloe thought it was because Hannah understood the urgency.

"I can't walk another three miles!" Hannah cried. "I just can't."

"It's not three miles," said Johnny. "It's three kilometers."

"Yeah, yeah. Why can't we just wait for Emil? How far could he have gone?"

Johnny didn't say.

"Let's wait," Hannah said, not budging. "He'll be back, won't he?"

Johnny wouldn't say.

But now the older group got vocal.

"You're not answering, Johnny."

"Where's Emil, Johnny?"

"What kind of driver splits at precisely the time he's supposed to stay put?"

"You did tell him three hours. Why isn't he here?"

"You think he got tired of waiting and left?"

"I don't know," Johnny said.

"He ought to be fired for doing that!"

"Yes, I'll be sure never to hire him again," said Johnny. "But in the meantime, we really should go. Come on, Hannah."

"Wait," Denise said, as if she just remembered the important part. "What about our things?"

Johnny's back was to her. "What things?"

"What do you mean, what things, Johnny?" Denise was shrill. "Like, our everything!"

"Denise is right," Dennis said. "We left our backpacks, our cameras on the bus."

Now Blake spoke in a dull voice. "Backpacks with our journals."

"Backpacks with all my money!" That was Hannah. She struggled up. The initial shock was wearing off for everyone. Even Mason had turned white. His mouth clamped together. "He'll be right back, Johnny, right?" Mason said. "We have to get our backpacks. We simply have to."

"Money? Forget money." That was Yvette. The handwringing had started. The quicksilver fury was only a breath away. "He has our passports!"

Chloe thought Mason seemed oddly quiet. He didn't even nod in agreement. He still looked white.

"Yes," Artie said. "Our passports. Which means we won't be able to leave Warsaw, travel anywhere, leave the hotel, exchange money, *go home.*"

Now, suddenly, Hannah wasn't the only one crying. Yvette and Denise joined in.

"We have cash in our bag!" Denise said. "Seventy-seven dollars."

Dennis comforted her with his arm. "Don't worry," he said. "The passports are more important."

"Seventy-seven dollars?" said Chloe. "I had Moody's fifteen hundred dollars in my backpack." In panic she stared at Mason, at Blake.

"I had all of my own money in mine," Hannah said. "Two hundred dollars."

The boys didn't say how much of their own spending cash they had brought. Mason spoke in a shaky voice. "He'll come back. Right, Johnny? Any minute he'll be back."

Blake glared at his brother, at Chloe—and at Johnny, and said nothing.

The girls and boys had left all their valuables in their backpacks on the bus. Johnny had specifically told them there was no museum shop and nothing to buy. He'd been right about that. So they left everything. Their passports, their Eurail tickets, their money, Chloe's makeup, the favorite Dior lipstick she got as a birthday gift, Rock-n-Roll red, her favorite green cashmere cardigan, their journals. The daily recollections of the things that mattered most, all in their packs, all in Emil's vanished van.

It was about three seconds, maybe four, before seven of the nine people turned on Johnny. Hannah just sat, staring vacantly down the highway, her stone face like the concrete road. And Chloe couldn't find a place in her heart to turn on Johnny. Give her time, maybe, but time with him was one thing she didn't have.

"Who is this Emil, Johnny?"

"Did he take off with our stuff?"

"Is he a thief?"

"What did you do to us?"

"We trusted you completely. What's happening? Tell us!"

And then from Blake: "How come *your* backpack is on your back, Johnny? Why didn't you leave yours on the bus, too, like us?"

Yeah, yeah, yeah, yeah, sang the Greek chorus.

Johnny didn't step away from their furious accusations. He faced them head on as he had faced the homeless man in Sestokai. He barely even blinked. "It's going to be fine," he said. "I promise you. But we need to get back to Warsaw. Emil is an airport shuttle driver, and he probably got an emergency call. So don't worry. I know where he lives. I'll get your things back. It's just a misunderstanding. But we must catch the train."

"Why would he take our things?"

"I'm sure he didn't take them. He ran to another job."

"Are you sure about that?" Blake said.

"Reasonably sure," replied Johnny, gesturing to Hannah to get up. "We have to hurry."

"Why? If your friend's just on an airport run and it's all a big mix-up, why the urgency to rush back to Warsaw?"

"Do you want to get your things back sooner rather than later?"

Everyone but Blake agreed that sooner was best.

"Then let's go. Blake, get your girlfriend up."

"Don't tell me what to do," Blake muttered, stretching out his hand to Hannah.

"Johnny, is this some kind of a hustle job?" Yvette asked. "Were we robbed? Tell us. Is he going to sell our passports and cameras on the black market?"

"You give him too much credit. He's a lummox, not a fox."

Johnny started walking. Doggedly they followed him. He was almost jogging. No one could keep up, not the men, not the women. He was five hundred paces ahead of them on a road with no shoulder, occasional cars whizzing by, while they trailed behind, too out of breath to even gossip about him. Perhaps that was the point.

But Mason did tell Chloe some things he had overheard earlier that morning, an exchange between Johnny and Emil about money, that now seemed a lot more important.

They barely made the train. Johnny had to hold the doors open, buy everyone's tickets, slip the conductor some money to wait. "So *he* still has money," Blake said under his breath.

There was a drunken party (of course) in the compartment next to theirs, making it difficult to talk, or think, or figure anything out. The train was lurchy, stopped every kilometer at a new station, took forever to pull out, moved slowly and was unbearably hot.

On the train, the suppositions, the phenomenal conjectures, the wild imaginings about Emil's character, purpose and nefarious connection to Johnny kept them all jarred on adrenaline.

Nine of them fit into one compartment. Hannah sat on Blake's lap. Johnny, the tenth, went elsewhere. I'll find another seat, he said, and vanished. I'll see you on the other side. Did he say that or did Chloe wish he had said that?

After an hour of heavy gossip—with Mason and Chloe not volunteering what Mason had heard about Johnny's financial straits—Blake said there was a good chance they'd never see Johnny again. "Who's to say they both weren't in on it? One tells us to leave all our stuff behind. The other one runs off. Johnny jumps off the train, they meet up and split the loot. We'll never see him again, I guarantee it." Blake spoke with corrosive glee, as if the loss of their money and prized possessions and passports, the ruination of their entire trip, would be worth it if they never saw that boy again. And this was after his taking them through the fields of Treblinka—as if this most astounding thing had meant nothing. Chloe would rather spend a night in the blackout of Malkinia Gorna than have what Blake said be true.

"Do you really think it could be true?" Denise asked.

"It's the most likely scenario."

"Blake, don't say that. Please." A frightened Chloe. "You don't really think he could've robbed us. Wise up, will you." She shot up. "I'll be right back."

"Mason, go with her," Blake said. "There are drunks on the train."

"I'll be fine, Mase," said Chloe. "Stay. I'll go the other way from the drunks." But she would walk toward the drunks and into a tar pit of moonshine until she found him. Blake couldn't be right about him. He simply couldn't. Churning with anxiety, balancing through the narrow corridor, holding the rails, pitching from side to side, she walked and peered into every compartment.

She found him in the food lounge. He was smoking, drinking a beer, staring out the window. He looked worried and forlorn. All Chloe felt was deep relief. Nothing else mattered. He was here. Blake was wrong.

"Johnny."

"Chloe," he said. "Sit. So, what are they saying?"

She sat down, heavy-hearted, full-hearted. As if Johnny's mess was Chloe's mess too, and not on the receiving end, but on the Bonnie and Clyde end. This is how perfectly lawful women dived into lawlessness, Chloe thought without regret. They were ambushed in the middle of Poland, and were glad for it.

"Come back to our compartment, Johnny," she said. "Everyone's afraid you ditched us. Please come back. Set their minds at ease."

"Who's everyone? Blake?" Johnny smirked. "First, I'm the odd guy out. No room for me. But also, I don't want to sit in the compartment with you when I know you need to trashtalk me. Blake needs to cool off. Or he's bound to say something we'll all regret, and then where will we be? Trapped in a tiny compartment, and no way out." He shook his head.

"Is there a way out?" Chloe herself didn't see it.

"Depends on what you're talking about."

"Anything. Everything."

"No," he said. Sliding his hand across the table, he took hold of her balled-up hand.

They sat for a few minutes in silence, struggling through their labored breathing.

Chloe told him about what Mason had caught of Johnny's conversation with Emil. "Does this have anything to do with that?"

"I don't know." Johnny sighed.

"You told us to leave our stuff behind, and it all got pinched."

"It looks bad, I agree."

"Does it look bad because it *is* bad, or does it just look bad?"

He released his gentle hold on her fist. "It is bad," said Johnny.

She fought the impulse to throw her hands to her face. All her life with her mother she fought the impulse to facepalm and she fought it off successfully now, thanks to all that practice.

"Don't worry," he said. "I'll make it right."

How could what Blake said be true? That this unfathomable stranger with crazy eyes, a boy with a wild voice, a teenager just like them, could have colluded with a toughened con artist to steal their passports and money and then split the treasure? Lowering her voice, her agitation and suspicion waging a war inside her embattled heart, Chloe pressed on. "Were you and Emil in on it together? Did you tell us to leave our stuff behind, knowing he was going to take everything?"

"No, that's not what happened. Tell Blake to go write his books and leave me out of it. I'm a real person, not an invented character in his head. That's not what happened."

"I didn't say it was Blake."

"You didn't have to."

"So what happened?"

"What happened, Chloe," Johnny said, "is that I do owe Emil some long-standing dough."

"What for?"

"Just stuff he and I were working on a while back. It's not relevant. Clearly he was afraid he wasn't going to get paid. So he took matters into his own hands. But I'll take care of it."

"How?"

"I just will, that's how. I need to get to Warsaw ASAP, and then I'll take care of it."

"You know your tour friends want to call the police as soon as we get there."

"No." Johnny shook his head emphatically. He slipped out of his seat and went across to sit next to Chloe. He took her by the arms, turned her to him. In another life, it would be the gesture of a man about to lean in and kiss a woman, a woman for whom he felt raw desire, and who felt a raw desire for him. But this wasn't another life. And in this life, his eyes blazing, lips parted, skin flushed, Johnny didn't kiss Chloe. He squeezed her and said, "Please. Please go and convince them not to call the cops. Tell them to give me a night and a day to get your stuff back. If you go to the consulate or get the police involved, I won't be able to do a thing, I won't be able to help you, do you understand?"

She didn't understand.

"I'll have to disappear. Emil is most certainly off the grid by now. The cops won't find him. He's got fake IDs, fake passports. He'll be gone by tomorrow morning if he thinks the police are looking for him."

"But we need our passports and money back, Johnny!" she exclaimed, as if by shouting she could make him understand.

"The cops might pick him up but they'll never find the goods. And if the cops pick me up, there goes my whole future, my army commission, my Ranger training. I just need a day. If I don't get your passports back by tomorrow, you can go to the police and the consulate."

"Passports and money."

"Passports and money," Johnny echoed, less certainly. He got up. "Let's go. We'll be in Warsaw soon. Let's go talk to them."

She walked in front of him, wobbling down the narrow train corridor. Behind her she heard him say, "What about you and me, Chloe Divine?"

One disaster at a time, she wanted to say to him.

"Is there a you and me?" he asked.

She didn't answer him. They were at their compartment.

The boy with the silver tongue persuaded the mob to give him a day before the lynching. Then he stepped outside between the train cars to smoke his last cigarette.

"Why is he so sure he can get it back?" Blake asked Chloe.

"He doesn't seem that sure," Chloe said.

"Why doesn't he want the police involved?"

"How should I know? He didn't say."

"You didn't ask? You were gone long enough. I figured you must have asked him some things."

Chloe resisted the temptation to give Blake a dirty look. "It took me a while to find him."

"It's all so sketchy," Blake said. "So suspicious, so not right."

"So write about it," said Hannah. "You wanted to come to Europe to find your story. Here it is. Write it down."

"Oh, I would, Hannah," Blake said, "but unfortunately all my journals, including my story notebooks, got stolen by a real thief—so I can't."

Johnny didn't stay with them. There was no room for him. There was barely any room for two beds, although this was supposedly a family-sized room. But even if there had been room, as they got off the train and onto the platform, Blake said—to no one in particular, but Chloe knew it was meant for her, "I hope he doesn't think for a second he can spend the night with us." Chloe wanted to protest, but couldn't find the words. Did she think Johnny might be able to? Just a few short days ago, a lifetime ago, in Carnikava, he was able to. So many things weren't possible anymore. Could Johnny sleep on the floor while she and Mason lay down in the bed that a night earlier she and Johnny had hallowed (or was it dishonored?) with their syrupy exertions? Or was it lying down with Mason that would dishonor Johnny? Chloe didn't know anything. She wanted him to stay despite all reason.

Fortunately and achingly, Johnny preempted trouble. He said he wasn't staying, he just needed to go back to the room to get his duffel.

"That's peculiar," Blake said. "Why didn't you take your duffel with you? You never go anywhere without it."

"I left it in the hotel," Johnny said, his tone non-confrontational. "It's too heavy for me to cart around." He paused, confrontationally? "Besides, why would I take it? You didn't take your suitcases."

"We took our backpacks."

"I took my backpack."

"You told us to leave ours on the bus."

"Mine had maps of Treblinka, and I was your tour guide. It had my train schedule, which I never go anywhere without. That came in handy, didn't it?"

"You know what would've come in handy?" said Blake. "Not getting robbed."

Johnny left, promising he would return tomorrow morning with their passports. She couldn't wave to him, or run to him, or beg him not to go.

If paying for the room at Castle Inn was difficult to reconcile before Treblinka, imagine how it felt now when almost all their money was gone. Chloe had secreted away a small amount in a pocket of her suitcase, but she had been afraid to keep all her cash at a hotel. Nothing seemed safe. Now look where all that caution got her. She didn't want to think about it, what would happen if Johnny didn't return with Moody's money. When Hannah asked how much money she had squirreled away, Chloe didn't want to say. She was afraid everyone, including her, would burst into tears. After Johnny left, Hannah insisted that they count the meager dollars they had hidden. Together they counted and recounted. Four hundred dollars left. Two thousand dollars was missing in total from their communal coffers. "We have to call Moody," Hannah said. "We have to call her immediately and tell her we were robbed."

"How is that any of her business?" said Chloe. "What is she going to do?" The boys had dispersed into chairs. They were staying out of it.

"Give us more money."

Chloe laughed.

"Well, what are we going to do, Chloe? Four hundred is not enough for Barcelona! I told you we should've gotten a credit card."

"What bank would give us one? I'm barely eighteen, and we have no regular jobs and make no money." Chloe was hostile and fed-up. "And even if we did manage to get one from some sucker bank that gives credit to jobless students, it would've been stolen along with everything else. What part of 'robbed' don't you understand?"

"Ah, you're right," Hannah said, waving her off, shoulders slumping. She sounded defeated. "Maybe we should just go home."

"The trouble is, Hannah," said Blake, no longer staying out of it, "that we can't do anything, go anywhere, even home, without our passports. If he doesn't get them back, we're screwed. We are completely dependent on a guy who caused all our current trouble to begin with. The consulate can issue new documents, but that takes five days, a week maybe. Where would we stay? And on what?"

"It's not his fault," Chloe said. Mason, Blake, and Hannah remained silent.

It was nine at night. Famished and exhausted, they splurged a few zloty at Pizza Hut around the corner, where not twelve hours earlier they had been standing waiting for the longest day to begin. They ate ravenously, without talking. Afterward no one wanted to walk around on the lit-up nighttime cobblestones. And Chloe had already walked them, a night ago. She couldn't lift her eyes at anyone. How could her night with him have been only a day away from this moment? It was both too vivid and too far away.

They went back to the hotel, Hannah complaining about why Chloe and Mason would get the biggest bed when she and Blake were taller and larger. How inappropriately quickly Chloe agreed to relinquish the big bed! Though Blake wasn't nearly as pleased as Hannah to climb into the spacious sheets. Chloe and Mason crawled into the glorified twin and everyone was asleep in seconds.

In the middle of the night Chloe woke up because she was thirsty, and when she looked over to the other bed, she was almost sure Blake was lying on his back with his eyes open to the ceiling. She wanted to whisper to him, but couldn't find the words to whisper. He was upset with her, and she couldn't defend anything. She climbed back into bed next to Mason and lay quietly, burning with fever, with life and death, reconstructing one by one the kisses that had fallen upon her body, recalling the clearing piled with bodies, begging for troubled sleep, which was so much more preferable than troubled wake.

28

Warsaw

THE NEXT MORNING THEY HAD TO DECIDE: EITHER STAY IN the room one more night or check out by eleven. Johnny was nowhere to advise.

"Let's check out," Blake said. "We can't afford it. And we'll never see him again. We should ask at the front desk where the American consulate is."

"Stop. Let's go get some coffee and wait. He said he'd be back."

"He said a lot of things."

The first words of the morning were already heated. How were they going to spend the rest of today? Mason agreed with Hannah: Chloe should call her grandmother and ask for replacement money.

"What *is* that, Mase?" Chloe wanted to know. She was stroppy, unpleasant. "There's no such thing as replacement money. There's just money. And why would she give us more? She's not a money tree. She already gave us two thousand dollars, and paid for our airfares and our Eurails. She's done."

"So what do you propose we do?"

"Let's wait for him."

Hannah refused to eat, and didn't want them to bring her anything back. She stayed in the room, locked in the bathroom, while the three of them went out. Warsaw was hot, sunny, beautiful, huge. Enormous Palace Square, long straight boulevards leading away from it, the River Vistula twice the width of the Daugava. No one cared how nice the city was. They got coffee and sweet buns with jam, then returned to stand by the front door of the hotel.

What if Blake was right? What if Johnny didn't come back? Chloe didn't believe this was how everything would end. Johnny vanished, the trip ruined.

To pass the merciless time, she and Blake bickered about what to do with their luggage. Chloe said there was nothing to do. They would check out, put it into hotel storage and wait. When Blake asked how long she intended to wait, she said as long as it took for him to come back.

"While we wait, do I have to remind you that we don't have four hundred dollars to pay Castle Inn for two nights' lodging? Makes you regret not staying in the hostel, doesn't it?"

Chloe regretted nothing. But with gritted teeth, she resented much.

Johnny appeared at the hotel half an hour after checkout. They were still in the lobby. Chloe was so happy to see him, she nearly sobbed. See, she wanted to say to Blake. You were wrong about him. He did come back. See? She didn't dare look in Blake's direction.

"I have your passports," Johnny said. He looked as if he hadn't slept all night.

"Do you have our money?" Hannah asked in reply. "That's really what we're interested in."

"I don't have all your money," he said, giving them back the passports and the boys' wallets. There was not a dollar left in them but the Eurail cards were there, and their driver's licenses. The girls' Eurails were gone. Another blight. "I have enough for the room, if you haven't already paid."

"What about our backpacks?" asked Blake. His journals were irreplaceable.

"Yes, Johnny, my brother is right," Mason said. "We really need the backpacks." He looked keenly disappointed. Chloe couldn't figure out what was in Mason's backpack that was irreplaceable.

"I'm sorry, dudes," Johnny said. "Chris and I found Emil's bus parked at the airport, broke in, ransacked it. There was nothing in it. He'd already cleaned it out."

"What about our money?" Hannah repeated.

"Here's four hundred dollars. I haven't been able to get the rest yet," Johnny said. "Hannah, don't worry. I'll play all day. How much did you lose, total?"

"You make it sound as if we lost it gambling, Johnny," Blake said. "As if it's our fault. The only thing we gambled on was you. And we lost there, didn't we?"

"So you admit we were robbed?" That was Hannah, assailing him.

Johnny tilted his head sideways in grudging acknowledgment of the plain truth. Chloe stood back, behind her friends. She needed a buffer of anger between Johnny and her sick happiness at seeing him again.

"Did you see Emil?" Blake asked. "Did you confront him?"

"I *really* need my backpack back, dude," Mason said quietly. "Is there anything you can do about that?"

Johnny shook his head. "Sorry, man. Really. I had to transgress some serious Polish laws to look for them, and then to get your passports back. Asshole was fast. He'd already sold them. Lucky for us, Chris knew the guy he sold them to. We had to burgle him to get you back the most important things. So you can travel again. Denise and Yvette were upset about their Nikons, too. Their husbands had to explain the priorities to them."

"So you got us into a situation where we were robbed, where everything we had was taken from us," Blake said. "And now you're chiding us for not being grateful to you for returning the bare minimum? That's rich, man. That is fucking rich."

"Passports are not the bare minimum," said Johnny. "And you didn't have everything taken from you. You can buy new journals."

"Can't replace what was in the old ones, can I?"

"I don't know, dude. I'm not a writer. But I promise you, I have a plan. I will sing all day on every corner in Warsaw. One way or another, Emil will seek me out. And even if he doesn't, I'll get you your money."

"I had two hundred dollars!" cried Hannah. "It took me two months to earn that. I *need* that money." She put her face into her hands. "Please."

"I know you do, Hannah," Johnny said. "I'll get it. Trust me one more time, please."

Chloe watched him. She didn't know what to say that wouldn't give her away. That she didn't care about the money? That she barely even cared about the passports? If she couldn't go back home, maybe she could stay in the primordial present with him, in the space of Alps and juniper berries, of honey and salt mines, of loamy earth. Maybe if she didn't have her passport, he wouldn't leave. Because a soldier, even a future one, didn't leave his girl behind. Wasn't that right?

Reluctantly she took her passport from him. With regret she held it in her hands.

"Do yourselves a favor," Johnny said. "Buy yourselves some cheap backpacks and never part with them."

"Advice we could've used fucking yesterday," Blake said.

Johnny didn't lean into an argument. "It would probably be safer for you to cut loose and head down to Krakow."

"Why? What do you mean it's not safe?"

What do you mean head to Krakow, thought Chloe. You mean with you, right? Head to Krakow with you?

"How can we go to Krakow?" Hannah cried. "We have no money."

"Patience, and you will. Don't worry, my friends," Johnny said, with a brief profound glance at Chloe. "I'll sing for your supper tonight."

"You mean sing for your life," Blake muttered, turning away. "And we're not your friends."

They meandered around the Old Town, walked down ancient stone steps to the River Vistula, paced through Market Square, looking at paintings, antique photographs, clay sculptures of fat funny Polish men. They bought nothing except new backpacks, the cheapest they could find. Otherwise no dresses, no ties, no souvenirs, no ice cream. When they got hungry, they got two sandwiches and two Cokes and shared them. Slowly they walked to the church that held Chopin's heart in its crypt. Not a replica, and not a metaphor, but his actual heart. He had died in Paris but asked for his heart to be brought back to his beloved Poland. And it was. They sat for a long time in that cold, starkly beautiful gray cathedral. Afterward they schlepped to the vast flat plaza of the Tomb of the Unknown Soldier.

They found Johnny there, in a corner under the trees, just him and his acoustic. He was singing Polish war songs, judging by the tearful reaction of some of the veterans in full military dress, who had gathered to hear him. When he saw Chloe, he played the Artur Gold waltz he had sung for her in the Treblinka woods. Chloe wanted to give him all the money she didn't have anymore. She needn't have worried. The teary veterans had turned out their pockets. A few songs later he called them over. He handed them the equivalent of four hundred dollars. "Took me all afternoon to make this," he said. But it was already five in the evening. They were still twelve hundred short. Chloe gave two hundred of it to Hannah to stop her from fretting.

"What about the rest of it? For Barcelona?"

"He's doing what he can," Chloe said. "We can turn on him after he stops working."

They had pizza again, because it was cheap, and then sought Johnny out in the crowded Old Town streets, which were still sunny although it was evening. They could hear him from blocks away. This time he was amped up; he held in his hands an electric guitar, and his friend Chris was on makeshift drums behind him, a floor tom and a snare.

Two hours later, Johnny was still shredding the electric, still singing. He had found a great corner in the Market Square, and while the happy people sat and drank in the cafés that lined the cobblestones, he played them slower music to chill by, to drink by, to love by.

Chloe, Mason, Hannah, and Blake stood like posts after they found him, leaning against a blue wall. Everything was fuzzy, real and unreal at the same time. After a break in the set, he called them over and stuffed a few bills into Chloe's hand.

"Here," Johnny said. "Get yourself some food, a beverage, grab a seat, chill, take a load off." He had given them hundreds of zloty. Two hundred more dollars. Things didn't seem quite as hopeless. They bought three plates of sausage and potatoes, three beers, sat, ate, and listened to him sing.

He knew everything, played everything. His repertoire included Sam Cooke and the Bee Gees, Deep Purple and Metallica, Fleetwood Mac and the Yardbirds. He sang Van Morrison, Pink Floyd, he sang "Crazy Little Thing Called Love." He sang Bowie's and Nirvana's "The Man Who Sold the World," Smashing Pumpkins and Eddie Vedder, and "Jolene," "Jolene," "Jolene," "Jolene." He killed Johnny Cash covering Trent Reznor's "Hurt" and followed it up with "The House of the Rising Sun," so vocally astonishing that the crowd instantly demanded an encore of it, and got it.

Dusk was falling when Hannah stood up and said, "Chloe, can you come with me to the store over there? I want to see if I can find something for my mother. No, Blake, no, Mase, you two stay. We'll be right back. We'll browse. I hardly want to spend a penny of my money. But I have to buy something for my mother." When they were barely ten feet away, she said to Chloe, "I don't really want to buy anything. I just want to talk to you. Let's stand in front of the dress racks, like we're shopping." Chloe was glad.

Though she didn't really want to talk. All she wanted was to listen to Johnny sing "Eighteen Till I Die."

"Chloe, listen to me."

Chloe pretended to. "What's going on?" She was gazing at Johnny. What in the world was like him? He didn't rob them. Emil did. He wasn't responsible for someone else's actions. He wasn't even a thief. He hadn't stolen her heart. She had given it to him.

"My period is over a month late," said Hannah.

Chloe turned and faced her friend. She paled. She became white like Hannah.

"No."

"Very unfuckingfortunately, yes."

"Hannah …"

The tall girl put her face into her shaking hands. She said nothing as she dry heaved. Chloe said nothing. After a few minutes Chloe embraced her, but had to let go quickly, because Hannah buckled as if about to crumple, and Blake, watching them, rose from the café table. Waving him off, Chloe straightened Hannah out.

"Could it just be late? Maybe …"

"No. It's real. Face it. I didn't want to. I don't want to now. But I'm going to have to. And so do you."

"You haven't taken a test, have you? I'm telling you, it can't be! You told me yourself, Blake and you are very careful …" Chloe stopped speaking.

"It's not going to help me if you remain in denial, Chloe," Hannah said. "Wake up, will you? Have you not noticed I'm puking every minute of every day? Have you really been that deaf and blind? God! What's going on with you?"

Chloe didn't think Hannah was in any state to hear what was going on with her. She muttered a muted apology. She didn't know what to say, what to ask. The things that swirled in her brain were incompatible with one another: shock, deep worry, raw compassion, pity, and a slight small sadness flitting around, banging its head against the ceiling like the last ladybug of autumn. Oh no, the ladybug cried as it threw itself against the sheetrock in a suicide attempt, will Blake have to marry Hannah now? And who was Chloe most sorry for in that scenario? The ladybug crashed. It hoped to die before it had to answer that question.

"All right," Chloe said. "It's all right. Hannah, listen to me. We'll work it out. It'll be okay."

"No, it isn't. It's going to be the opposite of okay."

"We'll figure it out. We'll talk to Blake when we get home, we'll decide what to do."

Hannah's gaze was deep in the cobblestones. The top of her bleached white head faced Chloe, who waited a while for Hannah to speak and then leaned forward and kissed her friend's hair.

"Come on, poodle," she said. "One way or another it'll be okay."

Hannah said nothing. Johnny was singing "Smoke on the Water." Poles and tourists alike were going nuts. Blake and Mason sat at the tables, twenty feet away. It was crazy loud.

"I haven't told you everything," Hannah said.

Chloe almost thought she'd misheard. "What you just told me is *not* everything?"

"It's not Blake's," Hannah said.

And then Chloe fell quiet. Really quiet. What was there to say? Through it she heard Johnny's primal scream that no matter what happened, he would never forget smoke on the water. This is what happens when you sleep with more than one person at a time, Chloe thought. Like a bee that leaves a part of itself with every sting, you disperse the essence of your true self among human beings, you divide your good soul into smaller and smaller fragments of what you once were and hoped to be, until all you've got left is suffering, and all anybody who knew you and loved you has left is suffering.

Wasn't she a fine one to throw that stone, Chloe thought, living in her own melting glasshouse. *That's not fair!* she wanted to cry. She and Mason were just two kids fumbling toward ecstasy. Everything with him had been heavy lead-up. The opening act. Not the main show. The ecstasy was with Johnny two nights ago. That was the above and beyond Lollapalooza.

Like all human beings, when faced with someone else's pain, Chloe couldn't help but dive into an ocean of her own. She blinked, came to. She tried to find something to say to Hannah that sounded like either help or comfort. But the problem was that Johnny stood near his microphone, the electric guitar in his hands untouched, and, unaccompanied, cried out straight into her heart the first verse of "Go Your Own Way." Except Chloe could swear he sang that loving her *was* the right thing to do. And then the heavy strum of his guitar. And then the chorus. Chloe didn't realize it, but tears were trickling down her face.

Don't go your own way. Don't do it.

"Why are *you* crying?" Hannah said. "Don't cry."

"I thought I drove you to Bangor to break up with him?" Chloe said. "I thought it was all over."

Everything is waiting for you, my love. Everything is waiting for you, just don't leave me. Chloe wiped her face. Johnny was rasping, gargling shards of glass in his mouth. Instead of a chorus there was operatic gravel pulled through his open throat over and over and over.

Don't go your own way, beautiful girl. Stay with me.

"It was," Hannah said. "I thought it was. I wanted it to be. But he called and wanted to see me one more time. The last time. And then one more time after that. And then one more. I tried, Chloe, I really did. But you don't know how persuasive men can be."

Sometimes not even that persuasive, thought Chloe. Gently they blow on you and you float away like anthers of a dandelion. Or they blow you away with "In the Midnight Hour." Yes, they do, oh yes, they do.

"Do you know what Martyn said to me?" Hannah got a mixed-up, dreamy look. "Young people like me didn't understand themselves, he told me, and that was fortunate for him, because we could still be hypnotized by those who did."

Chloe blinked to focus. "Dear God, Hannah."

"I know. Isn't it something?" She put her hand on her chest. "I guess that's what I am: hypnotized."

Chloe rubbed her face. Not for a moment did she stop hearing Johnny looking for another place to take her when it was all over, as dusk fell, as darkness descended on the things that mattered most.

"It could still be Blake's, though, couldn't it?" Chloe asked. Why was her tinged voice so small?

Hannah shrugged neutrally. "Blake and I ... no. He was such a gentleman. He either wore something, or pulled out. And we cooled it off until after the prom. I wanted it that way. It'd be more special after, I told him. We kept it at everything but. Like you and Mason. Blake said he didn't know how you two managed it. By the time we got together again, it was July, after graduation, not even a month ago. I'm over a month late, not five minutes late. It was the end of May or early June that this thing happened. I'm telling you. It's not Blake's."

"Well," Chloe mumbled, suddenly cold. She shivered even though it was hot in Warsaw, hot and over the top. Anarchy, mad beasts, semi-quavers, a thousand lifetimes, dancing men about to be hanged, and heartbreak, all in one reconstructed colorful plaza. "Math has always been Blake's weakest subject. Let's hope he can't count." It wasn't true. The psychology of young restless women was Blake's weakest subject.

"Yeah." Hannah's shoulders were heavy. "Look, I know how this seems."

"Okay."

"I can't excuse it or justify it. I just have to work through it, okay?"

"Okay."

"Just be my friend, Chloe."

"I am, poodle," Chloe said. "Maybe you can talk to Martyn?"

"Oh God. Blake might be able to help me with Planned Parenthood in Augusta, drive me four hours in his mother's car, pay for it maybe, but Martyn? Never. He'll want me to keep it, and then what am I going to do?"

Chloe didn't see another option. "What do *you* want? To go to Augusta?"

"I don't understand. Is that code for something?"

"Yes, Hannah. It's code for what do you want to do about your baby?"

"Shh! And don't call it a baby. It's a pregnancy, that's all. I don't know what to do. I want to go to school. I want to move away. I certainly don't want to live with Blake in Fryeburg. Which option will help me achieve that?"

"Talking to Martyn."

"But I can't! He'll want to marry me. I can't! That's even worse."

"Don't worry," Chloe said. "He'll hypnotize you. He'll make you okay with it."

"Stop joking."

"Who's joking? Look"—she pointed—"get hold of yourself, Blake's coming. We'll talk about this later, ok—"

Suddenly Chloe stopped speaking as if her tongue had been sliced out. Across the square in the far corner, near a beer bar, she spotted the dark messy shape of Emil, standing almost invisibly in black clothes, against the wall, watching Johnny with ominous eyes, watching the people throwing money into Johnny's guitar case.

Chloe didn't even say excuse me to Hannah. She bolted.

"Emil!" she yelled, sprinting as fast as she could across the square.

Behind her, she heard Blake yelling no no.

Through the microphone she heard Johnny yelling NO NO.

She paid them no mind. She chased Emil down one of the side streets. And the bastard ran! A two-hundred pound dude ran from a girl. He didn't stop to confront her. He ran like the craven thief that he was through the alleys, hoping to find a place to hide.

Behind her, she heard Johnny yelling, heard Johnny and Blake shouting things. They were running after her, perhaps to protect her. Or stop her. She didn't know. She wouldn't stop. Or be protected.

All she knew was that a bad man did something terrible, and one way or another she was going to force a reckoning.

Unable to lose Chloe, Emil made a wrong turn and got cornered in a dead end. He stopped running and spun around.

"Leave me alone, you bloody maniac," he panted, putting his arms out. "You're going to get sodding hurt."

"I'm already hurt," she blurted. "Give me my money, and I'll leave you alone." She ran up to him, panting herself, unable to catch her breath.

"I don't know what you're on about."

Because she was unable to speak, on furious impulse, she grabbed his buttoned shirt. It ripped. They grappled as he tried to pry her off him. "What are you doing?" he yelled in his perfect English. "Get the fuck away from me, you crazy bitch."

"No! Give me my money!" She pounded Emil's chest.

"It's not your money, sweetheart," Emil said, grabbing her arms and shoving her away.

"Hey! Don't touch her!" Blake and Johnny were in the alley. Now that they were here, she became only more incensed, as if she now had back-up. Blake shoved Emil in the chest. Emil staggered back, nearly falling. Blake and Johnny got between him and Chloe, like a wall. A standing, panting wall.

"It *is* my money!" she shouted.

"She's right, dickweed," Blake said. "One way or another you're going to give us back what's ours."

"No! It's *my* fucking money." Emil spat and pointed to Johnny, his own face a mask of distorted aggression. Chloe was glad Blake and Johnny were in front of her. "You're such a fucking bastard. You stole from me again, got me into heavy shit *again*. You'll pay for that, I promise you."

"You're fucked up," Johnny said. "You mean I took back what you stole? I told you I'd pay you. Why didn't you listen?"

"Because I didn't fucking believe you."

"Well, you should believe me now," said Johnny. "Because you'll never see another cent from me."

"You're all mouth and no trousers, mate, like always. I never saw any money from you. But you were happy to take my candy, though, weren't you? Did you have one of your cronies steal the passports off Rolando? He paid me big time for those! When I find out who your local is, he's dead, you hear me? Is it Chris? That boy is fucked—because of you."

"Why don't you quit with the threats," Blake said, "and give us back our money and our backpacks, and we'll be on our way, and you can get back to doing whatever you were doing before we came along. What was it, mugging old ladies? Hop to it, cowboy."

"Your bags are at the bottom of fucking Vistula," Emil said, not budging. "Go jump in after them."

"You're going to give me our money and our fucking backpacks," Blake repeated.

Chloe became afraid. She almost wanted to pull Blake back to safety.

The three men squared off, threateningly close, face to face, glare to glare.

"Nothing's yours. It's all mine now. Your friend here owes me."

"But *I* don't fucking owe you!" Blake yelled. "*She* doesn't fucking owe you!"

Yeah, Chloe wanted to echo, jumping up and down, trying to squeeze in between them. Yeah!

"His friends are my enemies. Everything you have is mine."

"Emil," Johnny said. "You took their passports, their cameras, their cash. You took their backpacks that had their personal shit. You took more than I ever owed you. And you didn't wait a single fucking day. I came back to Warsaw to pay you."

"I don't give a toss why you came back. I don't believe you. And I couldn't wait. How about that?" Emil swung. Johnny ducked. Emil swung at Blake. Blake didn't duck fast enough. Emil's fist caught him on the cheekbone under the eye. Blake swung at Emil, but Emil danced back as if in a ring. Blake went for him again, and now it was Johnny who got between them.

"Blake, no," Johnny said quietly. "Just flank him."

Panting, Blake stepped sideways, one of his arms reaching back to keep Chloe away. She knew she was too close. But Blake was too close.

"Just give us our stuff," Blake said, wiping the blood off his face with his sleeve, "and we won't bother you."

"I will fucking bother *you*," Emil said. "Stay out of it. It has nothing to do with you."

"You take our passports and two grand of our money? I'd say it has something to do with me."

Everybody's fists were clenched, except for Johnny's. His hands were straight like motionless boards. He was barely breathing. Blake's heaving wide denim shoulders were in front of Chloe. Chloe tried to push him out of the way, to get into Emil's face again.

"In one second I'll call for the cops," she yelled. "You can explain to them why you robbed nine people."

Emil laughed. "Yes, please! Do it. Johnny loves the coppers, don't you, Johnny-boy?"

"Shut the fuck up." That was Johnny. "Give them back their money. I'm not asking, Emil. I'm done asking."

"*You* give her back what you took from her," Emil said, shoving a threatening but stock-still Johnny in the chest with both fists. "This is all on you."

Johnny's body faltered, but his feet didn't move from their spot on the stones. What had he called it in Sestokai? An immovable stance. "*I* didn't take her fucking money." They were verbally hot, their bodies inching closer. And Blake wasn't stepping away.

"Yes you did. You're the one who robbed everybody, me included." Emil had no means of escape, yet he stared fearlessly into Johnny's face. "I don't give a shit how you two threaten me. Tell your friend to stand down unless he wants some serious hurt. You're never getting the money." Emil glanced darkly at Blake. "You'll be lucky to leave here with your life, Yank. You picked the wrong horse to back."

"I'm backing nobody," Blake said. "And don't tell me to stand down. I just want my fucking money. You know you're not getting out of here without giving it up, so why are you being such an asswipe?"

"Emil," Johnny said, "don't look at him. Look at *me*. This has nothing to do with him."

"Then why'd you involve him, toe-rag?"

"Shut the fuck up and give them their money." Johnny leaned to Blake. "Blake, *please*." Not taking his eyes off Emil, he gestured sideways with his head. "*Chloe*."

Blake stepped away from Emil and Johnny and toward Chloe.

"Chloe, move back," he hissed, blocking her with his body. "I won't be able to do this if I'm worrying about you."

Chloe pressed her small self against the wall, but didn't move far.

Emil and Johnny circled each other like wolves. Emil's fists were clenched. Not Johnny's.

"You stole thousands of dollars," Johnny said. "You sold their passports for another two thousand dollars. You'll get ten years for that alone. And I don't owe you two grand total."

"You're so right about that, mate. Spot on. You owe me forty-seven hundred dollars. So I'm still fucking short. And

Rolando wants either his passports back or his money. So there's that."

"Since they're not his passports, he's fucked because he's getting neither."

"Oh, he is."

"So pay him. Stop thieving. Pay somebody."

"*You* pay somebody!"

"I don't owe you forty-seven hundred fucking dollars!" Now Johnny was yelling.

"Did you forget penalties and interest?"

"What are you, a fucking bank?"

"Worse than that, old chap. I'm the connected guy you owe money to."

"You're a thief!" Chloe yelled. "You're going to jail for this!"

"Chloe, shh!" Blake stood in front of her.

"Ask your boy here about jail. He knows all about—"

Johnny's fist flew out. Emil tried to weave out of the way, but Johnny was quick. There was a dull thump, and Emil was on his back on the ground, holding his face. Blood streamed from his nose through his fingers. Blake tried to shield Chloe so she wouldn't see. But she saw. Clutching Blake's arm, she gaped at Emil's broken face in fascinated revulsion.

Emil wasn't safe. But he didn't know it. Or maybe he knew it and didn't care. Grunting, guttural, livid, he struggled up, his nose gushing blood, and took a boxing stance against Johnny, who was taller but thinner. They weren't in the same weight class. In Emil's hands flicked a long thin switchblade.

Johnny opened his steady hands to show Emil what was in his. He also wielded a knife, this one much more intimidating, with a long double-edged black blade.

"A World War II military fighting knife," Johnny said. "The sharpest, strongest, the best. You think you can throw your little pocket job?" He moved into a throwing stance. "Go ahead. But if you miss, mine is going straight into your throat."

Chloe choked back a scream.

Emil hesitated for only a second. Then he threw his knife. Johnny jerked his head back, and the knife flew past his face, landing on the stones.

"Now what are you going to do, you dumb fuck?" said Johnny. But he didn't throw his knife. He took two long strides to Emil, turned his body sideways and kicked out his leg. Emil was ready. He tried to grab it, but the alligator-boot caught Emil in his throat between his clenched fists. This time Emil went down and stayed down.

Chloe was gasping for breath. She and Blake stood stunned, staring at the limp man on the ground. Johnny studied Emil for a few moments and then flipped him over onto his stomach, faceplanted him into the stone, and yanked off his backpack. He rummaged around until he found what he was looking for: a wad of cash, a wallet, a lighter, cigarettes. Johnny took everything. He even took Emil's ring of keys and dropped it into a sewer grate. He also took some small ziplock bags filled with things Chloe couldn't quite see. He pulled both sets of shoelaces out of Emil's Adidas sneakers, made a quick but elaborate handcuff knot, slipped Emil's wrists into the loops, yanked them tight and then tied the ends together in a gunner's knot over a pipe in the wall. Emil stayed unconscious. Chloe couldn't tell if he was breathing. Blake remained by her side; they were both silent as they watched Johnny. Chloe had never witnessed such violence. It alternately terrified and thrilled her. It was electrifying to be in the presence of someone who could make his body into a weapon that knocked a two-hundred-pound man flat to the concrete.

"Blake, you okay?" she whispered, reaching out to touch the cut in his cheek.

"I'm better than he is," Blake said, gesturing to Emil. "I'm fine. It's a scratch."

Finally Johnny slid the knife under his jeans and back into his boot, and jumped up. Facing them, he appraised Blake's face. He wasn't panting or even heavily breathing. His face wasn't red like Chloe's felt. He was somber and utterly calm.

"Let's go," he said. "You did good, Blake. But he's not dead. If I'd thrown my knife, he'd be dead, and we'd be safe for a second, but then there'd be a manhunt. Too many people saw us chase him. As it is, we have very little time."

"To do what?"

"To leave Warsaw. Once he comes to, he'll try to scream. He won't be able to with his throat injury, but guaranteed some nosy passersby will get the cops, and the rest will all be shit. First place they'll look for us is the train station. So come on. Chloe, you okay? You ran so fast before. Why dawdle now?"

Chloe didn't think she was dawdling. She thought she was hurrying. "Leave Warsaw? But it's night."

"We'll take the midnight train to Krakow."

"We have no money."

"You have two Eurail tickets. And I'll give you money." He ran ahead. For Chloe there was no choice. She raced after him, Blake on her heels.

"Every single thing you get us into turns to shit," Blake said into Johnny's back when they had almost caught up. Johnny had slowed to a fast walk as they entered the more crowded streets. "Even this. We're fugitives now, is that it?"

"I'd love to chat with you about all the things you think are wrong with me," Johnny replied, "but I can't. Unless you want to leave them, you still have to get your suitcases from the hotel. Emil is going to wake up. You do understand that you and I beat him and robbed him, right?"

Chloe gave Blake an angry shove. "What's wrong with you?" she whispered. "He got our money back. Be happy."

"Happy? He's the reason it was stolen to begin with!" Blake didn't care if Johnny heard.

"Tonight we acquitted ourselves well," Johnny said, striding fast. "I still have to pay my man Chris. He totally saved my ass. Whatever I'm short, I'll make up to you in Krakow."

"You're always coming up a little fucking short, aren't you?"

Johnny didn't glance back. "I'm trying to make good on a lot of shit, Blake," he said. "Cut me some fucking slack."

Slack was something Blake had none of. Chloe saw that. The pace with which Johnny was walking told Chloe that they needed to get out of Warsaw stat, and that he would leave them all behind if he had to. He would leave Chloe behind. He would go his own way, leave nothing but smoke on the water. Whatever happened, Chloe would not be left behind. The gallows awaited. She sped up.

29

The Dragon and the Honey

THE NIGHT TRAIN TO KRAKOW WAS ABOMINABLE. IT WAS loud, lurching, and smelled of fermented alcohol and fermented people. It was a crossroads on the River Styx. Every which way was hell.

To make matters worse, their sliding door wouldn't stay latched. It kept popping open. They would hear chaos from down the corridor, wailing dogs and children, fighting adults, unrestrained laughter, maniacal sermons, all in a foreign tongue, which made it all the more frightening because it left Chloe to imagine the reasons for the purgatory fires.

Inside the compartment was not a walk in the park either.

"So what did Emil mean," Blake asked Johnny after they settled in, "about you knowing jail?"

"I dunno." Johnny leaned back, pulling his beret down over his eyes. "I don't remember him saying it."

"Really? It was the last thing the douchebag said before you gave him an injury that might permanently stop him from talking. It's rather surprising that you can't remember why you wanted to knife him in the throat."

"It wasn't because of his words, that's for fucking sure," Johnny said.

"So was there jail or wasn't there? Is that why you didn't want the police involved?" Blake held a cold can of Coke to his swelling face.

"I didn't know this was an interrogation cell," Johnny said, less mildly. "I thought I was on a train, trying to sleep. I was awake all night last night, you know, getting your shit back."

"Didn't get my shit back," interjected Mason.

"Mase, what did you have in there?" asked Chloe.

"Nothing. Just things. My journal." Mason sighed and stopped speaking.

"Or mine," Blake said. "And I'm just asking a question, Johnny, trying to have a conversation."

Johnny refused to explain his connection to Emil, refused to illuminate on their history, or why he owed Emil money, or where he had vanished for twelve months, leaving Chloe to imagine the rest, the worst. She wanted to ask Johnny if he was sure he left Emil alive, if he was *sure*? She was afraid he would lie and say yes. What was more frightening: to be lied to or to not know? Chloe decided to be lied to was worse, so she didn't ask. She wished someone would start talking about something light, but no one did, not even Johnny. She wished the unreliable lights would go out for just a minute, so Johnny could lean across and kiss her lips like before. But they didn't. And he didn't.

The five of them were alone in the fluorescently lit-up compartment, alone with themselves, alone with their thoughts. No one was writing in journals that no longer existed. Blake, his eye and cheek turning black and blue, looked as if he would never write another word in his life. Mason was lost somewhere far beyond the train to Krakow. He was spread out on the seats next to Chloe, his head away from her, his eyes closed. Chloe knew what Hannah was thinking. Hannah's expression was but a poor mask to the torment inside her, both physical and eternal. Hannah had barely reacted to any of it: to the story of Emil, to their escape from Warsaw, or even to the injury to Blake's face. She looked happy only when Johnny counted out Emil's stack of dollars, which numbered in the twelve hundreds, before giving Chris seven hundred of it. How Hannah protested! "Without him, you'd have no passports," Johnny explained. "I owe him more than this." Though the way Chris genuflected, agog before the inadequate greenbacks, made Chloe think the boy had never held more than a twenty in his hopeless life.

Chloe wondered aloud why Emil would carry the stolen money on his person. Johnny replied that Emil carried it on himself for the same reason they had carried it on themselves.

"What's the moral here?" Mason asked.

"That you can be robbed anywhere," said Johnny. "By anyone. So be meek like sheep but wise like serpents. Never leave behind what you can't part with."

Mason made a throaty noise that surprised Chloe; he sounded as if he was about to cry.

"Mason, what's the matter?"

"Nothing. Just tired."

Blake pointed out that they had never, not once, been robbed in Fryeburg.

"Duh," Johnny said. "That's because no one gets robbed in the Garden of Eden."

For an hour Chloe thought about what Johnny said, while Johnny slept, and Hannah and Mason pretended to sleep. So did Blake. Only Chloe's eyes were open, engraving the sleeping Johnny Rainbow onto the walls of her lungs so that later on, with every breath, she could exhale him.

She wanted to be far away from all the trouble, and for Johnny to be far from it, and for both of them to be far from it together. Whenever she thought ahead to Krakow, her heart stopped in her chest, for it didn't take her long to remember that after Krakow there was no more of anything. He was headed to Italy, and they to Spain. She sat and prayed for the train to break down, to become lost in the untrammeled wilderness. Johnny slept at the window across from her, next to Hannah. His head bobbed back and forth. With every lurch his feet bumped against Chloe's feet. She wanted to cry, to park on a bench, to ask him to sing, to beg for faith that it would all work out all right in the end, for him, for her, for them. She wanted to climb into his sleeping lap and hold his chocolate head to her breasts. Oh God. You and me, Johnny Rainbow. What else is left? Nothing. Just you and me.

He woke up after a particularly rough jolt, woke up refreshed and smiling. He stepped out for a minute, and when he returned, he was sociable, friendly, all his cares put away, all the dark days forgotten.

"It's amazing what a little sleep can do for a person's disposition," he said cheerfully.

"Maybe *that's* what's wrong. Blake hasn't slept," Chloe quipped, and Blake opened his eyes, one of them bruised, and scowled at her as if she had betrayed him. She flushed and was guilty, but also wanted to giggle. She just wanted everything to be normal, to be like it was. She wanted to tickle Blake out of his bad mood that had lasted half of Europe, wanted to shake and joke Mason out of his stupor. Only poor Hannah's plight continued to confound her. It was unsaveable by comedy.

Blake asked if Johnny was *ever* going to give them their money. Johnny handed Blake almost six hundred dollars over Hannah's lap.

"We're still short by more than five hundred," said Hannah, who was always awake and alert when money was changing hands.

"Whatever, Hannah, this is fine," Blake said. "He doesn't have to get us the rest. We'll be fine."

"No, no," said Johnny. "I know I'm a little short. I'll get it for you by tomorrow night."

"How? By robbing somebody else?"

"Nice," Johnny said. His disposition soured.

"Blake, stop!" That was Chloe.

"Yeah, Blakie, I know you think you're being funny, but you're not funny," said Hannah. "Johnny will sing." She half-smiled, listing sideways against Johnny. "Johnny, I wish you could make everything else in the world all right by your singing, like you did today."

Well, yes, singing. Also by high-kicking a fiend in the throat. But by singing, too, sure.

Amiably Johnny straightened Hannah out.

"Some things you can't fix with a song," he said. "Not many. But *some*."

"That is so true," said Hannah.

Chloe watched Johnny watching Hannah. It was as if he knew.

"Hey, dudes, dudettes, cheer up," Johnny said with an unperturbed smile. "It has all worked out. We're out of Warsaw. You still have nearly two weeks left. Everything is almost back to its old self again."

"Really?" Hannah said eagerly, and then more skeptically, "You think so?" As if he were a palmreader.

"I said almost. Wait till you see Krakow. You'll forget everything. I'll take you to Oskar Schindler's factory, if we have time. And the following day, after Auschwitz, maybe you'll have a chance to visit Katowice."

"Won't be time," Blake said curtly.

"Well, true. But if you have half a day, you should visit the great war museum there. There used to be a German prison camp in Katowice. For Soviet officers. Quite a place. Only photographs remain of it."

"I think we're done with many things," Blake said, "among them war museums."

"Except for Auschwitz."

Hannah groaned. "Do we *have* to? Blake is right. I feel like we've seen everything in Treblinka."

"Auschwitz is not a field," Johnny said. "There are things there that once you see, you will never unsee."

"That's true of many things on this joytrip," Blake said.

"You decide what's best," Johnny said, unbaited. "You have a long haul ahead of you to Barcelona. Krakow is a fantastic city, but you're right, you might want to limit your time there and maximize your time in Spain." He didn't look at Chloe when he spoke, and she didn't look at him. "When you're in Barcelona, don't forget to compare your travails to Saint Eulalia," he went on. "Eulalia was a thirteen-year-old virgin who was put in a barrel by the Romans. The inside of the barrel was lined with knives, and they rolled this barrel around the city. Which is why the tortured girl is the city's patron saint. Because her innocent blood runs on every street."

"Sometimes I feel a little like Saint Eulalia," said Hannah.

And Chloe thought, hmm, really? And when she glanced across at Johnny, she saw he was thinking it too. He knows! He absolutely knows. She almost smiled, but Blake was watching her, and she didn't. She stared away into the darkness past the window.

Why was it, she wondered, that in books love was the only thread stitching together a narrative, but in real life, it was only part of the tapestry? In real life there was hunger and irritation. There was rejoicing. There was anger, a desire to read, to sleep, to sing, a quest for revenge, physical ailments, much discomfort. Mosquito bites and runny noses, fainting at the worst times, missing trains and buses, being robbed, fighting in alleys, being stoned. There was terror, real and imagined, and a meadow full of ghostly dread. There was living with a baby inside you fathered by a man you didn't love, riding trains next to another man you didn't love.

And there was love, too, galloping like a paladin through the boggy bayou. There was love.

"Blake," Hannah said, "why are you so grumpy? Is Johnny right? Do you just need a little nap and you'll feel better?"

"Johnny is not right."

"So what is it, then? Is it your face?"

"It's not my face. Not a lot to be happy about, that's all."

Hannah said nothing. Hannah could hardly disagree. She and Chloe shared a blink, a dim nod.

"Chloe," Johnny said, "I noticed that Blake stopped calling you Haiku. Am I wrong?"

"I don't know." She wouldn't acknowledge either man with a glance that signaled admission or confession. And Blake didn't justify his lack of teasing moniker usage, which only signaled both admission and confession to everyone. Good thing no one cared.

"Chloe, did your mother ever tell you any scary Eastern fables as bedtime stories?" Johnny draped one leg over the other, stretching his arms across the long seat.

"No. Do you mean fables from Pembina? Also no."

"Did you ever hear of a fable from the Orient about a traveler chased by a wild beast?"

She shook her head. The others pretended not to hear, but everyone was listening.

"Escaping from the beast, the man jumps into the deadfall, a hole in the ground dug out as a trap for bears. But at the bottom of this well, there is a dragon that opens its fiery jaws to swallow him. The traveler clings to the side of the ditch, afraid to climb out and be torn apart by the beast, and afraid to jump down, where the mouth of the dragon awaits him. He grabs on to a root in the earth and hangs on for his life. After a while his hands grow tired, and he knows that soon he will have to let go and surrender to the destruction above or below. Still he hangs on. And then he sees that two mice have settled on the stem of the twig he clings to and are going round and round, gnawing at it. Soon the twig will snap, and he will fall. Desperate and doomed, he hangs on and glances around. He sees nearby a few drops of honey on the leaves of the twig. Leaning sideways, he reaches them with his tongue, licks them and murmurs, 'Ah! How *sweet*!'"

Chloe, heart thumping, waited. The others waited, less patiently. Johnny smiled.

"My grandfather," he said, "tells this story once a year at Christmas dinner. He raises his glass in a toast and says to all forty of us, your mother and grandmother, the only woman I have shared my life with, is my drop of honey. Merry Christmas."

There was a silence filled with screeching wheels, moaning old women, belches, sniffles, and out of tune laments. Someone was crying as if they were dying.

Hannah frowned. "What does that have to do with us, Johnny?"

"Searching anywhere and everywhere for the honey, you don't think it applies to us?" Turning his head, he locked eyes with Hannah.

She looked quickly away. "Are you saying that everything happens for a reason?"

"No," he said. "But I am saying be careful where you look for it, because no one was made wretched in a brothel." He paused. "Except maybe my father." After a shrug, he went on. "And I mean more about the eternal questions. Where is the drop of honey in your life? Are you the honey in anyone else's?"

"I completely disagree with your premise," Blake said. "I don't think life is a beast above and a dragon below and gnawing mice. Life is walking through a meadow. Occasionally there may be rain."

"But is there honey, Blake?" asked Johnny.

No one spoke for the rest of the ride.

The train, slow as a sloth and yet not slow enough, finally pulled into Krakow station at six in the morning. With all of Blake's travel guides gone, they had to rely on Johnny to find them a cheap, clean place to stay. He said he knew just the hotel, safe and reasonable, just off Krakow's main square, the thirteenth century Rynek Glowny. He brought them to a hotel of roses on a historic street full of shops and cafés. It was a nice place, tall and narrow, in a corner building with a long gray lobby.

"Thanks," Blake said to Johnny just after Chloe had signed for the room. "That's it then. We'll see you." Chloe's sleep had been so brief, the previous day so fraught and long that for a moment she didn't understand what Blake was saying to Johnny.

Even Johnny didn't understand. "Yes, you'll see me upstairs," he said.

Blake shook his head. "No. This is where you and us part ways." Glowering at each other, they stood with their suitcases in front of the morning clerk behind the tall desk. The young woman eyed them warily, the girls pale, the boys unshaven, all of them miserable. "You said yourself we don't need you for Auschwitz," Blake said to Johnny. "And we don't have an extra day to go on an Oskar Schindler tour with you, no matter how much we'd like to. Auschwitz is all we have time for, I'm afraid. If you want, we can meet up with you later, or tomorrow, for the money."

Now it was Johnny's turn to shake his head. "I'm out of here tonight," he said. "I have to be in Italy by tomorrow morning."

Chloe, now sharply awake and aware, wanted to cry why, but managed to keep her mouth shut.

"Whatever," Blake said.

"Bro, wait," Mason said, pulling Blake away, and then quieter, "What are you doing?"

Yanking his arm away from his brother, Blake shrugged. "Saying goodbye to him. What are you doing?"

"He's got to sleep somewhere, like us. What, we're going to split up now, after everything?"

"That is exactly right," Blake said, enunciating every word. "We're going to split up now. After everything."

"Hold on, Blakie," Hannah said. She made a gesture to Johnny as if to say, don't worry, it'll be fine, he'll calm down. "Be reasonable."

"I am being reasonable."

"Why should he rent a separate room, pay more money? It makes no sense."

Blake was quiet, breathing deeply. "It doesn't matter to me if he sleeps on the street," he said coldly. "We were robbed, Hannah. Because of him." He turned to Johnny. "All of our things were stolen, because of you. We still don't have over five hundred dollars of our money, because of you. Our irreplaceable things, the ones no money can buy, are gone forever—because of you. There is no fucking way I'm sleeping in the same room with you. I know you understand why." Blake and Johnny stared mutely at each other. "Trouble is, *they* don't." He glanced at Mason. "He's bound to open our throats, Hannah, and take off with what's left, though granted, there isn't much. He pretty much took everything." And then Blake stared at Chloe.

Chloe would never look at Blake again!

Johnny stepped away, bowing his head in assent. "It's fine," he said. "I got stuff to do all day. Don't forget, if you want to get to Auschwitz, the buses leave at 8 a.m. You don't have much time to get ready. It's almost seven."

"Wait," Mason said.

"Wait!" Hannah said.

Chloe wanted to cry wait, but she couldn't find her voice. This can't be how it ends! He can't just walk out of her life like this. No. No. Please. No.

Blake stepped away too, from Johnny, from Hannah, from his brother, and he was already far from Chloe. "No more waiting," he said. "You choose, friends, brother, girlfriends. Him or me. Because the two of us are not staying in the same room. That will never happen."

"Bro, it wasn't his fault," Mason said. "He just got mixed up with the wrong people. And he helped us. Give him a break."

"Yeah, Blakie, come on."

Chloe said nothing.

"This is so fucked up," Blake said, taking another step away from them. "Him. Or. Me."

Stepping forward, Johnny raised his hands in surrender. "It's absolutely fine. Blake is right. You're right, dude. I know how you feel." Johnny looked sad and guilty, but he didn't look away. "I'm really sorry for the trouble I caused. I didn't mean for any of it to happen. I liked you guys and only wanted to have fun with you. No sweat. Really. Oh, and don't even worry about meeting up with me later. As soon as I have it, I'll leave five hundred dollars in an envelope behind the front desk. Is the room under Chloe Divine?" He cast her a gaze of stormy despair. "I'll leave it for Chloe Divine, then." He hugged Hannah. "Take care, girl," he said to her. "Don't be too hard on yourself. But do try to hold yourself to some standards. If only so you can tell when you fail."

"What does that mean?" Hannah said.

"What the *hell* does that mean?" Blake said, but Johnny was already shaking Mason's hand. He didn't shake Blake's hand, obviously. Nor did he come near Chloe.

"Don't forget to visit the Temple of Sagrada Familia," he said to them. "It's the most visited place in Spain."

"Yeah, we got it," said Blake. "I read all about it in the books your chum stole from me."

"The temple rises nearly a thousand feet above sea level," Johnny went on with a last tormented glimpse at Chloe. He nodded to her and smiled, hoisting the green duffel onto his shoulder. "As God made the mountain, the saying goes, so man made the structure. Be well, all of you. And so long."

30

Instead of Auschwitz

THEY DIDN'T GO TO AUSCHWITZ. THEY CLIMBED TO THEIR
tiny room on the fourth floor, sat down for just a sec on their
hard beds with the itchy blankets, and didn't open their eyes
until late afternoon.

For a few absent-minded moments they teased each other
for falling asleep before Hannah ran to the bathroom and Chloe
remembered Johnny. Her chest and stomach and legs went
numb, numb, numb, stabbed with a kind of Novocaine through
which sorrow seeped. It was impossible! She didn't give him her
home address. She didn't even know his real name! This couldn't
be. The teasing stopped.

They showered and dressed, stared at the Krakow
newspaper, hurried each other along, complained of life-ending
hunger (not Hannah). Around six, they walked out of the hotel
of roses, hair brushed, faces clean, denim clad, except for Chloe
who, while brushed and clean, wore the coral minidress she'd
bought in Warsaw, bought to wear for Johnny, while he was in
Majdanek and she roamed the streets, trying to make herself
look pretty. Here she was, with her bejeweled sandals and
exposed bare legs and halter necklines, hair shining, lips glossy,
and no Johnny. She wished for a cardigan to cover herself. All
she had on was the sleeveless coral dress and her new small
backpack that contained in it all the things she couldn't part
with. Except for him.

They strolled down two blocks of a narrow treeless pastel-colored street to the immense wide plaza with the enormous basilica. They were too late to enter St. Mary's to take a look around. The last scheduled visit was at six. They had just missed it.

"Ain't it our luck," said Mason. "Once again I'm thwarted in my mission."

"What mission is that?" said Blake. "To visit every damn church in Europe?"

"Oh, nice. Blaspheme the holy church."

"It would've been worth it to go," Blake said. "I remember reading something about the opulent altar inside. It's from the fifteenth century. It's supposed to be the tallest indoor Gothic structure in the world."

"Thanks, bro, for letting me know what I'm missing."

"Welcome, bro."

Some things never changed.

The main square in Krakow's Old Town is the vast Rynek Glowny, a medieval renaissance Gothic space surrounded by light modern townhouses. It's an open-door market, with hundreds of eateries, dozens of tent vendors, millions of pigeons. Chloe had been in Livu Square in Riga, and in Old Town Square in Warsaw. Krakow's plaza was the largest. But it was the first one without Johnny in it. So it felt the smallest. She heard music in the far corner, a saxophonist playing an incongruous "Fly Like an Eagle." There was music, yet there was no music.

They bought a map and a guide, in bad Bilingual. You pay peanuts, you get monkeys, Blake said, but Hannah thought even there, they'd overpaid. "We're not staying, and we slept all day," she said, "so why throw our money away on a guide for a city we'll never see?"

"Perhaps we'll decide after reading this shoddily produced masterpiece," said Blake, "that one more day in Krakow will be worth it."

They were starving, yet had a lot to do, so they decided to divide their duties. Hannah went to buy herself and Chloe a phone card to call their mothers. Hannah hadn't called hers once. She said she wanted to tell her about Zhenya.

"Zhenya is what you want to tell your mother about?" Chloe whispered.

"Zhenya is all I can tell her about," Hannah whispered back.

Mason went to buy and mail a Krakow postcard back home to his friends. Blake found a small picnic table next to a beer bar by the far shady side of Cloth Hall, a closed-door market, and planted himself there with the map. He said he would do his best to salvage Krakow for the four of them. Chloe was sent to buy a feast for dinner.

"Something filling and Polish," Blake said to her.

"Something filling and non-Polish," Mason said to her.

Hannah said she wasn't hungry.

"Blake," Chloe said before she walked away, "don't forget to get us to Oskar Schindler, okay?" Her voice almost didn't crack.

"We have no time for Schindler and his enamel factory," Blake called back, sitting by himself at the picnic table, straddling the seat, studying the map. "But we might have time to walk to the river and see the dragon's lair. Would you like that?" He smiled. "I thought you might. Apparently it's a must-see."

By the time Chloe returned with the food, Mason had joined Blake at the table. The brothers were trying to outdo each other in useless conversation. It all started, they told her, because Mason had put on a striped henley. "I know Sponge Bob thinks the best time to wear a striped sweater is all the time," Blake said, "but the talking sponge is wrong, bro."

Mason waved him off. "Eat your foreign food and shut up. Just remember that diarrhea is Europe's third leading cause of death."

"Ha! Dude, when?"

"Well," Mason replied, trying to stay serious, "in 1900."

Blake laughed. "A *hundred* years ago? I'll take my chances. But on the same subject, did you know that constipation is Latin for crowding together?"

"Is not!"

"If I'm lyin', I'm dyin'."

"You're such a bullshit artist. You lie like a rug!" They both guffawed.

"Will you stop being two, you two?" Chloe said, setting the white bags down on the table. "Where's Hannah?"

"Still talking to her mom, I guess," Blake said. "Wait, there she is. Hannah! Here!" He waved. Hannah hurried across the square. "Look how funny she's walking," Blake said, amused. "Like she's waddling."

Chloe made no comment, not even under her breath. Especially not under her breath. "I got you *zurek*, Blake," she said, drawing his attention away, parceling out the food. "It's some kind of weird stew. You'll love it."

She held the pizza and pierogi in her hands. Mason was helping her unwrap the bread and the potato latkes.

Out of breath, Hannah neared the table. "Ugh, no, not pizza. I can't stand that tomato sauce."

"Pizza?" Mason said in a mimic tease. "Chloe, didn't you hear Hannah tell you she didn't want ethnic food?"

"Funny stuff, bro," Blake said. "Funny stuff. Hannah, since when don't you like pizza? You love tomato sauce."

Chloe quickly handed Hannah a paper plate with a potato pierogi and a crusty loaf. "Here, take, sit. Eat."

"I wish it wasn't fried," Hannah said, eyeing the greasy fare.

And then she spoke the following words: "Chloe, when was the last time you talked to your mom?"

"I don't know. Riga, I guess. After the orphanage. I called to tell her about the boy I found." In the ruins of old forts near white sand beaches. Chloe struggled to open her Coke. Her hands trembled slightly.

"You mean Raymonds?"

"Of course Raymonds."

"Oh. Did you ask her if you got your UMaine room assignment yet?"

Very carefully, Chloe lowered her unopened can of Coke to the table. She said nothing.

"Because my mom says I got mine in the mail," Hannah continued, "but for some reason I was given a random roommate. Not you. When you call your mom, can you find out who they gave you? Clearly she's going to have to call housing tomorrow to get it taken care of. Why would they do that? We were so specific that we wanted each other. We filled out our housing forms together just last month."

There was a hard marbled silence, the kind where the only sounds are of taxis and strangers, of wailing sirens and cooing pigeons, of vendors and buskers (though not *the* busker). The kind where there is so much to say, and yet not a single word can be spoken. Blake was eating voraciously. Neither Chloe, nor Mason, nor Hannah ate or moved. The plate with the tepid pizza dangled in Chloe's hand.

Mason took it from her, and placed it fastidiously in front of himself. With a napkin he dabbed the cheese on top to absorb some of the grease. "Are you *ever* going to tell her, Chloe?" asked Mason.

A puzzled Chloe turned her head toward her boyfriend. She didn't even have time to wonder properly before Mason spoke again. "Or should *I*?" He took a big bite of his slice.

"Tell me what?" said Hannah.

"Yeah." Blake's happy mouth was swallowing the thick *zurek*. "Tell her what?"

But Mason's mouth was full of pizza. He didn't reply.

Chloe lowered her hands. She had been waiting all these months to talk to Hannah, waiting for the right time. And yet this couldn't be a worse time. Simply could not be. Can I have a do-over, she thought with sadness. Can I rewind back to July, when we were on my dock, our feet dangling in the water, splashing each other, laughing in the afternoon, dreaming of Europe, mapping, planning, giggling like when we were kids and Hannah and I were the closest thing to sisters. I want that back. I want to ruin *that* moment.

She took a deep deep breath, a slow-motion pause before the train wreck. For some reason she couldn't take her eyes off Mason sitting next to her, enjoying his pizza. What do *you* know about it? she wanted to ask. What are you implying? That *you* know? She frowned, suspicious and troubled. Was that possible? She almost spoke her first words to Mason instead of Hannah. But she checked herself. Hannah deserved an answer.

"Hannah," Chloe said. "I'm sorry, poodle. But I'm not going to the University of Maine. That's why you have a different roommate."

Sparrows, shopkeepers, tourists, singers. Why did they fight, remember each other's offenses? Why didn't they go play? Chloe felt such regret.

"What?" Hannah said.

"What?" Blake said. He stopped eating. He put down his spoon. He stopped smiling, making num-num noises. He stopped.

"I'm going to another university." She turned her gaze to Mason's unraised head. "Mason, did you know this?"

"Mason, did you know this?" Blake echoed.

Mason wiped his mouth. "What are you glaring at *me* for? I'm not the one not going to UMaine. Though technically, of course, I'm not."

"Mason," Chloe repeated, more and more distressed, "*did* you know?"

"Yeah." He shrugged. "So?"

"You knew and you said nothing?"

"What did you want me to say?"

"What—I don't know, but … why didn't you talk to me?"

"Why didn't you talk to *me*?" Mason said, not looking at Chloe, staring ahead at Blake. "I was waiting for you to say something. Any minute, I thought, she's bound to tell me. Any second now, she'll let me know." Mason studied his pizza crust like it was a rare unearthed fossil. Chloe stared at Mason's spiky-haired head. She wouldn't and couldn't look at Hannah, or at Blake.

"Where are you going, Chloe?" Blake said in a voice so quiet.

Beyond the stunned *what*, Hannah had yet to speak.

"University of San Diego."

Blake's hands dropped to his sides. His shoulders slumped. Chloe almost wanted to say I'm sorry to him. She remembered her place, and didn't.

"Bro," Blake said, "you knew this and you didn't tell me?"

"Why would I?" said Mason.

Hannah found her voice, a loud one. "But you might have thought to tell *me*, Mason, no?"

"What are you yelling at *me* for?" Mason raised his own voice. "I'm just the messenger."

"Um, you mean the dead opposite of messenger?"

"Hey, yell at her! It wasn't my secret to tell. Be mad at Chloe. She's the one who didn't say anything."

She's a cat, Chloe wanted to say.

"She's the one who's leaving," said Blake.

The brief silence that followed wasn't the silence to process, to suffer, to grieve. It was the silence of the universe before the hurricane.

"Oh my God!" Hannah jumped up. "What is *wrong* with you?" she said to Chloe. "What's wrong with you?" She started to cry.

"I'm sorry, Hannah." Chloe wrung her hands. She wanted to rush to her friend, but didn't dare. She was afraid Hannah would punch her. In any case Blake was already doing the consoling. "I was going to tell you. Really. I just couldn't find the right time." You know how that is, sometimes? Chloe thought. When you have to tell somebody very dear something very important but just can't find the nerve or the right moment? You can imagine something like that, can't you, poodle?

"How long have you known?"

"Since May."

"Since May!" Hannah cried. "And you couldn't find a good time to tell me? We made plans to come here, and you knew! We filled out our housing applications together, and you knew! Couldn't you have told me then, before we wrote down our personal hygiene habits?"

"I could've, of course. I should've. I'm sorry." What could Chloe say? I didn't tell you because I was afraid you wouldn't come with me to Treblinka?

And yet Mason had known, and said nothing. Nothing! How was that possible? Chloe was so piercingly baffled by that, she couldn't cope with the injuries forming into an avalanche inside her.

"Oh my God!" Hannah wiped her blotchy face. "Your mother must be beside herself. How could you do this to her?"

The pierogi, the potato latkes, Blake's *zurek* lay unfinished on the table. Only Mason had polished off the last crumb of his pizza slice and was now picking off the doughy edges of Blake's fried pierogi.

"My mother is the one who suggested it," said Chloe. That must be how Mason found out. Her mother had told his mother over a Friday ShopRite spree and then swore her to secrecy. Some secrecy!

What was more shocking? That she was leaving, or that Lang approved? By Hannah's face, Chloe knew the answer. Lang's approval was the worst of all.

"San Diego's just a better fit for me, Hannah. I'm sorry."

Hannah waved her off, waved Blake off. She had to sit down.

Rainy Bangor, cold Bangor, Arctic Bangor, mosquitoes, fog, damp, snowshoes. L.L.Bean coats and ski pants. Ice skating under the moonlight on their frozen lake, the eight lake houses with their Christmas lights on, strands of rainbows flickering on the blue ice. Who was she on the ice with? Everyone or just Blake? Chloe couldn't remember. She had skated into his arms and they both fell. It must have been Blake.

"What a traitor you are," Hannah said. "What an unbelievable traitor. I thought you were my friend."

"I am your friend."

"You were never my friend."

"I was always your friend," Chloe said. "I love you. I'd do anything for you."

"Except go to school with me, like we planned our whole lives, like we dreamed our whole lives."

Chloe swallowed miserably. "Are you *my* friend, Hannah?"

"Obviously not."

"Okay. But if you were my friend, wouldn't you wish for me what I want for myself?" When there was no answer from a sniffling Hannah, Chloe continued. "Let me go to the place that's perfect for me. Please. Be happy I'm happy."

"Why should I be? You're happy that I'm unhappy."

"What? No," said Chloe. "I'm very unhappy you've been unhappy."

"You're unhappy, Hannah?" Blake asked. "Why?"

"Real friends don't do this," Hannah said. "Real friends talk to each other."

What about real boyfriends? Chloe thought fleetingly. Do real boyfriends talk to their girlfriends? "I tried to talk to you," she said to Hannah. "You didn't listen. All you wanted to talk about was yourself and your problems."

"What problems, Hannah?" asked Blake.

"I got me some new problems now, don't I," Hannah snapped. "Rooming with a complete stranger. Great, just great, Chloe."

"Great, just great." Chloe mimicked Hannah, losing a bit of her temper, her heart freshly wounded by Mason. Any second now, the avalanche would break off the mountain and take them all down. "Can you for a second get off that high stallion you're riding? You were just telling me how you might not even go to UMaine, or did you forget that? You were telling me this just yesterday. You'd leave me there by myself in a second. For all I know, you're about to. For all I know, you're not even going, and this is nothing but bullshit." Well done, Chloe. Best defense was offense, right?

"Wait," said Blake. Now he turned fully to Hannah, looking raw. "Why would you not go to UMaine? What problems?"

Hannah wouldn't say.

"Answer me," said Blake.

Hannah wouldn't answer. Her head was down, but when she raised it, her angry red gaze was at Mason. She pointed at him, stabbing the air with her shaking finger. "You are *such* a fucking asshole," she said. "This is all your goddamn fault."

"Whoa," Mason said. "Hang on just a sec—"

"You kept your stupid lying cheating mouth shut for this long, why couldn't you keep it shut for a few days longer? She would've told me herself. When we came back, she would've definitely told me, I'm almost sure. You are *so* screwed up, Mason." Hannah was loud. "Why are you pissed off all the time? You have it so good. Why didn't you just let it be? It's not her fault you forgot your idiot statue and let her go with Johnny on the train. It's not Johnny's fault you lost the statue. You cart around that thing with you like porn, ready at any moment to jerk off to it. Maybe it's fucking karma, did you think of that, huh? I bet you didn't. And it's not Chloe's fault either. If you're all about truth, and paying your pretend piety at the Riga cathedrals, why don't you tell Chloe where you got that two dollar item from. Who gave it to you, Mason? Go ahead. I can't *wait* to hear this one." Hannah folded her trembling arms around her chest and panted.

"You know, Mason," said Chloe, "I can't wait to hear this one either."

She continued to stand, but her thighs felt weak, as if the muscles in them had liquefied. Fake-casually, Chloe leaned forward and rested her palm—and therefore all her weight—on the picnic table. Something had to support her when she listened to Mason's answer.

But Mason, like Hannah, refused to answer. "Don't turn this around to me," he said. "Chloe's leaving has nothing to do with me."

"Is that *so*?" Hannah said with a sneer.

"Maybe if you were a better friend to her, she'd be going with you to UMaine instead of across the country."

"Maybe if you were a better boyfriend, you mean! Or even any kind of a boyfriend, anything at all, really. Maybe if you were more than a passing acquaintance!"

"Who gave you the statue, Mason?" said Chloe.

"All right, everyone." That was Blake, spitting into the hot wind. "This isn't worth it, let's all calm down ..."

"Who gave you the statue, Mason?" Chloe repeated.

"*Please*, it's not worth it, Chloe," said Blake.

Mason jumped away from the table. "I'm not going to do this," he said. "Blake, let's go. The girls need to cool off."

"Come on, tell her, Mase," Hannah said, mocking him. "Or should *I* tell her?"

"Somebody tell me," said Chloe.

"I'm not going to talk about it!" Mason's blue eyes were desperate and blazing.

"Hannah, why are you causing trouble?" Blake said. He didn't look at Chloe, or at his brother, or at Hannah when he said it.

Mason and Chloe, standing, faced each other.

"Mason Haul," Chloe said, her voice nearly failing her. "Are you refusing to answer my direct question? For the fourth time, *who* gave you the statue?"

Before Chloe was Mason's averted face, his fallen countenance, his bent head. "It was Mackenzie, Chloe," he said at last. "I'm real sorry."

Chloe tried to take a breath, but her lungs had deflated. She put one palm out to stop him from saying another word, while the other calmed her anguished chest.

"You did this deliberately," she gasped out. "You engineered this so we'd all have to go home."

"No, I didn't! That's crazy."

Blake stared at Chloe with deep pity. "Look what you did, Hannah," he said to his girlfriend. "Are you happy now?"

"Hey, don't look at me," Hannah said. "I'm just the messenger."

"Go to hell!" Mason furiously swiped the unopened soda can off the table. It popped, hissing out oozing Coke.

"Oh, worry not, I'm already there," said Hannah.

"What does *that* mean?" Panting and flummoxed like Chloe, Blake took Hannah by the shoulders and turned her to him. "Why are you saying these things?"

Mason, Mason, Chloe thought. All the fun you had with girls who weren't me. All the afternoons and nights you spent with the cheer squad at their dances and cancer walks, at their parties and charades. I've always been bad at charades. Perhaps that was why I was never invited.

All those afternoons away, the mornings you couldn't come with me to Lupe's, the offended nights when I took clever jabs at your fan club. Your flushed face each time you came to bat and they cheered your name, Mason, Mason. Your relentless desire for postcards in every town we visited, your quest for a pen, for a stamp, for a mail box, you just *had* to send those postcards back home, no matter how out of the way, no matter how inconvenient. It wasn't the postcards that were inconvenient. It was me.

All of it, all at once, in a big O.

The *other* big O. The one I never had with you.

The O of, oh, I finally get it now. I was, finally, the last to know.

Oh.

Congratulations, Chloe.

Chloe stood and condemned Mason with a look and then without saying another word to him spun toward Hannah. "You cannot be trusted," Chloe said. Not to Mason. To Hannah! "You're *such* a fraud. All you do is keep secrets. If you suspected this about him, why didn't you tell me? Don't you know that's what friends do? But you wouldn't know that, would you?"

Hannah shrugged. Satisfaction was on her face. "I thought you knew. Everybody *else* knew."

"For fuck's sake, Hannah!" Mason yelled. "Blake, I *swear* to God … shut her up. In a second, I'm going to say things I won't be able to take back." But it was too late. He clenched his fists. "You're a fucking vampire. Why can't you leave us alone? Haven't you sucked enough blood?"

"Oh, she *definitely* has," said Chloe.

"Mason!" Blake said. "Stop! You're out of line."

"*I'm* out of line? Did you hear Chloe?"

"She doesn't answer to me. But yes, Chloe, you too."

"I don't answer to you either, bro," Mason said. "Control your girl, or somebody will have to."

"She's done nothing wrong!" Blake yelled, putting his arm around Hannah, as if to protect her from them. "You control *your*self or somebody will have to."

Chloe laughed and took a taunting half-bow in Hannah's direction. "Well played, Hannah! Nicely done. You got Blake defending your honor now. Wow. What a scam."

"Ahh!" Blake pulled his angry arm off Hannah's shoulder. "Will somebody *please* fucking tell me what you're talking about."

How hostile, how frozen the unforgiving ground. It was a theft of the blue sky. All the lilies in the field were choked in gasoline.

"Well, Hannah," said Chloe, her slender empty body shaking. "Here it is. The moment I know you've been waiting for. Your turn for a reckoning. Do *you* want to tell him?" A smile balefully stretched across Chloe's white lips. "Or should *I* tell him?"

"Tell me what?" said Blake.

"Tell him what?" Mason said quickly, sounding relieved they were off the subject of him and Mackenzie.

Hannah fixed on Chloe. "I can't be*lieve* you're doing this to me," she said with hatred, and took two short steps away from Blake. They were all standing now, the flies fighting over the unbroken bread between them.

"Doing what?" Blake said. "What's Chloe doing?"

"I'm not doing *anything*," Chloe said, opening her hands. "I'm just the messenger."

Gasoline immolating all the lilies in the field.

"Blake, it's over between us," Hannah blurted. "It's been over between us for months. I'm sorry I didn't tell you, but that's just how it is. There is someone else. You must have suspected. I'm sorry," she added, as if it was the last thing she meant.

"What?" he said. He almost smiled. He thought she was joking.

"*That's* what you're telling him?" Chloe cried. "Shame on you."

"You mean there's something she *isn't* telling me?" Blake said tonelessly, as if he finally understood that Hannah wasn't joking. To steady himself, he grabbed the wooden table.

"Holy shit, you're a piece of work, aren't you?" Mason said to Hannah, walking around the table to his brother's side and placing a supportive arm around Blake. "Dude, I kept telling you she was trouble. You wouldn't listen."

"How can we be over?" Blake said to Hannah. "We're here right now. Together."

"He makes a good point, Hannah," Chloe said, all pitiless bitterness. "Since it's been over for months, you might as well go ahead and tell him the rest of it."

"Stop it!" Hannah cried. "Stop it, stop it! Stop it!" She slammed her palms against her ears.

Chloe raised her eyes to Mason. "You know how sometimes there's the rest of it?"

Mason hanged his head. "I'm so sorry, Chloe," he whispered.

Gasping for air, Chloe sank down.

Across the table Blake stood—judging *her*! Not his wayward girlfriend, not Mason, but Chloe! "Dying by the sword is such a bitch," he said to her quietly.

"Talking to the wrong person is a bitch," Chloe retorted. "Talk to your brother. Your words are meant for him."

Blake faced Hannah, this time unsupported by the table, or by Mason. "Tell me the rest of it. What else is there?"

"Nothing, Blakie. Don't listen to her." She reached for him.

"You kept this a secret from me last night in bed," Blake said, moving away from her extended hands. "And the night before. And for months and months. You went to the prom with me. Did other things with me. And to me. You'd think you might have mentioned that we were over. So I wouldn't waste any more of my fucking time."

"Why?" Hannah said. "Mason didn't mention it to Chloe. And yet they're over."

"The hell with Mason and Chloe," Blake said to Hannah, pointing to her eyes and then to his own. "Eyes on me. Tell me what else."

"There is nothing else! You knew it couldn't last! This isn't news. I was leaving. Like Chloe is leaving. We were over."

"Tell me what else," he repeated. Blake wasn't red in the face, or panting. He was eerily quiet.

Mouthing *I hate you* to Chloe, Hannah swallowed. She squared her shoulders and straightened her spine. "Don't be upset, okay?" she said, quivering with a small charming smile. "But I'm having a baby."

Blake staggered away from Hannah. And they had thought the robbery was the worst thing that could happen to them. Silly they. The money was returned. But there was no return from this brutality.

For a long while Blake, leaning against the table, stood mute.

"Blake, say something," Hannah whispered. "Please."

"I give up," he said, in hoarse outrage. "I give the fuck up on you."

Everything was squalor. They stood in vomit and retched, the ice fishing and dangling feet forgotten, while all around them balloons were popping and little kids were chasing kites and butterflies and happy parents tossed their melting ice cream cones because it was hot hot hot.

Why was there so much discord in Poland? All the wars started here. What was it about this country? It seemed so placid on the outside. And yet look at the havoc it has caused. It was now Poland's fault what had happened. Poor almost blameless Poland.

Eventually someone said, in a broken voice, what about Barcelona, as if already crying.

"I'll go with you to Barcelona, Chloe," Mason said. "I promised you I would, and I will."

Chloe stared at his earnest face as if she didn't know him, saw him through the kaleidoscope of cheering bases and flirting flyers, through the smiling vapid prism of the detested muscular Mackenzie, and suddenly Chloe didn't want to see Mason's face for another second, another *breath*, much less a week in her beachy naked fading ruined Barcelona dream.

"That's not the only thing you promised me, Mason," Chloe said, trying hard not to cry. "That's right, look away," she added. "What else can you do, really? So you can't look at me, but you'll go to Barcelona with me?"

He mumbled something she didn't hear.

She thought he said they should talk in private, away from … away from what? Away from whom? This was as private as it would ever get, with shattered Blake and bankrupt Hannah by their side in a public square filled with other people's joy. Every frozen season of Chloe's life had the four of them breaking fishing holes in the ice and gliding on their backs and making angels. And now there was nothing.

She backed away from the table, her pitying eyes on Blake, her frigid eyes on Mason, her guilty, angry, conflicted eyes on Hannah, she covered her face as if to shield it from a knife assault, in tremor she raised her hands, praying, surrendering, protecting herself against them, and then turned and ran as fast as she could in her Polish sundress and strappy sandals.

31

The Clock in Trieste

HER ENTRAILS ARE IN KNOTS. IT HAS BEEN MERE MINUTES IN burnished sunlight, but her whole body feels chafed, raw from exertion. She wanders, pretending to think, but she is single-mindedly, purposefully, frantically searching for Johnny. She doesn't know what to do. She had run back to the hotel of roses and asked the clerk if anyone had left an envelope for her. They had not. Afraid to encounter her arid bunch, Chloe escapes down a side street, around the university, around, around. How does she fix this? How does she make it right? She thinks that if only she can find him, he can help her figure it out. Everything will be easier to bear if they can figure it out together.

There is an ancient, small, windy feel to Krakow that appeals to Chloe's heart, and if only she were better disposed to being a traveler, she might perhaps fall in love with this seventh century city of narrow streets and immense fortresses. There is sun and music everywhere on a hot summer night. Oh, to open her eyes and see, instead of running in a state of siege. Stopping, listening for the seduction of his riding-a-Harley voice, hurrying on. Where is the black dog that will make her burn, that will leave its scorch marks on her? She roams the streets in circles.

Seconds, minutes, hours?

If he is here, he won't be far from where the people are. She won't give up. She won't give up.

The beautiful young Krakow women are tall and in heels. They wear lots of red lipstick and silver jewelry. They don't have tear-streaked faces. They carry designer purses not shoddy backpacks with stray lipstick of the expired Revlon variety and maybe a gummy bear.

There is also Mason's Eurail card, which she is holding for safe-keeping, how handy, and a hundred or so dollars Johnny had given her yesterday. Maybe more. For something to do, and to force herself to feel both less frenzied and less weary, Chloe sits down on a retaining wall and counts her money. Three beggars stop and ask her for some of it. None of them is Johnny. She has one hundred and seventy-five dollars. A Eurail card. Her passport. She wishes she had some underwear. A toothbrush. To be proactive, she looks for a drugstore to buy a toothbrush. The underwear remains a problem. But it's after seven in the evening, and the shops are closed. Soon it will get dark. And then what?

She may be guilty, but Mason is wrong. He is the one who broke their tacit agreement for a low-key easy beautiful union. Minimum fuss, minimum pain. That was their motto. Not anymore. She is angry with him for this most of all.

She doesn't want to think about how awful she acted, how upset she got, how she said things she can't take back.

She doesn't want to think about how she hurt Blake. She gets angry at this, defends herself to herself, mouthing inaudible words on a street corner. She didn't hurt him. Hannah hurt him. She was just the messenger. But why did she have to be so vindictive? Hannah would've gotten to the truth soon enough, wouldn't she? Like Chloe would've. Like Mason would've. Why did they mangle each other like this?

How does she go back to them, to the room? How does she speak to them, sleep with them?

No, that's a lie, what she said she felt. The broken contract is *not* what she finds unforgiveable. What she finds unforgiveable is that Mason would choose to step out on her with someone who wasn't just beneath him, but beneath the amoeba floating in the lake, beneath the algae. Why would Mason drift toward the most insipid of creatures? He must hear Chloe's contempt echoing off all the stones it took to build Krakow. How long had it been going on? She didn't want to ask, because she was afraid to know. What if he had said two years? Two Christmases, two winters in the snow, two summers in the lake, all of his varsity career. Chloe feels all her good intentions toward Mason swirling slowly down the clogged drain of her heart.

So what are her choices?

She can go home. Change her flight, fly home tomorrow. Accept defeat, get ready for the rest of her life.

She can go to Barcelona alone.

That seems insurmountable. She has never been anywhere alone.

She can go to Barcelona with Mason as he had offered.

Impossible.

She can go to Barcelona with Hannah.

The question is, dear Chloe, would Hannah ever again go anywhere with you?

She can go to Barcelona with Blake.

Chloe laughs out loud when she thinks this, perched on her little stone wall. Passersby flinch and speed up. They must think she has escaped and is roaming the streets until she is picked up by the soothing people in white.

Blake is a decent traveling companion. He is super easy. He is open to everything and, until Johnny came along, was in a fine mood from morning to night. He is funny, hungry, game and ready, and he buys her pastries and carries her shit, her bag and books and water. He doesn't get burned in the sun, and he doesn't cheat on her with the queen airhead of all flying bimbos. He is her friend and, alas, the only halfway palatable option to *seni*, *rochas* and empanadas in Saint Eulalia's city is the most impossible of all.

She has to find Johnny. That's all there is to it. She jumps up, scaring off more passersby, and starts walking with a purpose to nowhere. She either finds him or she goes home. There is no other way. Now it's really up to her.

Krakow is the city of poetry. Literally. Poetry is graffitied on Krakow's millennial stone walls. Chloe walks by the same street twice before she realizes she is duplicating her steps. *Mark the distant city glow / With gloomy splendor red*. A couplet from Sir Walter Scott. She longs to hear a different kind of canto. She will not despair. This city abounds with mystery and life. It has no whiff of disillusionment. She will not despair. She will find him.

Krakow is a city of women in colorful clothes sitting on wood crates selling cabbages. Most are old. They sit mutely in yellow dresses and sell carrots they brought from the villages. They don't have stalls, they perch on stools, low to the pavement, and the street musicians share the city walls with them. The old men stand nearby drinking vodka, toothlessly smiling. In the baskets between the women's feet lie radishes and lettuce, cucumbers and tomatoes, and roses by the bunch. On every street there is a blue trolley with an old woman selling what looks like huge pretzels with poppy seeds. They're called *obwarzanek*. They look delicious. Chloe doesn't want to stop.

The drunken scent of overripe roses mixes with dill and fermented cabbage on every corner. *Bigos* and roses. Krakow is a phantasmagoria of glittering gold of the setting sun sparkling in the stained glass windows. Chloe is light-headed and hungry and thirsty and alone, intoxicated with a nameless fear of all things unknown and the charged possibility of all impossible things.

She doesn't hear him at all, yet she hears him on every corner. She is walking through the desert, and he is her mirage. The canal in the middle of Krakow carries for her his unforgettable voice, echoing it through the parapets and the stained glass windows. She swears she can hear his dramatic tenor amplified by the acoustics of the ancient city, his unbreakable voice waxing about rides and trains and daisies and girls he can't leave behind.

She follows a figure she thinks is him down the park slope of the castle with the dragon's lair, because some women are sauntering and yelling into a young man's back from a distance, inviting him to familiarize himself with their melody or perhaps with their white necks. It's not him. It's another man with a ponytail in a black shirt.

The sun sets nice and late. The streetlamps switch on. It is dusk. Then it's night. She looks for him in the lit-up darkness.

He is nowhere.

She simply can't believe it. She doesn't find him.

It is almost midnight when she slowly steps inside the long gray lobby of the rose hotel. It's empty. The young clerk is asleep on duty behind the desk.

Chloe clears her throat to wake the girl up, and asks if the room key is hanging or if her companions are upstairs. The woman tells Chloe that her companions have been upstairs since ten.

With her head hung low, Chloe leans against the counter. She must go up. She is beaten.

"Is there an envelope for me?" she asks.

"You asked me earlier," the woman says. "There was nothing."

"I know. Is there still nothing?"

The woman theatrically slides off her chair, takes two steps to the cubbies behind her, looks inside.

"No. Just a newspaper and your bill for tomorrow. Wait—here's something." She removes something stuck to the back of the newspaper. "Are you Chloe Divine?"

Chloe picks up her heart from the floor and puts it back into her chest before she answers. Yes, she says. I am Chloe Divine. The woman hands her a cream envelope.

On it, in clear, strong all-caps handwriting, is her name. CHLOE DIVINE. Underlined twice. HOTEL OF THE ROSES, KRAKOW. Is it her imagination or is the underlining stronger under her last name *Divine*? She'll be sure to spend many hours dissecting the art of underlining. Maybe there's a course she can take in college.

Very carefully she grips the envelope with her fingers. She thanks the woman, and walks steadily out the front door. She goes into Rynek Glowny square, where, even though it's late, the party is just starting. Everything is illuminated and shiny and bright. Musicians, boom boxes, dancing women, drunken men everywhere. And then there is Chloe. She fits into a narrow crevice by the wall of St. Mary's, near a floor bulb that shines up from the cobblestones, and after holding onto the thick envelope for a few seconds, carefully peels it open.

Inside she finds six 50-euro bills ($400), a Xeroxed page with numbers on it, and a note. The note also has numbers. But also letters that form words. Everything is a symbol—numbers, letters. Everything stands for something else. Chloe tries to find the meaning in it all. Her mother is right once again. Human beings spend their lives infusing finite things with divine significance, with infinite meaning.

The numbers don't make sense, as numbers sometimes do not.

After she reads his letter again, she looks across the square and checks the time. Breathing shallowly, her back against the wall, she watches the clock hands on the tower move from 11:40 to 11:59 before she reads the letter for the third time.

12:02.

Riga, Warsaw, Barcelona. St. Mary's Basilica and Oskar Schindler and the field in Treblinka. Europe is why no one said a word to anyone about anything, remorselessly guilty before everyone and everything, for months, maybe years, hiding the essence of themselves to spare what they thought were their unbreakable bonds.

If she goes back to the room, there will be a scene. If she goes to the room, she won't be able to leave. They won't let her. In the room there's a suitcase. Shampoo. A toothbrush. Her books. Her Doc Martens. Her belt and jean jacket, and Blake and Mason and Hannah. Her woolly cardigan. Underwear.

On the street there is nothing, not even a sensible T-shirt to throw over her insensible cleavage.

On the street there is nothing but Johnny.

Dear Chloe,

In Trieste, there's a clock – on a tower by the sea, on Piazza Unita Italia.

I will wait for you by the fountain under that clock at ten tomorrow night. I will wait for two hours, until midnight. I will wait tomorrow night, and the night after. But then I will have to go.

I left you some numbers that may be helpful, if you dare.

Near Trieste overlooking the sea there is a castle on a cliff. The bus that goes to the castle is number 136. If I see you, I will tell you why that matters.

But now I'll tell you another thing that matters.

Pi never terminates, never repeats, never ends. I want to believe 3:14 is human, and 3:15 is divine, and we live in the irrational space between the two, the space with five trillion numbers and counting, the space with no patterns. We lumber on senselessly, transcendentally, to infinity.

But pi is not the key to infinity.

It's the key to eternity.

And sometimes, if we are lucky, we get to Proverbs 3:15.

I ask you, Chloe Divine, do you dare disturb the universe?

Johnny Rainbow

She grabbed a cab to the train station, waited barely twenty minutes and boarded the late-night express to Katowice, where she found a hostel at three in the morning close to the station. Perhaps it was not as terrifying as a field of blood, but only by a matter of degree.

She lay on the cot, fully dressed, with her backpack under her head. She slept poorly, and was up at six without being woken. The train she had to catch was leaving at eight. Johnny's Xeroxed numbers, now deciphered, said so. She had just enough time to buy herself some coffee and two sweet rolls, just like Johnny had taught her, and once on the train, she found a seat next to the window in a spotless compartment for four, placed her little fake-leather brown backpack between her and the sparkling glass, leaned against it, waited fifteen minutes to show the conductor Mason's Eurail pass, closed her eyes and didn't open them again until she was a half-hour away from Vienna, Austria.

In Vienna, she missed an unnervingly punctual train to Udine, and had to wait over an hour for the next one. But she bought a toothbrush, a T-shirt and some underwear, and felt grateful for the delay.

She spent the next six hours with the light on her face, and the staggering Alps in her eyes, the dales and foothills violent with lilac lupines, seeing things that even she, accustomed to the glory of the White Mountains, had never seen.

She thought about Hannah and Blake, about how Hannah had pursued him, and how he had fallen for her. How much Chloe had envied her at the time, that Hannah had snagged someone who felt about her the way Blake seemed to feel about her, even early on, on the cusp of forming the union that had brought them three years later to another picnic bench, this time in Krakow, where what began so promisingly at a high school barbecue dissolved into Hannah's being pregnant at eighteen with another man's child.

Chloe's heart hurt through the Alps all the way to Udine as she tried to forget Blake's astonished devastated face.

She got into Udine at eight in the evening and caught a train to Trieste. It took nearly two hours. There was an intimation of a sea to the right of her window, but she couldn't be sure about the black void with the moon behind the clouds. She had noticed a change in the trains in Vienna and again here in Udine. There was a marked upgrade from what she had been recently riding. For one, there were no drunks in the cars, no noise, no unmodulated anything. The floors were swept. The seats were clean. The lights didn't go out. No one kissed her. Every last detail was from Emily Post.

Once in Trieste, she reached Piazza Unita in twenty minutes by foot, walking along the rough and unquiet harbor. To reach the fountain took three more minutes. It was nearly eleven. He had said he would wait until midnight.

But he wasn't there.

I will wait until midnight. But those were just symbols of his intent. They weren't real. He was real. But he wasn't here. That was real. She hadn't asked herself what would happen if he didn't wait. What if she miscounted those damn numbers, blundered up the days by one, and yesterday was in fact the day after tomorrow, and he had already left her behind? What if she hadn't missed the train in Vienna?

She was sure of nothing. Was everything just a lie?

She waited for him until midnight.

What if nothing in her brightest life would ever compare to the carved-out moment in blackness on the Polish train with him when he kissed her? The ebony night flying by with his lips on her lips would remain vivid like fireworks, then intermittently, and then never again. That was the dread fear.

She asked an Italian closing up his café on the piazza for help. He directed her to a hostel nearby, clean, not that Chloe cared. Twenty American dollars bought her a bed in a dorm, another ten a hot shower, and five more a combination lock on the bathroom door, "for the just in case," as the hostel manager put it.

Chloe didn't know if she was starved or exhausted.

She was frightened she had been such a fool.

She had found a Bible in the hostel lounge. Placed there by the Gideons.

She sneaked it back to her bed and slept with the Gideon Bible pressed to her chest.

Proverbs 3:15.

She is more precious than rubies: and all the things thou canst desire are not to be compared unto her.

32

A Town Called Heartbreak

In the morning she wandered around Trieste, moody and gloomy, both she and the city. At ten she was back at the piazza with the clock, thinking maybe she had made a mistake and he meant morning, not night. Did he write noon and she read night?

No. At noon she left, cold and damp. She changed the last of her zloty into euro and found a department store where she bought herself a pair of jeans and a green sweater. Her flouncy coral minidress was suddenly ludicrous, like black tie at a backyard barbecue. She bought a pair of cheap sneakers, an umbrella and waterproof mascara because it hadn't stopped raining. Half the money he had given her was gone. After changing into her new, less absurd clothes, she found a corner café with tall tin ceilings where she had a pastry and a cappuccino. She just wanted to stay somewhere warm. She sat in the café for an hour waiting for the rain to end. When it didn't, she left and walked on, her sneakers soaked by the next block. There was an embankment that led to the sea, but the sea was invisible, because the gray air was so thick and low upon it. All the twisty little alleys and wide boulevards of Trieste were wet with rain. There were hardly any people on the streets. There was certainly no Johnny.

He had told her Trieste was a beautiful historic city, and perhaps it was. She listened for music, for troubadours. She found a sax player, and asked him if he knew a guy with an angel's voice. He didn't understand. She gave him a euro. She found an oboe player who spoke English. "You mean, *I* don't have an angel voice?" he said. She gave him some money too.

She kept hearing music, songs, but it was almost wishful thinking, like dreams close to waking, yet nothing in her hands, nothing in her eyes.

She found him by the granite harbor.

He was walking ahead of her in the pouring rain without an umbrella, his guitar case wet, his green duffel dripping. When she saw his back, in the soaked leather jacket, the beret on his head, the black hair untied, she cried. Johnny, she thought she said, Johnny, she whispered. Johnny!

He didn't turn around. Oh my God, was it not him? But his guitar, his duffel! She ran to catch up with him. Johnny! She cut him off on the sidewalk, stood in front of him.

"Johnny." She tried not to shake.

"Chloe Divine," he said. "I can't believe you came."

He looked terrible. He was haggard, his eyes black-circled, his skin the color of fog, his red lips blue. She couldn't understand it. When he hugged her, his body shook. He had looked aimless from the back, and when she stepped in front of him and called his name, he seemed surprised she had made it. *I can't believe you came*, is what he said, but that could mean anything. I can't believe you came when I wasn't expecting you at all, is what he could've meant.

"Are you okay?" Her troubled heart didn't know what to think, what to feel.

"Yeah, just cold." He wiped the rain off her face. It was rain, right?

"What happened to you?" she asked. "You told me you'd wait for me till midnight."

"When, yesterday?"

"Yes, yesterday."

"I don't remember yesterday," he said. "It was today I said I'd wait."

"You said tomorrow."

"Yes. Today was tomorrow yesterday."

"But you said you don't remember yesterday."

"I meant today. When did you get here?"

"Yesterday," said Chloe.

"I don't know how you managed it." There was truth in his face, in his weak arms draped around her. "Sorry you waited and I didn't come."

"Where were you?"

He struggled to recall. "I met my dad. I was late for him, too, I think. He was pretty pissed at me. Like you? Then I caught up with some friends."

"You have friends in Trieste?"

"I have friends everywhere."

"Why was your dad here?"

"We were supposed to go visit my mother together. Remember I told you about my mother?"

"Yes, of course. I didn't know you were going with your dad. Did you go?"

"Of course I didn't go yet," he said quietly. "Tarcento is far from here."

They stood in the rain.

"Did you play today?" Chloe asked him.

"Why, did you look for me?"

"Everywhere." Her voice broke.

"I didn't play today." He sounded so sad when he said it.

"So what did you do yesterday, and today? Were you with your dad?"

"No. I was with my friends. I was really out of it. I slept a lot. Which is why I must look like shit." He nudged her. "Kind of like you after Kaunas, remember?" He smiled nostalgically, as if Kaunas was years ago.

They stood on the street. He made no motion to move or to speak. He twitched a little.

"So what do you want to do now?" she said. "Are you hungry?"

"Starved. Problem is, I got no money."

"How can that be? What happened to it?"

"Well, I gave most of it to you."

She was skeptical. He hadn't even given her what he had promised them. He gave her four hundred dollars, not five hundred. And she'd spent nearly a third of it on jeans and toothbrushes and hostels. They never talked like this, discussing mundane things, almost bickering. "I owed my friends some money," he went on. "After I paid them we hung out. Then I had no more money. How much do you have left?"

"A few hundred. I had to buy some clothes. I—" She broke off. "Do you want to get out of the rain? I can tell you what happened. Where were you headed?" she asked him as they started walking.

"I don't know," he said. "I really didn't think you would come." His long arm went around her, but they were both too wet to hold on to each other. Pulling away, he held her red umbrella over their heads.

"Where's all your stuff?" he said.

She opened her hands. She pointed to her backpack. She said nothing. His dark eyes cleared a bit, turned up at the corners, glistened.

"Maybe after you feed me," Johnny said, pressing his shoulder into her shoulder, "I'll play a little to get us some cash, we don't need that much, and then we can ride a ferry to a place I hope you'll never forget."

She was hardly going to forget the hostels either.

"A ferry … or a bus?"

He smiled, as if recollecting his not-so-distant words to her. "Ah, yes. Bus number 136. We could. But wouldn't you rather go by sea?"

"I don't know where we're going. Why were you wandering the streets, Johnny?"

"I wasn't wandering."

"Where were you going?"

"To find a place to play."

"But it's raining."

"The ferry costs money, food costs money, and I've got none."

"Why didn't you ask your dad for some?"

Johnny's body got skittish. "My dad is long out of the business of giving me cash. Moms would give me some, but she doesn't have any herself. Plus she's far away. A pickle, really. Dad offered to feed me, though."

He didn't look as if he'd taken his father up on the offer. He didn't look as if he'd eaten or washed or played since Warsaw. Chloe didn't know what was the matter with him.

"Nothing, princess. I'm just beat. And hungry."

How can you be beat if you slept all day? she thought. But after they found a Greek-Italian place, and he had spanakopita and avgolemono soup and tagliatelle with sausage, he livened up. He was still weak tea, but at least he was Johnny tea.

He listened with great interest to her story of the picnic table at Krakow Square. "So that's how you were able to leave them," he said. "I don't know how you engineered that."

"Maybe the same way you engineered a tour on which all of our things got stolen," she said.

Unoffended, he laughed soundlessly. "That helped me almost not at all. And put quite a damper on our day in Treblinka." He clucked and tsk-tsked and asked more questions about Mason and Blake and Hannah. "What a waste of beautiful Krakow," he said in conclusion, shaking his head slightly and then groaning from the effort. "Everyone sore and undone." He didn't seem to be surprised by any of it, except by Blake's relative silence.

"Why shouldn't he be silent?" Why was Chloe annoyed by this? She was still smarting from before. Johnny didn't jump when he saw her, didn't run into her arms, didn't turn around when she called his name. Well, the last one was easy to figure out. He didn't turn around because it wasn't his name. But what about the rest of it? "What was Blake supposed to say?"

Johnny didn't stipulate.

"I left before the worst," she said. "He probably said it all after."

"I'm surprised he didn't say it before you left. Never mind. I suspected from the beginning Hannah was a heartless guttersnipe."

"Don't say that. She's not a guttersnipe."

He took her hand across the café table. "What do you think of Trieste? It's been raining non-stop since I got here. A drag, right? It's usually such a lush tropical multi-everything city." He leaned forward, bringing his stubbled face down to her hands, kissing one by one the tips of her fingers. "The place I plan to take you to, high on a cliff," he said, "I want it to take your breath away. But we've got a few challenges ahead of us, princess. We can't go there without some money. That's one. And two, I have to, have to, have to, be on the 8 a.m. plane in two days. And three, I have to, have to, have to, visit my mother before I fly back."

"Is that all we have?" she said, flinching from the sting of regret. "Not even three days? And it's raining." We would've had more, she thought. We would've had one more day, one more night had you not taken it from us by your mystifying absence.

"There is that. But Trieste is a great city for music lovers. You'll see. Rain or shine, they come. And you'll help. Let's get some hot coffee for the road, with some butterscotch whiskey in it, and we'll be all set."

"Whiskey? Won't that hurt your voice?"

He grinned like Johnny Vaudeville. "You mean won't that make it better? Fret not. Wasn't it Mason's favorite philosopher Bart Simpson who said that whiskey was the solution to all life's problems?"

"Um, you're misquoting both Mason and Bart," Chloe said. "Bart said alcohol was both the cause *and* the solution to all life's problems."

Johnny laughed, almost back to his old self.

"Very wise is Bart," said Johnny. "Like a little Yoda is he."

The unrelenting downpour continued the evening Johnny sang to take Chloe to a cliff by the sea. There was an ugly wind, whipping the rain into a circus of misery. She still hadn't seen the waters of the Adriatic.

The streets were empty, but they found one near Piazza Unita that was only a quarter empty and made their perch under a partial enclosure. She held the red umbrella over his head and guitar. With her green sweater, she thought she looked like a Christmas tree. She felt the shiver in her veins even before he began to sing, before he reached for the notes he reached only by birthright.

Where was Van Gogh to paint them in their ragtag threads, with the red umbrella over Johnny and his Gibson, Chloe a small green trembling stalk? The air cold cold. He sang. Without an amp, without a mic, without incompetent Chris on the drums, without electric strings or Robert Plant. She was wrong about that. Acoustic Robert Plant was channeled through Johnny's electric throat all the way to heaven. Did Chloe get what she came for? Joe Cocker unchained his heart. Springsteen was blinded by the light. Radiohead was high and dry, Bryan Adams got his six-string at the five-and-dime, and Freddie Mercury wanted to live forever. Johnny wanted to be young the rest of his life. And all the stars were shining. *E lucevan le stelle.* Yeah, yeah, yeah, he said. Come and get me. I said come get me. And you got me. Yeah, yeah, yeah. You got me.

"Where do we go now?" she asked, after he finished counting the change and the bills in his bucket of tears.

"Do you see how well we did?" He was himself again and happy. "We made nearly three hundred more euro. That's enough for food *and* a fairytale." Crouching, he smiled up at her. "They give more for the effort it takes me to sing in this weather and for them to stand and listen."

"I liked when they begged you for an encore of 'You Can't Always Get What You Want,'" Chloe said.

Jumping up, he took her by the hand. "But when you try real hard, you get what you need." Pulling her close, he lifted her face to his. "Now I take you to see some magic." They kissed under the red umbrella.

"Does the ferry operate in a storm?" she asked in a croaky voice.

"Ha. This isn't a storm. It's a little rain. We can always take a taxi now that we're flush. But let's bounce and see if we get lucky."

They ran. And the ferry still ran. They got lucky. The lights of the boat lit up a swathe of black stormy water, but that was all. The fog had come in over the cliffs, and no matter how they peered ahead, they couldn't see anything in the night, not even shore lights.

"How far are we going?"

"Just ten lousy kilometers," Johnny said. "A half-hour ride at most. Not tonight of course. Sad you can't see it in its splendor."

"See what?" she said. "You'll just have to paint me a picture with your words, Johnny." They huddled on the deck of the boat. She hoped that wherever they were going had a shower and some blankets. Though knowing him, they might be camping out in the woods, in the pre-Alpian mountains. "Tell me about bus 136, the bus we're not taking."

He smiled. "We're forging our own way to enchantment," he said. "But many years ago my grandparents fell in love on a bus, and the number of that bus was 136." He paused. "Don't you find that remarkable?"

"It'd be remarkable, yes, if we were actually taking it," Chloe grumbled, cold, wet, seeing nothing in front of her.

His spirits high, he kissed her damp neck. "Despite the snowy fog," he whispered, "there will be time for you and me. I wish the seas were silent, but alas. We'll put on flannel pajamas another day when we are old. There will be plenty of time then for Ovaltine by the fire. Right now, our bodies rage with disquiet. It's as it's supposed to be. Because in front of us, on a peak above the sea, stands a white Gothic castle."

"Is that where we're going to? A castle?"

He chuckled. "No, because when you're in it, you can't see it, and I want you to be able to see it from our balcony. We'll stay in a room with a view." He grinned at his own literary allusions.

She gazed into the darkness and tried her hardest to make out a shape, a shadow.

"Can you glimpse it? It's made out of limestone, and it's been bleached by the sun and the Adriatic. It's white and it juts out into the blue waters."

Her discomfort faded. "I can't see white nor blue, or jutting."

"Yes, but I'm painting it for you with my words, as you wished. Do you know a guy named T.S. Eliot? Of course you do. Well, a long time ago, the dude wrote a poem called, I can't remember, something about Alfred Prufrock, great name, right, and the poem was one of those weird jobs like he was on acid when he wrote it, but I never forgot the first lines." Tonight Johnny frowned, struggling to remember. Nothing came. With a little laugh, he shrugged. "Never mind. But around the same time, maybe a little earlier, a besotted archduke of Austria named Max built a castle for his young beloved named Charlotte. And he called it Castello di Miramare. A view by the sea. A Lovers' Castle. Where the peerless prince, or is it the pauper, brings his flower girl of Barcelona to show her what beauty is, though he is sure she already knows."

33

The Love Song of J. Alfred Prufrock

WHAT WORDS DO YOU USE TO EXPRESS THE INEXPRESSIBLE? The white mystery in the insistent rain, the empty hotel on a hill, the blurred headlights of cars racing through the tunnel and around the curve of the black road, red tail-lights vanishing around the bend. And across the road, downhill on a promontory into the sea, the lit-up silver walls of an enormous castle with towers and battlements, only slightly blurred by the rain. What a sight it must be during the day. What a sight it is now. Everything went flying flying the moment he stepped into her life, squeezing himself between her and the hefty Latvian.

He calls her into the hot shower after he drops his things on the floor. She has no things. Just her little bag, and him. The room is a small square with two large twin beds pushed together to make a king, brass headboards, red satin bedspreads. A bed is all the room has space for.

Trust me, he whispers as he pulls her in under the running water and lathers clean her body and his body. His long-fingered hands, pliant and chord-progression-ready, soap her back in circles, her breasts in circles. She didn't realize her breasts needed to be so clean. Trust me, there really is a castle outside our balcony door.

How does she tell him she's seen it, but also that she doesn't care about the view? Only what's inside the shower is real. The rest is myth. Even what's inside the shower is myth. But myth forcefully alive. He stands naked, hard, tall, too thin. He can't wait until the bed. Drying off is too long to wait. Even the conditioner is not yet washed away from his hair. Rinsing the conditioner is too long to wait. He lifts her up onto himself under the hot water. She grabs on, threads her arms around his slippery wet neck. Her back is pushed against the tiles.

They stay until the water runs cold.

Still damp they pull back the bedspreads and fall onto the white sheets. The beds can't sustain the toil of their efforts. The frames glide apart on the wooden floor.

Nothing in Chloe's life has been like this. She is dazzled not only by the kiss and the endless assault on her good senses, but by the alarming awareness that she has no sense left. There is nothing she won't do. There is nothing she doesn't want him to do. She marvels at the sweat of the labor of love that drips from his body, his hair, his face, onto her. What man has ever been so overcome for a girl?

They hope the water tank has had time to reheat. It has not. But they're burning up. They let the water run cold over their sticky breathless bodies to cool down. Wrapped in sheets they step out onto the wet balcony. It's misty. The visibility is Johnny.

Isn't it beautiful, he says.

It is, she says. I wish we had more time.

We have more than we ever thought we'd have, he says. We thought Warsaw would be all we'd have.

And even that was stolen, she says.

Yes. He kisses her deeply, their ghostly bodies pressed together. Had Mason not gone back for the statue … When you see him, will you please thank him for his idol worship?

You mean bimbo worship, says Chloe, and Johnny laughs, pulling her back inside.

Look how lush and fertile you look, how amazing, he murmurs, cupping her, fondling her as she straddles him. I can't believe you tried to hide your body from me.

Please don't call me fertile, she says. Last thing in the world I need. Look at Hannah.

Ah, he whispers, pulling her over him, his mouth closing in on her breasts, but if you had my child, I'd have to marry you, wouldn't I?

If I had your child, she replies in a moan, you'd have to tell me your real name, wouldn't you?

He laughs, his palms sliding down over her hips. Yes. The boy would be called Johnny Junior.

Seconds, minutes, hours. She caresses him endlessly with her hands, with her mouth. She keeps persuading him with her own immoderate desire to answer her need in the affirmative.

Please don't stop, she pleads in whispers. I don't want this to ever end.

I am only one man, he mutters. I can only do so much. Give me five more minutes.

She tries not to emit a wretched cry. She doesn't want him to think she is not in bliss. But she can't help it. Will there be another five minutes for you and me, she whispers, bringing his soaking body to lie flat on top of her, gripping his wet loose hair.

Yes, Chloe. We made *this* happen. We'll make other things happen too. You'll see. That's what love does. It makes possible impossible things.

She cradles his head to her face.

Is this what it feels like to fall in love?

Then why does it feel so much like dread?

Nothing but hunger and terror.

Is it being abandoned by God, or aflame with God? And what is so wrong with her that she can't tell the difference?

Everything else vanishes. Not a speck remains of her old life, her old priorities. Nothing else matters.

That's what it feels like, he says in assent. Love comes in and reorders the furniture. Love comes in, Chloe, does it not?

She moans. She can barely speak. But I always have everything under control.

Even this?

Yes. In this I am like my mother. This thing that's happening, it isn't me. This isn't how my mother taught me to be.

And all the while Chloe is speaking, Johnny is a smiling pendulum.

You think your mother has it under control? he asks.

I'd prefer not to talk about my mother at this precise moment, but yes.

Really. Then tell me, how often have you seen your mother's family?

Not often, she replies, her arms around him. Almost never.

How many times have you been to North Dakota?

Never.

Hmm. Sounds to me as if your mother ran off the tracks the day she met your father. So much so that she was willing to forsake all five generations of her family. Your mother was willing to sever her ancestral ties to follow her heart to the lake in Maine.

What are you talking about, Chloe says dumbly, staring up at him.

Sounds as if the Red River flooded Pembina, no?

Johnny, that can't be!

Why?

They're my parents. They can't feel this way. Not *this* way.

He shakes his head, perspiration dripping from his hair. The fire that brought them together made you. My mom and dad made me. My grandparents made my dad, and my dad changed the world.

What? She can barely listen.

Yes. My father altered the world as it was, and made it into a new thing that it is.

What are you talking about?

Nothing, nothing. A story for another time maybe.

Are you going to change the world, Johnny Rainbow? She almost sobs right then and there. Crush it with your mammoth glittering cry.

He kisses her. You want me to sing you songs of love? I'll sing until I shred my throat. I'll sing until you feel it.

He sings until she feels it.

He does everything until she feels it.

She doesn't know what time it is. They've unplugged the hotel clock, hidden his watch in his duffel. They don't want to know. Soon, it might be dawn. And then tomorrow. A whole life is waiting to be lived in these brief days. There is no time for time.

It's still raining and black out. It's been night for so long, it feels like winter in Maine, and yet nothing like it. It's warm. And there is a naked boy in her bed, under red satin covers, as if they're on a parade in a bordello. He has closed his eyes, finally, the last love having drained his vital powers.

Sitting up in bed, she huddles around her knees. They've pushed the beds back together, and she wants to turn her head to look at his beautiful sleeping body but can't. His motionless form in her periphery prompts her to imagine what it might be like if he was dead. If he was the un-Johnny.

He is joining the army. He plans to become a Ranger. Rangers jump out of airplanes. Go behind enemy lines. Men die when they go to war. She puts her hands over her face.

A few minutes later he is up too. What's the matter, he says. She has rings under her eyes, puffiness from the salt of her afflictions.

Perhaps she can love him six or seventy more times before she answers him. I'm afraid I'll never see you again after these three days when you tell me that you will love me forever is what she wants to say but can't.

Gray morning comes. It has stopped raining.

She notices his hands shake as he bends over the bed to tie his army boots. He's having trouble making a knot. Can't hold the ends of the laces together.

"What's the matter with your hands?" she asks from the pillow.

"Nothing, why?"

The fact that he pretends it's not happening worries her more. She sits up. "Johnny, your hands are shaking."

"No. They're fine. I just need coffee and a croissant." He hops to his feet. "I'll be right back."

"Wait, I'll get dressed. I'll come with you."

"No, you stay." He smiles. "Stay naked in bed. Just how I like you. Chill a bit. I don't think you slept at all. I felt you frantic next to me. Was I dreaming?"

She demurs from replying.

"I'll be back in a flash with breakfast in bed."

And sure enough he is back in a flash, chipper, delightful, and his hands don't shake anymore. His eyes are bloodshot. She's a fine one to talk, her own eyes not exactly Miss America ready either.

"Do you see how it's cleared up?" he asks. "The sun is out. You don't have any Visine, do you? My eyes get super bloodshot when I don't get enough sleep."

She had packed all kinds of weird nonsense in her cosmetic bag. Which is now with her former friends. Or in the trash somewhere. She doesn't know. She doesn't care.

"What do you want to do today?"

"Nothing."

"Do you want to eat? Look—jam, croissants."

"No."

"You are so foxy cute. Come on, you need some sustenance. Those breasts of yours aren't going to grow themselves."

"No."

"Chloe!"

"Johnny."

Low low he sings. In between love, he sings to her. Like it is love itself.

"It is actual love," he says when she remarks upon this. "I've been trying to seduce you with song since the first moment I opened my mouth."

That can't be. First time he opened his mouth was on the smelly train.

He says nothing.

"You didn't sing."

"I thought you'd call for the conductor, have me thrown out. I wooed you in other ways."

"Wooed me? Hardly."

"Are you here with me now, or aren't you?"

She laughs at him as if he's the main act at the Comedy Store. "You think I'm here because of the things you said to me on the Liepaja train?"

"Did you abandon your life and come with me to Miramare, a thousand miles away from dumb Barcelona, or didn't you?"

They nestle, marry, join, conjoin, smelt and melt, solids, liquids, air, all material things, all ephemeral things, the spirit and the flesh in the hillside hotel with the castle outside their open door, the rippling sea, the marble clouds, and inside, their enraptured entwined bodies.

If I didn't sing, he asks, would you still love me?

She is half-conscious, her heart fractured, her mouth parched; she doesn't answer, not because she doesn't know, but because she can't speak.

I think you would, he says. Do you know how I know? His fingers trace the outline of her breasts, circle her raw nipples, caress her neck, her hips, her lips.

She doesn't answer. She is on the fainting bed.

"Because you don't sing," he whispers. "And yet I love you."

Spooned together in one of the twin beds, they gaze at the castle on the rocky highlands. "You think," he says, "that the archduke built Miramare on a peninsula thrust into the sea, so that his bride could have an incomparable view of Trieste and Croatia on one side and Grado and Venice on the other. But what you don't know from where we lie, is that you can stand on a hill anywhere on the lower Adriatic and see our miraculous castello in the hazy distance. Anywhere. The view is of the castle, not the other way around." He lowers his voice to a husk. "The view is of us."

He promised her he would show her the famed castle grounds, that they would walk amid the rows of juniper and spruce. Reluctantly she dons her Polish coral love dress, finally less absurd, and they head out past the lemon trees to the temperamental sea, blue one minute like a robin's egg, malachite green the next.

There is a café in the lush but unkempt garden. It serves speck-filled baguettes, pasta with sauce, and giant cannoli. It has tables by the seaside under the overgrown trellis gazebo. The thousands of cats living in the garden are underfoot begging for food. Chloe and Johnny eat quickly. They want to go swim. And other things. But she has to admit, it's nice to sit out here with him, al fresco, just the two of them, holding hands, making small talk, giggling in post-coital embarrassment (her not him).

"Tell me," Johnny says, "is Mason the first boy you've been with?"

"Yes, of course," she says, and hesitates, which he catches because he catches everything. She doesn't want to tell him the truth, how naïve she is, how unsullied. It wasn't for lack of trying. She was afraid of getting caught in the back seat of Mason's mother's car like they were that one time behind Subway when they almost went all the way but not quite, and there was never a bed, because Burt was never out of the house, and neither was Lang. She wants Johnny to think she is not a child. That she's done things, knows things.

"First boy for everything?"

"Not the first boy I've kissed," she says, a little bristly even though she's eating the cannoli cream he's feeding her with his fingers.

"Oh?"

"Yeah. There've been others. I'm not a neophyte."

Leaning forward he licks a bit of cream from the corner of her mouth. "You think I want you to have more experience?"

That is a stumbling block. She certainly thinks so, but from his expression she guesses the answer is no.

"Who else was there?"

"Nobody." She starts to clean up their mess, feeding scraps to the begging cats. She wants to go. She tries to change the subject, but Johnny won't let her.

"Why so secretive, princess? Divulge away." They pull in their metal chairs. "What does it matter to me who it was? I don't know anybody from your high school. Do I?" Why is he smiling like that?

She divulges nothing as she throws their garbage into the trash. She doesn't even breathe, in case her breathing gives her away. He relents, has mercy on her. Pursues her in other ways, lets this one drop. "Do you want to go swimming?"

"God, yes."

They giggle about waiting an hour after eating, an old wives' tale. When she asks where the beach is, he laughs. "Right here." He points to the pedestrian path off the highway, and she repeats her question, and he points again. "We plunge into the sea straight from the road. That's the Italian way."

And they do, in a secluded spot under a ginkgo biloba and a palm tree, because Chloe has brought no bathing suit. He swims in his boxer briefs and she dives into the mild Adriatic in her red bra and blue polka dot underwear, almost like a bikini, and the way Johnny gazes at her in the water, and grabs her, and kisses her, she might as well be not wearing anything.

Later, when he is briefly unconscious during a break between very late and very early, Chloe flies back down the years, to one June night with music and "She Will Be Loved" and dashboard lights and picnic tables hidden under awnings, and all the other kids doing something else, laughing somewhere else, and only Chloe and Blake by the barbecue grill near Hastings. He had been in charge of the grill, so they had gone together to clean it and close it up for the night and when they were done, they plopped down on the picnic bench and shared a beer in secret. They giggled, chewing mint gum to hide the smell of alcohol; they had to share the gum too, because Chloe only had one stick.

Earlier the kids had bellowed songs that didn't sound like music, screaming, mangling the words. Chloe pretended she knew the words to "Billy, Don't be a Hero," and Hannah and Blake sang "Total Eclipse of the Heart," and Mason sang "Two Out of Three Ain't Bad," prophetic in retrospect, since there ain't no way he was ever gonna love her. It was nothing but screeching fun of fifteen-year-olds with little adult supervision, and a cooler full of beer that someone smuggled in and covered with Cokes, and they all drank and then sang even louder, and Blake was the one who had sung "She Will Be Loved."

Chloe almost forgot that part, Blake singing it, wanting to make her feel beautiful. She has tried hard to forget. It is not even a memory anymore, but part of her identity: the smell of oak and cut grass, warm beer, mosquitoes feasting on her bare legs, and Blake on top of the picnic table as the chorus went around and around and around in the core of her soul. Back then, she didn't belong to someone else yet.

"She Will Be Loved."

"She Will Be Loved."

And later, after singing and cleaning the grill and polishing off a can of Bud, they were sitting at the table arguing like always, debating the construction of verbals or the best way to catch a bass, or the perfection of roses. There was no one nearby, it was dark. The multi-colored string lights draped over the tent sparkled like dim stars. They were straddling the bench in the furthest edge of the common, snug between the Hastings wall, the corner of the lit-up tent and the narrow passageway that led to the rear gate. Chloe might have said something like you and Hannah looked so cute together singing "Total Eclipse of the Heart" ... when Blake said turn around, bright eyes, leaned forward, head bent, and kissed her lingeringly on the mouth. He hardly even had to lean forward. She blamed it on sitting too close and that wicked half-can of beer. They had been nearly chest to chest, face to face, forearms touching on the table, casual, intimate, laughing, arguing and close, and the kiss was drunken and long and open. His hands went in her hair. Her body went weak.

Someone dropped a tray of cups a few feet away, there was a drum roll, a loud saxophone, a mob of cackling taunting teenagers. He pulled away. There was barely a blink exchanged between them after the open lips and tilted faces.

One long slow blink, maybe. But that was all.

He got up to go help, and she tottered over to the clearing to find the others, Hannah, and Taylor and Mackenzie and Mason, and Madison and Megan. Hannah said what were you doing over there alone with Blake, and Chloe said I don't know what you mean. They started playing capture the flag, as if it hadn't already been captured.

As it turned out, no it had not, because a few minutes later Hannah dragged Blake away with her under the trees, and Chloe was left alone. That's when Mason took her hand. That summer, the four of them fell into another rhythm, one where the tall slender blonde beauty made time with the brawny, scruffy, completely dear giant, and the mousy girl with the bangs, the breasts and the silent passions ended up with the unexpected prize of the jock, the all-star and the tri-county batting champion.

Chloe and Blake never spoke of that night, and he never looked at her like that again, or sat close to her, or paused between sentences, or tilted his head, or anything. She was his brother's girl, and that was that. Talk about a heavy castle door falling shut in the distance across the moat.

After many months the image faded: stumbling around the commons by herself after Hannah had pulled Blake away to the distant birches, Chloe's mouth swollen from the bruising of his open crazy kiss. Stumbling around until Mason took her hand.

Why didn't she want to confess any of this to Johnny in the violet silence?

Maybe because she didn't want him to say, the wrong guy took your hand. Because it wasn't true. It had been just an impulse, a kid thing, not real. Mason was real. Hannah was real.

When he is up, Johnny never stops talking, joking, humming, strumming, moon gazing, navel too, philosophizing, proselytizing, copying, originating, prophesying. He keeps calling himself her eternal footman. He keeps saying their carnal love has been attained.

There are caresses, kisses, embraces. There is whistling, madness in the bed, there is anguish and weeping into sleeves and bare arms and handkerchiefs. Awake, he is the strongest most full-bodied, scarlet wine, all day and night, all the transitory minutes, a parade of rhythmic rhyming battalions, a million men in one boy body with incense and flame at the altar of her, as if Chloe is the one who makes Johnny holy.

Suddenly without any falling, there is a leap into sleep, one minute reciting the classics, singing Byron and Pope, the next on his back in the lilac petals of lullabies, gentle, peaceful, not a collapse, just off. OFF.

Like a switch of life.

One moment a spectacle, an orgy, the next pale silence. Barely even breathing.

He is tough to awaken.

Up all the livelong hours of the insane night, then lifeless. Mute lips, dull eyes, candle wax drying and cold.

When he wakes, his hands tremble. Pale of face he rises and vanishes, down the corridor, behind another door away from her, outside, he says, to smoke. Animation increases by degrees upon his return.

I don't do well when I first wake up, he tells her when she asks, and she does ask.

She can't sleep. If someone threw her off a cliff into the sea it would feel less like fear. She hasn't been able to close her eyes to oblivion since the rain the night before. She stares either into his peaceful face or the highway outside. The bleached Miramare is so close, she can pitch a paper airplane into one of its open windows. The bed creaks. Probably everyone at the small inn has heard their unrestrained coupling. She doesn't care. That's what she's become. From three shirts to hide the curves of her flesh to the Twickenham nude at the football stadium, running and shouting his name naked from the field. Johnny, Johnny …

JOHNNY!

He bolts upright in the red bed.

"Oh, thank God, you're awake." She jostles him. "Come on, what's your actual name?"

He falls back. "Johnny."

"I'm serious."

"Me too."

Then why didn't you turn around in Trieste when I called
your name, she wants to ask, but doesn't want to draw attention
to the washed-out Johnny that wasn't him.

"Come on. What are you hiding?"

"Nothing." A teasing smile plays on his face. "Maybe I'm a
descendant of the Founding Fathers. Or of the Pilgrims."

"Are you?"

"Maybe."

"Be serious. Why can't you tell me your name?"

"Tell me yours."

"Chloe Divine."

"Divine indeed," he murmurs, his hands gliding up her
thighs. A panting swallow. "Well, I'm like a rainbow."

"Let me see proof. I can show you proof. Let's see yours."

"Chloe," he says solemnly, "sometimes you have to have faith
even if you don't have proof. Especially if you don't."

"I want to make sure my faith is not misplaced, that's all,"
she says. "I just want to know who you are."

He shows her his ID. On this ID card, issued by—he flashes
it too fast, she doesn't catch it—is his name. Johnny Rainbow.
It's probably fake. She's heard of that. People getting fake IDs
to get liquor. Hard to acquire in little Fryeburg, but some kids
in North Conway had gone to Boston once and returned with
laminated plastic. On Saturday nights they would show it off to
all the squares.

"You're telling me your name is Johnny Rainbow?"

"For realsies."

"So if I marry you, I'll be Chloe Rainbow?"

He laughs with joy, pounding his Lone Star tattoo, pulling
her down on himself embracing her. "Chloe Divine Rainbow.
The greatest name in all the world! I want to marry you just so
you can carry that name for a long time."

"*That's* why you want to marry me."

Tickling her, he rolls her over on her stomach and caresses
her spine. He kisses her shoulder blades, the nape of her neck,

the nape of her everything. I want life and bliss, he murmurs, your dizzying breasts reanimating my loins and lungs.

In between pleading and singing they are vised together as Chloe has never imagined a vise: she is the plaything between an acetylene torch and a jackhammer. Gentler, gentler, she begs him. To him who loves me and washes me from my sin, gentler, gentler.

Gentler what? Gentler hands, softer mouth, less ...

Gentler mouth, like you're kissing me to the beat of your excited heart, one and two, and one and two, and one and two, gentle, rhythmic, soft, yes, like that, now a little faster, a little faster, Johnny, be less gentle, be more, more, more ...

More of everything. Who ever touched her like that? Who ever will again? More of him who is the Alpha and the Omega, the beginning and the end. The mystery of all the stars is in your golden mouth, Johnny. You hold the sun in your voice, a drumbeat of life in the gifts placed upon your lips. I want to recite you with my blood. I want to engrave you on my body.

I want to kneel before you.

I kneel before you.

Wide-eyed he gazes at her afterward, kisses her under the endless thunder of the ice floes breaking up in the turbulent spring rivers. Every minute awake is poured out like this, drenched in lava, overflowed in seas.

Through the convulsions, the spasms of the dying night, he sings by the open windows, plays his guitar naked in their uncovered bed. Someone below yells encore, encore. He has enraptured the crowds. Chloe is almost sure it's not she who moans encore, encore. He has been singing, kneeling behind her on the floor, his drumming hands keeping immobile her arching hips. She stifles her desperate moans, he holds back nothing, and obligingly there is an encore, a rout, panting lovers, fools, kings, nectar and poison all at once. How could anything else ever be like this, feel like this, and all the while, he sings into her quivering shoulder blades and into the night air, he sings save me from the dark before I utterly perish.

Save me from the dark before I come undone.

Very soon dawn. Very soon gone. They make stupid promises all the young make. Of course we'll write. Of course we'll call. Keeping in touch is easier than ever. This isn't *Little House on the Prairie*. We don't need the Rural Free Delivery Route of 1903. And I'm not overseas forever. I'll be back. My first tour is only twelve months. Then I'm back. Yes, I'll train with the Rangers, but we'll write letters. I'll get furlough next summer. We'll meet up. I promise. I'll meet you in San Diego. Give me your address there. Give me your address in Maine too. Don't worry. I won't lose it. I never lose anything, or forget anything. I promise I'll get in touch. One day, Chloe Divine, you will see me walking down your country road, returning for you. I promise. On and on and on and on and on.

He kisses the bliss and sorrow from her eyes.

Don't cry, beautiful girl. Love does break your heart, don't it? Do you want me to tell you whose heart you've broken?

No, she says. Do you know why I cry? Because even as I live it with you so happy, I fear it will never come again.

To be fair, he says, right now you don't seem that happy.

Covering them both with one damp sheet, he pulls her out onto the balcony and shows her the Adriatic, still and crystal, the distant shores of Croatia, the blue sunrise mist over Trieste, the white limestone walls of the medieval castle for princes and princesses.

We are at Lover's Fortress. Nothing can touch us here, nothing can hurt us.

Tell me about the duke and duchess, about Max and Charlotte, she says. Please tell me they lived happily ever after.

He hesitates as they stare out onto the leafy firs partially obstructing the view of Miramare.

Oh no. What happened to them?

Maximillian was tried for treason and shot, and Charlotte of Belgium went mad and was committed to a sanatorium where she eventually died.

Chloe never wants less for the sun to rise.

Don't weep, Johnny says. Life is beautiful.

34

My Rags of Heart

"Onward, my bride," he says in the early morning. "I have only one mother, and I have to see her today before I fly."

"Do you have to?"

"To see my mother?"

"To fly."

He smiles. She doesn't.

"You don't have to come with me," Johnny says. "You haven't slept. I can go by myself. Stay here. I'll be back late tonight." He takes his duffel and his guitar. In other words, everything but her.

"Yeah, famous last words," she says, springing out of bed. "Of course I'm going with you. Into the mountains, right? To get lost in the Alps, where no one will ever find us?"

He smiles again, as if she is ever so funny!

Castello di Miramare not only has a boat dock and a bus stop but also a rail station. It has everything. They catch a train to Gemona, and from there a train to Tarcento. The trains are pristine, quiet, and a little Italian lady wheels a shiny cart around, selling espresso and Napoleons. They load up on both plus a bagful of biscotti. "Shouldn't we bring something for your mom?" Chloe asks. "Not good to arrive empty-handed."

"The only thing she craves we can't bring her," says Johnny. "But if we have any left, we'll give her some of our biscotti."

"When was the last time you saw her?"

"Over a year ago," he replies. He is next to the window. He asked and she let him. She'd let him take her in an open car if that's what he wanted. She huddles next to his arm.

"Why so long?"

"I couldn't come."

She remembers Johnny owing Emil money for twelve months and not being able to pay. "Why not?"

"I was busy."

"Too busy to see your mother? No wonder she's mad."

"She's not mad. Well, she might be a little mad I'm only staying for one day." Changing the subject, he says he wishes they had time to go to Cividale. It has a pastry shop from heaven, he says, and has the best speck.

Chloe wants to say she wishes they had time for a lot more than a speck of ham.

"Am I going to meet your mom?"

"I don't know. We'll play it by ear. Sometimes she's okay. Other times … we'll see."

"Tell me something about her so I don't embarrass myself with stupid questions," says Chloe. "Is she nice?"

"Is my mother nice?"

"I mean …" Chloe means to say is she nice to strange girls? Strange girls with bare legs and without a stitch of makeup, wearing green sweaters over improper coral dresses, girls you drag in behind you, hiding them, letting a mother know after one glance why you are so late and why you can stay so briefly.

"Yes, she's nice."

"How long has she been in Tarcento?"

"Two years. She might be leaving soon, my father said."

"Really? She's all better?"

"He didn't say."

"So why would she be leaving?"

"He didn't say."

Chloe clears her throat. "So what's the matter with her?" She takes his cool hand. "Why is she in Tarcento?"

"She's convalescing."

"From what?"

He continues to stare out the window. So does she, over his shoulder. He is right to stare. Northeastern Italy is lousy with sweeping vistas of endless mountains and flowing rivers carving out a myriad gorges. The architect said *one* valley, *one* snow-capped peak, one rocky glen, one chalet, and the builder replied, not enough. I will give you thousands. And it still won't be enough.

"The problem with my mother," Johnny says, "is she never quite figured out what kind of woman she wanted to be. So now she's spent the last ten years of her life trying to recover from the ill effects of her ignorance."

"What do you mean what she wanted to be? Like a career woman or a wife?" And why would she be convalescing from that?

"Yes, but what kind of career woman, what kind of wife."

"Wasn't she a singer?"

"Yes. She did once want to be a star."

Well, so what. Chloe's mother once wanted to be a dancer. But she wasn't living by herself in an Italian hamlet.

"My dad was quite a catch. But she thought *she* was the catch, you see. She was much younger than he was and misunderstood some basic things. So they fell in love. You know the way people sometimes do."

Chloe's heart shrinks into a tight fist, but Johnny isn't looking at her.

"Falling in love is the easy part," he says. "You give yourself to me on Italian shores. You give me your naked body, and I'm young and you're young. It's not even a riddle. The answer is yes a thousand times scrawled across all the stars in the heavens. It was for my dad, too."

Chloe swallows. "What did you mean when you said to Hannah that your dad was made wretched in a brothel? You weren't, um, talking about your mother, were you?"

Johnny laughs. "Some son I'd be if I were. No. That was before my mother. That's not what I'm talking about. That one is definitely a story for another time."

She waits to hear anything he deigns to bring forth from his mouth.

"The question is, do you have staying power past the rapture?" Johnny asks. "Do you give renewable pleasure? Do you suffer, believe, endure? Do you fail? Are you the real thing or a temporary flicker? So here's the problem. My mother was the temporary flicker. But the really unfortunate part is that both she and my dad mistook it for an eternal flame. They should've never gotten married, because one must know the difference, and they did not. My mother just didn't have the goods. Not like your mother."

"What?" Chloe hoots. "My mother doesn't have … *goods*."

"Your green cabin on the lake is the real thing."

"How—how do you know?" How would he know!

"Because I know when it's missing. It's been missing my whole life. My mother wanted from my dad what he couldn't give her. But she couldn't be what he needed either. For a long time I believed it was because he was a terrible husband, and I loved my mother, and still do, and so I blamed him and modeled my whole life on wanting to be only one thing—not him. But after he and my mom split up and he remarried, I saw the way he was with his new wife. She dotes on him and he responds with love and kindness. Kind is not a word I'd have ever used to describe my old man. But the way he walks through the door and laughs at Kerri's stupid jokes and watches her play guitar. He never looked at my mother like that when she sang."

"Even though she was beautiful?"

"Even though she was beautiful."

"Your mother wasn't devoted to your father?"

"My mother," says Johnny, "was a beauty queen." As if that answers Chloe's question. "She wanted my father to be devoted to her."

"Who wouldn't want that," Chloe mutters.

"Exactly. Mother was like, take me out dancing, to parties, to your social functions. Let me get dressed up. Let me see you adore me in public while I make you proud by being a bauble on your arm. And my dad was like, yeah, okay, hotcakes, but I'm starved, and the kids are failing math. While you and I are tripping the light fantastic, who's gluing the Egyptian pyramid for Johnny's school project?"

"He's sort of right about that," Chloe says. In her house, her mother takes care of all she can take care of, and her dad takes care of the rest.

"But my mom didn't care about chicken cutlets or pyramids," Johnny says. "Plus she hated to cook, hated math, hated school projects. She liked to sing. And she liked to look pretty. And then she started liking other things. With gin in them. And my dad was away a lot, working. So sometimes he acted as if she wasn't the runner-up in a beauty pageant. He wanted his kids to be fed and the beds to be made. And my mother was like, I'm a beauty queen! And he was like, I don't give a fuck, feed my kids! And she was like, if you care so much, then be home more, and he was like, I'd be home more if you made it more of a home. That's the part my mother didn't get most of all—that she was stunning and yet he wasn't home. If he wasn't home for her, then who would he ever be home for? Well, we found out. His new wife who bakes him pies."

"I assume, um, not a beauty queen?" says Chloe.

"Blonde and petite and quite fetching. That's what I mean about deciding what kind of a person you want to be. Because on that decision rest all your life's expectations. And if they're not met, then whoa. And woe."

Rocky glens and mountains into the horizons fly by their windows. "I just want to be loved and cherished," says Chloe. "That's what I want."

Turning away from the canyons and the roaring waters, he kisses her. "You are adorable. You say it as if you've just discovered the Dead Sea Scrolls." He smiles. "That's what everybody wants. Welcome to the human race, Princess of the Orient. Your fellowship is seven billion souls."

She can tell he wants to say more, but doesn't. Not just then. They pass through old hamlets and villages, streams below, snowy mountains above. Italy is taking her breath away. Italy, right?

"Why is it so hard?" she finally asks. "To be loved? Seems such a simple matter."

"What are you, a statue?" asks Johnny. "A movie? A flavor of ice cream? Make yourself into chocolate; who won't love you then?" He lifts his arms, crooking them above his head, glancing at her with bemusement, as if he can't believe she doesn't know the answer to this simplest of all trivia questions.

"Are you laughing at me?"

"No." He cups her face. "You're just naïve, china doll. You may have school smarts, but you've got another decade of living before you be all growed up."

"All right, old man, you haven't had another decade of living either. You're like two minutes older."

"But I know this. Before you can be loved, you have to make yourself into a civilized being, not a wild brute, a human being capable of loving another, of giving another person something they need. I said the same thing to my mother, but she didn't ever want to hear it. Let your father give me things, and then we shall see, she said."

"Is that the trick we must learn," mutters Chloe, eyes past his black stubble to the fields beyond.

"Yes, to love another is the trick we must learn," he says, leaning sideways and kissing her green shoulder. "What a magic trick it is."

Tarcento is a stony Italian town on the fast-flowing, transparent green meandering Torre River, a narrow tributary of the pre-

Alpian Isonzo. The elms and the firs cover it like a canopy, the range of ancient mountains surround the town on all four sides like a forest or a fortress. The river is full of large rocks and whirling basins. Chloe thinks it might be very good for fishing. They cross the stone bridge and then walk for miles on the road hugging the river. They walk hand in hand because they are lovers. Chloe's body aches in all the places he has recently been and now is not. Squeezing his long thin hand, she prays as she walks that this will not be a permanent state of her being, throbbing on empty without him.

The turn-off they're looking for is a dirt road that leads to the Tarcento Pensione nested on the banks of the wild Torre. The grounds the house stands on are park-like. Immaculate like the Italian trains. The only clue to what kind of a place it is, is the carefully camouflaged fence, hidden by bushes and trees. Chloe doesn't want to make *any* comparisons, favorable or otherwise, to other camouflaged fences she has been told about recently by the surreal Adonis at her side. This fence has a gate and an intercom, and though the gate is locked, Chloe needs to assume that Johnny's mother is not a prisoner and can leave if she wants to, but chooses not to. The Italian voice on the intercom says gravely, "*Ciao, chi e questo?*"

Johnny replies in Italian. The only words Chloe understands are Ingrid Camala or something like that. Maybe Coomala. Kumala? The gate clicks, unlocks, and slowly swings open. They walk down the winding path to the pastel blue house, Chloe thinking all the while that no gates or fences can keep someone in when the choppy river is but an embankment away. For God's sake, hasn't anyone here read the biography of Virginia Woolf? Before they get to the house, Johnny stops walking, turns to Chloe, and runs his palm over her silky hair, perhaps meant as tenderness, or perhaps to smooth her out before the presentation. "Are you ready?" he says. He kisses her. He doesn't sound anxious, but who can tell? "It'll be fine. Remember, best to speak as little as possible. Our role here is not to talk. It's just to listen, if we can bear it."

Chloe doesn't know if she can bear it. Can *he* bear it? Depends on what your mother wants to say, she thinks, as they walk up the porch steps of the house.

The staff at the Tarcento Pensione all know Johnny. The nurses squeal as they rush to embrace him. They ask a flurry of questions in a gorgeous rolling Romance tongue about his well-being, or perhaps about how long it has been since he was here last, or perhaps about the splendid hardness of his naked body. Chloe doesn't know for certain they're actual nurses. They're dressed a little wantonly for Chloe's taste, in tight white dresses that some might call uniforms. These so-called nurses to the one, even the really old one, suddenly acquire shiny lips and flushed cheeks. Chloe stands back disapprovingly, watching them effuse all over her Johnny. He leans back into her with a toothy grin. "Did you hear, by the way, how they keep calling me Johnny?"

"Oh, I'm hearing many things," she says.

He agrees with a cheerful squeeze. "Italians are a very friendly people."

"Clearly. And they said Yanni, or Anni. Could be anyone."

Even one of the doctors on duty comes out to shake Johnny's hand. The doctor, because he's a male, nods to Chloe, but the female staff eye her as if she is a vagrant who's wandered in.

Finally Johnny is released from their clutches. "Wow," she says as they walk down the short corridor past the reception counter.

"Are you saying wow because you're impressed with the facilities?" he asks, swinging his arm around her.

"That too."

The house is a glorified bed and breakfast, spacious, cosy, homey, rustic, Italian, soft lighting, beautifully furnished, classical music playing. The only difference between an inn and this place is the doctors on standby waiting to dispense the meds and the pretend nurses doing whatever the heck it is they do.

"My mother is outside," he says. "She is taking her lunch in the garden. They asked me if we wanted some food. I'm kind of starved, are you? They said they had some speck from Cividale." He smiles. "At least we'll get some of my favorite thing in the world."

"Really, favorite," Chloe says in a grumble.

"Okay, like fourth or fifth favorite." He nuzzles her cheek as they descend the veranda steps in the back. The landscaped lawn leading to the river is enormous and wooded. Secluded foliaged spots are everywhere, with little tables under the gazebos set on the grass or on stone patios. There are comfortable reading chairs, a hammock, a bench swing. It is beautiful and comforting. Only one or two people are out in the garden, including a print-clad female shape in the far distance, facing the river, her back to the house.

"How can your mom afford to live in a place like this?" she asks him as they cross the wide lawn. "This is very lux."

"My grandparents help pay for it," Johnny says. At the edge of the grass he stops walking and takes her by the shoulders. After lightly kissing her lips, he shows her to an Adirondack chair nearby. "My mom is just over there." The motionless print-clad shape is now but a bush away. "Can you sit here for a few minutes while I go talk to her?" he says quietly. "I don't want her to think I came late and not alone. Do you mind?"

She nods as she half-frowns. "But you did come late and, um, not alone."

"Well, I know. I just need a few minutes with her. To make sure she's okay. Then I'll introduce you."

"Of course," she says, perching down in the wooden chair. "I'll be right here." *Right here, where I can hear everything.* She leans back. The place is so tranquil, the sound of the river like white noise, set on extra loud, and she hasn't had any sleep in two nights. She might pass out in the stillness. She doesn't want to miss a word, but she fears that any moment life is going to stop making sense. She pinches her arms to stay awake.

Chloe can't see Johnny's mother well from where she is sitting. Ingrid's back is to her and she is partly obscured by a blooming rhododendron. She looks full-bodied. She gets up when Johnny approaches, exclaims, "My son!" and maternally embraces him. She is quite heavy, and she wears a loose long geometric-print kaftan that makes her look twice as large. "You're finally here," she says. "Sit down, sit down, no, wait, let me look at you. I haven't seen you in so long." The mother examines the son, palpates his unshaven face, caresses his head, tugs disapprovingly on his ponytail, judges his black jacket. "I don't know *what* your father is going on about. My God, did he go on for days about how terrible you looked in Trieste. You don't look so bad." She pats his cheek, a little roughly, almost like a half-slap. "I've seen you look a lot worse than this."

"Thanks, Mom."

They sit, she back in her chaise longue, he in an upright straight-back lawn chair. He places the guitar on one side of him, the duffel on the other. She takes hold of his hand, kisses it, won't let go of it. "I'm so happy to see you," she says. "How've you been?"

"Good, Mom. You?"

"You talk to your sisters? Your brother?"

"I haven't had the chance. Thought I'd do it when I'm back Stateside. Dad said everybody is good."

She waves her hand. "Your sister is annoying me."

"Which one?"

"Take your pick. One wants to go to graduate school for, get this, business! Like she's not even my daughter. And the other one wants to get married immediately. God. Both of them are just going to wreck their lives."

"They'll be fine. Dad said Tomboy is good."

"How good can he possibly be? He's staying with your grandparents for the summer. Your grandmother will ruin him.

She could never say no to you, and look at you now in your alligator boots. Now she's hooked her claws into my baby boy. He'll be a disaster by the time I come back."

"When are you coming back? Dad said maybe soon?"

"Your father doesn't know anything. I'm not well. I can't just up and go. We'll see. I'm still recuperating."

Johnny chews his lip. "I brought you some biscotti," he says, handing her a white paper bag.

She takes it indifferently. "That's not what I want. What about … are you having lunch with me? Because you know what Churchill says. There's no celebration without wine."

Johnny rubs his bristly face. "First of all, that's not how the quote goes. It's: there's no celebration without *food*. And Churchill didn't say it. Either one."

"Oh, Churchill would say it about the wine, if I know my political leaders."

Johnny stays quiet.

"Well? Did you bring it, or didn't you?"

"Bring what?"

She points to the duffel. "That little flask you carry with you everywhere you go. That's gotta have something good in it."

Intensely he presses his hands together. "Mom, no. They'll throw me out."

"They don't have to see." She reaches for his bag between their chairs. With a deft foot he pushes it behind him.

"Can we not start immediately?" he says. "Can we not begin like this?"

She backs off, stares at him coldly. "What's gotten into you?"

"Nothing."

"So why didn't you come with your father like you were supposed to?"

"I was busy."

"Exactly. Don't make excuses."

"No excuses. I was busy."

"Did you catch a ride?" Ingrid asks knowingly, as if the expression doesn't mean what Chloe thinks it means but something else more sinister. "You don't have to make excuses with *me*, of all people," she continues. "*I* know what's going on. I've made them all myself—better than you."

"Well, you *have* had more practice."

Chloe sucks in her breath. Yeesh! Didn't he tell her their job was not to speak but to listen? He blew that one in five seconds. It hurts her to hear him get so instantly hostile with his mother. It's too familiar. What is it about parents and children, Chloe thinks.

Ingrid also sucks in her breath.

"I'm sorry, Mom," says Johnny. "I'm here for such a short time. I want to have a nice visit. I don't want to fight again. Please."

"Who's fighting? I made a polite request …"

"And I said no. Just because you ask politely doesn't mean the answer will be yes. That's what you and Dad taught me, isn't it?"

She harrumphs. "You can't ask your father anything, polite or not. You know that better than anyone."

"Yes. How was his visit?"

"Excellent. Better than this. He stayed for two days. We had a wonderful time. Just like the old days, first he was his charming old self and then poof, he vanished." Ingrid's voice is not operatic but throaty and ragged, as if scorched by too many cigarettes or too much screaming, or by other things, perhaps, in hidden flasks.

"Why do you sound so hoarse, Mom?"

"I had some large polyps removed," she replies. "I'm fine, nothing to even talk about. Enough about me. How have *you* been is the question."

"I told you, good."

"When did you get out?"

"Uh, about a week ago, I guess."

Ingrid lowers her voice. Fully awake, Chloe strains to hear. And she thought she could have a nap! "How did they treat you in Kurosta?" she asks. "I can't tell you how upset I was—"

"It's all fine," Johnny cuts her off. "Look at me. Not a hair harmed on my head. In fact, they let me keep my hair. And Dad's guitar, and I had all the books I wanted. How bad could it be? I read a lot. The time flew by."

"Yeah, sure," she says. "I want you to know, I was *very* upset with your father. I couldn't believe he let you rot there for a whole fucking year."

"What are you talking about? He didn't *let* me. It's only because of him that I'm out. I would've gotten five to ten mandatory if it wasn't for his connections. And five years not in a halfway house, a juvy derelict place, but up a very real river."

"You mean like this?" She waves her dismissive arm to the splendor around her.

He takes a breath. "You can leave any time you want. You don't want to."

"I came to Italy only to keep an eye on you," she says. "I didn't do very well, did I?"

"We all could use someone to watch over us, don't you think?"

Ingrid sighs deeply. She has not let go of Johnny's hand the entire time they've been speaking. "Are you still singing?"

"Yeah, why not."

"Your father says you sound pretty good."

"How would he know?"

"He heard you in Trieste. You didn't want to come with him to see me, but you were working the street. He said you were good."

Johnny shrugs.

"He is very worried about you," Ingrid says. "Because, son, you don't know this, and we don't want to, but I'm going to tell you something about dead children."

"I don't want to know."

Chloe sits up. Or sinks down.

"You're never okay after. You never get over it."

Chloe stays sunk. Diminished, you learn to live with it, Chloe wants to say.

"I'm fine, Mom," Johnny says. "There's nothing to worry about anymore."

"So I asked your father," Ingrid continued, "if he was trying to save you any which way he could, then why in hell was he sending you to Afghanistan?"

"Boy, sounds like you two had quite a time together."

"Oh, we did. We brawled like we did back in Washington. Remember?"

"How could I forget?"

"Exactly. I told him he was making a huge mistake forcing you into the army. I told him you'd sort yourself out in other ways. And do you know what he said?"

"I can't imagine."

"He said, what, like you sorted *your*self out?" Ingrid sneers. "Didn't take him long to get back to his old insults. But I told him the army is not the place for you. You aren't cut out for it the way he was. You're too gentle a boy. You're too sensitive, feel things too much. You know, son, in *my* family we weren't fighters. Not my brothers or my uncles. That's your father's side, the damn pugilists. But you're still half-mine, aren't you?"

"Yes, Mom."

Letting go of him, she wrings her hands, slightly histrionically. It passes, fades, but Chloe is jarred by it. It seems so desperate. "Why," says Ingrid, "why did you have to inherit the very worst from your father, and all the worst from me?"

"I didn't inherit the worst from you, Mom," says Johnny, hanging his head.

"No?"

"No."

Mother and son don't look at each other. They both stare down into the grass. Ingrid leans into Johnny. Their heads touch. "My life is an unimaginable nightmare," she breathes out wrenchingly. "If you only knew."

"I know."

She separates from him, eventually brightens.

"Are they bringing you lunch? Ring the bell. They're so slow. I don't know what the hell they're doing. Not making you lunch, that's for fucking sure. Ring the bell!"

She grabs a small silver bell beside her chair and rings it like a fire alarm, non-stop. Johnny holds his hand over it to stop it from trilling. "They said a few minutes."

"How long can you stay?"

Johnny hesitates to answer. "Didn't Dad tell you?"

"Tell me what?"

"I have to be on the plane back to Washington at eight tomorrow morning. I report for training at 6 p.m. the day after."

Ingrid emits a throaty groan of disappointment and pain. She falls silent. For a long time they don't speak. Without something to concentrate on, Chloe starts to fade away in the rustling of leaves, in the roll of the river.

Then Ingrid speaks. "You've always been this way," she says. Her voice is cold. "Pushing every single thing in your life until the last possible second, and then another minute past that. After not visiting me for over a year, you're only staying for one day?"

"Well, I could hardly visit when I was … why didn't you come visit me? Exactly. You couldn't. Do I blame you?"

"Absolutely. Like it's my fault."

"Isn't it?" Johnny sighs. "Look, we have all afternoon, all evening. We'll have lunch, we'll take a walk. Do you still like the river? We'll go down there."

And here is Chloe shaking her sleepy head. Don't go down to the river, don't. With half-closed eyes she spots a woman walking from the veranda carrying a large tray with a silver pot, silver plates, tall glasses, a lonely rose in a vase. When the woman passes her chair, Chloe smells smoked ham and crusty warm bread and olive oil and coffee. The smells are good, the food is good. But Chloe can't help it anymore, she can't help anything. She falls into a black well.

She hears them whispering over her before she opens her eyes.

"Why did you bring her here? Who is she?"

"I told you—Chloe."

"So what's wrong with her that she is passed out in the middle of the afternoon? Even your sick mother is awake."

"She's not passed out, Mom. She's asleep."

"Why is she asleep?"

"I don't know. She got tired?"

"Why?"

"I don't know. Why don't you ask her?"

"I would but she's asleep."

"Chloe," Johnny calls softly. "Chloe." There's love in his voice.

She opens her eyes and looks up. Both mother and son are looming over her. There is love in his eyes. The mother studies her with unfriendly intent. Remembering her manners, Chloe struggles up from the low-to-the-ground Adirondack. Johnny gives her his hand to help. The mother notes the gesture, watches it grimly. How long was Chloe out? Hours? All the food is gone and the shadows are longer.

"Chloe, this is my mother. Mom, this is Chloe."

Chloe remembers that the young must never extend their hand to the adults first, so she doesn't. But Ingrid says, "What, she's too good to shake my hand?"

"*She* is right here," says Johnny.

Chloe sticks out her hand. "Hello, Mrs. …"

She waits. With paused breath, she waits.

"Call me Ingrid," Ingrid says. "No formalities here. Just Ingrid. And anyway, didn't he tell you? I'm not a Mrs. anymore. His father made sure of that. Sent me away and got himself another Mrs. in a hurry."

Ingrid is bloated of face and body. She may have been attractive once. Her bone structure still retains the prominent thing all beautiful faces retain forever—as if they had once been sculpted. She has thick straight black hair, shiny and short. She wears no makeup. Her olive skin is sallow and stretched out with lines before their time and her full lips are dry and blue. She may be forty-five, but she looks sixty-five. Her almond eyes are dull and black with agonies Chloe doesn't understand. She is tall for a woman. Both mother and son dwarf Chloe, who wishes they'd all sit down so she wouldn't feel so self-conscious and undersized, and, as if reading her mind, Johnny directs them to Ingrid's chaise, pulls up another straight-back chair next to his own, and they sit in a little triangular circle under the elms.

Ingrid stares at Chloe interminably. She stares at her the way Chloe imagines Lang must stare at some of her friends who stop by the house after having made poor clothing choices. She feels sorry for every girl that's ever entered her home. Ingrid scrutinizes the substantial swell of Chloe's breasts under the fitted green sweater, as if she can see the imprints of her son's paws on Chloe's fragile white flesh. It's excruciating!

And then Ingrid speaks.

"I have a question for you," she says to Chloe. "Let's assume we are all lost in the woods. Each and every one of us. In your opinion, what do you think is better, to live in a wood out of which there is no exit and not care there is no exit, or to live in a wood in which you've lost your way, and to know you've lost your way, and to rush about looking for the road, for the way out, knowing it's out there, but being unable to find it, and becoming only more and more hopelessly confused and lost?"

Chloe is hopelessly confused herself, and scared. She can't remember the question. Johnny is no help. He's not saying a word, just looking down at his guitar, strumming it quietly. Chloe stammers. "I'd say better not to be in the woods at all."

"That isn't one of the options," says Ingrid. "The woods is what we all live in, like fish in the sea."

"Mom, all right, come on."

"Either way," Ingrid continues, "at the end of the woods is death. The reaper awaits us all. So my question remains. Since you know that death is ahead either way, is it better *not* to know you're lost or to keep trying to machete your way through the brambles?"

"I don't know," Chloe whispers, peering at Johnny for guidance which he's not providing. "Is this a trick question? Is there no right answer?"

"I just want to know what you think," Ingrid says. "What side of the equation you're on about the meaning of life."

When did Chloe acquire such a prominent stutter! "I want to say, um, that it's better to be on the … um, road."

"Are you on the road?"

Chloe nods. She doesn't know anything anymore.

Ingrid leans back in her chair, puts her feet up, folds her arms in satisfaction.

"Very good," she says. "Now, what about my son? Is he on the road?"

"Mom!"

"I'm making conversation, Junior. You brought her here. So let me talk to her. Let me see what this girl of yours is made of."

Did Ingrid say Junior? Or is Chloe so panicked she misheard?

"I don't know," Chloe says.

Ingrid gives Johnny a critical glare and Chloe a pitying one. "But if you had to guess."

She can't guess and doesn't want to!

"All right, I'll tell you," says Ingrid. "He is lost. But he's still trying to claw his way out. Two more questions. Say you're in the woods trying to claw your way out, but you're blind. Would that be terrifying?"

Barely, Chloe acknowledges that it would be. *This* is terrifying.

"So my last question is not: what *will* he do to rid himself of the terror," says Ingrid, "but what *won't* he?"

Chloe wants to cry. Shaking his head, Johnny remains steady.

Ingrid leans forward to Chloe. "There is *nothing* my son won't do," she says, "to rid himself of the terror."

"Honestly, Mom, you have to stop," Johnny says.

"Has he told you about the dragon pit and the honey?" she asks. "Has he told you the story of his father's parents?" Ingrid spits out the words *father's parents*. Also *story*.

Chloe nods. Or shudders.

"So what do you see happening here?" The large woman circles the air in a cynical sphere between Chloe and Johnny. "I want to say you must know it's just for fun, but since my son has *never* brought anyone to parade in front of me before, I have to assume at least one of you feels it's more than just fun. Possibly both of you by the dumbstruck looks on your faces."

Chloe heeds well Johnny's earlier admonition and says nothing.

"Are you in love? How darling. How retro of you." Her puffy face lifts to the sky. "Are you like me with his father? Thinking you can have what his grandparents had?"

"Mom, leave her alone. Come on, we came to visit you. Be nice."

"No one can have it." As if Johnny hasn't spoken.

"You're wrong, Mom. Everyone can have it!"

"Your father couldn't."

"Not with you."

They argue. Chloe can't even watch them, twitching on the outside, cringing inside. She wants to put her hands over her ears.

"We talked about this, Mom. A million times. Grandma and Grandpa gave each other an extravagant thing. A marriage."

"What does it even mean, marriage?" Ingrid scoffs. "It's a farce. To comfort each other to the end of your days. What shite!"

Johnny throws Chloe a tiny look, as if to say, do you see what I mean?

Ingrid catches the glance. "You think your father's found the holy grail with his new wife?" She shakes her head. "How long has it been, ten minutes? He'll be moving on at the one hour mark." She leans to Chloe as if the young woman has suddenly become her confidante. "Men don't understand this," she says, "but marriage is being there not just when they feel like it, but even when they don't feel like it. Especially when they don't feel like it. There is hardly more he can give away of himself. He has to give away everything. He takes on your burdens. He helps you carry the cross. He binds his life to yours."

"Yes," says Johnny. "But not just him. You too must do this."

"Pfft. Why would *anyone* do this? What the hell do you get in return?"

"Each other?" Chloe replies in a timid voice. "You don't have to face the world alone again." She inhales. For bravery. "Those woods you were talking about before; married you're not alone in them, even if you might be a little bit lost. You're lost together."

"Oh! But aren't you a dear sweet romantic!" Ingrid gazes at Chloe with nothing but bitter pity. "Johnny, wherever did you find such a simple thing?"

Chloe wants to disappear. She looks around, at the trees, at the river down the rocky shore. "It's beautiful here," she says quietly. "So peaceful." She doesn't look at mother and child.

"Yeah, yeah. It's all bullshit. Those damn show-offs lived out their love story, and now the rest of us have to suffer because of it, trying to duplicate the stupid fucking thing." She swears like a sailor. It must make her feel better. But Chloe is not used to it, her own mother and father always so proper around her, so … parental. "*My rags of heart can like, wish and adore,*" Ingrid whispers haltingly, her low voice breaking, "*but after one such love can love no more.*"

"Don't listen to my mother, Chloe." Johnny stands up, leaning unsteadily on the neck of his guitar. "*Everything* is a love story. You can make a love story out of anything. Where there is a story, there will be love."

"Not like theirs," says Ingrid.

"Better! Because it will be your own."

"Not like theirs."

"Mom, stop saying that!" In exasperation Johnny bangs his father's guitar on the grass. "It's not *true*," he says adamantly, almost hisses. "What they had, okay, they had, but that was a long time ago, and we all still have to live. We have to fight new wars, build our own homes, love new people. Make our own mistakes. Break hearts anew. As many stories as there are human beings, Mom." He stands up tall and forces himself to stay composed. "*I'm* not going to be weighted down by it," Johnny says. "No one is—except you. Tomboy doesn't care a lick about it. I swear, he looked shocked when he read what Beck wrote, that Grandpa had been to Poland. No one knows anything anymore. No one cares. Not about the war, or Coral Gables, or the wine country, or Majdanek, or anything."

"You care, son," Ingrid says.

"Yes, but I'm making my own drama!"

Now that she has Johnny thoroughly agitated, Ingrid is soothed. She turns her attention back to Chloe. "Aww, look at the way she's looking at you. As if she thinks *you're* the one." She makes a derisive sound. "Trust me, sweetheart, he is *not* the one."

"Mom!"

"Do you want me to tell you why?"

"Chloe, get up." Johnny throws his guitar into the black case, tries to zip it up. His hands are shaking. "We have to get going. Sorry, Mom. We can't stay. Have to be at Trieste airport at six in the morning. Come on, Chloe."

Chloe rises. "It was really nice to meet you, Ingrid."

Ingrid languishes in her chaise, zen-calm. "Do you see the temper?" she says to Chloe. "He pretends it's not there, but do you see? He's just like his father. That's why they're kindling and matches when they're together. The apple doesn't fall far from the tree. Don't waste your time, dear. He'll promise you all the heavenly glories. But he'll be catching a ride from someone other than you as soon as he says goodbye."

Johnny staggers back from his mother. No one knows what to do. Ingrid isn't put off, isn't ashamed. She sits serenely, almost gleefully, staring at Chloe.

"He's not opening every door for you and pushing your rolling pedestal in front of him. He's not the one. He's got another master, baby girl. And you know what they say about masters. You can serve only one."

"Mom!"

"And he serves the devil."

Johnny grabs Chloe's hand. Trembling, nearly convulsing, he bends to kiss his mother's cheek, misses and catches the air instead. Ingrid remains unfettered. She squeezes Johnny's arm.

"I should know, son, right?" she says. "I serve him too."

35

Jimmy Eat World Pain

JOHNNY WALKS SO QUICKLY, CHLOE CAN BARELY KEEP UP. SHE hurries after him, through the house, not stopping to wave goodbye to the clucking nurses. They're down the path, out the gate and a mile on the winding road before he speaks.

"I don't know what I was thinking," he says. "I thought she might be happy I found someone. I'm sorry about that."

"Don't worry about it," Chloe says. "She was disappointed you couldn't stay. She wasn't herself."

"Oh no." Johnny shakes his head. "She was herself. Never happy until everybody around her is wretched."

They wait for the train in silence. They are on the train in silence. He closes his eyes for the half-hour it takes them to get into Gemona. Resting her head against his arm, she looks out the window. She'll have plenty of time to sleep when he's gone from her life starting tomorrow. The long leg between Gemona and Ronchi is dark. They get food on the train, chit-chat about nonsense. They get off at Ronchi instead of Trieste because it's closer to the airport and find a brown bed and breakfast next to the station. Dog Inn or something. The barely one-star room is a closet with a twin bed and white wooden shutters. She is grateful for the private shower, but the showerhead points right at the toilet seat, and there is no curtain. Not ideal. Nothing is ideal. Not like it was. Before Tarcento.

Naked in bed they speak. Rather, he speaks and she listens. She finds herself losing her power of speech the closer it gets to the implacable time it all ends. The sorrow of it is tearing up her throat.

"Don't worry about the things my mother said. She goes off on these rants. That's why she's convalescing. That's why she's on meds."

"Did they forget to give her the meds today or something?" Chloe asks.

"Oh no, that was her medicated up to the eyeballs."

"Which things should I not be worried about?" Ingrid said so many things. None of which Chloe wants to remember. Was it when the mother told the young girl to look elsewhere for true love, as if the glimpse of what Johnny had offered Chloe wasn't paradise? Or was it when she said that both mother and son served a dark master stronger than love. And there was Chloe, thinking nothing was stronger than love.

"About me being away for a year," Johnny replies.

Ah. That's what he is worried about? What Chloe thinks about a place called Kurosta? Doesn't he know that Chloe is too swept up thinking about Miramare and tomorrow after 8:01?

"You know how parents tend to exaggerate," he says. "It was a small infraction. Last year I got caught with some stuff when I was in Latvia. I want to say it was a bum beef but … I was moving some product for Emil from Warsaw to Riga and wasn't careful enough. Mouthed off to a cop, got stopped, searched, and well, you know the rest."

"I really don't." She hears her own voice as if through broken headphones. It doesn't sound like her. It's distant and rough and adult.

"I had to do a little time. When they searched me, they took my shit."

"What shit?"

He holds her close. "Just shit I was moving for Emil. I had weed on me, some meth, some molly, some coke. A little H. The whole package. But when they took it, obviously I couldn't deliver it to its destination, or bring the money back to Emil since there was no money. Hence my problem. I held my mud, no one else got snagged, and I was under eighteen at the time, which is one of the reasons Emil had used me. He knew if I got caught they'd slap me on the wrist with a few months and a juvy sentence. But Mom and Dad majorly overreacted. Which is why Afghanistan."

"Johnny," Chloe draws out, trying not to sound too alarmed. "You spent a year of your precious life in jail! That's not a slap on the wrist."

"Could've been worse."

"Yeah. Could've been better too." Chloe thinks back to other words he has spoken. "But didn't you say you got kicked out of the School of Performing Arts for similar trouble?"

"That was child's play, just some weed I was holding. I wasn't even really selling, not full price, it was just for spending money."

"What about Juilliard? Wasn't that also …"

"Look, yes, I've had one or two run-ins with the law." He is still holding her, but his arms are tense and stiff. Any minute he might fling her away from him.

"I'm just saying," she says softly, "that maybe *that's* why your mom and dad …"

"I know what you're saying, but these are unrelated events! It wasn't like a pattern."

"Okay."

"What does that mean?"

"Nothing. I'm agreeing with you. That's what okay means."

Here it comes. The flinging away. He sits up on the bed. She does too. "I was a wild kid doing stupid things. That's all. The kinds of things everybody does. Come on, you didn't have troublemakers in your high school?"

"Well, sure …"

"There you go."

They weren't the one I love, she wants to say.

"And you're telling me your folks don't overreact?"

"Three times before brunch," says Chloe. "But getting arrested for drug possession and drug dealing, I don't know if you can overreact to that." Just react.

"Yes, you can. It's idiotic. Anyway, it's in the past. I'm going into the army. They don't allow that shit there. It's over with. That's why I don't want you to worry about it."

"I'm not worried," says Chloe.

"Really?" Still huddled around his knees he turns his face to her, his searching bottomless eyes scrutinizing her pallid expression. "Truth."

"Truth." She pauses. She recalls his jerky unhinged motions, his flask, his weed, his bloodshot eyes, his constant jittery wakefulness, the large geometric tattoos on the insides of his forearms, almost as if the blue ink is a decoy for needle marks. Her hands shake. "Should I be worried?"

"One hundred percent no."

They kiss. Fall back on the bed. Is the kiss the only thing that's true?

Thank you, she whispers.

You're welcome. For what?

For showing me everything.

He makes a twist with his mouth. This isn't everything, he says, playing with the tassels that circle the red lamp. The whole tiny place is like a dirty brothel with electric blue walls. This is blindness. This is fire. It's not everything.

And then he says no more. As if the castle and the beaches and the promise of an Adriatic moonlit swim speak for themselves. She'd cry if she only knew what he's talking about, but he gazes at her with such tenderness, such yearning.

I've seen everything, he says.

What did you see? Shark teeth? Tornadoes? Palm trees bending in the tropical wind?

He lies on his back, tattooed forearms behind his head, drifting off. No, don't go to sleep, Johnny! Stay with me. Talk to me.

Someday you'll understand, he says, opening his eyes.

Tell me now. Tell what you mean.

Dear Chloe, beautiful girl among the sequoias, look at where we were. You and Mason could have had bliss in a hotel by the moon and the castle. Don't shake your head. Yes. You and he could have had reckless nights with no protection and no defenses when he said he loved you forever.

Vehemently she shakes her head.

Look at us. We're just kids. What are we prepared to do? Do you know what love is? Being willing to change your life. What are you willing to give up for me? More important, what are you not willing to give up for me?

She wants to say, *everything*. I will give up everything for you.

You're going to lie on your back, he says, and you're going to whisper to me that I'm your boy.

You are. You are my boy.

And then you're going to rise from our shameless bed, walk through the door and bounce forth into the rest of your life. You've got so much to live for. But I'll still be here, flat on my back, in another cheap hotel, watching my life flicker out on the ceiling. So when you ask what we could do differently, you already know the answer. Nothing. You know how I know? Because we are doing nothing.

Chloe turns away.

What can I do, she says finally. She croaks it. Tell me. I'll do it.

But he is just like his mother. He replies to her in riddles.

Do you know what my grandmother gave up? Her child. My dad. She had to choose between a dream so faint it was barely a memory and her own flesh-and-blood boy. Would you do that?

Would that I had a boy to give up, whispers Chloe. I don't. I have only you.

One day others will pine for you, Chloe. They'll hand you flowers and wail at your door. Like me, they'll show you beaches, moons, castles. One day you'll have to choose for real between what you think you want and what you truly want. That's when you will know what love is.

What about you and me, Johnny?

Is there a you and me?

What are you saying? That we're not real?

That's not it at all, he says. That's not what I mean at all. We are all that's real. We've already had so much.

Not enough, she says. Not enough by a life.

He shakes his head. But if this is all the life you've been allotted, then we had enough, didn't we? One day to live all the things that we must live, to soften our hearts, to bring us joy. One day to swim, to eat, to drink, to laugh. One day to kiss the one you love.

He kisses her.

She hides her fallen face from him.

One day is enough for us to know all happiness, Chloe Divine, he whispers into her shoulder blades, caressing her hair. She stares at the stone wall outside their white shutters. He turns her around to him, straddles her, kisses the space between her breasts as he speaks, his soft warm lips kissing her between each small word, like the aching pulse of a love song. One day is enough to celebrate, to bless this life, Johnny murmurs into Chloe's soul. That's about all that my grandparents had before they were separated, they both thought forever. And then they split apart mountains to find each other again. That's what I'm saying to you. Even if death takes me—he waves to the nebulous beyond—as it takes us all, I won't let it destroy the significance of our present days. I read that when I was in prison. Ask yourself: what single thing gives your life meaning that grisly death will not destroy? Chloe, I promise you this, I swear to you, one way or another, I will find a way to make what I do today have infinite meaning tomorrow.

These nocturnal torments are carving up her heart.

He tells her that sometimes he fears the gray February mornings. She misunderstands. She thinks he said great.

He tells her it's true, at times he can't find his way, and becomes afflicted, and the blight of it makes him do stupid things.

There's clearly so much she doesn't know.

In Trieste under the rain and the red umbrella he had played a song she had never heard and so it barely registered, and it wasn't the most popular with the soaked crowds, who thinned out during it, but it was a shame because he sang it with such intensity as if it was something private and deeply personal. When she asked him about it in Miramare, he said it was from a new album by a British band called Jimmy Eat World, and the song was called "Pain."

The song was about tragic flaws, and a false sense of pride in your own so-called accomplishments ("like singing," he told her), but mostly it was about how the little white pill took your pain away.

That's the part she scratched out on the wailing wall inside her. Johnny soaked with rain, shouting furiously in perfect pitch at the indifferent crowd. How the little white pill took his pain away.

Is your mother right? Are you lost in the woods? Can you find the road? Do you care?

My mother is wrong about everything. He says it with no conviction.

Is the forest your mother's version of the dragon and the honey, Chloe wants to know. Except without the honey?

He doesn't say no. He doesn't say anything.

Johnny, what plagues you, she whispers, what black agonies?

Not a blemish upon my soul when I'm with you, he replies, enfolding her in his arms. Hold open for your own splendor, Chloe, and be helpless.

Stolen heart, o stolen everything.

Taken heart, o taken everything.

As if she isn't helpless and wretched and open already.

As if he doesn't carry the taste of her enslaved flesh on his lyric mouth.

As if the luxuries in front of which he falls to his knees do not already belong to him.

Prairies, plains, deserts, swarming amorous flowering fields, not woods is where I want to walk with you.

Except for when he kisses her, her eyes remain open at night.

It's barely dawn when they leave the Dog Inn.

A final ride, a short cab to Trieste International Airport.

They're silent as Italy passes them by.

I'll come back, he says. Are you listening? Can you hear my voice?

I hear.

I promise I'll come back.

I promise I'll be waiting.

His arm is around her. He holds her hand. This is for my dad, too. Not just me. He staked his reputation on me going to Afghanistan. He's waiting for me. He said, don't let me down. I promised him I wouldn't. Johnny Rainbow keeps his promises. I know I mouth off and everything. But deep down, I really do want to make him proud. Like he made his father proud.

Of course, Chloe says. That's what we all want. To make our parents proud.

He presses his mouth into the palms of her hands. She prays not to break down. It takes them so long to separate. His plane leaves at eight, and here it is seven-thirty, and he's not on it. Last call. Like in a bar. His back is to the boarding gate. Chloe stands as straight as she can, watching him stride backwards, his face to her, the way he strode backwards, his face to her, when they were in the forest on the way to the killing field.

In a song he calls out to her from across the crowded airport lounge, his crazy tenor vibrating, other travelers stopping to gape, to listen. This one goes out to the one I love. If he would stop walking, they'd throw money at his feet. Her eyes pooling up, she shakes her head. Don't do that, Johnny, please.

A tall man in an oversized military coat stands like an official at the gate. The man watches Johnny, doesn't move, doesn't blink, doesn't speak. Johnny walks past, half-nods to the man, and brings up his hand in a salute. Ironic? From a distance, Chloe can't tell.

Right before he disappears from her view, he turns around one last time. She stands watching until the last drop of him dries up before her eyes. The only thing left for him to do is make a grand exit. He turns completely around, not just a jaunty glance back. His whole lanky body faces her, guitar on his back, army duffel dropped to his side on the floor. He stands motionless for a moment as other passengers file past him down the gray chute, and then he bends at the waist as if doubling over, one arm flying up for balance, and takes the deepest bow Chloe has ever seen anyone take. In tribute and farewell he leans so far forward that his black ponytail flips over and his guitar case slides, nearly hitting the floor.

Johnny remains that way for a few moments and then straightens up. All his teeth on display, his coal eyes shining, he blows her a kiss, nods to the official, yanks up his duffel, spins around, and marches on.

The man in the military coat follows him down the accordion highway.

Part Three

The Blue Suitcase

*Give me the waters of Lethe that numb the heart, if they exist,
I will still not have the power to forget you.*

Ovid, *The Poems of Exile: Tristia and the Black Sea Letters*

36

Freshman Summer

San Diego University Freshman Course Load

Fall Semester:
Intro to Mixed Martial Arts
Jewish Faith and Practice
Class Voice I
World War II
Studies in European Literature

Spring Semester:
Women's Self-defense
Modern Middle East
Class Voice II
Social Ethics
Bootcamp
Nursery Management

Mission Florist

Dear Mom,

I was offered two internships, one during the week, one on the weekends. During the week, a paralegal at a prestigious law firm. Tell

Dad so he'll be pleased. On the weekends, a job at Mission Florist, the most well-known florist in San Diego. It supplies all the hotels, country clubs and wedding venues. I took a course in nursery management to satisfy a core requirement and the professor suggested I apply at Mission. He thinks I have a natural talent. If it's okay with you and Dad, I was thinking of taking two additional classes in the summer: landscape design and plant biology. I'd have to stay here. I'd get paid at the jobs, and the university will let me have summer housing—for an additional fee. I can pay for that, but not for the extra course work. If I want to have two majors, philosophy and plant science, I really need to take the extra classes. Please, can you and Dad help? Talk it over and let me know. Maybe you can come and visit again, if Dad can get another break from work. I'll show you an awesome beach I found. It's definitely for families, so don't worry.

Love,

Chloe

P.S. I'm glad little Ray likes Maine. It's so different from Liepaja. Give him a hug from me. How long is he staying? If you come in the summer, you should bring him. He'll love San Diego.

P.P.S. Please please forward me all my mail, even what you think is junk.

Fort Benning

Lieutenant Commander Scott: Lieutenant Commander Scott here.

Chloe: Oh, hello. Um …

Lieutenant Commander Scott: How can I help you?

Chloe: Um, yes, I'm calling because I'm looking for a soldier who enlisted in your officer program last summer.

Lieutenant Commander Scott: Did he enlist or did he join the officer candidate school?

Chloe: Um, yes, he enlisted in the officer school.

Lieutenant Commander Scott (after a pause): Is this some kind of a joke?

Chloe: I'm terribly sorry. He said he might be joining the Park Rangers ...

Lieutenant Commander Scott: Do you mean the 75th Ranger Regiment?

Chloe: Yes, that's what I meant.

Lieutenant Commander Scott (with a sigh): His name, miss?

Chloe: He told me his name was Johnny Rainbow. But ...

Lieutenant Commander Scott: Johnny *Rainbow*?

Chloe: I don't think ...

Lieutenant Commander Scott: Yeah. We don't have anyone here by that name.

Chloe: Right. But what I was saying was ...

Lieutenant Commander Scott: Can I help you with something else?

Chloe: He has a Lone Star tattoo on his chest.

Lieutenant Commander Scott: I don't know what that is.

Chloe: Like the star of Texas. On his chest.

Lieutenant Commander Scott: Young lady, my men are dressed when they come here, and they are dressed when they train. I don't keep track of my men's tattoos.

Chloe: Right. Of course. But I think his father might be someone important. Someone who has pull or ... influence or something.

Lieutenant Commander Scott: I don't know anyone like that. I don't know anyone with a tattoo or a father like that or anyone named Rainbow. The name is not in our rolls.

Chloe: I think his name was Junior. That's why they called him Johnny. Johnny, Junior. Something like that. Which means he had his father's name. Who, I think, may have been a four-star general.

Lieutenant Commander Scott: Was he a four-lonestar general, miss?

(Silence from Chloe.)

Lieutenant Commander Scott: So let's see if I have the facts straight. You're looking for a soldier who may have either enlisted or joined the OCS, or gone into the Rangers, you're not sure, a soldier with a tattoo of a star on his chest who answers to the name John, but also Junior, and whose father may or may not be a high-ranking commander?

Chloe: He has long black hair! Tied in a ponytail.

Lieutenant Commander Scott: Certainly not in Fort Benning. Our men have no hair.

Chloe: He sings. He has the most amazing voice. You wouldn't forget it if you heard—

Lieutenant Commander Scott: Did he come here to be a soldier or is he going to music and dance camp down the road?

(Silence from Chloe.)

Lieutenant Commander Scott: Will there be anything else?

Chloe: There is nothing else.

37

Sophomore Summer

San Diego University Sophomore Course Load

FALL SEMESTER:
Judo Multi-level
Hiking/camping
Prophetic Traditions of Israel
Ethics of War and Peace
Studies in Modern European Philosophy
Romanticism
Introduction to Horticulture and Green Design

SPRING SEMESTER:
Aikido Multi-level
Topics in Russian and Eastern European History
Studies in World Literature
Plant Diversity
Landscape Design
Continental Philosophy
Legal Reasoning

Yesterday's Café

Chloe got up her nerve (plus her mother forced her) and walked up the road, past Hannah's old place, to Blake and Mason's. Hannah's mother had married the manager of L.L.Bean, sold her house, and moved with him to a small bungalow on the enormous Conway Lake. A black Ford F-150 was parked outside the Hauls' pebbled drive. Janice's Subaru wasn't there. Chloe knocked quickly, thinking—or hoping?—that no one was home, despite the noise of a nail gun from the back. She'd just as soon leave the small gift and a note by the door and hightail it out.

She heard pine needles crunching under work boots. Blake came around the stilts of the back deck, tool belt on, nail gun in his hands. His mouth had nails in it. He spit them out before he spoke.

"Ah," he said, coming forward but stopping a good distance away. "You're back." He was reserved, almost formal. "Hey."

"Yeah." She failed in spoken word. Mental note to oneself: take damn interpersonal communications next semester. "Hey. How's everything? Whatcha doing?"

"Fixing the ramp to the lake for my dad. What's going on with you?"

"Yeah, yeah, oh, excellent."

"Your mother gives my mother periodic reports on you," he said.

"She does?" Mental note to oneself: talk to mother about blabbing! Intensely discomfited, she chewed her lip and stared at her flip-flops and his work boots. He had cut off his hair. It was short, streaked with blond. His face still had a week or two of growth on it. His unshaven face was so familiar, it felt wrong to be this awkward. "I brought you something from San Diego," she said. She couldn't look directly at him.

"Is it a fridge magnet? I've always wanted one of those."

She pulled the bottle from behind her. "It's a local beer," she said. "Called Ruination."

"Yes, I see that." He took it from her hands and read the label. "San Diego's liquid poem to the glory of the hop." He smiled. There. That was better. "Nice. Thanks. Do you want to share it?" His sand-color eyes softened.

She stepped back. "No. I'm late for work. I just wanted to stop by, say hi." She was already halfway down the drive.

"Where'd you find a job?"

"My friend Taylor, remember her, got me rehired at the Waterpark in North Conway."

"Sure, I remember her," Blake said. "Her squeeze Joey and I are bowling partners."

"That's great. Say hello to your mom and dad—"

"Not Mason?"

"Oh, him too, of course, yeah, sure, absolutely, uh, I'll see you."

She turned and walked speedily down the road, trying not to kick up too much dust or run or trip over her discomfort.

She saw Blake standing by the edge of the shallow receiving pool where she was wading waist deep in water holding a long red flotation bar, waiting for the next writhing body to eject from the flume slide.

He wore navy swim trunks and a T-shirt. She wore her lifeguard red.

"What are you doing here?" she asked.

"Came to pick you up. When are you off?"

"Not for another two hours."

He looked at his watch, then took off his T-shirt and jumped into the shallow pool with her.

"Don't distract me," she said, after a short stare, keeping her gaze on the water-slide exit. That was literally her entire job. She couldn't look away. She was there to catch the kids as they exited the ride. Blake had lost weight. No more happy Blake pie weight around the middle. Is it because he was less happy or ate fewer pies? He got narrower at the waist, wider through the chest and shoulders. He was tanned as if he worked shirtless outside all day. "My mother said she was coming to pick me up."

"I know. I told her I'd do it."

"Oh. And she was okay with that?"

"Why wouldn't she be?"

Chloe changed the subject. "Have you met the little guy yet? Ray."

"Um, have *you* met the little guy yet? He's been living with your parents since last year. Where've you been?"

She stammered. Thank God for the slippery kids. She returned to her duties. He stood in the water by her side.

"So you like San Diego, then?"

"It doesn't feel like home, if that's what you're asking," she replied. "But I love it there, yes. Weather is fantastic. Seventy-five all year round. Never rains. Even the Pacific is almost warm that far south. Lots of beaches."

"You always liked the beach." His mouth twisted. Hers too.

Kids came down, one, two, three, seven. He stood back and to the side, rowing his hands through the water. It was a beautiful, sunny June day.

"How's everyone?" she asked. Vague enough.

"Who do you mean?"

She got flustered.

He took pity on her and volunteered about Mason. He was working as a manager for one of the White Mountains ski resorts, up in Crawford Notch.

"Is he still living at home?"

Blake hesitated.

"Just tell it to me straight," she said, her red bar out to catch the kids. "I'm fine." This is not what heartbreak is.

"They're living up there."

"They?"

"He and—"

Chloe busied herself helping a boy to the stairs. She *was* fine, but she didn't want to hear about it. Could Blake see her condemning expression?

"When did you get so fit?" he asked. "Though you're still not tanned, I see."

She shrugged it off. "Can't lose the Irish." The fit came from all the self-defense classes she was taking. She didn't mention his weight loss or his increased brawniness or his brown chest. She didn't want him to think she noticed.

"Is it true you never made it to Barcelona?" he asked.

"It's true," said Chloe. "I never did."

"So where'd you go then, after you split?"

"Italy."

They fell quiet.

"I'll get out," he said. "Dry off."

"I'll be another hour."

"That's fine."

In an hour, she climbed out of the pool, toweled off, punched out, threw a white terry cover-up over her wet red bathing suit, and met him waiting for her by the bench near the exit.

They walked to his black truck. He opened the door for her.

"Is it new? It's swanky." Lang had told Chloe a little bit about Blake doing well.

"Not new, but swanky. I have drinks in the cooler. Want a Coke?"

She was impressed by his attention to amenities. Gladly she took a Coke. "Did you get the truck with your prize money? Congratulations, by the way."

"Thank you. But I didn't get the dumb money yet. Soon, I hope." He grinned. "You surprised I won?"

"Pretty stunned, actually, yeah."

"That I wrote it in the first place?"

"That too." It had taken him an extra year, but he had done it. She should've known he'd eventually write it. He had said he would. "So when do I get a copy?"

"Oh, not until it's properly published. That won't be till next summer."

"No! I don't want to wait that long. You must have a manuscript lying around?"

"Uh-uh. You won't like the bad guy in it. Wait for the book." He had been driving for a few minutes when Chloe noticed he was going north on 16 instead of south. "Yes, I know," he said. "You don't want to drive up to Crawford, to visit Mason?"

She whirled to face him. "Stop kidding." She watched the road, waiting for him to make a U-turn. "Why is he all the way up in Crawford Notch? I thought you and he were going to be the Haul Brothers together."

"We're still Haul brothers," Blake said. "We're just not the Haul Brothers." He sighed with resigned disappointment. "Truth is, Mason wanted to do something else. He loves the skiing, the winter sports. Likes managing the slopes." He continued to drive in the wrong direction.

"Blake, turn around. I'm not going to visit him. Ain't gonna happen."

"I know," he said, one hand coolly on the wheel. "But I thought you might want to say hi to your friend Hannah."

Only slightly less aghast. "Where—in Bangor?"

"Oh no," Blake said, "our dear Hannah is not in Bangor anymore. She's in Jackson."

"Jackson, where Lupe lives? Why? It's got like fifty people in it."

"Fifty-three with her, the baby and young Zhenya."

"What are you talking about? Stop playing mind games! You're freaking me out. What Zhenya?"

"Why is your voice so high?"

"Because you're confusing me. Can you stop driving for a second?"

"No can do." He pointed to the narrow road. "No shoulder."

Chloe knew that Hannah had gone to Bangor, but little beyond that. Despite one or two half-hearted attempts, she had not spoken to her friend in nearly two years. Since Krakow. As they drove toward Jackson, Blake filled her in. After they had come back from Poland ("Of course we flew back right away. What else were we going to do?"), he had offered to pay for Hannah's abortion. Hannah opted for door number two and decided to approach Martyn, to let him know it was happening. *"The least she could do* is how she put it," Blake told Chloe. Martyn used his formidable powers of hypnotic persuasion to convince Hannah that there was no reason to terminate the pregnancy, that if she stayed with him, he would take care of her schooling, the baby, everything. He even offered to help sponsor Zhenya from Liepaja to come stay with them in Bangor. The only thing he asked of Hannah was that they get married. He didn't want his baby to be illegitimate. How old school of him, how quaint, Blake and Chloe clucked. So Hannah and Martyn got married, after some doing Zhenya was shipped to Bangor, baby Hayley was born, and …

"It sounds like they lived happily ever after," said Chloe. "Don't tell me she got sick of him already."

"She didn't get a chance to. The dude croaked."

Chloe coughed up her Coke. "What?"

"He was like a hundred years old," Blake said. "That parrot became an ex-parrot eight months ago. Heart attack."

"No!"

Blake continued driving, palming the gear shift in the console. "Our Hannah thought that as his widow she would come into his money, but during probate she discovered that the place they were living in was university housing. It wasn't his. And his debt was in the hundreds of thousands. Apparently, Martyn had quite the gambling problem. Stock market options. Kept it well hidden. Bottom line, negative red. He may have paid a few grand to sponsor Zhenya, but that was about all. So now she has nowhere to live, his massive debt to sort through, and a baby and a Latvian to feed."

"Blake …" Chloe didn't know what to say. "That's awful. What's in Jackson?"

"Yesterday's Café."

"What's that?"

"Where she works. She's a waitress at Yesterday's Café."

"But where's she living?"

"Back with her mother and her new stepdad in their cottage, barely bigger than Lupe's garage."

"Crap."

"Oh yeah."

He made a right into Jackson. Shaking her head, Chloe reached for the wheel.

"Blake, no."

"Just go say hello."

"With you? We're just going to waltz in there? Arm in arm?"

"No, *I'm* not going. I'll wait in the truck."

"Have you visited her even once?"

"She invited me and Mason to her wedding. She wanted me to give her away."

"Did you *go?*" She gasped out the question.

"Let go of my wheel. Do I look like the kind of guy who'd go?"

Chloe didn't know how to answer that.

"Of course I didn't fucking go," he said. "What kind of a chump do you think I am?"

She sighed with relief. "So when did you see her?"

"Recently. She stopped by the house to congratulate me on the success of my Spring Fair. Cried. Pretty hard. Apologized. Up, down, left, right. Said she treated me real bad and I didn't deserve it. Maybe she thought I'd argue with her."

"Did you?"

"I told her she was right, I didn't deserve it."

Chloe studied him, trying to discern how he felt. He was still the same Blake, almost. Friendly, transparent about the little things, inscrutable about the big. Except there was a hardness to his eyes that wasn't there before, a small unsmiling disillusionment with mankind. Maybe Hannah had hoped little

Hayley would bring the sunshine back? "Did she bring the baby with her?"

"She wanted to. I told her to leave the girl with her mom."

"Wow."

"What, too tough? I gave her some money. She protested. Not too hard. I think what she really wanted was for us to get back together. She told me she was saving up, and then she and her girls were moving, either to New York or New Orleans, one of the New cities. I wasn't really paying attention. Maybe she was hoping I'd ask her to stay."

"Did you?"

"Nope." He made an L with his left hand and placed it to his forehead. "I sent a buddy of mine to check on her a few weeks ago. Orville. Nice guy, unfortunate name."

"Like you're sending me to check on her now? Blake, stop the car, please."

He pulled into a dirt lot near the downmarket bar and grill.

"You have to go see her, Chloe," Blake said.

"I know. I plan to, I do. I just … I'm damp, I don't want to go into the air-conditioning."

"Oh, don't worry, there's no air-conditioning at Yesterday's."

"You and I have so much to catch up on." Chloe forced a smile. "We didn't even talk about your book or Blake Haul's amazing fundraising fair."

"Stop buttering me up, I'm not toast. Go." He took two twenties out of his pocket and stuffed them into Chloe's hand. "Have a burger with her. Leave her the rest of the money for a tip. I'll be here. Wait, not a burger. She's a vegetarian now. Go!"

Chloe sat at a little table near the exit. She was studying the menu—very thoroughly—when she felt a long, tall shape at her elbow. She looked up. Hannah stood like a statue, unsmiling in her beige uniform.

"Hi," she said. "How did you know I was here?"

"Blake told me. Hi, Hannah." Chloe managed a smile, guilty, uncomfortable, happy to see her friend, sad to see her under such circumstances. "How are you?"

"Where is he?"

"Outside."

Hannah made a desolate face. "He's still mad at me. But it gives me hope, you know, that there's love there. Because you're never mad at people you don't care about. Don't you think?"

Chloe bleated back something inarticulate. She didn't know if she would call what Blake was at Hannah mad. You're mad at your girlfriend because she forgets you're going to the movies on Friday night and makes other plans. Having unprotected sex with an old dude and then getting knocked up while supposedly being faithful to you was a different kettle of fish entirely.

"Hang on, I'll take my break. Can I get you a grilled cheese? I'll have one too. I don't eat meat anymore."

While she waited, Chloe peered out the small window. She wanted to shake her fist at Blake lounging in his truck, head back, listening to the radio, but he was facing the road, not the restaurant.

Hannah returned with two crisp hot sandwiches and two coffees. "I only have like ten minutes," she said, sitting sideways, as if at any minute ready to bolt. "Can you believe what happened to me?"

I can't even believe what happened to me, Chloe thought. "No. How's your baby?"

"She's good. She's with my mom." Hannah sighed. She still looked ephemeral, delicate, forlorn. In other words, irresistible. "It's terrible. Mom doesn't want me there, and I don't want to be there. She's remarried, and I'm completely intruding. Blake told you everything? Isn't it sick about Martyn? How could it happen? To be in such debt is ghastly!"

Chloe squeezed her mouth together. "Also to be dead."

"Chloe, he *owed* more money than my mother earned in twenty years! And all his creditors are now after me. It's a nightmare."

"It'll be okay—"

"How? I've got Zhenya with me now, too. At my mom's. What was I thinking? Good news is, she's almost old enough to babysit. Bad news is, she wants to be out with her American friends. And I'm like, no way. You're eleven. So we're fighting. At my mother's house."

Chloe began to tell Hannah about Ray. He was only eight years old. He didn't want to be anywhere but with Lang and Jimmy.

"I know, right?" Hannah said. "I wish my mom hadn't moved. It was so nice on our lake. And your mom helped me a lot with the sponsorship papers. She filled them out for Ray and Zhenya at the same time. I couldn't have done it without her. If we were still there, she could help me look after the kids. She's so great. She's always home."

"Well, not always …"

"Do you have any idea how Blake is feeling?"

"About what?"

"About what? Chloe! About me, the baby, the whole situation."

"You mean about you getting married to someone else?"

"No, about what's happening to me *now*."

Their sandwiches lay untouched, their coffee undrunk. Chloe sat and listened, shaking her head or nodding in the appropriate places. It was as if Chloe didn't exist. It was as if Europe, Johnny, Mason, San Diego weren't even a blip on the friend radar. Chloe tried to keep the sting of their suffocating one-way friendship from watering up her eyes. When it was time to go, she left Blake's money on the table.

"Aww, don't cry," Hannah said. "You said yourself it'll be fine. Maybe you can come visit me and the baby?" She grabbed the two twenties and hid them in her apron. "She's fifteen months now. Super cute."

Chloe swatted away a rogue tear. Why did growing up mean having to accept that people you loved kept disappointing you?

"But bring Blake with you," Hannah added. "Don't come on your own. I want him to forgive me. I *need* him to forgive me. I know he won't be able to resist the baby when he sees her. He can barely resist me."

Chloe thought Blake would want to talk about Hannah, but it was the last thing he wanted to talk about. He slammed the truck into reverse and peeled out into the open road.

"Thanks a lot," she said.

"Better you than me."

"Why is *that* the choice? Why is that the *only* choice?"

He laughed. "You think that was hard work? Try writing."

"Sorry, no. That was harder than hauling junk out of people's homes."

"How would you know? Try sitting in one place for hours and hours. Your back hurts, your ass hurts, your arms go numb, your eyes stop focusing. You chew the pencils to nubs, so now you got wood chips floating around in your gut, and then the words don't come. Outside the sun is shining and you want to be fishing or swimming or … I mean, I'm glad I wrote it, but man, I wouldn't want to inflict that on someone I hate." He didn't specify who that might be.

Chloe felt sorry for herself for only a second. Blake told her Hannah never even asked him about *The Blue Suitcase*. When he told her his story had won first prize, she said what story?

"She didn't!"

"Oh yeah. She did."

But then again, Blake was running around town, working a little, bowling a lot, and Chloe was on a break from awesome, while Hannah was waitressing an empty lunch shift before she went home to her mother's where her two kids waited, one of them a tween.

"So if you don't marry Hannah," Chloe said, "what else are you going to do with your money?"

"Don't joke, I'm not in the mood," he said lightly. "The dough, when it arrives, is already spoken for."

"For what? You got the truck. Mason is doing his own thing."

"My dad, if you must know," Blake said. "His back keeps getting worse. He's nearly paralyzed."

"Sorry." She had been too flip.

"The operation is crazy bucks. My mom's insurance covers most of it, I guess"—Blake raised his voice—"except for the *twenty thousand dollar* lifetime deductible. Plus thousands more for rehab. Who the hell has all that?"

"Well," said Chloe. "I guess the answer is, you do."

Blake didn't even sigh as he drove, one hand on the wheel, one arm bent through the open window. "After I'd get paid, who knows when, my mom and I would still be short. And Mason never has any money. And Dad's really been struggling. So I got this idea to have a fundraising fair on the Academy grounds. Games, rides, prizes, some food and drink, and charge a few bucks for admission. I talked to the president, and he agreed to let us have the Academy for a weekend, provided that afterward we made it look like we were never there. So a month ago we had our first Annual Haul Spring Fair, sponsored by Chevy." Blake smiled happily. "The mayor was so proud that I'd won the competition, he made the town put up a banner over Main Street. 'Congratulations Blake Haul' or something like that, and the local radio interviewed me and the local paper did a piece on me, so we had pretty good attendance. Like ten thousand people."

"No!"

"Yeah, it was epic. We made fifty grand."

Chloe loudly verbalized her astonishment.

"I know, right? Well, thirty in the clear after expenses. But amazing, still."

"No wonder Hannah wants you back."

"What did I say about jokes? Dad's going under the knife in August. Maybe I'll get my money by the time we have to pay for his rehab. But now Mom thinks she's found her true calling. She went around for months asking local businesses to contribute garbage cans, drinks, games, cookies, burger joints, zeppoles, pizza. She loved it. She wants to do it every year. She's a born saleswoman."

"Your dad is not going to need an annual operation, is he?"

Blake smiled. "Let's hope not. Mom says there'll always be a kid out there who needs help. *Your* mom, because she's a troublemaker, says to my mom we should have a fundraiser for Hannah and her daughters."

"Be cheaper just to get back together with her."

"How many times do I have to tell you that unlike your mother, you're not funny?"

Chloe faced him as he drove, observed his familiar profile, his easygoing expression. "So who are you making time with these days? Taylor told me you and Melissa hooked up."

"Did she actually use the term hooked up, or is that your San Diego surfer girl talking?"

"She actually said hooked up."

He was keeping it light. "Yeah, for a while. Then we moved on."

"Who'd you move on to? Taylor said you were sweet on Crystal." Taylor said he had broken up with Crystal in April.

"She was cute."

"Still is. I like her better than Melissa."

"Your approval of my girls means a lot to me, Chloe," Blake said.

They drove through Fryeburg. The banner with Congratulations Blake Haul! still spanned Main Street.

They were past the rock with the whale, which meant almost at the turn to their road, when Blake said, "Have you heard from him?"

And Chloe almost said *who*.

"No." She said no more. What more was there to say? And he didn't follow up. What else was there to ask? He walked her to the front door in silence. There was a patter of feet, a swinging screen door and a dark-haired little boy ran out and hugged Blake around the waist.

"Blake! Football? You promised!" Eight-year-old Ray had learned English well. He begged like a pro.

Blake ruffled the boy's hair. "Not today, bud. Maybe tomorrow. I got stuff to do."

Lang came to the front door carrying a covered plate of cookies. "Hello, dear," she said, but not to Chloe—to Blake. "Do you want to stay for dinner? I made plenty. Rib eye tonight. Your favorite."

"No, thank you, Mrs. Devine, my mom is making what she thinks are burritos."

"Ah. Well, here. Lemon bars for you."

Blake gladly took the plate.

Chloe stared at her mother. "Lemon bars?"

Lang was already inside the house. Chloe glanced at Ray, expectant by her side. She was right from the moment she first laid eyes on him. He was the sweetest kid. A little needy maybe, but, well, who wasn't?

"So, Ray," she said. "How about I go put on my beating Ray shoes and you go get the ball so I can kick your butt?"

Lone Star

"Chloe, come inside, it's almost dinner time. Why are you pacing the road? Are you waiting for your father to come home? He'll be another twenty minutes. He's bringing Latvian pie for you from Moody."

"No."

"Are you waiting for Blake?"

"What? No!"

"So what are you doing?"

"Nothing."

Chloe couldn't even mope in peace.

Aside from staring at the empty road, she searched for him from the comfort of her favorite red chair by the window with the white curtains and her glorious pendulous violet fuchsias blooming outside in the shade of the firs. With the PowerBook on her lap, she googled until her fingers went stiff. Johnny Rainbow this, Lone Star that. Johnny Rainbow no hits. Every search with the name Lone Star produced a million hits. There was of course the local Lone Star Pawn and Gun in Fryeburg. There was also Lone Star beer, and Lone Star steak, and Lone Star wine bar. Lone Star saloon, Lone Star campus, Lone Star kickball, Lone Star country road 92, and there was even a band named Lonestar, which got Chloe excited, as they had just put out a greatest hits CD, which would imply that there had been songs to choose from. But they were not Johnny and had nothing to do with Johnny.

Lone Star hiking club. How many search pages back should one go? Six? Twelve? All of them?

Why hadn't she asked him why he had a tattoo of the star of Texas engraved on his chest? She thought she *had* asked him.

Evenings and nights crawled by in endless searching. Lone Star college. Lone Star fertilizer.

Lone Star mercantile shop.

Lone Star music.

That was almost promising. She called them, but they'd never heard of a Johnny Rainbow.

"There is a very strong possibility that isn't his real name," her mother called from the kitchen. Ray, not Chloe, was helping her make dinner. Chloe was busy.

"I don't want to talk to you about it, Mom," said Chloe. "You don't know everything." Chloe hoped her mother didn't know everything. Why had Chloe told her everything! The only thing her mother had said two years ago after she heard the whole sobbing rant was were you careful. That's it. Were you careful?

No, Mom, Chloe had replied. We were wildly reckless. Flagrantly irresponsible. Careful is the last thing we were. We lived it like we were dying. Don't talk to me about this anymore. I can't bear it. Because I've already bled, but what I want is to bleed out, is that histrionic enough for you? Is that super careful enough for you?

Lone Star emergency vehicles.

Lone Star girl. That was her.

Lone Star Texas eclectic gifts.

Lone Star burritos. Maybe there was a girl in a taco joint, and he got the tat to remember her by. Maybe Lone Star was his Winona Forever.

Zane Grey was the Lone Star Ranger. Did Johnny have anything to do with Zane Grey?

Lone Star chili cookoff. Did he cook chili? Did he even like chili? There were so many things about him she did not know and could not know and was now afraid she would never know.

She googled Johnny Rainbow and Lone Star together. Nothing came up.

But you know what did come up?

Lone Star shootout.

Lone Star cookout. They were having a barbecue in Texas. The best spare ribs won.

Lone Star scavenger hunt. Chloe was the scavenger.

Her mother observed her for the month of July. Then she said, "Didn't you tell me you two went to visit his mother?"

"So?"

"Maybe she knows her son's name?"

Chloe wasn't sure Ingrid would want to speak to her. "No one there spoke English."

"You're right. Better not call."

"Ugh. Don't exasperate me, Mom." A minute later, "It was two years ago. She's probably not there."

"You're right. It's hopeless. Stop looking."

"Mom, I think Dad is calling for you to see what Ray is up to. Go see."

"Chloe, I think Blake is at the door, asking if you want to go to the movies with him and Taylor and Joey. Should I tell him you can't because you're googling?"

Chloe slammed shut her laptop.

Later that night, after the movies, when everyone was asleep, Chloe googled the Tarcento Pensione to find its phone number. The first item that came up was not a phone number, but a news alert about a something in Italian. *Incendio doloso. Gravi danni.* She used her barely-trustworthy online translator. Arson. Heavy damage. At dawn she walked outside into the dewy fuchsias and dialed the number she had found. There was no answer.

She kept calling. In August she finally reached someone who spoke a little English at the parish church of St. Peter in Tarcento. The man told her that after the fire, the pensione had closed because the insurance money didn't cover the cost of rebuilding it. No, he didn't know where the people who lived there had gone. Chloe asked if anyone had died. The man said no. It was a miracle that everyone survived. He told her to go with God. *Andare con Dio.*

That was that.

Fishing

Blake and Chloe were in the boat together, just like in childhood. It was mid-August, almost time for her to fly back to her other life. They were sitting in the anchored boat, bobbing lightly, late afternoon, trying to catch a perch or a bass. Pickings had been slim. Perhaps because they kept scaring away the fish. No matter how many times he said shh to her, he'd then make her laugh and ruin the silence.

Right before he pulled up anchor and rowed back to shore, he took a breath. "You asked before why I seemed off, and I didn't want to be rude, but now I'll tell you. I don't want you to go back to school and have it stay unsaid between us, what pissed me off, and still does. Okay?"

"Okay, I guess." They had been sitting so affably.

"I thought we were friends," Blake said. "I mean, I understand what happened in Poland was awful, for you and Mason, for me and Hannah. I was upset with you for lying to me for so long—to all of us, I mean. You were leaving us, going west to almost Mexico."

"Not for good," she said. "Look at me, I'm right here."

He looked. "Whatever. I understood why you couldn't tell *me*, since you hadn't told your best friend or your boyfriend, but it doesn't mean I wasn't upset about it."

"I know." She hung her head, but only briefly, because she wanted to watch him struggle to get the main part out, the part he wanted to get to.

"But that's not what upset me," he continued. "What really upset me was that after you came back from your little adventure, after you ditched us all in the middle of Europe without a word—"

"I left a note," Chloe said. "I told you not to worry about me."

"Yeah, okay. As I was saying. After all that, you came back home, a full week after us, and not five minutes later flew out to San Diego and didn't say goodbye to anyone. Didn't *speak* to anyone. I mean, I can understand maybe Mason, because he'd done you wrong, and I can almost understand Hannah, though you could've said sorry even to her for being so sneaky and underhanded."

"Do you really care that I didn't say goodbye to Hannah?" Chloe asked quietly.

"Let me finish. But what did *I* do to you? I thought we were friends. And then you left, and didn't come back for Thanksgiving, didn't come back for Christmas, and didn't even come back last summer!"

"I was working … I have two majors. It wasn't personal …"

"I thought we would clear the air then, but no. You didn't come back, you didn't write, you didn't call my house, you didn't send me a birthday card. I turned twenty. And nothing."

"We celebrated your twenty-first, didn't we?" Chloe was guilty as charged. He had turned twenty-one last month. She and Taylor and Joey took him boating and had gotten him so drunk on the shores of Lake Sebago that Chloe had to drive him home in his F-150. It was a great day. She was hoping he'd forgiven her for her previous absence from his life. Guess not.

"Your mom must have told you I'd won the story prize," Blake continued, "but you didn't send so much as an email saying congrats, old buddy. You and I have been friends since we could walk, and you acted as if you weren't my friend anymore."

Blake looked away. He lugged the anchor out of the water, bent over the little wooden boat. She watched his broad back in a white T-shirt as she tried to fight through her remorse, yet find words to explain why she had shut him out too.

Silently he rowed back. She sat in the nose of the boat, in front of him.

"Look, I'm sorry," she finally said. "I didn't think you'd care very much, but that wasn't right. I just didn't think about it in the terms you put it."

"How did you think about it?"

"I was really mad at you," said Chloe.

"What did I do?"

"You didn't behave like my friend, Blake", she said. "You want to talk about friendship? Let's. You knew Mason didn't like me anymore, you knew he had a hard-on for another girl, and you said nothing. That's not how friends behave in my book." Chloe felt she made a pretty good case for herself.

Blake stopped rowing. He hooked the oars onto the sides of the boat and leaned toward her, slightly breathless, completely unsmiling, and incredulous.

"You must be fucking kidding me," he said. "Chloe, of all the things to be upset with me about. You have some nerve. Mason never told me a thing. I had my suspicions, just like you must have had yours, and I did think he didn't act enough like your boyfriend, but he and I didn't have midnight chats about it. But you know who did have midnight chats about things? You and Hannah. You knew Hannah was fucking around! You knew she was going to motels with Professor X, you *knew* and yet you let me go to Europe with you! You let me believe everything was all right. You knew for sure what she was up to, and yet you never said to her, if you don't do the right thing and break up with him, I'm going to tell him myself."

"She was my best friend!"

"And Mason is *still* my fucking brother!"

Their loud voices, brimming with injured hearts, echoed up and down the tranquil little lake. Anyone sitting in a lawn chair could have heard every word of the injustice, as if through a megaphone.

"She was supposed to tell you, talk to you," said Chloe.

"You know she didn't. Because we went to Europe. You think I would've gone if I'd known she was knocked up?"

"*I* didn't know that myself!" Her head shook from side to side in protest. "She told me in Warsaw. But you absolutely knew Mason was pining for the airhead back home."

"We were in Riga by then. What was I supposed to do?"

"What was *I* supposed to do?"

"Maybe if you hadn't been completely subsumed by other things, you would've known what to do."

"Well, what's your excuse? You weren't subsumed by other things and yet look!"

"How do you know I wasn't subsumed?"

"By effing what?"

He didn't say.

They backed off, regrouped.

"It's not rational for you to be upset with me about Mason," Blake said.

"I'm not upset with you. I didn't start this conversation."

"If you're not upset, then why didn't you talk to me for almost two years?"

There was wounded pride in his eyes, and hurt, and incomprehension. He was right. She was subsumed. She had been focused only on what she left behind in Trieste. Which was everything.

"I'm sorry," she said. "I didn't know what to say to you, or to Hannah. Or Mason, of course." She still didn't. She hadn't seen Mason all summer.

"Did you think we ruined your dream trip?"

That wasn't it at all. Her trip wasn't ruined. Her life was changed.

"No." My heart is broken, though not dead. The empty ring inside me is still filled with agony. "I wanted to begin my adult life. That's all. Sorry."

"Okay," he said, but cold. He picked up the oars.

"And I didn't stay away last summer," she said. "I told you I was working two jobs, taking classes. It wasn't deliberate."

"Yeah, sure."

"I'll keep in touch from now on. I promise."

"Whatever."

She was silent for a moment. Then she dipped her hand into the water and splashed him. He didn't react. She splashed him again. He blinked, said hey. "You can't do that," she said, splashing him again. "You either accept my apology, or don't, but if you accept it, you can't sit and brood. That's not what friends do."

"Oh, now you're all about what friends do. And who's brooding?"

"You."

"Stop splashing, I can't see where I'm rowing."

"Stop brooding and I'll stop splashing."

"Okay."

"Blake!"

"What?"

"Do you accept my apology?"

"No."

"What do you mean, no?" She splashed him again. He put down the oars and stood up. Without saying another word, he took one wobbly step over to her, picked her up, and before she had a chance to protest, threw her in the lake. Then he sat back down and picked up the oars. She thought he would jump in after her, like he used to when they were kids, but he didn't.

"What are you doing?" she called, blowing water out of her mouth and nose.

"Stop splashing me, or you can swim back home."

"You're going to leave me in the middle of the lake?"

"It's forty yards to shore, Miss Melodrama."

"Help me get into the boat right now."

"Are you going to stop splashing?"

"Are you going to accept my apology and stop brooding?"

"No."

"Then I'm not going to stop splashing."

Calmly he moved the boat away from her, and resumed rowing.

"Blake!"

He's impossible, she thought, and didn't call out his name again. She simply turned over onto her back in the lake and drifted toward her dock, her arms every once in a while fanning through the water to propel her body forward.

Bartering

A few days before Chloe left for California, Blake drove her to Jackson to say goodbye to Hannah.

"Are you going to stay in the truck again?"

"I'm going to visit my girl by the covered bridge," he said.

"What girl?"

"Jealous, are we?"

Chloe rolled her eyes.

"Lupe in the yellow shack."

"You still see her? Splain."

"Nothing to splain. I started bringing her Meals on Wheels after you left, and then she wanted me to come read to her every other Tuesday, and then she wanted me to take her to the doctor every Friday, and then do her shopping, and fix her roof and her windows and install her new oven. Then she made me pie in that oven. On and on. She pays me almost a full-time nut. I'm with her four days a week. She needs my help. She has no one."

"She has three sons!"

"They're in California, like you. What if *your* mother needs help? You're going to help her lying in your little bikini on Mission Bay beach?"

Chloe scoffed. "Like I would ever wear a bikini."

"I don't know *what* you do over there," he said, leaning over and reaching across her to open the door and let her out, his entire large Blake arm nearly sweeping against both her breasts. He didn't touch her at all.

"Chloe, I beg you, if you're still my friend, talk to him for me. Please." Forgetting about her other tables, Hannah parked across from Chloe, grasping her hands. Her face plain, beautiful, her eyes moist, pleading, her hair all slicked back, oh God, what boy could resist that face and those eyes, childbirth be damned.

"What could I possibly say to him?"

"You're a college student. Figure something out."

"Having book smarts doesn't make me smart." Chloe nearly went moist-eyed herself.

"Yes, but he still listens to you."

"No, he doesn't. Where do you get that? He's not too thrilled with me either."

"Oh, please. You know you can do no wrong. But I really screwed up. Tell him I'm sorry."

"He knows."

"Tell him again. Tell him I miss him. I'm going to be good to him. We had it so good once."

Chloe's head went from side to side, in a swing not a shake. "What if he thinks you just want to get out of your mom's house?"

"Well, I do."

"Right. But maybe that's not enough to build a whole relationship on?"

"Who says? And we don't have to build. We already built. We need to rebuild."

"It's been leveled," Blake said on the way home when Chloe tried to persuade him of Hannah's sincerity. "Can't build on scorched earth, baby. Gotta get what's left of your shit and get the fuck out. It can never, and I mean *never*, happen."

Chloe shook her head. "Blake, you don't think people deserve a second chance? Everybody makes mistakes. Come on. Don't be such a hard-ass."

"I see where you're coming from. Second chances. Mistakes. She's ready to turn over a new leaf, maybe?"

"Absolutely!"

"Ready to give me what I need?"

"Goes without saying."

"Willing to commit to a real relationship?"

"That's the point."

"So let me ask you, this new Hannah who wants to try again, with a baby by another daddy and a waif she's dragged here all the way from Latvia, do you think that turning over a new leaf includes her giving my friend Orville head a few weeks ago when he gave her a ride home from Yesterday's?"

"What?"

"Oh yeah."

"It's a lie. Who told you?"

"Orville."

"What—why would he tell you that?"

"Because I told him she wanted to get back together with me."

"No!"

"Oh yeah."

"I don't understand."

"What's not clear? He gave her a ride home, and she wanted to say thank you."

Chloe, completely flustered, turned toward the side window. "Why did your dumb friend say yes?" she muttered.

Blake was silent a moment. "Are you asking why a twentysomething dude with a 24/7 hard-on would say yes to a blowjob from a pretty girl? Have you ever met a dude, Chloe? Any dude?"

"Wait, hang on …" She tried to compose her words. "I'm saying, I didn't know this was a thing."

"Me neither! Would that I did. I'd have had a completely different high school experience. Because I was always driving chicks around. Back and forth. Blake, take me here, Blake, take me there. Come pick me up. If only I'd known this secret barter system for rides. I would've slept with a smile on my face every night."

They arrived at her house. He pulled into the clearing, stopped the car, idled it. "Well, here we are," he said.

"Yes." She unlatched her seatbelt, took her purse from the well. "Thanks for the ride."

"That's it? Thanks for the ride? I thought I explained to you how these things work."

Chloe fixed him with an appropriate blinkless stare. "I'm leaving the truck right now."

Laughing he circled her wrist. "I'm kidding."

She unfurled herself from his fingers. "Yeah, sure."

"What, you don't think I'm kidding?" He was so twinkly cute.

"You said it yourself. Are you a dude or aren't you?"

"Well, I'm not a dude with you," he said, getting out of the car to walk her to her front door because her father was a cop and cops didn't like their daughters dropped off at the curb like UPS packages. "I'm Blake."

Back at her other life, Chloe scrutinized the audition message boards on her laptop. Her mother was in the kitchen. A thousand meaningless posts. Come see this band, come buy my Les Paul, my steel drums, audition for my band, piano for sale, cat for sale, cat lost, looking for a lead singer, looking for a new lead singer ...

Looking over Chloe's shoulder, Lang said she'd look into that one, auditions at the Blue Moon in Santa Fe, because it was posted three weeks in a row. A cover band called Lone Star looking for a singer, a small but intensely loyal following. Auditions this Friday at the university practice rooms down in the basement.

"Mom, *how* is this helpful? We don't even know if Lone Star was the name of his band." He lifts up his shirt on the train and, beaming, shows her the tattoo and says how do you know I don't already have a band? She has just told him he is going to own the world with his voice. Johnny Rainbow and the Hail of Bullets. He is going to live forever.

"Maybe it's his old band," her mother said. "Maybe they're auditioning for a new singer."

"What, they're looking for a singer, five years later?"

"Why not?" Lang said to Chloe. "You are."

38

Junior Summer

San Diego University Junior Year Course Load

FALL SEMESTER:
Tai Chi Multi-level
Advanced Voice
Plant Pathology
Plant Propagation
Topics in Modern Europe
Modern U.S. Fiction

SPRING SEMESTER:
Kung Fu
Advanced Hiking
Applied Entomology
Herbaceous Landscape Plants
Studies in Continued Continental Philosophy
Law and Society
Holocaust: Death of God or Death of Humanity
Introduction to the Brain

She has forgotten an introductory science class to satisfy her graduation requirement and apparently plant biology doesn't satisfy.

So half-asleep she soldiers on through an 8:30 a.m. class on Mondays, Wednesdays, and Fridays, learning about the amygdala and the hippocampus.

Of some interest is the transfer of information between neurons. The end with the dendrites receives the information. The other, with an electrical charge, sends it. The neurons don't touch; it's all about the strength of the electrical impulse in the synapse and the sensitivity of the branchy receptors.

Eureka! Now she understands why she can never remember anything. The distance between her neurons is a micrometer too long.

She has been combing through twenty days of her life, trying to find a star, a proton, a quantum particle that might point her in the direction of the boy who had promised her himself in the palm of her hand. In the Introduction to the Brain, she learns why she can't find him. And maybe why he can't find her. The neuron that holds the data she needs is spaced too far apart from the neuron that throbs to receive it. In the end, Chloe and Johnny, the forever lovers, are felled by nothing more than biology.

All the philosophy courses Chloe doggedly takes—because that's what pre-law undergrads do, that's what abandoned lovers do—can't answer the unsolvable riddle.

Here's one he and his mother would like. Chloe knows how much those two enjoy unsolvable riddles.

What if she doesn't wait and he comes for her?

What if she waits and he never comes?

The riddle, not for Ingrid or Johnny but for Chloe, is: which is worse?

Johnny!

Promise me you'll never forget me, you whispered to me the night before the day you left me.

I promised you I never would.

How I wish to God I had.

How I wish to God I could.

Why did you make me a promise you couldn't keep?

Despite her neurological limitations, Chloe tries hard to remember something, anything. She keeps returning to the traveling butterflies who accompanied them to the mass graveyard at Treblinka. She doesn't know why her mind keeps sifting through that barren ground.

The bus, the walk, the woods, something about those people and their incessant chatter keeps ringing a dim bell inside the belfry of her head. Look here, the bell thuds. There is something here.

Chloe fears it's something irretrievable. On the bus, while their mouths had been going like go-cart wheels, Chloe was either staring out the window or gaping at Johnny as he talked about Majdanek and cyanide. Yet through it, Yvette's voice, or Denise's, keeps poking in with something revealing. But try as Chloe might, she can't catch the end of the string of their words. Yet the bell keeps chiming. There is something there.

Lupe

The Haul Spring Fair conceived by Blake and sponsored by Chevy grew a tad in its second year. Attendance jumped from ten to thirty thousand people. Old vendors returned, new vendors called him directly, wanting to participate, to license a booth, to sell their products. His mother remained the treasurer and publicist, and his father, with his brand-new titanium back and a new sponsored-by-Chevy Chevy, gifted to him as a promotional gimmick, drove around town, shaking hands and lugging lumber. Burt described it all to Chloe in rich detail when she came to call on Blake after she returned home for the summer. The Hauls built a new deck and two new carports. The wheelchair ramp to the lake had been dismantled. "Her next car, she tells me, is going to be a Cadillac," a beaming Burt told Chloe. "My wife, in a Cadillac!"

"Sit down." Janice pulled on Burt's sleeve. "Why stand at the door like a horse?"

"I've been sitting for ten years," the man said. "From now on, I'm doing *everything* standing up." He grabbed Janice around the waist.

"Burt, the children!" Janice squealed. "You'll have to excuse him, he—"

Blake strode out, in new jeans and a white button-down shirt with the sleeves rolled up. He was even wider in the shoulders than he had been last summer. Through their emails she knew that he was roofing and hauling granite blocks for outdoor fireplaces. "I leave you with her for two minutes, and what happens?" he said. He smiled. His face was clean-shaven. "Hey, Chloe."

"Hey, Blake. Is it true you now have even your dad running errands for you? I'm so sorry, Mr. Haul."

"Oh, I don't mind," said Burt, gazing adoringly at his son. "I'd carry his water for him, if he'd let me."

Blake gave Chloe a nudge. "Did you hear that?" He grabbed his wallet and keys.

"So where are you two headed? Why don't you eat first? Blake, you can show her the pictures from the fair. Janice, fetch the album."

"We can't eat *here*, Dad, because we're going to eat elsewhere."

"Is that why you told me to get dressed up?" she asked, in a miniskirt and a sleeveless blouse.

"And I'm so glad you didn't listen." He winked. "Let's go."

"Chloe," said Janice, "come for dinner on Sunday. Mason will be here with Mackenzie and their new baby boy."

"No, Ma, Chloe won't be able to make it," said Blake, thank God.

"Blakie, wait, don't rush the girl out, I want to show her a picture of the baby—"

"Gotta go. Bye, Mom, bye, Dad."

"Wait! Do you have your phone? He always forgets his phone …"

"Lost it last week, don't worry." He waved, prodding Chloe to his truck.

"Are you going to tell me where you're taking me?"

"Nope."

"I swear, it better not be to your brother's house to see his new baby."

"There's an idea."

"How's Hannah?"

"What, Taylor doesn't give you a full report on us?"

"She's lost touch with Hannah." Taylor was otherwise quite good at keeping Chloe updated. "She told me she's going to start a clipping service for every time she sees your mug in the local paper. Why are you working so hard?"

"I don't work that hard," Blake said. "I fix some roofs and fire pits, read to some blind old ladies, swim, fish."

"Renovate houses, write books, run fairs that make tens of thousands of dollars for local businesses and charities."

"My mother does all the work. I just make the money. She gives it away. To St. Elizabeth's, Meals on Wheels, MADD, Planned Parenthood."

She did a doubletake. "What?"

He chuckled. "Just making sure you're paying attention. My mother loves playing the queen. Yea here, nay there. The other day she got a request from the South Maine Bowling Association asking for new shirts for their bowling league. She's like, how is that charity? And they were like, because we can't afford them."

Chloe laughed. "Where are you taking me?" They were heading into the White Mountains, past Jackson, past Bartlett.

"You'll see. I have a big day planned."

Chloe was happy to be back home. She told Blake she was thinking of not working at all this summer. Just sleeping and repairing her ruined rose bushes. Watching the road. Watching the Internet. "Um, maybe reading *The Blue Suitcase*?"

He shook his head. "First, I don't have physical books yet. In August, if we're lucky. But second, what if, after you read it, you won't want to hang out?"

"Perhaps that's a worthy sacrifice to make for art. Blake, what the heck did you put in that story? Now I'm *dying* to read it."

They turned into the mile-long winding drive of the Mount Washington Hotel, an enormous white, red-roofed resort spread over a hundred acres at the foot of the White Mountains.

"You're taking me to a hotel?" She was being silly.

"To a restaurant in a hotel to be more precise."

They valeted his truck! That must be a first, not to self-park. "Aren't you fancy," she whispered to him, as her door was opened.

"Good afternoon, sir, good afternoon, madam," the valet said to Blake and Chloe. "Are you checking in? Will you be needing a luggage rack?"

Chloe giggled. They called him sir! They asked if they were checking in! "Um, sir, will you be needing a luggage rack?" she teased, as Blake pressed his palm into her back guiding her inside the long gilded lobby. He was treating her to a nice lunch.

"I thought it'd be a welcome change from the dorm fare you've been noshing on. I've acquired quite a sophisticated palate while you've been away. I eat lamb sliders now."

They sat outside on the veranda with a view of the rolling golf course and the full sweep of the mountains. White cloth napkins grazed their laps. It was funny to be so elegant. "You clean up nice, Blake Haul," she said.

"You too, Chloe Divine."

"So are you going to tell me what you and Hannah are up to, or am I going to have to guess?" she asked after he ordered for both of them (!).

"Me and Hannah? I'm good, and she's … well, you'll see for yourself. She's the last part of our afternoon today. But what's going on with you? I saw on your schedule you're taking advanced hiking. Among other things."

She was baffled. "Since when do you look at my schedule?"

"Since your mother showed it to me last time I was over."

"Since when do you go to my mother's house when I'm not there?"

"Since every week when I ask her if she needs anything from the store, and she invites me for dinner."

Chloe stopped sipping her ice tea.

"She does? And do you?"

"Once a week."

"Wait. You eat dinner with my parents once a week?"

"Your parents and Ray. He's a great kid. Makes your mom and dad happy. You did well there, finding him."

"Blake, you're bullshitting me."

"You're changing the subject."

"You mean there's another subject other than you having dinner at my house every week?"

"Absolutely. There's the much more important matter of your schedule." He pulled out a crumpled piece of paper from the pocket of his jeans. It had her course list on it.

"So you don't have your cell phone, but my class schedule is in your pocket?"

"Correct. Advanced Voice? Holocaust studies? Tai Chi?"

The lamb sliders came and distracted Chloe from having to answer Blake's unanswerable question. She knew why she was taking these courses. Affixed to the past, she was polishing away at the edges of an empty cup. Did Blake and her mother discuss this? She almost lost her appetite. Almost, because the sliders with the mint yoghurt sauce were delectable. She didn't respond to his teasing or judging or whatever it was he was doing. They talked about other things.

Over the toffee chocolate bread pudding, Blake said, "You won't believe who died."

"This is how you tell me? Over bread pudding? Who?"

"Lupe."

"Oh no! I'm so sorry. Poor thing. What happened?"

"She was nearly a hundred; maybe that? I loved that old broad. Remember she told me not to go to Europe? Boy, should I have listened to her. It's as if she knew. She said all the drama I could want was right here."

Chloe didn't say there was drama everywhere.

"You want to hear drama?" He leaned toward her over the amazing pudding they were sharing.

She leaned forward too. "What did Hannah do now?"

"That's later. Now it's Lupe's turn. In her will, Lupe left everything to me."

"What do you mean everything?"

"I mean *everything.*"

Chloe stopped mid-gooey-toffee slurp. "Like what? What did she have? She lived in a shack next to somebody else's house."

"So you'd think. Turns out somebody else's house was hers, and the shack, and the ten acres of property leading to the river, and also an antique store in North Conway, and a bed and breakfast in Crawford Notch, near here. Plus a shitload of investments."

"No way!"

"Yeah way. Who knew, right?"

Chloe sat back. "Haven't you done well for yourself. And you thought Hannah couldn't stay away from you after you won a ten thousand dollar prize and made thirty grand fundraising."

"Yeah, more on that later. Eat, before I devour it."

"For three years you lifted Lupe's immobile legs into the car, and now look. Aww." She smiled. "There's a moral in there somewhere."

"Maybe at first glance." He licked the spoon. His eyes were merry, his short hair a little longer, streaked blonder. He had shaved well but missed a small patch where his broad neck met his collarbone. Chloe didn't want to stare at it and make him self-conscious. He was trying so hard. "Lupe's sons, all three of them, raced in from California for the reading of the will, and you can imagine *their* reaction. They're taking me to court.

Trying to overturn the will, to say she died intestate. You should read the documents. It's so bizarre. They're saying I coerced her and sexually dominated her."

Chloe narrowed her eyes. "Are you much known for that?"

"Well, sure, but not with her. She was mad old."

Chloe laughed.

"It's so stupid," Blake said. "I don't even want her stuff."

"Don't say that. You do."

"I don't. It's nothing but trouble. I had to get a lawyer and everything. Hey, maybe you can be my lawyer?" Blake made a frustrated gesture with his hands. "I put shoes on a cute old lady, and suddenly I'm the bad guy. Makes you not want to do anything for anybody."

"Don't worry, they won't win," said Chloe. "I'd love to be your lawyer, Blake. But I have to go to law school first."

"Are you," he asked, almost carefully, "going to law school?"

"Thinking about it, why?"

"Are you taking your LSATs?"

"This October."

"Where, San Diego Law?"

"Thinking about it."

"What, they don't have law schools on the East Coast? Not even one?"

"Maybe one," she said with a return twinkle. Harvard Law was only a few hours away. "But it's why SDU offered me their prized undergrad scholarship in the first place. So I could eventually attend their prized law school."

"Is that what you want to be when you grow up?" he asked, his mouth full of the last bite of bread pudding. "A lawyer in San Diego? Or do you still want to be a florist?" He pitched his baritone higher to sound like her. "Oh, because I sure love the laaaaaw, but flowers are so preeetty."

And she laughed, and the way he looked at her while she was laughing made her feel slightly unsteady even though she was sitting down.

After lunch they wandered around the expansive country club grounds of the hotel. Chloe wondered what the rooms were like, but of course wouldn't *think* of wondering this out loud. She bet they were pretty lux, though. Blake showed her the ballroom with the floor to ceiling Georgian windows and asked if she thought this was a nice place for a white wedding. Or even an off-white wedding, he quipped.

"I don't know," Chloe said. "Who's getting married this time?"

He wouldn't say.

They drove into Crawford Notch to Lupe's bed and breakfast, a cozy maroon guesthouse up in the woody hills. They picked half a meadow of lupines and daisies. Blake said he had plans for the guesthouse if he won in court, but wouldn't tell Chloe what they were yet. On the way back, they bought an ice cream and stopped by Lupe's farm in Jackson. It was quite a spread. There was a large main house and acres of flat and landscaped lawn stretching to the woods that led to the river. There was a four-car garage, and another guesthouse.

"Blake, give up everything else, but definitely fight for this house," said Chloe. "It's pretty special."

"What in the world would I need a house this size for?"

"Eventually you'll want to fill it with little Blakes, no?" She knocked into him as they paced back and forth in front of the property, enjoying their ice cream. "Taylor told me ..."

"Oh, so with Taylor you communicate aplenty." He knocked into her, but gentler.

"What do you mean? You and I emailed all year. Anyway, Taylor told me you were hot and heavy with some chick named Fiona. Where do you even find these girls?"

"Fiona? In a bowling alley." Blake grinned. "The indigent bowling alley with no money for league shirts. She bowled a 270."

"Blake! You went out with a chick because she bowled a 270?"

"What, I need another reason?"

He was impossible. Chloe didn't mention the other thing Taylor had told her: that Fiona was inconsolable, because Blake had broken it off with her in April, out of the blue, just when she thought they were taking their relationship to the next level. Taylor said that Blake invariably seemed to find a girl in the fall and lose her by springtime. That dude has no staying power, Taylor solemnly told Chloe.

"So what's going on with Hannah?"

Blake put an arm around her shoulder and led her toward his truck. "All right," he said. "For the climax of our afternoon, no pun intended, I'll show you Hannah."

A few miles off the main drag in North Conway, out in the boonies, Blake pulled up in front of a modest one-story ranch house by the river.

This time they both walked up the steps to the front porch, littered with kids' toys. Blake knocked.

A few seconds later Hannah appeared at the door. Her hands were covered in flour, her hair, longer and unbleached, fell around her shoulders. Her giant pregnant stomach bumped the screen.

"Oh, look who's back." Her face was full of harried happiness. "Hi, you two. Blake, bad boy, you said you'd call before you stopped by. I'd invite you in, but the house is a wreck. Next time, give me a half-hour warning, will you? Chloe, look at the porch swing we just got. Nice, right? Sit. I'll get you an ice tea." She turned back inside. "Hayley, stop breaking all my eggs!"

"Hannah, wait," Blake said. "We can't sit or stay." His hand circled Chloe's upper arm to keep her from moving toward the swing. "We have to get back. Chloe just wanted to say hi. She approves of my idea, by the way."

"I'm so glad!" Hannah smiled. Hannah. Smiled.

Also stunning: the enormity of Hannah's belly.

Squealing banging noise came from inside the house. "Zhenya, I'll be a sec, keep an eye on the baby!" Hannah shook her head in mild exasperation. "Those kids. Blake, let me know if you need anything. A deposition, or whatever. A statement. I'll write whatever you need. Chloe, can you believe it about those bastards suing Blake? He should be suing them for abandoning their own mother."

"Chloe agreed to be my lawyer," Blake said. "So I can't lose." He squeezed Chloe's arm. He hadn't let go of her yet. "Here." He handed Hannah the field of flowers he and Chloe had picked.

"For me? Thank you, Blake." She kissed him lightly on the cheek. He patted her huge belly.

"When are you due?" Chloe stammered.

"October. I know, I'm a rhino." Hannah beamed. "It's twins."

Chloe needed Blake's hand on her to keep her from reeling. Not from the news. From the joy with which the news was relayed.

"Blakie, I told Orville no way am I getting married," Hannah continued, "until I lose the baby weight. Look at me. I must be two hundred pounds. They don't make wedding dresses in hippo size. Did you check out the ballroom at Mount Washington, by the way? What did you think?"

"We did, but Chloe didn't like it," Blake said. "She thinks something is buried in the parquet. Like chinchillas. That's what she said the place smelled like. Dead chinchillas. Right, Chloe?"

"Blake! Don't listen to him, Hannah. It was perfect. A great place for a, um, wedding." Blake squeezed her arm until she nearly laughed out loud.

In Blake's truck and down the block, Chloe spun to face him. He couldn't hide his howling delight.

"You're terrible!" She slapped his shoulder. "Why didn't you tell me?"

"And miss the shock on your face when you saw her? That was priceless."

"She's having Orville's twins?!"

"Yup. The sucker. I guess he didn't want anyone else giving her rides home anymore. And she's quite grateful for that, as you can see."

"Blake!"

"You know what, Miss Judgy, you should bless their union. I do. Every day I light a candle of thanks. It all worked out. I'm dating girls who know how to bowl, Orville is working two jobs and walking around like he's won the lottery. Hannah too. Who would've thunk? You won't believe what a strict mother she is, by the way. Zhenya doesn't leave the house unless Hannah says she can leave the house."

Chloe watched the passing road all the way to Fryeburg. How unpredictable life was, how surprising, how mystifying. "What's this wacky idea of yours I approve of?"

"If the law is on my side, I'm going to give Lupe's bed and breakfast to Orville and Hannah as a wedding present. They can make a good living there. Did you see its great location?"

Chloe stopped staring at the road and stared at Blake instead.

"Does my mother know any of this about you?" Lupe, Hannah, bed and breakfasts, Orville. Bouquets of lupines for his erstwhile love.

"Know what?" he said. "How young women thank me for car rides?" He raised his eyebrows. "Absolutely."

"Blake!"

★

"Mom," Chloe said to her mother, "is it true what Blake told me? He eats dinner here once a week?"

"Oh, that boy likes to exaggerate," said Lang. "He comes by once in a while …"

"He said every week, Mom."

Her mother demurred. Her father, already sitting at the dinner table, called Chloe over to his side. "You don't want us to feed him, Chloe-bear?" Jimmy asked, kissing his daughter's temple. "How was your day with him?"

"Fine, but—why does he do that? Why do you do that?"

"What, eat?"

"Why don't you invite Hannah or Mason or Taylor over for dinner?"

"For your information," Jimmy said, "your mother would love to have more of your friends over. But Mason is married and busy, and Hannah is pregnant with twins and planning yet another wedding. We're hoping this one takes."

"Go wash your hands," Lang said, opening the back door. "Ray, dinner!"

The four of them sat down, blessed their food, broke bread.

"Geez, Mom. What do you talk about?"

"When?"

"At dinner! With Blake!"

"Don't shout, girl," Jimmy said. "Nobody's deaf."

"Nothing much," Lang said, cutting up Ray's steak. "This. That. He's quite impressed by the deep coral petals of your roses."

"That's not creepy at all, Mom. Why do you talk to him about my schedule at SDU?"

"He asks. What am I supposed to do, lie?" Lang glanced at Jimmy. "Why is she being so ornery about this?"

"Who knows, sweet potato. Pass the salt."

"Because it's weird, Mom. It's supremely weird. How would Burt and Janice feel if I went over there for dinner?"

"Oh, you absolutely should!" Lang exclaimed. "I mean, Janice is not the best cook, you might want to eat a bite here first, but they love you. They're always asking how you are."

"And you tell them."

"Why shouldn't we tell them about our daughter double majoring at a private university," Jimmy said, "possibly heading to Harvard Law School, working two jobs? We can't be proud?"

"Yes, but Mom also tells him about my karate courses and my voice classes."

"*I* don't tell him!" Lang was indignant. "He saw it himself on your class schedule."

"Ahhh!"

The Armchair Detective

"What are you doing?" her mother asked later that night, later that week, later that month. "What are you looking up with such zeal?"

"Nothing."

During the year, to keep two jobs, two majors, twenty-one special dispensation credits and a summa cum laude average, Chloe's searching was by necessity limited. But in the summer, she came home, unpacked, grabbed a Coke from the fridge, and from her reclining La-Z-Boy explored Google's oceanic depths, searching for one lost boy.

Her mother came back with a piece of upside-down pineapple cake, a fruit salad, cheese and crackers. "You know it's a beautiful day out, right?"

"I know. Taylor's coming by in a little while. What are you worried about? Where's Ray?"

"Dad took him to work. Remember this morning he asked if you wanted to come too?"

"I was sleeping, so no."

"Because you were up all night googling."

"Mom, please."

"Chloe Lin Divine, your father and I have discussed it, and we would like for you to be home less. Curfew is sunrise. Can you do that for us? Dad's been leaving his cans of beer right in the fridge, hoping you'll pinch three or four. You're almost twenty-one. You're allowed to go a little crazy."

"Why would I need to steal Dad's beer, Mom? Blake's already twenty-one. He can get me all the beer I need."

"How much beer do you need, sunshine?"

"None."

"You see, that's the problem, right there."

A lot of dead ends on a rural afternoon.

In-A-Gadda-Da-Vida

Blake knocked on her door crazy early one July morning. Even Jimmy hadn't gone to work yet. She heard them exchanging manly pleasantries below, heard her father leave. Blake didn't leave.

"Chloe, it's Blake," her mother called up into the attic.

"Who?"

Oh, nice, she heard Blake say.

She had gone to sleep at three, having been online until all hours, consumed with the cold molecules of the binary universe. All things are numbers. 1,0,1,0,1,0. He is either here, or he's not here. Those are the options. Here. Not here. 1. 0.

"What's wrong?" Chloe said, stumbling downstairs in boxer shorts and tank, meeting him by the screen door standing all big in jeans and work boots, ready for the day. His fitted green T-shirt had a picture of yellow Tweety Bird on it.

"Are you ready?"

"For what?"

"Don't pretend. We agreed yesterday we were going on the Cog Railway."

"We did what?"

"You said you couldn't believe you'd lived here your whole life and never been, and reminisced about how the four of us once tried to go, but missed the turn and went all the way to Berlin around the mountain. Do you remember? How we missed the train?"

She rubbed her eyes, tried to look alive. She remembered how they had missed the train.

"Hurry up if you want breakfast."

"You didn't say you were going to take me *today*!"

"Yes, I said how about tomorrow."

"And what did I do?"

"Well, you laughed, as if you thought I was joking, but I wasn't. So hop to it, rabbit."

"You don't think we've been on enough trains?"

Blake paused, blinked at her cheerfully. "Listen, Chloe-bear. I'm going to take you for a ride on a long red train, all the way up the tallest mountain in the Appalachian range. It leaves at ten. Hurry up."

Chloe looked helplessly at her mother, but she would find no quarter there. Lang was getting the cooler ready! With drinks and potato chips, which Chloe didn't realize needed to be chilled, but whatever. She was also making sandwiches, and filling plastic bags with carrots and chocolate-chip cookies.

"Mom, are Blake and I heading into the Alaskan wilderness? Stop it. For God's sake."

"You'll get hungry. And this way you don't have to spend Blake's hard-earned money. You don't have any of your own. You're jobless."

Chloe opened her hands in barely awake befuddlement.

"Chloe Divine, don't make the poor boy wait any longer than necessary," Lang said. "Go get dressed, young lady. But not *over*dressed. It's going to be hot today. Dress like Blake. Honey, would you like some coffee while you wait for her? I made it fresh."

"Yes, thank you, Mrs. Devine."

Twenty minutes later Lang and Ray were at the door, waving goodbye. "Don't hurry back! Stay out as long as you like! We're having leftovers for dinner."

"Leftovers?" Chloe muttered. "I don't think I've ever heard my mother use that word in a sentence before."

They raced to the mountains. They made it in time for the ten o'clock, just. The red train was half-full. Chloe was hungry, hungry and resentful that her mother was as usual right about the food. As she sat next to Blake, eating her mother's lovingly prepared ham and cheese sandwiches, she remembered Johnny saying to her, you're so lucky, Chloe, so lucky that someone follows you to the end of the road to make sure you're okay. He had said it to her on the train to Tarcento. But at the pensione, Ingrid had mentioned that she came to Italy only to be close to Johnny in case he needed her, and Johnny's father had come to Kurosta, to Treblinka, to Trieste, and Chloe herself saw a man waiting by the gate of the plane that took him away, and she wondered if Johnny perhaps had been lucky himself that he had someone to follow him to the end of the road to make sure he was okay.

Was he okay?

Would she ever know?

Would he ever come for her down the dirt road, with a rifle on his shoulder and a guitar on his back, in officer's duds, a beret on his head, whistling a tune through the pines, as he promised?

"Chloe, why are you crying? Is it the sandwich?"

She swiped the tears from her eyes. The train chugged slowly uphill, the mountain full of green, the view astonishing, the day clear and sunny.

"Blake, did you mean it," she asked, "when you said that you should've listened to Lupe and never gone to Europe?"

He opened his hands. "You're crying now because of something I said a month ago?"

She confessed she didn't know why she was crying.

And Blake, who used to sing—before Europe—placidly started humming something catchy and vaguely familiar. She listened to him, her head turned to the mountains. There was a place in Southern California, down San Diego way, where the dudes played guitar and sang all night in some dark and low café.

She wanted to tell him it wasn't like that, that she spent her days in San Diego in flannel pajamas on Moonlight Beach, being where she dreamed she'd be but being only half a Chloe, living only half a life.

Blake's steady comforting voice was making big talk masked as small talk. Was there was someone special out west? No, no one special, she assured him. She now knew the answer to a question she never wanted to ask. Nothing in her ordinary life ever did compare to Johnny Rainbow.

She kept herself busy in the relentless sunshine, work, school, parties on the weekend, study circles, boys who followed her around. Sometimes she thought she was forgetting and grew all proud of herself, drinking forbidden beer and staying up all night, until one boy at the end of sophomore year said as he was leaving, you keep wanting from me what I don't have, like you think I'm somebody else. This set her back the entire junior run. And now, here they were.

"But there is someone?"

She told Blake she went out a few times with two surfers and a double-major geek like herself, and Blake said, "What, all three at the same time?"

She laughed despite herself.

"And?"

"And what?" She didn't want to tell him what she found out the hard way: that surfer dudes had the most beautiful bodies but were the worst lovers, as if external beauty precluded them from being anything but horizontal monuments, *like statues or chocolate ice cream*. And the double major's modus vivendi was memorizing the names of the stars at the end of his telescope. Omitting the surfers, Chloe told Blake about the philosophic astronomer, who had rhapsodized to her about ontological relativity.

"About what?"

"Ontological relativity," she repeated. "The understanding that nothing can be separated from language, which is symbolic. So there is no actual way of knowing the meaning of any concrete thing, because every concrete thing, like stars and the universe—"

"Stars aren't objective? The universe isn't concrete?"

"Yes, let me—"

"And friendship?"

"No, not concrete. But to finish, since everything is understood only by using language, which is a symbol—"

"I don't agree," Blake said. "Not everything is understood by using language. Sometimes nothing is understood by using language. And other times *nothing* is understood by using anything at all. Nothing is understood."

She tried not to sigh. "You're just proving Felix's point."

"His name is *Felix*, and he's seducing you with ontological relativity? Doofus. No, I'm proving the opposite point. Some things are understood without any language at all. And some things are not understood despite the most advanced language skills."

"Okay, but then, as Felix said, it's all subjective, all relative, and there is no way to actually know anything about anything."

"Hmm," Blake said. "The dude is taking a university course on this?"

"Try a whole major."

"That doesn't sound to you like a waste of his parents' money? He should read a book, available for free at his local library, about the ghost in the machine."

Chloe studied Blake with surprise and amusement. The ghost was the soul, the machine the body. Was there separation between the two, or wasn't there? Two millennia of philosophers argued this point. And poets. *Love's mysteries in souls do grow. But yet the body is his book.*

"What do *you* possibly know about the ghost in the machine?"

"I'm a published writer now," he replied loftily. "I'm paid to know all kinds of things."

That was so endearing. Impulsively leaning over, she kissed his stubbly cheek. "You are so funny," she said.

When the train stopped and they alighted, they found the mesa of the mountain peak disappointingly crowded with other people. Tourists drove their cars to the top of the mountain and parked in a large paved lot. It wasn't as transformative as Chloe had hoped. They could've been on the ugly concrete of an outlet mall. It was like driving cars on a virgin beach. She and Blake carried their cooler to a remote bench, set up a picnic, and stared out beyond into the blue mist vistas. They sat for an hour.

"How does the dude even know he's alive," Blake asked, "if he doesn't know the meaning of anything? What does it even mean to be alive?"

Chloe didn't know. Once she was alive.

She felt pretty alive at the moment, sitting with Blake on the highest Appalachian peak, drinking Coke and eating Lang's ham sandwiches.

"What were you humming earlier?" she asked him as they headed back. "It was nice."

He shrugged and said he didn't know the meanings of all ontological humming symbols, but possibly the humming could be interpreted to mean "Rosalita."

"'Rosalita'? Are you flipping kidding me?" That was Taylor, floating in the lake. They had been drifting for two hours, Chloe in a red ring and Taylor in a blue one, kicking up the water, kicking away the fish. "Why didn't you tell me?"

"Why didn't I tell you what?"

"Honey, have you heard the chorus of 'Rosalita'?"

"No, but so what? Stop reading into stupid things. He didn't even know what he was humming. It could've been 'In-A-Gadda-Da-Vida' for all he cared."

Taylor laughed and dived under her tube. "Girl, you are the squarest chick in this county. Possibly in two adjacent states. What's wrong with you? Do you even know what 'In-A-Gadda-Da-Vida' means?"

"No. And I don't want to."

"I didn't think so. You should be so lucky if that delicious dude sang you that song—"

Chloe cut her off. She knew all about the Iron Butterfly gypsy tune. "He wasn't singing to *me*, I told you. He was humming to himself."

"Swell difference. Well, in 'Rosalita' he sings that you are his stone desire."

"Stop! Why can't someone just hum, non-ontologically? Why does it have to mean things?"

"He just wants to be your lover, baby."

"Which song is that or are you making unsupported observations?"

"Correct," said Taylor. "Blind friend, have you seen how yummy he is, how jacked? The other day when they were at our house working on a transmission, I overheard him telling my Joey that his favorite tool was the demolition hammer. I nearly came right then and there."

"Taylor!"

"Chloe, Fiona still calls me up bawling three times a week. That boy's got game. Swear to me on your boobs, you haven't once thought of him using the demolition hammer on you—"

"Taylor, I swear on all things holy, if you say *one* more word ..."

Blake calling to the girls from his dock. Hey, what are you two giggling about? Everyone on the lake can hear you.

God, Chloe hoped not. The girls giggled all the more.

Chloe did only one actual thing in July. She turned twenty-one. The rest of the time she slept, ate, swam, played with Ray, floated, bowled, fished, drank Blake's beer, tailgated off Blake's truck, visited Hannah, and occasionally opened a celebrity magazine. She wanted to be and not to think, and most of the time she succeeded, except at night.

At night she tried to convince herself that it was all for the best. Sometimes she tried to hypnotize herself into believing it was better he didn't come looking for her, better she didn't find him.

That way she was never disillusioned.

Or disappointed, or bored.

There wasn't any bickering.

(Or Christmas.)

No shopping in crowded malls, waiting for the car to be brought around, being hot in your parka, knowing as soon as you got outside you would freeze.

No getting fuel in the rain, no flat tires.

His hands never smelled of gasoline.

They were never broke. Or had to get up in the middle of the night to let the dogs out, or because she heard a noise.

She never heard a noise.

She pretended she wanted a routine with him, but she wouldn't trade it for the sublime with him, not when their fused celestial bodies had imagined that everything else would one day be perfect too. Or that nothing could be as perfect.

Either way it wasn't real.

Just a fairytale, a dream divine, a breath barely taken.

Her lungs filled with his fake name and, for one shining day, life became extraordinary.

And even before she exhaled, he was already receding. Every moment with him was the one before the one before the one before the last.

But every once in a while when her body ached with loneliness, Chloe craved not the aria burst of Italian fire, but the elevator muzak of daily love. Every once in a while she longed to find someone else in the woods. She slept and wandered, hopelessly lost in the brambles, in every new face searching for him and the way out.

Faith

"Mom, do you think he'll ever come looking for me?"

"No, my love," said Lang.

Chloe wouldn't speak to her mother afterward, wouldn't listen to her explanations.

"Ask me another question," Lang said.

"Like I'd ever."

"I think the best you can hope for," Lang said, "is to find out what happened to him, and for that you'd have to learn who he is. Every year that goes by makes the task more difficult."

"Should I keep trying?"

Her mother sat at the table, hulling strawberries. Jimmy Devine loved coming home to the smell of warm treacly jam. The screen door to the back was open, the birds were chirping, the lake glistened through the birches, it was peaceful, mid-summer, it smelled fantastic, it was green and warm. Her mother's silence filled Chloe with so much sadness, she had to turn away.

"My angel beloved," Lang said from behind her. "My darling child. What do you hope for?"

"He promised me he would come back," Chloe whispered. "Can you understand that?"

"I can. But he hasn't."

"He could've lost my number! I gave it to him on a piece of paper. You know how some people are with pieces of paper. They always lose them. Look at Blake."

Lang nodded. "Perhaps he lost yours. Is that what you hope for?"

"Clearly."

"Okay. Say you find him. He is Brad Jones, son of Bill Jones, grandson of Bud Jones, distracted phone number loser. Then what?"

Chloe's face was turned toward the window, to outside. She heard her mother's voice from behind her. "If he wanted you to know his real name, wouldn't he have told you?"

"He was trying to reinvent himself," Chloe said. "He told me that his name was not his name to disclose. He was trying to protect his father."

"How hard is it, do you think, to get in touch with you?"

"I don't know. I've been trying to get in touch with him, and I haven't been successful, have I?"

"He would've had to forget your father was chief of police of a small town."

"No, Mom," Chloe snapped. "All he would've had to do was forget the name of my small town."

Lang lowered her head. "Or that you go to the University of San Diego."

"There are four universities in San Diego!"

"You've searched through fifty states for Lone Star. He can't look through four universities? He can't look you up on Facebook? You're plain and prominent enough there."

"He doesn't have a computer. He doesn't have a Facebook account. A thousand things. Mason is not on Facebook. Neither are you. Neither is Blake. For God's sake!"

"What if he just moved on, Chloe?"

"Do you know how much you're not helping?"

"I'm trying to help you work through the possible endings. Do you want to learn he's forgotten you, and moved on?"

"I don't want riddles from you too, Mother."

"Not riddles. Questions."

"Stop with the questions."

"What if he died in that damn Afghanistan, what if his life ended years before your story begins?"

Chloe burst into tears.

Lang put down the strawberries. She got up and walked to Chloe, who, besieged with fright and desperation, actually let her mother touch her. Let her mother hug her. On Lang's shoulder, she bent her head and bawled.

"My sweetest girl," Lang said, gentle as a hummingbird, "I want to help you. But you haven't thought it through."

"You're being truly terrible right now," said Chloe, sniffling. "You're being the worst. I'm going to write a story about you for advanced composition. Just wait till you see how you come off. Terrible, that's how." She didn't stop her mother from touching her, embracing her.

"Leave it be, angel. Let it go, my love. Go swim, and I'll make you your favorite honey cake."

In the lake Chloe lay on the water float, eyes to the sky, and she lay in the hammock as the sun set, eyes to the sky, and she sat like a mute at the dinner table, eyes at her plate with her father asking every minute, "Chloe-bear, what's the matter?" She lay on her bed up in the loft and stared at the wooden rafters, and tried to listen to her mother's voice of reason, to her own voice of reason. She tried to heed the passing of time. She felt distant from San Diego, from Blake, from her parents, from herself. She flew to the only place she felt connected to in the universe, over the oceans and the distant miles to the room near the castle by the sea. All the windows were open because it was stifling hot, and she saw the stars over the Adriatic, and the swell of the green water, even at night, heard the occasional car passing, the laughter of women at a nearby bar. It was so vivid, and his parched voice murmuring. *Chloe, sometimes you have to have faith even if you don't have proof. Especially if you don't. Look at my grandparents.*

Binary Boys and Sentient Girls

They were standing face to face on her dock when Taylor and Joey drove up in his Explorer to have a swim and a picnic.

"What have you wrought, Chloe," Blake said, waving to their friends. "Nobody works because of you. Taylor is going to get fired from Applebee's. Joey hasn't fixed a car in days. You've corrupted everybody with your indolent summer."

"Who wants to work, this is way more fun," Taylor said, putting down the towels. "What are you two up to?" And it must have looked strange. They had been standing close to the edge of the dock facing each other, Chloe all coiled up in her *moroto dori* Aikido position of full frontal offensive, and Blake at complete ease as if loitering.

"She is trying to show me what she has learned so far after one hundred and seventy thousand dollars worth of schooling," said Blake, "and I'm refraining from knocking her into the water for the ..."

He trailed off as she struck out, attacking with her arms, and he twisted out of her way and with the back of his forearm swatted her off the dock and into the lake. "For the—what is it, Haiku, twenty-first time, or twenty-second?" He catapulted into the water and swam after her. She swam away, giggling.

Taylor watched them, nodding wisely, as if the high school graduate understood in its entirety the ontological relativity of all metaphysical arguments. "Hey, did you know," she said officiously as if reading from an educational manual for professors, "that your best chance of finding a compatible mate is sixteen blocks from the home where you grew up?" She plunked herself cross-legged onto the dock and opened her *Redbook* magazine.

"Taylor! Shut up," Chloe said from the water. "Put down the magazine and go jump in the lake."

"Nice. Do you want to hear the rest or no?"

"No!" Blake and Chloe both exclaimed, and laughed.

"The part I don't get, Taylor," said Blake, "is why such a specific number? Why not five blocks? Or thirty-three? And what if there's no one remotely attractive enough who lives sixteen blocks away? What do you do then? How far does Joey live from you? I thought he was from New Hampshire."

"This isn't about me," Taylor said. "This is about you." Even Joey had had enough and picked her up and threw her into the lake, *Redbook* magazine and all.

Nothing is like bobbing on Blake's floating dock in the deep part of the lake on an August afternoon. In a blue tankini Chloe lies on her back and he is spread out next to her in black swim trunks. She pretends to tan, but she's just looking up at the sky. It's quiet except for their occasional speaking; he murmurs something; she echoes back. Dad is working. Janice and Burt are at Home Depot. Mom and Ray are at the waterpark. Blake and Chloe had offered to take him, but Lang said no. She wanted to. Stay here, she said. Relax. You've done enough. Chloe ponders this, because she knows she's done nothing. Literally nothing. They had swum, dived, argued about distilled spirits and the best soil for jacarandas and almost made a bet that Chloe could grow and keep a palm tree in the Maine weather if Blake would build her a greenhouse for it. They wondered whether there was any time before she flew back to drive down to the ocean and Chloe said, I see the ocean twice a week in San Diego, and he said yes, because it's all about you. And then he added, it's not even about the ocean, it's about the drive. You know how much I like to drive. But I also like gratitude. And smiling she played along and said, why would I want to thank you for driving me to a place I don't want to go, and he said, geez, maybe just to be polite? And she tried hard not to laugh, her body shaking from the effort. How do you know you don't want to thank me, he said. What if you really really do—and suddenly in front of her eyes there appears a mountain and a glen full of cacti, long and tall, saguaros maybe, and not one, but myriad! What an odd vision, she thinks, and there is tremendous heat. She is hot, parched, panting, sweating. Nothing makes sense. And then Chloe hears Blake say, "Binary boys like sentient girls."

She opens her eyes and moans. She is sitting up on the dock, leaning back on her arms. She is naked. Her blue tankini floats in the water. His blond streaked head is pressed deep into her bare breasts, into her wet nipples, his big work hands fondle her, his lips are hot in her white neck, and she is moaning, and then he pushes her down onto her back and opens her legs. And vanishes. She looks up and sees nothing but sky. Her fingers grip the edge of the dock. Her body writhes in agitated, desperately longed-for incineration. The mountains in the distance are embroidered with her scarlet cries. She reaches down, grabs hold of his shaggy head, begs him, slower slower, she doesn't want it to end, the indiscreet things he is doing to her with his mouth are making her body curve upward, and then he gets up and stands over her, naked himself, throttle on full. She gasps, reaches for him, and—

"Chloe, are you okay? You're whimpering."

She reels away from him on the bobbing dock. She is wobbling, she is panting. She doesn't say a word. Any moment she will keel over and pitch into the water. That would be a blessing. Was she only dreaming? It's not possible! It was so real! She glances down, to check for her bathing suit. It's disappointingly on, the blue nylon fabric covering what was just fully exposed to his eyes, to his hands, to his mouth. She feels so let down. Her body, her soul stretching over her bones like fine fevered jello, Chloe can't look at him in her mortification and regret.

"What's happening?" he says (in pretend confusion?).

She lies back down. She doesn't want him to see her tremble. Big-bodied and half-naked he lies next to her. He looks normal, pleasing, twinkling, not ... full on, the way he was in her reverie, and he looks *at* her normal too, not the way he just looked at her in the reverie when all the outrageous gifts of the universe were about to be bestowed upon her body, on the lake, in full view of eight summer homes, parents coming back, young Latvian boys running into the water, moms bringing out pitchers of lemonade, dads displaying the hunky new tools they brought back from the DIY store, maybe an impact drill or a sabre saw. Holy mother, hear my prayer. The mad beast with a thousand mouths. She can never look at him again. What's wrong with her? It's Blake!

Finally Chloe dares to speak. "Did you just say to me that binary boys like sentient girls, or did I dream that?"

"I don't know how to answer that," Blake says, after a measured pause of staring up at the drifting clouds. "Did you dream it because you wanted me to say it?"

"No, I want ontological absolutism. Just so that I don't ascribe to you things you didn't say." Or ascribe to you brazen things you didn't do.

"I didn't say it," Blake says. "Though I can say it right now if you want me to, because it's true and I believe it. But I don't always say true things that I believe." Another gaze into the blue heavens. "Like that one."

She dives into the water to cool herself down, and starts swimming to shore. "Must have been some dream," he says into her back, diving in after her.

Why does that word—sentient—bang the drum of her heart, the drum of her everything, with such wanton longing? Is it because it's a responsive word? If the girl begs to be touched, then here is a binary boy ready to touch her.

Nonchalant and Indifferent

Ray was trampling her flowers, pretending he was weeding, while Chloe and Blake straddled the picnic bench under the pines by the lake. Indifferent to the havoc Ray was wreaking in her prized garden, turned to each other, they were playing cat's cradle with a long piece of string.

She was very good at the game, and he wasn't good at all but, as always, pretended to be. Ray was hiding from them in the bushes, they were chatting with each other, the light was waning, the mosquitoes rising, the summer almost gone, when Chloe, her mouth full of a teasing smile, looked into Blake's face, only inches away, and recalled the pose, the proximity, almost the same light, a third of a life ago. She inhaled a short *ahh* of pungent memory, blushed, and then caught the look in his eye. He was relaxed in body, but intense of expression. They stared at each other. She said nothing. He said nothing. There wasn't a breath, just a thickening of the dusky air, and an inclination forward. He tilted his head. At her elbow, Ray nudged her. "Okay, I weed your stupid flowers," he proclaimed. "Now what do you want me to do?"

"Go inside and fetch us some lemonade, bud," said Blake, not taking his eyes off Chloe. His forearm rested on the table against her forearm. Their four hands were intertwined in the string.

Lang came outside. "Not lemonade, it's time for dinner, you three. Blake, are you staying?"

Chloe blinked, exhaled, moved away. Blake held her elbow to steady her off the bench. He stood up. "Thank you, Mrs. Devine, but no. I'm coming tomorrow for Chloe's last night. Tonight I'm having dinner with my own mother. She says she hasn't seen me. My books were supposed to arrive today. I hope to be able to give your daughter a copy before she flies back. Maybe you can read it on the plane, Chloe?"

"I'd like that," Chloe said. "I'll be right in, Mom. I just need a minute."

Lang ushered Ray inside, and Blake turned smiling to Chloe. They sat back down at the picnic table, more demurely. Chloe took a breath. Before anything else could happen, she had to ask Blake a question. Not a riddle. An actual question. She didn't know if he knew the answer. She didn't know if he would tell her even if he did. But she was out of options.

"Blake," she said, "I need to ask you something …"

He leaned forward. "Yes?" The smile still played on his face.

"Do you remember the bus ride to Treblinka?"

Slightly he stiffened. "What about it?"

"Do you remember Yvette or Denise telling you about how they knew Johnny's uncle?"

He moved away. "I think so." His smile faded.

"They mentioned a town, either where they met the uncle or knew him from."

"Yes, so?"

"Do you by any chance remember the name of that town? It was something like Casual, or Nonchalant, or …"

She wished she could take it back. His wounded face grew so immediately cold. She regretted asking for the ten seconds it took him to rise from the bench, to step away from her toward the clearing, to get ready to leave, to run, go back to his house, to not look back. But she didn't regret asking after he spoke.

"Carefree," Blake said, his face anything but.

Chloe sucked in her breath, afraid to miss a syllable. "Carefree where?"

"Carefree, Arizona."

What relief. He remembered. "Thank you," she mouthed to him. "Thank you."

Without saying a word, he started to walk away.

"Bye?" she said into his back.

"Bye," he said, the pine needles crunching under his boots.

"Blake," she called after him. "Are you upset or something?"

"I'm not upset or something," he said. "See ya."

But he didn't see her. He begged off the farewell dinner the following night, saying he had other plans, and he didn't bring her a copy of *The Blue Suitcase*, and he didn't answer his cell, but that could've been because he'd lost it again. When she called his house, his mother said he wasn't there. When Chloe had walked halfway uphill to check, his truck wasn't under the carport.

The morning she was leaving for Logan to fly back to San Diego, he had gone out, he wasn't even home!

"Please tell him I said goodbye, Mrs. Haul," said a dejected Chloe, standing at his screen door.

"I will, honey. He'll be sorry he missed you. But we'll see you at Christmas, right?"

"My parents are coming to San Diego instead, Mrs. Haul. Please remind Blake to send me his book when he finally gets his copies."

"What do you mean, they came days ago." Janice shook her head. "That boy. Sometimes I don't know about him. Wait here. He probably thought he already gave you one. You know how absent-minded he can be. Do you know he lost his phone again? Third time this summer. Boys, right?"

Janice brought out the slim tome. Glossy white cover, with nothing on the front but an embossed electric blue suitcase and Blake's name.

She was walking back to her house, clutching the book to her chest like in high school, when his black truck came barreling up the hill. She waved and stepped to the side of the narrow road so he wouldn't run her over. The truck slowed down, almost reluctantly, Chloe thought. She approached the driver's window. He rolled it down, almost reluctantly. They didn't speak for a moment.

"I got your book," she said, showing him.

"Ah, good," he said. "I was sure you'd left already. Isn't your plane in a few hours?"

"Five hours," Chloe said, frowning at his grim face, at his not getting out of the truck, at his not even putting the truck into park, judging by the vehicle's irregular spin of black tires. "Why didn't you bring me a copy like you said you would?"

"I was going to send it to you." His unsmiling eyes, the color of wet sand today, looked somewhere left of her face, left of her inquiring gaze.

Her father yelled for her from down the hill. Come on, Chloe, we have to go, you'll miss your plane.

"Better run along," Blake said.

"Why are you upset with me?"

"I'm not upset."

"Come on."

"Why should I be upset? You owe me nothing. You made that clear. I'm fine."

Her blood went up. Hostile but not knowing what to say, not having a defense for herself, she stepped off the narrow path, into the underbrush, to let him pass, to let him go.

"Don't you know anything?" he said. "Don't they teach you anything in that damn school of yours?"

Clearly not how to find your way out, or make your way back, or use detective skills, or be the kind of girl a boy might come back for, or the kind of girl who wouldn't go around disappointing her closest, most intimate friends. And worst of all, the very worst of all, teach her not to be the kind of girl who was so overjoyed to get a single word that meant something or might lead somewhere that she didn't even have any regrets except one. That she hadn't asked Blake sooner.

"They teach me everything I need to know, thank you very much."

"Not the important things."

"And what in your opinion are those?" Chloe said, snide as snide can be. Both her parents were yelling now.

"That the dude who goes off to war never comes back." Blake raised his hand before Chloe spoke again. "*Never*. I can't believe you don't know that basic fact."

"No, that's not true, his grandparents … you don't know about them, don't—"

"It's been three years!" Blake's voice broke with strangled emotion. "A thousand days. I may not know much about chicks or the fucking meaning of life, but I'm a guy, and I know this— that if I wanted to find you again, and there was breath still left in my body, there would be nothing that could stop me. *Nothing!*"

She opened her mouth to speak.

"Save it," he said. "I don't give a shit anymore. I'm done, Chloe. I'm fucking done."

"Blake …"

He cut her off. Not by arguing, or yelling, or raising his hands, or getting out of the truck, or grabbing her or shaking her, or anything her. He cut her off by stepping on the gas and dusting her with the wheels of his F-150 as he revved away, not looking back.

The Blue Suitcase

A young, extremely good-looking man named Alastair thought he was going to haul junk for a living, but he became a private detective instead. He lived in Maine, and ran his small business with his brother Marley. They thought they would do well since private eyes were a rare commodity in their area. But the business struggled. No one was interested in their services.

One day, a local woman named Lenora DuPrix called to hire them for a "small but very important job."

Lenora was a stern humorless woman who had recently lost her mother. Lenora told the brothers that she had hired a junk-hauling company to clear the unwanted things from her mother's house, but they accidentally, or on purpose, took something that was never meant to be taken. This is where Alastair and Marley came in. Lenora wanted the brothers to locate the junk dealers and retrieve the missing article: a shiny hardshell electric blue Samsonite suitcase.

She offered them a thousand dollars for this seemingly simple job, but when they called the number for the junk dealers, they discovered it was a bogus business. There was no such thing as BCN Junk Professionals in Denmark, Maine. There was not even a house at the fake street address the two men had given Lenora.

Alastair and Marley were ready to give up. Lenora wasn't. She increased the price for the recovery of the suitcase. She offered them fifty thousand dollars plus all expenses. At first the amount seemed startlingly large. It was two years' profit.

But then Alastair asked what was in the suitcase. After Lenora told him, he began to suspect fifty thousand dollars wasn't nearly enough. The suitcase contained all the jewelry that had been given to the mother by the father over seven decades of their marriage. The mother had been partial to rubies, her birthstone. Most of the bracelets, necklaces, rings and pins were rubies. The jewelry had tremendous sentimental value. It was irreplaceable. But it also had actual value. It was worth over a million dollars. Lenora suspected that the men who took it were not junk dealers but jewel thieves who had come to rob her.

Alastair and Marley set out to find the purveyors of this theft. They learned that near the fake address in Denmark, two men with foreign accents had recently rented a broken-down shack in the woods. A few weeks ago they vanished. One of the men, a creepy guy with a long greasy ponytail, went by the name of Giancarlo. The other one was called Rubio, but he was the assistant, not the ringleader, according to the landlady. They told the landlady they had come from Latvia, but she thought they were lying. They looked vaguely Mediterranean. She said she was glad they were gone because the neighbors kept complaining about the noise and the filth. Late at night they would get drunk, break bottles and sing very loudly, even though they were both terrible singers, absolutely atrocious.

During a search through and around the dump of the rented house, Alastair and Marley found an empty matchbook from a restaurant in Riga. They asked Lenora for additional funds to cover international travel and followed this thin trail to Latvia. They met many unsavory characters, dark shady men doing dark shady things. They learned there was active black market for precious gems.

Pretending they wanted to buy some expensive jewelry at a discount price, our heroes were finally led to Giancarlo. He was a real charmer. They hated him immediately. They confronted him about the blue suitcase.

At first Giancarlo fiercely denied ever laying his hands on this suitcase. After Alastair and Marley persisted, he admitted that he and Rubio did indeed take it from Lenora, and then as a joke, swore on Rubio's life that there had been nothing in it of any value. When he saw that the brothers were in no mood for jokes, Giancarlo changed his story slightly. He told them that he took the Samsonite, but didn't realize he wasn't supposed to. He and Rubio were paid to clean the house of junk, and that is what they did. He was very sorry for the inconvenience. He had sold the blue suitcase to another junk dealer in Warsaw. For a price he agreed to take the brothers to him.

Giancarlo was a snake-oil salesman, and Alastair and Marley knew it. They had no choice but to trust him. They gave him half of the agreed upon sum, and traveled with him to Poland. In Warsaw, Giancarlo had the brothers cornered, beaten and robbed in an alley, and all remaining expense money from Lenora stolen. They searched for Giancarlo in Warsaw, but the man disappeared. The brothers concluded that Giancarlo knew very well what was inside the blue suitcase and wanted the contents of it for himself. And who wouldn't?

Enraged, injured, and now with a personal stake in the outcome, they agreed between themselves that a fifty thousand dollar payment was not nearly enough to balance the grave risk to their life and limb. They decided that if and when they eventually recovered the suitcase, they would take some of the rubies for themselves. To justify this course of action, the brothers reasoned that if they were truly terrible men with no scruples, they would keep the entire suitcase for themselves, as Giancarlo was clearly planning to, and never return to Maine, or see Lenora again. While stuck in Warsaw with no cash and no leads, they fantasized about what they would do with a million dollars worth of rubies.

The brothers had no choice but to call Lenora to ask for another infusion of cash. While they waited for the wire to come through, they tried to figure out from where in Europe Giancarlo could possibly conduct his nefarious business. While Googling for some possibilities at an Internet café, Alastair keyed in the initials of the fake Maine junk company, BCN, into the search engine, and the very first item that came up was Barcelona International Airport. BCN.

It was nothing more than a hunch, but the brothers had no other leads. They decided to follow it. Giancarlo looked as if he could be from Spain. They headed south.

In the underbelly of Barcelona, Alastair and Marley encountered a network of jewelry thieves far more elaborate than in Riga or Warsaw. They could not ferret out Giancarlo. He was too well protected on his own turf. Our two heroes were beaten up, plied with drugs, thrown off trains. They refused to give up. They contrived a plan to lure away Giancarlo's bodyguards with a clever deployment of irresistible strippers, and then to impersonate them (bodyguards not strippers). Once Giancarlo was in their clutches, they would persuade him by all interrogatory means in their power to return the stolen suitcase. The mission had become very personal for the brothers.

They succeeded in this thrilling and elaborate sleight of hand. The bodyguards were seduced, tied up and muzzled, and Alastair and Marley, in masquerades, accosted Giancarlo, who himself was a masquerade. They dragged him into an alley, tackled him and beat him, demanding he surrender what was never his.

A bloodied but unbowed Giancarlo gleefully informed Alastair and Marley that yes, he and his partner Rubio travelled all over the United States, posing as junk dealers and preying on the gullible daughters of recently deceased mothers. They removed jewelry from their homes, and then brought it to Europe to sell over their vast underground network. Giancarlo admitted he cleaned out Lenora's mother's house, and he had taken the blue suitcase because he assumed from its prominent position in the bedroom that it contained valuable items. But neither the suitcase nor its contents were here with him in Barcelona. The suitcase never made it to Europe.

"I already told you this in Riga," Giancarlo said, "and you didn't believe me. You should've listened to me, you morons. The suitcase contained nothing valuable. Only old papers. Think of all the trouble you could've saved yourselves and me, if you had only returned to the States immediately, when you learned weeks ago you were chasing nothing but a phantom."

Alastair and Marley hadn't believed him then, and they believed him even less now. They resumed beating him until Giancarlo pleaded for his life. Swearing on every church, cross, saint, Buddhist temple, he vowed what he was telling them was true. He was so disgusted with the worthless Samsonite that he never even took it to Europe. He left it where he opened it, in the woods right behind the rented shack.

Alastair and Marley refused to believe him. They had walked around the small cottage in Denmark and nothing blue caught their eye in the forest. They knew that if there were no rubies, they would get no money. Enraged at Giancarlo's repeated assertions to the impossibility of their demand, they continued to physically insist Giancarlo produce what he didn't have. During this night of endless assault and interrogation, they dragged him to a remote Barcelona beach on the Mediterranean coast. Their desperate ploy of waterboarding to get him to disclose the location of the suitcase went on one minute too long. Giancarlo drowned and died in the shallow waters.

Now they were truly out of options. They disposed of Giancarlo's body in the sea, and returned home to Maine, defeated and penniless. Before they went to see Lenora to tell her of their failure, they decided to drive to the Denmark shack one last time to confirm for themselves that Giancarlo had been lying.

They spotted the electric blue suitcase almost right away. They didn't know how they had missed it the first time. It was almost in plain sight, in the woods, a few yards away from the house. It lay on its side in a ditch, partly covered with old leaves and moss. The thieves hadn't even bothered locking it after they ransacked it; the locks were still flapping open.

What a horror. Giancarlo had been telling the truth! To the brim, the small case was filled with nothing but papers. Junk. There was no million dollars worth of jewels, no rubies. After latching it and cleaning it off, Alastair and Marley took it to Lenora's house, ready to confess everything.

Through the curtain of her living room, Lenora saw them walking to her front door, carrying the blue case. She dashed out, grabbed it out of their hands, asked tremulously if it was full when they found it, and when they said yes, she started to weep. She ran back inside the house, carrying the case like a baby in her arms. Bewildered, they followed her inside. They found her sitting on the floor of the living room, face streaked with tears, suitcase open at her legs, papers spilling out. She was on the phone with her sisters. "They found it," she cried. "By God, they found it!"

Alastair and Marley stood baffled. One thing had to be true: either Lenora or they had gone insane. She wiped her face, got up off the floor, went to her desk and wrote them a check. She handed it to Alastair. The check was for a hundred thousand dollars—double what she had agreed to pay them.

"If I told you the suitcase had in it nothing but letters," Lenora said, "would you have risked your life and searched all over Europe to find it and bring it back for me and my sisters? I know human beings, and I knew that if you believed the case had a million dollars worth of jewelry, you would bluster and chafe at being grossly underpaid. Which would make you turn Eastern Europe upside down to find it. And I was right."

The brothers were aghast. They did a lot more than turn Europe upside down. They killed a man. Granted, he deserved to be dead, but still. They didn't want his death to be on their hands.

"What's really in that thing?" Alastair asked.

"Love," Lenora replied. "Nothing but love."

She took out an envelope from the desk. The envelope contained a letter from her mother. Alastair and Marley read it.

"My dear daughters," the letter began. "Of all the things in my house, I beg you, implore you, command you, preserve the contents of the blue suitcase with your entire hearts, with your entire souls. Everything else is vanity. In the suitcase is each and every one of the letters your father wrote to me over our seventy-four years of married life. I leave you these letters to let you see with your own eyes how he loved me once. I leave you love instead of rubies."

39

Senior Summer

San Diego University Senior Schedule

FALL SEMESTER:
Fitness Triathlon
Kant's Deontological Ethics
Special Topics in Music Theory
Armed Conflict in American History
Philosophy of Law
Internship Law Society

SPRING SEMESTER:
Judo Multi-level
Belief and Unbelief
Plants and Landscapes
Post Tonal Music
Drugs in U.S. Society
Philosophy of Love
Philosophy of God

Dani Falco

Dear Chloe,

I'm glad you liked my story. Thanks for letting me know—again. As I said before, it means a lot that you liked it.

To answer your other question, I haven't been in touch because I've been super busy. Besides working, I spent most of February and March in court, trying to clear my name from accusations of thievery and greed. We settled a few weeks ago. Best thing really. I was done with the MF lot of them. I get to keep Lupe's Jackson house and the bed and breakfast for Hannah and Orville. I'm also elbow deep in the Spring Fair prep. We're expecting fifty thousand people this year. Mother has quit her school job to administrate. Dad and I are building a stage. Nick Santino and The Maine are performing.

I must run, I'm supposed to be babysitting my nephew, not emailing. Best of luck with deciding on law school. I'm sure SDU will be perfect if you stay on. You'll make a pretty good lawyer and a fine florist wherever you go.

P.S. I know you're sorry and confused and whatever, but you gotta work out your shit, Chloe, all the shit. Or not. I'm good either way. I've got nothing more to add on the subject. Stop asking.

Blake

Dear Chloe,

I hear you, sister, you sound swamped. You're almost at the end though, a college grad. So exciting. As for your question, we've seen a bit of Blake, not much, because he's been wrapped up in that lawsuit. They settled out of court, but Joey says Blake should've never done it because he definitely would've won. From Joey I heard he's been keeping time with Dani Falco from seventh period trig, remember her? She was the one with the braids and the thick glasses. Apparently, she let her hair out and got contacts, so.

They didn't break up in April. Dani told her brother who told his best friend who told Joey that it was getting serious between them. FWIW, don't be surprised if there's an announcement soon, said Dani's brother's best friend to Joey.

Write, if you have time, but otherwise, I'll see you in a month. I think Joey might propose soon too! Fingers crossed. Can't believe you're driving back by yourself. That's mofo scary! You're a ninja.

Love,

Taylor

Lone Star at the Flying Monkey

Blake's casual but costly mention of Carefree, Arizona, leads Chloe to an oblique Tumblr post deep in the search pages, with a sad face next to the title, *Lone Star at the Flying Monkey.*

Come back, Lone Star, the post reads. *How we miss you on rowdy Saturday nights. Please come back.* No address, except *the copper state.* She researches that one. Apparently it's the other nickname for Arizona. Well, Carefree is in a copper state. And when she googles further, she finds this: a Flying Monkey joint in downtown Phoenix. About an hour from Carefree. A small lead. But a lead nonetheless.

After graduation weekend, her parents fly back home with Ray, while Chloe jams her boxes into the used red VW Beetle her parents had bought her for sophomore year Christmas and takes off one morning after sunrise for the copper state.

There are a million reasons to let him go, and only one to drive through the rain shadow dust of the parched Mojave Desert north of Yuma, all dirt and brown sand. The ink isn't dry on her degree, the ink isn't dry on her twenty days on another continent. His rendition of "The One I Love" still crowds her soul. Kierkegaard is right. Each human being has infinite reality. She can barely remember what he looks like, but she cannot forget what she felt like when she looked at him. The ragtag troubadour has not given Chloe back her only heart.

The Flying Monkey is a dive bar with a stage in the back. The burly dude with tattoos on his neck and his gut falling out of his easy-fit jeans looks as if he hasn't slept or shaved since the Lone Star days. His name is Lou.

"Johnny Rainbow? Boy, you're *really* dredging up the past," he says. "I haven't seen him in years. He's not in town, cause I woulda heard about it. I didn't, so."

"You remember Lone Star?" Chloe holds on to the edge of the counter. It's mid-afternoon, almost opening time. The clean glasses are stacked in pyramids along the bar. It's quiet. It smells of fermented hops and old smoke.

"*Him.* I remember him," Lou corrects her. "Who could forget? What a piece of work he was. Did some wild shit. But I never in my life heard a voice like his. Before or since."

"That's him," says Chloe.

"He was the only thing on that stage. For years I had people coming in asking about the kid who sang Red Hot Chili Peppers' 'Johnny Kick a Hole in the Sky.' He was something, that animal man."

She cries, she cries. "Do you remember his name?"

Lou frowns. "Are you being funny with me or something? You know his name. Johnny Rainbow."

"I mean his real name."

"Nah, have no idea." He busies himself with wiping the counter.

"What happened to his band?"

Lou shrugs with hostile indifference. "What always happens? The lead singer and the guitarist chick start banging other people and their dreams of stardom vanish with the latest bonk."

Chloe wants to know if that is what happened.

"It was a long time ago, girly," Lou says. "I got a lot of bands coming through here, I can't remember why they all stopped playing."

Chloe listens to him, appraises him. For some reason this overflowing man sounds too clipped in his speech. Chloe peruses the options why. "Is that what happened here?" she repeats, gleaning something.

"I don't remember."

"You don't remember Lone Star or you don't remember what happened?"

Lou mumbles. She asks him to repeat. He mumbles. She asks him to repeat.

"Look, sweetheart, what do you want? Do I remember him? Sure I remember him. I told you. You hear him sing, you don't forget a thing like that."

Chloe stays motionless and mute.

"But that's not enough. Are you here on his behalf or something? Is he looking for a gig again? I'm not interested. I was glad for the business he brought. But that boy was trouble. With a capital T. A larger door means nothing if the cops are shutting me down, or worse, throwing me in jail for illegal shit conducted on my premises."

"Are you saying you let Johnny go because he was doing things in your club?"

"I'm not saying that." He glares at her suspiciously. His bulbous nose inflates. "Who did you say you are?"

"I'm not sent by him, or by anyone. This isn't entrapment. I'm just trying to find him."

"Get in line, girly," Lou says. "Look, I can tell you I didn't want to fire him. He was a sweet kid. Sure, Lou. Sorry, Lou. I know the rules, I know the law. Don't worry. Won't happen again. And then the next weekend, bam. More trouble. More dudes coming to my place, dealing, using, fights, cops, just awful. And on Mondays I'd haul his ass in here and say, now look here, Johnny, and he'd be all smiles and charm, disarming me with his pipes. Sorry, Lou, won't happen again, Lou. Blah, blah. In the end, he made it impossible for me to keep him."

"What did he do?"

"Some asshole keeled over in the john of my fine establishment. Johnny sold him the rock and the Mexican mud for a speedball, and a hundred people saw it. That was the end. It's all fun and games until a junkie expires in a toilet stall. That black tar bitch is satanic. Takes everything in its path. He came in once or twice after that, apologizing, but I was done. Told him to straighten himself out before he came to me again. Haven't heard from him since."

Yeah, Chloe wants to say. Me neither. "Is he from around here?"

"Not sure." Again, too clipped.

"But what about his name?"

Lou chews on a toothpick as he eyeballs her. "Johnny Rainbow is his name."

"Come on."

"I don't know nothing else."

"So how did you pay him? Didn't you need his social security number, an address maybe?"

Lou laughs. "Clearly you never sang in a bar band. I pay cash from door receipts. They like it, I like it, that's how it's done."

"So you don't know where he lives?"

"Nope."

"Or his real name?"

"Nope."

"Well," says Chloe, "without one of those two things, I can't find him."

Lou studies her. "Personally," he says, "I think he didn't give out his real name because he didn't want to embarrass his family if he got caught. And trust me, they always get caught."

"Who's his family?"

"How should I know? Just a hunch, I tell you."

"Who is his family?"

"Girl, you're not listening to me."

She *is* listening. To all the things he's saying and not saying. She fails to suppress a sigh, an eyeroll, a fistclench, a pained frustrated ugly breath. "So you refuse to say or do or remember anything?" Chloe raises her voice. She sounds desperate because she is. "I'm asking you. I'm begging you. I've been looking for him for four years. I have no one else to go to if you don't help me. I'm going to have to get in my car and drive three thousand miles back home. I came here for one afternoon, just trying—" She breaks off. Takes a deep breath. "To find him."

Lou leans over the bar, elbows on the counter, chewing his toothpick. His eyes are blank.

"Thank you," she says, grabbing her bag. "You've been very helpful." She starts to walk away.

She hears his voice behind her. "Come back," he says with a sigh. "Stop wigging out."

Chloe quickly approaches the bar. That was wigging out?

The man scribbles down a few words on a napkin. He places the napkin on the counter but won't let go of it. "No, I can't give it to you," he says. "You have two seconds to look at the words before I get rid of it. If something bad happens because I gave this out to a stranger, I won't have a business no more. Don't shake your head. I don't know who you are. You could be a stalker, or a killer. You could be an ex-convict with a death wish. It's happened. It gets found out I gave you this, forget about my business, I might not even keep my life. And I'm not fucking kidding you about that. So read up, girly. Two seconds."

Her hands reaching for it, Chloe stares at the napkin with five short words scribbled on it, her heart pummeling her chest. Before she can explain to Lou about dendrites and synapses, he snatches the napkin from her, flicks on his lighter and holds the flame to the paper over the bar sink. In fifteen seconds, the water washes the ashes down the drain. Not a trace of the address remains.

"Now I'm going to tell you a story," Lou says. "One Saturday night, an *extremely* well-known locally prominent gentleman and his wife came to my bar to watch Johnny perform. They sat in the corner in the back like they didn't want to be noticed. I was so honored to have them, I talked about it for months. I brought them my best whiskey and of course never charged

them, would never charge them. The wife saved my niece's
life. Horrible car accident, no one could stop the bleeding. But
she did. Because she was holy. Anyway, right after they came,
Johnny suddenly started working the stage with a six thousand
dollar microphone and wearing twelve grand worth of alligator
boots. I asked him where he got the mic because I'm in the
business, I know a dope mic when I see it, and he said it was a
gift from his family."

"What makes you think those two people were his family?"

"A hunch. A coincidence of the sick boots and the couple's
appearance in my bar. This isn't the kind of place those two
frequent, let me tell you. But I may be wrong, girly."

Chloe wants to say he is definitely wrong about one thing.
That is not a coincidence. It's a correlation.

"Go," he says to her. "Get out of here before you forget."

She walks out into the sunshine. It blinds her for a few
minutes. San Diego has nothing on Phoenix on cloudless days.
San Diego is tempered by the ocean. Not Phoenix, all in a scorch.

Johnny Kick a Hole in the Sky

It's a long way from downtown Phoenix to the address etched
into the cold stone inside her heart. Every dusty road looks
the same. It's desert flat, streets on a grid, measured lights,
civilization, and suddenly nothing but mountain. She makes a
left and drives north at ten miles an hour on a road called Pima.
It's an old Indian road, and the canal the Hohokam built three
hundred years ago to water the desert still runs between the
road and the sagebrush hills. The cars behind Chloe roll down
their windows and curse her loudly as they speed by her on the
left. A man on a galloping horse passes her by!

Though she wears nothing but a tank and shorts, she is
overdressed. Chloe has never been this hot in her life. The
miserably inadequate AC in the Beetle stopped working long
ago. Now it pumps out nothing but hot air. Soon the engine will

set itself on fire, like every other thing here. Every other thing except the cold stone inside her heart.

She stops before she makes a right onto the road Lou made her memorize. She doesn't have the courage to make the turn, to go up the hill. Right now, she thinks, she can make the choice to just keep going. North on Pima, straight to the interstate, go east, drive on, not know. The fear of turning onto the road is so great that Chloe starts to hyperventilate. What would Lou think if he saw her now. He thought she was histrionic before when, in a calm soft voice, she had asked him a simple question.

She imagines driving on. She imagines driving up. She imagines not knowing. She imagines knowing. She doesn't know what to do. She wishes her mother were here to tell her.

It depends on the outcome, she hears Lang say. Which Chloe doesn't know.

Can she live with it, unknowing?

Can she live, unknowing?

Her palm is unsteady. It takes her several tries to shift into drive. Whatever happens, she cannot live the way she has been living, in purgatory. *Top of Jomax* is the only way out of the hell of her suspended haunted life.

After making the right, she drives up the sloping narrow unpaved road overgrowing with deer grass and pink muhly. The road stretches up and up and up for a mile into the desert foothills. There are only a handful of houses on it, four sprinkled at the bottom and one sprawling adobe mansion at the very top. That's where Chloe stops, as Lou's napkin had instructed her. *Top of Jomax, off Pima*. She had left San Diego at eight in the morning, and it's almost four. The Arizona sun still seems to be at its zenith. Go, Arizona sun.

There is no one outside. It's a hundred and twenty degrees; of course there is no one outside. In five minutes everything is singed.

But she is wrong. In the front yard of the adobe house near a sunlit mountain, a woman in her forties crouches in a sombrero hat, gardening. The porch radio is playing something Spanish on the guitar. Perhaps "Bamboléo."

Chloe gets out of the car. The door slams shut. The sombrero lady glances up. "Excuse me, please," Chloe says, walking to the white rail fence. "Can you help me?"

The woman stands up from crouching and sways as if she's light-headed. She is tall and blonde. She wears khaki shorts and a long-sleeve linen shirt to protect her from the sun. For some reason Chloe becomes light-headed herself.

"Yes?" The woman isn't rude, but she isn't not rude either. Perhaps she thinks Chloe is a Jehovah's Witness.

Chloe raises her hands to show she has no pamphlets, nothing to hawk, nothing to proselytize. "I'm looking for a friend of mine," she says. "I'm sorry to bother you. I'm having trouble locating his exact address."

"Who's your friend?"

"Johnny Rainbow?"

The woman blinks. She says nothing, but Chloe can almost swear she takes a half-stagger back on her garden clogs. It could be a mirage. Under the desert sun, in the waves of heat and light, everything appears slightly jittery.

"No one here by that name," she says. "Wrong house."

"Jane." A voice sounds from the covered porch off the wide center promenade, a soft voice, but one that demands to be heard.

"It's all right, Mom," Jane calls out. "It's nothing."

"Jane," the voice repeats.

Chloe watches a small platinum-haired woman, dressed in cream linen, walk carefully holding on to the railing down three steps and toward them through the garden. She also wears a hat. She is so tiny and fragile she seems translucent.

The daughter steps toward the mother and immediately puts a protective arm around her. "Mom, it's fine. I'll take care of it. Go back in the shade. You know it's not good for you to be out—"

The woman lifts her hand to stop her daughter from speaking.

The daughter stops speaking.

The woman continues slowly through the garden to the road and stops on her side of the low fence in front of Chloe. For a few moments she doesn't speak, she simply appraises the young girl with her seafoam eyes. She is silent, like the daughter, but unlike the daughter, she gazes on Chloe with a distant sisterly compassion. "Why the question mark at the end of his name?" the old woman finally says. "Don't you know who your friend is?" Her voice carries a trace of a distant accent, a faint Slavic rounding of Teutonic English.

"He didn't tell me his real name," Chloe says, and instantly regrets admitting it. She is certain they judge her now, as in, perhaps if he cared more, he would've told her.

Jane has joined her mother in front of Chloe. The two women, one tall, the other small, exchange a brief glance. The daughter shakes her head. "They still come to our house looking for him," she says. Irritation is in her voice. "When will it stop?"

"Imagine if he had told them his actual name," the old woman says, speaking gentler than her daughter, though not by much. She levels her eyes at Chloe. "My grandson's name was Anthony," she says. "He died a long time ago."

Chloe's legs buckle.

"I'm not looking for Anthony," she mutters. "I'm looking for Johnny Rainbow."

The women don't speak.

"Maybe I have the wrong house," Chloe whispers. "The wrong name."

The women don't speak.

She tries to stand erect. She leans on a fence post, she hangs her head. Her shoulders slump. It is minutes before she is able to compose herself to speak again. And through it, they stay quiet, as if they understand. All she is praying for is not to break down in front of his family. She remembers this from losing Jimmy. Vocal grief of strangers is unfair and hard to endure. "In Afghanistan?" she says, not looking up.

"No," the old woman replies. "Though I agree with you, that would've been better. To die in a blaze of glory. Our boy never saw Afghanistan. Three weeks into OCS training he was booted from the program. Not even his father could fix it that time."

He was caught with a half-pound of rock—thirty baggies of crack cocaine. Plus two dozen other assorted sins. He went off the grid after that. "We searched for him everywhere," Jane says. "We hired private detectives in twenty states."

"Eventually we found him," says the old woman. Chloe almost hears the words ahead of the whisper-soft voice. "He overdosed in a motel room somewhere in California."

"In Death Valley," Jane says. "Near Funeral Mountains maybe? It was hopeless. Nothing anyone could do for him. How his father tried."

Silence rolls back and forth between them on the parched ground. Chloe has not looked up. Her tears fall onto the sand and instantly dry, sizzling as they evaporate. When she does look up, she stares off to the side of the two women, to where the trains are, where the guitar lies, where the sea and the moon and the rain in Trieste is, to the mouth near the mic, the mouth near her mouth, the twinkling, smiling dark eyes.

Jane puts her hand around her mother. "Come on, Mom. Please. Get out of the sun. Excuse us," she says to Chloe. "She can't be out here this long. It's too hot for her."

"Stop mothering me," says the woman. "Not your job." She addresses Chloe. "When did you know our Anthony?"

"We met in Europe before he went to Fort Benning. We visited his mother." She cannot keep her voice from breaking. "How is she?"

"Outlived him," Jane replies. "Though not by much."

And all this time Chloe thought she would find him walking down the road. All these years she hoped to see him on the mesa above the ocean, on the moonlit beach. When, she asks. When.

Not three months after he enlisted. Before Halloween.

Not three months after he left her. She waited for him for four years, and he had been gone the whole time, the bow, the air kiss, the march to the plane, the vanishing.

"He was going to be a rock star," Chloe whispers.

"Yes, he could've been anything," the old woman says. "He had almost every gift."

Mother and daughter start toward their house. Chloe concentrates on the desert flowers because her eye is drawn to the things she loves. She appraises the blue hydrangeas, and wants to compliment the women on the excellent fertilization and watering of the sandy soil. Hydrangeas are difficult to grow this big and beautiful, especially in the desert. I'm really sorry, Chloe wants to say, but her throat won't cooperate.

"Would you like some lemonade before you go?" the old woman asks Chloe. "It's terribly hot out."

Chloe shakes her head. She watches them make their slow way to the porch. The daughter fusses over the mother, getting her comfortable in the chair, pouring her a lemonade from a pitcher, adjusting her hat. The old woman is annoyed but tender.

What now?

Now everything.

Now anything.

Now nothing.

He had everything.

He lived, he flew, he wasn't a smudge. He was somebody. Look how he was loved. All they wanted was to see him happy.

And he chose nothing.

Chloe might fall down from her great sadness.

She blinks away the sun and sees a man come out into the courtyard from the heavy double doors of the house. The man is tall and white-haired, slightly stooped from age, from the weight of his nine decades on earth, but only slightly.

"Who is that?" he says to the women in a gruff deep voice, stopping in the garden and squinting at Chloe.

"It's nobody, Dad, just another girl about Anthony Jr.," Jane says.

"Did you ask this nobody her name?"

"Uh, no …"

"I told you to ask their name," he says. "Why doesn't anyone ever listen to me?" He steps forward. "What is your name, child?"

"Chloe," says Chloe. "Chloe Divine."

With rebuke the man turns to his daughter. "You were going to let her drive off, and yet she is the one we've been waiting for." Guiltily Jane looks away from her father, and glares at Chloe! As if it's Chloe's fault Jane didn't ask for her name. "Wait here," the man says and disappears back inside. Chloe isn't sure if he is speaking to her or his daughter. But whoever he is addressing, they wait. Because he tells them to, and his voice brooks no argument.

The man's wife beckons Chloe to come inside the garden. "I know it's a shock," she says when Chloe is at the foot of the porch steps. "We were like you once. It's been almost four years for us. Only five minutes for you. We learned to live with it."

"Not his father," Jane says, and twists deeply away. She doesn't look at Chloe again.

The mother tips her head in pained assent.

Chloe wants to tell them about her brother, wants to say that she knows something about learning to live with the unlivable. That's not what this feels like. This feels like the washing away of all waters. Chloe is charred by the remorseless sun.

Carrying something in his hand, the man reappears after some long awkward minutes. Coming to stand in front of Chloe, he hands her an envelope. She clings to the railing. She looks up at him. Under the external age, under the machine, it is the ghost of Johnny's eyes that peers down at her from a different face, a broad, calm, watchful, sanguine face. She can't look away from the man. She doesn't even blink away from him. Johnny's eyes are staring down at her!

On the small greeting card envelope, in Johnny's block letter scrawl, her name is written, as if in the stars. CHLOE DIVINE.

"Among the things left in the room where he was found, there was this," the man tells her. "It's been waiting for you to come and claim it."

Her hands shake.

The envelope is flimsy. It feels as if there is nothing in it except a postcard or a photograph. One or the other, but not both. That is even worse. Either a picture or a letter. What does she want? Him. She wants him alive. Not even for herself. For himself. She wants him not to fall down, not to give up, not to die alone in a bed in a motel. In a minute she won't be able to stand upright. She needs to leave.

"We saved it because he had saved it," the man says. "His father took most of his things. Like the guitar and his clothes. We have the rest. The boots, the mic. And this letter. Look, he was trying to remember your address. We couldn't figure it out. We couldn't tell if it was Maine or Mississippi or Montana. And the name of the town, what is that? Looks like Firetown? Firegrad?"

"Fryeburg," Chloe says. She had been right. He couldn't remember it. The crack cocaine neurons were a micrometer too far apart.

The thin envelope clenched in her trembling hand, the tips of her fingers numb, Chloe manages a smile and a thank you. She bows her head in a farewell to his family, the one she has heard so much about and yet not enough, so much and yet nothing. Taking a deep breath, she starts away, and then turns back with a last question. "What was his full name?" she calls to the man. "I never knew it."

"Anthony Alexander Barrington III," the man says, his voice like gravel, and like gravel it crackles.

She stares into the man's eyes for one last moment. No wonder Johnny wanted a different name. He thought it might give him a different life.

And it did.

Chloe gets into her car, after several attempts starts it, drives downhill, brakes at the corner of Jomax and Pima, and then doesn't move. For she doesn't know how long, she sits in the driver's seat, her forehead against the wheel and cries.

Without opening the envelope, she drives three hundred miles north and east through the desert, the Petrified Forest and the prairie until she can't drive anymore and it's midnight. In Gallup where she stops, all the better motels have no vacancies. She finds a ground floor room on Highway 66 in a joint with blood stains on the shower curtain and electrical wires poking live out of the wall.

She knows she won't be able to sleep until she opens Johnny's letter. But she also knows that once she opens it, she won't be able to sleep. Fully clothed, she lies on the musty bed, and stares at the ceiling, flying back through the years to another ceiling she had stared at, desperately wishing for a life that could never be, for a love that could never be. Even as she had lived it, she wept, because she knew in her deepest heart it would never come again. He was next to her then, his naked body on his stomach, sprawled out, asleep. She crawled on top of him and laid her head on his back. She kissed him between his shallowly rising shoulder blades. She kissed his neck, his loose black hair. She whispered to him about life, herself, love, joy, about all the abundant gifts he was endowed with.

The place where you died, did it look like this, she asks the empty room, the empty ceiling. Dirty bedspreads, a broken Coke machine down the hall, the slimy bathroom, the algae-filled pool invitingly lit up as if anyone would dare dive into it. Is this like the last cheap hotel where you gave up your one precious life?

You wanted to be young until the angels came and asked you to fly. You're nineteen forever now, stumbling over the words, flexing your hips, hip hopping your elbows to the beat of the aurochs. The promises you made me were all for naught, because a promise is for tomorrow, and you didn't have one.

All you had was a set in Warsaw's Old Town Square when the money poured in every time you killed a chord change, every time your unearthly voice soared above the Royal Castle. It was sure good to be alive with you, Johnny Rainbow. Except now all your dreams are used up and wasted, all cut and cut and cut into smaller and smaller irrational fractions, into little white lines until there is nothing left, of them, or of you.

She forgot to ask where he is buried. It is too painful to realize this. She should've asked. Now it's too late. It doesn't matter. Is she going to bring him purple lupines? An armful of red roses? Is she going to plant for him lilies of the field?

Four times someone tries to break into her room. The flimsy lock and chain nearly can't contain the door. Bereft, Chloe falls asleep in the clothes she was dressed in when she found out he died, all her makeup long melted off by heat and tears, the envelope on her heart unopened, the heart full of cold stone pain.

When she wakes up nothing is different or feels different, except it's morning and she is in Gallup, New Mexico. She cleans herself up as best she can in the disgusting bathroom, steps outside, and sits on the old wooden bench by her door. It is a dry morning, the sun high and hot, the sky hazy blue. Highway 66 in front of her, a boulder mountain behind her. Train tracks run along the highway. To the left of her is a sign for a café, but only a sign. There is no café. There is, however, a radiator repair shop next door. If she needs her radiator repaired, she's come to the right place.

She sits and waits. The cars whizz by, the freight trains clang.

She sits and waits for her life to begin, to end.

The sun beats mercilessly against the sky.

On the bench, she holds the frayed white envelope and gazes at the historic road, at the train tracks, at the prairie.

What she holds in her hands is what he left behind for her. He told her that he refused to let the minutes pass without filling them with meaning. Death wasn't going to snatch the essence from their present days. That's what he promised her. That he would find a way to make his life matter.

And here it is.

White paper covering either a postcard or a photograph.

To prepare herself for every eventuality, Chloe has spent the drive to New Mexico, last night on the bed, and all this morning imagining what the contents of the envelope might hold, so that whatever it is can come as a shock, but not a surprise. Like his death.

Is it a postcard with words from him? Is it a photograph? Johnny in a uniform holding his rifle. Johnny in a leather jacket, hair tied back, Chuck Berrying his guitar. Johnny with his dad, also an Anthony Alexander, during a better time for them. A small boy on top of his dad's proud shoulders, his twin sisters in tow, the beauty queen mother beaming by their side. Perhaps it's a picture of his grandparents when they were young, ruining things for everybody with their crazy love. Wishful thinking all, like sweet coffee or buttercup orchids.

It's not important what it is, she decides. What's most important is the words written on it. It could be a postcard from Death Valley, just for something to scribble on. He had nothing else on hand in Stovepipe Wells, the last motel of his life. The front image is immaterial. The image he is about to paint for her with his words—that is the material part. That is ontological.

It's brutal outside. She sits alone in the courtyard, in part shade so she won't blister or burn her pale swollen face. Her red Beetle is parked in front of her, the hotel pool solid green behind the chain-link fence across the concrete. There is a dying ocotillo in a brown pot next to where she sits. She notices these things. She notices everything. Another hour of grief ticks by before she heaves a laden breath and tears open the last of the magic stars one by one going dark inside her heart. From the envelope she teases out a photograph.

She is wrong on all counts.

The front image is not immaterial.

It isn't a postcard of the bakeries in Warsaw or the fields in Treblinka. It is a photograph from a green slope on the Riga Canal. The incongruity of the image crashes against her hard expectations. Her mind can't reconcile the thing she is seeing with the thing she thought she would see.

It is a photograph of her in Riga.

Sometime in the balmy late afternoon on the Riga Canal, sometime before the end, before they knew it was the end, before everything came tumbling down off the funeral mountain, Chloe sat perched on the grass with her bare legs crossed, her painted feet flat on the ground. Hannah, Mason, and Blake sat on the grass beside her. Johnny must have snapped the shot from the boat full of tourists, when all she heard from a watery distance was, *Chloe, Chloe* …

No one was aware of the silver Olympus that clicked and caught one sixtieth of a second of the four of them after a lifetime together and before a lifetime apart, after a long day of walking, hot, sweaty, tired, slightly grimy, in need of a pool or an ocean, relaxed and at peace. Halfway smiling at whatever it was Chloe was saying, Hannah was inspecting her bitten nails. Mason, one careless hand on Chloe's foot, was studying the open map.

Only Blake was turned fully to Chloe. He gazed up at her entranced, while she was laughing and unsuspecting. Probably a good way to describe much of her character. Her teeth gleaming, she was caught by Johnny, chortling at her own joke. But Blake wasn't smiling. He was fixated on her, unlaughing and unarmored. Because Hannah was in the nails and Mason was in the map, and Chloe was in herself, Blake stared at Chloe open-eyed, clear-eyed, overflowing. Between his gaze and her face was the opulent swell of her summer breasts, squeezed into an aqua sundress, the décolletage spilling out, taking up half the picture frame. Since no one was watching him, or so he thought, Blake's eyes had freedom to gawp anywhere they wished. But in this click in time, it wasn't her breasts he was devouring, but her laughing face.

By the side of Highway 66, her mouth falling open, Chloe stares at Blake staring at her. He is caught, starkly, in plain sight. He is inhaling her. All the tulips bloom in Latvia under his fertile adoring gaze. There is no question that anyone who ever felt anything for anyone else would look at Blake's face in that frozen blink of transcendental eternity and know that he loved her.

Chloe is astonished.

She is afraid to turn the photograph over. What if there is nothing written on it? Does there need to be something on the other side? What if instead of a letter from Johnny, she has only this?

But why?

Why would this mean anything to him? Why would he take it, why would he save it? Why in the world would he preserve it in amber, develop it, carry it, put it in an envelope, and die bequeathing it to her, will it to her life? Instead of a love letter, this! Why?

She stares into Blake's face as the sun rises in the desert sky, reaching high noon, blistering the ocotillo next to her baffled throat.

Holding her breath, she turns the photograph over.

In Johnny's meandering unsteady hand are the following words. She squints to make them out, tears making them nearly unreadable. It is dated October 2004. She can't take it. She almost can't read on.

I love you, Chloe. I wish I could do it over again, I wish I could keep myself.

I give you this so you will be free of me. Make your own story. Take your own bus 136. Your whole life it's been front and center of you. Everything you need, want, long for, inches away from your oblivious heart. Open your eyes – and see. You're not alone. He is the answer. 3:15. All the things that he desires canst ever compare unto you.

Johnny Rainbow

Chloe weeps for him for twenty-five hundred miles through fifteen states of the Union as she races back home. She weeps bent over her knees on the brown bench in New Mexico, her body shaking so much it feels as if she will never stand up, get in the car, get going. She mourns him through the prairies of Albuquerque and the mountains of Santa Fe, through northwest Texas where the sandy heat parches her blotchy face, the flying insects eat her, and the wind blows grit inside her smallest pores. She hides in a ditch to escape a tornado in Oklahoma and just as well, for the tears are blinding her off the road. Of all the unsung regrets, she feels most sharply the waste of his unfinished chapters, the weight of his uncharted oceans.

After surviving the twister, she has waffles for dinner and burgers for breakfast, she has fries and onion rings and hard strawberries barely in season. In Tennessee, during the length of that entire and entirely too long state, she realizes that faith alone was not enough to return him to her, that something more was needed, something Johnny didn't have, a way out.

By the time she reaches Kentucky she is numb, drained of tears. She has pecan pie, and the most delicious bacon hash, so delicious that she stays an extra half-day so she can get hungry in Louisville and have it again. She calls her mother, and can barely get the words out about what happened before she has to hang up.

She eats her second helping of heavenly bacon hash as a tearful tribute to him.

In West Virginia, Chloe brutally grasps that she has wasted four years of her life obsessing over a phantom. The spear of grief turns into wobbling self-pity.

In Maryland, looking for answers and comfort, she drives extra slowly, reading all the white signs posted on the green lawns of churches. Maryland is brim-full of Appalachian houses of worship with signs out front, each pithier than the next, each giving a kernel of old wisdom to live by. One finally does it for her. IT'S NEVER TOO LATE TO BE WHAT YOU MIGHT HAVE BEEN. It is too late for Johnny. But not too late for Chloe. When he played in Warsaw, Johnny had written out this exact George Eliot quote on a Post-it note and stuck it on the inside of his guitar case so when the passersby bent to throw him some money, they could read those eleven words and walk away maybe a little straighter than before.

That is what happens to Chloe. Faster and straighter, Chloe drives her red VW bug home to Maine. She comes to understand why she has driven like Jimmy Dean ever since she left Gallup, tearing up the pavement. Because she is terrified. Terrified that while she was being so disastrously dull-witted, Blake has found someone else. He has been through every girl within a six-town radius. Looking for someone other than her? Anyone but her, as he would say. What if one of the floozies has ingratiated herself permanently into his Biblical life? Didn't Taylor write there would be some announcement soon from Dani and Blake? What if it is too late? Chloe can't endure the thought of it. She wishes she could fly.

Johnny's days have not been squandered. He left a permanent mark on all who loved him. Afflicted Johnny has nonetheless managed to find a way to fill Chloe's finite life with infinite meaning. He left Chloe Blake. He filled her cup to overflowing with himself and when it was bone empty, he left her for the one who loved her most. No wonder Johnny never fought back even when Blake was being impossible. Johnny knew why. He knew everything from the beginning.

All her education didn't make her heart smart enough to see bliss. Pining away after the lost gold of Pima when the mansion of kings was three houses up from her green cabin.

A cloud of dust rises up around the red bug as she flies downhill and screeches into the clearing in front of her house. The screen door slams as she storms in. "Mom?" She runs through the empty house.

Lang is by the lake with her begonias. There is a kiss, a deep hug, a constricted I'm sorry, a comment about Chloe looking awful, as if she has driven three thousand sleepless miles. Chloe interrupts with the only question resonating through her body. "Mom, where's Blake?"

"I don't know. He went out earlier."

"Where? With who?"

"I don't know. To the store? He was walking."

"Walking to the store? It's six miles away."

"Well, maybe not to the store, then, but to Leary's. How did you miss him when you drove by?" Lang squints, wipes her sweaty head with gardening gloves leaving long dirt streaks on her forehead. "What's the fuss anyway?"

Carefully holding it by the edges, Chloe thrusts the discolored Riga photograph into her mother's face. Lang studies it—rather calmly, a panting Chloe thinks. "You. Blake. Mason. Hannah. So?"

"No. Mom. What do you *see*?"

"I don't know. You're wearing a dress?"

"God! Turn it over!"

Taking off her work gloves, Lang turns it over. She reads Johnny's words. She remains composed. She stares into her daughter's agitated face. She pats Chloe with her mother paw. "Darling," she says. "Do you know how much I love you?" She opens wide her arms. "This much. But really, you're as dense as a thicket. Have you not read Blake's award-winning novella? Who do you think the letters in the blue suitcase were for? I mean, the man wrote you a love story, how many ways does he have to keep saying it?"

"You knew this?"

"Um, everybody knew this, Chloe. Why do you think Burt stayed our friend after your uncle nearly killed him? And do you know how hard it was for us to see Burt and Janice after your brother died? It was one of the hardest things we ever had to do. All these years we kept our families together for you two. We always knew Blake was the one. I personally think he may be too good for you." Lang smiled. "Never mind. Even the tortoise eventually gets to the finish line. Go find him. He's at Leary's."

"Do you think he still …"

"I don't know, darling. Go find him."

"Oh my God, Mom, we parted so badly, and he's barely emailed me, hardly stayed in touch, what do I say, what do I do?"

Lang spins her daughter around and pushes her yonder. "I'm out of answers. Go find your own."

Before she goes, Chloe turns around and hugs her mother. "I love you," she whispers, and bolts.

She was going to drive to him in a desperate hurry, but her hands are shaking and she can't get behind the wheel. She walks instead, then runs, until her heart is about to give out. Slowing down, she walks, pants, and runs again.

Down the single lane dirt road on a straight stretch just before the train tracks, she hears him whistling through the firs, hears him before she sees him, as he merrily strolls toward her, carrying a rusted tire iron on his shoulder. Look who is walking down the hill for me.

He sees her from a distance, focuses on her, nods, slows down and puts his hand to his eyes, as if shielding himself from the mirage, perhaps not believing it's her. Thank God she stopped running, though she is still gasping, panting.

"I thought that was you smoking past me like a maniac," he calls out. "Where's the fire?"

She wishes for a bench in the middle of the road to fall onto. She stands, fists to her chest, separated from his friendly, lightly smiling, confounded face by ten yards of Maine air. He is so familiar, so wide-shouldered, so beloved. She wants to fall to her knees and beg his forgiveness. There is no one else the world entire she is happier to see at that moment than Blake, strolling toward her, rocking on his heels, humming, smiling, long lost singers and broken hearts notwithstanding. The passion ghosts fade into the great divide that cleaves the Miramare past with the non-existent Arizona future. Blake is the present, the real, the yesterday, the tomorrow, the everything.

She wants to stick out her hand to show him the photo she clutches in her balled-up fingers. Is it true, she wants to ask. Look at it, Blake, look what Johnny has given me, is it true? But she doesn't need to ask him anything. His face tells her it's true. Her eyes fill with tears. He drops the tire iron, spits out his gum.

"Who's Dani Falco?" she asks when he is almost near.

"Not you." He stops in front of her, his eyes emotional and ablaze, muscle tee full of Blake labor, jeans ripped, brown boots muddy and large. He cups her face full into his hands and kisses her. Her head tips back, her arms drop. Suffering mingles with the sea and the sun, the day is on fire, and she is a sweet salty foreign girl, with abandon kissing a man in the woods before he tears off her dress.

"Whoa," she whispers, mouth agape, flinging both arms around his neck. "Just whoa." The summer, shouting things at her through the pines, is so full of promise. The whole spilling over life, trickling warm tears, hope and mad desire, sorrow and relief, and alive air, is so full of promise.

"Oh Blake," she says. "Will you ever forgive me?"

"I have waited for you for so long, Chloe Divine," he says, taking her into his big arms, lifting her off the ground, swinging her, spinning her, embracing her so tightly, she can hardly breathe and hardly cry. His lips kiss her exposed white throat, the palms of his hands press into her back. He holds her to his heart. "I want Mount Washington Resort," he whispers.

"For lunch?"

"For a week."

Chloe can't speak. She is breathless.

"Behold, everything old is brand-new," he says.

She wipes her face and opens her eyes. And beholds.

Do not weep, Johnny says. Life is beautiful.

The End

Other bestselling novels
by Paullina Simons

Tully

Red Leaves

Eleven Hours

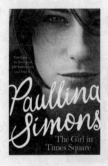
The Girl in
Times Square

Road to Paradise

A Song in
the Daylight

The Bronze Horseman series

The epic story of Tatiana and Alexander …

  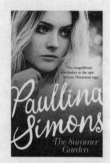

… and how it all began.

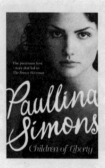